KURT VONNEGUT

KURT VONNEGUT

NOVELS & STORIES 1963–1973

———————————

Cat's Cradle
God Bless You, Mr. Rosewater
Slaughterhouse-Five
Breakfast of Champions
Stories

———————————

Sidney Offit, editor

THE LIBRARY OF AMERICA

Library of America, a nonprofit organization,
champions our nation's cultural heritage
by publishing America's greatest writing in
authoritative new editions and providing resources
for readers to explore this rich, living legacy.

Contents

CAT'S CRADLE

For Kenneth Littauer,
a man of gallantry and taste.

Nothing in this book is true.

"Live by the *foma** that make you brave and kind and healthy and happy."

The Books of Bokonon. I: 5

* *Harmless untruths*

I

The Day the World Ended

CALL ME JONAH. My parents did, or nearly did. They called me John.

Jonah—John—if I had been a Sam, I would have been a Jonah still—not because I have been unlucky for others, but because somebody or something has compelled me to be certain places at certain times, without fail. Conveyances and motives, both conventional and bizarre, have been provided. And, according to plan, at each appointed second, at each appointed place this Jonah was there.

Listen:

When I was a younger man—two wives ago, 250,000 cigarettes ago, 3,000 quarts of booze ago . . .

When I was a much younger man, I began to collect material for a book to be called *The Day the World Ended*.

The book was to be factual.

The book was to be an account of what important Americans had done on the day when the first atomic bomb was dropped on Hiroshima, Japan.

It was to be a Christian book. I was a Christian then.

I am a Bokononist now.

I would have been a Bokononist then, if there had been anyone to teach me the bittersweet lies of Bokonon. But Bokononism was unknown beyond the gravel beaches and coral knives that ring this little island in the Caribbean Sea, the Republic of San Lorenzo.

We Bokononists believe that humanity is organized into teams, teams that do God's Will without ever discovering what they are doing. Such a team is called a *karass* by Bokonon, and the instrument, the *kan-kan*, that brought me into my own particular *karass* was the book I never finished, the book to be called *The Day the World Ended*.

2

Nice, Nice, Very Nice

"If you find your life tangled up with somebody else's life for no very logical reasons," writes Bokonon, "that person may be a member of your *karass*."

At another point in *The Books of Bokonon* he tells us, "Man created the checkerboard; God created the *karass*." By that he means that a *karass* ignores national, institutional, occupational, familial, and class boundaries.

It is as free-form as an amoeba.

In his "Fifty-third Calypso," Bokonon invites us to sing along with him:

> Oh, a sleeping drunkard
> Up in Central Park,
> And a lion-hunter
> In the jungle dark,
> And a Chinese dentist,
> And a British queen—
> All fit together
> In the same machine.
> Nice, nice, very nice;
> Nice, nice, very nice;
> Nice, nice, very nice—
> So many different people
> In the same device.

3

Folly

Nowhere does Bokonon warn against a person's trying to discover the limits of his *karass* and the nature of the work God Almighty has had it do. Bokonon simply observes that such investigations are bound to be incomplete.

In the autobiographical section of *The Books of Bokonon* he writes a parable on the folly of pretending to discover, to understand:

I once knew an Episcopalian lady in Newport, Rhode Island, who asked me to design and build a doghouse for her Great Dane. The lady claimed to understand God and His Ways of Working perfectly. She could not understand why anyone should be puzzled about what had been or about what was going to be.

And yet, when I showed her a blueprint of the doghouse I proposed to build, she said to me, "I'm sorry, but I never could read one of those things."

"Give it to your husband or your minister to pass on to God," I said, "and, when God finds a minute, I'm sure he'll explain this doghouse of mine in a way that even *you* can understand."

She fired me. I shall never forget her. She believed that God liked people in sailboats much better than He liked people in motorboats. She could not bear to look at a worm. When she saw a worm, she screamed.

She was a fool, and so am I, and so is anyone who thinks he sees what God is Doing [writes Bokonon].

4

A Tentative Tangling of Tendrils

Be that as it may, I intend in this book to include as many members of my *karass* as possible, and I mean to examine all strong hints as to what on Earth we, collectively, have been up to.

I do not intend that this book be a tract on behalf of Bokononism. I should like to offer a Bokononist warning about it, however. The first sentence in *The Books of Bokonon* is this:

"All of the true things I am about to tell you are shameless lies."

My Bokononist warning is this:

Anyone unable to understand how a useful religion can be founded on lies will not understand this book either.

So be it.

About my *karass*, then.

It surely includes the three children of Dr. Felix Hoenikker, one of the so-called "Fathers" of the first atomic bomb. Dr. Hoenikker himself was no doubt a member of my *karass*, though he was dead before my *sinookas*, the tendrils of my life, began to tangle with those of his children.

The first of his heirs to be touched by my *sinookas* was Newton Hoenikker, the youngest of his three children, the younger of his two sons. I learned from the publication of my fraternity, *The Delta Upsilon Quarterly*, that Newton Hoenikker, son of the Nobel Prize physicist, Felix Hoenikker, had been pledged by my chapter, the Cornell Chapter.

So I wrote this letter to Newt:

"Dear Mr. Hoenikker:

"Or should I say, Dear *Brother* Hoenikker?

"I am a Cornell DU now making my living as a free-lance writer. I am gathering material for a book relating to the first atomic bomb. Its contents will be limited to events that took place on August 6, 1945, the day the bomb was dropped on Hiroshima.

"Since your late father is generally recognized as having been one of the chief creators of the bomb, I would very much appreciate any anecdotes you might care to give me of life in your father's house on the day the bomb was dropped.

"I am sorry to say that I don't know as much about your illustrious family as I should, and so don't know whether you have brothers and sisters. If you do have brothers and sisters, I should like very much to have their addresses so that I can send similar requests to them.

"I realize that you were very young when the bomb was dropped, which is all to the good. My book is going to emphasize the *human* rather than the *technical* side of the bomb, so recollections of the day through the eyes of a 'baby,' if you'll pardon the expression, would fit in perfectly.

"You don't have to worry about style and form. Leave all that to me. Just give me the bare bones of your story.

"I will, of course, submit the final version to you for your approval prior to publication.

"Fraternally yours—"

5

Letter from a Pre-med

To which Newt replied:

"I am sorry to be so long about answering your letter. That sounds like a very interesting book you are doing. I was so young when the bomb was dropped that I don't think I'm going to be much help. You should really ask my brother and sister, who are both older than I am. My sister is Mrs. Harrison C. Conners, 4918 North Meridian Street, Indianapolis, Indiana. That is my home address, too, now. I think she will be glad to help you. Nobody knows where my brother Frank is.

He disappeared right after Father's funeral two years ago, and nobody has heard from him since. For all we know, he may be dead now.

"I was only six years old when they dropped the atomic bomb on Hiroshima, so anything I remember about that day other people have helped me to remember.

"I remember I was playing on the living-room carpet outside my father's study door in Ilium, New York. The door was open, and I could see my father. He was wearing pajamas and a bathrobe. He was smoking a cigar. He was playing with a loop of string. Father was staying home from the laboratory in his pajamas all day that day. He stayed home whenever he wanted to.

"Father, as you probably know, spent practically his whole professional life working for the Research Laboratory of the General Forge and Foundry Company in Ilium. When the Manhattan Project came along, the bomb project, Father wouldn't leave Ilium to work on it. He said he wouldn't work on it at all unless they let him work where he wanted to work. A lot of the time that meant at home. The only place he liked to go, outside of Ilium, was our cottage on Cape Cod. Cape Cod was where he died. He died on a Christmas Eve. You probably know that, too.

"Anyway, I was playing on the carpet outside his study on the day of the bomb. My sister Angela tells me I used to play with little toy trucks for hours, making motor sounds, going 'burton, burton, burton' all the time. So I guess I was going 'burton, burton, burton' on the day of the bomb; and Father was in his study, playing with a loop of string.

"It so happens I know where the string he was playing with came from. Maybe you can use it somewhere in your book. Father took the string from around the manuscript of a novel that a man in prison had sent him. The novel was about the end of the world in the year 2000, and the name of the book was *2000 A.D.* It told about how mad scientists made a terrific bomb that wiped out the whole world. There was a big sex orgy when everybody knew that the world was going to end, and then Jesus Christ Himself appeared ten seconds before the bomb went off. The name of the author was Marvin Sharpe Holderness, and he told Father in a covering letter that he was in prison for killing his own brother. He sent the manuscript to Father because he couldn't figure out what kind of explosives to put in the bomb. He thought maybe Father could make suggestions.

"I don't mean to tell you I read the book when I was six. We had it around the house for years. My brother Frank made it his personal property, on account of the dirty parts. Frank kept it hidden in what he called his 'wall safe' in his bedroom. Actually, it wasn't a safe but just an old stove flue with a tin lid. Frank and I must have read the orgy part a thousand times when we were kids. We had it for years, and then my sister Angela found it. She read it and said it was nothing but a piece of dirty rotten filth. She burned it up, and the string with it. She was a mother to Frank and me, because our real mother died when I was born.

"My father never read the book, I'm pretty sure. I don't think he ever read a novel or even a short story in his whole life, or at least not since he was a little boy. He didn't read his mail or magazines or newspapers, either. I suppose he read a lot of technical journals, but to tell you the truth, I can't remember my father reading anything.

"As I say, all he wanted from that manuscript was the string. That was the way he was. Nobody could predict what he was going to be interested in next. On the day of the bomb it was string.

"Have you ever read the speech he made when he accepted the Nobel Prize? This is the whole speech: 'Ladies and Gentlemen. I stand before you now because I never stopped dawdling like an eight-year-old on a spring morning on his way to school. Anything can make me stop and look and wonder, and sometimes learn. I am a very happy man. Thank you.'

"Anyway, Father looked at that loop of string for a while, and then his fingers started playing with it. His fingers made the string figure called a 'cat's cradle.' I don't know where Father learned how to do that. From *his* father, maybe. His father was a tailor, you know, so there must have been thread and string around all the time when Father was a boy.

"Making that cat's cradle was the closest I ever saw my father come to playing what anybody else would call a game. He had no use at all for tricks and games and rules that other people made up. In a scrapbook my sister Angela used to keep up, there was a clipping from *Time* magazine where somebody asked Father what games he played for relaxation, and he said, 'Why should I bother with made-up games when there are so many real ones going on?'

"He must have surprised himself when he made a cat's cradle out of the string, and maybe it reminded him of his own childhood. He all of a sudden came out of his study and did something he'd never done before. He tried to play with me. Not only had he never played with me before; he had hardly ever even spoken to me.

"But he went down on his knees on the carpet next to me, and he showed me his teeth, and he waved that tangle of string in my face. 'See? See? See?' he asked. 'Cat's cradle. See the cat's cradle? See where the nice pussycat sleeps? Meow. Meow.'

"His pores looked as big as craters on the moon. His ears and nostrils were stuffed with hair. Cigar smoke made him smell like the mouth of Hell. So close up, my father was the ugliest thing I had ever seen. I dream about it all the time.

"And then he sang. 'Rockabye catsy, in the tree top'; he sang, 'when the wind blows, the cray-dull will rock. If the bough breaks, the cray-dull will fall. Down will come cray-dull, catsy, and all.'

"I burst into tears. I jumped up and I ran out of the house as fast as I could go.

"I have to sign off here. It's after two in the morning. My roommate just woke up and complained about the noise from the typewriter."

6

Bug Fights

Newt resumed his letter the next morning. He resumed it as follows:

"Next morning. Here I go again, fresh as a daisy after eight hours of sleep. The fraternity house is very quiet now. Everybody is in class but me. I'm a very privileged character. I don't have to go to class any more. I was flunked out last week. I was a pre-med. They were right to flunk me out. I would have made a lousy doctor.

"After I finish this letter, I think I'll go to a movie. Or if the sun comes out, maybe I'll go for a walk through one of the gorges. Aren't the gorges beautiful? This year, two girls jumped into one holding hands. They didn't get into the sorority they wanted. They wanted Tri-Delt.

"But back to August 6, 1945. My sister Angela has told me many times that I really hurt my father that day when I wouldn't admire the cat's cradle, when I wouldn't stay there on the carpet with my father and listen to him sing. Maybe I did hurt him, but I don't think I could have hurt him much. He was one of the best-protected human beings who ever lived. People couldn't get at him because he just wasn't interested in people. I remember one time, about a year before he died, I tried to get him to tell me something about my mother. He couldn't remember anything about her.

"Did you ever hear the famous story about breakfast on the day Mother and Father were leaving for Sweden to accept the Nobel Prize? It was in *The Saturday Evening Post* one time. Mother cooked a big breakfast. And then, when she cleared off the table, she found a quarter and a dime and three pennies by Father's coffee cup. He'd tipped her.

"After wounding my father so terribly, if that's what I did, I ran out into the yard. I didn't know where I was going until I found my brother Frank under a big spiraea bush. Frank was twelve then, and I wasn't surprised to find him under there. He spent a lot of time under there on hot days. Just like a dog, he'd make a hollow in the cool earth all around the roots. And you never could tell what Frank would have under the bush with him. One time he had a dirty book. Another time he had a bottle of cooking sherry. On the day they dropped the bomb Frank had a tablespoon and a Mason jar. What he was doing was spooning different kinds of bugs into the jar and making them fight.

"The bug fight was so interesting that I stopped crying right away—forgot all about the old man. I can't remember what all

Frank had fighting in the jar that day, but I can remember other bug fights we staged later on: one stag beetle against a hundred red ants, one centipede against three spiders, red ants against black ants. They won't fight unless you keep shaking the jar. And that's what Frank was doing, shaking, shaking the jar.

"After a while Angela came looking for me. She lifted up one side of the bush and she said, 'So there you are!' She asked Frank what he thought he was doing, and he said, 'Experimenting.' That's what Frank always used to say when people asked him what he thought he was doing. He always said, 'Experimenting.'

"Angela was twenty-two then. She had been the real head of the family since she was sixteen, since Mother died, since I was born. She used to talk about how she had three children—me, Frank, and Father. She wasn't exaggerating, either. I can remember cold mornings when Frank, Father, and I would be all in a line in the front hall, and Angela would be bundling us up, treating us exactly the same. Only I was going to kindergarten; Frank was going to junior high; and Father was going to work on the atom bomb. I remember one morning like that when the oil burner had quit, the pipes were frozen, and the car wouldn't start. We all sat there in the car while Angela kept pushing the starter until the battery was dead. And then Father spoke up. You know what he said? He said, 'I wonder about turtles.' 'What do you wonder about turtles?' Angela asked him. 'When they pull in their heads,' he said, 'do their spines buckle or contract?'

"Angela was one of the unsung heroines of the atom bomb, incidentally, and I don't think the story has ever been told. Maybe you can use it. After the turtle incident, Father got so interested in turtles that he stopped working on the atom bomb. Some people from the Manhattan Project finally came out to the house to ask Angela what to do. She told them to take away Father's turtles. So one night they went into his laboratory and stole the turtles and the aquarium. Father never said a word about the disappearance of the turtles. He just came to work the next day and looked for things to play with and think about, and everything there was to play with and think about had something to do with the bomb.

"When Angela got me out from under the bush, she asked me what had happened between Father and me. I just kept saying over and over again how ugly he was, how much I hated him. So she slapped me. 'How dare you say that about your father?' she said. 'He's one of the greatest men who ever lived! He won the war today! Do you realize that? He won the war!' She slapped me again.

"I don't blame Angela for slapping me. Father was all she had. She didn't have any boy friends. She didn't have any friends at all. She had only one hobby. She played the clarinet.

"I told her again how much I hated my father; she slapped me again; and then Frank came out from under the bush and punched her in the stomach. It hurt her something awful. She fell down and she rolled around. When she got her wind back, she cried and she yelled for Father.

"'He won't come,' Frank said, and he laughed at her. Frank was right. Father stuck his head out a window, and he looked at Angela and me rolling on the ground, bawling, and Frank standing over us, laughing. The old man pulled his head indoors again, and never even asked later what all the fuss had been about. People weren't his specialty.

"Will that do? Is that any help to your book? Of course, you've really tied me down, asking me to stick to the day of the bomb. There are lots of other good anecdotes about the bomb and Father, from other days. For instance, do you know the story about Father on the day they first tested a bomb out at Alamogordo? After the thing went off, after it was a sure thing that America could wipe out a city with just one bomb, a scientist turned to Father and said, 'Science has now known sin.' And do you know what Father said? He said, 'What is sin?'

"All the best,
"Newton Hoenikker"

7

The Illustrious Hoenikkers

Newt added these three postscripts to his letter:

"P.S. I can't sign myself 'fraternally yours' because they won't let me be your brother on account of my grades. I was only a pledge, and now they are going to take even that away from me.

"P.P.S. You call our family 'illustrious,' and I think you would maybe be making a mistake if you called it that in your book. I am a midget, for instance—four feet tall. And the last we heard of my brother Frank, he was wanted by the Florida police, the F.B.I., and the Treasury Department for running stolen cars to Cuba on war-surplus L.S.T.'s. So I'm pretty sure 'illustrious' isn't quite the word you're after. 'Glamorous' is probably closer to the truth.

"P.P.P.S. Twenty-four hours later. I have reread this letter and I can see where somebody might get the impression that I don't do anything but sit around and remember sad things and pity myself. Actually, I am a very lucky person and I know it. I am about to marry a wonderful little girl. There is love enough in this world for everybody, if people will just look. I am proof of that."

8

Newt's Thing with Zinka

Newt did not tell me who his girl friend was. But about two weeks after he wrote to me everybody in the country knew that her name was Zinka—plain Zinka. Apparently she didn't have a last name.

Zinka was a Ukrainian midget, a dancer with the Borzoi Dance Company. As it happened, Newt saw a performance by that company in Indianapolis, before he went to Cornell. And then the company danced at Cornell. When the Cornell performance was over, little Newt was outside the stage door with a dozen long-stemmed American Beauty roses.

The newspapers picked up the story when little Zinka asked for political asylum in the United States, and then she and little Newt disappeared.

One week after that, little Zinka presented herself at the Russian Embassy. She said Americans were too materialistic. She said she wanted to go back home.

Newt took shelter in his sister's house in Indianapolis. He gave one brief statement to the press. "It was a private matter," he said. "It was an affair of the heart. I have no regrets. What happened is nobody's business but Zinka's and my own."

One enterprising American reporter in Moscow, making inquiries about Zinka among dance people there, made the unkind discovery that Zinka was not, as she claimed, only twenty-three years old.

She was forty-two—old enough to be Newt's mother.

9

Vice-president in Charge of Volcanoes

I loafed on my book about the day of the bomb.

About a year later, two days before Christmas, another story carried me through Ilium, New York, where Dr. Felix Hoenikker had done most of his work; where little Newt, Frank, and Angela had spent their formative years.

I stopped off in Ilium to see what I could see.

There were no live Hoenikkers left in Ilium, but there were plenty of people who claimed to have known well the old man and his three peculiar children.

I made an appointment with Dr. Asa Breed, Vice-president in charge of the Research Laboratory of the General Forge and Foundry Company. I suppose Dr. Breed was a member of my *karass*, too, though he took a dislike to me almost immediately.

"Likes and dislikes have nothing to do with it," says Bokonon —an easy warning to forget.

"I understand you were Dr. Hoenikker's supervisor during most of his professional life," I said to Dr. Breed on the telephone.

"On paper," he said.

"I don't understand," I said.

"If I actually supervised Felix," he said, "then I'm ready now to take charge of volcanoes, the tides, and the migrations of birds and lemmings. The man was a force of nature no mortal could possibly control."

10

Secret Agent X-9

Dr. Breed made an appointment with me for early the next morning. He would pick me up at my hotel on his way to work, he said, thus simplifying my entry into the heavily-guarded Research Laboratory.

So I had a night to kill in Ilium. I was already in the beginning and end of night life in Ilium, the Del Prado Hotel. Its bar, the Cape Cod Room, was a hang-out for whores.

As it happened—"as it was *meant* to happen," Bokonon would say—the whore next to me at the bar and the bartender serving me had both gone to high school with Franklin Hoenikker, the bug tormentor, the middle child, the missing son.

The whore, who said her name was Sandra, offered me delights unobtainable outside of Place Pigalle and Port Said. I said I wasn't interested, and she was bright enough to say that she wasn't really interested either. As things turned out, we had both overestimated our apathies, but not by much.

Before we took the measure of each other's passions, however, we talked about Frank Hoenikker, and we talked about the old man, and we talked a little about Asa Breed, and we talked about the General Forge and Foundry Company, and we talked about the Pope and birth control, about Hitler and the Jews. We talked about phonies. We talked about truth. We talked about gangsters; we talked about business. We talked about the nice poor people who went to the electric chair; and we talked about the rich bastards who didn't. We talked about religious people who had perversions. We talked about a lot of things.

We got drunk.

The bartender was very nice to Sandra. He liked her. He respected her. He told me that Sandra had been chairman of the Class Colors Committee at Ilium High. Every class, he explained, got to pick distinctive colors for itself in its junior year, and then it got to wear those colors with pride.

"What colors did you pick?" I asked.

"Orange and black."

"Those are good colors."

"I thought so."

"Was Franklin Hoenikker on the Class Colors Committee, too?"

"He wasn't on anything," said Sandra scornfully. "He never got on any committee, never played any game, never took any girl out. I don't think he ever even talked to a girl. We used to call him Secret Agent X-9."

"X-9?"

"You know—he was always acting like he was on his way between two secret places; couldn't ever talk to anybody."

"Maybe he really *did* have a very rich secret life," I suggested.

"Nah."

"Nah," sneered the bartender. "He was just one of those kids who made model airplanes and jerked off all the time."

II

Protein

"He was supposed to be our commencement speaker," said Sandra.

"Who was?" I asked.

"Dr. Hoenikker—the old man."

"What did he say?"

"He didn't show up."

"So you didn't get a commencement address?"

"Oh, we got one. Dr. Breed, the one you're gonna see tomorrow, he showed up, all out of breath, and he gave some kind of talk."

"What did he say?"

"He said he hoped a lot of us would have careers in science," she said. She didn't see anything funny in that. She was remembering a lesson that had impressed her. She was repeating it gropingly, dutifully. "He said, the trouble with the world was . . ."

She had to stop and think.

"The trouble with the world was," she continued hesitatingly, "that people were still superstitious instead of scientific. He said if everybody would study science more, there wouldn't be all the trouble there was."

"He said science was going to discover the basic secret of life someday," the bartender put in. He scratched his head and frowned. "Didn't I read in the paper the other day where they'd finally found out what it was?"

"I missed that," I murmured.

"I saw that," said Sandra. "About two days ago."

"That's right," said the bartender.

"What *is* the secret of life?" I asked.

"I forget," said Sandra.

"Protein," the bartender declared. "They found out something about protein."

"Yeah," said Sandra, "that's it."

12

End of the World Delight

An older bartender came over to join in our conversation in the Cape Cod Room of the Del Prado. When he heard that I was writing a book about the day of the bomb, he told me what the day had been like for him, what the day had been like in the very bar in which we sat. He had a W. C. Fields twang and a nose like a prize strawberry.

"It wasn't the Cape Cod Room then," he said. "We didn't have all these fugging nets and seashells around. It was called the Navajo Tepee in those days. Had Indian blankets and cow skulls on the walls. Had little tom-toms on the tables. People were supposed to beat on the tom-toms when they wanted service. They tried to get me to wear a war bonnet, but I wouldn't do it. Real Navajo Indian came in here one day; told me Navajos didn't live in tepees. 'That's a fugging shame,' I told him. Before that it was the Pompeii Room, with busted plaster all over the place; but no matter what they call the room, they never change the fugging light fixtures. Never change the fugging people who come in or the fugging town outside, either. The day they dropped Hoenikker's fugging bomb on the Japanese a bum came in and tried to scrounge a drink. He wanted me to give him a drink on account of the world was coming to an end. So I mixed him an 'End of the World Delight.' I gave him about a half-pint of crème de menthe in a hollowed-out pineapple, with whipped cream and a cherry on top. 'There, you pitiful son of a bitch,' I said to him, 'don't ever say I never did anything for you.' Another guy came in, and he said he was quitting his job at the Research Laboratory; said anything a scientist worked on was sure to wind up as a weapon, one way or another. Said he didn't want to help politicians with their fugging wars anymore. Name was Breed. I asked him if he was any relation to the boss of the fugging Research Laboratory. He said he fugging well was. Said he was the boss of the Research Laboratory's fugging son."

13

The Jumping-off Place

Ah, God, what an ugly city Ilium is!

"Ah, God," says Bokonon, "what an ugly city every city is!"

Sleet was falling through a motionless blanket of smog. It was early morning. I was riding in the Lincoln sedan of Dr. Asa Breed. I was vaguely ill, still a little drunk from the night before. Dr. Breed was driving. Tracks of a long-abandoned trolley system kept catching the wheels of his car.

Breed was a pink old man, very prosperous, beautifully dressed. His manner was civilized, optimistic, capable, serene. I, by contrast, felt bristly, diseased, cynical. I had spent the night with Sandra.

My soul seemed as foul as smoke from burning cat fur.

I thought the worst of everyone, and I knew some pretty sordid things about Dr. Asa Breed, things Sandra had told me.

Sandra told me everyone in Ilium was sure that Dr. Breed had been in love with Felix Hoenikker's wife. She told me that most people thought Breed was the father of all three Hoenikker children.

"Do you know Ilium at all?" Dr. Breed suddenly asked me.

"This is my first visit."

"It's a family town."

"Sir?"

"There isn't much in the way of night life. Everybody's life pretty much centers around his family and his home."

"That sounds very wholesome."

"It is. We have very little juvenile delinquency."

"Good."

"Ilium has a very interesting history, you know."

"That's very interesting."

"It used to be the jumping-off place, you know."

"Sir?"

"For the Western migration."

"Oh."

"People used to get outfitted here."

"That's very interesting."

"Just about where the Research Laboratory is now was the old stockade. That was where they held the public hangings, too, for the whole county."

"I don't suppose crime paid any better then than it does now."

"There was one man they hanged here in 1782 who had murdered twenty-six people. I've often thought somebody ought to do a book about him sometime. George Minor Moakely. He sang a song on the scaffold. He sang a song he'd composed for the occasion."

"What was the song about?"

"You can find the words over at the Historical Society, if you're really interested."

"I just wondered about the general tone."

"He wasn't sorry about anything."

"Some people are like that."

"Think of it!" said Dr. Breed. "Twenty-six people he had on his conscience!"

"The mind reels," I said.

14

When Automobiles Had Cut-glass Vases

My sick head wobbled on my stiff neck. The trolley tracks had caught the wheels of Dr. Breed's glossy Lincoln again.

I asked Dr. Breed how many people were trying to reach the General Forge and Foundry Company by eight o'clock, and he told me thirty thousand.

Policemen in yellow raincapes were at every intersection, contradicting with their white-gloved hands what the stop-and-go signs said.

The stop-and-go signs, garish ghosts in the sleet, went

through their irrelevant tomfoolery again and again, telling the glacier of automobiles what to do. Green meant go. Red meant stop. Orange meant change and caution.

Dr. Breed told me that Dr. Hoenikker, as a very young man, had simply abandoned his car in Ilium traffic one morning.

"The police, trying to find out what was holding up traffic," he said, "found Felix's car in the middle of everything, its motor running, a cigar burning in the ash tray, fresh flowers in the vases . . ."

"Vases?"

"It was a Marmon, about the size of a switch engine. It had little cut-glass vases on the doorposts, and Felix's wife used to put fresh flowers in the vases every morning. And there that car was in the middle of traffic."

"Like the *Marie Celeste*," I suggested.

"The Police Department hauled it away. They knew whose car it was, and they called up Felix, and they told him very politely where his car could be picked up. Felix told them they could keep it, that he didn't want it any more."

"Did they?"

"No. They called up his wife, and she came and got the Marmon."

"What was her name, by the way?"

"Emily." Dr. Breed licked his lips, and he got a faraway look, and he said the name of the woman, of the woman so long dead, again. "Emily."

"Do you think anybody would object if I used the story about the Marmon in my book?" I asked.

"As long as you don't use the end of it."

"The *end* of it?"

"Emily wasn't used to driving the Marmon. She got into a bad wreck on the way home. It did something to her pelvis . . ." The traffic wasn't moving just then. Dr. Breed closed his eyes and tightened his hands on the steering wheel.

"And that was why she died when little Newt was born."

15

Merry Christmas

The Research Laboratory of the General Forge and Foundry Company was near the main gate of the company's Ilium works, about a city block from the executive parking lot where Dr. Breed put his car.

I asked Dr. Breed how many people worked for the Research Laboratory. "Seven hundred," he said, "but less than a hundred are actually doing research. The other six hundred are all housekeepers in one way or another, and I am the chiefest housekeeper of all."

When we joined the mainstream of mankind in the company street, a woman behind us wished Dr. Breed a merry Christmas. Dr. Breed turned to peer benignly into the sea of pale pies, and identified the greeter as one Miss Francine Pefko. Miss Pefko was twenty, vacantly pretty, and healthy—a dull normal.

In honor of the dulcitude of Christmastime, Dr. Breed invited Miss Pefko to join us. He introduced her as the secretary of Dr. Nilsak Horvath. He then told me who Horvath was. "The famous surface chemist," he said, "the one who's doing such wonderful things with films."

"What's new in surface chemistry?" I asked Miss Pefko.

"God," she said, "don't ask me. I just type what he tells me to type." And then she apologized for having said "God."

"Oh, I think you understand more than you let on," said Dr. Breed.

"Not me." Miss Pefko wasn't used to chatting with someone as important as Dr. Breed and she was embarrassed. Her gait was affected, becoming stiff and chickenlike. Her smile was glassy, and she was ransacking her mind for something to say, finding nothing in it but used Kleenex and costume jewelry.

"Well . . . ," rumbled Dr. Breed expansively, "how do you like us, now that you've been with us—how long? Almost a year?"

"You scientists *think* too much," blurted Miss Pefko. She laughed idiotically. Dr. Breed's friendliness had blown every fuse in her nervous system. She was no longer responsible. "You *all* think too much."

A winded, defeated-looking fat woman in filthy coveralls trudged beside us, hearing what Miss Pefko said. She turned to examine Dr. Breed, looking at him with helpless reproach. She hated people who thought too much. At that moment, she struck me as an appropriate representative for almost all mankind.

The fat woman's expression implied that she would go crazy on the spot if anybody did any more thinking.

"I think you'll find," said Dr. Breed, "that everybody does about the same amount of thinking. Scientists simply think about things in one way, and other people think about things in others."

"Ech," gurgled Miss Pefko emptily. "I take dictation from Dr. Horvath and it's just like a foreign language. I don't think I'd understand—even if I was to go to college. And here he's maybe talking about something that's going to turn everything upside-down and inside-out like the atom bomb.

"When I used to come home from school Mother used to ask me what happened that day, and I'd tell her," said Miss Pefko. "Now I come home from work and she asks me the same question, and all I can say is—" Miss Pefko shook her head and let her crimson lips flap slackly—"I dunno, I dunno, I dunno."

"If there's something you don't understand," urged Dr. Breed, "ask Dr. Horvath to explain it. He's very good at explaining." He turned to me. "Dr. Hoenikker used to say that any scientist who couldn't explain to an eight-year-old what he was doing was a charlatan."

"Then I'm dumber than an eight-year-old," Miss Pefko mourned. "I don't even know what a charlatan is."

16

Back to Kindergarten

We climbed the four granite steps before the Research Laboratory. The building itself was of unadorned brick and rose six stories. We passed between two heavily-armed guards at the entrance.

Miss Pefko showed the guard on the left the pink *confidential* badge at the tip of her left breast.

Dr. Breed showed the guard on our right the black *top-secret* badge on his soft lapel. Ceremoniously, Dr. Breed put his arm around me without actually touching me, indicating to the guards that I was under his august protection and control.

I smiled at one of the guards. He did not smile back. There was nothing funny about national security, nothing at all.

Dr. Breed, Miss Pefko, and I moved thoughtfully through the Laboratory's grand foyer to the elevators.

"Ask Dr. Horvath to explain something sometime," said Dr. Breed to Miss Pefko. "See if you don't get a nice, clear answer."

"He'd have to start back in the first grade—or maybe even kindergarten," she said. "I missed a lot."

"We *all* missed a lot," Dr. Breed agreed. "We'd *all* do well to start over again, preferably with kindergarten."

We watched the Laboratory's receptionist turn on the many educational exhibits that lined the foyer's walls. The receptionist was a tall, thin girl—icy, pale. At her crisp touch, lights twinkled, wheels turned, flasks bubbled, bells rang.

"Magic," declared Miss Pefko.

"I'm sorry to hear a member of the Laboratory family using that brackish, medieval word," said Dr. Breed. "Every one of those exhibits explains itself. They're designed so as *not* to be mystifying. They're the very antithesis of magic."

"The very what of magic?"

"The exact opposite of magic."

"You couldn't prove it by me."

Dr. Breed looked just a little peeved. "Well," he said, "we don't *want* to mystify. At least give us credit for that."

17

The Girl Pool

Dr. Breed's secretary was standing on her desk in his outer office tying an accordion-pleated Christmas bell to the ceiling fixture.

"Look here, Naomi," cried Dr. Breed, "we've gone six months without a fatal accident! Don't you spoil it by falling off the desk!"

Miss Naomi Faust was a merry, desiccated old lady. I suppose she had served Dr. Breed for almost all his life, and her life, too. She laughed. "I'm indestructible. And, even if I did fall, Christmas angels would catch me."

"They've been known to miss."

Two paper tendrils, also accordion-pleated, hung down from the clapper of the bell. Miss Faust pulled one. It unfolded stickily and became a long banner with a message written on it. "Here," said Miss Faust, handing the free end to Dr. Breed, "pull it the rest of the way and tack the end to the bulletin board."

Dr. Breed obeyed, stepping back to read the banner's message. "Peace on Earth!" he read out loud heartily.

Miss Faust stepped down from her desk with the other tendril, unfolding it. "Good Will Toward Men!" the other tendril said.

"By golly," chuckled Dr. Breed, "they've dehydrated Christmas! The place looks festive, very festive."

"And I remembered the chocolate bars for the Girl Pool, too," she said. "Aren't you proud of me?"

Dr. Breed touched his forehead, dismayed by his forgetfulness. "Thank God for that! It slipped my mind."

"We mustn't ever forget that," said Miss Faust. "It's a tradition now—Dr. Breed and his chocolate bars for the Girl Pool at Christmas." She explained to me that the Girl Pool was the typing bureau in the Laboratory's basement. "The girls belong to anybody with access to a dictaphone."

All year long, she said, the girls of the Girl Pool listened to the faceless voices of scientists on dictaphone records—records brought in by mail girls. Once a year the girls left their cloister of cement block to go a-caroling—to get their chocolate bars from Dr. Asa Breed.

"They serve science, too," Dr. Breed testified, "even though they may not understand a word of it. God bless them, every one!"

18

The Most Valuable Commodity on Earth

When we got into Dr. Breed's inner office, I attempted to put my thoughts in order for a sensible interview. I found that my mental health had not improved. And, when I started to ask Dr. Breed questions about the day of the bomb, I found that the public-relations centers of my brain had been suffocated by booze and burning cat fur. Every question I asked implied that the creators of the atomic bomb had been criminal accessories to murder most foul.

Dr. Breed was astonished, and then he got very sore. He drew back from me and he grumbled, "I gather you don't like scientists very much."

"I wouldn't say that, sir."

"All your questions seem aimed at getting me to admit that scientists are heartless, conscienceless, narrow boobies, indifferent to the fate of the rest of the human race, or maybe not really members of the human race at all."

"That's putting it pretty strong."

"No stronger than what you're going to put in your book, apparently. I thought that what you were after was a fair,

objective biography of Felix Hoenikker—certainly as significant a task as a young writer could assign himself in this day
and age. But no, you come here with preconceived notions
about mad scientists. Where did you ever get such ideas? From
the funny papers?"

"From Dr. Hoenikker's son, to name one source."

"Which son?"

"Newton," I said. I had little Newt's letter with me, and I
showed it to him. "How small is Newt, by the way?"

"No bigger than an umbrella stand," said Dr. Breed, reading
Newt's letter and frowning.

"The other two children are normal?"

"Of course! I hate to disappoint you, but scientists have
children just like anybody else's children."

I did my best to calm down Dr. Breed, to convince him that
I was really interested in an accurate portrait of Dr. Hoenikker.
"I've come here with no other purpose than to set down exactly what you tell me about Dr. Hoenikker. Newt's letter was
just a beginning, and I'll balance off against it whatever you
can tell me."

"I'm sick of people misunderstanding what a scientist is,
what a scientist does."

"I'll do my best to clear up the misunderstanding."

"In this country most people don't even understand what
pure research is."

"I'd appreciate it if you'd tell me what it is."

"It isn't looking for a better cigarette filter or a softer face
tissue or a longer-lasting house paint, God help us. Everybody
talks about research and practically nobody in this country's
doing it. We're one of the few companies that actually hires
men to do pure research. When most other companies brag
about their research, they're talking about industrial hack tech-
nicians who wear white coats, work out of cookbooks, and
dream up an improved windshield wiper for next year's
Oldsmobile."

"But here . . . ?"

"Here, and shockingly few other places in this country, men
are paid to increase knowledge, to work toward no end but
that."

"That's very generous of General Forge and Foundry Company."

"Nothing generous about it. New knowledge is the most valuable commodity on earth. The more truth we have to work with, the richer we become."

Had I been a Bokononist then, that statement would have made me howl.

19

No More Mud

"Do you mean," I said to Dr. Breed, "that nobody in this Laboratory is ever told what to work on? Nobody even *suggests* what they work on?"

"People suggest things all the time, but it isn't in the nature of a pure-research man to pay any attention to suggestions. His head is full of projects of his own, and that's the way we want it."

"Did anybody ever try to suggest projects to Dr. Hoenikker?"

"Certainly. Admirals and generals in particular. They looked upon him as a sort of magician who could make America invincible with a wave of his wand. They brought all kinds of crackpot schemes up here—still do. The only thing wrong with the schemes is that, given our present state of knowledge, the schemes won't work. Scientists on the order of Dr. Hoenikker are supposed to fill the little gaps. I remember, shortly before Felix died, there was a Marine general who was hounding him to do something about mud."

"Mud?"

"The Marines, after almost two-hundred years of wallowing in mud, were sick of it," said Dr. Breed. "The general, as their spokesman, felt that one of the aspects of progress should be that Marines no longer had to fight in mud."

"What did the general have in mind?"

"The absence of mud. No more mud."

"I suppose," I theorized, "it might be possible with mountains of some sort of chemical, or tons of some sort of machinery . . ."

"What the general had in mind was a little pill or a little machine. Not only were the Marines sick of mud, they were sick of carrying cumbersome objects. They wanted something *little* to carry for a change."

"What did Dr. Hoenikker say?"

"In his playful way, and *all* his ways were playful, Felix suggested that there might be a single grain of something—even a microscopic grain—that could make infinite expanses of muck, marsh, swamp, creeks, pools, quicksand, and mire as solid as this desk."

Dr. Breed banged his speckled old fist on the desk. The desk was a kidney-shaped, sea green steel affair. "One Marine could carry more than enough of the stuff to free an armored division bogged down in the Everglades. According to Felix, one Marine could carry enough of the stuff to do that under the nail of his little finger."

"That's impossible."

"You would say so, I would say so—practically everybody would say so. To Felix, in his playful way, it was entirely possible. The miracle of Felix—and I sincerely hope you'll put this in your book somewhere—was that he always approached old puzzles as though they were brand new."

"I feel like Francine Pefko now," I said, "and all the girls in the Girl Pool, too. Dr. Hoenikker could never have explained to me how something that could be carried under a fingernail could make a swamp as solid as your desk."

"I told you what a good explainer Felix was . . ."

"Even so . . ."

"He was able to explain it to me," said Dr. Breed, "and I'm sure I can explain it to you. The puzzle is how to get Marines out of the mud—right?"

"Right."

"All right," said Dr. Breed, "listen carefully. Here we go."

20

"Ice-nine"

"There are several ways," Dr. Breed said to me, "in which certain liquids can crystallize—can freeze—several ways in which their atoms can stack and lock in an orderly, rigid way."

That old man with spotted hands invited me to think of the several ways in which cannonballs might be stacked on a courthouse lawn, of the several ways in which oranges might be packed into a crate.

"So it is with atoms in crystals, too; and two different crystals of the same substance can have quite different physical properties."

He told me about a factory that had been growing big crystals of ethylene diamine tartrate. The crystals were useful in certain manufacturing operations, he said. But one day the factory discovered that the crystals it was growing no longer had the properties desired. The atoms had begun to stack and lock —to freeze—in a different fashion. The liquid that was crystallizing hadn't changed, but the crystals it was forming were, as far as industrial applications went, pure junk.

How this had come about was a mystery. The theoretical villain, however, was what Dr. Breed called "a seed." He meant by that a tiny grain of the undesired crystal pattern. The seed, which had come from God-only-knows-where, taught the atoms the novel way in which to stack and lock, to crystallize, to freeze.

"Now think about cannonballs on a courthouse lawn or about oranges in a crate again," he suggested. And he helped me to see that the pattern of the bottom layer of cannonballs or of oranges determined how each subsequent layer would stack and lock. "The bottom layer is the seed of how every cannonball or every orange that comes after is going to behave, even to an infinite number of cannonballs or oranges.

"Now suppose," chortled Dr. Breed, enjoying himself, "that there were many possible ways in which water could crystallize, could freeze. Suppose that the sort of ice we skate upon and put into highballs—what we might call *ice-one*—is only one of several types of ice. Suppose water always froze as *ice-one* on Earth because it had never had a seed to teach it how to form *ice-two*, *ice-three*, *ice-four* . . . ? And suppose," he rapped on his desk with his old hand again, "that there were one form, which we will call *ice-nine*—a crystal as hard as this desk—with a melting point of, let us say, one-hundred degrees Fahrenheit, or, better still, a melting point of one-hundred-and-thirty degrees."

"All right, I'm still with you," I said.

Dr. Breed was interrupted by whispers in his outer office, whispers loud and portentous. They were the sounds of the Girl Pool.

The girls were preparing to sing in the outer office.

And they did sing, as Dr. Breed and I appeared in the doorway. Each of about a hundred girls had made herself into a choirgirl by putting on a collar of white bond paper, secured by a paper clip. They sang beautifully.

I was surprised and mawkishly heartbroken. I am always moved by that seldom-used treasure, the sweetness with which most girls can sing.

The girls sang "O Little Town of Bethlehem." I am not likely to forget very soon their interpretation of the line:

"The hopes and fears of all the years are here with us tonight."

21

The Marines March On

When old Dr. Breed, with the help of Miss Faust, had passed out the Christmas chocolate bars to the girls, we returned to his office.

There, he said to me, "Where were we? Oh yes!" And that old man asked me to think of United States Marines in a Godforsaken swamp.

"Their trucks and tanks and howitzers are wallowing," he complained, "sinking in stinking miasma and ooze."

He raised a finger and winked at me. "But suppose, young man, that one Marine had with him a tiny capsule containing a seed of *ice-nine*, a new way for the atoms of water to stack and lock, to freeze. If that Marine threw that seed into the nearest puddle . . . ?"

"The puddle would freeze?" I guessed.

"And all the muck around the puddle?"

"It would freeze?"

"And all the puddles in the frozen muck?"

"They would freeze?"

"And the pools and the streams in the frozen muck?"

"They would freeze?"

"You *bet* they would!" he cried. "And the United States Marines would rise from the swamp and march on!"

22

Member of the Yellow Press

"There *is* such stuff?" I asked.

"No, no, no, no," said Dr. Breed, losing patience with me again. "I only told you all this in order to give you some insight into the extraordinary novelty of the ways in which Felix was likely to approach an old problem. What I've just told you is what he told the Marine general who was hounding him about mud.

"Felix ate alone here in the cafeteria every day. It was a rule that no one was to sit with him, to interrupt his chain of thought. But the Marine general barged in, pulled up a chair, and started talking about mud. What I've told you was Felix's offhand reply."

"There—there really *isn't* such a thing?"

"I just told you there wasn't!" cried Dr. Breed hotly. "Felix died shortly after that! And, if you'd been listening to what

I've been trying to tell you about pure research men, you wouldn't ask such a question! Pure research men work on what fascinates them, not on what fascinates other people."

"I keep thinking about that swamp. . . ."

"You can *stop* thinking about it! I've made the only point I wanted to make with the swamp."

"If the streams flowing through the swamp froze as *ice-nine*, what about the rivers and lakes the streams fed?"

"They'd freeze. But there is no such thing as *ice-nine*."

"And the oceans the frozen rivers fed?"

"They'd freeze, of course," he snapped. "I suppose you're going to rush to market with a sensational story about *ice-nine* now. I tell you again, it does not exist!"

"And the springs feeding the frozen lakes and streams, and all the water underground feeding the springs?"

"They'd freeze, damn it!" he cried. "But if I had known that you were a member of the yellow press," he said grandly, rising to his feet, "I wouldn't have wasted a minute with you!"

"And the rain?"

"When it fell, it would freeze into hard little hobnails of *ice-nine*—and that would be the end of the world! And the end of the interview, too! Good-bye!"

23

The Last Batch of Brownies

Dr. Breed was mistaken about at least one thing: there was such a thing as *ice-nine*.

And *ice-nine* was on earth.

Ice-nine was the last gift Felix Hoenikker created for mankind before going to his just reward.

He did it without anyone's realizing what he was doing. He did it without leaving records of what he'd done.

True, elaborate apparatus was necessary in the act of creation, but it already existed in the Research Laboratory. Dr. Hoenikker had only to go calling on Laboratory neighbors—borrowing this and that, making a winsome neighborhood nuisance of himself—until, so to speak, he had baked his last batch of brownies.

He had made a chip of *ice-nine*. It was blue-white. It had a melting point of one-hundred-fourteen-point-four-degrees Fahrenheit.

Felix Hoenikker had put the chip in a little bottle; and he put the bottle in his pocket. And he had gone to his cottage on Cape Cod with his three children, there intending to celebrate Christmas.

Angela had been thirty-four. Frank had been twenty-four. Little Newt had been eighteen.

The old man had died on Christmas Eve, having told only his children about *ice-nine*.

His children had divided the *ice-nine* among themselves.

24

What a "Wampeter" Is

Which brings me to the Bokononist concept of a *wampeter*.

A *wampeter* is the pivot of a *karass*. No *karass* is without a *wampeter*, Bokonon tells us, just as no wheel is without a hub.

Anything can be a *wampeter*: a tree, a rock, an animal, an idea, a book, a melody, the Holy Grail. Whatever it is, the members of its *karass* revolve about it in the majestic chaos of a spiral nebula. The orbits of the members of a *karass* about their common *wampeter* are spiritual orbits, naturally. It is souls and not bodies that revolve. As Bokonon invites us to sing:

> Around and around and around we spin,
> With feet of lead and wings of tin . . .

And *wampeters* come and *wampeters* go, Bokonon tells us.

At any given time a *karass* actually has two *wampeters*—one waxing in importance, one waning.

And I am almost certain that while I was talking to Dr. Breed in Ilium, the *wampeter* of my *karass* that was just coming into bloom was that crystalline form of water, that blue-white gem, that seed of doom called *ice-nine*.

While I was talking to Dr. Breed in Ilium, Angela, Franklin, and Newton Hoenikker had in their possession seeds of *ice-nine*, seeds grown from their father's seed—chips, in a manner of speaking, off the old block.

What was to become of those three chips was, I am convinced, a principal concern of my *karass*.

25

The Main Thing About Dr. Hoenikker

So much, for now, for the *wampeter* of my *karass*.

After my unpleasant interview with Dr. Breed in the Research Laboratory of the General Forge and Foundry Company, I was put into the hands of Miss Faust. Her orders were to show me the door. I prevailed upon her, however, to show me the laboratory of the late Dr. Hoenikker first.

En route, I asked her how well she had known Dr. Hoenikker. She gave me a frank and interesting reply, and a piquant smile to go with it.

"I don't think he was knowable. I mean, when most people talk about knowing somebody a lot or a little, they're talking about secrets they've been told or haven't been told. They're talking about intimate things, family things, love things," that nice old lady said to me. "Dr. Hoenikker had all those things in his life, the way every living person has to, but they weren't the main things with him."

"What *were* the main things?" I asked her.

"Dr. Breed keeps telling me the main thing with Dr. Hoenikker was truth."

"You don't seem to agree."

"I don't know whether I agree or not. I just have trouble understanding how truth, all by itself, could be enough for a person."

Miss Faust was ripe for Bokononism.

26

What God Is

"Did you ever talk to Dr. Hoenikker?" I asked Miss Faust.

"Oh, certainly. I talked to him a lot."

"Do any conversations stick in your mind?"

"There was one where he bet I couldn't tell him anything that was absolutely true. So I said to him, 'God is love.'"

"And what did he say?"

"He said, 'What is God? What is love?'"

"Um."

"But God really *is* love, you know," said Miss Faust, "no matter what Dr. Hoenikker said."

27

Men from Mars

The room that had been the laboratory of Dr. Felix Hoenikker was on the sixth floor, the top floor of the building.

A purple cord had been stretched across the doorway, and a brass plate on the wall explained why the room was sacred:

IN THIS ROOM, DR. FELIX HOENIKKER,
NOBEL LAUREATE IN PHYSICS, SPENT THE LAST
TWENTY-EIGHT YEARS OF HIS LIFE. "WHERE HE
WAS, THERE WAS THE FRONTIER OF KNOWLEDGE."
THE IMPORTANCE OF THIS ONE MAN IN THE
HISTORY OF MANKIND IS INCALCULABLE.

Miss Faust offered to unshackle the purple cord for me so that I might go inside and traffic more intimately with whatever ghosts there were.

I accepted.

"It's just as he left it," she said, "except that there were rubber bands all over one counter."

"Rubber bands?"

"Don't ask me what for. Don't ask me what any of all this is for."

The old man had left the laboratory a mess. What engaged my attention at once was the quantity of cheap toys lying around. There was a paper kite with a broken spine. There was a toy gyroscope, wound with string, ready to whirr and balance itself. There was a top. There was a bubble pipe. There was a fish bowl with a castle and two turtles in it.

"He loved ten-cent stores," said Miss Faust.

"I can see he did."

"Some of his most famous experiments were performed with equipment that cost less than a dollar."

"A penny saved is a penny earned."

There were numerous pieces of conventional laboratory equipment, too, of course, but they seemed drab accessories to the cheap, gay toys.

Dr. Hoenikker's desk was piled with correspondence.

"I don't think he ever answered a letter," mused Miss Faust. "People had to get him on the telephone or come to see him if they wanted an answer."

There was a framed photograph on his desk. Its back was toward me and I ventured a guess as to whose picture it was. "His wife?"

"No."

"One of his children?"

"No."

"Himself?"

"No."

So I took a look. I found that the picture was of an humble little war memorial in front of a small-town courthouse. Part of the memorial was a sign that gave the names of those villagers who had died in various wars, and I thought that the sign must be the reason for the photograph. I could read the names, and I half expected to find the name Hoenikker among them. It wasn't there.

"That was one of his hobbies," said Miss Faust.

"What was?"

"Photographing how cannonballs are stacked on different courthouse lawns. Apparently how they've got them stacked in that picture is very unusual."

"I see."

"He was an unusual man."

"I agree."

"Maybe in a million years everybody will be as smart as he was and see things the way he did. But, compared with the average person of today, he was as different as a man from Mars."

"Maybe he really *was* a Martian," I suggested.

"That would certainly go a long way toward explaining his three strange kids."

28

Mayonnaise

While Miss Faust and I waited for an elevator to take us to the first floor, Miss Faust said she hoped the elevator that came would not be number five. Before I could ask her why this was a reasonable wish, number five arrived.

Its operator was a small and ancient Negro whose name was

Lyman Enders Knowles. Knowles was insane, I'm almost sure —offensively so, in that he grabbed his own behind and cried, "Yes, yes!" whenever he felt that he'd made a point.

"Hello, fellow anthropoids and lily pads and paddlewheels," he said to Miss Faust and me. "Yes, yes!"

"First floor, please," said Miss Faust coldly.

All Knowles had to do to close the door and get us to the first floor was to press a button, but he wasn't going to do that yet. He wasn't going to do it, maybe, for years.

"Man told me," he said, "that these here elevators was Mayan architecture. I never knew that till today. And I says to him, 'What's that make me—mayonnaise?' Yes, yes! And while he was thinking that over, I hit him with a question that straightened him up and made him think twice as hard! Yes, yes!"

"Could we please go down, Mr. Knowles?" begged Miss Faust.

"I said to him," said Knowles, "'This here's a *re*-search laboratory. *Re*-search means *look again*, don't it? Means they're looking for something they found once and it got away somehow, and now they got to *re*-search for it? How come they got to build a building like this, with mayonnaise elevators and all, and fill it with all these crazy people? What is it they're trying to find again? Who lost what?' Yes, yes!"

"That's very interesting," sighed Miss Faust. "Now, could we go down?"

"Only way we *can* go is down," barked Knowles. "This here's the top. You ask me to go up and wouldn't be a thing I could do for you. Yes, yes!"

"So let's go down," said Miss Faust.

"Very soon now. This gentleman here been paying his respects to Dr. Hoenikker?"

"Yes," I said. "Did you know him?"

"*Intimately*," he said. "You know what I said when he died?"

"No."

"I said, 'Dr. Hoenikker—he ain't dead.'"

"Oh?"

"Just entered a new dimension. Yes, yes!"

He punched a button, and down we went.

"Did you know the Hoenikker children?" I asked him.

"Babies full of rabies," he said. "Yes, yes!"

29

Gone, but Not Forgotten

There was one more thing I wanted to do in Ilium. I wanted to get a photograph of the old man's tomb. So I went back to my room, found Sandra gone, picked up my camera, hired a cab.

Sleet was still coming down, acid and gray. I thought the old man's tombstone in all that sleet might photograph pretty well, might even make a good picture for the jacket of *The Day the World Ended*.

The custodian at the cemetery gate told me how to find the Hoenikker burial plot. "Can't miss it," he said. "It's got the biggest marker in the place."

He did not lie. The marker was an alabaster phallus twenty feet high and three feet thick. It was plastered with sleet.

"By God," I exclaimed, getting out of the cab with my camera, "how's that for a suitable memorial to a father of the atom bomb?" I laughed.

I asked the driver if he'd mind standing by the monument in order to give some idea of scale. And then I asked him to wipe away some of the sleet so the name of the deceased would show.

He did so.

And there on the shaft in letters six inches high, so help me God, was the word:

MOTHER

30

Only Sleeping

"Mother?" asked the driver, incredulously.
I wiped away more sleet and uncovered this poem:

> Mother, Mother, how I pray
> For you to guard us every day.
> —ANGELA HOENIKKER

And under this poem was yet another:

> You are not dead,
> But only sleeping.
> We should smile,
> And stop our weeping.
> —FRANKLIN HOENIKKER

And underneath this, inset in the shaft, was a square of cement bearing the imprint of an infant's hand. Beneath the imprint were the words:

> Baby Newt.

"If that's Mother," said the driver, "what in hell could they have raised over Father?" He made an obscene suggestion as to what the appropriate marker might be.

We found Father close by. His memorial—as specified in his will, I later discovered—was a marble cube forty centimeters on each side.

"FATHER," it said.

31

Another Breed

As we were leaving the cemetery the driver of the cab worried about the condition of his own mother's grave. He asked if I would mind taking a short detour to look at it.

It was a pathetic little stone that marked his mother—not that it mattered.

And the driver asked me if I would mind another brief detour, this time to a tombstone salesroom across the street from the cemetery.

I wasn't a Bokononist then, so I agreed with some peevishness. As a Bokononist, of course, I would have agreed gaily to go anywhere anyone suggested. As Bokonon says: "Peculiar travel suggestions are dancing lessons from God."

The name of the tombstone establishment was Avram Breed and Sons. As the driver talked to the salesman I wandered among the monuments—blank monuments, monuments in memory of nothing so far.

I found a little institutional joke in the showroom: over a stone angel hung mistletoe. Cedar boughs were heaped on her pedestal, and around her marble throat was a necklace of Christmas tree lamps.

"How much for her?" I asked the salesman.

"Not for sale. She's a hundred years old. My great-grandfather, Avram Breed, carved her."

"This business is that old?"

"That's right."

"And you're a Breed?"

"The fourth generation in this location."

"Any relation to Dr. Asa Breed, the director of the Research Laboratory?"

"His brother." He said his name was Marvin Breed.

"It's a small world," I observed.

"When you put it in a cemetery, it is." Marvin Breed was a sleek and vulgar, a smart and sentimental man.

32

Dynamite Money

"I just came from your brother's office. I'm a writer. I was interviewing him about Dr. Hoenikker," I said to Marvin Breed.

"There was one queer son of a bitch. Not my brother; I mean Hoenikker."

"Did you sell him that monument for his wife?"

"I sold his kids that. He didn't have anything to do with it. He never got around to putting any kind of marker on her grave. And then, after she'd been dead for a year or more, Hoenikker's three kids came in here—the big tall girl, the boy, and the little baby. They wanted the biggest stone money could buy, and the two older ones had poems they'd written. They wanted the poems on the stone."

"You can laugh at that stone, if you want to," said Marvin Breed, "but those kids got more consolation out of that than anything else money could have bought. They used to come and look at it and put flowers on it I-don't-know-how-many-times a year."

"It must have cost a lot."

"Nobel Prize money bought it. Two things that money bought: a cottage on Cape Cod and that monument."

"Dynamite money," I marveled, thinking of the violence of dynamite and the absolute repose of a tombstone and a summer home.

"What?"

"Nobel invented dynamite."

"Well, I guess it takes all kinds . . ."

Had I been a Bokononist then, pondering the miraculously intricate chain of events that had brought dynamite money to that particular tombstone company, I might have whispered, "Busy, busy, busy."

Busy, busy, busy, is what we Bokononists whisper whenever we think of how complicated and unpredictable the machinery of life really is.

But all I could say as a Christian then was, "Life is sure funny sometimes."

"And sometimes it isn't," said Marvin Breed.

33

An Ungrateful Man

I asked Marvin Breed if he'd known Emily Hoenikker, the wife of Felix; the mother of Angela, Frank, and Newt; the woman under that monstrous shaft.

"Know her?" His voice turned tragic. "Did I *know* her, mister? Sure, I knew her. I knew Emily. We went to Ilium High together. We were co-chairmen of the Class Colors Committee then. Her father owned the Ilium Music Store. She could play every musical instrument there was. I fell so hard for her I gave up football and tried to play the violin. And then my big brother Asa came home for spring vacation from M.I.T., and I made the mistake of introducing him to my best girl." Marvin Breed snapped his fingers. "He took her away from me just like that. I smashed up my seventy-five-dollar violin on a big brass knob at the foot of my bed, and I went down to a florist shop and got the kind of box they put a dozen roses in, and I put the busted fiddle in the box, and I sent it to her by Western Union messenger boy."

"Pretty, was she?"

"Pretty?" he echoed. "Mister, when I see my first lady angel, if God ever sees fit to show me one, it'll be her wings and not her face that'll make my mouth fall open. I've already seen the prettiest face that ever could be. There wasn't a man in Ilium County who wasn't in love with her, secretly or otherwise. She could have had any man she wanted." He spit on his own floor. "And she had to go and marry that little Dutch son of a bitch! She was engaged to my brother, and then that sneaky little bastard hit town." Marvin Breed snapped his fingers again. "He took her away from my big brother like that.

"I suppose it's high treason and ungrateful and ignorant and backward and anti-intellectual to call a dead man as famous as Felix Hoenikker a son of a bitch. I know all about how harmless and gentle and dreamy he was supposed to be, how he'd never hurt a fly, how he didn't care about money and power and fancy clothes and automobiles and things, how he wasn't like the rest of us, how he was better than the rest of us, how he was so innocent he was practically a Jesus—except for the Son of God part . . ."

Marvin Breed felt it was unnecessary to complete his thought. I had to ask him to do it.

"But what?" he said, "But what?" He went to a window looking out at the cemetery gate. "But what," he murmured at the gate and the sleet and the Hoenikker shaft that could be dimly seen.

"But," he said, "but how the hell innocent is a man who helps make a thing like an atomic bomb? And how can you say a man had a good mind when he couldn't even bother to do anything when the best-hearted, most beautiful woman in the world, his own wife, was dying for lack of love and understanding . . ."

He shuddered, "Sometimes I wonder if he wasn't born dead. I never met a man who was less interested in the living. Sometimes I think that's the trouble with the world: too many people in high places who are stone-cold dead."

34

"Vin-dit"

It was in the tombstone salesroom that I had my first *vin-dit*, a Bokononist word meaning a sudden, very personal shove in the direction of Bokononism, in the direction of believing that God Almighty knew all about me, after all, that God Almighty had some pretty elaborate plans for me.

The *vin-dit* had to do with the stone angel under the mistletoe. The cab driver had gotten it into his head that he had to have that angel for his mother's grave at any price. He was standing in front of it with tears in his eyes.

Marvin Breed was still staring out the window at the cemetery gate, having just said his piece about Felix Hoenikker. "The little Dutch son of a bitch may have been a modern holy man," he added, "but Goddamn if he ever did anything he didn't want to, and Goddamn if he didn't get everything he ever wanted.

"Music," he said.

"Pardon me?" I asked.

"That's why she married him. She said his mind was tuned to the biggest music there was, the music of the stars." He shook his head. "Crap."

And then the gate reminded him of the last time he'd seen Frank Hoenikker, the model-maker, the tormentor of bugs in jars. "Frank," he said.

"What about him?"

"The last I saw of that poor, queer kid was when he came out through that cemetery gate. His father's funeral was still going on. The old man wasn't underground yet, and out through that gate came Frank. He raised his thumb at the first car that came by. It was a new Pontiac with a Florida license plate. It stopped. Frank got in it, and that was the last anybody in Ilium ever saw of him."

"I hear he's wanted by the police."

"That was an accident, a freak. Frank wasn't any criminal. He didn't have that kind of nerve. The only work he was any good at was model-making. The only job he ever held on to was at Jack's Hobby Shop, selling models, making models, giving people advice on how to make models. When he cleared out of here, went to Florida, he got a job in a model shop in Sarasota. Turned out the model shop was a front for a ring that stole Cadillacs, ran 'em straight on board old L.S.T.'s and shipped 'em to Cuba. That's how Frank got balled up in all that. I expect the reason the cops haven't found him is he's dead. He just heard too much while he was sticking turrets on the battleship *Missouri* with Duco Cement."

"Where's Newt now, do you know?"

"Guess he's with his sister in Indianapolis. Last I heard was he got mixed up with that Russian midget and flunked out of pre-med at Cornell. Can you imagine a midget trying to become a doctor? And, in that same miserable family, there's that great big, gawky girl, over six feet tall. That man, who's so famous for having a great mind, he pulled that girl out of high school in her sophomore year so he could go on having some woman take care of him. All she had going for her was the clarinet she'd played in the Ilium High School band, the Marching Hundred.

"After she left school," said Breed, "nobody ever asked her out. She didn't have any friends, and the old man never even thought to give her any money to go anywhere. You know what she used to do?"

"Nope."

"Every so often at night she'd lock herself in her room and she'd play records, and she'd play along with the records on her clarinet. The miracle of this age, as far as I'm concerned, is that that woman ever got herself a husband."

"How much do you want for this angel?" asked the cab driver.

"I've told you, it's not for sale."

"I don't suppose there's anybody around who can do that kind of stone cutting any more," I observed.

"I've got a nephew who can," said Breed. "Asa's boy. He was all set to be a heap-big *re*-search scientist, and then they dropped the bomb on Hiroshima and the kid quit, and he got drunk, and he came out here, and he told me he wanted to go to work cutting stone."

"He works here now?"

"He's a sculptor in Rome."

"If somebody offered you enough," said the driver, "you'd take it, wouldn't you?"

"Might. But it would take a lot of money."

"Where would you put the name on a thing like that?" asked the driver.

"There's already a name on it—on the pedestal." We couldn't see the name, because of the boughs banked against the pedestal.

"It was never called for?" I wanted to know.

"It was never *paid* for. The way the story goes: this German immigrant was on his way West with his wife, and she died of smallpox here in Ilium. So he ordered this angel to be put up over her, and he showed my great-grandfather he had the cash to pay for it. But then he was robbed. Somebody took practically every cent he had. All he had left in this world was some land he'd bought in Indiana, land he'd never seen. So he moved on—said he'd be back later to pay for the angel."

"But he never came back?" I asked.

"Nope." Marvin Breed nudged some of the boughs aside with his toe so that we could see the raised letters on the pedestal. There was a last name written there. "There's a screwy name for you," he said. "If that immigrant had any descendants, I expect they Americanized the name. They're probably Jones or Black or Thompson now."

"There you're wrong," I murmured.

The room seemed to tip, and its walls and ceiling and floor were transformed momentarily into the mouths of many tunnels—tunnels leading in all directions through time. I had a Bokononist vision of the unity in every second of all time and all wandering mankind, all wandering womankind, all wandering children.

"There you're wrong," I said, when the vision was gone.

"You know some people by that name?"

"Yes."

The name was my last name, too.

35

Hobby Shop

On the way back to the hotel I caught sight of Jack's Hobby Shop, the place where Franklin Hoenikker had worked. I told the cab driver to stop and wait.

I went in and found Jack himself presiding over his teeny-weeny fire engines, railroad trains, airplanes, boats, houses, lamp-posts, trees, tanks, rockets, automobiles, porters, conductors, policemen, firemen, mommies, daddies, cats, dogs, chickens, soldiers, ducks, and cows. He was a cadaverous man, a serious man, a dirty man, and he coughed a lot.

"What kind of a boy was Franklin Hoenikker?" he echoed, and he coughed and coughed. He shook his head, and he showed me that he adored Frank as much as he'd ever adored anybody. "That isn't a question I have to answer with words. I can *show* you what kind of a boy Franklin Hoenikker was." He coughed. "You can look," he said, "and you can judge for yourself."

And he took me down into the basement of his store. He lived down there. There was a double bed and a dresser and a hot plate.

Jack apologized for the unmade bed. "My wife left me a week ago." He coughed. "I'm still trying to pull the strings of my life back together."

And then he turned on a switch, and the far end of the basement was filled with a blinding light.

We approached the light and found that it was sunshine to a fantastic little country built on plywood, an island as perfectly rectangular as a township in Kansas. Any restless soul, any soul seeking to find what lay beyond its green boundaries, really would fall off the edge of the world.

The details were so exquisitely in scale, so cunningly textured and tinted, that it was unnecessary for me to squint in order to believe that the nation was real—the hills, the lakes, the rivers, the forests, the towns, and all else that good natives everywhere hold so dear.

And everywhere ran a spaghetti pattern of railroad tracks.

"Look at the doors of the houses," said Jack reverently.

"Neat. Keen."

"They've got real knobs on 'em, and the knockers really work."

"God."

"You ask what kind of a boy Franklin Hoenikker was; he built this." Jack choked up.

"All by himself?"

"Oh, I helped some, but anything I did was according to his plans. That kid was a genius."

"How could anybody argue with you?"

"His kid brother was a midget, you know."

"I know."

"He did some of the soldering underneath."

"It sure looks real."

"It wasn't easy, and it wasn't done overnight, either."

"Rome wasn't built in a day."

"That kid didn't have any home life, you know."

"I've heard."

"This was his real home. Thousands of hours he spent down here. Sometimes he wouldn't even run the trains; just sit and look, the way we're doing."

"There's a lot to see. It's practically like a trip to Europe, there are so many things to see, if you look close."

"He'd see things you and I wouldn't see. He'd all of a sudden tear down a hill that would look just as real as any hill you ever saw—to you and me. And he'd be right, too. He'd put a lake where that hill had been and a trestle over the lake, and it would look ten times as good as it did before."

"It isn't a talent everybody has."

"That's right!" said Jack passionately. The passion cost him another coughing fit. When the fit was over, his eyes were watering copiously. "Listen, I told that kid he should go to college and study some engineering so he could go to work for American Flyer or somebody like that—somebody big, somebody who'd really back all the ideas he had."

"Looks to me as if you backed him a good deal."

"Wish I had, wish I could have," mourned Jack. "I didn't have the capital. I gave him stuff whenever I could, but most of this stuff he bought out of what he earned working upstairs for me. He didn't spend a dime on anything but this—didn't drink, didn't smoke, didn't go to movies, didn't go out with girls, wasn't car crazy."

"This country could certainly use a few more of those."

Jack shrugged. "Well . . . I guess the Florida gangsters got him. Afraid he'd talk."

"Guess they did."

Jack suddenly broke down and cried. "I wonder if those dirty sons of bitches," he sobbed, "have any idea what it was they killed!"

36

Meow

During my trip to Ilium and to points beyond—a two-week expedition bridging Christmas—I let a poor poet named Sherman Krebbs have my New York City apartment free. My second wife had left me on the grounds that I was too pessimistic for an optimist to live with.

Krebbs was a bearded man, a platinum blond Jesus with spaniel eyes. He was no close friend of mine. I had met him at a cocktail party where he presented himself as National Chairman of Poets and Painters for Immediate Nuclear War. He begged for shelter, not necessarily bomb proof, and it happened that I had some.

When I returned to my apartment, still twanging with the puzzling spiritual implications of the unclaimed stone angel in Ilium, I found my apartment wrecked by a nihilistic debauch. Krebbs was gone; but, before leaving, he had run up three-hundred-dollars' worth of long-distance calls, set my couch on fire in five places, killed my cat and my avocado tree, and torn the door off my medicine cabinet.

He wrote this poem, in what proved to be excrement, on the yellow linoleum floor of my kitchen:

> I have a kitchen.
> But it is not a complete kitchen.
> I will not be truly gay
> Until I have a
> Dispose-all.

There was another message, written in lipstick in a feminine hand on the wallpaper over my bed. It said: "No, no, no, said Chicken-licken."

There was a sign hung around my dead cat's neck. It said, "Meow."

I have not seen Krebbs since. Nonetheless, I sense that he was in my *karass*. If he was, he served it as a *wrang-wrang*. A *wrang-wrang*, according to Bokonon, is a person who steers people away from a line of speculation by reducing that line, with the example of the *wrang-wrang*'s own life, to an absurdity.

I might have been vaguely inclined to dismiss the stone angel as meaningless, and to go from there to the meaninglessness of all. But after I saw what Krebbs had done, in particular what he had done to my sweet cat, nihilism was not for me.

Somebody or something did not wish me to be a nihilist. It was Krebbs's mission, whether he knew it or not, to disenchant me with that philosophy. Well done, Mr. Krebbs, well done.

37

A Modern Major General

And then, one day, one Sunday, I found out where the fugitive from justice, the model-maker, the Great God Jehovah and Beelzebub of bugs in Mason jars was—where Franklin Hoenikker could be found.

He was alive!

The news was in a special supplement to the New York *Sunday Times*. The supplement was a paid ad for a banana republic. On its cover was the profile of the most heartbreakingly beautiful girl I ever hope to see.

Beyond the girl, bulldozers were knocking down palm trees, making a broad avenue. At the end of the avenue were the steel skeletons of three new buildings.

"The Republic of San Lorenzo," said the copy on the cover, "on the move! A healthy, happy, progressive, freedom-loving, beautiful nation makes itself extremely attractive to American investors and tourists alike."

I was in no hurry to read the contents. The girl on the cover was enough for me—more than enough, since I had fallen in love with her on sight. She was very young and very grave, too —and luminously compassionate and wise.

She was as brown as chocolate. Her hair was like golden flax.

Her name was Mona Aamons Monzano, the cover said. She was the adopted daughter of the dictator of the island.

I opened the supplement, hoping for more pictures of this sublime mongrel Madonna.

I found instead a portrait of the island's dictator, Miguel "Papa" Monzano, a gorilla in his late seventies.

Next to "Papa's" portrait was a picture of a narrow-shouldered, fox-faced, immature young man. He wore a snow white military blouse with some sort of jeweled sunburst hanging on it. His eyes were close together; they had circles under them. He had apparently told barbers all his life to shave the sides and back of his head, but to leave the top of his hair alone. He had a wiry pompadour, a sort of cube of hair, marcelled, that arose to an incredible height.

This unattractive child was identified as Major General Franklin Hoenikker, *Minister of Science and Progress in the Republic of San Lorenzo.*

He was twenty-six years old.

38

Barracuda Capital of the World

San Lorenzo was fifty miles long and twenty miles wide, I learned from the supplement to the New York *Sunday Times.* Its population was four hundred fifty thousand souls, ". . . all fiercely dedicated to the ideals of the Free World."

Its highest point, Mount McCabe, was eleven thousand feet above sea level. Its capital was Bolivar, ". . . a strikingly modern city built on a harbor capable of sheltering the entire United States Navy." The principal exports were sugar, coffee, bananas, indigo, and handcrafted novelties.

"And sports fishermen recognize San Lorenzo as the unchallenged barracuda capital of the world."

I wondered how Franklin Hoenikker, who had never even finished high school, had got himself such a fancy job. I found a partial answer in an essay on San Lorenzo that was signed by "Papa" Monzano.

"Papa" said that Frank was the architect of the "San Lorenzo Master Plan," which included new roads, rural electrification, sewage-disposal plants, hotels, hospitals, clinics, railroads—the works. And, though the essay was brief and tightly edited, "Papa" referred to Frank five times as: ". . . the *blood son* of Dr. Felix Hoenikker."

The phrase reeked of cannibalism.

"Papa" plainly felt that Frank was a chunk of the old man's magic meat.

39

Fata Morgana

A little more light was shed by another essay in the supplement, a florid essay titled, "What San Lorenzo Has Meant to One American." It was almost certainly ghost-written. It was signed by Major General Franklin Hoenikker.

In the essay, Frank told of being all alone on a nearly swamped sixty-eight-foot Chris-Craft in the Caribbean. He didn't explain what he was doing on it or how he happened to be alone. He did indicate, though, that his point of departure had been Cuba.

"The luxurious pleasure craft was going down, and my meaningless life with it," said the essay. "All I'd eaten for four days was two biscuits and a sea gull. The dorsal fins of man-eating sharks were cleaving the warm seas around me, and needle-teethed barracuda were making those waters boil.

"I raised my eyes to my Maker, willing to accept whatever His decision might be. And my eyes alit on a glorious mountain peak above the clouds. Was this Fata Morgana—the cruel deception of a mirage?"

I looked up Fata Morgana at this point in my reading; learned that it was, in fact, a mirage named after Morgan le Fay, a fairy who lived at the bottom of a lake. It was famous for appearing in the Strait of Messina, between Calabria and Sicily. Fata Morgana was poetic crap, in short.

What Frank saw from his sinking pleasure craft was not cruel Fata Morgana, but the peak of Mount McCabe. Gentle seas then nuzzled Frank's pleasure craft to the rocky shores of San Lorenzo, as though God wanted him to go there.

Frank stepped ashore, dry shod, and asked where he was. The essay didn't say so, but the son of a bitch had a piece of *ice-nine* with him—in a thermos jug.

Frank, having no passport, was put in jail in the capital city of Bolivar. He was visited there by "Papa" Monzano, who wanted to know if it were possible that Frank was a blood relative of the immortal Dr. Felix Hoenikker.

"I admitted I was," said Frank in the essay. "Since that moment, every door to opportunity in San Lorenzo has been opened wide to me."

40

House of Hope and Mercy

As it happened—"As it was *supposed* to happen," Bokonon would say—I was assigned by a magazine to do a story in San Lorenzo. The story wasn't to be about "Papa" Monzano or Frank. It was to be about Julian Castle, an American sugar millionaire who had, at the age of forty, followed the example of Dr. Albert Schweitzer by founding a free hospital in a jungle, by devoting his life to miserable folk of another race.

Castle's hospital was called the House of Hope and Mercy in the Jungle. Its jungle was on San Lorenzo, among the wild coffee trees on the northern slope of Mount McCabe.

When I flew to San Lorenzo, Julian Castle was sixty years old.

He had been absolutely unselfish for twenty years.

In his selfish days he had been as familiar to tabloid readers as Tommy Manville, Adolf Hitler, Benito Mussolini, and Barbara Hutton. His fame had rested on lechery, alcoholism, reckless driving, and draft evasion. He had had a dazzling talent for spending millions without increasing mankind's stores of anything but chagrin.

He had been married five times, had produced one son.

The one son, Philip Castle, was the manager and owner of the hotel at which I planned to stay. The hotel was called the Casa Mona and was named after Mona Aamons Monzano, the blonde Negro on the cover of the supplement to the New York *Sunday Times*. The Casa Mona was brand new; it was one of the three new buildings in the background of the supplement's portrait of Mona.

While I didn't feel that purposeful seas were wafting me to San Lorenzo, I did feel that love was doing the job. The Fata Morgana, the mirage of what it would be like to be loved by Mona Aamons Monzano, had become a tremendous force in my meaningless life. I imagined that she could make me far happier than any woman had so far succeeded in doing.

41

A "Karass" Built for Two

The seating on the airplane, bound ultimately for San Lorenzo from Miami, was three and three. As it happened—"As it was *supposed* to happen"—my seatmates were Horlick Minton, the new American Ambassador to the Republic of San Lorenzo, and his wife, Claire. They were white-haired, gentle, and frail.

Minton told me that he was a career diplomat, holding the rank of Ambassador for the first time. He and his wife had so far served, he told me, in Bolivia, Chile, Japan, France, Yugoslavia, Egypt, the Union of South Africa, Liberia, and Pakistan.

They were lovebirds. They entertained each other endlessly with little gifts: sights worth seeing out the plane window, amusing or instructive bits from things they read, random recollections of times gone by. They were, I think, a flawless example of what Bokonon calls a *duprass*, which is a *karass* composed of only two persons.

"A true *duprass*," Bokonon tells us, "can't be invaded, not even by children born of such a union."

I exclude the Mintons, therefore, from my own *karass*, from Frank's *karass*, from Newt's *karass*, from Asa Breed's *karass*, from Angela's *karass*, from Lyman Enders Knowles's *karass*, from Sherman Krebbs's *karass*. The Mintons' *karass* was a tidy one, composed of only two.

"I should think you'd be very pleased," I said to Minton.

"What should I be pleased about?"

"Pleased to have the rank of Ambassador."

From the pitying way Minton and his wife looked at each other, I gathered that I had said a fat-headed thing. But they humored me. "Yes," winced Minton, "I'm very pleased." He smiled wanly. "I'm *deeply* honored."

And so it went with almost every subject I brought up. I couldn't make the Mintons bubble about anything.

For instance: "I suppose you can speak a lot of languages," I said.

"Oh, six or seven—between us," said Minton.

"That must be very gratifying."

"What must?"

"Being able to speak to people of so many different nationalities."

"Very gratifying," said Minton emptily.

"Very gratifying," said his wife.

And they went back to reading a fat, typewritten manuscript that was spread across the chair arm between them.

"Tell me," I said a little later, "in all your wide travels, have you found people everywhere about the same at heart?"

"Hm?" asked Minton.

"Do you find people to be about the same at heart, wherever you go?"

He looked at his wife, making sure she had heard the question, then turned back to me. "About the same, wherever you go," he agreed.

"Um," I said.

Bokonon tells us, incidentally, that members of a *duprass* always die within a week of each other. When it came time for the Mintons to die, they did it within the same second.

42
Bicycles for Afghanistan

There was a small saloon in the rear of the plane and I repaired there for a drink. It was there that I met another fellow American, H. Lowe Crosby of Evanston, Illinois, and his wife, Hazel.

They were heavy people, in their fifties. They spoke twangingly. Crosby told me that he owned a bicycle factory in Chicago, that he had had nothing but ingratitude from his employees. He was going to move his business to grateful San Lorenzo.

"You know San Lorenzo well?" I asked.

"This'll be the first time I've ever seen it, but everything I've heard about it I like," said H. Lowe Crosby. "They've got discipline. They've got something you can count on from one year to the next. They don't have the government encouraging everybody to be some kind of original pissant nobody ever heard of before."

"Sir?"

"Christ, back in Chicago, we don't make bicycles any more. It's all human relations now. The eggheads sit around trying to figure out new ways for everybody to be happy. Nobody can get fired, no matter what; and if somebody does accidentally make a bicycle, the union accuses us of cruel and inhuman practices and the government confiscates the bicycle for back taxes and gives it to a blind man in Afghanistan."

"And you think things will be better in San Lorenzo?"

"I know damn well they will be. The people down there are poor enough and scared enough and ignorant enough to have some common sense!"

Crosby asked me what my name was and what my business was. I told him, and his wife Hazel recognized my name as an Indiana name. She was from Indiana, too.

"My God," she said, "are you a *Hoosier?*"

I admitted I was.

"I'm a Hoosier, too," she crowed. "Nobody has to be ashamed of being a Hoosier."

"I'm not," I said. "I never knew anybody who was."

"Hoosiers do all right. Lowe and I've been around the world twice, and everywhere we went we found Hoosiers in charge of everything."

"That's reassuring."

"You know the manager of that new hotel in Istanbul?"

"No."

"He's a Hoosier. And the military-whatever-he-is in Tokyo . . ."

"Attaché," said her husband.

"He's a Hoosier," said Hazel. "And the new Ambassador to Yugoslavia . . ."

"A Hoosier?" I asked.

"Not only him, but the Hollywood Editor of *Life* magazine, too. And that man in Chile . . ."

"A Hoosier, too?"

"You can't go anywhere a *Hoosier* hasn't made his mark," she said.

"The man who wrote *Ben Hur* was a Hoosier."

"And James Whitcomb Riley."

"Are you from Indiana, too?" I asked her husband.

"Nope. I'm a Prairie Stater. 'Land of Lincoln,' as they say."

"As far as that goes," said Hazel triumphantly, "Lincoln was a Hoosier, too. He grew up in Spencer County."

"Sure," I said.

"I don't know what it is about Hoosiers," said Hazel, "but they've sure got something. If somebody was to make a list, they'd be amazed."

"That's true," I said.

She grasped me firmly by the arm. "We Hoosiers got to stick together."

"Right."

"You call me 'Mom.'"

"What?"

"Whenever I meet a young Hoosier, I tell them, 'You call me *Mom*.'"

"Uh huh."

"Let me hear you say it," she urged.

"Mom?"

She smiled and let go of my arm. Some piece of clockwork had completed its cycle. My calling Hazel "Mom" had shut it off, and now Hazel was rewinding it for the next Hoosier to come along.

Hazel's obsession with Hoosiers around the world was a textbook example of a false *karass*, of a seeming team that was meaningless in terms of the ways God gets things done, a textbook example of what Bokonon calls a *granfalloon*. Other examples of *granfalloons* are the Communist party, the Daughters of the American Revolution, the General Electric Company, the International Order of Odd Fellows—and any nation, anytime, anywhere.

As Bokonon invites us to sing along with him:

> If you wish to study a *granfalloon*,
> Just remove the skin of a toy balloon.

43

The Demonstrator

H. Lowe Crosby was of the opinion that dictatorships were often very good things. He wasn't a terrible person and he wasn't a fool. It suited him to confront the world with a certain barn-yard clownishness, but many of the things he had to say about undisciplined mankind were not only funny but true.

The major point at which his reason and his sense of humor left him was when he approached the question of what people were really supposed to do with their time on Earth.

He believed firmly that they were meant to build bicycles for him.

"I hope San Lorenzo is every bit as good as you've heard it is," I said.

"I only have to talk to one man to find out if it is or not," he said. "When 'Papa' Monzano gives his word of honor about anything on that little island, that's it. That's how it is; that's how it'll be."

"The thing I like," said Hazel, "is they all speak English and they're all Christians. That makes things so much easier."

"You know how they deal with crime down there?" Crosby asked me.

"Nope."

"They just don't have any crime down there. 'Papa' Monzano's made crime so damn unattractive, nobody even thinks about it without getting sick. I heard you can lay a billfold in the middle of a sidewalk and you can come back a week later and it'll be right there, with everything still in it."

"Um."

"You know what the punishment is for stealing something?"

"Nope."

"The hook," he said. "No fines, no probation, no thirty days in jail. It's the hook. The hook for stealing, for murder, for arson, for treason, for rape, for being a peeping Tom. Break a law—any damn law at all—and it's the hook. Everybody can understand that, and San Lorenzo is the best-behaved country in the world."

"What is the hook?"

"They put up a gallows, see? Two posts and a cross beam. And then they take a great big kind of iron fishhook and they hang it down from the cross beam. Then they take somebody who's dumb enough to break the law, and they put the point of the hook in through one side of his belly and out the other and they let him go—and there he hangs, by God, one damn sorry law-breaker."

"Good God!"

"I don't say it's good," said Crosby, "but I don't say it's bad, either. I sometimes wonder if something like that wouldn't clear up juvenile delinquency. Maybe the hook's a little extreme for a democracy. Public hanging's more like it. String up a few teen-age car thieves on lampposts in front of their houses with signs around their necks saying, 'Mama, here's your boy.' Do that a few times and I think ignition locks would go the way of the rumble seat and the running board."

"We saw that thing in the basement of the waxworks in London," said Hazel.

"What thing?" I asked her.

"The hook. Down in the Chamber of Horrors in the basement; they had a wax person hanging from the hook. It looked so real I wanted to throw up."

"Harry Truman didn't look anything like Harry Truman," said Crosby.

"Pardon me?"

"In the waxworks," said Crosby. "The statue of Truman didn't really look like him."

"Most of them did, though," said Hazel.

"Was it anybody in particular hanging from the hook?" I asked her.

"I don't think so. It was just somebody."

"Just a demonstrator?" I asked.

"Yeah. There was a black velvet curtain in front of it and you had to pull the curtain back to see. And there was a note pinned to the curtain that said children weren't supposed to look."

"But kids did," said Crosby. "There were kids down there, and they all looked."

"A sign like that is just catnip to kids," said Hazel.

"How did the kids react when they saw the person on the hook?" I asked.

"Oh," said Hazel, "they reacted just about the way the grownups did. They just looked at it and didn't say anything, just moved on to see what the next thing was."

"What was the next thing?"

"It was an iron chair a man had been roasted alive in," said Crosby. "He was roasted for murdering his son."

"Only, after they roasted him," Hazel recalled blandly, "they found out he hadn't murdered his son after all."

44

Communist Sympathizers

When I again took my seat beside the *duprass* of Claire and Horlick Minton, I had some new information about them. I got it from the Crosbys.

The Crosbys didn't know Minton, but they knew his reputation. They were indignant about his appointment as Ambassador. They told me that Minton had once been fired by the State Department for his softness toward communism, and that Communist dupes or worse had had him reinstated.

"Very pleasant little saloon back there," I said to Minton as I sat down.

"Hm?" He and his wife were still reading the manuscript that lay between them.

"Nice bar back there."

"Good. I'm glad."

The two read on, apparently uninterested in talking to me. And then Minton turned to me suddenly, with a bittersweet smile, and he demanded, "Who was he, anyway?"

"Who was who?"

"The man you were talking to in the bar. We went back there for a drink, and, when we were just outside, we heard you and a man talking. The man was talking very loudly. He said I was a Communist sympathizer."

"A bicycle manufacturer named H. Lowe Crosby," I said. I felt myself reddening.

"I was fired for pessimism. Communism had nothing to do with it."

"I got him fired," said his wife. "The only piece of real evidence produced against him was a letter I wrote to the New York *Times* from Pakistan."

"What did it say?"

"It said a lot of things," she said, "because I was very upset about how Americans couldn't imagine what it was like to be something else, to be something else and proud of it."

"I see."

"But there was one sentence they kept coming back to again and again in the loyalty hearing," sighed Minton. "'Americans,'" he said, quoting his wife's letter to the *Times*, "'are forever searching for love in forms it never takes, in places it can never be. It must have something to do with the vanished frontier.'"

45

Why Americans Are Hated

Claire Minton's letter to the *Times* was published during the worst of the era of Senator McCarthy, and her husband was fired twelve hours after the letter was printed.

"What was so awful about the letter?" I asked.

"The highest possible form of treason," said Minton, "is to say that Americans aren't loved wherever they go, whatever they do. Claire tried to make the point that American foreign policy should recognize hate rather than imagine love."

"I guess Americans *are* hated a lot of places."

"*People* are hated a lot of places. Claire pointed out in her letter that Americans, in being hated, were simply paying the normal penalty for being people, and that they were foolish to think they should somehow be exempted from that penalty. But the loyalty board didn't pay any attention to that. All they knew was that Claire and I both felt that Americans were unloved."

"Well, I'm glad the story had a happy ending."

"Hm?" said Minton.

"It finally came out all right," I said. "Here you are on your way to an embassy all your own."

Minton and his wife exchanged another of those pitying *du-prass* glances. Then Minton said to me, "Yes. The pot of gold at the end of the rainbow is ours."

46

The Bokononist Method for Handling Caesar

I talked to the Mintons about the legal status of Franklin Hoenikker, who was, after all, not only a big shot in "Papa" Monzano's government, but a fugitive from United States justice.

"That's all been written off," said Minton. "He isn't a United States citizen any more, and he seems to be doing good things where he is, so that's that."

"He gave up his citizenship?"

"Anybody who declares allegiance to a foreign state or serves in its armed forces or accepts employment in its government loses his citizenship. Read your passport. You can't lead the sort of funny-paper international romance that Frank has led and still have Uncle Sam for a mother chicken."

"Is he well liked in San Lorenzo?"

Minton weighed in his hands the manuscript he and his wife had been reading. "I don't know yet. This book says not."

"What book is that?"

"It's the only scholarly book ever written about San Lorenzo."

"*Sort* of scholarly," said Claire.

"Sort of scholarly," echoed Minton. "It hasn't been published yet. This is one of five copies." He handed it to me, inviting me to read as much as I liked.

I opened the book to its title page and found that the name of the book was *San Lorenzo: The Land, the History, the People.*

The author was Philip Castle, the son of Julian Castle, the hotel-keeping son of the great altruist I was on my way to see.

I let the book fall open where it would. As it happened, it fell open to the chapter about the island's outlawed holy man, Bokonon.

There was a quotation from *The Books of Bokonon* on the page before me. Those words leapt from the page and into my mind, and they were welcomed there.

The words were a paraphrase of the suggestion by Jesus: "Render therefore unto Caesar the things which are Caesar's."

Bokonon's paraphrase was this:

"Pay no attention to Caesar. Caesar doesn't have the slightest idea what's *really* going on."

47

Dynamic Tension

I became so absorbed in Philip Castle's book that I didn't even look up from it when we put down for ten minutes in San Juan, Puerto Rico. I didn't even look up when somebody behind me whispered, thrilled, that a midget had come aboard.

A little while later I looked around for the midget, but could not see him. I did see, right in front of Hazel and H. Lowe Crosby, a horse-faced woman with platinum blonde hair, a woman new to the passenger list. Next to hers was a seat that appeared to be empty, a seat that might well have sheltered a midget without my seeing even the top of his head.

But it was San Lorenzo—the land, the history, the people—that intrigued me then, so I looked no harder for the midget. Midgets are, after all, diversions for silly or quiet times, and I was serious and excited about Bokonon's theory of what he called "Dynamic Tension," his sense of a priceless equilibrium between good and evil.

When I first saw the term "Dynamic Tension" in Philip Castle's book, I laughed what I imagined to be a superior laugh. The term was a favorite of Bokonon's, according to young Castle's book, and I supposed that I knew something that Bokonon didn't know: that the term was one vulgarized by Charles Atlas, a mail-order muscle-builder.

As I learned when I read on, briefly, Bokonon knew exactly who Charles Atlas was. Bokonon was, in fact, an alumnus of his muscle-building school.

It was the belief of Charles Atlas that muscles could be built without bar bells or spring exercisers, could be built by simply pitting one set of muscles against another.

It was the belief of Bokonon that good societies could be built only by pitting good against evil, and by keeping the tension between the two high at all times.

And, in Castle's book, I read my first Bokononist poem, or "Calypso." It went like this:

> "Papa" Monzano, he's so very bad,
> But without bad "Papa" I would be so sad;
> Because without "Papa's" badness,
> Tell me, if you would,
> How could wicked old Bokonon
> Ever, ever look good?

48

Just Like Saint Augustine

Bokonon, I learned from Castle's book, was born in 1891. He was a Negro, born an Episcopalian and a British subject on the island of Tobago.

He was christened Lionel Boyd Johnson.

He was the youngest of six children, born to a wealthy family. His family's wealth derived from the discovery by Bokonon's grandfather of one quarter of a million dollars in buried pirate treasure, presumably a treasure of Blackbeard, of Edward Teach.

Blackbeard's treasure was reinvested by Bokonon's family in asphalt, copra, cacao, livestock, and poultry.

Young Lionel Boyd Johnson was educated in Episcopal schools, did well as a student, and was more interested in ritual than most. As a youth, for all his interest in the outward trappings of organized religion, he seems to have been a carouser, for he invites us to sing along with him in his "Fourteenth Calypso":

> When I was young,
> I was so gay and mean,
> And I drank and chased the girls
> Just like young St. Augustine.
> Saint Augustine,
> He got to be a saint.
> So, if I get to be one, also,
> Please, Mama, don't you faint.

49

A Fish Pitched Up by an Angry Sea

Lionel Boyd Johnson was intellectually ambitious enough, in 1911, to sail alone from Tobago to London in a sloop named the *Lady's Slipper*. His purpose was to gain a higher education.

He enrolled in the London School of Economics and Political Science.

His education was interrupted by the First World War. He enlisted in the infantry, fought with distinction, was commissioned in the field, was mentioned four times in dispatches. He was gassed in the second Battle of Ypres, was hospitalized for two years, and then discharged.

And he set sail for home, for Tobago, alone in the *Lady's Slipper* again.

When only eighty miles from home, he was stopped and searched by a German submarine, the *U-99*. He was taken prisoner, and his little vessel was used by the Huns for target practice. While still surfaced, the submarine was surprised and captured by the British destroyer, the *Raven*.

Johnson and the Germans were taken on board the destroyer and the *U-99* was sunk.

The *Raven* was bound for the Mediterranean, but it never got there. It lost its steering; it could only wallow helplessly or make grand, clockwise circles. It came to rest at last in the Cape Verde Islands.

Johnson stayed in those islands for eight months, awaiting some sort of transportation to the Western Hemisphere.

He got a job at last as a crewman on a fishing vessel that was carrying illegal immigrants to New Bedford, Massachusetts. The vessel was blown ashore at Newport, Rhode Island.

By that time Johnson had developed a conviction that something was trying to get him somewhere for some reason. So he stayed in Newport for a while to see if he had a destiny there. He worked as a gardener and carpenter on the famous Rumfoord Estate.

During that time, he glimpsed many distinguished guests of the Rumfoords, among them, J. P. Morgan, General John J. Pershing, Franklin Delano Roosevelt, Enrico Caruso, Warren Gamaliel Harding, and Harry Houdini. And it was during that time that the First World War came to an end, having killed ten million persons and wounded twenty million, Johnson among them.

When the war ended, the young rakehell of the Rumfoord family, Remington Rumfoord, IV, proposed to sail his steam yacht, the *Scheherazade*, around the world, visiting Spain, France, Italy, Greece, Egypt, India, China, and Japan. He invited Johnson to accompany him as first mate, and Johnson agreed.

Johnson saw many wonders of the world on the voyage.

The *Scheherazade* was rammed in a fog in Bombay harbor, and only Johnson survived. He stayed in India for two years, becoming a follower of Mohandas K. Gandhi. He was arrested for leading groups that protested British rule by lying down on railroad tracks. When his jail term was over, he was shipped at Crown expense to his home in Tobago.

There, he built another schooner, which he called the *Lady's Slipper II.*

And he sailed her about the Caribbean, an idler, still seeking the storm that would drive him ashore on what was unmistakably his destiny.

In 1922, he sought shelter from a hurricane in Port-au-Prince, Haiti, which country was then occupied by United States Marines.

Johnson was approached there by a brilliant, self-educated, idealistic Marine deserter named Earl McCabe. McCabe was a corporal. He had just stolen his company's recreation fund. He offered Johnson five hundred dollars for transportation to Miami.

The two set sail for Miami.

But a gale hounded the schooner onto the rocks of San Lorenzo. The boat went down. Johnson and McCabe, absolutely naked, managed to swim ashore. As Bokonon himself reports the adventure:

> A fish pitched up
> By the angry sea,
> I gasped on land,
> And I became me.

He was enchanted by the mystery of coming ashore naked on an unfamiliar island. He resolved to let the adventure run its full course, resolved to see just how far a man might go, emerging naked from salt water.

It was a rebirth for him:

> Be like a baby,
> The Bible say,
> So I stay like a baby
> To this very day.

How he came by the name of Bokonon was very simple. "Bokonon" was the pronunciation given the name Johnson in the island's English dialect.

As for that dialect . . .

The dialect of San Lorenzo is both easy to understand and difficult to write down. I say it is easy to understand, but I speak only for myself. Others have found it as incomprehensible as Basque, so my understanding of it may be telepathic.

Philip Castle, in his book, gave a phonetic demonstration of the dialect and caught its flavor very well. He chose for his sample the San Lorenzan version of "Twinkle, Twinkle, Little Star."

In American English, one version of that immortal poem goes like this:

> Twinkle, twinkle, little star,
> How I wonder what you are,
> Shining in the sky so bright,
> Like a tea tray in the night,
> Twinkle, twinkle, little star,
> How I wonder what you are.

In San Lorenzan dialect, according to Castle, the same poem went like this:

> *Tsvent-kiul, tsvent-kiul, lett-pool store,*
> *Ko jy tsvantoor bat voo yore.*
> *Put-shinik on lo shee zo brath,*
> *Kam oon teetron on lo nath,*
> *Tsvent-kiul, tsvent-kiul, lett-pool store,*
> *Ko jy tsvantoor bat voo yore.*

Shortly after Johnson became Bokonon, incidentally, the lifeboat of his shattered ship was found on shore. That boat was later painted gold and made the bed of the island's chief executive.

"There is a legend, made up by Bokonon," Philip Castle wrote in his book, "that the golden boat will sail again when the end of the world is near."

50

A Nice Midget

My reading of the life of Bokonon was interrupted by H. Lowe Crosby's wife, Hazel. She was standing in the aisle next to me. "You'll never believe it," she said, "but I just found two more Hoosiers on this airplane."

"I'll be damned."

"They weren't born Hoosiers, but they *live* there now. They live in Indianapolis."

"Very interesting."

"You want to meet them?"

"You think I should?"

The question baffled her. "They're your fellow Hoosiers."

"What are their names?"

"Her name is Conners and his name is Hoenikker. They're brother and sister, and he's a midget. He's a nice midget, though." She winked. "He's a smart little thing."

"Does he call you Mom?"

"I almost asked him to. And then I stopped, and I wondered if maybe it wouldn't be rude to ask a midget to do that."

"Nonsense."

51

O.K., Mom

So I went aft to talk to Angela Hoenikker Conners and little Newton Hoenikker, members of my *karass*.

Angela was the horse-faced platinum blonde I had noticed earlier.

Newt was a very tiny young man indeed, though not grotesque.

He was as nicely scaled as Gulliver among the Brobdingnagians, and as shrewdly watchful, too.

He held a glass of champagne, which was included in the price of his ticket. That glass was to him what a fishbowl would have been to a normal man, but he drank from it with elegant ease—as though he and the glass could not have been better matched.

The little son of a bitch had a crystal of *ice-nine* in a thermos bottle in his luggage, and so did his miserable sister, while under us was God's own amount of water, the Caribbean Sea.

When Hazel had got all the pleasure she could from introducing Hoosiers to Hoosiers, she left us alone. "Remember," she said as she left us, "from now on, call me *Mom*."

"O.K., Mom," I said.

"O.K., Mom," said Newt. His voice was fairly high, in keeping with his little larynx. But he managed to make that voice distinctly masculine.

Angela persisted in treating Newt like an infant—and he forgave her for it with an amiable grace I would have thought impossible for one so small.

Newt and Angela remembered me, remembered the letters I'd written, and invited me to take the empty seat in their group of three.

Angela apologized to me for never having answered my letters.

"I couldn't think of anything to say that would interest anybody reading a book. I could have made up something about that day, but I didn't think you'd want that. Actually, the day was just like a regular day."

"Your brother here wrote me a very good letter."

Angela was surprised. "Newt did? How could Newt remember anything?" She turned to him. "Honey, you don't remember anything about that day, do you? You were just a baby."

"I remember," he said mildly.

"I wish I'd *seen* the letter." She implied that Newt was still too immature to deal directly with the outside world. Angela was a God-awfully insensitive woman, with no feeling for what smallness meant to Newt.

"Honey, you should have showed me that letter," she scolded.

"Sorry," said Newt. "I didn't think."

"I might as well tell you," Angela said to me, "Dr. Breed told me I wasn't supposed to co-operate with you. He said you weren't interested in giving a fair picture of Father." She showed me that she didn't like me for that.

I placated her some by telling her that the book would probably never be done anyway, that I no longer had a clear idea of what it would or should mean.

"Well, if you ever *do* do the book, you better make Father a saint, because that's what he was."

I promised that I would do my best to paint that picture. I asked if she and Newt were bound for a family reunion with Frank in San Lorenzo.

"Frank's getting married," said Angela. "We're going to the engagement party."

"Oh? Who's the lucky girl?"

"I'll show you," said Angela, and she took from her purse a billfold that contained a sort of plastic accordion. In each of the accordion's pleats was a photograph. Angela flipped through the photographs, giving me glimpses of little Newt on a Cape Cod beach, of Dr. Felix Hoenikker accepting his Nobel Prize, of Angela's own homely twin girls, of Frank flying a model plane on the end of a string.

And then she showed me a picture of the girl Frank was going to marry.

She might, with equal effect, have struck me in the groin.

The picture she showed me was of Mona Aamons Monzano, the woman I loved.

52

No Pain

Once Angela had opened her plastic accordion, she was reluctant to close it until someone had looked at every photograph.

"There are the people I love," she declared.

So I looked at the people she loved. What she had trapped in plexiglass, what she had trapped like fossil beetles in amber, were the images of a large part of our *karass*. There wasn't a *granfallooner* in the collection.

There were many photographs of Dr. Hoenikker, father of a bomb, father of three children, father of *ice-nine*. He was a little person, the purported sire of a midget and a giantess.

My favorite picture of the old man in Angela's fossil collection showed him all bundled up for winter, in an overcoat, scarf, galoshes, and a wool knit cap with a big pom-pom on the crown.

This picture, Angela told me, with a catch in her throat, had been taken in Hyannis just about three hours before the old man died. A newspaper photographer had recognized the seeming Christmas elf for the great man he was.

"Did your father die in the hospital?"

"Oh, no! He died in our cottage, in a big white wicker chair facing the sea. Newt and Frank had gone walking down the beach in the snow . . ."

"It was a very warm snow," said Newt. "It was almost like walking through orange blossoms. It was very strange. Nobody was in any of the other cottages . . ."

"Ours was the only one with heat," said Angela.

"Nobody within miles," recalled Newt wonderingly, "and Frank and I came across this big black dog out on the beach, a Labrador retriever. We threw sticks into the ocean and he brought them back."

"I'd gone back into the village for more Christmas tree bulbs," said Angela. "We always had a tree."

"Did your father enjoy having a Christmas tree?"

"He never said," said Newt.

"I think he liked it," said Angela. "He just wasn't very demonstrative. Some people aren't."

"And some people are," said Newt. He gave a small shrug.

"Anyway," said Angela, "when we got back home, we found him in the chair." She shook her head. "I don't think he suffered any. He just looked asleep. He couldn't have looked like that if there'd been the least bit of pain."

She left out an interesting part of the story. She left out the fact that it was on that same Christmas Eve that she and Frank and little Newt had divided up the old man's *ice-nine*.

53

The President of Fabri-Tek

Angela encouraged me to go on looking at snapshots.

"That's me, if you can believe it." She showed me an adolescent girl six feet tall. She was holding a clarinet in the picture, wearing the marching uniform of the Ilium High School band. Her hair was tucked up under a bandsman's hat. She was smiling with shy good cheer.

And then Angela, a woman to whom God had given virtually nothing with which to catch a man, showed me a picture of her husband.

"So that's Harrison C. Conners." I was stunned. Her husband was a strikingly handsome man, and looked as though he knew it. He was a snappy dresser, and had the lazy rapture of a Don Juan about the eyes.

"What—what does he do?" I asked.

"He's president of Fabri-Tek."

"Electronics?"

"I couldn't tell you, even if I knew. It's all very secret government work."

"Weapons?"

"Well, war anyway."

"How did you happen to meet?"

"He used to work as a laboratory assistant to Father," said Angela. "Then he went out to Indianapolis and started Fabri-Tek."

"So your marriage to him was a happy ending to a long romance?"

"No. I didn't even know he knew I was alive. I used to think he was nice, but he never paid any attention to me until after Father died.

"One day he came through Ilium. I was sitting around that big old house, thinking my life was over. . . ." She spoke of the awful days and weeks that followed her father's death. "Just me and little Newt in that big old house. Frank had disappeared, and the ghosts were making ten times as much noise as Newt and I were. I'd given my whole life to taking care of Father, driving him to and from work, bundling him up when it was cold, unbundling him when it was hot, making him eat, paying his bills. Suddenly, there wasn't anything for me to do. I'd never had any close friends, didn't have a soul to turn to but Newt.

"And then," she continued, "there was a knock on the door —and there stood Harrison Conners. He was the most beautiful thing I'd ever seen. He came in, and we talked about Father's last days and about old times in general."

Angela almost cried now.

"Two weeks later, we were married."

54

Communists, Nazis, Royalists, Parachutists, and Draft Dodgers

Returning to my own seat in the plane, feeling far shabbier for having lost Mona Aamons Monzano to Frank, I resumed my reading of Philip Castle's manuscript.

I looked up *Monzano, Mona Aamons* in the index, and was told by the index to see *Aamons, Mona*.

So I saw *Aamons, Mona*, and found almost as many page references as I'd found after the name of "Papa" Monzano himself.

And after *Aamons, Mona* came *Aamons, Nestor*. So I turned to the few pages that had to do with Nestor, and learned that he was Mona's father, a native Finn, an architect.

Nestor Aamons was captured by the Russians, then liberated

by the Germans during the Second World War. He was not returned home by his liberators, but was forced to serve in a *Wehrmacht* engineer unit that was sent to fight the Yugoslav partisans. He was captured by Chetniks, royalist Serbian partisans, and then by Communist partisans who attacked the Chetniks. He was liberated by Italian parachutists who surprised the Communists, and he was shipped to Italy.

The Italians put him to work designing fortifications for Sicily. He stole a fishing boat in Sicily, and reached neutral Portugal.

While there, he met an American draft dodger named Julian Castle.

Castle, upon learning that Aamons was an architect, invited him to come with him to the island of San Lorenzo and to design for him a hospital to be called the House of Hope and Mercy in the Jungle.

Aamons accepted. He designed the hospital, married a native woman named Celia, fathered a perfect daughter, and died.

55

Never Index Your Own Book

As for the life of *Aamons, Mona*, the index itself gave a jangling, surrealistic picture of the many conflicting forces that had been brought to bear on her and of her dismayed reactions to them.

"*Aamons, Mona*:" the index said, "adopted by Monzano in order to boost Monzano's popularity, 194–199, 216 n.; childhood in compound of House of Hope and Mercy, 63–81; childhood romance with P. Castle, 72 f; death of father, 89 ff; death of mother, 92 f; embarrassed by role as national erotic symbol, 80, 95 f, 166 n., 209, 247 n., 400–406, 566 n., 678; engaged to P. Castle, 193; essential naïveté, 67–71, 80, 95 f, 116 n., 209, 274 n., 400–406, 566 n., 678; lives with Bokonon, 92–98, 196–197; poems about, 2 n., 26, 114, 119, 311, 316, 477 n., 501, 507, 555 n., 689, 718 ff, 799 ff, 800 n., 841, 846 ff, 908 n., 971,

974; poems by, 89, 92, 193; returns to Monzano, 199; returns to Bokonon, 197; runs away from Bokonon, 199; runs away from Monzano, 197; tries to make self ugly in order to stop being erotic symbol to islanders, 80, 95 f, 116 n., 209, 247 n., 400–406, 566 n., 678; tutored by Bokonon, 63–80; writes letter to United Nations, 200; xylophone virtuoso, 71."

I showed this index entry to the Mintons, asking them if they didn't think it was an enchanting biography in itself, a biography of a reluctant goddess of love. I got an unexpectedly expert answer, as one does in life sometimes. It appeared that Claire Minton, in her time, had been a professional indexer. I had never heard of such a profession before.

She told me that she had put her husband through college years before with her earnings as an indexer, that the earnings had been good, and that few people could index well.

She said that indexing was a thing that only the most amateurish author undertook to do for his own book. I asked her what she thought of Philip Castle's job.

"Flattering to the author, insulting to the reader," she said. "In a hyphenated word," she observed, with the shrewd amiability of an expert, " '*self-indulgent.*' I'm always embarrassed when I see an index an author has made of his own work."

"Embarrassed?"

"It's a revealing thing, an author's index of his own work," she informed me. "It's a shameless exhibition—to the *trained* eye."

"She can read character from an index," said her husband.

"Oh?" I said. "What can you tell about Philip Castle?"

She smiled faintly. "Things I'd better not tell strangers."

"Sorry."

"He's obviously in love with this Mona Aamons Monzano," she said.

"That's true of every man in San Lorenzo I gather."

"He has mixed feelings about his father," she said.

"That's true of every man on earth." I egged her on gently.

"He's insecure."

"What mortal isn't?" I demanded. I didn't know it then, but that was a very Bokononist thing to demand.

"He'll never marry her."

"Why not?"

"I've said all I'm going to say," she said.

"I'm gratified to meet an indexer who respects the privacy of others."

"Never index your own book," she stated.

A *duprass*, Bokonon tells us, is a valuable instrument for gaining and developing, in the privacy of an interminable love affair, insights that are queer but true. The Mintons' cunning exploration of indexes was surely a case in point. A *duprass*, Bokonon tells us, is also a sweetly conceited establishment. The Mintons' establishment was no exception.

Sometime later, Ambassador Minton and I met in the aisle of the airplane, away from his wife, and he showed that it was important to him that I respect what his wife could find out from indexes.

"You know why Castle will never marry the girl, even though he loves her, even though she loves him, even though they grew up together?" he whispered.

"No, sir, I don't."

"Because he's a homosexual," whispered Minton. "She can tell that from an index, too."

56

A Self-supporting Squirrel Cage

When Lionel Boyd Johnson and Corporal Earl McCabe were washed up naked onto the shore of San Lorenzo, I read, they were greeted by persons far worse off than they. The people of San Lorenzo had nothing but diseases, which they were at a loss to treat or even name. By contrast, Johnson and McCabe had the glittering treasures of literacy, ambition, curiosity, gall, irreverence, health, humor, and considerable information about the outside world.

From the "Calypsos" again:

Oh, a very sorry people, yes,
Did I find here.
Oh, they had no music,
And they had no beer.
And, oh, everywhere
Where they tried to perch
Belonged to Castle Sugar, Incorporated,
Or the Catholic church.

This statement of the property situation in San Lorenzo in 1922 is entirely accurate, according to Philip Castle. Castle Sugar was founded, as it happened, by Philip Castle's great-grandfather. In 1922, it owned every piece of arable land on the island.

"Castle Sugar's San Lorenzo operations," wrote young Castle, "never showed a profit. But, by paying laborers nothing for their labor, the company managed to break even year after year, making just enough money to pay the salaries of the workers' tormentors.

"The form of government was anarchy, save in limited situations wherein Castle Sugar wanted to own something or to get something done. In such situations the form of government was feudalism. The nobility was composed of Castle Sugar's plantation bosses, who were heavily armed white men from the outside world. The knighthood was composed of big natives who, for small gifts and silly privileges, would kill or wound or torture on command. The spiritual needs of the people caught in this demoniacal squirrel cage were taken care of by a handful of butterball priests.

"The San Lorenzo Cathedral, dynamited in 1923, was generally regarded as one of the man-made wonders of the New World," wrote Castle.

57
The Queasy Dream

That Corporal McCabe and Johnson were able to take command of San Lorenzo was not a miracle in any sense. Many
people had taken over San Lorenzo—had invariably found it
lightly held. The reason was simple: God, in His Infinite
Wisdom, had made the island worthless.

Hernando Cortes was the first man to have his sterile con-
quest of San Lorenzo recorded on paper. Cortes and his men
came ashore for fresh water in 1519, named the island, claimed
it for Emperor Charles the Fifth, and never returned.
Subsequent expeditions came for gold and diamonds and rubies and spices, found none, burned a few natives for entertainment and heresy, and sailed on.

"When France claimed San Lorenzo in 1682," wrote Castle,
"no Spaniards complained. When Denmark claimed San
Lorenzo in 1699, no Frenchmen complained. When the Dutch
claimed San Lorenzo in 1704, no Danes complained. When
England claimed San Lorenzo in 1706, no Dutchmen complained. When Spain reclaimed San Lorenzo in 1720, no
Englishmen complained. When, in 1786, African Negroes took
command of a British slave ship, ran it ashore on San Lorenzo,
and proclaimed San Lorenzo an independent nation, an empire
with an emperor, in fact, no Spaniards complained.

"The emperor was Tum-bumwa, the only person who ever
regarded the island as being worth defending. A maniac, Tum-
bumwa caused to be erected the San Lorenzo Cathedral and
the fantastic fortifications on the north shore of the island, fortifications within which the private residence of the so-called
President of the Republic now stands.

"The fortifications have never been attacked, nor has any
sane man ever proposed any reason why they should be attacked. They have never defended anything. Fourteen hundred
persons are said to have died while building them. Of these
fourteen hundred, about half are said to have been executed in
public for substandard zeal."

Castle Sugar came into San Lorenzo in 1916, during the sugar boom of the First World War. There was no government at all. The company imagined that even the clay and gravel fields of San Lorenzo could be tilled profitably, with the price of sugar so high. No one complained.

When McCabe and Johnson arrived in 1922 and announced that they were placing themselves in charge, Castle Sugar withdrew flaccidly, as though from a queasy dream.

58

Tyranny with a Difference

"There was at least one quality of the new conquerors of San Lorenzo that was really new," wrote young Castle. "McCabe and Johnson dreamed of making San Lorenzo a Utopia.

"To this end, McCabe overhauled the economy and the laws.

"Johnson designed a new religion."

Castle quoted the "Calypsos" again:

> I wanted all things
> To seem to make some sense,
> So we all could be happy, yes,
> Instead of tense.
> And I made up lies
> So that they all fit nice,
> And I made this sad world
> A par-a-dise.

There was a tug at my coat sleeve as I read. I looked up.

Little Newt Hoenikker was standing in the aisle next to me. "I thought maybe you'd like to go back to the bar," he said, "and hoist a few."

So we did hoist and topple a few, and Newt's tongue was loosened enough to tell me some things about Zinka, his

Russian midget dancer friend. Their love nest, he told me, had been in his father's cottage on Cape Cod.

"I may not ever have a marriage, but at least I've had a honeymoon."

He told me of idyllic hours he and his Zinka had spent in each other's arms, cradled in Felix Hoenikker's old white wicker chair, the chair that faced the sea.

And Zinka would dance for him. "Imagine a woman dancing just for me."

"I can see you have no regrets."

"She broke my heart. I didn't like that much. But that was the price. In this world, you get what you pay for."

He proposed a gallant toast. "Sweethearts and wives," he cried.

59

Fasten Your Seat Belts

I was in the bar with Newt and H. Lowe Crosby and a couple of strangers, when San Lorenzo was sighted. Crosby was talking about pissants. "You know what I mean by a pissant?"

"I know the term," I said, "but it obviously doesn't have the ding-a-ling associations for me that it has for you."

Crosby was in his cups and had the drunkard's illusion that he could speak frankly, provided he spoke affectionately. He spoke frankly and affectionately of Newt's size, something nobody else in the bar had so far commented on.

"I don't mean a little feller like this." Crosby hung a ham hand on Newt's shoulder. "It isn't size that makes a man a pissant. It's the way he thinks. I've seen men four times as big as this little feller here, and they were pissants. And I've seen little fellers—well, not this little actually, but pretty damn little, by God—and I'd call them real men."

"Thanks," said Newt pleasantly, not even glancing at the monstrous hand on his shoulder. Never had I seen a human being better adjusted to such a humiliating physical handicap. I shuddered with admiration.

"You were talking about pissants," I said to Crosby, hoping to get the weight of his hand off Newt.

"Damn right I was." Crosby straightened up.

"You haven't told us what a pissant is yet," I said.

"A pissant is somebody who thinks he's so damn smart, he never can keep his mouth shut. No matter what anybody says, he's got to argue with it. You say you like something, and, by God, he'll tell you why you're wrong to like it. A pissant does his best to make you feel like a boob all the time. No matter what you say, he knows better."

"Not a very attractive characteristic," I suggested.

"My daughter wanted to marry a pissant once," said Crosby darkly.

"Did she?"

"I squashed him like a bug." Crosby hammered on the bar, remembering things the pissant had said and done. "Jesus!" he said, "we've all been to college!" His gaze lit on Newt again. "You go to college?"

"Cornell," said Newt.

"Cornell!" cried Crosby gladly. "My God, I went to Cornell."

"So did he." Newt nodded at me.

"Three Cornellians—all in the same plane!" said Crosby, and we had another *granfalloon* festival on our hands.

When it subsided some, Crosby asked Newt what he did.

"I paint."

"Houses?"

"Pictures."

"I'll be damned," said Crosby.

"Return to your seats and fasten your seat belts, please," warned the airline hostess. "We're over Monzano Airport, Bolivar, San Lorenzo."

"Christ! Now wait just a Goddamn minute here," said Crosby, looking down at Newt. "All of a sudden I realize you've got a name I've heard before."

"My father was the father of the atom bomb." Newt didn't say Felix Hoenikker was *one* of the fathers. He said Felix was *the* father.

"Is that so?" asked Crosby.

"That's so."

"I was thinking about something else," said Crosby. He had to think hard. "Something about a dancer."

"I think we'd better get back to our seats," said Newt, tightening some.

"Something about a Russian dancer." Crosby was sufficiently addled by booze to see no harm in thinking out loud. "I remember an editorial about how maybe the dancer was a spy."

"Please, gentlemen," said the stewardess, "you really must get back to your seats and fasten your belts."

Newt looked up at H. Lowe Crosby innocently. "You sure the name was Hoenikker?" And, in order to eliminate any chance of mistaken identity, he spelled the name for Crosby.

"I could be wrong," said H. Lowe Crosby.

60

An Underprivileged Nation

The island, seen from the air, was an amazingly regular rectangle. Cruel and useless stone needles were thrust up from the sea. They sketched a circle around it.

At the south end of the island was the port city of Bolivar.

It was the only city.

It was the capital.

It was built on a marshy table. The runways of Monzano Airport were on its water front.

Mountains arose abruptly to the north of Bolivar, crowding the remainder of the island with their brutal humps. They were called the Sangre de Cristo Mountains, but they looked like pigs at a trough to me.

Bolivar had had many names: Caz-ma-caz-ma, Santa Maria, Saint Louis, Saint George, and Port Glory among them. It was given its present name by Johnson and McCabe in 1922, was named in honor of Simón Bolívar, the great Latin-American idealist and hero.

When Johnson and McCabe came upon the city, it was built of twigs, tin, crates, and mud—rested on the catacombs of a trillion happy scavengers, catacombs in a sour mash of slop, feculence, and slime.

That was pretty much the way I found it, too, except for the new architectural false face along the water front.

Johnson and McCabe had failed to raise the people from misery and muck.

"Papa" Monzano had failed, too.

Everybody was bound to fail, for San Lorenzo was as unproductive as an equal area in the Sahara or the Polar Icecap.

At the same time, it had as dense a population as could be found anywhere, India and China not excluded. There were four hundred and fifty inhabitants for each uninhabitable square mile.

"During the idealistic phase of McCabe's and Johnson's reorganization of San Lorenzo, it was announced that the country's total income would be divided among all adult persons in equal shares," wrote Philip Castle. "The first and only time this was tried, each share came to between six and seven dollars."

61

What a Corporal Was Worth

In the customs shed at Monzano Airport, we were all required to submit to a luggage inspection, and to convert what money we intended to spend in San Lorenzo into the local currency, into *Corporals*, which "Papa" Monzano insisted were worth fifty American cents.

The shed was neat and new, but plenty of signs had already been slapped on the walls, higgledy-piggledy.

ANYBODY CAUGHT PRACTICING BOKONONISM IN SAN LORENZO, said one, WILL DIE ON THE HOOK!

Another poster featured a picture of Bokonon, a scrawny

old colored man who was smoking a cigar. He looked clever and kind and amused.

Under the picture were the words: WANTED DEAD OR ALIVE, 10,000 CORPORALS REWARD!

I took a closer look at that poster and found reproduced at the bottom of it some sort of police identification form Bokonon had had to fill out way back in 1929. It was reproduced, apparently, to show Bokonon hunters what his fingerprints and handwriting were like.

But what interested me were some of the words Bokonon had chosen to put into the blanks in 1929. Wherever possible, he had taken the cosmic view, had taken into consideration, for instance, such things as the shortness of life and the longness of eternity.

He reported his avocation as: "Being alive."

He reported his principal occupation as: "Being dead."

THIS IS A CHRISTIAN NATION! ALL FOOT PLAY WILL BE PUNISHED BY THE HOOK, said another sign. The sign was meaningless to me, since I had not yet learned that Bokononists mingled their souls by pressing the bottoms of their feet together.

And the greatest mystery of all, since I had not read all of Philip Castle's book, was how Bokonon, bosom friend of Corporal McCabe, had come to be an outlaw.

62

Why Hazel Wasn't Scared

There were seven of us who got off at San Lorenzo: Newt and Angela, Ambassador Minton and his wife, H. Lowe Crosby and his wife, and I. When we had cleared customs, we were herded outdoors and onto a reviewing stand.

There, we faced a very quiet crowd.

Five thousand or more San Lorenzans stared at us. The islanders were oatmeal colored. The people were thin. There wasn't a fat person to be seen. Every person had teeth missing. Many legs were bowed or swollen.

Not one pair of eyes was clear.

The women's breasts were bare and paltry. The men wore loose loincloths that did little to conceal penes like pendulums on grandfather clocks.

There were many dogs, but not one barked. There were many infants, but not one cried. Here and there someone coughed—and that was all.

A military band stood at attention before the crowd. It did not play.

There was a color guard before the band. It carried two banners, the Stars and Stripes and the flag of San Lorenzo. The flag of San Lorenzo consisted of a Marine Corporal's chevrons on a royal blue field. The banners hung lank in the windless day.

I imagined that somewhere far away I heard the blamming of a sledge on a brazen drum. There was no such sound. My soul was simply resonating the beat of the brassy, clanging heat of the San Lorenzan clime.

"I'm sure glad it's a Christian country," Hazel Crosby whispered to her husband, "or I'd be a little scared."

Behind us was a xylophone.

There was a glittering sign on the xylophone. The sign was made of garnets and rhinestones.

The sign said, MONA.

63

Reverent and Free

To the left side of our reviewing stand were six propeller-driven fighter planes in a row, military assistance from the United States to San Lorenzo. On the fuselage of each plane was painted, with childish bloodlust, a boa constrictor which was crushing a devil to death. Blood came from the devil's ears, nose, and mouth. A pitchfork was slipping from satanic red fingers.

Before each plane stood an oatmeal-colored pilot; silent, too.

Then, above that tumid silence, there came a nagging song like the song of a gnat. It was a siren approaching. The siren was on "Papa's" glossy black Cadillac limousine.

The limousine came to a stop before us, tires smoking.

Out climbed "Papa" Monzano, his adopted daughter, Mona Aamons Monzano, and Franklin Hoenikker.

At a limp, imperious signal from "Papa," the crowd sang the San Lorenzan National Anthem. Its melody was "Home on the Range." The words had been written in 1922 by Lionel Boyd Johnson, by Bokonon. The words were these:

> Oh, ours is a land
> Where the living is grand,
> And the men are as fearless as sharks;
> The women are pure,
> And we always are sure
> That our children will all toe their marks.
> San, San Lo-ren-zo!
> What a rich, lucky island are we!
> Our enemies quail,
> For they know they will fail
> Against people so reverent and free.

64

Peace and Plenty

And then the crowd was deathly still again.

"Papa" and Mona and Frank joined us on the reviewing stand. One snare drum played as they did so. The drumming stopped when "Papa" pointed a finger at the drummer.

He wore a shoulder holster on the outside of his blouse.

The weapon in it was a chromium-plated .45. He was an old, old man, as so many members of my *karass* were. He was in poor shape. His steps were small and bounceless. He was still a fat man, but his lard was melting fast, for his simple uniform was loose. The balls of his hoptoad eyes were yellow. His hands trembled.

His personal bodyguard was Major General Franklin Hoenikker, whose uniform was white. Frank—thin-wristed, narrow-shouldered—looked like a child kept up long after his customary bedtime. On his breast was a medal.

I observed the two, "Papa" and Frank, with some difficulty —not because my view was blocked, but because I could not take my eyes off Mona. I was thrilled, heartbroken, hilarious, insane. Every greedy, unreasonable dream I'd ever had about what a woman should be came true in Mona. There, God love her warm and creamy soul, was peace and plenty forever.

That girl—and she was only eighteen—was rapturously serene. She seemed to understand all, and to be all there was to understand. In *The Books of Bokonon* she is mentioned by name. One thing Bokonon says of her is this: "Mona has the simplicity of the all."

Her dress was white and Greek.

She wore flat sandals on her small brown feet.

Her pale gold hair was lank and long.

Her hips were a lyre.

Oh God.

Peace and plenty forever.

She was the one beautiful girl in San Lorenzo. She was the national treasure. "Papa" had adopted her, according to Philip Castle, in order to mingle divinity with the harshness of his rule.

The xylophone was rolled to the front of the stand. And Mona played it. She played "When Day Is Done." It was all tremolo—swelling, fading, swelling again.

The crowd was intoxicated by beauty.

And then it was time for "Papa" to greet us.

65

A Good Time to Come to San Lorenzo

"Papa" was a self-educated man, who had been major-domo to Corporal McCabe. He had never been off the island. He spoke American English passably well.

Everything that any one of us said on the reviewing stand was bellowed out at the crowd through doomsday horns.

Whatever went out through those horns gabbled down a wide, short boulevard at the back of the crowd, ricocheted off the three glass-faced new buildings at the end of the boulevard, and came cackling back.

"Welcome," said "Papa." "You are coming to the best friend America ever had. America is misunderstood many places, but not here, Mr. Ambassador." He bowed to H. Lowe Crosby, the bicycle manufacturer, mistaking him for the new Ambassador.

"I know you've got a good country here, Mr. President," said Crosby. "Everything I ever heard about it sounds great to me. There's just one thing . . ."

"Oh?"

"I'm not the Ambassador," said Crosby. "I wish I was, but I'm just a plain, ordinary businessman." It hurt him to say who the real Ambassador was. "This man over here is the big cheese."

"Ah!" "Papa" smiled at his mistake. The smile went away suddenly. Some pain inside of him made him wince, then made him hunch over, close his eyes—made him concentrate on surviving the pain.

Frank Hoenikker went to his support, feebly, incompetently. "Are you all right?"

"Excuse me," "Papa" whispered at last, straightening up some. There were tears in his eyes. He brushed them away, straightening up all the way. "I beg your pardon."

He seemed to be in doubt for a moment as to where he was, as to what was expected of him. And then he remembered. He shook Horlick Minton's hand. "Here, you are among friends."

"I'm sure of it," said Minton gently.

"Christian," said "Papa."

"Good."

"Anti-Communists," said "Papa."

"Good."

"No Communists here," said "Papa." "They fear the hook too much."

"I should think they would," said Minton.

"You have picked a very good time to come to us," said "Papa." "Tomorrow will be one of the happiest days in the history of our country. Tomorrow is our greatest national holiday, The Day of the Hundred Martyrs to Democracy. It will also be the day of the engagement of Major General Hoenikker to Mona Aamons Monzano, to the most precious person in my life and in the life of San Lorenzo."

"I wish you much happiness, Miss Monzano," said Minton warmly. "And I congratulate *you*, General Hoenikker."

The two young people nodded their thanks.

Minton now spoke of the so-called Hundred Martyrs to Democracy, and he told a whooping lie. "There is not an American schoolchild who does not know the story of San Lorenzo's noble sacrifice in World War Two. The hundred brave San Lorenzans, whose day tomorrow is, gave as much as freedom-loving men can. The President of the United States has asked me to be his personal representative at ceremonies tomorrow, to cast a wreath, the gift of the American people to the people of San Lorenzo, on the sea."

"The people of San Lorenzo thank you and your President and the generous people of the United States of America for their thoughtfulness," said "Papa." "We would be honored if you would cast the wreath into the sea during the engagement party tomorrow."

"The honor is mine."

"Papa" commanded us all to honor him with our presence at the wreath ceremony and engagement party next day. We were to appear at his palace at noon.

"What children these two will have!" "Papa" said, inviting us to stare at Frank and Mona. "What blood! What beauty!"

The pain hit him again.

He again closed his eyes to huddle himself around that pain.

He waited for it to pass, but it did not pass.

Still in agony, he turned away from us, faced the crowd and the microphone. He tried to gesture at the crowd, failed. He tried to say something to the crowd, failed.

And then the words came out. "Go home," he cried strangling. "Go home!"

The crowd scattered like leaves.

"Papa" faced us again, still grotesque in pain. . . .

And then he collapsed.

66

The Strongest Thing There Is

He wasn't dead.

But he certainly looked dead; except that now and then, in the midst of all that seeming death, he would give a shivering twitch.

Frank protested loudly that "Papa" wasn't dead, that he *couldn't* be dead. He was frantic. "'Papa'! You can't die! You can't!"

Frank loosened "Papa's" collar and blouse, rubbed his wrists. "Give him air! Give 'Papa' air!"

The fighter-plane pilots came running over to help us. One had sense enough to go for the airport ambulance.

The band and the color guard, which had received no orders, remained at quivering attention.

I looked for Mona, found that she was still serene and had withdrawn to the rail of the reviewing stand. Death, if there was going to be death, did not alarm her.

Standing next to her was a pilot. He was not looking at her, but he had a perspiring radiance that I attributed to his being so near to her.

"Papa" now regained something like consciousness. With a

hand that flapped like a captured bird, he pointed at Frank. "You . . ." he said.

We all fell silent, in order to hear his words.

His lips moved, but we could hear nothing but bubbling sounds.

Somebody had what looked like a wonderful idea then— what looks like a hideous idea in retrospect. Someone—a pilot, I think—took the microphone from its mount and held it by "Papa's" bubbling lips in order to amplify his words.

So death rattles and all sorts of spastic yodels bounced off the new buildings.

And then came words.

"You," he said to Frank hoarsely, "you—Franklin Hoenikker —you will be the next President of San Lorenzo. Science—you have science. Science is the strongest thing there is."

"Science," said "Papa." "Ice." He rolled his yellow eyes, and he passed out again.

I looked at Mona.

Her expression was unchanged.

The pilot next to her, however, had his features composed in the catatonic, orgiastic rigidity of one receiving the Congressional Medal of Honor.

I looked down and I saw what I was not meant to see.

Mona had slipped off her sandal. Her small brown foot was bare.

And with that foot, she was kneading and kneading and kneading—obscenely kneading—the instep of the flyer's boot.

67

"Hy-u-o-ook-kuh!"

"Papa" didn't die—not then.

He was rolled away in the airport's big red meat wagon.

The Mintons were taken to their embassy by an American limousine.

Newt and Angela were taken to Frank's house in a San Lorenzan limousine.

The Crosbys and I were taken to the Casa Mona hotel in San Lorenzo's one taxi, a hearselike 1939 Chrysler limousine with jump seats. The name on the side of the cab was Castle Transportation Inc. The cab was owned by Philip Castle, the owner of the Casa Mona, the son of the completely unselfish man I had come to interview.

The Crosbys and I were both upset. Our consternation was expressed in questions we had to have answered at once. The Crosbys wanted to know who Bokonon was. They were scandalized by the idea that anyone should be opposed to "Papa" Monzano.

Irrelevantly, I found that I had to know at once who the Hundred Martyrs to Democracy had been.

The Crosbys got their answer first. They could not understand the San Lorenzan dialect, so I had to translate for them. Crosby's basic question to our driver was: "Who the hell is this pissant Bokonon, anyway?"

"Very bad man," said the driver. What he actually said was, "*Vorry ball moan.*"

"A Communist?" asked Crosby, when he heard my translation.

"Oh, sure."

"Has he got any following?"

"Sir?"

"Does anybody think he's any good?"

"Oh, no, sir," said the driver piously. "Nobody that crazy."

"Why hasn't he been caught?" demanded Crosby.

"Hard man to find," said the driver. "Very smart."

"Well, people must be hiding him and giving him food or he'd be caught by now."

"Nobody hide him; nobody feed him. Everybody too smart to do that."

"You sure?"

"Oh, sure," said the driver. "Anybody feed that crazy old man, anybody give him place to sleep, they get the hook. Nobody want the hook."

He pronounced that last word: "*hy-u-o-ook-kuh.*"

68

"Hoon-yera Mora-toorz"

I asked the driver who the Hundred Martyrs to Democracy had been. The boulevard we were going down, I saw, was called the Boulevard of the Hundred Martyrs to Democracy.

The driver told me that San Lorenzo had declared war on Germany and Japan an hour after Pearl Harbor was attacked.

San Lorenzo conscripted a hundred men to fight on the side of democracy. These hundred men were put on a ship bound for the United States, where they were to be armed and trained.

The ship was sunk by a German submarine right outside of Bolivar harbor.

"*Dose, sore,*" he said, "*yeeara lo hoon-yera mora-toorz tut zamoo-cratz-ya.*"

"Those, sir," he'd said in dialect, "are the Hundred Martyrs to Democracy."

69

A Big Mosaic

The Crosbys and I had the curious experience of being the very first guests of a new hotel. We were the first to sign the register of the Casa Mona.

The Crosbys got to the desk ahead of me, but H. Lowe Crosby was so startled by a wholly blank register that he couldn't bring himself to sign. He had to think about it a while.

"You sign," he said to me. And then, defying me to think he was superstitious, he declared his wish to photograph a man who was making a huge mosaic on the fresh plaster of the lobby wall.

The mosaic was a portrait of Mona Aamons Monzano. It was twenty feet high. The man who was working on it was young and muscular. He sat at the top of a stepladder. He wore nothing but a pair of white duck trousers.

He was a white man.

The mosaicist was making the fine hairs on the nape of Mona's swan neck out of chips of gold.

Crosby went over to photograph him; came back to report that the man was the biggest pissant he had ever met. Crosby was the color of tomato juice when he reported this. "You can't say a damn thing to him that he won't turn inside out."

So I went over to the mosaicist, watched him for a while, and then I told him, "I envy you."

"I always knew," he sighed, "that, if I waited long enough, somebody would come and envy me. I kept telling myself to be patient, that, sooner or later, somebody envious would come along."

"Are you an American?"

"That happiness is mine." He went right on working; he was incurious as to what I looked like. "Do you want to take my photograph, too?"

"Do you mind?"

"I think, therefore I am, therefore I am photographable."

"I'm afraid I don't have my camera with me."

"Well, for Christ's sake, get it! You're not one of those people who trusts his memory, are you?"

"I don't think I'll forget that face you're working on very soon."

"You'll forget it when you're dead, and so will I. When I'm dead, I'm going to forget everything—and I advise you to do the same."

"Has she been posing for this or are you working from photographs or what?"

"I'm working from or what."

"What?"

"I'm working from or what." He tapped his temple. "It's all in this enviable head of mine."

"You know her?"

"That happiness is mine."

"Frank Hoenikker's a lucky man."

"Frank Hoenikker is a piece of shit."

"You're certainly candid."

"I'm also rich."

"Glad to hear it."

"If you want an expert opinion, money doesn't necessarily make people happy."

"Thanks for the information. You've just saved me a lot of trouble. I was just about to make some money."

"How?"

"Writing."

"I wrote a book once."

"What was it called?"

"*San Lorenzo*," he said, "*the Land, the History, the People.*"

70

Tutored by Bokonon

"You, I take it," I said to the mosaicist, "are Philip Castle, son of Julian Castle."

"That happiness is mine."

"I'm here to see your father."

"Are you an aspirin salesman?"

"No."

"Too bad. Father's low on aspirin. How about miracle drugs? Father enjoys pulling off a miracle now and then."

"I'm not a drug salesman. I'm a writer."

"What makes you think a writer isn't a drug salesman?"

"I'll accept that. Guilty as charged."

"Father needs some kind of book to read to people who are dying or in terrible pain. I don't suppose you've written anything like that."

"Not yet."

"I think there'd be money in it. There's another valuable tip for you."

"I suppose I could overhaul the 'Twenty-third Psalm,' switch it around a little so nobody would realize it wasn't original with me."

"Bokonon tried to overhaul it," he told me. "Bokonon found out he couldn't change a word."

"You know him, too?"

"That happiness is mine. He was my tutor when I was a little boy." He gestured sentimentally at the mosaic. "He was Mona's tutor, too."

"Was he a good teacher?"

"Mona and I can both read and write and do simple sums," said Castle, "if that's what you mean."

71

The Happiness of Being an American

H. Lowe Crosby came over to have another go at Castle, the pissant.

"What do you call yourself," sneered Crosby, "a beatnik or what?"

"I call myself a Bokononist."

"That's against the law in this country, isn't it?"

"I happen to have the happiness of being an American. I've been able to say I'm a Bokononist any time I damn please, and, so far, nobody's bothered me at all."

"I believe in obeying the laws of whatever country I happen to be in."

"You are not telling me the news."

Crosby was livid. "Screw you, Jack!"

"Screw you, Jasper," said Castle mildly, "and screw Mother's Day and Christmas, too."

Crosby marched across the lobby to the desk clerk and he said, "I want to report that man over there, that pissant, that so-called artist. You've got a nice little country here that's trying to attract the tourist trade and new investment in industry. The way that man talked to me, I don't ever want to see San

Lorenzo again—and any friend who asks me about San Lorenzo, I'll tell him to keep the hell away. You may be getting a nice picture on the wall over there, but, by God, the pissant who's making it is the most insulting, discouraging son of a bitch I ever met in my life."

The clerk looked sick. "Sir . . ."

"I'm listening," said Crosby, full of fire.

"Sir—he owns the hotel."

72

The Pissant Hilton

H. Lowe Crosby and his wife checked out of the Casa Mona. Crosby called it "The Pissant Hilton," and he demanded quarters at the American embassy.

So I was the only guest in a one-hundred-room hotel.

My room was a pleasant one. It faced, as did all the rooms, the Boulevard of the Hundred Martyrs to Democracy, Monzano Airport, and Bolivar harbor beyond. The Casa Mona was built like a bookcase, with solid sides and back and with a front of blue-green glass. The squalor and misery of the city, being to the sides and back of the Casa Mona, were impossible to see.

My room was air-conditioned. It was almost chilly. And, coming from the blamming heat into that chilliness, I sneezed.

There were fresh flowers on my bedside table, but my bed had not yet been made. There wasn't even a pillow on the bed. There was simply a bare, brand-new Beautyrest mattress. And there weren't any coat hangers in the closet; and there wasn't any toilet paper in the bathroom.

So I went out in the corridor to see if there was a chambermaid who would equip me a little more completely. There wasn't anybody out there, but there was a door open at the far end and very faint sounds of life.

I went to this door and found a large suite paved with dropcloths. It was being painted, but the two painters weren't painting when I appeared. They were sitting on a shelf that ran the width of the window wall.

They had their shoes off. They had their eyes closed. They were facing each other.

They were pressing the soles of their bare feet together.

Each grasped his own ankles, giving himself the rigidity of a triangle.

I cleared my throat.

The two rolled off the shelf and fell to the spattered drop-cloth. They landed on their hands and knees, and they stayed in that position—their behinds in the air, their noses close to the ground.

They were expecting to be killed.

"Excuse me," I said, amazed.

"Don't tell," begged one querulously. "Please—please don't tell."

"Tell what?"

"What you saw!"

"I didn't see anything."

"If you tell," he said, and he put his cheek to the floor and looked up at me beseechingly, "if you tell, we'll die on the *hy-u-o-ook-kuh*!"

"Look, friends," I said, "either I came in too early or too late, but, I tell you again, I didn't see anything worth mentioning to anybody. Please—get up."

They got up, their eyes still on me. They trembled and cowered. I convinced them at last that I would never tell what I had seen.

What I had seen, of course, was the Bokononist ritual of *boko-maru*, or the mingling of awarenesses.

We Bokononists believe that it is impossible to be sole-to-sole with another person without loving the person, provided the feet of both persons are clean and nicely tended.

The basis for the foot ceremony is this "Calypso":

> We will touch our feet, yes,
> Yes, for all we're worth,
> And we will love each other, yes,
> Yes, like we love our Mother Earth.

73

Black Death

When I got back to my room I found that Philip Castle—mosaicist, historian, self-indexer, pissant, and hotel-keeper—was installing a roll of toilet paper in my bathroom.

"Thank you very much," I said.

"You're entirely welcome."

"This is what I'd call a hotel with a real heart. How many hotel owners would take such a direct interest in the comfort of a guest?"

"How many hotel owners have just one guest?"

"You used to have three."

"Those were the days."

"You know, I may be speaking out of turn, but I find it hard to understand how a person of your interests and talents would be attracted to the hotel business."

He frowned perplexedly. "I don't seem to be as good with guests as I might, do I?"

"I knew some people in the Hotel School at Cornell, and I can't help feeling they would have treated the Crosbys somewhat differently."

He nodded uncomfortably. "I know. I know." He flapped his arms. "Damned if I know why I built this hotel—something to do with my life, I guess. A way to be busy, a way not to be lonesome." He shook his head. "It was be a hermit or open a hotel—with nothing in between."

"Weren't you raised at your father's hospital?"

"That's right. Mona and I both grew up there."

"Well, aren't you at all tempted to do with your life what your father's done with his?"

Young Castle smiled wanly, avoiding a direct answer. "He's a funny person, Father is," he said. "I think you'll like him."

"I expect to. There aren't many people who've been as un-selfish as he has."

"One time," said Castle, "when I was about fifteen, there

was a mutiny near here on a Greek ship bound from Hong Kong to Havana with a load of wicker furniture. The mutineers got control of the ship, didn't know how to run her, and smashed her up on the rocks near 'Papa' Monzano's castle. Everybody drowned but the rats. The rats and the wicker furniture came ashore."

That seemed to be the end of the story, but I couldn't be sure. "So?"

"So some people got free furniture, and some people got bubonic plague. At Father's hospital, we had fourteen hundred deaths inside of ten days. Have you ever seen anyone die of bubonic plague?"

"That unhappiness has not been mine."

"The lymph glands in the groin and the armpits swell to the size of grapefruit."

"I can well believe it."

"After death, the body turns black—coals to Newcastle in the case of San Lorenzo. When the plague was having everything its own way, the House of Hope and Mercy in the Jungle looked like Auschwitz or Buchenwald. We had stacks of dead so deep and wide that a bulldozer actually stalled trying to shove them toward a common grave. Father worked without sleep for days, worked not only without sleep but without saving many lives, either."

Castle's grisly tale was interrupted by the ringing of my telephone.

"My God," said Castle, "I didn't even know the telephones were connected yet."

I picked up the phone. "Hello?"

It was Major General Franklin Hoenikker who had called me up. He sounded out of breath and scared stiff. "Listen! You've got to come out to my house right away. We've got to have a talk! It could be a very important thing in your life!"

"Could you give me some idea?"

"Not on the phone, not on the phone. You come to my house. You come right away! Please!"

"All right."

"I'm not kidding you. This is a really important thing in your life. This is the most important thing ever." He hung up.

"What was that all about?" asked Castle.

"I haven't got the slightest idea. Frank Hoenikker wants to see me right away."

"Take your time. Relax. He's a moron."

"He said it was important."

"How does he know what's important? I could carve a better man out of a banana."

"Well, finish your story anyway."

"Where was I?"

"The bubonic plague. The bulldozer was stalled by corpses."

"Oh, yes. Anyway, one sleepless night I stayed up with Father while he worked. It was all we could do to find a live patient to treat. In bed after bed after bed we found dead people.

"And Father started giggling," Castle continued.

"He couldn't stop. He walked out into the night with his flashlight. He was still giggling. He was making the flashlight beam dance over all the dead people stacked outside. He put his hand on my head, and do you know what that marvelous man said to me?" asked Castle.

"Nope."

"'Son,' my father said to me, 'someday this will all be yours.'"

74

Cat's Cradle

I went to Frank's house in San Lorenzo's one taxicab.

We passed through scenes of hideous want. We climbed the slope of Mount McCabe. The air grew cooler. There was mist.

Frank's house had once been the home of Nestor Aamons, father of Mona, architect of the House of Hope and Mercy in the Jungle.

Aamons had designed it.

It straddled a waterfall; had a terrace cantilevered out into the mist rising from the fall. It was a cunning lattice of very light steel posts and beams. The interstices of the lattice were variously open, chinked with native stone, glazed, or curtained by sheets of canvas.

The effect of the house was not so much to enclose as to announce that a man had been whimsically busy there.

A servant greeted me politely and told me that Frank wasn't home yet. Frank was expected at any moment. Frank had left orders to the effect that I was to be made happy and comfortable, and that I was to stay for supper and the night. The servant, who introduced himself as Stanley, was the first plump San Lorenzan I had seen.

Stanley led me to my room; led me around the heart of the house, down a staircase of living stone, a staircase sheltered or exposed by steel-framed rectangles at random. My bed was a foam-rubber slab on a stone shelf, a shelf of living stone. The walls of my chamber were canvas. Stanley demonstrated how I might roll them up or down, as I pleased.

I asked Stanley if anybody else was home, and he told me that only Newt was. Newt, he said, was out on the cantilevered terrace, painting a picture. Angela, he said, had gone sightseeing to the House of Hope and Mercy in the Jungle.

I went out onto the giddy terrace that straddled the waterfall and found little Newt asleep in a yellow butterfly chair.

The painting on which Newt had been working was set on an easel next to the aluminum railing. The painting was framed in a misty view of sky, sea, and valley.

Newt's painting was small and black and warty.

It consisted of scratches made in a black, gummy impasto. The scratches formed a sort of spider's web, and I wondered if they might not be the sticky nets of human futility hung up on a moonless night to dry.

I did not wake up the midget who had made this dreadful thing. I smoked, listening to imagined voices in the water sounds.

What awakened little Newt was an explosion far away below. It caromed up the valley and went to God. It was a cannon on the water front of Bolivar, Frank's major-domo told me. It was fired every day at five.

Little Newt stirred.

While still half-snoozing, he put his black, painty hands to his mouth and chin, leaving black smears there. He rubbed his eyes and made black smears around them, too.

"Hello," he said to me, sleepily.

"Hello," I said. "I like your painting."

"You see what it is?"

"I suppose it means something different to everyone who sees it."

"It's a cat's cradle."

"Aha," I said. "Very good. The scratches are string. Right?"

"One of the oldest games there is, cat's cradle. Even the Eskimos know it."

"You don't say."

"For maybe a hundred thousand years or more, grownups have been waving tangles of string in their children's faces."

"Um."

Newt remained curled in the chair. He held out his painty hands as though a cat's cradle were strung between them. "No wonder kids grow up crazy. A cat's cradle is nothing but a bunch of X's between somebody's hands, and little kids look and look and look at all those X's . . ."

"And?"

"*No damn cat, and no damn cradle.*"

75

Give My Regards to Albert Schweitzer

And then Angela Hoenikker Conners, Newt's beanpole sister, came in with Julian Castle, father of Philip, and founder of the House of Hope and Mercy in the Jungle. Castle wore a baggy white linen suit and a string tie. He had a scraggly mustache. He was bald. He was scrawny. He was a saint, I think.

He introduced himself to Newt and to me on the canti-

levered terrace. He forestalled all references to his possible
saintliness by talking out of the corner of his mouth like a
movie gangster.

"I understand you are a follower of Albert Schweitzer," I
said to him.

"At a distance. . . ." He gave a criminal sneer. "I've never
met the gentleman."

"He must surely know of your work, just as you know of
his."

"Maybe and maybe not. You ever see him?"

"No."

"You ever expect to see him?"

"Someday maybe I will."

"Well," said Julian Castle, "in case you run across Dr.
Schweitzer in your travels, you might tell him that he is *not* my
hero." He lit a big cigar.

When the cigar was going good and hot he pointed its red
end at me. "You can tell him he isn't my hero," he said, "but
you can also tell him that, thanks to him, Jesus Christ *is*."

"I think he'll be glad to hear it."

"I don't give a damn if he is or not. This is something between Jesus and me."

76

Julian Castle Agrees with Newt that
Everything Is Meaningless

Julian Castle and Angela went to Newt's painting. Castle
made a pinhole of a curled index finger, squinted at the painting through it.

"What do you think of it?" I asked him.

"It's *black*. What is it—hell?"

"It means whatever it means," said Newt.

"Then it's hell," snarled Castle.

"I was told a moment ago that it was a cat's cradle," I said.

"Inside information always helps," said Castle.

"I don't think it's very nice," Angela complained. "I think it's ugly, but I don't know anything about modern art. Sometimes I wish Newt would take some lessons, so he could know for sure if he was doing something or not."

"Self-taught, are you?" Julian Castle asked Newt.

"Isn't everybody?" Newt inquired.

"Very good answer." Castle was respectful.

I undertook to explain the deeper significance of the cat's cradle, since Newt seemed disinclined to go through that song and dance again.

And Castle nodded sagely. "So this is a picture of the meaninglessness of it all! I couldn't agree more."

"Do you *really* agree?" I asked. "A minute ago you said something about Jesus."

"Who?" said Castle.

"Jesus Christ?"

"Oh," said Castle. "*Him.*" He shrugged. "People have to talk about something just to keep their voice boxes in working order, so they'll have good voice boxes in case there's ever anything really meaningful to say."

"I see." I knew I wasn't going to have an easy time writing a popular article about him. I was going to have to concentrate on his saintly deeds and ignore entirely the satanic things he thought and said.

"You may quote me:" he said. "Man is vile, and man makes nothing worth making, knows nothing worth knowing."

He leaned down and he shook little Newt's painty hand. "Right?"

Newt nodded, seeming to suspect momentarily that the case had been a little overstated. "Right."

And then the saint marched to Newt's painting and took it from its easel. He beamed at us all. "Garbage—like everything else."

And he threw the painting off the cantilevered terrace. It sailed out on an updraft, stalled, boomeranged back, sliced into the waterfall.

There was nothing little Newt could say.

Angela spoke first. "You've got paint all over your face, honey. Go wash it off."

77

Aspirin and "Boko-maru"

"Tell me, Doctor," I said to Julian Castle, "how is 'Papa' Monzano?"

"How would I know?"

"I thought you'd probably been treating him."

"We don't speak . . ." Castle smiled. "He doesn't speak to me, that is. The last thing he said to me, which was about three years ago, was that the only thing that kept me off the hook was my American citizenship."

"What have you done to offend him? You come down here and with your own money found a free hospital for his people. . . ."

"'Papa' doesn't like the way we treat the whole patient," said Castle, "particularly the whole patient when he's dying. At the House of Hope and Mercy in the Jungle, we administer the last rites of the Bokononist Church to those who want them."

"What are the rites like?"

"Very simple. They start with a responsive reading. You want to respond?"

"I'm not that close to death just now, if you don't mind."

He gave me a grisly wink. "You're wise to be cautious. People taking the last rites have a way of dying on cue. I think we could keep you from going all the way, though, if we didn't touch feet."

"Feet?"

He told me about the Bokononist attitude relative to feet.

"That explains something I saw in the hotel." I told him about the two painters on the window sill.

"It works, you know," he said. "People who do that really do feel better about each other and the world."

"Um."

"*Boko-maru.*"

"Sir?"

"That's what the foot business is called," said Castle. "It works. I'm grateful for things that work. Not many things *do* work, you know."

"I suppose not."

"I couldn't possibly run that hospital of mine if it weren't for aspirin and *boko-maru.*"

"I gather," I said, "that there are still several Bokononists on the island, despite the laws, despite the *hy-u-o-ook-kuh.* . . ."

He laughed. "You haven't caught on, yet?"

"To what?"

"Everybody on San Lorenzo is a devout Bokononist, the *hy-u-o-ook-kuh* notwithstanding."

78

Ring of Steel

"When Bokonon and McCabe took over this miserable country years ago," said Julian Castle, "they threw out the priests. And then Bokonon, cynically and playfully, invented a new religion."

"I know," I said.

"Well, when it became evident that no governmental or economic reform was going to make the people much less miserable, the religion became the one real instrument of hope. Truth was the enemy of the people, because the truth was so terrible, so Bokonon made it his business to provide the people with better and better lies."

"How did he come to be an outlaw?"

"It was his own idea. He asked McCabe to outlaw him and his religion, too, in order to give the religious life of the people more zest, more tang. He wrote a little poem about it, incidentally."

Castle quoted this poem, which does not appear in *The Books of Bokonon*:

> So I said good-bye to government,
> And I gave my reason:
> That a really good religion
> Is a form of treason.

"Bokonon suggested the hook, too, as the proper punishment for Bokononists," he said. "It was something he'd seen in the Chamber of Horrors at Madame Tussaud's." He winked ghoulishly. "That was for zest, too."

"Did many people die on the hook?"

"Not at first, not at first. At first it was all make-believe. Rumors were cunningly circulated about executions, but no one really knew anyone who had died that way. McCabe had a good old time making bloodthirsty threats against the Bokononists—which was everybody.

"And Bokonon went into cozy hiding in the jungle," Castle continued, "where he wrote and preached all day long and ate good things his disciples brought him.

"McCabe would organize the unemployed, which was practically everybody, into great Bokonon hunts.

"About every six months McCabe would announce triumphantly that Bokonon was surrounded by a ring of steel, which was remorselessly closing in.

"And then the leaders of the remorseless ring would have to report to McCabe, full of chagrin and apoplexy, that Bokonon had done the impossible.

"He had escaped, had evaporated, had lived to preach another day. Miracle!"

79

Why McCabe's Soul Grew Coarse

"McCabe and Bokonon did not succeed in raising what is generally thought of as the standard of living," said Castle. "The truth was that life was as short and brutish and mean as ever.

"But people didn't have to pay as much attention to the awful truth. As the living legend of the cruel tyrant in the city and the gentle holy man in the jungle grew, so, too, did the happiness of the people grow. They were all employed full time as actors in a play they understood, that any human being anywhere could understand and applaud."

"So life became a work of art," I marveled.

"Yes. There was only one trouble with it."

"Oh?"

"The drama was very tough on the souls of the two main actors, McCabe and Bokonon. As young men, they had been pretty much alike, had both been half-angel, half-pirate.

"But the drama demanded that the pirate half of Bokonon and the angel half of McCabe wither away. And McCabe and Bokonon paid a terrible price in agony for the happiness of the people—McCabe knowing the agony of the tyrant and Bokonon knowing the agony of the saint. They both became, for all practical purposes, insane."

Castle crooked the index finger of his left hand. "And then, people really did start dying on the *hy-u-o-ook-kuh*."

"But Bokonon was never caught?" I asked.

"McCabe never went that crazy. He never made a really serious effort to catch Bokonon. It would have been easy to do."

"Why didn't he catch him?"

"McCabe was always sane enough to realize that without the holy man to war against, he himself would become meaningless. 'Papa' Monzano understands that, too."

"Do people still die on the hook?"

"It's inevitably fatal."

"I mean," I said, "does 'Papa' really have people executed that way?"

"He executes one every two years—just to keep the pot boiling, so to speak." He sighed, looking up at the evening sky. "Busy, busy, busy."

"Sir?"

"It's what we Bokononists say," he said, "when we feel that a lot of mysterious things are going on."

"You?" I was amazed. "A Bokononist, too?"

He gazed at me levelly. "You, too. You'll find out."

80

The Waterfall Strainers

Angela and Newt were on the cantilevered terrace with Julian Castle and me. We had cocktails. There was still no word from Frank.

Both Angela and Newt, it appeared, were fairly heavy drinkers. Castle told me that his days as a playboy had cost him a kidney, and that he was unhappily compelled, perforce, to stick to ginger ale.

Angela, when she got a few drinks into her, complained of how the world had swindled her father. "He gave so much, and they gave him so little."

I pressed her for examples of the world's stinginess and got some exact numbers. "General Forge and Foundry gave him a forty-five-dollar bonus for every patent his work led to," she said. "That's the same patent bonus they paid anybody in the company." She shook her head mournfully. "Forty-five dollars—and just think what some of those patents were for!"

"Um," I said. "I assume he got a salary, too."

"The most he ever made was twenty-eight thousand dollars a year."

"I'd say that was pretty good."

She got very huffy. "You know what movie stars make?"

"A lot, sometimes."

"You know Dr. Breed made ten thousand more dollars a year than Father did?"

"That was certainly an injustice."

"I'm sick of injustice."

She was so shrilly exercised that I changed the subject. I asked Julian Castle what he thought had become of the painting he had thrown down the waterfall.

"There's a little village at the bottom," he told me. "Five or ten shacks, I'd say. It's 'Papa' Monzano's birthplace, incidentally. The waterfall ends in a big stone bowl there.

"The villagers have a net made out of chicken wire stretched across a notch in the bowl. Water spills out through the notch into a stream."

"And Newt's painting is in the net now, you think?" I asked.

"This is a poor country—in case you haven't noticed," said Castle. "Nothing stays in the net very long. I imagine Newt's painting is being dried in the sun by now, along with the butt of my cigar. Four square feet of gummy canvas, the four milled and mitered sticks of the stretcher, some tacks, too, and a cigar. All in all, a pretty nice catch for some poor, poor man."

"I could just scream sometimes," said Angela, "when I think about how much some people get paid and how little they paid Father—and how much he gave." She was on the edge of a crying jag.

"Don't cry," Newt begged her gently.

"Sometimes I can't help it," she said.

"Go get your clarinet," urged Newt. "That always helps."

I thought at first that this was a fairly comical suggestion. But then, from Angela's reaction, I learned that the suggestion was serious and practical.

"When I get this way," she said to Castle and me, "sometimes it's the only thing that helps."

But she was too shy to get her clarinet right away. We had to keep begging her to play, and she had to have two more drinks.

"She's really just wonderful," little Newt promised.

"I'd love to hear you play," said Castle.

"All right," said Angela finally as she rose unsteadily. "All right—I will."

When she was out of earshot, Newt apologized for her. "She's had a tough time. She needs a rest."

"She's been sick?" I asked.

"Her husband is mean as hell to her," said Newt. He showed us that he hated Angela's handsome young husband, the extremely successful Harrison C. Conners, President of Fabri-Tek. "He hardly ever comes home—and, when he does, he's drunk and generally covered with lipstick."

"From the way she talked," I said, "I thought it was a very happy marriage."

Little Newt held his hands six inches apart and he spread his fingers. "See the cat? See the cradle?"

81

A White Bride for the Son of a Pullman Porter

I did not know what was going to come from Angela's clarinet. No one could have imagined what was going to come from there.

I expected something pathological, but I did not expect the depth, the violence, and the almost intolerable beauty of the disease.

Angela moistened and warmed the mouthpiece, but did not blow a single preliminary note. Her eyes glazed over, and her long, bony fingers twittered idly over the noiseless keys.

I waited anxiously, and I remembered what Marvin Breed had told me—that Angela's one escape from her bleak life with her father was to her room, where she would lock the door and play along with phonograph records.

Newt now put a long-playing record on the large phonograph in the room off the terrace. He came back with the record's slipcase, which he handed to me.

The record was called *Cat House Piano*. It was of unaccompanied piano by Meade Lux Lewis.

Since Angela, in order to deepen her trance, let Lewis play his first number without joining him, I read some of what the jacket said about Lewis.

"Born in Louisville, Ky., in 1905," I read, "Mr. Lewis didn't turn to music until he had passed his 16th birthday and then the instrument provided by his father was the violin. A year later young Lewis chanced to hear Jimmy Yancey play the piano. 'This,' as Lewis recalls, 'was the real thing.' Soon," I read, "Lewis was teaching himself to play the boogie-woogie piano, absorbing all that was possible from the older Yancey, who remained until his death a close friend and idol to Mr. Lewis. Since his father was a Pullman porter," I read, "the Lewis family lived near the railroad. The rhythm of the trains soon became a natural pattern to young Lewis and he composed the boogie-woogie solo, now a classic of its kind, which became known as 'Honky Tonk Train Blues.'"

I looked up from my reading. The first number on the record was done. The phonograph needle was now scratching its slow way across the void to the second. The second number, I learned from the jacket, was "Dragon Blues."

Meade Lux Lewis played four bars alone—and then Angela Hoenikker joined in.

Her eyes were closed.

I was flabbergasted.

She was great.

She improvised around the music of the Pullman porter's son; went from liquid lyricism to rasping lechery to the shrill skittishness of a frightened child, to a heroin nightmare.

Her glissandi spoke of heaven and hell and all that lay between.

Such music from such a woman could only be a case of schizophrenia or demonic possession.

My hair stood on end, as though Angela were rolling on the floor, foaming at the mouth, and babbling fluent Babylonian.

When the music was done, I shrieked at Julian Castle, who was transfixed, too, "My God—life! Who can understand even one little minute of it?"

"Don't try," he said. "Just pretend you understand."

"That's—that's very good advice," I went limp.

Castle quoted another poem:

> Tiger got to hunt,
> Bird got to fly;
> Man got to sit and wonder, "Why, why, why?"
> Tiger got to sleep,
> Bird got to land;
> Man got to tell himself he understand.

"What's that from?" I asked.

"What could it possibly be from but *The Books of Bokonon*?"

"I'd love to see a copy sometime."

"Copies are hard to come by," said Castle. "They aren't printed. They're made by hand. And, of course, there is no such thing as a completed copy, since Bokonon is adding things every day."

Little Newt snorted. "Religion!"

"Beg your pardon?" Castle said.

"See the cat?" asked Newt. "See the cradle?"

82

"Zah-mah-ki-bo"

Major General Franklin Hoenikker didn't appear for supper.

He telephoned, and insisted on talking to me and to no one else. He told me that he was keeping a vigil by "Papa's" bed; that "Papa" was dying in great pain. Frank sounded scared and lonely.

"Look," I said, "why don't I go back to my hotel, and you and I can get together later, when this crisis is over."

"No, no, no. You stay right there! I want you to be where I can get hold of you right away!" He was panicky about my slipping out of his grasp. Since I couldn't account for his interest in me, I began to feel panic, too.

"Could you give me some idea what you want to see me about?" I asked.

"Not over the telephone."

"Something about your father?"

"Something about *you*."

"Something I've done?"

"Something you're *going* to do."

I heard a chicken clucking in the background of Frank's end of the line. I heard a door open, and xylophone music came from some chamber. The music was again "When Day Is Done." And then the door was closed, and I couldn't hear the music any more.

"I'd appreciate it if you'd give me some small hint of what you expect me to do—so I can sort of get set," I said.

"*Zah-mah-ki-bo.*"

"What?"

"It's a Bokononist word."

"I don't know any Bokononist words."

"Julian Castle's there?"

"Yes."

"Ask him," said Frank. "I've got to go now." He hung up.

So I asked Julian Castle what *zah-mah-ki-bo* meant.

"You want a simple answer or a whole answer?"

"Let's start with a simple one."

"Fate—inevitable destiny."

83

Dr. Schlichter von Koenigswald Approaches the Break-even Point

"Cancer," said Julian Castle at dinner, when I told him that "Papa" was dying in pain.

"Cancer of what?"

"Cancer of about everything. You say he collapsed on the reviewing stand today?"

"He sure did," said Angela.

"That was the effect of drugs," Castle declared. "He's at the point now where drugs and pain just about balance out. More drugs would kill him."

"I'd kill myself, I think," murmured Newt. He was sitting on a sort of folding high chair he took with him when he went visiting. It was made of aluminum tubing and canvas. "It beats sitting on a dictionary, an atlas, and a telephone book," he'd said when he erected it.

"That's what Corporal McCabe did, of course," said Castle. "He named his major-domo as his successor, then he shot himself."

"Cancer, too?" I asked.

"I can't be sure; I don't think so, though. Unrelieved villainy just wore him out, is my guess. That was all before my time."

"This certainly is a cheerful conversation," said Angela.

"I think everybody would agree that these are cheerful times," said Castle.

"Well," I said to him, "I'd think you would have more reasons for being cheerful than most, doing what you are doing with your life."

"I once had a yacht, too, you know."

"I don't follow you."

"Having a yacht is a reason for being more cheerful than most, too."

"If you aren't 'Papa's' doctor," I said, "who is?"

"One of my staff, a Dr. Schlichter von Koenigswald."

"A German?"

"Vaguely. He was in the S.S. for fourteen years. He was a camp physician at Auschwitz for six of those years."

"Doing penance at the House of Hope and Mercy is he?"

"Yes," said Castle, "and making great strides, too, saving lives right and left."

"Good for him."

"Yes. If he keeps going at his present rate, working night and day, the number of people he's saved will equal the number of people he let die—in the year 3010."

So there's another member of my *karass*: Dr. Schlichter von Koenigswald.

84

Blackout

Three hours after supper Frank still hadn't come home. Julian Castle excused himself and went back to the House of Hope and Mercy in the Jungle.

Angela and Newt and I sat on the cantilevered terrace. The lights of Bolivar were lovely below us. There was a great, illuminated cross on top of the administration building of Monzano Airport. It was motor-driven, turning slowly, boxing the compass with electric piety.

There were other bright places on the island, too, to the north of us. Mountains prevented our seeing them directly, but we could see in the sky their balloons of light. I asked Stanley, Frank Hoenikker's major-domo, to identify for me the sources of the auroras.

He pointed them out, counterclockwise. "House of Hope and Mercy in the Jungle, 'Papa's' palace, and Fort Jesus."

"Fort Jesus?"

"The training camp for our soldiers."

"It's named after Jesus Christ?"

"Sure. Why not?"

There was a new balloon of light growing quickly to the north. Before I could ask what it was, it revealed itself as headlights topping a ridge. The headlights were coming toward us. They belonged to a convoy.

The convoy was composed of five American-made army trucks. Machine gunners manned ring mounts on the tops of the cabs.

The convoy stopped in Frank's driveway. Soldiers dismounted at once. They set to work on the grounds, digging foxholes and machine-gun pits. I went out with Frank's major-domo to ask the officer in charge what was going on.

"We have been ordered to protect the next President of San Lorenzo," said the officer in island dialect.

"He isn't here now," I informed him.

"I don't know anything about it," he said. "My orders are to dig in here. That's all I know."

I told Angela and Newt about it.

"Do you think there's any real danger?" Angela asked me.

"I'm a stranger here myself," I said.

At that moment there was a power failure. Every electric light in San Lorenzo went out.

85

A Pack of "Foma"

Frank's servants brought us gasoline lanterns; told us that power failures were common in San Lorenzo, that there was no cause for alarm. I found that disquiet was hard for me to set aside, however, since Frank had spoken of my *zah-mah-ki-bo*.

He had made me feel as though my own free will were as irrelevant as the free will of a piggy-wig arriving at the Chicago stockyards.

I remembered again the stone angel in Ilium.

And I listened to the soldiers outside—to their clinking, chunking, murmuring labors.

I was unable to concentrate on the conversation of Angela and Newt, though they got onto a fairly interesting subject. They told me that their father had had an identical twin. They had never met him. His name was Rudolph. The last they had heard of him, he was a music-box manufacturer in Zurich, Switzerland.

"Father hardly ever mentioned him," said Angela.

"Father hardly ever mentioned anybody," Newt declared.

There was a sister of the old man, too, they told me. Her name was Celia. She raised giant schnauzers on Shelter Island, New York.

"She always sends a Christmas card," said Angela.

"With a picture of a giant schnauzer on it," said little Newt.

"It sure is funny how different people in different families turn out," Angela observed.

"That's very true and well said," I agreed. I excused myself from the glittering company, and I asked Stanley, the major-domo, if there happened to be a copy of *The Books of Bokonon* about the house.

Stanley pretended not to know what I was talking about. And then he grumbled that *The Books of Bokonon* were filth. And then he insisted that anyone who read them should die on the hook. And then he brought me a copy from Frank's bedside table.

It was a heavy thing, about the size of an unabridged dictionary. It was written by hand. I trundled it off to my bedroom, to my slab of rubber on living rock.

There was no index, so my search for the implications of *zah-mah-ki-bo* was difficult; was, in fact, fruitless that night.

I learned some things, but they were scarcely helpful. I learned of the Bokononist cosmogony, for instance, wherein *Borasisi*, the sun, held *Pabu*, the moon, in his arms, and hoped that *Pabu* would bear him a fiery child.

But poor *Pabu* gave birth to children that were cold, that did not burn; and *Borasisi* threw them away in disgust. These were the planets, who circled their terrible father at a safe distance.

Then poor *Pabu* herself was cast away, and she went to live with her favorite child, which was Earth. Earth was *Pabu*'s favorite because it had people on it; and the people looked up at her and loved her and sympathized.

And what opinion did Bokonon hold of his own cosmogony?

"*Foma*! Lies!" he wrote. "A pack of *foma*!"

86

Two Little Jugs

It's hard to believe that I slept at all, but I must have—for, otherwise, how could I have found myself awakened by a series of bangs and a flood of light?

I rolled out of bed at the first bang and ran to the heart of the house in the brainless ecstasy of a volunteer fireman.

I found myself rushing headlong at Newt and Angela, who were fleeing from beds of their own.

We all stopped short, sheepishly analyzing the nightmarish sounds around us, sorting them out as coming from a radio, from an electric dishwasher, from a pump—all restored to noisy life by the return of electric power.

The three of us awakened enough to realize that there was humor in our situation, that we had reacted in amusingly human ways to a situation that seemed mortal but wasn't. And, to demonstrate my mastery over my illusory fate, I turned the radio off.

We all chuckled.

And we all vied, in saving face, to be the greatest student of human nature, the person with the quickest sense of humor.

Newt was the quickest; he pointed out to me that I had my passport and my billfold and my wristwatch in my hands. I had no idea what I'd grabbed in the face of death—didn't know I'd grabbed anything.

I countered hilariously by asking Angela and Newt why it was that they both carried little Thermos jugs, identical red-and-gray jugs capable of holding about three cups of coffee.

It was news to them both that they were carrying such jugs. They were shocked to find them in their hands.

They were spared making an explanation by more banging outside. I was bound to find out what the banging was right away; and, with a brazenness as unjustified as my earlier panic, I investigated, found Frank Hoenikker outside tinkering with a motor-generator set mounted on a truck.

The generator was the new source of our electricity. The

gasoline motor that drove it was backfiring and smoking. Frank was trying to fix it.

He had the heavenly Mona with him. She was watching him, as always, gravely.

"Boy, have I got news for you!" he yelled at me, and he led the way back into the house.

Angela and Newt were still in the living room, but, somehow, somewhere, they had managed to get rid of their peculiar Thermos jugs.

The contents of those jugs, of course, were parts of the legacies from Dr. Felix Hoenikker, were parts of the *wampeter* of my *karass*, were chips of *ice-nine*.

Frank took me aside. "How awake are you?"

"As awake as I ever was."

"I hope you're really wide awake, because we've got to have a talk right now."

"Start talking."

"Let's get some privacy." Frank told Mona to make herself comfortable. "We'll call you if we need you."

I looked at Mona, meltingly, and I thought that I had never needed anyone as much as I needed her.

87

The Cut of My Jib

About this Franklin Hoenikker—the pinch-faced child spoke with the timbre and conviction of a kazoo. I had heard it said in the Army that such and such a man spoke like a man with a paper rectum. Such a man was General Hoenikker. Poor Frank had had almost no experience in talking to anyone, having spent a furtive childhood as Secret Agent X-9.

Now, hoping to be hearty and persuasive, he said tinny things to me, things like, "I like the cut of your jib!" and "I want to talk cold turkey to you, man to man!"

And he took me down to what he called his "den" in order

that we might, ". . . call a spade a spade, and let the chips fall where they may."

So we went down steps cut into a cliff and into a natural cave that was beneath and behind the waterfall. There were a couple of drawing tables down there; three pale, bare-boned Scandinavian chairs; a bookcase containing books on architecture, books in German, French, Finnish, Italian, English.

All was lit by electric lights, lights that pulsed with the panting of the motor-generator set.

And the most striking thing about the cave was that there were pictures painted on the walls, painted with kindergarten boldness, painted with the flat clay, earth, and charcoal colors of very early man. I did not have to ask Frank how old the cave paintings were. I was able to date them by their subject. The paintings were not of mammoths or saber-toothed tigers or ithyphallic cave bears.

The paintings treated endlessly the aspects of Mona Aamons Monzano as a little girl.

"This—this is where Mona's father worked?" I asked.

"That's right. He was the Finn who designed the House of Hope and Mercy in the Jungle."

"I know."

"That isn't what I brought you down here to talk about."

"This is something about your father?"

"This is about *you*." Frank put his hand on my shoulder and he looked me in the eye. The effect was dismaying. Frank meant to inspire camaraderie, but his head looked to me like a bizarre little owl, blinded by light and perched on a tall white post.

"Maybe you'd better come to the point."

"There's no sense in beating around the bush," he said. "I'm a pretty good judge of character, if I do say so myself, and I like the cut of your jib."

"Thank you."

"I think you and I could really hit it off."

"I have no doubt of it."

"We've both got things that mesh."

I was grateful when he took his hand from my shoulder. He meshed the fingers of his hands like gear teeth. One hand represented him, I suppose, and the other represented me.

"We need each other." He wiggled his fingers to show me how gears worked.

I was silent for some time, though outwardly friendly.

"Do you get my meaning?" asked Frank at last.

"You and I—we're going to *do* something together?"

"That's right!" Frank clapped his hands. "You're a worldly person, used to meeting the public; and I'm a technical person, used to working behind the scenes, making things go."

"How can you possibly know what kind of a person I am? We've just met."

"Your clothes, the way you talk." He put his hand on my shoulder again. "I like the cut of your jib!"

"So you said."

Frank was frantic for me to complete his thought, to do it enthusiastically, but I was still at sea. "Am I to understand that . . . that you are offering me some kind of job here, here in San Lorenzo?"

He clapped his hands. He was delighted. "That's right! What would you say to a hundred thousand dollars a year?"

"Good God!" I cried. "What would I have to do for that?"

"Practically nothing. And you'd drink out of gold goblets every night and eat off of gold plates and have a palace all your own."

"What's the job?"

"President of the Republic of San Lorenzo."

88

Why Frank Couldn't Be President

"Me? President?" I gasped.

"Who else is there?"

"Nuts!"

"Don't say no until you've really thought about it." Frank watched me anxiously.

"No!"

"You haven't really thought about it."

"Enough to know it's crazy."

Frank made his fingers into gears again. "We'd work *together.* I'd be backing you up all the time."

"Good. So, if I got plugged from the front you'd get it, too."

"Plugged?"

"Shot! Assassinated!"

Frank was mystified. "Why would anybody shoot you?"

"So he could get to be President."

Frank shook his head. "Nobody in San Lorenzo *wants* to be President," he promised me. "It's against their religion."

"It's against *your* religion, too? I thought *you* were going to be the next President."

"I . . ." he said, and found it hard to go on. He looked haunted.

"You what?" I asked.

He faced the sheet of water that curtained the cave. "Maturity, the way I understand it," he told me, "is knowing what your limitations are."

He wasn't far from Bokonon in defining maturity. "Maturity," Bokonon tells us, "is a bitter disappointment for which no remedy exists, unless laughter can be said to remedy anything."

"I know I've got limitations," Frank continued. "They're the same limitations my father had."

"Oh?"

"I've got a lot of very good ideas, just the way my father did," Frank told me and the waterfall, "but he was no good at facing the public, and neither am I."

89

"Duffle"

"You'll take the job?" Frank inquired anxiously.

"No," I told him.

"Do you know anybody who *might* want the job?" Frank was giving a classic illustration of what Bokonon calls *duffle*. *Duffle*, in the Bokononist sense, is the destiny of thousands upon thousands of persons when placed in the hands of a *stuppa*. A *stuppa* is a fogbound child.

I laughed.

"Something's funny?"

"Pay no attention when I laugh," I begged him. "I'm a notorious pervert in that respect."

"Are you laughing at me?"

I shook my head. "No."

"Word of honor?"

"Word of honor."

"People used to make fun of me all the time."

"You must have imagined that."

"They used to yell things at me. I didn't imagine *that*."

"People are unkind sometimes without meaning to be," I suggested. I wouldn't have given him my word of honor on that.

"You know what they used to yell at me?"

"No."

"They used to yell at me, 'Hey, X-9, where you going?'"

"That doesn't seem too bad."

"That's what they used to call me," said Frank in sulky reminiscence, "'Secret Agent X-9.'"

I didn't tell him I knew that already.

"'Where are you going, X-9?'" Frank echoed again.

I imagined what the taunters had been like, imagined where Fate had eventually goosed and chivvied them to. The wits who had yelled at Frank were surely nicely settled in deathlike jobs at General Forge and Foundry, at Ilium Power and Light, at the Telephone Company. . . .

And here, by God, was Secret Agent X-9, a Major General,

offering to make me king . . . in a cave that was curtained by a tropical waterfall.

"They really would have been surprised if I'd stopped and told them where I was going."

"You mean you had some premonition you'd end up here?" It was a Bokononist question.

"I was going to Jack's Hobby Shop," he said, with no sense of anticlimax.

"Oh."

"They all knew I was going there, but they didn't know what really went on there. They would have been really surprised— especially the girls—if they'd found out what *really* went on. The girls didn't think I knew anything about girls."

"What *really* went on?"

"I was screwing Jack's wife every day. That's how come I fell asleep all the time in high school. That's how come I never achieved my full potential."

He roused himself from this sordid recollection. "Come on. Be President of San Lorenzo. You'd be real good at it, with your personality. Please?"

90

Only One Catch

And the time of night and the cave and the waterfall—and the stone angel in Ilium. . . .

And 250,000 cigarettes and 3,000 quarts of booze, and two wives and no wife. . . .

And no love waiting for me anywhere. . . .

And the listless life of an ink-stained hack. . . .

And *Pabu*, the moon, and *Borasisi*, the sun, and their children. . . .

All things conspired to form one cosmic *vin-dit*, one mighty shove into Bokononism, into the belief that God was running my life and that He had work for me to do.

And, inwardly, I *sarooned*, which is to say that I acquiesced to the seeming demands of my *vin-dit*.

Inwardly, I agreed to become the next President of San Lorenzo.

Outwardly, I was still guarded, suspicious. "There must be a catch," I hedged.

"There isn't."

"There'll be an election?"

"There never has been. We'll just announce who the new President is."

"And nobody will object?"

"Nobody objects to anything. They aren't interested. They don't care."

"There *has* to be a catch!"

"There's kind of one," Frank admitted.

"I knew it!" I began to shrink from my *vin-dit*. "What is it? What's the catch?"

"Well, it isn't really a catch, because you don't have to do it, if you don't want to. It *would* be a good idea, though."

"Let's hear this great idea."

"Well, if you're going to be President, I think you really ought to marry Mona. But you don't have to, if you don't want to. You're the boss."

"She would *have* me?"

"If she'd have me, she'd have you. All you have to do is ask her."

"Why should she say yes?"

"It's predicted in *The Books of Bokonon* that she'll marry the next President of San Lorenzo," said Frank.

91

Mona

Frank brought Mona to her father's cave and left us alone. We had difficulty in speaking at first. I was shy.

Her gown was diaphanous. Her gown was azure. It was a simple gown, caught lightly at the waist by a gossamer thread. All else was shaped by Mona herself. Her breasts were like pomegranates or what you will, but like nothing so much as a young woman's breasts.

Her feet were all but bare. Her toenails were exquisitely manicured. Her scanty sandals were gold.

"How—how do you do?" I asked. My heart was pounding. Blood boiled in my ears.

"It is not possible to make a mistake," she assured me.

I did not know that this was a customary greeting given by all Bokononists when meeting a shy person. So, I responded with a feverish discussion of whether it was possible to make a mistake or not.

"My God, you have no idea how many mistakes I've already made. You're looking at the world's champion mistakemaker," I blurted—and so on. "Do you have any idea what Frank just said to me?"

"About *me*?"

"About everything, but *especially* about you."

"He told you that you could have me, if you wanted."

"Yes."

"That's true."

"I—I—I . . ."

"Yes?"

"I don't know what to say next."

"*Boko-maru* would help," she suggested.

"What?"

"Take off your shoes," she commanded. And she removed her sandals with the utmost grace.

I am a man of the world, having had, by a reckoning I once made, more than fifty-three women. I can say that I have seen women undress themselves in every way that it can be done. I have watched the curtains part on every variation of the final act.

And yet, the one woman who made me groan involuntarily did no more than remove her sandals.

I tried to untie my shoes. No bridegroom ever did worse. I got one shoe off, but knotted the other one tight. I tore a thumbnail on the knot; finally ripped off the shoe without untying it.

Then off came my socks.

Mona was already sitting on the floor, her legs extended, her round arms thrust behind her for support, her head tilted back, her eyes closed.

It was up to me now to complete my first—my first—my first, Great God . . .

Boko-maru.

92

On the Poet's Celebration of His First "Boko-maru"

These are not Bokonon's words. They are mine.

> Sweet wraith,
> Invisible mist of . . .
> I am—
> My soul—
> Wraith lovesick o'erlong,
> O'erlong alone:
> Wouldst another sweet soul meet?
> Long have I
> Advised thee ill
> As to where two souls
> Might tryst.
> My soles, my soles!
> My soul, my soul,
> Go there,
> Sweet soul;
> Be kissed.
> Mmmmmmm.

93

How I Almost Lost My Mona

"Do you find it easier to talk to me now?" Mona inquired.

"As though I'd known you for a thousand years," I confessed. I felt like crying. "I love you, Mona."

"I love you." She said it simply.

"What a fool Frank was!"

"Oh?"

"To give you up."

"He did not love me. He was going to marry me only because 'Papa' wanted him to. He loves another."

"Who?"

"A woman he knew in Ilium."

The lucky woman had to be the wife of the owner of Jack's Hobby Shop. "He told you?"

"Tonight, when he freed me to marry you."

"Mona?"

"Yes?"

"Is—is there anyone else in your life?"

She was puzzled. "Many," she said at last.

"That you *love*?"

"I love everyone."

"As—as much as me?"

"Yes." She seemed to have no idea that this might bother me.

I got off the floor, sat in a chair, and started putting my shoes and socks back on.

"I suppose you—you perform—you do what we just did with—with other people?"

"*Boko-maru*?"

"*Boko-maru*."

"Of course."

"I don't want you to do it with anybody but me from now on," I declared.

Tears filled her eyes. She adored her promiscuity; was angered that I should try to make her feel shame. "I make people happy. Love is good, not bad."

"As your husband, I'll want all your love for myself."

She stared at me with widening eyes. "A *sin-wat*!"

"What was that?"

"A *sin-wat*!" she cried. "A man who wants all of somebody's love. That's very bad."

"In the case of marriage, I think it's a very good thing. It's the only thing."

She was still on the floor, and I, now with my shoes and socks back on, was standing. I felt very tall, though I'm not very tall; and I felt very strong, though I'm not very strong; and I was a respectful stranger to my own voice. My voice had a metallic authority that was new.

As I went on talking in ball-peen tones, it dawned on me what was happening, what was happening already. I was already starting to rule.

I told Mona that I had seen her performing a sort of vertical *boko-maru* with a pilot on the reviewing stand shortly after my arrival. "You are to have nothing more to do with him," I told her. "What is his name?"

"I don't even know," she whispered. She was looking down now.

"And what about young Philip Castle?"

"You mean *boko-maru*?"

"I mean anything and everything. As I understand it, you two grew up together."

"Yes."

"Bokonon tutored you both?"

"Yes." The recollection made her radiant again.

"I suppose there was plenty of *boko-maruing* in those days."

"Oh, yes!" she said happily.

"You aren't to see him any more, either. Is that clear?"

"No."

"No?"

"I will not marry a *sin-wat*." She stood. "Good-bye."

"Good-bye?" I was crushed.

"Bokonon tells us it is very wrong not to love everyone exactly the same. What does *your* religion say?"

"I—I don't have one."

"I *do*."

I had stopped ruling. "I see you do," I said.

"Good-bye, man-with-no-religion." She went to the stone staircase.

"Mona . . ."

She stopped. "Yes?"

"Could I have your religion, if I wanted it?"

"Of course."

"I want it."

"Good. I love you."

"And I love you," I sighed.

94

The Highest Mountain

So I became betrothed at dawn to the most beautiful woman in the world. And I agreed to become the next President of San Lorenzo.

"Papa" wasn't dead yet, and it was Frank's feeling that I should get "Papa's" blessing, if possible. So, as *Borasisi*, the sun, came up, Frank and I drove to "Papa's" castle in a Jeep we commandeered from the troops guarding the next President.

Mona stayed at Frank's. I kissed her sacredly, and she went to sacred sleep.

Over the mountains Frank and I went, through groves of wild coffee trees, with the flamboyant sunrise on our right.

It was in the sunrise that the cetacean majesty of the highest mountain on the island, of Mount McCabe, made itself known to me. It was a fearful hump, a blue whale, with one queer stone plug on its back for a peak. In scale with a whale, the plug might have been the stump of a snapped harpoon, and it seemed so unrelated to the rest of the mountain that I asked Frank if it had been built by men.

He told me that it was a natural formation. Moreover, he declared that no man, as far as he knew, had ever been to the top of Mount McCabe.

"It *doesn't* look very tough to climb," I commented. Save

for the plug at the top, the mountain presented inclines no more forbidding than courthouse steps. And the plug itself, from a distance at any rate, seemed conveniently laced with ramps and ledges.

"Is it sacred or something?" I asked.

"Maybe it was once. But not since Bokonon."

"Then why hasn't anybody climbed it?"

"Nobody's felt like it yet."

"Maybe I'll climb it."

"Go ahead. Nobody's stopping you."

We rode in silence.

"What *is* sacred to Bokononists?" I asked after a while.

"Not even God, as near as I can tell."

"Nothing?"

"Just one thing."

I made some guesses. "The ocean? The sun?"

"Man," said Frank. "That's all. Just man."

95

I See the Hook

We came at last to the castle.

It was low and black and cruel.

Antique cannons still lolled on the battlements. Vines and bird nests clogged the crenels, the machicolations, and the balistrariae.

Its parapets to the north were continuous with the scarp of a monstrous precipice that fell six hundred feet straight down to the lukewarm sea.

It posed the question posed by all such stone piles: how had puny men moved stones so big? And, like all such stone piles, it answered the question itself. Dumb terror had moved those stones so big.

The castle was built according to the wish of Tum-bumwa, Emperor of San Lorenzo, a demented man, an escaped slave.

Tum-bumwa was said to have found its design in a child's picture book.

A gory book it must have been.

Just before we reached the palace gate the ruts carried us through a rustic arch made of two telephone poles and a beam that spanned them.

Hanging from the middle of the beam was a huge iron hook. There was a sign impaled on the hook.

"This hook," the sign proclaimed, "is reserved for Bokonon himself."

I turned to look at the hook again, and that thing of sharp iron communicated to me that I really was going to rule. I would chop down the hook!

And I flattered myself that I was going to be a firm, just, and kindly ruler, and that my people would prosper.

Fata Morgana.

Mirage!

96

Bell, Book, and Chicken in a Hatbox

Frank and I couldn't get right in to see "Papa." Dr. Schlichter von Koenigswald, the physician in attendance, muttered that we would have to wait about half an hour.

So Frank and I waited in the anteroom of "Papa's" suite, a room without windows. The room was thirty feet square, furnished with several rugged benches and a card table. The card table supported an electric fan. The walls were stone. There were no pictures, no decorations of any sort on the walls.

There were iron rings fixed to the wall, however, seven feet off the floor and at intervals of six feet. I asked Frank if the room had ever been a torture chamber.

He told me that it had, and that the manhole cover on which I stood was the lid of an oubliette.

There was a listless guard in the anteroom. There was also a

Christian minister, who was ready to take care of "Papa's" spiritual needs as they arose. He had a brass dinner bell and a hatbox with holes drilled in it, and a Bible, and a butcher knife—all laid out on the bench beside him.

He told me there was a live chicken in the hatbox. The chicken was quiet, he said, because he had fed it tranquilizers.

Like all San Lorenzans past the age of twenty-five, he looked at least sixty. He told me that his name was Dr. Vox Humana, that he was named after an organ stop that had struck his mother when San Lorenzo Cathedral was dynamited in 1923. His father, he told me without shame, was unknown.

I asked him what particular Christian sect he represented, and I observed frankly that the chicken and the butcher knife were novelties insofar as my understanding of Christianity went.

"The bell," I commented, "I can understand how that might fit in nicely."

He turned out to be an intelligent man. His doctorate, which he invited me to examine, was awarded by the Western Hemisphere University of the Bible of Little Rock, Arkansas. He made contact with the University through a classified ad in *Popular Mechanics*, he told me. He said that the motto of the University had become his own, and that it explained the chicken and the butcher knife. The motto of the University was this:

MAKE RELIGION LIVE!

He said that he had had to feel his way along with Christianity, since Catholicism and Protestantism had been outlawed along with Bokononism.

"So, if I am going to be a Christian under those conditions, I have to make up a lot of new stuff."

"*Zo*," he said in dialect, "*yeff jy bam gong be Kret-yeen hooner yoze kon-steez-yen, jy hay my yup oon lot nee stopf.*"

Dr. Schlichter von Koenigswald now came out of "Papa's" suite, looking very German, very tired. "You can see 'Papa' now."

"We'll be careful not to tire him," Frank promised.

"If you could kill him," said Von Koenigswald, "I think he'd be grateful."

97

The Stinking Christian

"Papa" Monzano and his merciless disease were in a bed that was made of a golden dinghy—tiller, painter, oarlocks and all, all gilt. His bed was the lifeboat of Bokonon's old schooner, the *Lady's Slipper*; it was the lifeboat of the ship that had brought Bokonon and Corporal McCabe to San Lorenzo so long ago.

The walls of the room were white. But "Papa" radiated pain so hot and bright that the walls seemed bathed in angry red.

He was stripped from the waist up, and his glistening belly wall was knotted. His belly shivered like a luffing sail.

Around his neck hung a chain with a cylinder the size of a rifle cartridge for a pendant. I supposed that the cylinder contained some magic charm. I was mistaken. It contained a splinter of *ice-nine.*

"Papa" could hardly speak. His teeth chattered and his breathing was beyond control.

"Papa's" agonized head was at the bow of the dinghy, bent back.

Mona's xylophone was near the bed. She had apparently tried to soothe "Papa" with music the previous evening.

"'Papa'?" whispered Frank.

"Good-bye," "Papa" gasped. His eyes were bugging, sightless.

"I brought a friend."

"Good-bye."

"He's going to be the next President of San Lorenzo. He'll be a much better president than I could be."

"Ice!" "Papa" whimpered.

"He asks for ice," said Von Koenigswald. "When we bring it, he does not want it."

"Papa" rolled his eyes. He relaxed his neck, took the weight of his body from the crown of his head. And then he arched his neck again. "Does not matter," he said, "who is President of . . ." He did not finish.

I finished for him. "San Lorenzo?"

"San Lorenzo," he agreed. He managed a crooked smile. "Good luck!" he croaked.

"Thank you, sir," I said.

"Doesn't matter! Bokonon. Get Bokonon."

I attempted a sophisticated reply to this last. I remembered that, for the joy of the people, Bokonon was always to be chased, was never to be caught. "I will get him."

"Tell him . . ."

I leaned closer, in order to hear the message from "Papa" to Bokonon.

"Tell him I am sorry I did not kill him," said "Papa."

"I will."

"*You* kill him."

"Yessir."

"Papa" gained control enough of his voice to make it commanding. "I mean *really*!"

I said nothing to that. I was not eager to kill anyone.

"He teaches the people lies and lies and lies. Kill him and teach the people truth."

"Yessir."

"You and Hoenikker, you teach them science."

"Yessir, we will," I promised.

"Science is magic that *works*."

He fell silent, relaxed, closed his eyes. And then he whispered, "Last rites."

Von Koenigswald called Dr. Vox Humana in. Dr. Humana took his tranquilized chicken out of the hatbox, preparing to administer Christian last rites as he understood them.

"Papa" opened one eye. "Not you," he sneered at Dr. Humana. "Get out!"

"Sir?" asked Dr. Humana.

"I am a member of the Bokononist faith," "Papa" wheezed. "Get out, you stinking Christian."

98

Last Rites

So I was privileged to see the last rites of the Bokononist faith.

We made an effort to find someone among the soldiers and the household staff who would admit that he knew the rites and would give them to "Papa." We got no volunteers. That was hardly surprising, with a hook and an oubliette so near.

So Dr. von Koenigswald said that he would have a go at the job. He had never administered the rites before, but he had seen Julian Castle do it hundreds of times.

"Are you a Bokononist?" I asked him.

"I agree with one Bokononist idea. I agree that all religions, including Bokononism, are nothing but lies."

"Will this bother you as a scientist," I inquired, "to go through a ritual like this?"

"I am a very bad scientist. I will do anything to make a human being feel better, even if it's unscientific. No scientist worthy of the name could say such a thing."

And he climbed into the golden boat with "Papa." He sat in the stern. Cramped quarters obliged him to have the golden tiller under one arm.

He wore sandals without socks, and he took these off. And then he rolled back the covers at the foot of the bed, exposing "Papa's" bare feet. He put the soles of his feet against "Papa's" feet, assuming the classical position for *boko-maru*.

99

"Dyot meet mat"

"*Gott mate mutt*," crooned Dr. von Koenigswald.

"*Dyot meet mat*," echoed "Papa" Monzano.

"God made mud," was what they'd said, each in his own dialect. I will here abandon the dialects of the litany.

"God got lonesome," said Von Koenigswald.

"God got lonesome."

"So God said to some of the mud, 'Sit up!'"

"So God said to some of the mud, 'Sit up!'"

"'See all I've made,' said God, 'the hills, the sea, the sky, the stars.'"

"'See all I've made,' said God, 'the hills, the sea, the sky, the stars.'"

"And I was some of the mud that got to sit up and look around."

"And I was some of the mud that got to sit up and look around."

"Lucky me, lucky mud."

"Lucky me, lucky mud." Tears were streaming down "Papa's" cheeks.

"I, mud, sat up and saw what a nice job God had done."

"I, mud, sat up and saw what a nice job God had done."

"Nice going, God!"

"Nice going, God!" "Papa" said it with all his heart.

"Nobody but You could have done it, God! I certainly couldn't have."

"Nobody but You could have done it, God! I certainly couldn't have."

"I feel very unimportant compared to You."

"I feel very unimportant compared to You."

"The only way I can feel the least bit important is to think of all the mud that didn't even get to sit up and look around."

"The only way I can feel the least bit important is to think of all the mud that didn't even get to sit up and look around."

"I got so much, and most mud got so little."

"I got so much, and most mud got so little."
"*Deng you vore da on-oh!*" cried Von Koenigswald.
"*Tz-yenk voo vore lo yon-yo!*" wheezed "Papa."
What they had said was, "Thank you for the honor!"
"Now mud lies down again and goes to sleep."
"Now mud lies down again and goes to sleep."
"What memories for mud to have!"
"What memories for mud to have!"
"What interesting other kinds of sitting-up mud I met!"
"What interesting other kinds of sitting-up mud I met!"
"I loved everything I saw!"
"I loved everything I saw!"
"Good night."
"Good night."
"I will go to heaven now."
"I will go to heaven now."
"I can hardly wait . . ."
"I can hardly wait . . ."
"To find out for certain what my *wampeter* was . . ."
"To find out for certain what my *wampeter* was . . ."
"And who was in my *karass* . . ."
"And who was in my *karass* . . ."
"And all the good things our *karass* did for you."
"And all the good things our *karass* did for you."
"Amen."
"Amen."

100

Down the Oubliette Goes Frank

But "Papa" didn't die and go to heaven—not then.

I asked Frank how we might best time the announcement of my elevation to the Presidency. He was no help, had no ideas; he left it all up to me.

"I thought you were going to back me up," I complained.

"As far as anything *technical* goes." Frank was prim about it. I wasn't to violate his integrity as a technician; wasn't to make him exceed the limits of his job.

"I see."

"However you want to handle people is all right with me. That's *your* responsibility."

This abrupt abdication of Frank from all human affairs shocked and angered me, and I said to him, meaning to be satirical, "You mind telling me what, in a purely technical way, is planned for this day of days?"

I got a strictly technical reply. "Repair the power plant and stage an air show."

"Good! So one of my first triumphs as President will be to restore electricity to my people."

Frank didn't see anything funny in that. He gave me a salute. "I'll try, sir. I'll do my best for you, sir. I can't guarantee how long it'll be before we get juice back."

"That's what I want—a juicy country."

"I'll do my best, sir." Frank saluted me again.

"And the air show?" I asked. "What's that?"

I got another wooden reply. "At one o'clock this afternoon, sir, six planes of the San Lorenzan Air Force will fly past the palace here and shoot at targets in the water. It's part of the celebration of the Day of the Hundred Martyrs to Democracy. The American Ambassador also plans to throw a wreath into the sea."

So I decided, tentatively, that I would have Frank announce my apotheosis immediately following the wreath ceremony and the air show.

"What do you think of that?" I said to Frank.

"You're the boss, sir."

"I think I'd better have a speech ready," I said. "And there should be some sort of swearing-in, to make it look dignified, official."

"You're the boss, sir." Each time he said those words they seemed to come from farther away, as though Frank were descending the rungs of a ladder into a deep shaft, while I was obliged to remain above.

And I realized with chagrin that my agreeing to be boss had freed Frank to do what he wanted to do more than anything else, to do what his father had done: to receive honors and creature comforts while escaping human responsibilities. He was accomplishing this by going down a spiritual oubliette.

IOI

Like My Predecessors, I Outlaw Bokonon

So I wrote my speech in a round, bare room at the foot of a tower. There was a table and a chair. And the speech I wrote was round and bare and sparsely furnished, too.

It was hopeful. It was humble.

And I found it impossible not to lean on God. I had never needed such support before, and so had never believed that such support was available.

Now, I found that I had to believe in it—and I did.

In addition, I would need the help of people. I called for a list of the guests who were to be at the ceremonies and found that Julian Castle and his son had not been invited. I sent messengers to invite them at once, since they knew more about my people than anyone, with the exception of Bokonon.

As for Bokonon:

I pondered asking him to join my government, thus bringing about a sort of millennium for my people. And I thought of ordering that the awful hook outside the palace gate be taken down at once, amidst great rejoicing.

But then I understood that a millennium would have to offer something more than a holy man in a position of power, that there would have to be plenty of good things for all to eat, too, and nice places to live for all, and good schools and good health and good times for all, and work for all who wanted it— things Bokonon and I were in no position to provide.

So good and evil had to remain separate; good in the jungle, and evil in the palace. Whatever entertainment there was in that was about all we had to give the people.

There was a knock on my door. A servant told me the guests had begun to arrive.

So I put my speech in my pocket and I mounted the spiral staircase in my tower. I arrived at the uppermost battlement of my castle, and I looked out at my guests, my servants, my cliff, and my lukewarm sea.

IO2

Enemies of Freedom

When I think of all those people on my uppermost battlement, I think of Bokonon's "hundred-and-nineteenth Calypso," wherein he invites us to sing along with him:

> "Where's my good old gang done gone?"
> I heard a sad man say.
> I whispered in that sad man's ear,
> "Your gang's done gone away."

Present were Ambassador Horlick Minton and his lady; H. Lowe Crosby, the bicycle manufacturer, and his Hazel; Dr. Julian Castle, humanitarian and philanthropist, and his son, Philip, author and innkeeper; little Newton Hoenikker, the picture painter, and his musical sister, Mrs. Harrison C. Conners; my heavenly Mona; Major General Franklin Hoenikker; and twenty assorted San Lorenzo bureaucrats and military men.

Dead—almost all dead now.

As Bokonon tells us, "It is never a mistake to say good-bye."

There was a buffet on my battlements, a buffet burdened with native delicacies: roasted warblers in little overcoats made of their own blue-green feathers; lavender land crabs taken from their shells, minced, fried in coconut oil, and returned to their shells; fingerling barracuda stuffed with banana paste; and, on unleavened, unseasoned cornmeal wafers, bite-sized cubes of boiled albatross.

The albatross, I was told, had been shot from the very barti-zan in which the buffet stood.

There were two beverages offered, both un-iced: Pepsi-Cola and native rum. The Pepsi-Cola was served in plastic Pilseners. The rum was served in coconut shells. I was unable to identify the sweet bouquet of the rum, though it somehow reminded me of early adolescence.

Frank was able to name the bouquet for me. "Acetone."

"Acetone?"

"Used in model-airplane cement."

I did not drink the rum.

Ambassador Minton did a lot of ambassadorial, gourmand saluting with his coconut, pretending to love all men and all the beverages that sustained them. But I did not see him drink. He had with him, incidentally, a piece of luggage of a sort I had never seen before. It looked like a French horn case, and proved to contain the memorial wreath that was to be cast into the sea.

The only person I saw drink the rum was H. Lowe Crosby, who plainly had no sense of smell. He was having a good time, drinking acetone from his coconut, sitting on a cannon, block-ing the touchhole with his big behind. He was looking out to sea through a huge pair of Japanese binoculars. He was look-ing at targets mounted on bobbing floats anchored offshore.

The targets were cardboard cutouts shaped like men.

They were to be fired upon and bombed in a demonstration of might by the six planes of the San Lorenzan Air Force.

Each target was a caricature of some real person, and the name of that person was painted on the target's back and front.

I asked who the caricaturist was and learned that he was Dr. Vox Humana, the Christian minister. He was at my elbow.

"I didn't know you were talented in that direction, too."

"Oh, yes. When I was a young man, I had a very hard time deciding what to be."

"I think the choice you made was the right one."

"I prayed for guidance from Above."

"You got it."

H. Lowe Crosby handed his binoculars to his wife. "There's old Joe Stalin, closest in, and old Fidel Castro's anchored right next to him."

"And there's old Hitler," chuckled Hazel, delighted. "And there's old Mussolini and some old Jap."

"And there's old Karl Marx."

"And there's old Kaiser Bill, spiked hat and all," cooed Hazel. "I never expected to see *him* again."

"And there's old Mao. You see old Mao?"

"Isn't *he* gonna get it?" asked Hazel. "Isn't *he* gonna get the surprise of his life? This sure is a cute idea."

"They got practically every enemy that freedom ever had out there," H. Lowe Crosby declared.

103

A Medical Opinion on the Effects of a Writers' Strike

None of the guests knew yet that I was to be President. None knew how close to death "Papa" was. Frank gave out the official word that "Papa" was resting comfortably, that "Papa" sent his best wishes to all.

The order of events, as announced by Frank, was that Ambassador Minton would throw his wreath into the sea, in honor of the Hundred Martyrs; and then the airplanes would shoot the targets in the sea; and then he, Frank, would say a few words.

He did not tell the company that, following his speech, there would be a speech by me.

So I was treated as nothing more than a visiting journalist, and I engaged in harmless *granfalloonery* here and there.

"Hello, Mom," I said to Hazel Crosby.

"Why, if it isn't my boy!" Hazel gave me a perfumed hug, and she told everybody, "This boy's a Hoosier!"

The Castles, father and son, stood separate from the rest of the company. Long unwelcome at "Papa's" palace, they were curious as to why they had now been invited there.

Young Castle called me "Scoop." "Good morning, Scoop. What's new in the word game?"

"I might ask the same of you," I replied.

"I'm thinking of calling a general strike of all writers until mankind finally comes to its senses. Would you support it?"

"Do writers have a right to strike? That would be like the police or the firemen walking out."

"Or the college professors."

"Or the college professors," I agreed. I shook my head. "No, I don't think my conscience would let me support a strike like that. When a man becomes a writer, I think he takes on a sacred obligation to produce beauty and enlightenment and comfort at top speed."

"I just can't help thinking what a real shaking up it would give people if, all of a sudden, there were no new books, new plays, new histories, new poems . . ."

"And how proud would you be when people started dying like flies?" I demanded.

"They'd die more like mad dogs, I think—snarling and snapping at each other and biting their own tails."

I turned to Castle the elder. "Sir, how does a man die when he's deprived of the consolations of literature?"

"In one of two ways," he said, "petrescence of the heart or atrophy of the nervous system."

"Neither one very pleasant, I expect," I suggested.

"No," said Castle the elder. "For the love of God, *both* of you, *please* keep writing!"

104

Sulfathiazole

My heavenly Mona did not approach me and did not encourage me with languishing glances to come to her side. She made a hostess of herself, introducing Angela and little Newt to San Lorenzans.

As I ponder now the meaning of that girl—recall her indifference to "Papa's" collapse, to her betrothal to me—I vacillate between lofty and cheap appraisals.

Did she represent the highest form of female spirituality?

Or was she anesthetized, frigid—a cold fish, in fact, a dazed addict of the xylophone, the cult of beauty, and *boko-maru*?

I shall never know.

Bokonon tells us:

> A lover's a liar,
> To himself he lies.
> The truthful are loveless,
> Like oysters their eyes!

So my instructions are clear, I suppose. I am to remember my Mona as having been sublime.

"Tell me," I appealed to young Philip Castle on the Day of the Hundred Martyrs to Democracy, "have you spoken to your friend and admirer, H. Lowe Crosby, today?"

"He didn't recognize me with a suit and shoes and necktie on," young Castle replied. "We've already had a nice talk about bicycles. We may have another."

I found that I was no longer amused by Crosby's wanting to build bicycles in San Lorenzo. As chief executive of the island I wanted a bicycle factory very much. I developed sudden respect for what H. Lowe Crosby was and could do.

"How do you think the people of San Lorenzo would take to industrialization?" I asked the Castles, father and son.

"The people of San Lorenzo," the father told me, "are interested in only three things: fishing, fornication, and Bokononism."

"Don't you think they could be interested in progress?"

"They've seen some of it. There's only one aspect of progress that really excites them."

"What's that?"

"The electric guitar."

I excused myself and I rejoined the Crosbys.

Frank Hoenikker was with them, explaining who Bokonon was and what he was against. "He's against science."

"How can anybody in his right mind be against science?" asked Crosby.

"I'd be dead now if it wasn't for penicillin," said Hazel. "And so would my mother."

"How old *is* your mother?" I inquired.

"A hundred and six. Isn't that wonderful?"

"It certainly is," I agreed.

"And I'd be a widow, too, if it wasn't for the medicine they gave my husband that time," said Hazel. She had to ask her husband the name of the medicine. "Honey, what was the name of that stuff that saved your life that time?"

"Sulfathiazole."

And I made the mistake of taking an albatross canapé from a passing tray.

105

Pain-killer

As it happened—"As it was *supposed* to happen," Bokonon would say—albatross meat disagreed with me so violently that I was ill the moment I'd choked the first piece down. I was compelled to canter down the stone spiral staircase in search of a bathroom. I availed myself of one adjacent to "Papa's" suite.

When I shuffled out, somewhat relieved, I was met by Dr. Schlichter von Koenigswald, who was bounding from "Papa's" bedroom. He had a wild look, and he took me by the arms and he cried, "What is it? What was it he had hanging around his neck?"

"I beg your pardon?"

"He took it! Whatever was in that cylinder, 'Papa' took—and now he's dead."

I remembered the cylinder "Papa" had hung around his neck, and I made an obvious guess as to its contents. "Cyanide?"

"Cyanide? Cyanide turns a man to cement in a second?"

"Cement?"

"Marble! Iron! I have never seen such a rigid corpse before. Strike it anywhere and you get a note like a marimba! Come look!" Von Koenigswald hustled me into "Papa's" bedroom.

In the bed, in the golden dinghy, was a hideous thing to see. "Papa" was dead, but his was not a corpse to which one could say, "At rest at last."

"Papa's" head was bent back as far as it would go. His weight rested on the crown of his head and the soles of his feet, with the rest of his body forming a bridge whose arch thrust toward the ceiling. He was shaped like an andiron.

That he had died of the contents of the cylinder around his neck was obvious. One hand held the cylinder and the cylinder was uncapped. And the thumb and index finger of the other hand, as though having just released a little pinch of something, were stuck between his teeth.

Dr. von Koenigswald slipped the tholepin of an oarlock from its socket in the gunwale of the gilded dinghy. He tapped "Papa" on his belly with the steel oarlock, and "Papa" really did make a sound like a marimba.

And "Papa's" lips and nostrils and eyeballs were glazed with a blue-white frost.

Such a syndrome is no novelty now, God knows. But it certainly was then. "Papa" Monzano was the first man in history to die of *ice-nine*.

I record that fact for whatever it may be worth. "Write it all down," Bokonon tells us. He is really telling us, of course, how futile it is to write or read histories. "Without accurate records of the past, how can men and women be expected to avoid making serious mistakes in the future?" he asks ironically.

So, again: "Papa" Monzano was the first man in history to die of *ice-nine*.

106

What Bokononists Say When They Commit Suicide

Dr. von Koenigswald, the humanitarian with the terrible deficit of Auschwitz in his kindliness account, was the second to die of *ice-nine*.

He was talking about rigor mortis, a subject I had introduced.

"Rigor mortis does not set in in seconds," he declared. "I turned my back to 'Papa' for just a moment. He was raving . . ."

"What about?" I asked.

"Pain, ice, Mona—everything. And then 'Papa' said, 'Now I will destroy the whole world.'"

"What did he mean by that?"

"It's what Bokononists always say when they are about to commit suicide." Von Koenigswald went to a basin of water, meaning to wash his hands. "When I turned to look at him," he told me, his hands poised over the water, "he was dead—as hard as a statue, just as you see him. I brushed my fingers over his lips. They looked so peculiar."

He put his hands into the water. "What chemical could possibly . . ." The question trailed off.

Von Koenigswald raised his hands, and the water in the basin came with them. It was no longer water, but a hemisphere of *ice-nine*.

Von Koenigswald touched the tip of his tongue to the blue-white mystery.

Frost bloomed on his lips. He froze solid, tottered, and crashed.

The blue-white hemisphere shattered. Chunks skittered over the floor.

I went to the door and bawled for help.

Soldiers and servants came running.

I ordered them to bring Frank and Newt and Angela to "Papa's" room at once.

At last I had seen *ice-nine*!

107

Feast Your Eyes!

I let the three children of Dr. Felix Hoenikker into "Papa" Monzano's bedroom. I closed the door and put my back to it. My mood was bitter and grand. I knew *ice-nine* for what it was. I had seen it often in my dreams.

There could be no doubt that Frank had given "Papa" *ice-nine*. And it seemed certain that if *ice-nine* were Frank's to give, then it was Angela's and little Newt's to give, too.

So I snarled at all three, calling them to account for monstrous criminality. I told them that the jig was up, that I knew about them and *ice-nine*. I tried to alarm them about *ice-nine*'s being a means to ending life on earth. I was so impressive that they never thought to ask how I knew about *ice-nine*.

"Feast your eyes!" I said.

Well, as Bokonon tells us: "God never wrote a good play in His Life." The scene in "Papa's" room did not lack for spectacular issues and props, and my opening speech was the right one.

But the first reply from a Hoenikker destroyed all magnificence.

Little Newt threw up.

108

Frank Tells Us What to Do

And then we all wanted to throw up.

Newt certainly did what was called for.

"I couldn't agree more," I told Newt. And I snarled at Angela and Frank, "Now that we've got Newt's opinion, I'd like to hear what you two have to say."

"Uck," said Angela, cringing, her tongue out. She was the color of putty.

"Are those your sentiments, too?" I asked Frank. "'Uck'? General, is that what you say?"

Frank had his teeth bared, and his teeth were clenched, and he was breathing shallowly and whistlingly between them.

"Like the dog," murmured little Newt, looking down at Von Koenigswald.

"What dog?"

Newt whispered his answer, and there was scarcely any wind behind the whisper. But such were the acoustics of the stone-walled room that we all heard the whisper as clearly as we would have heard the chiming of a crystal bell.

"Christmas Eve, when Father died."

Newt was talking to himself. And, when I asked him to tell me about the dog on the night his father died, he looked up at me as though I had intruded on a dream. He found me irrelevant.

His brother and sister, however, belonged in the dream. And he talked to his brother in that nightmare; told Frank, "You gave it to him.

"That's how you got this fancy job, isn't it?" Newt asked Frank wonderingly. "What did you tell him—that you had something better than the hydrogen bomb?"

Frank didn't acknowledge the question. He was looking around the room intently, taking it all in. He unclenched his teeth, and he made them click rapidly, blinking his eyes with every click. His color was coming back. This is what he said.

"Listen, we've got to clean up this mess."

109

Frank Defends Himself

"General," I told Frank, "that must be one of the most co-
gent statements made by a major general this year. As my technical advisor, how do you recommend that *we*, as you put it so
well, 'clean up this mess'?"

Frank gave me a straight answer. He snapped his fingers. I
could see him dissociating himself from the causes of the mess;
identifying himself, with growing pride and energy, with the
purifiers, the world-savers, the cleaners-up.

"Brooms, dustpans, blowtorch, hot plate, buckets," he commanded, snapping, snapping, snapping his fingers.

"You propose applying a blowtorch to the bodies?" I asked.

Frank was so charged with technical thinking now that he
was practically tap dancing to the music of his fingers. "We'll
sweep up the big pieces on the floor, melt them in a bucket on
a hot plate. Then we'll go over every square inch of floor with
a blowtorch, in case there are any microscopic crystals. What
we'll do with the bodies—and the bed . . ." He had to think
some more.

"A funeral pyre!" he cried, really pleased with himself. "I'll
have a great big funeral pyre built out by the hook, and we'll
have the bodies and the bed carried out and thrown on."

He started to leave, to order the pyre built and to get the
things we needed in order to clean up the room.

Angela stopped him. "How *could* you?" she wanted to know.

Frank gave her a glassy smile. "Everything's going to be all
right."

"How *could* you give it to a man like 'Papa' Monzano?"
Angela asked him.

"Let's clean up the mess first; then we can talk."

Angela had him by the arms, and she wouldn't let him go.
"How *could* you!" She shook him.

Frank pried his sister's hands from himself. His glassy smile
went away and he turned sneeringly nasty for a moment—a
moment in which he told her with all possible contempt, "I

bought myself a job, just the way you bought yourself a tomcat husband, just the way Newt bought himself a week on Cape Cod with a Russian midget!"

The glassy smile returned.

Frank left; and he slammed the door.

110

"The Fourteenth Book"

"Sometimes the *pool-pah*," Bokonon tells us, "exceeds the power of humans to comment." Bokonon translates *pool-pah* at one point in *The Books of Bokonon* as "shit storm" and at another point as "wrath of God."

From what Frank had said before he slammed the door, I gathered that the Republic of San Lorenzo and the three Hoenikkers weren't the only ones who had *ice-nine*. Apparently the United States of America and the Union of Soviet Socialist Republics had it, too. The United States had obtained it through Angela's husband, whose plant in Indianapolis was understandably surrounded by electrified fences and homicidal German shepherds. And Soviet Russia had come by it through Newt's little Zinka, that winsome troll of Ukrainian ballet.

I was without comment.

I bowed my head and closed my eyes; and I awaited Frank's return with the humble tools it would take to clean up one bedroom—one bedroom out of all the bedrooms in the world, a bedroom infested with *ice-nine*.

Somewhere, in that violet, velvet oblivion, I heard Angela say something to me. It wasn't in her own defense. It was in defense of little Newt. "Newt didn't give it to her. She *stole* it."

I found the explanation uninteresting.

"What hope can there be for mankind," I thought, "when there are such men as Felix Hoenikker to give such playthings as *ice-nine* to such short-sighted children as almost all men and women are?"

And I remembered *The Fourteenth Book of Bokonon*, which I had read in its entirety the night before. *The Fourteenth Book* is entitled, "What Can a Thoughtful Man Hope for Mankind on Earth, Given the Experience of the Past Million Years?"

It doesn't take long to read *The Fourteenth Book*. It consists of one word and a period.

This is it:

"Nothing."

III

Time Out

Frank came back with brooms and dustpans, a blowtorch, and a kerosene hot plate, and a good old bucket and rubber gloves.

We put on the gloves in order not to contaminate our hands with *ice-nine*. Frank set the hot plate on the heavenly Mona's xylophone and put the honest old bucket on top of that.

And we picked up the bigger chunks of *ice-nine* from the floor; and we dropped them into that humble bucket; and they melted. They became good old, sweet old, honest old water.

Angela and I swept the floor, and little Newt looked under furniture for bits of *ice-nine* we might have missed. And Frank followed our sweeping with the purifying flame of the torch.

The brainless serenity of charwomen and janitors working late at night came over us. In a messy world we were at least making our little corner clean.

And I heard myself asking Newt and Angela and Frank in conversational tones to tell me about the Christmas Eve on which the old man died, to tell me about the dog.

And, childishly sure that they were making everything all right by cleaning up, the Hoenikkers told me the tale.

The tale went like this:

On that fateful Christmas Eve, Angela went into the village for Christmas tree lights, and Newt and Frank went for a walk on the lonely winter beach, where they met a black Labrador retriever. The dog was friendly, as all Labrador retrievers are, and he followed Frank and little Newt home.

Felix Hoenikker died—died in his white wicker chair looking out at the sea—while his children were gone. All day the old man had been teasing his children with hints about *ice-nine*, showing it to them in a little bottle on whose label he had drawn a skull and crossbones, and on whose label he had written: "Danger! *Ice-nine*! Keep away from moisture!"

All day long the old man had been nagging his children with words like these, merry in tone: "Come on now, stretch your minds a little. I've told you that its melting point is a hundred fourteen-point-four degrees Fahrenheit, and I've told you that it's composed of nothing but hydrogen and oxygen. What could the explanation be? Think a little! Don't be afraid of straining your brains. They won't break."

"He was always telling us to stretch our brains," said Frank, recalling olden times.

"I gave up trying to stretch my brain when I-don't-know-how-old-I-was," Angela confessed, leaning on her broom. "I couldn't even listen to him when he talked about science. I'd just nod and pretend I was trying to stretch my brain, but that poor brain, as far as science went, didn't have any more stretch than an old garter belt."

Apparently, before he sat down in his wicker chair and died, the old man played puddly games in the kitchen with water and pots and pans and *ice-nine*. He must have been converting water to *ice-nine* and back to water again, for every pot and pan was out on the kitchen countertops. A meat thermometer was out, too, so the old man must have been taking the temperature of things.

The old man meant to take only a brief time out in his chair, for he left quite a mess in the kitchen. Part of the disorder was a saucepan filled with solid *ice-nine*. He no doubt meant to melt it up, to reduce the world's supply of the blue-white stuff to a splinter in a bottle again—after a brief time out.

But, as Bokonon tells us, "Any man can call time out, but no man can say how long the time out will be."

112

Newt's Mother's Reticule

"I should have known he was dead the minute I came in," said Angela, leaning on her broom again. "That wicker chair, it wasn't making a sound. It always talked, creaked away, when Father was in it—even when he was asleep."

But Angela had assumed that her father was sleeping, and she went on to decorate the Christmas tree.

Newt and Frank came in with the Labrador retriever. They went out into the kitchen to find something for the dog to eat. They found the old man's puddles.

There was water on the floor, and little Newt took a dishrag and wiped it up. He tossed the sopping dishrag onto the counter.

As it happened, the dishrag fell into the pan containing *ice-nine.*

Frank thought the pan contained some sort of cake frosting, and he held it down to Newt, to show Newt what his carelessness with the dishrag had done.

Newt peeled the dishrag from the surface and found that the dishrag had a peculiar, metallic, snaky quality, as though it were made of finely-woven gold mesh.

"The reason I say 'gold mesh,'" said little Newt, there in "Papa's" bedroom, "is that it reminded me right away of Mother's reticule, of how the reticule felt."

Angela explained sentimentally that when a child, Newt had treasured his mother's gold reticule. I gathered that it was a little evening bag.

"It felt so funny to me, like nothing else I'd ever touched," said Newt, investigating his old fondness for the reticule. "I wonder whatever happened to it."

"I wonder what happened to a *lot* of things," said Angela. The question echoed back through time—woeful, lost.

What happened to the dishrag that felt like a reticule, at any rate, was that Newt held it out to the dog, and the dog licked it. And the dog froze stiff.

Newt went to tell his father about the stiff dog and found out that his father was stiff, too.

113

History

Our work in "Papa's" bedroom was done at last.

But the bodies still had to be carried to the funeral pyre. We decided that this should be done with pomp, that we should put it off until the ceremonies in honor of the Hundred Martyrs to Democracy were over.

The last thing we did was stand Von Koenigswald on his feet in order to decontaminate the place where he had been lying. And then we hid him, standing up, in "Papa's" clothes closet.

I'm not quite sure why we hid him. I think it must have been to simplify the tableau.

As for Newt's and Angela's and Frank's tale of how they divided up the world's supply of *ice-nine* on Christmas Eve—it petered out when they got to details of the crime itself. The Hoenikkers couldn't remember that anyone said anything to justify their taking *ice-nine* as personal property. They talked about what *ice-nine* was, recalling the old man's brain-stretchers, but there was no talk of morals.

"Who did the dividing?" I inquired.

So thoroughly had the three Hoenikkers obliterated their memories of the incident that it was difficult for them to give me even that fundamental detail.

"It wasn't Newt," said Angela at last. "I'm sure of that."

"It was either you or me," mused Frank, thinking hard.

"You got the three Mason jars off the kitchen shelf," said Angela. "It wasn't until the next day that we got the three little Thermos jugs."

"That's right," Frank agreed. "And then you took an ice pick and chipped up the *ice-nine* in the saucepan."

"That's right," said Angela. "I did. And then somebody brought tweezers from the bathroom."

Newt raised his little hand. "I did."

Angela and Newt were amazed, remembering how enterprising little Newt had been.

"I was the one who picked up the chips and put them in the Mason jars," Newt recounted. He didn't bother to hide the swagger he must have felt.

"What did you people do with the dog?" I asked limply.

"We put him in the oven," Frank told me. "It was the only thing to do."

"History!" writes Bokonon. "Read it and weep!"

114

When I Felt the Bullet Enter My Heart

So I once again mounted the spiral staircase in my tower; once again arrived at the uppermost battlement of my castle; and once more looked out at my guests, my servants, my cliff, and my lukewarm sea.

The Hoenikkers were with me. We had locked "Papa's" door, and had spread the word among the household staff that "Papa" was feeling much better.

Soldiers were now building a funeral pyre out by the hook. They did not know what the pyre was for.

There were many, many secrets that day.

Busy, busy, busy.

I supposed that the ceremonies might as well begin, and I told Frank to suggest to Ambassador Horlick Minton that he deliver his speech.

Ambassador Minton went to the seaward parapet with his memorial wreath still in its case. And he delivered an amazing speech in honor of the Hundred Martyrs to Democracy. He dignified the dead, their country, and the life that was over for them by saying the "Hundred Martyrs to Democracy" in island dialect. That fragment of dialect was graceful and easy on his lips.

The rest of his speech was in American English. He had a written speech with him—fustian and bombast, I imagine. But, when he found he was going to speak to so few, and to fellow Americans for the most part, he put the formal speech away.

A light sea wind ruffled his thinning hair. "I am about to do a very un-ambassadorial thing," he declared. "I am about to tell you what I really feel."

Perhaps Minton had inhaled too much acetone, or perhaps he had an inkling of what was about to happen to everybody but me. At any rate, it was a strikingly Bokononist speech he gave.

"We are gathered here, friends," he said, "to honor *lo Hoon-yera Mora-toorz tut Zamoo-cratz-ya*, children dead, all dead, all murdered in war. It is customary on days like this to call such lost children *men*. I am unable to call them men for this simple reason: that in the same war in which *lo Hoon-yera Mora-toorz tut Zamoo-cratz-ya* died, my own son died.

"My soul insists that I mourn not a man but a child.

"I do not say that children at war do not die like men, if they have to die. To their everlasting honor and our everlasting shame, they *do* die like men, thus making possible the manly jubilation of patriotic holidays.

"But they are murdered children all the same.

"And I propose to you that if we are to pay our sincere respects to the hundred lost children of San Lorenzo, that we might best spend the day despising what killed them; which is to say, the stupidity and viciousness of all mankind.

"Perhaps, when we remember wars, we should take off our clothes and paint ourselves blue and go on all fours all day long and grunt like pigs. That would surely be more appropriate than noble oratory and shows of flags and well-oiled guns.

"I do not mean to be ungrateful for the fine, martial show we are about to see—and a thrilling show it really will be . . ."

He looked each of us in the eye, and then he commented very softly, throwing it away, "And hooray say I for thrilling shows."

We had to strain our ears to hear what Minton said next.

"But if today is really in honor of a hundred children murdered in war," he said, "is today a day for a thrilling show?

"The answer is yes, on one condition: that we, the celebrants, are working consciously and tirelessly to reduce the stupidity and viciousness of ourselves and of all mankind."

He unsnapped the catches on his wreath case.

"See what I have brought?" he asked us.

He opened the case and showed us the scarlet lining and the golden wreath. The wreath was made of wire and artificial laurel leaves, and the whole was sprayed with radiator paint.

The wreath was spanned by a cream-colored silk ribbon on which was printed, "PRO PATRIA."

Minton now recited a poem from Edgar Lee Masters' *The Spoon River Anthology*, a poem that must have been incomprehensible to the San Lorenzans in the audience—and to H. Lowe Crosby and his Hazel, too, for that matter, and to Angela and Frank.

> I was the first fruits of the battle of Missionary Ridge.
> When I felt the bullet enter my heart
> I wished I had staid at home and gone to jail
> For stealing the hogs of Curl Trenary,
> Instead of running away and joining the army.
> Rather a thousand times the county jail
> Than to lie under this marble figure with wings,
> And this granite pedestal
> Bearing the words, "*Pro Patria*."
> What do they mean, anyway?

"What do they mean, anyway?" echoed Ambassador Horlick Minton. "They mean, 'For one's country.'" And he threw away another line. "Any country at all," he murmured.

"This wreath I bring is a gift from the people of one country to the people of another. Never mind which countries. Think of people. . . .

"And children murdered in war . . .

"And any country at all.

"Think of peace.

"Think of brotherly love.

"Think of plenty.

"Think of what a paradise this world would be if men were kind and wise.

"As stupid and vicious as men are, this is a lovely day," said Ambassador Horlick Minton. "I, in my own heart and as a representative of the peace-loving people of the United States of America, pity *lo Hoon-yera Mora-toorz tut Zamoo-cratz-ya* for being dead on this fine day."

And he sailed the wreath off the parapet.

There was a hum in the air. The six planes of the San Lorenzan Air Force were coming, skimming my lukewarm sea. They were going to shoot the effigies of what H. Lowe Crosby had called "practically every enemy that freedom ever had."

115

As It Happened

We went to the seaward parapet to see the show. The planes were no larger than grains of black pepper. We were able to spot them because one, as it happened, was trailing smoke.

We supposed that the smoke was part of the show.

I stood next to H. Lowe Crosby, who, as it happened, was alternately eating albatross and drinking native rum. He exhaled fumes of model airplane cement between lips glistening with albatross fat. My recent nausea returned.

I withdrew to the landward parapet alone, gulping air. There were sixty feet of old stone pavement between me and all the rest.

I saw that the planes would be coming in low, below the footings of the castle, and that I would miss the show. But nausea made me incurious. I turned my head in the direction of their now snarling approach. Just as their guns began to hammer, one plane, the one that had been trailing smoke, suddenly appeared, belly up, in flames.

It dropped from my line of sight again and crashed at once into the cliff below the castle. Its bombs and fuel exploded.

The surviving planes went booming on, their racket thinning down to a mosquito hum.

And then there was the sound of a rockslide—and one great tower of "Papa's" castle, undermined, crashed down to the sea.

The people on the seaward parapet looked in astonishment at the empty socket where the tower had stood. Then I could hear rockslides of all sizes in a conversation that was almost orchestral.

The conversation went very fast, and new voices entered in. They were the voices of the castle's timbers lamenting that their burdens were becoming too great.

And then a crack crossed the battlement like lightning, ten feet from my curling toes.

It separated me from my fellow men.

The castle groaned and wept aloud.

The others comprehended their peril. They, along with tons of masonry, were about to lurch out and down. Although the crack was only a foot wide, people began to cross it with heroic leaps.

Only my complacent Mona crossed the crack with a simple step.

The crack gnashed shut; opened wider, leeringly. Still trapped on the canted deathtrap were H. Lowe Crosby and his Hazel and Ambassador Horlick Minton and his Claire.

Philip Castle and Frank and I reached across the abyss to haul the Crosbys to safety. Our arms were now extended imploringly to the Mintons.

Their expressions were bland. I can only guess what was going through their minds. My guess is that they were thinking of dignity, of emotional proportion above all else.

Panic was not their style. I doubt that suicide was their style either. But their good manners killed them, for the doomed crescent of castle now moved away from us like an ocean liner moving away from a dock.

The image of a voyage seems to have occurred to the voyaging Mintons, too, for they waved to us with wan amiability.

They held hands.

They faced the sea.

Out they went; then down they went in a cataclysmic rush, were gone!

116

The Grand Ah-whoom

The ragged rim of oblivion was now inches from my curling toes. I looked down. My lukewarm sea had swallowed all. A lazy curtain of dust was wafting out to sea, the only trace of all that fell.

The palace, its massive, seaward mask now gone, greeted the north with a leper's smile, snaggle-toothed and bristly. The bristles were the splintered ends of timbers. Immediately below me a large chamber had been laid open. The floor of that chamber, unsupported, stabbed out into space like a diving platform.

I dreamed for a moment of dropping to the platform, of springing up from it in a breath-taking swan dive, of folding my arms, of knifing downward into a blood-warm eternity with never a splash.

I was recalled from this dream by the cry of a darting bird above me. It seemed to be asking me what had happened. "Poo-tee-phweet?" it asked.

We all looked up at the bird, and then at one another.

We backed away from the abyss, full of dread. And, when I stepped off the paving stone that had supported me, the stone began to rock. It was no more stable than a teeter-totter. And it tottered now over the diving platform.

Down it crashed onto the platform, made the platform a chute. And down the chute came the furnishings still remaining in the room below.

A xylophone shot out first, scampering fast on its tiny wheels. Out came a bedside table in a crazy race with a bounding blowtorch. Out came chairs in hot pursuit.

And somewhere in that room below, out of sight, something mightily reluctant to move was beginning to move.

Down the chute it crept. At last it showed its golden bow. It was the boat in which dead "Papa" lay.

It reached the end of the chute. Its bow nodded. Down it tipped. Down it fell, end over end.

"Papa" was thrown clear, and he fell separately.

I closed my eyes.

There was a sound like that of the gentle closing of a portal as big as the sky, the great door of heaven being closed softly. It was a grand AH-WHOOM.

I opened my eyes—and all the sea was *ice-nine*.

The moist green earth was a blue-white pearl.

The sky darkened. *Borasisi*, the sun, became a sickly yellow ball, tiny and cruel.

The sky was filled with worms. The worms were tornadoes.

117

Sanctuary

I looked up at the sky where the bird had been. An enormous worm with a violet mouth was directly overhead. It buzzed like bees. It swayed. With obscene peristalsis, it ingested air.

We humans separated; fled my shattered battlements; tumbled down staircases on the landward side.

Only H. Lowe Crosby and his Hazel cried out. "American! American!" they cried, as though tornadoes were interested in the *granfalloons* to which their victims belonged.

I could not see the Crosbys. They had descended by another staircase. Their cries and the sounds of others, panting and running, came gabbling to me through a corridor of the castle. My only companion was my heavenly Mona, who had followed noiselessly.

When I hesitated, she slipped past me and opened the door to the anteroom of "Papa's" suite. The walls and roof of the anteroom were gone. But the stone floor remained. And in its center was the manhole cover of the oubliette. Under the wormy sky, in the flickering violet light from the mouths of tornadoes that wished to eat us, I lifted the cover.

The esophagus of the dungeon was fitted with iron rungs. I replaced the manhole cover from within. Down those iron rungs we went.

And at the foot of the ladder we found a state secret. "Papa" Monzano had caused a cozy bomb shelter to be constructed there. It had a ventilation shaft, with a fan driven by a stationary bicycle. A tank of water was recessed in one wall. The water was sweet and wet, as yet untainted by *ice-nine*. And there was a chemical toilet, and a short-wave radio, and a Sears, Roebuck catalogue; and there were cases of delicacies, and liquor, and candles; and there were bound copies of the *National Geographic* going back twenty years.

And there was a set of *The Books of Bokonon*.

And there were twin beds.

I lighted a candle. I opened a can of Campbell's chicken gumbo soup and I put it on a Sterno stove. And I poured two glasses of Virgin Islands rum.

Mona sat on one bed. I sat down on the other.

"I am about to say something that must have been said by men to women several times before," I informed her. "However, I don't believe that these words have ever carried quite the freight they carry now."

"Oh?"

I spread my hands. "Here we are."

118

The Iron Maiden and the Oubliette

The Sixth Book of *The Books of Bokonon* is devoted to pain, in particular to tortures inflicted by men on men. "If I am ever put to death on the hook," Bokonon warns us, "expect a very human performance."

Then he speaks of the rack and the peddiwinkus and the iron maiden and the *veglia* and the oubliette.

> In any case, there's bound to be much crying.
> But the oubliette alone will let you think while dying.

And so it was in Mona's and my rock womb. At least we could think. And one thing I thought was that the creature comforts of the dungeon did nothing to mitigate the basic fact of oubliation.

During our first day and night underground, tornadoes rattled our manhole cover many times an hour. Each time the pressure in our hole would drop suddenly, and our ears would pop and our heads would ring.

As for the radio—there was crackling, fizzing static and that was all. From one end of the short-wave band to the other not one word, not one telegrapher's beep, did I hear. If life still existed here and there, it did not broadcast.

Nor does life broadcast to this day.

This I assumed: tornadoes, strewing the poisonous blue-white frost of *ice-nine* everywhere, tore everyone and everything above ground to pieces. Anything that still lived would die soon enough of thirst—or hunger—or rage—or apathy.

I turned to *The Books of Bokonon*, still sufficiently unfamiliar with them to believe that they contained spiritual comfort somewhere. I passed quickly over the warning on the title page of *The First Book*:

"Don't be a fool! Close this book at once! It is nothing but *foma*!"

Foma, of course, are lies.
And then I read this:

In the beginning, God created the earth, and he looked upon it in His cosmic loneliness.

And God said, "Let Us make living creatures out of mud, so the mud can see what We have done." And God created every living creature that now moveth, and one was man. Mud as man alone could speak. God leaned close as mud as man sat up, looked around, and spoke. Man blinked. "What is the *purpose* of all this?" he asked politely.

"Everything must have a purpose?" asked God.

"Certainly," said man.

"Then I leave it to you to think of one for all this," said God. And He went away.

I thought this was trash.

"Of course it's trash!" says Bokonon.

And I turned to my heavenly Mona for comforting secrets a good deal more profound.

I was able, while mooning at her across the space that separated our beds, to imagine that behind her marvelous eyes lurked mysteries as old as Eve.

I will not go into the sordid sex episode that followed. Suffice it to say that I was both repulsive and repulsed.

The girl was not interested in reproduction—hated the idea. Before the tussle was over, I was given full credit by her, and by myself, too, for having invented the whole bizarre, grunting, sweating enterprise by which new human beings were made.

Returning to my own bed, gnashing my teeth, I supposed that she honestly had no idea what lovemaking was all about. But then she said to me, gently, "It would be very sad to have a little baby now. Don't you agree?"

"Yes," I agreed murkily.

"Well, that's the way little babies are made, in case you didn't know."

119

Mona Thanks Me

"Today I will be a Bulgarian Minister of Education," Bokonon tells us. "Tomorrow I will be Helen of Troy." His meaning is crystal clear: Each one of us has to be what he or she is. And, down in the oubliette, that was mainly what I thought—with the help of *The Books of Bokonon*.

Bokonon invited me to sing along with him:

We do, doodley do, doodley do, doodley do,
What we must, muddily must, muddily must, muddily must;

Muddily do, muddily do, muddily do, muddily do,
Until we bust, bodily bust, bodily bust, bodily bust.

I made up a tune to go with that and I whistled it under my breath as I drove the bicycle that drove the fan that gave us air, good old air.

"Man breathes in oxygen and exhales carbon dioxide," I called to Mona.

"What?"

"Science."

"Oh."

"One of the secrets of life man was a long time understanding: Animals breathe in what animals breathe out, and vice versa."

"I didn't know."

"You know now."

"Thank you."

"You're welcome."

When I'd bicycled our atmosphere to sweetness and freshness, I dismounted and climbed the iron rungs to see what the weather was like above. I did that several times a day. On that day, the fourth day, I perceived through the narrow crescent of the lifted manhole cover that the weather had become somewhat stabilized.

The stability was of a wildly dynamic sort, for the tornadoes were as numerous as ever, and tornadoes remain numerous to this day. But their mouths no longer gobbled and gnashed at the earth. The mouths in all directions were discretely withdrawn to an altitude of perhaps a half of a mile. And their altitude varied so little from moment to moment that San Lorenzo might have been protected by a tornado-proof sheet of glass.

We let three more days go by, making certain that the tornadoes had become as sincerely reticent as they seemed. And then we filled canteens from our water tank and we went above.

The air was dry and hot and deathly still.

I had heard it suggested one time that the seasons in the temperate zone ought to be six rather than four in number: summer, autumn, locking, winter, unlocking, and spring. And I remembered that as I straightened up beside our manhole, and stared and listened and sniffed.

There were no smells. There was no movement. Every step I took made a gravelly squeak in blue-white frost. And every squeak was echoed loudly. The season of locking was over. The earth was locked up tight.

It was winter, now and forever.

I helped my Mona out of our hole. I warned her to keep her hands away from the blue-white frost and to keep her hands away from her mouth, too. "Death has never been quite so easy to come by," I told her. "All you have to do is touch the ground and then your lips and you're done for."

She shook her head and sighed. "A very bad mother."

"What?"

"Mother Earth—she isn't a very good mother any more."

"Hello? Hello?" I called through the palace ruins. The awesome winds had torn canyons through that great stone pile. Mona and I made a half-hearted search for survivors—half-hearted because we could sense no life. Not even a nibbling, twinkle-nosed rat had survived.

The arch of the palace gate was the only man-made form untouched. Mona and I went to it. Written at its base in white paint was a Bokononist "Calypso." The lettering was neat. It was new. It was proof that someone else had survived the winds.

The "Calypso" was this:

Someday, someday, this crazy world will have to end,
And our God will take things back that He to us did lend.
And if, on that sad day, you want to scold our God,
Why go right ahead and scold Him. He'll just smile and nod.

120

To Whom It May Concern

I recalled an advertisement for a set of children's books called *The Book of Knowledge*. In that ad, a trusting boy and girl looked up at their father. "Daddy," one asked, "what makes the sky blue?" The answer, presumably, could be found in *The Book of Knowledge*.

If I had had my daddy beside me as Mona and I walked down the road from the palace, I would have had plenty of questions to ask as I clung to his hand. "Daddy, why are all the trees broken? Daddy, why are all the birds dead? Daddy, what makes the sky so sick and wormy? Daddy, what makes the sea so hard and still?"

It occurred to me that I was better qualified to answer those tough questions than any other human being, provided there were any other human beings alive. In case anyone was interested, I knew what had gone wrong—where and how.

So what?

I wondered where the dead could be. Mona and I ventured more than a mile from our oubliette without seeing one dead human being.

I wasn't half so curious about the living, probably because I sensed accurately that I would first have to contemplate a lot of dead. I saw no columns of smoke from possible campfires; but they would have been hard to see against an horizon of worms.

One thing did catch my eye: a lavender corona about the queer plug that was the peak on the hump of Mount McCabe. It seemed to be calling me, and I had a silly, cinematic notion of climbing that peak with Mona. But what would it mean?

We were walking into the wrinkles now at the foot of Mount McCabe. And Mona, as though aimlessly, left my side, left the road, and climbed one of the wrinkles. I followed.

I joined her at the top of the ridge. She was looking down raptly into a broad, natural bowl. She was not crying.

She might well have cried.

In that bowl were thousands upon thousands of dead. On the lips of each decedent was the blue-white frost of *ice-nine*.

Since the corpses were not scattered or tumbled about, it was clear that they had been assembled since the withdrawal of the frightful winds. And, since each corpse had its finger in or near its mouth, I understood that each person had delivered himself to this melancholy place and then poisoned himself with *ice-nine*.

There were men, women, and children, too, many in the attitudes of *boko-maru*. All faced the center of the bowl, as though they were spectators in an amphitheater.

Mona and I looked at the focus of all those frosted eyes, looked at the center of the bowl. There was a round clearing there, a place in which one orator might have stood.

Mona and I approached the clearing gingerly, avoiding the morbid statuary. We found a boulder in it. And under the boulder was a penciled note which said:

To whom it may concern: These people around you are almost all of the survivors on San Lorenzo of the winds that followed the freezing of the sea. These people made a captive of the spurious holy man named Bokonon. They brought him here, placed him at their center, and commanded him to tell them exactly what God Almighty was up to and what they should now do. The mountebank told them that God was surely trying to kill them, possibly because He was through with them, and that they should have the good manners to die. This, as you can see, they did.

The note was signed by Bokonon.

121

I Am Slow to Answer

"What a cynic!" I gasped. I looked up from the note and gazed around the death-filled bowl. "Is *he* here somewhere?"

"I do not see him," said Mona mildly. She wasn't depressed or angry. In fact, she seemed to verge on laughter. "He always said he would never take his own advice, because he knew it was worthless."

"He'd *better* be here!" I said bitterly. "Think of the gall of the man, advising all these people to kill themselves!"

Now Mona did laugh. I had never heard her laugh. Her laugh was startlingly deep and raw.

"This strikes you as *funny*?"

She raised her arms lazily. "It's all so simple, that's all. It solves so much for so many, so simply."

And she went strolling up among the petrified thousands, still laughing. She paused about midway up the slope and faced me. She called down to me, "Would you wish any of these alive again, if you could? Answer me quickly.

"Not quick enough with your answer," she called playfully, after half a minute had passed. And, still laughing a little, she touched her finger to the ground, straightened up, and touched the finger to her lips and died.

Did I weep? They say I did. H. Lowe Crosby and his Hazel and little Newton Hoenikker came upon me as I stumbled down the road. They were in Bolivar's one taxicab, which had been spared by the storm. They tell me I was crying. Hazel cried, too, cried for joy that I was alive.

They coaxed me into the cab.

Hazel put her arm around me. "You're with your mom, now. Don't you worry about a thing."

I let my mind go blank. I closed my eyes. It was with deep, idiotic relief that I leaned on that fleshy, humid, barn-yard fool.

122

The Swiss Family Robinson

They took me to what was left of Franklin Hoenikker's house at the head of the waterfall. What remained was the cave under the waterfall, which had become a sort of igloo under a translucent, blue-white dome of *ice-nine*.

The ménage consisted of Frank, little Newt, and the Crosbys. They had survived in a dungeon in the palace, one far shallower and more unpleasant than the oubliette. They had moved out the moment the winds had abated, while Mona and I had stayed underground for another three days.

As it happened, they had found the miraculous taxicab waiting

for them under the arch of the palace gate. They had found a
can of white paint, and on the front doors of the cab Frank had
painted white stars, and on the roof he had painted the letters
of a *granfalloon*: U.S.A.

"And you left the paint under the arch," I said.

"How did you know?" asked Crosby.

"Somebody else came along and wrote a poem."

I did not inquire at once as to how Angela Hoenikker
Conners and Philip and Julian Castle had met their ends, for I
would have had to speak at once about Mona. I wasn't ready
to do that yet.

I particularly didn't want to discuss the death of Mona since,
as we rode along in the taxi, the Crosbys and little Newt
seemed so inappropriately gay.

Hazel gave me a clue to the gaiety. "Wait until you see how
we live. We've got all kinds of good things to eat. Whenever
we want water, we just build a campfire and melt some. The
Swiss Family Robinson—that's what we call ourselves."

123

Of Mice and Men

A curious six months followed—the six months in which I
wrote this book. Hazel spoke accurately when she called our
little society the Swiss Family Robinson, for we had survived a
storm, were isolated, and then the living became very easy indeed. It was not without a certain Walt Disney charm.

No plants or animals survived, it's true. But *ice-nine* pre-
served pigs and cows and little deer and windrows of birds and
berries until we were ready to thaw and cook them. Moreover,
there were tons of canned goods to be had for the grubbing in
the ruins of Bolivar. And we seemed to be the only people left
on San Lorenzo.

Food was no problem, and neither were clothing or shelter,
for the weather was uniformly dry and dead and hot. Our

health was monotonously good. Apparently all the germs were dead, too—or napping.

Our adjustment became so satisfactory, so complacent, that no one marveled or protested when Hazel said, "One good thing anyway, no mosquitoes."

She was sitting on a three-legged stool in the clearing where Frank's house had stood. She was sewing strips of red, white, and blue cloth together. Like Betsy Ross, she was making an American flag. No one was unkind enough to point out to her that the red was really a peach, that the blue was nearly a Kelly green, and that the fifty stars she had cut out were six-pointed stars of David rather than five-pointed American stars.

Her husband, who had always been a pretty good cook, now simmered a stew in an iron pot over a wood fire nearby. He did all our cooking for us; he loved to cook.

"Looks good, smells good," I commented.

He winked. "Don't shoot the cook. He's doing the best he can."

In the background of this cozy conversation were the nagging dah-dah-dahs and dit-dit-dits of an automatic SOS transmitter Frank had made. It called for help both night and day.

"Save our soulllls," Hazel intoned, singing along with the transmitter as she sewed, "save our soulllllls."

"How's the writing going?" Hazel asked me.

"Fine, Mom, just fine."

"When you going to show us some of it?"

"When it's ready, Mom, when it's ready."

"A lot of famous writers were Hoosiers."

"I know."

"You'll be one of a long, long line." She smiled hopefully. "Is it a funny book?"

"I hope so, Mom."

"I like a good laugh."

"I know you do."

"Each person here has some specialty, something to give the rest. You write books that make us laugh, and Frank does science things, and little Newt—he paints pictures for us all, and I sew, and Lowie cooks."

"'Many hands make much work light.' Old Chinese proverb."

"They were smart in a lot of ways, those Chinese were."

"Yes, let's keep their memory alive."

"I wish now I'd studied them more."

"Well, it was hard to do, even under ideal conditions."

"I wish now I'd studied everything more."

"We've all got regrets, Mom."

"No use crying over spilt milk."

"As the poet said, Mom, 'Of all the words of mice and men, the saddest are, "It might have been." '"

"That's so beautiful, and so true."

124

Frank's Ant Farm

I hated to see Hazel finishing the flag, because I was all balled up in her addled plans for it. She had the idea that I had agreed to plant the fool thing on the peak of Mount McCabe.

"If Lowe and I were younger, we'd do it ourselves. Now all we can do is give you the flag and send our best wishes with you."

"Mom, I wonder if that's really a good place for the flag."

"What other place *is* there?"

"I'll put on my thinking cap." I excused myself and went down into the cave to see what Frank was up to.

He was up to nothing new. He was watching an ant farm he had constructed. He had dug up a few surviving ants in the three-dimensional world of the ruins of Bolivar, and he had reduced the dimensions to two by making a dirt and ant sandwich between two sheets of glass. The ants could do nothing without Frank's catching them at it and commenting upon it.

The experiment had solved in short order the mystery of how ants could survive in a waterless world. As far as I know, they were the only insects that did survive, and they did it by forming with their bodies tight balls around grains of *ice-nine*. They would generate enough heat at the center to kill half their number and produce one bead of dew. The dew was drinkable. The corpses were edible.

"Eat, drink, and be merry, for tomorrow we die," I said to Frank and his tiny cannibals.

His response was always the same. It was a peevish lecture on all the things that people could learn from ants.

My responses were ritualized, too. "Nature's a wonderful thing, Frank. Nature's a wonderful thing."

"You know why ants are so successful?" he asked me for the thousandth time. "They co-*op*-er-ate."

"That's a hell of a good word—co-operation."

"Who *taught* them how to make water?"

"Who taught *me* how to make water?"

"That's a silly answer and you know it."

"Sorry."

"There was a time when I took people's silly answers seriously. I'm past that now."

"A milestone."

"I've grown up a good deal."

"At a certain amount of expense to the world." I could say things like that to Frank with an absolute assurance that he would not hear them.

"There was a time when people could bluff me without much trouble because I didn't have much self-confidence in myself."

"The mere cutting down of the number of people on earth would go a long way toward alleviating your own particular social problems," I suggested. Again, I made the suggestion to a deaf man.

"You *tell* me, you *tell* me who told these ants how to make water," he challenged me again.

Several times I had offered the obvious notion that God had taught them. And I knew from onerous experience that he would neither reject nor accept this theory. He simply got madder and madder, putting the question again and again.

I walked away from Frank, just as *The Books of Bokonon* advised me to do. "Beware of the man who works hard to learn something, learns it, and finds himself no wiser than before," Bokonon tells us. "He is full of murderous resentment of

people who are ignorant without having come by their ignorance the hard way."

I went looking for our painter, for little Newt.

125

The Tasmanians

When I found little Newt, painting a blasted landscape a
quarter of a mile from the cave, he asked me if I would drive
him into Bolivar to forage for paints. He couldn't drive himself.
He couldn't reach the pedals.

So off we went, and, on the way, I asked him if he had any
sex urge left. I mourned that I had none—no dreams in that
line, nothing.

"I used to dream of women twenty, thirty, forty feet tall," he
told me. "But now? God, I can't even remember what my
Ukrainian midget looked like."

I recalled a thing I had read about the aboriginal Tasmanians,
habitually naked persons who, when encountered by white
men in the seventeenth century, were strangers to agriculture,
animal husbandry, architecture of any sort, and possibly even
fire. They were so contemptible in the eyes of white men, by
reason of their ignorance, that they were hunted for sport
by the first settlers, who were convicts from England. And
the aborigines found life so unattractive that they gave up
reproducing.

I suggested to Newt now that it was a similar hopelessness
that had unmanned us.

Newt made a shrewd observation. "I guess all the excitement in bed had more to do with excitement about keeping
the human race going than anybody ever imagined."

"Of course, if we had a woman of breeding age among us,
that might change the situation radically. Poor old Hazel is
years beyond having even a Mongolian idiot."

Newt revealed that he knew quite a bit about Mongolian idiots. He had once attended a special school for grotesque children, and several of his schoolmates had been Mongoloids. "The best writer in our class was a Mongoloid named Myrna—I mean penmanship, not what she actually wrote down. God, I haven't thought about her for years."

"Was it a good school?"

"All I remember is what the headmaster used to say all the time. He was always bawling us out over the loudspeaker system for some mess we'd made, and he always started out the same way: 'I am sick and tired . . .'"

"That comes pretty close to describing how I feel most of the time."

"Maybe that's the way you're supposed to feel."

"You talk like a Bokononist, Newt."

"Why shouldn't I? As far as I know, Bokononism is the only religion that has any commentary on midgets."

When I hadn't been writing, I'd been poring over *The Books of Bokonon*, but the reference to midgets had escaped me. I was grateful to Newt for calling it to my attention, for the quotation captured in a couplet the cruel paradox of Bokononist thought, the heartbreaking necessity of lying about reality, and the heartbreaking impossibility of lying about it.

Midget, midget, midget, how he struts and winks,
For he knows a man's as big as what he hopes and thinks!

126

Soft Pipes, Play On

"Such a *depressing* religion!" I cried. I directed our conversation into the area of Utopias, of what might have been, of what should have been, of what might yet be, if the world would thaw.

But Bokonon had been there, too, had written a whole book

about Utopias, *The Seventh Book*, which he called "Bokonon's Republic." In that book are these ghastly aphorisms:

The hand that stocks the drug stores rules the world.

Let us start our Republic with a chain of drug stores, a chain of grocery stores, a chain of gas chambers, and a national game. After that, we can write our Constitution.

I called Bokonon a jigaboo bastard, and I changed the subject again. I spoke of meaningful, individual heroic acts. I praised in particular the way in which Julian Castle and his son had chosen to die. While the tornadoes still raged, they had set out on foot for the House of Hope and Mercy in the Jungle to give whatever hope and mercy was theirs to give. And I saw magnificence in the way poor Angela had died, too. She had picked up a clarinet in the ruins of Bolivar and had begun to play it at once, without concerning herself as to whether the mouthpiece might be contaminated with *ice-nine*.

"Soft pipes, play on," I murmured huskily.

"Well, maybe you can find some neat way to die, too," said Newt.

It was a Bokononist thing to say.

I blurted out my dream of climbing Mount McCabe with some magnificent symbol and planting it there. I took my hands from the wheel for an instant to show him how empty of symbols they were. "But what in hell would the right symbol *be*, Newt? What in hell would it *be*?" I grabbed the wheel again. "Here it is, the end of the world; and here I am, almost the very last man; and there it is, the highest mountain in sight. I know now what my *karass* has been up to, Newt. It's been working night and day for maybe half a million years to get me up that mountain." I wagged my head and nearly wept. "But what, for the love of God, is supposed to be in my hands?"

I looked out of the car window blindly as I asked that, so blindly that I went more than a mile before realizing that I had looked into the eyes of an old Negro man, a living colored man, who was sitting by the side of the road.

And then I slowed down. And then I stopped. I covered my eyes.

"What's the matter?" asked Newt.

"I saw Bokonon back there."

127

The End

He was sitting on a rock. He was barefoot. His feet were
frosty with *ice-nine*. His only garment was a white bedspread
with blue tufts. The tufts said Casa Mona. He took no note of
our arrival. In one hand was a pencil. In the other was paper.

"Bokonon?"

"Yes?"

"May I ask what you're thinking?"

"I am thinking, young man, about the final sentence for *The
Books of Bokonon*. The time for the final sentence has come."

"Any luck?"

He shrugged and handed me a piece of paper.

This is what I read:

If I were a younger man, I would write a history of human stupidity; and I would climb to the top of Mount McCabe and lie down
on my back with my history for a pillow; and I would take from the
ground some of the blue-white poison that makes statues of men; and
I would make a statue of myself, lying on my back, grinning horribly,
and thumbing my nose at You Know Who.

GOD BLESS YOU, MR. ROSEWATER

or Pearls Before Swine

For Alvin Davis,
the telepath,
the hoodlums' friend

"*The Second World War was over—and there I was at high noon, crossing Times Square with a Purple Heart on.*"

—ELIOT ROSEWATER

PRESIDENT, The Rosewater Foundation

All persons, living and dead,
are purely coincidental,
and should not be construed.

1

A SUM OF MONEY is a leading character in this tale about people, just as a sum of honey might properly be a leading character in a tale about bees.

The sum was $87,472,033.61 on June 1, 1964, to pick a day. That was the day it caught the soft eyes of a boy shyster named Norman Mushari. The income the interesting sum produced was $3,500,000 a year, nearly $10,000 a day—Sundays, too.

The sum was made the core of a charitable and cultural foundation in 1947, when Norman Mushari was only six. Before that, it was the fourteenth largest family fortune in America, the Rosewater fortune. It was stashed into a foundation in order that tax-collectors and other predators not named Rosewater might be prevented from getting their hands on it. And the baroque masterpiece of legal folderol that was the charter of the Rosewater Foundation declared, in effect, that the presidency of the Foundation was to be inherited in the same manner as the British Crown. It was to be handed down throughout all eternity to the closest and oldest heirs of the Foundation's creator, Senator Lister Ames Rosewater of Indiana.

Siblings of the President were to become officers of the Foundation upon reaching the age of twenty-one. All officers were officers for life, unless proved legally insane. They were free to compensate themselves for their services as lavishly as they pleased, but only from the Foundation's income.

• • •

As required by law, the charter prohibited the Senator's heirs having anything to do with the management of the Foundation's capital. Caring for the capital became the responsibility of a corporation that was born simultaneously with the Foundation. It was called, straightforwardly enough, The Rosewater Corporation. Like almost all corporations, it was dedicated to prudence and profit, to balance sheets. Its employees were very well paid. They were cunning and happy and energetic on that account. Their main enterprise was the churning of stocks and

193

bonds of other corporations. A minor activity was the management of a saw factory, a bowling alley, a motel, a bank, a brewery, extensive farms in Rosewater County, Indiana, and some coal mines in northern Kentucky.

The Rosewater Corporation occupied two floors at 500 Fifth Avenue, in New York, and maintained small branch offices in London, Tokyo, Buenos Aires and Rosewater County. No member of the Rosewater Foundation could tell the Corporation what to do with the capital. Conversely, the Corporation was powerless to tell the Foundation what to do with the copious profits the Corporation made.

• • •

These facts became known to young Norman Mushari when, upon graduating from Cornell Law School at the top of his class, he went to work for the Washington, D.C., law firm that had designed both the Foundation and the Corporation, the firm of McAllister, Robjent, Reed and McGee. He was of Lebanese extraction, the son of a Brooklyn rug merchant. He was five feet and three inches tall. He had an enormous ass, which was luminous when bare.

He was the youngest, the shortest, and by all odds the least Anglo-Saxon male employee in the firm. He was put to work under the most senile partner, Thurmond McAllister, a sweet old poop who was seventy-six. He would never have been hired if the other partners hadn't felt that McAllister's operations could do with just a touch more viciousness.

No one ever went out to lunch with Mushari. He took nourishment alone in cheap cafeterias, and plotted the violent overthrow of the Rosewater Foundation. He knew no Rosewaters. What engaged his emotions was the fact that the Rosewater fortune was the largest single money package represented by McAllister, Robjent, Reed and McGee. He recalled what his favorite professor, Leonard Leech, once told him about getting ahead in law. Leech said that, just as a good airplane pilot should always be looking for places to land, so should a lawyer be looking for situations where large amounts of money were about to change hands.

"In every big transaction," said Leech, "there is a magic moment during which a man has surrendered a treasure, and during which the man who is due to receive it has not yet done so. An alert lawyer will make that moment his own, possessing the treasure for a magic microsecond, taking a little of it, passing it on. If the man who is to receive the treasure is unused to wealth, has an inferiority complex and shapeless feelings of guilt, as most people do, the lawyer can often take as much as half the bundle, and still receive the recipient's blubbering thanks."

The more Mushari rifled the firm's confidential files relative to the Rosewater Foundation, the more excited he became. Especially thrilling to him was that part of the charter which called for the immediate expulsion of any officer adjudged insane. It was common gossip in the office that the very first president of the Foundation, Eliot Rosewater, the Senator's son, was a lunatic. This characterization was a somewhat playful one, but as Mushari knew, playfulness was impossible to explain in a court of law. Eliot was spoken of by Mushari's co-workers variously as "The Nut," "The Saint," "The Holy Roller," "John the Baptist," and so on.

"By all means," Mushari mooned to himself, "we must get this specimen before a judge."

From all reports, the person next in line to be President of the Foundation, a cousin in Rhode Island, was inferior in all respects. When the magic moment came, Mushari would represent him.

Mushari, being tone-deaf, did not know that he himself had an office nickname. It was contained in a tune that someone was generally whistling when he came or went. The tune was "Pop Goes the Weasel."

• • •

Eliot Rosewater became President of the Foundation in 1947. When Mushari began to investigate him seventeen years later, Eliot was forty-six. Mushari, who thought of himself as brave little David about to slay Goliath, was exactly half his age. And it was almost as though God Himself wanted little David to win, for confidential document after document proved that Eliot was crazy as a loon.

In a locked file inside the firm's vault, for instance, was an envelope with three seals on it—and it was supposed to be delivered unopened to whomever took over the Foundation when Eliot was dead.

Inside was a letter from Eliot, and this is what it said:

Dear Cousin, or whoever you may be—

Congratulations on your great good fortune. Have fun. It may increase your perspective to know what sorts of manipulators and custodians your unbelievable wealth has had up to now.

Like so many great American fortunes, the Rosewater pile was accumulated in the beginning by a humorless, constipated Christian farm boy turned speculator and briber during and after the Civil War. The farm boy was Noah Rosewater, my great-grandfather, who was born in Rosewater County, Indiana.

Noah and his brother George inherited from their pioneer father six hundred acres of farmland, land as dark and rich as chocolate cake, and a small saw factory that was nearly bankrupt. War came.

George raised a rifle company, marched away at its head.

Noah hired a village idiot to fight in his place, converted the saw factory to the manufacture of swords and bayonets, converted the farm to the raising of hogs. Abraham Lincoln declared that no amount of money was too much to pay for the restoration of the Union, so Noah priced his merchandise in scale with the national tragedy. And he made this discovery: Government objections to the price or quality of his wares could be vaporized with bribes that were pitifully small.

He married Cleota Herrick, the ugliest woman in Indiana, because she had four hundred thousand dollars. With her money he expanded the factory and bought more farms, all in Rosewater County. He became the largest individual hog farmer in the North. And, in order not to be victimized by meat packers, he bought controlling interest in an Indianapolis slaughterhouse. In order not to be victimized by steel suppliers, he bought controlling interest in a steel company in Pittsburgh. In order not to be victimized by coal suppliers, he bought controlling interest in several mines. In order not to be victimized by money lenders, he founded a bank.

And his paranoid reluctance to be a victim caused him to deal more and more in valuable papers, in stocks and bonds, and less and less in swords and pork. Small experiments with worthless papers convinced him that such papers could be sold effortlessly. While he continued to bribe persons in government to hand over treasuries and national resources, his first enthusiasm became the peddling of watered stock.

When the United States of America, which was meant to be a Utopia for all, was less than a century old, Noah Rosewater and a few men like him demonstrated the folly of the Founding Fathers in one respect: those sadly recent ancestors had not made it the law of the Utopia that the wealth of each citizen should be limited. This oversight was engendered by a weak-kneed sympathy for those who loved expensive things, and by the feeling that the continent was so vast and valuable, and the population so thin and enterprising, that no thief, no matter how fast he stole, could more than mildly inconvenience anyone.

Noah and a few like him perceived that the continent was in fact finite, and that venal office-holders, legislators in particular, could be persuaded to toss up great hunks of it for grabs, and to toss them in such a way as to have them land where Noah and his kind were standing.

Thus did a handful of rapacious citizens come to control all that was worth controlling in America. Thus was the savage and stupid and entirely inappropriate and unnecessary and humorless American class system created. Honest, industrious, peaceful citizens were classed as bloodsuckers, if they asked to be paid a living wage. And they saw that praise was reserved henceforth for those who devised means of getting paid enormously for committing crimes against which no laws had been passed. Thus the American dream turned belly up, turned green, bobbed to the scummy surface of cupidity unlimited, filled with gas, went *bang* in the noonday sun.

E pluribus unum is surely an ironic motto to inscribe on the currency of this Utopia gone bust, for every grotesquely rich American represents property, privileges, and pleasures that have been denied the many. An even more instructive motto, in the light of history made by the Noah Rosewaters, might be: *Grab much too much, or you'll get nothing at all.*

And Noah begat Samuel, who married Geraldine Ames Rockefeller. Samuel became even more interested in politics than his father had been, served the Republican Party tirelessly as a king-maker, caused that party to nominate men who would whirl like dervishes, bawl fluent Babylonian, and order the militia to fire into crowds whenever a poor man seemed on the point of suggesting that he and a Rosewater were equal in the eyes of the law.

And Samuel bought newspapers, and preachers, too. He gave them this simple lesson to teach, and they taught it well: *Anybody who thought that the United States of America was supposed to be a Utopia was a piggy, lazy, God-damned fool.* Samuel thundered that no American factory hand was worth more than eighty cents a day. And yet he could be thankful for the opportunity to pay a hundred thousand dollars or more for a painting by an Italian three centuries dead. And he capped this insult by giving paintings to museums for the spiritual elevation of the poor. The museums were closed on Sundays.

And Samuel begat Lister Ames Rosewater, who married Eunice Eliot Morgan. There was something to be said for Lister and Eunice: unlike Noah and Cleota and Samuel and Geraldine, they could laugh as though they meant it. As a curious footnote to history, Eunice became Woman's Chess Champion of the United States in 1927, and again in 1933.

Eunice also wrote an historical novel about a female gladiator, *Ramba of Macedon*, which was a best-seller in 1936. Eunice died in 1937, in a sailing accident in Cotuit, Massachusetts. She was a wise and amusing person, with very sincere anxieties about the condition of the poor. She was my mother.

Her husband, Lister, never was in business. From the moment of his birth to the time I am writing this, he has left the manipulation of his assets to lawyers and banks. He has spent nearly the whole of his adult life in the Congress of the United States, teaching morals, first as a Representative from the district whose heart is Rosewater County, and then as Senator from Indiana. That he is or ever was an Indiana person is a tenuous political fiction. And Lister begat Eliot.

Lister has thought about the effects and implications of his inherited wealth about as much as most men think about their left big toes. The fortune has never amused, worried, or tempted him. Giving ninety-five per cent of it to the Foundation you now control didn't cause him a twinge.

And Eliot married Sylvia DuVrais Zetterling, a Parisienne beauty who came to hate him. Her mother was a patroness of painters. Her father was the greatest living cellist. Her maternal grandparents were a Rothschild and a DuPont.

And Eliot became a drunkard, a Utopian dreamer, a tinhorn saint, an aimless fool.

Begat he not a soul.

Bon voyage, dear Cousin or whoever you are. Be generous. Be kind. You can safely ignore the arts and sciences. They never helped anybody. Be a sincere, attentive friend of the poor.

The letter was signed,

The late Eliot Rosewater.

His heart going like a burglar alarm, Norman Mushari hired a large safe-deposit box, and he put the letter into it. That first piece of solid evidence would not be lonesome long.

Mushari went back to his cubicle, reflected that Sylvia was in the process of divorcing Eliot, with old McAllister representing the defendant. She was living in Paris, and Mushari wrote a letter to her, suggesting that it was customary in friendly, civilized divorce actions for litigants to return each other's letters. He asked her to send him any letters from Eliot that she might have saved.

He got fifty-three such letters by return mail.

2

ELIOT ROSEWATER was born in 1918, in Washington, D.C. Like his father, who claimed to represent the Hoosier State, Eliot was raised and educated and entertained on the Eastern Seaboard and in Europe. The family visited the so-called "home" in Rosewater County very briefly every year, just long enough to reinvigorate the lie that it was home.

Eliot had unremarkable academic careers at Loomis and Harvard. He became an expert sailor during summers in Cotuit, on Cape Cod, and an intermediate skier during winter vacations in Switzerland.

He left Harvard Law School on December 8, 1941, to volunteer for the Infantry of the Army of the United States. He served with distinction in many battles. He rose to the rank of captain, was a company commander. Near the end of the war in Europe, Eliot suffered what was diagnosed as combat fatigue. He was hospitalized in Paris, where he wooed and won Sylvia.

After the war, Eliot returned to Harvard with his stunning wife, took his law degree. He went on to specialize in international law, dreamed of helping the United Nations in some way. He received a doctorate in that field, and was handed simultaneously the presidency of the new Rosewater Foundation. His duties, according to the charter, were exactly as flimsy or as formidable as he himself declared them to be.

Eliot chose to take the Foundation seriously. He bought a town house in New York, with a fountain in the foyer. He put a Bentley and a Jaguar in the garage. He hired a suite of offices in the Empire State Building. He had them painted lime, burnt-orange and oyster white. He proclaimed them the headquarters for all the beautiful, compassionate and scientific things he hoped to do.

He was a heavy drinker, but no one worried about it. No amount of booze seemed to make him drunk.

• • •

From 1947 until 1953, the Rosewater Foundation spent fourteen million dollars. Eliot's benefactions covered the full eleemosynary spectrum from a birth control clinic in Detroit to an El Greco for Tampa, Florida. Rosewater dollars fought cancer and mental illness and race prejudice and police brutality and countless other miseries, encouraged college professors to look for truth, bought beauty at any price.

Ironically, one of the studies Eliot paid for had to do with alcoholism in San Diego. When the report was submitted, Eliot was too drunk to read it. Sylvia had to come down to his office to escort him home. A hundred people saw her trying to lead him across the sidewalk to a waiting cab. And Eliot recited for them a couplet he had spent all morning composing:

> "Many, many good things have I bought!
> Many, many bad things have I fought!"

• • •

Eliot stayed contritely sober for two days after that, then disappeared for a week. Among other things, he crashed a convention of science-fiction writers in a motel in Milford, Pennsylvania. Norman Mushari learned about this episode from a private detective's report that was in the files of McAllister, Robjent, Reed and McGee. Old McAllister had hired the detective to retrace Eliot's steps, to find out if he had done things that might later legally embarrass the Foundation.

The report contained Eliot's speech to the writers word-for-word. The meeting, including Eliot's drunken interruption, had been taken down on tape.

"I love you sons of bitches," Eliot said in Milford. "You're all I read any more. You're the only ones who'll talk about the *really* terrific changes going on, the only ones crazy enough to know that life is a space voyage, and not a short one, either, but one that'll last for billions of years. You're the only ones with guts enough to *really* care about the future, who *really* notice what machines do to us, what wars do to us, what cities do to us, what big, simple ideas do to us, what tremendous misunderstandings, mistakes, accidents and catastrophes do to us. You're the only ones zany enough to agonize over time and distances without limit, over mysteries that will never die, over the fact that we are right now determining whether the space voyage for the next billion years or so is going to be Heaven or Hell."

• • •

Eliot admitted later on that science-fiction writers couldn't write for sour apples, but he declared that it didn't matter. He said they were poets just the same, since they were more sensitive to important changes than anybody who was writing well. "The hell with the talented sparrowfarts who write delicately of one small piece of one mere lifetime, when the issues are galaxies, eons, and trillions of souls yet to be born."

• • •

"I only wish Kilgore Trout were here," said Eliot, "so I could shake his hand and tell him that he is the greatest writer alive today. I have just been told that he could not come because he could not afford to leave his job! And what job does this society give its greatest prophet?" Eliot choked up, and, for a few moments, he couldn't make himself name Trout's job. "They have made him a stock clerk in a trading stamp redemption center in Hyannis!"

This was true. Trout, the author of eighty-seven paperback books, was a very poor man, and unknown outside the science-fiction field. He was sixty-six years old when Eliot spoke so warmly of him.

"Ten thousand years from now," Eliot predicted boozily, "the names of our generals and presidents will be forgotten, and the only hero of our time still remembered will be the author of *2BRO2B*." This was the title of a book by Trout, a title which, upon examination, turned out to be the famous question posed by Hamlet.

• • •

Mushari dutifully went looking for a copy of the book for his dossier on Eliot. No reputable bookseller had ever heard of Trout. Mushari made his last try at a smut-dealer's hole in the wall. There, amidst the rawest pornography, he found tattered copies of every book Trout had ever written. *2BRO2B*, which had been published at twenty-five cents, cost him five dollars, which was what *The Kama Sutra of Vitsayana* cost, too.

Mushari glanced through the *Kama Sutra*, the long-suppressed oriental manual on the art and techniques of love, read this:

> If a man makes a sort of jelly with the juices of the fruit cassia fistula and eugenie jambolina and mixes the powder of the plants soma, veronia anthelminica, eclipta prostata, lohopa-juihirka, and applies this mixture to the yoni of a woman with whom he is about to have intercourse, he will instantly cease to love her.

Mushari didn't see anything funny in that. He never saw anything funny in anything, so deeply immured was he by the utterly unplayful spirit of the law.

And he was witless enough, too, to imagine that Trout's books were very dirty books, since they were sold for such high prices to such queer people in such a place. He didn't understand that what Trout had in common with pornography wasn't sex but fantasies of an impossibly hospitable world.

• • •

So Mushari felt swindled as he wallowed through the garish prose, lusted for sex, learned instead about automation. Trout's favorite formula was to describe a perfectly hideous society, not unlike his own, and then, toward the end, to suggest ways in which it could be improved. In *2BR02B* he hypothecated an America in which almost all of the work was done by machines, and the only people who could get work had three or more Ph.D's. There was a serious overpopulation problem, too.

All serious diseases had been conquered. So death was voluntary, and the government, to encourage volunteers for death, set up a purple-roofed Ethical Suicide Parlor at every major intersection, right next door to an orange-roofed Howard Johnson's. There were pretty hostesses in the parlor, and Barca-Loungers, and Muzak, and a choice of fourteen painless ways to die. The suicide parlors were busy places, because so many people felt silly and pointless, and because it was supposed to be an unselfish, patriotic thing to do, to die. The suicides also got free last meals next door.

And so on. Trout had a wonderful imagination.

One of the characters asked a death stewardess if he would go to Heaven, and she told him that of course he would. He asked if he would see God, and she said, "Certainly, honey."

And he said, "I sure hope so. I want to ask Him something I never was able to find out down here."

"What's that?" she said, strapping him in.

"What in hell are people *for*?"

• • •

In Milford, Eliot told the writers that he wished they would learn more about sex and economics and style, but then he supposed that people dealing with really big issues didn't have much time for such things.

And it occurred to him that a really good science-fiction book had never been written about money. "Just think of the wild ways money is passed around on Earth!" he said. "You don't have to go to the Planet Tralfamadore in Anti-Matter Galaxy 508 G to find weird creatures with unbelievable powers. Look at the powers of an Earthling millionaire! Look at me! I was born naked, just like you, but my God, friends and neighbors, I have thousands of dollars a day to spend!"

He paused to make a very impressive demonstration of his magical powers, writing a smeary check for two hundred dollars for every person there.

"*There's* fantasy for you," he said. "And you go to the bank tomorrow, and it will all come true. It's insane that I should be able to do such a thing, with money so important." He lost his balance for a moment, regained it, and then nearly fell asleep on his feet. He opened his eyes with great effort. "I leave it to you, friends and neighbors, and especially to the immortal Kilgore Trout: think about the silly ways money gets passed around now, and then think up better ways."

• • •

Eliot lurched away from Milford, hitchhiked to Swarthmore, Pennsylvania. He went into a small bar there, announced that anyone who could produce a volunteer fireman's badge could drink with him free. He built gradually to a crying jag, during which he claimed to be deeply touched by the idea of an in-habited planet with an atmosphere that was eager to combine violently with almost everything the inhabitants held dear. He was speaking of Earth and the element oxygen.

"When you think about it, boys," he said brokenly, "that's what holds us together more than anything else, except maybe gravity. We few, we happy few, we band of brothers—joined in the serious business of keeping our food, shelter, clothing and loved ones from combining with oxygen. I tell you, boys, I used to belong to a volunteer fire department, and I'd belong to one now, if there were such a human thing, such a *humane* thing, in New York City." This was bunk about Eliot's having been a fireman. The closest he had ever come to that was during his annual childhood visits to Rosewater County, to the family fief. Sycophants among the townies had flattered little Eliot by making him mascot of the Volunteer Fire Department of Rosewater. He had never fought a fire.

"I tell you, boys," he went on, "if those Russian landing barges come barging in some day, and there isn't any way to stop 'em, all the phony bastards who get all the good jobs in this country by kissing ass will be down to meet the conquerers with vodka and caviar, offering to do any kind of work the Russians have in mind. And you know who'll take to the woods with hunting knives and Springfields, who'll go on fighting for a hundred years, by God? The volunteer firemen, that's who."

Eliot was locked up in Swarthmore on a drunk and disorderly charge. When he awoke the next morning, the police called his wife. He apologized to her, slunk home.

• • •

But he was off again in a month, carousing with firemen in Clover Lick, West Virginia, one night, and in New Egypt, New Jersey, the next. And on that trip he traded clothes with another man, swapped a four-hundred-dollar suit for a 1939 double-breasted blue chalkstripe, with shoulders like Gibraltar, lapels like the wings of the Archangel Gabriel, and with the creases in the trousers permanently sewed in.

"You must be crazy," said the New Egypt fireman.

"I don't want to look like me," Eliot replied. "I want to look like you. You're the salt of the earth, by God. You're what's good about America, men in suits like that. You're the soul of the U.S. Infantry."

And Eliot eventually traded away everything in his wardrobe but his tails, his dinner jacket, and one gray flannel suit. His sixteen-foot closet became a depressing museum of coveralls, overalls, Robert Hall Easter specials, field jackets, Eisenhower jackets, sweatshirts and so on. Sylvia wanted to burn them, but Eliot told her, "Burn my tails, my dinner jacket and my gray flannel suit instead."

• • •

Eliot was a flamboyantly sick man, even then, but there was no one to hustle him off for treatment, and no one was as yet entranced by the profits to be made in proving him insane. Little Norman Mushari was only twelve in those troubled days, was assembling plastic model airplanes, masturbating, and papering his room with pictures of Senator Joe McCarthy and Roy Cohn. Eliot Rosewater was the farthest thing from his mind.

Sylvia, raised among rich and charming eccentrics, was too European to have him put away. And the Senator was in the political fight of his life, rallying the Republican forces of reaction that had been shattered by the election of Dwight David Eisenhower. When told of his son's bizarre way of life, the Senator refused to worry, on the grounds that the boy was well-bred. "He's got fiber, he's got spine," the Senator said. "He's experimenting. He'll come back to his senses any time he's good and ready. This family never produced and never will produce a chronic drunk or a chronic lunatic."

Having said that, he went into the Senate Chamber to deliver his fairly famous speech on the Golden Age of Rome, in which he said, in part:

I should like to speak of the Emperor Octavian, of Caesar Augustus, as he came to be known. This great humanitarian, and he was a humanitarian in the profoundest sense of the word, took command of the Roman Empire in a degenerate period strikingly like our own. Harlotry, divorce, alcoholism, liberalism, homosexuality, pornography, abortion, venality, murder, labor racketeering, juvenile delinquency, cowardice, atheism, extortion, slander, and theft were the height of fashion. Rome was a paradise for gangsters, perverts, and the lazy working man, just as America is now. As in America now, forces of law and order were openly attacked by mobs, children were disobedient, had no respect for their parents or their country, and no decent woman was safe on any street, even at high noon! And cunning, sharp-trading, bribing foreigners were in the ascendency everywhere. And ground under the heels of the big city money-changers were the honest farmers, the backbone of the Roman Army and the Roman soul.

What could be done? Well, there were soft-headed liberals then as there are bubble-headed liberals now, and they said what liberals always say after they have led a great nation to such a lawless, self-indulgent, polyglot condition: "Things have never been better! Look at all the freedom! Look at all the equality! Look how sexual hypocrisy has been driven from the scene! Oh boy! People used to get all knotted up inside when they thought about rape or fornication. Now they can do both with glee!"

And what did the terrible, black-spirited, non-fun-loving conservatives of those happy days have to say? Well, there weren't many of them left. They were dying off in ridiculed old age. And their children had been turned against them by the liberals, by the purveyors of synthetic sunshine and moonshine, by the something-for-nothing political strip-teasers, by the people who loved everybody, including the barbarians, by people who loved the barbarians so much they wanted to open all the gates, have all the soldiers lay their weapons down, and let the barbarians come in!

That was the Rome that Caesar Augustus came home to, after defeating those two sex maniacs, Antony and Cleopatra, in the great sea battle of Actium. And I don't think I have to re-create the things he thought when he surveyed the Rome he was said to rule. Let us take a moment of silence, and let each think what he will of the stews of today.

There was a moment of silence, too, about thirty seconds that seemed to some like a thousand years.

And what methods did Caesar Augustus use to put this disorderly house in order? He did what we are so often told we must never, ever do, what we are told will never, ever work: he wrote morals into law, and he enforced those unenforceable laws with a police force that was cruel and unsmiling. He made it illegal for a Roman to behave like a pig. Do you hear me? It became illegal! And Romans caught acting like pigs were strung up by their thumbs, thrown down wells, fed to lions, and given other experiences that might impress them with the desirability of being more decent and reliable than they were. Did it work? You bet your boots it did! Pigs miraculously disappeared! And what do we call the period that followed this now-unthinkable oppression? Nothing more nor less, friends and neighbors, than "The Golden Age of Rome."

• • •

Am I suggesting that we follow this gory example? Of course I am. Scarcely a day has passed during which I have not said in one way or another: "Let us force Americans to be as good as they should be." Am I in favor of feeding labor crooks to lions? Well, to give those who get such satisfaction from imagining that I am covered with primordial scales a little twinge of pleasure, let me say, "Yes. Absolutely. This afternoon, if it can be arranged." To disappoint my critics, let me add that I am only fooling. I am not entertained by cruel and unusual punishments, not in the least. I am fascinated by the fact that a carrot and a stick can make a donkey go, and that this Space Age discovery may have some application in the world of human beings.

And so on. The Senator said that the carrot and the stick had been built into the Free Enterprise System, as conceived by the Founding Fathers, but that do-gooders, who thought people shouldn't ever have to struggle for anything, had buggered the logic of the system beyond all recognition.

In summation: *he said*, I see two alternatives before us. We can write morals into law, and enforce those morals harshly, or we can return to a true Free Enterprise System, which has the sink-or-swim justice of Caesar Augustus built into it. I emphatically favor the latter alternative. We must be hard, for we must become again a nation of swimmers, with the sinkers quietly disposing of themselves. I have spoken of another hard time in ancient history. In case you have forgotten the name of it, I shall refresh your memories: "The Golden Age of Rome," friends and neighbors, "The Golden Age of Rome."

As for friends who might have helped Eliot through his time of troubles: he didn't have any. He drove away his rich friends by telling them that whatever they had was based on dumb luck. He advised his artist friends that the only people who paid any attention to what they did were rich horses' asses with nothing more athletic to do. He asked his scholarly friends, "Who has time to read all the boring crap you write and listen to all the boring things you say?" He alienated his friends in the sciences by thanking them extravagantly for scientific advances he had read about in recent newspapers and magazines, by assuring them, with a perfectly straight face, that life was getting better and better, thanks to scientific thinking.

• • •

And then Eliot entered psychoanalysis. He swore off drinking, took pride in his appearance again, expressed enthusiasm for the arts and sciences, won back many friends.

Sylvia was never happier. But then, one year after the treatments had begun, she was astonished by a call from the analyst. He was resigning the case because, in his taut Viennese opinion, Eliot was untreatable.

"But you've cured him!"

"If I were a Los Angeles quack, dear lady, I would most demurely agree. However, I am not a Swami. Your husband has the most massively defended neurosis I have ever attempted to treat. What the nature of that neurosis is I can't imagine. In one solid year of work, I have not succeeded in even scratching its armor plate."

"But he always comes home from your office so cheerful!"

"Do you know what we talk about?"

"I thought it better not to ask."

"American history! Here is a very sick man, who, among other things, killed his mother, who has a terrifying tyrant for a father. And what does he talk about when I invite him to let his mind wander where it will? American history."

The statement that Eliot had killed his beloved mother was, in a crude way, true. When he was nineteen, he took his mother for a sail in Cotuit Harbor. He jibed. The slashing boom knocked his mother overboard. Eunice Morgan Rosewater sank like a stone.

"I ask him what he dreams about," the doctor continued, "and he tells me, 'Samuel Gompers, Mark Twain, and Alexander Hamilton.' I ask him if his father ever appears in his dreams, and he says, 'No, but Thorstein Veblen often does.' Mrs. Rosewater, I'm defeated. I resign."

• • •

Eliot seemed merely amused by the doctor's dismissal. "It's a cure he doesn't understand, so he refuses to admit it's a cure," he said lightly.

That evening, he and Sylvia went to the Metropolitan Opera for the opening of a new staging of *Aïda*. The Rosewater Foundation had paid for the costumes. Eliot looked sleekly marvelous, tall, tailcoated, his big, friendly face pink, and his blue eyes glittering with mental hygiene.

Everything was fine until the last scene of the opera, during which the hero and heroine were placed in an airtight chamber to suffocate. As the doomed pair filled their lungs, Eliot called out to them, "You will last a lot longer, if you don't try to sing." Eliot stood, leaned far out of his box, told the singers, "Maybe you don't know anything about oxygen, but I do. Believe me, you must not sing."

Eliot's face went white and blank. Sylvia plucked at his sleeve. He looked at her dazedly, then permitted her to lead him away as easily as she might have led a toy balloon.

3

Norman Mushari learned that, on the night of *Aïda*, Eliot disappeared again, jumped out of his homeward-bound cab at Forty-second Street and Fifth Avenue.

Ten days later, Sylvia got this letter, which was written on the stationery of the Elsinore Volunteer Fire Department, Elsinore, California. The name of the place set him off on a new line of speculation about himself, to the effect that he was a lot like Shakespeare's Hamlet.

Dear Ophelia—

Elsinore isn't quite what I expected, or maybe there's more than one, and I've come to the wrong one. The high school football players here call themselves "The Fighting Danes." In the surrounding towns they're known as "The Melancholy Danes." In the past three years they have won one game, tied two, and lost twenty-four. That's what happens, I guess, when Hamlet goes in as quarterback.

The last thing you said to me before I got out of the taxicab was that maybe we should get a divorce. I did not realize that life had become that uncomfortable for you. I do realize that I am a very slow realizer. I still find it hard to realize that I am an alcoholic, though even strangers know this right away.

Maybe I flatter myself when I think that I have things in common with Hamlet, that I have an important mission, that I'm temporarily mixed up about how it should be done. Hamlet had one big edge on me. His father's ghost told him exactly what he had to do, while I am operating without instructions. But from somewhere something is trying to tell me where to go, what to do there, and why to do it. Don't worry, I don't hear voices. But there is this feeling that I have a destiny far away from the shallow and preposterous posing that is our life in New York. And I roam.

And I roam.

Young Mushari was disappointed to read that Eliot did *not* hear voices. But the letter did end on a definitely cracked note. Eliot described the fire apparatus of Elsinore, as though Sylvia would be avid for such details.

They paint their fire engines here with orange and black stripes, like tigers. Very striking! They use detergent in their water, so that

the water will soak right through wallboard to get at a fire. That
certainly makes good sense, provided it doesn't harm the pumps and
hoses. They haven't been using it long enough to really know. I told
them they should write the pump manufacturer and tell him what
they're doing, and they said they would. They think I am a very big
volunteer fireman from back East. They are wonderful people. They
aren't like the sparrowfarts and dancing masters who come tapping at
the Rosewater Foundation's door. They're like the Americans I knew
in the war.

Be patient, Ophelia.

> Love,
> Hamlet.

Eliot went from Elsinore to Vashti, Texas, and was soon arrested. He wandered up to the Vashti firehouse, covered with
dust, needing a shave. He started talking to some idlers there
about how the government ought to divide up the wealth of
the country equally, instead of some people having more than
they could ever use, and others having nothing.

He rambled on, said such things as, "You know, I think the
main purpose of the Army, Navy, and Marine Corps is to get
poor Americans into clean, pressed, unpatched clothes, so rich
Americans can stand to look at them." He mentioned a revolution, too. He thought there might be one in about twenty
years, and he thought it would be a good one, provided infantry veterans and volunteer firemen led it.

He was thrown in jail as a suspicious character. They let him
go after a mystifying series of questions and answers. They
made him promise never to come back to Vashti again.

A week after that, he turned up in New Vienna, Iowa. He
wrote another letter to Sylvia on the stationery of the fire department there. He called Sylvia "*the most patient woman in
the world*," and he told her that her long vigil was almost over.

I know now, *he wrote*, where I must go. I am going there with all
possible speed! I will telephone from there! Perhaps I'll stay there
forever. It isn't clear to me yet what I must do when I get there. But
that will become clear, too, I'm sure. The scales are falling from my
eyes!

Incidentally, I told the fire department here that they might try putting detergent in their water, but that they should write the pump manufacturer first. They like the idea. They're going to bring it up at the next meeting. I've gone sixteen hours without a drink! I don't miss the poison at all! Cheers!

When Sylvia got that letter, she immediately had a recording device attached to her telephone, another nice break for Norman Mushari. Sylvia did this because she thought that Eliot had at last gone irrevocably bananas. When he called, she wanted to record every clue as to his whereabouts and condition, so that she could have him picked up.

The call came:

"Ophelia?"

"Oh, Eliot, Eliot—where are you, darling?"

"In America—among the rickety sons and grandsons of the pioneers."

"But where? But where?"

"Absolutely anywhere—in an aluminum and glass phone booth in a drab little American anywhere, with American nickels, dimes and quarters scattered on the little gray shelf before me. There is a message written with a ballpoint pen on the little gray shelf."

"And what does it say?"

"'*Sheila Taylor is a cock-teaser.*' I'm sure it's true."

There was an arrogant *blat* from Eliot's end. "Hark!" said Eliot. "A Greyhound bus has blatted its Roman trumpets flatulently outside the bus depot, which is also a candy store. Lo! One old American responds, comes tottering out. There is no one to bid him farewell, nor does he look up and down the street for someone to wish him well. He carries a brown paper parcel tied with twine. He is going somewhere, no doubt to die.

"He is taking leave of the only town he's ever known, the only life he's ever known. But he isn't thinking about saying goodbye to his universe. His whole being is intent on not offending the mighty bus driver, who looks down fumingly from his blue leather throne. Wupps! Too bad! The old American crawled aboard in fair shape, but now he can't find his ticket. He finds it at last, too late, too late. The driver is filled with rage. He slams the door, starts off with a savage clashing of gears, blows his horn at an old American woman crossing the street, rattles the window-panes. Hate, hate, hate."

"Eliot—is there a river there?"

"My telephone booth is in the broad valley of an open sewer called the Ohio. The Ohio is thirty miles to the south. Carp as big as atomic submarines fatten on the sludge of the sons and grandsons of the pioneers. Beyond the river lie the once green hills of Kentucky, the promised land of Dan'l Boone, now gulched and gashed by strip mines, some of which are owned by a charitable and cultural foundation endowed by an interesting old American family named Rosewater.

"On that side of the river, the Rosewater Foundation's holdings are somewhat diffuse. On this side, though, right around my phone booth, for a distance of about fifteen miles in any direction you care to go, the Foundation owns almost everything. The Foundation, however, has left the booming night-crawler business wide open. Signs on every home proclaim, 'Night-crawlers for Sale.'

"The key industry here, hogs and night-crawlers aside, is the making of saws. The saw factory is owned by the Foundation, of course. Because saws are so important here, the athletes of Noah Rosewater Memorial High School are known as 'The Fighting Sawmakers.' Actually, there aren't many sawmakers left. The saw factory is almost fully automatic now. If you can work a pinball machine, you can run the factory, make twelve thousand saws a day.

"A young man, a Fighting Sawmaker about eighteen years old, is strolling insouciantly past my phone booth now, wearing the sacred blue and white. He looks dangerous, but he wouldn't harm a soul. His two best subjects in school were Citizenship and Problems in Modern American Democracy, both taught by his basketball coach. He understands that anything violent he might do would not only weaken the Republic, but would ruin his own life, too. There is no work for him in Rosewater. There is damn little work for him anywhere. He often carries birth-control devices in his pocket, which many people find alarming and disgusting. The same people find it alarming and disgusting that the boy's father did *not* use birth-control devices. One more kid rotten-spoiled by postwar abundance, one more princeling with gooseberry eyes. He's meeting his girl now, a girl not much older than fourteen—a five-and-ten-cent-store Cleopatra, a four-letter word.

"Across the street is the firehouse—four trucks, three drunks, sixteen dogs, and one cheerful, sober young man with a can of metal polish."

"Oh, Eliot, Eliot—come home, come home."

"Don't you understand, Sylvia? I *am* home. I know now that this has always been home—the Town of Rosewater, the Township of Rosewater, the County of Rosewater, the State of Indiana."

• • •

"And what do you intend to *do* there, Eliot?"

"I'm going to *care* about these people."

"That's—that's very nice," said Sylvia bleakly. This was a pale and delicate girl, cultivated, wispy. She played the harpsichord, spoke six languages enchantingly. As a child and young woman, she had met many of the greatest men of her time in her parents' home—Picasso, Schweitzer, Hemingway, Toscanini, Churchill, de Gaulle. She had never seen Rosewater County, had no idea what a night-crawler was, did not know that land anywhere could be so deathly flat, that people anywhere could be so deathly dull.

"I look at these people, these Americans," Eliot went on, "and I realize that they can't even care about themselves any more—because they have no *use*. The factory, the farms, the mines across the river—they're almost completely automatic now. And America doesn't even need these people for war—not any more. Sylvia—I'm going to be an artist."

"An artist?"

"I'm going to love these discarded Americans, even though they're useless and unattractive. *That* is going to be my work of art."

4

ROSEWATER COUNTY, the canvas Eliot proposed to paint with love and understanding, was a rectangle on which other men—other Rosewaters, mainly—had already made some bold designs. Eliot's predecessors had anticipated Mondrian. Half the roads ran east and west and half the roads ran north and south. Bisecting the county exactly, and stopping at its borders, was a stagnant canal fourteen miles long. It was the one dash of reality added by Eliot's great grandfather to a stock and bond fantasy of a canal that would join Chicago, Indianapolis, Rosewater and the Ohio. There were now bullheads, crappies, redeyes, bluegills, and carp in the canal. It was to people interested in catching such fish that night-crawlers were sold.

The ancestors of many of the night-crawler merchants had been stockholders and bondholders in the Rosewater Inter-State Ship Canal. When the scheme failed utterly, some of them lost their farms, which were bought by Noah Rosewater. A Utopian community in the southwest corner of the county, New Ambrosia, invested everything it had in the canal, and lost. They were Germans, communists and atheists who practiced group marriage, absolute truthfuless, absolute cleanliness, and absolute love. They were now scattered to the winds, like the worthless papers that represented their equity in the canal. No one was sorry to see them go. Their one contribution to the county that was still viable in Eliot's time was their brewery, which had become the home of Rosewater Golden Lager Ambrosia Beer. On the label of each can of beer was a picture of the heaven on earth the New Ambrosians had meant to build. The dream city had spires. The spires had lightning-rods. The sky was filled with cherubim.

• • •

The town of Rosewater was in the dead center of the county. In the dead center of town was a Parthenon built of honest red brick, columns and all. Its roof was green copper. The canal ran through it, and so, in the bustling past, had the New York

Central, Monon, and Nickel Plate Railroads. When Eliot and Sylvia took up residence, only the canal and the Monon tracks remained, and the Monon was bankrupt, and its tracks were brown.

To the west of the Parthenon was the old Rosewater Saw Company, red brick, too, green-roofed, too. The spine of its roof was broken, its windows unglazed. It was a New Ambrosia for barn swallows and bats. Its four tower clocks were handless. Its big brass whistle was choked with nests.

To the east of the Parthenon was the County Courthouse, red brick, too, green-roofed, too. Its tower was identical with that of the old saw company. Three of its four clocks still had their hands, but they did not run. Like an abscess at the base of a dead tooth, a private business had somehow managed to establish itself in the cellar of the public building. It had a little red neon sign. "Bella's Beauty Nook," it said. Bella weighed three hundred fourteen pounds.

To the east of the courthouse was the Samuel Rosewater Veterans' Memorial Park. It had a flagpole and an honor roll. The honor roll was a four-by-eight sheet of exterior plywood painted black. It was hung on pipe, sheltered by a gable that was only two inches wide. It had all the names of Rosewater County people who had laid down their lives for their country.

• • •

The only other masonry structures were the Rosewater Mansion and its carriage house, set on an artificial elevation at the east end of the park and surrounded by a rank of iron spikes, and the Noah Rosewater Memorial High School, home of the Fighting Sawmakers, which bounded the park on the south. To the north of the park was the old Rosewater Opera House, a terrifyingly combustible frame wedding cake which had been converted to a firehouse. All else was shithouses, shacks, alcoholism, ignorance, idiocy and perversion, for all that was healthy and busy and intelligent in Rosewater County shunned the county seat.

The new Rosewater Saw Company, all yellow brick and no windows, was set in a cornfield midway between Rosewater and New Ambrosia. It was served by a gleaming new spur of the New York Central, and by a sizzling double-barreled high-way that missed the county seat by eleven miles. Near it were the Rosewater Motel and the Rosewater Bowl-A-Rama, and the great grain elevators and animal pens that were shipping points for fruits of the Rosewater Farms. And the few highly paid agronomists, engineers, brewers, accountants and administrators who did all that needed doing lived in a defensive circle of expensive ranch homes in another cornfield near New Ambrosia, a community named, for no reason whatsoever, "Avondale." All had gas-lit patios framed and terraced with railroad ties from the old Nickel Plate right-of-way.

• • •

Eliot stood in relation to the clean people of Avondale as a constitutional monarch. They were employees of the Rosewater Corporation, and the properties they managed were owned by the Rosewater Foundation. Eliot could not tell them what to do—but he was surely the King, and Avondale knew it.

So, when King Eliot and Queen Sylvia took up residence in the Rosewater Mansion, they were showered by figs from Avondale—invitations, visits, flattering notes and calls. All were deflected. Eliot required Sylvia to receive all prosperous visitors with an air of shallow, absent-minded cordiality. Every Avondale woman left the mansion stiffly, as though, as Eliot observed gleefully, she had a pickle up her ass.

• • •

Interestingly, the social-climbing technocrats of Avondale were able to bear the theory that the Rosewaters snubbed them because the Rosewaters felt superior to them. They even enjoyed the theory as they discussed it again and again. They were avid for lessons in authentic, upper-class snobbery, and Eliot and Sylvia seemed to be giving those.

But then the King and Queen got the Rosewater family crystal, silver and gold out of the dank vaults of the Rosewater County National Bank, began to throw lavish banquets for morons, perverts, starvelings and the unemployed.

They listened tirelessly to the misshapen fears and dreams of people who, by almost anyone's standards, would have been better off dead, gave them love and trifling sums of money.

The only social life they had that was untainted by pity had to do with the Rosewater Volunteer Fire Department. Eliot arose quickly to the rank of Fire Lieutenant, and Sylvia was elected President of the Ladies' Auxiliary. Though Sylvia had never before touched a bowling ball, she was made captain of the auxiliary's bowling team, too.

Avondale's clammy respect for the monarchy turned to incredulous contempt, and then to savagery. Yahooism, drinking, cuckolding, and self-esteem all took sharp upturns. The voices of Avondale acquired the tone of bandsaws cutting galvanized tin when discussing the King and Queen, as though a tyranny had been overthrown. Avondale was no longer a settlement of rising young executives. It was peopled by vigorous members of the true ruling class.

Five years later, Sylvia suffered a nervous collapse, burned the firehouse down. So sadistic had republican Avondale become about the royalist Rosewaters that Avondale laughed.

• • •

Sylvia was placed in a private mental hospital in Indianapolis, was taken there by Eliot and Charley Warmergran, the Fire Chief. They took her in the Chief's car, which was a red Henry J with a siren on top. They turned her over to a Dr. Ed Brown, a young psychiatrist who later made his reputation describing her illness. In the paper, he called Eliot and Sylvia "*Mr. and Mrs. Z*," and he called the town of Rosewater "*Hometown, U.S.A.*" He coined a new word for Sylvia's disease, "*Samaritrophia*," which he said meant, "*hysterical indifference to the troubles of those less fortunate than oneself.*"

• • •

Norman Mushari now read Dr. Brown's treatise, which was also in the confidential files of McAllister, Robjent, Reed and McGee. His eyes were moist and soft and brown, compelling him to see the pages as he saw the world, as though through a quart of olive oil.

Samaritrophia, *he read*, is the suppression of an overactive conscience by the rest of the mind. "You must all take instructions from me!" the conscience shrieks, in effect, to all the other mental processes.

The other processes try it for a while, note that the conscience is unappeased, that it continues to shriek, and they note, too, that the outside world has not been even microscopically improved by the unselfish acts the conscience had demanded.

They rebel at last. They pitch the tyrannous conscience down an oubliette, weld shut the manhole cover of that dark dungeon. They can hear the conscience no more. In the sweet silence, the mental processes look about for a new leader, and the leader most prompt to appear whenever the conscience is stilled, Enlightened Self-interest, *does* appear. Enlightened Self-interest gives them a flag, which they adore on sight. It is essentially the black and white Jolly Roger, with these words written beneath the skull and crossbones, "The hell with you, Jack, I've got mine!"

It seemed unwise to me, *Dr. Brown wrote and Norman Mushari read slaveringly*, to set the noisy conscience of Mrs. Z at liberty again. Neither could I take much satisfaction in discharging her while she was as heartless as Ilse Koch. I made it the goal of my treatments, then, to keep her conscience imprisoned, but to lift the lid of the oubliette ever so slightly, so that the howls of the prisoner might be very faintly heard. Through trial and error with chemotherapy and electric shock, this I achieved. I was not proud, for I had calmed a deep woman by making her shallow. I had blocked the underground rivers that connected her to the Atlantic, Pacific, and Indian Oceans, and made her content with being a splash pool three feet across, four inches deep, chlorinated, and painted blue.

Some doctor!

Some cure!

•   •   •

And some models the doctor was obliged to choose in determining how much guilt and pity Mrs. Z might safely be allowed to feel! The models were persons with reputations for being normal. The therapist, after a deeply upsetting investigation of normality at this time and place, was bound to conclude that a normal person, functioning well on the upper levels of a prosperous, industrialized society, can hardly hear his conscience at all.

So a logical person might conclude that I have been guilty of balderdash in announcing a new disease, samaritrophia, when it is virtually as common among healthy Americans as noses, say. I defend myself in this manner: samaritrophia is only a disease, and a violent one, too, when it attacks those exceedingly rare individuals who reach biological maturity still loving and wanting to help their fellow men.

I have treated only one case. I have never heard of anyone's treating another. In looking about myself, I can see only one other person who has the potential for a samaritrophic collapse. That person, of course, is Mr. Z. And so deep is his commitment to compassion, that, were he to come down with samaritrophia, I sense that he would kill himself, or perhaps kill a hundred others and then be shot down like a mad dog, before we could treat him.

• • •

Treat, treat, treat.

Some treat!

Mrs. Z, having been treated and cured in our health emporium, expressed a wish to, ". . . go out and have some fun for a change, to live it up . . ." before her looks were gone. Her looks were still staggeringly attractive, were marked by lines of affection unlimited, which she no longer deserved.

She wanted nothing more to do with Hometown or Mr. Z, announced that she was off to the gaiety of Paris, and to merry old friends there. She wished to buy new clothes, she said, and to dance and dance and dance until she fainted in the arms of a tall, dark stranger, into the arms, hopefully, of a double spy.

She often referred to her husband as, "My dirty, drunk uncle down South," although never to his face. She was not a schizophrenic, but, whenever her husband visited her, which he did three times a week, she manifested all of the sick cutenesses of paranoia. Shades of Clara Bow! She would pluck his cheek, coax kisses from him, kisses she gigglingly declined to receive. She told him she wanted to go to Paris for just a little while, to see her dear family, and that she would be back before he knew it. She wanted him to say farewell and give her love to all her dear, underprivileged friends in Hometown.

Mr. Z was not deceived. He saw her off to Paris at the Indianapolis Airport, and he told me when the plane was a speck in the sky that he would never see her again. "She certainly looked happy," he said to me. "She certainly will have a good time when she gets back there with the kind of company she deserves."

He had used the word "certainly" twice. It grated. And I knew intuitively that he was about to grate me with it again. He did. "A lot of credit," he said, "certainly goes to you."

• • •

I am informed by the woman's parents, who are understandably ungrateful to Mr. Z, that he writes and calls often. She does not open his letters. She will not come to the phone. And it is their satisfied opinion that, as Mr. Z had hoped, she is certainly happy.

Prognosis: Another breakdown by-and-by.

• • •

As for Mr. Z: He is certainly sick too, since he certainly isn't like any other man I ever knew. He will not leave Hometown, except for very short trips as far as Indianapolis and no farther. I suspect that he cannot leave Hometown. Why not?

To be utterly unscientific, and science becomes nauseating to a therapist after a case such as this: His Destination is there.

The good doctor's prognosis was correct. Sylvia became a popular and influential member of the international Jet Set, learned the many variations of the Twist. She became known as the Duchess of Rosewater. Many men proposed, but she was too happy to think of either marriage or divorce. And then she fell to pieces again in July of 1964.

She was treated in Switzerland. She was discharged six months later, silent and sad, almost unbearably deep again. Eliot and the pitiful people of Rosewater County again had a place in her consciousness. She wished to return to them, not out of yearning but out of a sense of duty. Her doctor warned her that a return might be fatal. He told her to remain in Europe, to divorce Eliot, and to build a quiet, meaningful life of her own.

So, very civilized divorce proceedings were begun, stage-managed by McAllister, Robjent, Reed and McGee.

• • •

Now it was time for Sylvia to fly to America for the divorce. And a meeting was held on a June evening in the Washington, D.C., apartment of Eliot's father, Senator Lister Ames Rosewater. Eliot was not there. He would not leave Rosewater County. Present were the Senator, Sylvia, Thurmond McAllister, the ancient lawyer, and his watchful young aide, Mushari.

• • •

The tone of the meeting was frank, sentimental, forgiving, sometimes hilarious, and fundamentally tragic always. There was brandy.

"In his heart," said the Senator, swirling his snifter, "Eliot doesn't love those awful people out there any more than I do.

He couldn't possibly love them, if he weren't drunk all the time. I've said it before, and I'll say it again: This is basically a booze problem. If Eliot's booze were shut off, his compassion for the maggots in the slime on the bottom of the human garbage pail would vanish."

He clapped his hands, shook his old head. "If only there had been a child!" He was a product of St. Paul's and Harvard, but it pleased him to speak with the split-banjo twang of a Rosewater County hog farmer. He tore off his steel-rimmed spectacles, stared at his daughter-in-law with suffering blue eyes. "If only! If only!" He put his spectacles back on, spread his hands in resignation. The hands were as speckled as box-turtles. "The end of the Rosewater family is now plainly in view."

"There *are* other Rosewaters," McAllister suggested gently.

Mushari squirmed, for he meant to represent those others soon.

"I'm talking about *real* Rosewaters!" cried the Senator bitterly. "The *hell* with Pisquontuit!" Pisquontuit, Rhode Island, a seaside resort, was where the only other branch of the family lived.

"A buzzard feast, a buzzard feast," the Senator moaned, writhing in a masochistic fantasy of how the Rhode Island Rosewaters would pick the Indiana Rosewaters' bones. He coughed hackingly. The cough embarrassed him. He was a chain-smoker, like his son.

He went to the mantelpiece, glared at a colored photograph of Eliot there. The picture had been taken at the end of the Second World War. It showed a much-decorated captain of the Infantry. "So clean, so tall, so purposeful—so clean, so clean!" He gnashed his crockery teeth. "What a noble mind is here o'erthrown!"

He scratched himself, though he did not itch. "How puffy and pasty he looks these days. I've seen healthier complexions on rhubarb pies! Sleeps in his underwear, eats a balanced diet of potato chips, Southern Comfort, and Rosewater Golden Lager Ambrosia Beer." He rattled his fingernails against the photograph. "Him! Him! Captain Eliot Rosewater—Silver Star, Bronze Star, Soldier's Medal, and Purple Heart with Cluster! Sailing champion! Ski champion! Him! Him! My God—the number of times life has said, 'Yes, yes, yes,' to him! Millions of dollars, hundreds of significant friends, the most beautiful, intelligent, talented, affectionate wife imaginable! A splendid education, an elegant mind in a big, clean body—and what is his reply when life says nothing but, 'Yes, yes, yes'?

" 'No, no, no.'

"Why? Will someone tell me why?"

No one did.

• • •

"I had a female cousin one time—a Rockefeller, as it happened—" said the Senator, "and she confessed to me that she spent the fifteenth, sixteenth, and seventeenth years of her life saying nothing but, 'No, thank you.' Which is all very well for a girl of that age and station. But it would have been a damned unattractive trait in a *male* Rockefeller, and an even more unsuitable one, if I may say so, in a male Rosewater."

He shrugged. "Be that as it may, we *do* now have a male Rosewater who says 'No' to all the good things life would like to give him. He won't even live in the mansion any more." Eliot had moved out of the mansion and into an office when it became clear that Sylvia was never coming back to him.

"He could have been Governor of Indiana by lifting an eyebrow, could have been President of the United States, even, at the price of a few beads of sweat. And what is he? I ask you, what *is* he?"

The Senator coughed again, then answered his own question: "A notary public, friends and neighbors, whose commission is about to expire."

• • •

This was fairly true. The only official document that hung on the mildewed beaverboard wall of Eliot's busy office was his commission as a notary public. So many of the people who brought their troubles to him needed, among such a multitude of other things, someone to witness their signatures.

Eliot's office was on Main Street, a block northeast of the brick Parthenon, across the street from the new firehouse, which the Rosewater Foundation had built. It was a shotgun attic that spanned a lunchroom and a liquor store. There were only two windows, in doghouse dormers. Outside of one was a sign that said, *EATS*. Outside the other was a sign that said, *BEER*. Both signs were electrified and equipped with blinkers. And, as Eliot's father ranted in Washington about him, him, him, Eliot slept like a baby, and the signs blinked off and on.

Eliot made of his mouth a Cupid's bow, murmured something sweetly, turned over, snored. He was an athlete gone to lard, a big man, six-feet-three, two hundred thirty pounds, pale, balding on all sides of a wispy scalplock. He was swaddled in the elephant wrinkles of war-surplus long underwear. Written in gold letters on each of his windows, and on his street-level door, too, were these words:

> ROSEWATER FOUNDATION
> HOW CAN WE HELP
> YOU?

5

ELIOT SLEPT SWEETLY ON, although he had troubles in droves.

It was the toilet in the foul little office lavatory that seemed to be having all the bad dreams. It sighed, it sobbed, it gurgled that it was drowning. Canned goods and tax forms and *National Geographic*s were piled on the toilet tank. A bowl and a spoon were soaking in cold water in the washbasin. The medicine cabinet over the basin was wide open. It was crammed with vitamins and headache remedies and hemorrhoid salves and laxatives and sedatives. Eliot used them all regularly, but they weren't for him alone. They were for all the vaguely ill people who came to see him.

Love and understanding and a little money were not enough for those people. They wanted medicine besides.

Papers were stacked everywhere—tax forms, Veteran's Administration forms, pension forms, relief forms, Social Security forms, parole forms. Stacks had toppled here and there, forming dunes. And between the stacks and dunes lay paper cups and empty cans of Ambrosia and cigarette butts and empty bottles of Southern Comfort.

Thumbtacked to the walls were pictures Eliot had clipped from *Life* and *Look*, pictures that now rustled in a light cool breeze running before a thunderstorm. Eliot found that certain pictures cheered people up, particularly pictures of baby animals. His visitors also enjoyed pictures of spectacular accidents. Astronauts bored them. They liked pictures of Elizabeth Taylor because they hated her so much, felt very superior to her. Their favorite person was Abraham Lincoln. Eliot tried to popularize Thomas Jefferson and Socrates, too, but people couldn't remember from one visit to the next who they were. "Which one is which?" they'd say.

The office had once belonged to a dentist. There was no clue of this previous occupancy save for the staircase leading up from the street. The dentist had nailed tin signs to the risers, each sign praising some aspect of his services. The signs were still there, but Eliot had painted out the messages. He had written a new one, a poem by William Blake. This was it, as broken up so as to fit twelve risers:

> The Angel
> that presided
> o'er my
> birth said,
> "Little creature,
> form'd of
> Joy & Mirth,
> Go love
> without the
> help of
> any Thing
> on Earth."

At the foot of the stairs, written in pencil on the wall, by the Senator himself, was the Senator's rebuttal, another poem by Blake:

> Love seeketh only Self to please,
> To bind another to Its delight,
> Joys in another's loss of ease,
> And builds a Hell in Heaven's despite.

• • •

Back in Washington, Eliot's father was wishing out loud that he and Eliot were both dead.

"I—I have a rather primitive idea," said McAllister.

"The last primitive idea you had cost me control of eighty-seven million dollars."

McAllister indicated with a tired smile that he wasn't about to apologize for the design of the Foundation. It had, after all, done exactly what it was meant to do, had handed the fortune from father to son, without the tax collector's getting a dime. McAllister could scarcely have guaranteed that the son would be conventional. "I should like to propose that Eliot and Sylvia make one last try for a reconciliation."

Sylvia shook her head. "No," she whispered. "I'm sorry. No." She was curled in a great wingchair. She had taken off her shoes. Her face was a flawless blue-white oval, her hair raven black. There were circles under her eyes. "No."

This was, of course, a medical decision, and a wise one, too. Her second breakdown and recovery had not turned her back into the old Sylvia of the early Rosewater County days. It had given her a distinctly new personality, the third since her marriage to Eliot. The core of this third personality was a feeling of worthlessness, of shame at being revolted by the poor and by Eliot's personal hygiene, and a suicidal wish to ignore her revulsions, to get back to Rosewater, to very soon die in a good cause.

So it was with self-conscious, medically-prescribed, superficial opposition to total sacrifice that she said again, "No."

• • •

The Senator swept Eliot's picture from the mantelpiece. "Who can blame her? One more roll in the hay with that drunk gypsy I call son?" He apologized for the coarseness of this last image. "Old men without hope have a tendency to be both crude and accurate. I beg your pardon."

Sylvia put her lovely head down, raised it again. "I don't think of him as that—as a drunk gypsy."

"I do, by God. Every time I'm forced to look at him I think to myself, 'What a staging area for a typhoid epidemic!' Don't try to spare my feelings, Sylvia. My son doesn't deserve a decent woman. He deserves what he's got, the sniveling camaraderie of whores, malingerers, pimps, and thieves."

"They're not that bad, Father Rosewater."

"As I understand it, that's their chief appeal to Eliot, that there's absolutely nothing good about them."

Sylvia, with two nervous breakdowns behind her, and with no well-formed dreams before her, said quietly, just as her doctor would have wanted her to, "I don't want to argue."

"You still *could* argue on Eliot's behalf?"

"Yes. If I don't make anything else clear tonight, at least let me make that clear: Eliot is right to do what he's doing. It's beautiful what he's doing. I'm simply not strong enough or good enough to be by his side any more. The fault is mine."

Pained mystification, and then helplessness, suffused the

Senator's face. "Tell me one good thing about those people Eliot helps."

"I can't."

"I thought not."

"It's a secret thing," she said, forced to argue, pleading for the argument to stop right there.

Without any notion of how merciless he was being, the Senator pressed on. "You're among friends now—suppose you tell us what this great secret is."

"The secret is that they're human," said Sylvia. She looked from face to face for some flicker of understanding. There was none. The last face into which she peered was Norman Mushari's. Mushari gave her a hideously inappropriate smile of greed and fornication.

Sylvia excused herself abruptly, went into the bathroom and wept.

• • •

Thunder was heard in Rosewater now, caused a brindle dog to come scrambling out of the firehouse with psychosomatic rabies. The dog stopped in the middle of the street, shivering. The street lights were faint and far apart. The only other illumination came from a blue bulb in front of the police station in the courthouse basement, a red bulb in front of the firehouse, and a white bulb in the telephone booth across the street from the Saw City Kandy Kitchen, which was the bus depot, too.

There was a *crash*. Lightning turned everything to blue-white diamonds.

The dog ran to the door of the Rosewater Foundation, scratched and howled. Upstairs, Eliot slept on. His sickly translucent drip-dry shirt, which hung from a ceiling fixture, swayed like a ghost.

• • •

Eliot had only one shirt. He had only one suit—a frowzy, blue, double-breasted chalkstripe now hanging on the knob of the lavatory door. It was a wonderfully made suit, for it still held together, though it was very old. Eliot had gotten it in trade from a volunteer fireman in New Egypt, New Jersey, way back in 1952.

Eliot had only one pair of shoes, black ones. They had a crackle finish as a result of an experiment. Eliot once tried to polish them with Johnson's *Glo-Coat*, which was a floorwax, not intended for shoes. One shoe was on his desk. The other was in the lavatory, on the rim of the washbasin. A maroon nylon sock, with garter attached, was in each shoe. One end of the garter of the sock in the shoe on the washbasin was in the water. It had saturated itself and its sock, too, through the magic of capillary action.

The only colorful, new articles in the office, other than the magazine pictures, were a family-size box of *Tide*, the washday miracle, and the yellow slicker and red helmet of a volunteer fireman, which hung on pegs by the office door. Eliot was a Fire Lieutenant. He could easily have been Captain or Chief, since he was a devoted and skilful fireman, and had given the Fire Department six new engines besides. It was at his own insistence that he held a rank no higher than Lieutenant.

Eliot, because he almost never left his office except to fight fires, was the man to whom all fire calls were sent. That was why he had two telephones by his cot. The black one was for Foundation calls. The red one was for fire calls. When a fire call came in, Eliot would push a red button mounted on the wall under his commission as a Notary Public. The button activated a doomsday bullhorn under the cupola on top of the firehouse. Eliot had paid for the horn, and the cupola, too.

There was an earsplitting thunderclap.

"Now, now—now, now," said Eliot in his sleep.

His black telephone was about to ring. Eliot would awake and answer it by the third ring. He would say what he said to every caller, no matter what the hour:

"This is the Rosewater Foundation. How can we help you?"

• • •

It was the Senator's conceit that Eliot trafficked with criminals. He was mistaken. Most of Eliot's clients weren't brave enough or clever enough for lives of crime. But Eliot, particularly when he argued with his father or his bankers or his lawyers, was almost equally mistaken about who his clients were.

He would argue that the people he was trying to help were the same sorts of people who, in generations past, had cleared the forests, drained the swamps, built the bridges, people whose sons formed the backbone of the infantry in time of war—and so on. The people who leaned on Eliot regularly were a lot weaker than that—and dumber, too. When it came time for their sons to go into the Armed Forces, for instance, the sons were generally rejected as being mentally, morally, and physically undesirable.

There was a tough element among the Rosewater County poor who, as a matter of pride, stayed away from Eliot and his uncritical love, who had the guts to get out of Rosewater County and look for work in Indianapolis or Chicago or Detroit. Very few of them found steady work in those places, of course, but at least they tried.

• • •

The client who was about to make Eliot's black telephone ring was a sixty-eight-year-old virgin who, by almost anybody's standards, was too dumb to live. Her name was Diana Moon Glampers. No one had ever loved her. There was no reason why anyone should. She was ugly, stupid, and boring. On the rare occasions when she had to introduce herself, she always said her full name, and followed that with the mystifying equation that had thrust her into life so pointlessly:

"My mother was a Moon. My father was a Glampers."

• • •

This cross between a Glampers and a Moon was a domestic servant in the tapestry-brick Rosewater Mansion, the legal residence of the Senator, a house he actually occupied no more than ten days out of any year. During the remaining 355 days of each year, Diana had the twenty-six rooms all to herself. She cleaned and cleaned and cleaned alone, without even the luxury of having someone to blame for making dirt.

When Diana was through for the day, she would retire to a room over the Rosewater's six-car garage. The only vehicles in the garage were a 1936 Ford *Phaeton*, which was up on blocks, and a red tricycle with a fire bell hanging from the handlebars. The tricycle had belonged to Eliot as a child.

After work, Diana would sit in her room and listen to her cracked green plastic radio, or she would fumble with her Bible. She could not read. Her Bible was a frazzled wreck. On the table beside her bed was a white telephone, a so-called Princess telephone, which she rented from the Indiana Bell Telephone Company for seventy-five cents a month, over and above ordinary service charges.

There was a thunderclap.

Diana yelled for help. She should have yelled. Lightning had killed her mother and father at a Rosewater Lumber Company picnic in 1916. She was sure lightning was going to kill her, too. And, because her kidneys hurt all the time, she was sure the lightning would hit her in the kidneys.

She snatched her Princess phone from its cradle. She dialed the only number she ever dialed. She whimpered and moaned, waiting for the person at the other end to answer.

It was Eliot. His voice was sweet, vastly paternal—as humane as the lowest note of a cello. "This is the Rosewater Foundation," he said. "How can we help you?"

• • •

"The electricity is after me again, Mr. Rosewater. I *had* to call! I'm so *scared*!"

"Call any time you want, dear. That's what I'm here for."

"The electricity is *really* gonna get me this time."

"Oh, darn that electricity." Eliot's anger was sincere. "That electricity makes me so mad, the way it torments you all the time. It isn't fair."

"I wish it would come ahead and kill me, instead of just talk about it all the time."

"This would be a mighty sad town, dear, if that ever happened."

"Who'd care?"

"*I'd* care."

"You care about everybody. I mean who else?"

"Many, many, many people, dear."

"Dumb old woman—sixty-eight years old."

"Sixty-eight is a wonderful age."

"Sixty-eight years is a long time for a body to live without having one nice thing ever happen to the body. Nothing nice ever happened to me. How could it? I was behind the door when the good Lord passed out the brains."

"That is not *true!*"

"I was behind the door when the good Lord passed out the strong, beautiful bodies. Even when I was young, I couldn't run fast, couldn't jump. I have never felt real good—not once. I have had gas and swole ankles and kiddley pains since I was a baby. And I was behind the door when the good Lord passed out the money and the good luck, too. And when I got nerve enough to come out from behind the door and whisper, 'Lord, Lord—dear, sweet Lord—here's little old me—' wasn't one nice thing left. He had to give me an old potato for a nose. He had to give me hair like steel wool, and had to give me a voice like a bullfrog."

"It isn't a bullfrog voice at all, Diana. It's a lovely voice."

"Bullfrog voice," she insisted. "There was this bullfrog up there in Heaven, Mr. Rosewater. The good Lord was going to send it down to this sad world to be born, but that old bullfrog was smart. 'Sweet Lord,' that smart old bullfrog said, 'if it's all the same to you, Sweet Lord, I'd just as soon not be born. It don't look like much fun for a *frog* down there.' So the Lord let that bullfrog hop around in Heaven up there, where nobody'd use it for bait or eat its legs, and the Lord gave *me* that bullfrog's voice."

•   •   •

There was another thunderclap. It raised Diana's voice an octave. "I should have said what that bullfrog said! This ain't such a hot world for Diana Moon Glamperses, neither!"

•   •   •

"Now, now, Diana—now, now," said Eliot. He took a small drink from a bottle of Southern Comfort.

"My kiddleys hurt me all day, Mr. Rosewater. They feel like a red-hot cannonball full of electricity was going through them real slow, and just turning round and round, with poisoned razorblades sticking out of it."

"That can't be very pleasant."

"It ain't."

"I *do* wish you'd go see a doctor about those darn kidneys, dear."

"I did. I went to Dr. Winters today, just like you told me. He treated me like I was a cow and he was a drunk veterinarian. And when he was through punching me and rolling me all around, why he just laughed. He said he wished everybody in Rosewater County had kiddleys as wonderful as mine. He said my kiddley trouble was all in my head. Oh, Mr. Rosewater, from now on you're the only doctor for me."

"I'm not a doctor, dear."

"I don't care. You've cured more hopeless diseases than all the doctors in Indiana put together."

"Now, now—"

"Dawn Leonard had boils for ten years, and you cured 'em. Ned Calvin had that twitch in his eye since he was a little boy, and you made it stop. Pearl Flemming came and saw you, and she threw her crutch away. And now my kiddleys have stopped hurting, just hearing your sweet voice."

"I'm glad."

"And the thunder and lightning's stopped."

It was true. There was only the hopelessly sentimental music of rainfall now.

• • •

"So you can sleep now, dear?"

"Thanks to you. Oh, Mr. Rosewater, there should be a big statue of you in the middle of this town—made out of diamonds and gold, and precious rubies beyond price, and pure uranimum. You, with your great name and your fine education and your money and the nice manners your mother taught you—you could have been off in some big city, riding around in Cadillacs with the highest muckety-mucks, while the bands played and the crowds cheered. You could have been so high and mighty in this world, that when you looked down on the plain, dumb, ordinary people of poor old Rosewater County, we would look like bugs."

"Now, now—"

"You gave up everything a man is supposed to want, just to help the little people, and the little people know it. God bless you, Mr. Rosewater. Good night."

6

"NATURE'S LITTLE DANGER SIGNALS—" Senator Rosewater said to Sylvia and McAllister and Mushari darkly. "How many did I miss? All of them, I guess."

"Don't blame yourself," said McAllister.

"If a man has but one child," said the Senator, "and the family is famous for producing unusual, strong-willed individuals, what standards can the man have for deciding whether or not his child is a nut?"

"Don't *blame* yourself!"

"I have spent my life demanding that people blame themselves for their misfortunes."

"You've made exceptions."

"Damn few."

"Include yourself among the damn few. That's where you belong."

"I often think that Eliot would not have turned out as he has, if there hadn't been all that whoop-dee-doo about his being mascot of the Fire Department when he was a child. God, how they spoiled him—let him ride on the seat of the Number One Pumper, let him ring the bell—taught him how to make the truck backfire by turning the ignition off and on, laughed like crazy when he blew the muffler off. They all smelled of booze, of course, too—" He nodded and blinked. "Booze and fire engines—a happy childhood regained. I don't know, I don't know, I just don't know. Whenever we went out there, I told him it was home—but I never thought he would be dumb enough to believe it."

• • •

"I blame myself," said the Senator.

"Good for you," said McAllister. "And, while you're at it, be sure to hold yourself responsible for everything that happened to Eliot during World War Two. It's your fault, without a doubt, that all those firemen were in that smoke-filled building."

McAllister was speaking of the proximate cause of Eliot's nervous breakdown near the end of the war. The smoke-filled building was a clarinet factory in Bavaria. It was supposedly infested by a hedgehog of S.S. troops.

Eliot led a platoon from his company in an assault on the building. His customary weapon was a Thompson submachinegun. But he went in with a rifle and fixed bayonet this time, because of the danger of shooting one of his own men in the smoke. He had never stuck a bayonet into anybody before, not in years of carnage.

He pitched a grenade into a window. When it went off, Captain Rosewater went through the window himself, found himself standing in a sea of very still smoke whose undulating surface was level with his eyes. He tilted his head back to keep his nose in air. He could hear Germans, but he couldn't see them.

He took a step forward, stumbled over one body, fell on another. They were Germans who had been killed by his grenade. He stood up, found himself face-to-face with a helmeted German in a gas mask.

Eliot, like the good soldier he was, jammed his knee into the man's groin, drove his bayonet into his throat, withdrew the bayonet, smashed the man's jaw with his rifle butt.

And then Eliot heard an American sergeant yelling somewhere off to his left. The visibility was apparently a lot better over there, for the sergeant was yelling, "Cease fire! Hold your fire, you guys. Jesus Christ—these aren't soldiers. They're firemen!"

It was true: Eliot had killed three unarmed firemen. They were ordinary villagers, engaged in the brave and uncontroversial business of trying to keep a building from combining with oxygen.

When the medics got the masks off the three Eliot had killed, they proved to be two old men and a boy. The boy was the one Eliot had bayoneted. He didn't look more than fourteen.

Eliot seemed reasonably well for about ten minutes after that. And then he calmly lay down in front of a moving truck.

The truck stopped in time, but the wheels were touching Captain Rosewater. When some of his horrified men picked him up, they found out Eliot was stiff, so rigid that they might have carried him by his hair and his heels.

He stayed like that for twelve hours, and would not speak or eat—so they shipped him back to Gay Paree.

• • •

"What did he seem like there in Paris?" the Senator wanted to know. "Did he seem sane enough to you then?"

"That's how I happened to meet him."

"I don't understand."

"Father's string quartet played for some of the mental patients in one of the American hospitals—and Father got talking to Eliot, and Father thought Eliot was the sanest American he had ever met. When Eliot was well enough to leave, Father had him to dinner. I remember Father's introduction: 'I want you all to meet the only American who has so far noticed the Second World War.'"

"What did he say that was so *sane*?"

"It was the impression he made, really—more than—than the particular things he said. I remember how my father described him. He said, 'This young Captain I'm bringing home —he despises art. Can you imagine? *Despises* it—and yet he does it in such a way that I can't help loving him for it. What he's saying, I think, is that art has failed him, which, I must admit, is a very fair thing for a man who has bayoneted a fourteen-year-old boy in the line of duty to say.'"

• • •

"I loved Eliot on sight."

"Isn't there some other word you could use?"

"Than what?"

"Than *love*."

"What better word *is* there?"

"It was a perfectly good word—until Eliot got hold of it. It's spoiled for me now. Eliot did to the word *love* what the Russians did to the word *democracy*. If Eliot is going to love everybody, no matter what they are, no matter what they do, then those of us who love particular people for particular reasons had better find ourselves a new word." He looked up at an oil painting of his deceased wife. "For instance—I loved *her* more than I loved our garbage collector, which makes me guilty of the most unspeakable of modern crimes: *Dis-crim-i-nay-tion.*"

•   •   •

Sylvia smiled wanly. "For want of a better word, could I go on using the old one—just for tonight?"

"On your lips it still has meaning."

"I loved him on sight in Paris—and I love him when I think of him now."

"You must have realized pretty early in the game that you had a nut on your hands."

"There was the drinking."

"There's the heart of the problem right there!"

"And there was that awful business with Arthur Garvey Ulm." Ulm was a poet Eliot had given ten thousand dollars to when the Foundation was still in New York.

"That poor Arthur told Eliot he wanted to be free to tell the truth, regardless of the economic consequences, and Eliot wrote him a tremendous check right then and there. It was at a cocktail party," said Sylvia. "I remember Arthur Godfrey was there—and Robert Frost—and Salvador Dali—and a lot of others, too.

"'You go tell the truth, by God. It's about time somebody did,' Eliot said to him. 'And if you need any more money to tell more truth, you just come back to me.'

"Poor Arthur wandered around the party in a daze, showing people the check, asking them if it could possibly be real. They all told him it was a perfectly wonderful check, and he came back to Eliot, made sure again that the check was not a joke. And then, almost hysterically, he begged Eliot to tell him what he should write about.

"'The truth!' said Eliot.

"'You're my patron—and I thought that as my patron you —you might—'

"'I'm not your patron. I'm a fellow-American who's paying you money to find out what the truth is. That's a very different sort of thing.'

"'Right, right,' said Arthur. 'That's the way it should be. That's the way I want it. I just thought there was maybe some special subject you—'

"'*You* pick the subject, and be good and fearless about it.'

"'Right.' And before he knew what he was doing, poor Arthur saluted, and I don't think he'd even been in the Army or Navy or anything. And he left Eliot, but he went around the party again, asking everybody what sorts of things Eliot was interested in. He finally came back to tell Eliot that he had once been a migratory fruit-picker, and that he wanted to write a cycle of poems about how miserable the fruit pickers were.

"Eliot drew himself up to his full height, looked down on Arthur, his eyes blazing, and he said, so that everybody could hear, 'Sir! Do you realize that the Rosewaters are the founders and the majority stockholders in the United Fruit Company?'"

"That wasn't true!" said the Senator.

"Of course it wasn't," said Sylvia.

"Did the Foundation have any United Fruit stock at all at that time?" the Senator asked McAllister.

"Oh—five thousand shares, maybe."

"Nothing."

"Nothing," McAllister agreed.

"Poor Arthur turned crimson, slunk away, came back again, asked Eliot very humbly who his favorite poet was. 'I don't know his name,' said Eliot, 'and I wish I did, because it's the only poem I ever thought enough of to commit to heart.'

"'Where did you see it?'

"'It was written on a wall, Mr. Ulm, of the men's room of a beer joint on the border between Rosewater and Brown Counties in Indiana, the Log Cabin Inn.'"

"Oh, this is weird, this is weird," said the Senator. "The Log Cabin Inn must have burned down—oh God—in 1934 or so. How weird that Eliot should remember it."

"Was he ever in it?" McAllister asked.

"Once—just once, now that I think back," said the Senator. "It was a dreadful robbers' roost, and we would never have stopped there if the car hadn't boiled over. Eliot must have been—ten?—twelve? And he probably *did* use the men's room, and he probably did see something written on the wall, something he never forgot." He nodded. "How weird, how weird."

"What was the poem?" said McAllister.

Sylvia apologized to the two old men for having to be coarse, and then she recited the two lines Eliot had recited loudly for Ulm:

> "We don't piss in your ashtrays,
>   So please don't throw cigarettes in our urinals."

● ● ●

"The poor poet fled in tears," said Sylvia. "For months after that I was in terror of opening small packages, lest one of them contain the ear of Arthur Garvey Ulm."

● ● ●

"Hates the arts," said McAllister. He clucked.

"He's a poet himself," said Sylvia.

"That's news to me," said the Senator. "I never saw any of it."

"He used to write me poems sometimes."

"He's probably happiest when writing on the walls of public lavatories. I often wondered who did it. Now I know. It's my poetic son."

"*Does* he write on lavatory walls?" McAllister asked.

"I heard that he did," said Sylvia. "It was innocent—it wasn't obscene. During the New York days, people told me Eliot was writing the same message in men's rooms all over town."

"Do you remember what it was?"

"Yes. '*If you would be unloved and forgotten, be reasonable.*' As far as I know, that was original with him."

● ● ●

At that moment Eliot was trying to read himself back to sleep with the manuscript of a novel by none other than Arthur Garvey Ulm.

The name of the book was *Get With Child a Mandrake Root*, a line from a poem by John Donne. The dedication read, "For Eliot Rosewater, my compassionate turquoise." And under that was another quotation from Donne:

> A compassionate turquoise which doth tell
> By looking pale, the wearer is not well.

A covering letter from Ulm explained that the book was going to be published by Palindrome Press in time for Christmas, and was going to be a joint selection, along with *The Cradle of Erotica*, of a major book club.

You have no doubt forgotten me, Compassionate Turquoise, *the letter said in part*. The Arthur Garvey Ulm you knew was a man well worth forgetting. What a coward he was, and what a fool he was to think he was a poet! And what a long, long time it took him to understand exactly how generous and kind your cruelty was! How much you managed to tell me about what was wrong with me, and what I should do about it, and how few words you used! Here then (fourteen years later) are eight hundred pages of prose by me. They could not have been created by me without you, and I do not mean your money. (Money is shit, which is one of the things I have tried to say in the book.) I mean your insistence that the truth be told about this sick, sick society of ours, and that the words for the telling could be found on the walls of restrooms.

Eliot couldn't remember who Arthur Garvey Ulm was, and so was even further from knowing what advice he might have given the man. The clues Ulm offered were so nebulous. Eliot was pleased that he had given someone useful advice, was thrilled even, when Ulm declared:

Let them shoot me, let them hang me, but I have told the truth. The gnashing of the teeth of the Pharisees, Madison Avenue phonies and Philistines will be music to my ears. With your divine assistance, I have let the Djin of truth about them out of the bottle, and they will never, never, never ever get it back in!

Eliot began to read avidly the truths Ulm expected to get killed for telling:

CHAPTER ONE

I twisted her arm until she opened her legs, and she gave a little scream, half joy, half pain (how do you figure a woman?), as I rammed the old avenger home.

Eliot found himself possessed of an erection. "Oh, for heaven's sakes," he said to his procreative organ, "how irrelevant can you be?"

•   •   •

"If only there had been a child," said the Senator again. And then the density of his regret was penetrated by this thought: That it was cruel of him to speak so to the woman who had failed to bear the magic child. "Excuse an old fool, Sylvia. I can understand why you might thank God there is no child."

Sylvia, returning from her cry in the bathroom, experimented with small gestures, all indicating that she would have loved such a baby, but that she might have pitied it, too. "I would never thank God for a thing like *that*."

"May I ask you a highly personal question?"

"It's what life does all the time."

"Do you think it is remotely possible that he will *ever* reproduce?"

"I haven't seen him for three years."

"I'm asking you to make an extrapolation."

"I can only tell you," she said, "that, toward the end of our marriage, love-making was something less than a mania with us both. He was once a sweet fanatic for love-making, but not for making children of his own."

The Senator clucked ruefully. "If only I had taken proper care of *my* child!" He winced. "I paid a call to the psychoanalyst Eliot used to go to in New York. Finally got around to it last year. I seem to get around to everything about Eliot twenty years too late. The thing is—the thing is—I—I've never been able to get it through my head that such a splendid animal could ever go so much to hell!"

Mushari concealed his hunger for clinical details of Eliot's ailment, waited tensely for someone to urge the Senator to continue. No one did, so Mushari exposed himself. "And what did the doctor say?"

The Senator, suspecting nothing, resumed his tale: "These people never want to talk about what *you* want to talk about. It's always something else. When he found out who I was, he didn't want to talk about Eliot. He wanted to talk about the Rosewater Law." The Rosewater Law was what the Senator thought of as his legislative masterpiece. It made the publication or possession of obscene materials a Federal offense, carrying penalties up to fifty thousand dollars and ten years in prison, without hope of parole. It was a masterpiece because it actually defined obscenity.

Obscenity, *it said*, is any picture or phonograph record or any written matter calling attention to reproductive organs, bodily discharges, or bodily hair.

"This psychoanalyst," the Senator complained, "wanted to know about *my* childhood. He wanted to go into my feelings about bodily hair." The Senator shuddered. "I asked him to kindly get off the subject, that my revulsions were shared, so far as I knew, by all decent men." He pointed to McAllister, simply wanting to point at someone, anyone. "There's your key to pornography. Other people say, 'Oh, how can you recognize it, how can you tell it from art and all that?' I've written the key into law! The difference between pornography and art is bodily hair!"

He flushed, apologized abjectly to Sylvia. "I beg your pardon, my dear."

Mushari had to prod him again. "And the doctor didn't say *anything* about Eliot?"

"The damn doctor said Eliot never told him a damn thing but well-known facts from history, almost all of them related to the oppression of odd-balls or the poor. He said any diagnosis he made of Eliot's disease would have to be irresponsible speculation. As a deeply worried father, I told the doctor, 'Go ahead and guess as much as you want to about my son. I won't hold you responsible. I'd be most grateful if you'd say anything, true or not, because I ran out of ideas about my boy, responsible or irresponsible, true or not, years ago. Stick your stainless steel spoon in this unhappy old man's brains, Doctor,' I told him, 'and stir.'

"He said to me, 'Before I tell you what my irresponsible thoughts are, I'll have to discuss sexual perversion some. I intend to involve Eliot in the discussion—so, if an involvement of that sort would affect you violently, let's have our talk come to an end right here.' 'Carry on,' I said. 'I'm an old futz, and the theory is that an old futz can't be hurt very much by anything anybody says. I've never believed it before, but I'll try to believe it now.'

"'Very well—' he said, 'let's assume that a healthy young man is supposed to be sexually aroused by an attractive woman not his mother or sister. If he's aroused by other things, another man, say, or an umbrella or the ostrich boa of the Empress Josephine or a sheep or a corpse or his mother or a stolen garterbelt, he is what we call a *pervert*.'

"I replied that I had always known such people were about, but that I'd never thought much about them because there didn't seem to be much *to* think about them.

"'Good,' he said. 'That's a calm, reasonable reaction, Senator Rosewater, that I'm frank to say surprises me. Let us hasten on to the admission that every case of perversion is essentially a case of crossed wires. Mother Nature and Society order a man to take his sex to such and such a place and do thus and so with it. Because of the crossed wires, the unhappy man enthusiastically goes straight to the wrong place, proudly, vigorously does some hideously inappropriate thing; and he can count himself lucky if he is simply crippled for life by a police force rather than killed by a mob.'

"I began to feel terror for the first time in many years," said the Senator, "and I told the doctor so.

"'Good,' he said again. 'The most exquisite pleasure in the practice of medicine comes from nudging a layman in the direction of terror, then bringing him back to safety again. Eliot certainly has his wires crossed, but the inappropriate thing to which the short circuit has caused him to bring his sexual energies isn't necessarily such a very bad thing.'

"'What *is* it?' I cried, thinking in spite of myself of Eliot stealing women's underwear, of Eliot snipping off locks of hair on subways, of Eliot as a Peeping Tom." The Senator from Indiana shuddered. "'Tell me, Doctor—tell me the worst. Eliot is bringing his sexual energies to what?'

"'To Utopia,' he said."

Frustration made Norman Mushari sneeze.

7

E LIOT'S EYELIDS were growing heavy as he read *Get With Child a Mandrake Root.* He was rumpling about in it at random, hoping to find by chance the words that were supposed to make Pharisees gnash their teeth. He found one place where a judge was damned for never having given his wife an orgasm, and another where an advertising executive in charge of a soap account got drunk, locked his apartment doors, and put on his mother's wedding dress. Eliot frowned, tried to think that that sort of thing was fair-to-middling Pharisee-baiting, failed to think so.

He read now the account executive's fiancée's seduction of her father's chauffeur. Suggestively, she bit off the breast-pocket buttons of his uniform jacket. Eliot Rosewater fell fast asleep.

The telephone rang three times.

"This is the Rosewater Foundation. How can we help you?"

"Mr. Rosewater—" said a fretful man, "you don't know me."

"Did someone tell you that mattered?"

"I'm nothing, Mr. Rosewater. I'm worse than nothing."

"Then God made a pretty bad mistake, didn't he?"

"He sure did when he made me."

"Maybe you brought your complaint to the right place."

"What kind of a place *is* it, anyway?"

"How did you happen to hear of us?"

"There's this big black and yellow sticker in the phone booth. Says, '*Don't Kill Yourself. Call the Rosewater Foundation*,' and it's got your number." Such stickers were in every phone booth in the county, and in the back windows of the cars and trucks of most of the volunteer firemen, too. "You know what somebody's written right under that in pencil?"

"No."

"Says, '*Eliot Rosewater is a saint. He'll give you love and money. If you'd rather have the best piece of tail in southern Indiana, call Melissa.*' And then it's got *her* number."

"You're a stranger in these parts?"

"I'm a stranger in all parts. But what *are* you anyway—some kind of religion?"

"Two-Seed-in-the-Spirit Predestinarian Baptist."

"What?"

"That's what I generally say when people insist I must have a religion. There happens to *be* such a sect, and I'm sure it's a good one. Foot-washing is practiced, and the ministers draw no pay. I wash my feet, and I draw no pay."

"I don't get it," said the caller.

"Just a way of trying to put you at ease, to let you know you don't have to be deadly serious with me. You don't happen to *be* a Two-Seed-in-the-Spirit Predestinarian Baptist, do you?"

"Jesus, no."

"There are two hundred people who *are*, and sooner or later I'm going to say to one of them what I've just said to you." Eliot took a drink. "I live in dread of that moment—and it's sure to come."

"You sound like a drunk. It sounded like you just took a drink."

"Be that as it may—what can we do to help you?"

"Who the hell *are* you?"

"The Government."

"The what?"

"The Government. If I'm not a Church, and I still want to keep people from killing themselves, I must be the Government. Right?"

The man muttered something.

"Or the Community Chest," said Eliot.

"Is this some kind of joke?"

"That's for me to know and you to find out."

"Maybe you think it's funny to put up signs about people who want to commit suicide."

"Are *you* about to?"

"And what if I was?"

"I wouldn't tell you the gorgeous reasons *I* have discovered for going on living."

"What *would* you do?"

"I'd ask you to name the rock-bottom price you'd charge to go on living for just one more week."

There was a silence.

"Did you hear me?" said Eliot.

"I heard you."

"If you're not going to kill yourself, would you please hang up? There are other people who'd like to use the line."

"You sound so crazy."

"You're the one who wants to kill himself."

"What if I said I wouldn't live through the next week for a million dollars?"

"I'd say, 'Go ahead and die.' Try a thousand."

"A thousand."

"Go ahead and die. Try a hundred."

"A hundred."

"Now you're making sense. Come on over and talk." He told him where his office was. "Don't be afraid of the dogs in front of the firehouse," he said. "They only bite when the fire horn goes off."

• • •

About the fire horn: To the best of Eliot's knowledge, it was the loudest alarm in the Western Hemisphere. It was driven by a seven-hundred-horsepower Messerschmitt engine that had a thirty-horsepower electric starter. It had been the main air-raid siren of Berlin during the Second World War. The Rosewater Foundation had bought it from the West German government and presented it to the town anonymously.

When it arrived by flatcar, the only clue as to the donor was a small tag that said, simply: "Compliments of a friend."

• • •

Eliot wrote in a cumbersome ledger he kept under his cot. It was bound in pebbled black leather, had three hundred ruled pages of eye-rest green. He called it his *Domesday Book*. It was in this book, from the very first day of the Foundation's operations in Rosewater, that Eliot entered the name of each client, the nature of the client's pains, and what the Foundation had done about them.

The book was nearly full, and only Eliot or his estranged wife could have interpreted all that was written there. What he wrote now was the name of the suicidal man who had called him, who had come to see him, who had just departed—departed a little sulkily, as though suspecting that he had been swindled or mocked, but couldn't imagine how or why.

"Sherman Wesley Little," wrote Eliot. "*Indy, Su-TDM-LO-V2-W3K3-K2CP-RF $300.*" Decoded, this meant that Little was from Indianapolis, was a suicidal tool-and-die maker who had been laid off, a veteran of the Second World War with a wife and three children, the second child suffering from cerebral palsy. Eliot had awarded him a Rosewater Fellowship of $300.

A prescription that was far more common than money in the Domesday Book was "AW." This represented Eliot's recommendation to people who were down in the dumps for every reason and for no reason in particular: "Dear, I tell you what to do—take an aspirin tablet, and wash it down with a glass of wine."

• • •

"FH" stood for "Fly Hunt." People often felt a desperate need to do something nice for Eliot. He would ask them to come at a specific time in order to rid his office of flies. During the fly season, this was an Augean task, for Eliot had no screens on his windows, and his office, moreover, was connected directly to the foul kitchen of the lunchroom below by means of a greasy hot-air register in the floor.

So the fly hunts were actually rituals, and were ritualized to such an extent that conventional fly-swatters were not used, and men and women hunted flies in very different ways. The men used rubber bands, and the women used tumblers of lukewarm water and soapsuds.

The rubber-band technique worked like this: A man would slice through a rubber band, making it a strand rather than a loop. He would stretch the strand between his hands, sight down the strand as though it were a rifle barrel, let it snap when a fly was in his sights. A well-hit fly would often be vaporized, accounting for the peculiar color of Eliot's walls and woodwork, which was largely dried fly purée.

The tumbler-and-soapsuds technique worked like this: A woman would look for a fly hanging upside down. She would then bring her tumbler of suds directly under the fly very slowly, taking advantage of the fact that an upside-down fly, when approached by danger, will drop straight down two inches or more, in a free fall, before using his wings. Ideally, the fly would not sense danger until it was directly below him, and he would obligingly drop into the suds to be caught, to work his way down through the bubbles, to drown.

Of this technique Eliot often said: "Nobody believes it until she tries it. Once she finds out it works, she never wants to quit."

• • •

In the back of the ledger was a very unfinished novel which Eliot had begun years before, on an evening when he understood at last that Sylvia would never come back to him.

Why do so many souls voluntarily return to Earth after failing and dying, failing and dying, failing and dying there? Because Heaven is such a null. Over Dem Pearly Gates these words should be emblazoned:

A LITTLE NOTHING, O GOD, GOES A LONG, LONG WAY.

But the only words written on the infinite portal of Paradise are the grafitti of vandal souls. "Welcome to the Bulgarian World's Fair!" says a penciled plaint on a pediment of pearl. "Better red than dead," another opines.

"You ain't a man till you've had black meat," suggests another. And this has been revised to read, "You ain't a man till you've *been* black meat."

"Where can I get a good lay around here?" asks a bawdy soul, drawing this reply: "Try 'Lay of the Last Minstrel,' by Alfred, Lord Tennyson."

My own contribution:

> Those who write on Heaven's walls
> Should mold their shit in little balls.
> And those who read these lines of wit
> Should eat these little balls of shit.

• • •

"Kublai Khan, Napoleon, Julius Caesar and King Richard the Lion Hearted all stink," a brave soul declares. The claim is unchallenged, nor are challenges from the parties insulted likely. The immortal soul of Kublai Khan now inhabits the meek meat of a veterinarian's wife in Lima, Peru. The immortal soul of Bonaparte peers out from the hot

and stuffy meat of the fourteen-year-old son of the Harbor Master of
Cotuit, Massachusetts. Great Caesar's ghost manages as best it can
with the syphilitic meat of a Pygmy widow in the Andaman Islands.
Coeur de Lion has found himself once again taken captive during
his travels, imprisoned this time in the flesh of Coach Letzinger, a
pitiful exhibitionist and freelance garbage man in Rosewater, Indiana.
Coach, with poor old King Richard inside, goes to Indianapolis on
the Greyhound bus three or four times a year, dresses up for the trip
in shoes, socks, garters, a raincoat, and a chromium-plated whistle
hung around his neck. When he gets to Indianapolis, Coach goes to
the silverware department of one of the big stores, where there are
always a lot of brides-to-be picking out silver patterns. Coach blows
his whistle, all the girls look, Coach throws open his raincoat, closes it
again, and runs like hell to catch the bus back to Rosewater.

• • •

Heaven is the bore of bores, *Eliot's novel went on*, so most wraiths
queue up to be reborn—and they live and love and fail and die, and
they queue up to be reborn again. They take pot luck, as the saying
goes. They don't gibber and squeak to be one race or another, one
sex or another, one nationality or another, one class or another. What
they want and what they get are three dimensions—and comprehen-
sible little packets of time—and enclosures making possible the crucial
distinction between inside and outside.

There is no inside here. There is no outside here. To pass through
the gates in either direction is to go from nowhere to nowhere and
from everywhere to everywhere. Imagine a billiard table as long and
broad as the Milky Way. Do not omit the detail of its being a flawless
slate slab to which green felt has been glued. Imagine a gate at dead
center on the slab. Anyone imagining that much will have comprehended all there is to know about Paradise—and will have sympathized
with those becoming ravenous for the distinction between inside and
outside.

• • •

Uncomfortable as it is here, however, there are a few of us who
do not care to be reborn. I am among that number. I have not been
on Earth since 1587 A.D., when, riding around in the meat of one
Walpurga Hausmännin, I was executed in the Austrian village of
Dillingen. The alleged crime of my meat was witchcraft. When I
heard the sentence, I certainly wanted out of that meat. I was about
to leave it anyway, having worn it for more than eighty-five years. But
I had to stay right with it when they tied it astride a sawhorse, put the

sawhorse on a cart, took my poor old meat to the Town Hall. There they tore my right arm and left breast with red-hot pincers. Then we went to the lower gate, where they tore my right breast. Then they took me to the door of the hospital, where they tore my right arm. And then they took me to the village square. In view of the fact that I had been a licensed and pledged midwife for sixty-two years, and yet had acted so vilely, they cut off my right hand. And then they tied me to a stake, burned me alive, and dumped my ashes into the nearest stream.

As I say, I haven't been back since.

•   •   •

It used to be that most of us who didn't want to go back to good old Earth were souls whose meat had been tortured in slow and fancy ways—a fact that should make very smug indeed proponents of corporal and capital punishments as deterrents to crime. But something curious has been happening of late. We have been gaining recruits to whom, by our standards of agony, practically nothing happened on Earth. They scarcely barked a shin down there, and yet they arrive up here in shell-shocked battalions, bawling, "Never again!"

"Who are these people?" I ask myself. "What is this unimaginably horrible thing that has happened to them?" And I realized that, in order to get proper answers, I am going to have to cease to be dead. I am going to have to let myself be reborn.

Word has just come that I am to be sent where the soul of Richard the Lion Hearted now lives, Rosewater, Indiana.

Eliot's black telephone rang.

"This is the Rosewater Foundation. How can we help you?"

"Mr. Rosewater—" said a woman chokingly, "this—this is Stella Wakeby." She panted, waiting for his reaction to the announcement.

"Well! Hello!" said Eliot heartily. "How nice to *hear* from you! What a pleasant surprise!" He didn't know who Stella Wakeby was.

"Mr. Rosewater—I—I never asked you for anything, did I?"

"No—no, you never did."

"A lot of people with a lot less troubles than I got bother you all the time."

"I never feel that anyone is *bothering* me. It is true—I do see some people more than others." He did so much business with Diana Moon Glampers, for instance, that he no longer recorded his transactions with her in the book. He took a chance now: "And I've often thought of the awful burdens you must have to carry."

"Oh, Mr. Rosewater—if you only *knew*—" And she burst into violent tears. "We always said we were *Senator* Rosewater people and not *Eliot* Rosewater people!"

"There, there."

"We've always stood on our own two feet, no matter what. Many's the time I passed you out on the street and looked the other way, not on account of I had anything against you. I just wanted you to know the Wakebys were *fine*."

"I understood—and I was always glad to get the good news." Eliot couldn't recall any woman's turning her face away from him, and he walked around the town so rarely that he couldn't have offered the overwrought Stella very many opportunities to react to him. He supposed correctly that she lived in frightful poverty on some back road, rarely showing herself and her rags, and only imagining that she had some sort of life in the town, too, and that everyone knew her. If she had passed Eliot on the street once, which she probably had, that once had become a thousand passings in her mind—each with its own dramatic lights and shadows.

"I couldn't sleep tonight, Mr. Rosewater—so I walked the road."

"And many's the time you've done it."

"Oh, God, Mr. Rosewater—full moon, half moon, and no moon at all."

"And tonight the rain."

"I like the rain."

"And so do I."

"And there was this light in my neighbor's house."

"Thank God for neighbors."

"And I knocked on the door, and they took me in. And I said, 'I just can't go another step without some kind of help. If I can't get some kind of help, I don't care if tomorrow never comes. I can't be a Senator Rosewater person any more!'"

"There, there—now, now."

"So they put me in the car, and they drove me to the nearest telephone, and they said, 'You call up Eliot. He'll help.' So that's what I've *done*."

"Would you like to come see me now, dear—or can you wait until tomorrow?"

"Tomorrow." It was almost a question.

"Wonderful! Any time that's convenient to you, dear."

"Tomorrow."

"Tomorrow, dear. It's going to be a very nice day."

"Thank *God*!"

"There, there."

"Ohhhhh, Mr. Rosewater, thank God for *you*!"

• • •

Eliot hung up. The telephone rang immediately.

"This is the Rosewater Foundation. How can we help you?"

"You might start by getting a haircut and a new suit," said a man.

"What?"

"Eliot—"

"Yes—?"

"You don't even recognize my voice?"

"I—I'm sorry—I—"

"It's your God-damned *Dad*!"

• • •

"Gee, *Father*!" said Eliot, lyrical with love, surprise and pleasure. "How *nice* to hear your voice."

"You didn't even recognize it."

"Sorry. You know—the calls just *pour* in."

"They do, eh?"

"*You* know that."

"I'm afraid I do."

"Gee—how *are* you, anyway?"

"Fine!" said the Senator with brisk sarcasm. "Couldn't be better!"

"I'm so glad to hear that."

The Senator cursed.

"What's the matter, Father?"

"Don't talk to me as though I were some drunk! Some pimp! Some moronic washerwoman!"

"What did I *say*?"

"Your whole damn tone!"

"Sorry."

"I can sense your getting ready to tell me to take an aspirin in a glass of wine. Don't talk *down* to me!"

"Sorry."

"I don't need anybody to make the last payment on my motor scooter." Eliot had actually done this for a client once. The client killed himself and a girlfriend two days later, smashed up in Bloomington.

"I know you don't."

"He knows I don't," said the Senator to somebody on his end of the line.

"You—you sound so *angry* and *unhappy*, Father." Eliot was genuinely concerned.

"It will pass."

"Is it anything special?"

"Little things, Eliot, little things—such as the Rosewater family's dying out."

"What makes you think it *is*?"

"Don't tell me you're pregnant."

"What about the people in Rhode Island?"

"You make me feel so much better. I'd forgotten all about them."

"Now you sound sarcastic."

"It must be a bad connection. Tell me some good news from out your way, Eliot. Buoy up this old futz."

"Mary Moody had twins."

"Good! Good! Wonderful! As long as *somebody's* reproducing. And what names has Miss Moody chosen for these new little citizens?"

"Foxcroft and Melody."

• • •

"Eliot—"

"Sir—?"

"I want you to take a good look at yourself."

Dutifully, Eliot looked himself over as best he could without a mirror. "I'm looking."

"Now ask yourself, 'Is this a dream? How did I ever get into such a disreputable condition?'"

Again dutifully, and without a trace of whimsicality, Eliot said to himself out loud, "Is this a dream? How did I ever get into such a disreputable condition?"

"Well? What is your answer?"

"Isn't a dream," Eliot reported.

"Don't you wish it *were*?"

"What would I wake up *to*?"

"What you can *be*. What you *used* to be!"

"You want me to start buying paintings for museums again? Would you be prouder of me, if I'd contributed two and a half million dollars to buy Rembrandt's *Aristotle Contemplating a Bust of Homer*?"

"Don't reduce the argument to an absurdity."

"I'm not the one who did *that*. Blame the people who put up that kind of money for that kind of picture. I showed a photograph of it to Diana Moon Glampers, and she said, 'Maybe I'm dumb, Mr. Rosewater, but I wouldn't give that thing house room.'"

"Eliot—"

"Sir—?"

"Ask yourself what Harvard would think of you now."

"I don't have to. I already know."

"Oh?"

"They're crazy about me. You should see the letters I get."

The Senator nodded to himself resignedly, knowing that the Harvard jibe was ill-considered, knowing Eliot told the truth when he spoke of letters from Harvard that were full of respect.

"After all—" said Eliot, "for goodness sakes, I've given those guys three hundred thousand dollars a year, regular as clockwork, ever since the Foundation began. You should *see* the letters."

•   •   •

"Eliot—"

"Sir—?"

"We come to a supremely ironic moment in history, for Senator Rosewater of Indiana now asks his own son, 'Are you or have you ever been a communist?'"

"Oh, I have what a lot of people would probably call

communistic thoughts," said Eliot artlessly, "but, for heaven's sakes, Father, nobody can work with the poor and not fall over Karl Marx from time to time—or just fall over the Bible, as far as that goes. I think it's terrible the way people don't share things in this country. I think it's a heartless government that will let one baby be born owning a big piece of the country, the way I was born, and let another baby be born without owning anything. The least a government could do, it seems to me, is to divide things up fairly among the babies. Life is hard enough, without people having to worry themselves sick about *money*, too. There's plenty for everybody in this country, if we'll only *share* more."

"And just what do you think that would do to incentive?"

"You mean fright about not getting enough to eat, about not being able to pay the doctor, about not being able to give your family nice clothes, a safe, cheerful, comfortable place to live, a decent education, and a few good times? You mean shame about not knowing where the Money River is?"

"The *what*?"

"The Money River, where the wealth of the nation flows. We were born on the banks of it—and so were most of the mediocre people we grew up with, went to private schools with, sailed and played tennis with. We can slurp from that mighty river to our hearts' content. And we even take slurping lessons, so we can slurp more efficiently."

"Slurping lessons?"

"From lawyers! From tax consultants! From customers' men! We're born close enough to the river to drown ourselves and the next ten generations in wealth, simply using dippers and buckets. But we still hire the experts to teach us the use of aqueducts, dams, reservoirs, siphons, bucket brigades, and the Archimedes' screw. And our teachers in turn become rich, and their children become buyers of lessons in slurping."

"I wasn't aware that I slurped."

Eliot was fleetingly heartless, for he was thinking angrily in the abstract. "Born slurpers never are. And they can't imagine what the poor people are talking about when they say they hear somebody slurping. They don't even know what it means when somebody mentions the Money River. When one of us claims that there is no such thing as the Money River I think to myself, 'My gosh, but that's a dishonest and tasteless thing to say.'"

•   •   •

"How stimulating to hear you talk of taste," said the Senator clankingly.

"You want me to start going to the opera again? You want me to build a perfect house in a perfect village, and sail and sail and sail?"

"Who cares what I want?"

"I admit this is no Taj Mahal. But should it be, with other Americans having such a rotten time?"

"Perhaps, if they stopped believing in crazy things like the Money River, and got to work, they would stop having such a rotten time."

"If there isn't a Money River, then how did I make ten thousand dollars today, just by snoozing and scratching myself, and occasionally answering the phone?"

"It's still possible for an American to make a fortune on his own."

"Sure—provided somebody tells him when he's young enough that there *is* a Money River, that there's nothing fair about it, that he had damn well better forget about hard work and the merit system and honesty and all that crap, and get to where the river is. 'Go where the rich and the powerful are,' I'd tell him, 'and learn their ways. They can be flattered and they can be scared. Please them enormously or scare them enormously, and one moonless night they will put their fingers to their lips, warning you not to make a sound. And they will lead you through the dark to the widest, deepest river of wealth ever known to man. You'll be shown your place on the riverbank, and handed a bucket all your own. Slurp as much as you want, but try to keep the racket of your slurping down. A poor man might hear.'"

The Senator cursed.

"Why did you say that, Father?" It was a tender question.

The Senator cursed again.

"I just wish there didn't have to be this *acrimony*, this tension, every time we talk. I love you so."

There was more cursing, made harsher by the fact that the Senator was close to tears.

"Why would you swear when I say I love you, Father?"

"You're the man who stands on a street corner with a roll of toilet paper, and written on each square are the words, 'I love you.' And each passer-by, no matter who, gets a square all his or her own. I don't want *my* square of toilet paper."

"I didn't realize it *was* toilet paper."

"Until you stop drinking, you're not going to realize anything!" the Senator cried brokenly. "I'm going to put your wife on the phone. Do you realize you've lost her? Do you realize what a good wife she was?"

• • •

"Eliot—?" Sylvia's was such a breathy and frightened greeting. The girl weighed no more than a wedding veil.

"Sylvia—" This was formal, manly, but uneven. Eliot had written to her a thousand times, had called and called. Until now, there had been no reply.

"I—I am aware that—that I have behaved badly."

"As long as the behavior was human—"

"Can I help being human?"

"No."

"Can anybody?"

"Not that I know of."

• • •

"Eliot—?"

"Yes?"

"How is everybody?"

"Here?"

"Anywhere."

"Fine."

"I'm glad."

• • •

"If—if I ask about certain people, I'll cry," said Sylvia.

"Don't ask."

"I still care about them, even if the doctors tell me I mustn't ever go there again."

"Don't ask."

"Somebody had a baby?"

"Don't ask."

"Didn't you tell your father somebody had a baby?"

"Don't ask."

"Who had a baby, Eliot?—I care, I care."

"Oh Christ, don't ask."

"I care, I care!"

"Mary Moody."

"Twins?"

"Of course." Eliot revealed here that he had no illusions about the people to whom he was devoting his life. "And fire-bugs, too, no doubt, no doubt." The Moody family had a long history of not only twinning but arson.

"Are they cute?"

"I haven't seen them." Eliot added with an irritability that had always been a private thing between himself and Sylvia. "They always are."

"Have you sent their presents yet?"

"What makes you think I still send presents?" This had reference to Eliot's old custom of sending a share of International Business Machines stock to each child born in the county.

"You don't do it any more?"

"I still do it." Eliot sounded sick of doing it.

"You seem tired."

"It must be a bad connection."

"Tell me some more news."

"My wife is divorcing me for medical reasons."

"Can't we skip that news?" This was not a flippant sugges-tion. It was a tragic one. The tragedy was beyond discussion.

"Hippity hop," said Eliot emptily.

•   •   •

Eliot took a drink of Southern Comfort, was uncomforted. He coughed, and his father coughed, too. This coincidence, where father and son matched each other unknowingly, incon-solable hack for hack, was heard not only by Sylvia, but by Norman Mushari, too. Mushari had slipped out of the living room, had found a telephone extension in the Senator's study. He was listening in with ears ablaze.

"I—I suppose I should say goodbye," said Sylvia guiltily. Tears were streaming down her cheeks.

"That would be up to your doctor to say."

"Give—give my love to everyone."

"I will, I will."

"Tell them I dream about them all the time."

"That will make them proud."

"Congratulate Mary Moody on her twins."

"I will. I'll be baptizing them tomorrow."

"Baptizing?" This was something new.

Mushari rolled his eyes.

"I—I didn't know you—you did things like that," said Sylvia carefully.

Mushari was gratified to hear the anxiety in her voice. It meant to him that Eliot's lunacy was not stabilized, but was about to make the great leap forward into religion.

"I couldn't get out of it," said Eliot. "She insisted on it, and nobody else would do it."

"Oh." Sylvia relaxed.

Mushari did not register disappointment. The baptism would hold up very well in court as evidence that Eliot thought of himself as a Messiah.

"I told her," said Eliot, and Mushari's mind, which was equipped with ratchets, declined to accept this evidence, "that I wasn't a religious person by any stretch of the imagination. I told her nothing I did would count in Heaven, but she insisted just the same."

"What will you say? What will you do?"

"Oh—I don't know." Eliot's sorrow and exhaustion dropped away for a moment as he became enchanted by the problem. A birdy little smile played over his lips. "Go over to her shack, I guess. Sprinkle some water on the babies, say, 'Hello, babies. Welcome to Earth. It's hot in the summer and cold in the winter. It's round and wet and crowded. At the outside, babies, you've got about a hundred years here. There's only one rule that I know of, babies—:

"'God damn it, you've got to be kind.'"

8

I T WAS AGREED that night that Eliot and Sylvia should meet for a final farewell in the Bluebird Room of the Marott Hotel in Indianapolis, three nights hence. This was a tremendously dangerous thing for two such sick and loving people to do. The agreement was reached in a chaos of murmurs and whispers and little cries of loneliness that came at the close of the telephone conversation.

"Oh, Eliot, should we?"

"I think we have to."

"Have to," she echoed.

"Don't you feel it—that—that we have to?"

"Yes."

"It's life."

Sylvia wagged her head. "Oh, damn love—damn love."

"This will be nice. I promise."

"I promise, too."

"I'll get a new suit."

"Please don't—not on my account."

"On account of the Bluebird Room, then."

"Good night."

"I love you, Sylvia. Good night."

There was a pause.

"Good night, Eliot."

"I love you."

"Good night. I'm frightened. Good night."

• • •

This conversation was a worry to Norman Mushari, who restored the telephone with which he had been eavesdropping to its cradle. It was crucial to his plans that Sylvia not get pregnant by Eliot. A child in her womb would have an unbreakable claim to control of the Foundation, whether Eliot was crazy or not. And it was Mushari's dream that control should go to Eliot's second cousin, Fred Rosewater, in Pisquontuit, Rhode Island.

Fred knew nothing of this, didn't even know for certain that he was related to the Indiana Rosewaters. The Indiana Rosewaters knew about him only because McAllister, Robjent, Reed and McGee, being thorough, had hired a genealogist and a detective to find out who their closest relatives bearing the name Rosewater were. Fred's dossier in the law firm's confidential files was fat, as was Fred, but the investigation had been discreet. Fred never imagined that he might be tapped for wealth and glory.

•   •   •

So, on the morning after Eliot and Sylvia agreed to meet, Fred felt like an ordinary or less-than-ordinary man, whose prospects were poor. He came out of the Pisquontuit Drug Store, squinted in the sunlight, took three deep breaths, went into the Pisquontuit News Store next door. He was a portly man, aslop with coffee, gravid with Danish pastry.

Poor, lugubrious Fred spent his mornings seeking insurance prospects in the drugstore, which was the coffee house of the rich, and the news store, which was the coffee house of the poor. He was the only man in town who had coffee in *both* places.

Fred bellied up to the news store's lunch counter, beamed at a carpenter and two plumbers sitting there. He climbed aboard a stool, and his great behind made the cushion seem no larger than a marshmallow.

"Coffee and Danish, Mr. Rosewater?" said the not-very-clean idiot girl behind the counter.

"Coffee and Danish sounds real good," Fred agreed heartily. "On a morning like this, by God, coffee and Danish sounds real good."

•   •   •

About Pisquontuit: It was pronounced "Pawn-it" by those who loved it, and "Piss-on-it" by those who didn't. There had once been an Indian chief named Pisquontuit.

Pisquontuit wore an apron, lived, as did his people, on clams, raspberries, and rose hips. Agriculture was news to Chief Pisquontuit. So, for that matter, were wampum, feather ornaments, and the bow and arrow.

Alcohol was the best news of all. Pisquontuit drank himself to death in 1638.

Four thousand moons later, the village that made his name immortal was populated by two hundred very wealthy families and by a thousand ordinary families whose breadwinners served, in one way and another, the rich.

The lives led there were nearly all paltry, lacking in subtlety, wisdom, wit or invention—were precisely as pointless and unhappy as lives led in Rosewater, Indiana. Inherited millions did not help. Nor did the arts and sciences.

• • •

Fred Rosewater was a good sailor and had attended Princeton University, so he was welcomed into the homes of the rich, though, for Pisquontuit, he was gruesomely poor. His home was a sordid little brown-shingle carpenter's special, a mile from the glittering waterfront.

Poor Fred worked like hell for the few dollars he brought home once in a while. He was working now, beaming at the carpenter and the two plumbers in the news store. The three workmen were reading a scandalous tabloid, a national weekly dealing with murder, sex, pets, and children—*mutilated* children, more often than not. It was called *The American Investigator*, "The World's Most Sparkling Newspaper." *The Investigator* was to the news store what *The Wall Street Journal* was to the drugstore.

"Improving your minds as usual, I see," Fred observed. He said it with the lightness of fruitcake.

The workmen had an uneasy respect for Fred. They tried to be cynical about what he sold, but they knew in their hearts that he was offering the only get-rich-quick scheme that was open to them: to insure themselves and die soon. And it was Fred's gloomy secret that without such people, tantalized by such a proposition, he would not have a dime. All of his business was with the working class. His cavorting with the sailboat rajahs next door was bluster, bluff. It impressed the poor to think that Fred sold insurance to the canny rich, too, but it was not true. The estate plans of the rich were made in banks and law offices far, far away.

"What's the foreign news today?" Fred inquired. This was another joke about *The Investigator*.

The carpenter held up the front page for Fred to see. The page was well filled by a headline and a picture of a fine looking young woman. The headline said this:

I WANT A MAN WHO
CAN GIVE ME A
GENIUS BABY!

The girl was a showgirl. Her name was Randy Herald.

"I'd be *pleased* to help the lady with her problem," said Fred, lightly again.

"My God," said the carpenter, cocking his head and gnashing his teeth, "wouldn't anybody?"

"You think I'm *serious*?" Fred sneered at Randy Herald. "I wouldn't trade my bride for twenty thousand Randy Heralds!" He was calculatingly maudlin now. "And I don't think you guys would trade *your* brides, either." To Fred, a bride was any woman with an insurable husband.

"I know your brides," he continued, "and any one of you would be crazy to trade." He nodded. "We are four lucky guys sitting here, and we'd better not forget it. Four wonderful brides we've got, boys, and we'd damn well better stop and thank God for 'em from time to time."

Fred stirred his coffee. "I wouldn't be anything without my bride, and I know it." His bride was named Caroline. Caroline was the mother of an unattractive, fat little boy, poor little Franklin Rosewater. Caroline had taken lately to drinking lunch with a rich Lesbian named Amanita Buntline.

"I've done what I can for her," Fred declared. "God knows it isn't enough. Nothing could be enough." There was a real lump in his throat. He knew that lump had to be there and it had to be real, or he wouldn't sell any insurance "It's something, though, something even a poor man can do for his bride."

Fred rolled his eyes mooningly. He was worth forty-two thousand dollars dead.

• • •

Fred was often asked, of course, whether he was related to the famous Senator Rosewater. Fred's self-effacing, ignorant reply was along the lines of, "Somewhere, somehow, I guess—way, way back." Like most Americans of modest means, Fred knew nothing about his ancestors.

There was this to know:

The Rhode Island branch of the Rosewater family was descended from George Rosewater, younger brother of the infamous Noah. When the Civil War came, George raised a company of Indiana riflemen, marched off with them to join the nearly legendary *Black Hat Brigade*. Under George's command was Noah's substitute, the Rosewater village idiot, Fletcher Moon. Moon was blown to hamburger by Stonewall Jackson's artillery at Second Bull Run.

During the retreat through the mud toward Alexandria, Captain Rosewater took time out to write his brother Noah this note:

Fletcher Moon kept up his end of the deal to the utmost of his ability. If you are put out about your considerable investment in him being used up so quickly, I suggest you write General Pope for a partial refund. Wish you were here.

George

To which Noah replied:

I am sorry about Fletcher Moon, but, as the *Bible* says, "A deal is a deal." Enclosed find some routine legal papers for you to sign. They empower me to run your half of the farm and the saw factory until your return, etc., etc. We are undergoing great privations here at home. Everything is going to the troops. A word of appreciation from the troops would be much appreciated.

Noah.

By the time of Antietam, George Rosewater had become a Lieutenant Colonel, and had, curiously, lost the little fingers from both hands. At Antietam, he had his horse shot out from under him, advanced on foot, grabbed the regimental colors from a dying boy, found himself holding only a shattered staff when Confederate cannister carried the colors away. He pressed on, killed a man with the staff. At the moment he was doing the killing, one of his own men fired off a musket that still had its ramrod jammed down the bore. The explosion blinded Colonel Rosewater for life.

•   •   •

George returned to Rosewater County a blind brevet brigadier. People found him remarkably cheerful. And his cheerfulness did not seem to fade one iota when it was explained to him by bankers and lawyers, who kindly offered to be his eyes, that he didn't own anything any more, that he had signed everything over to Noah. Noah, unfortunately, was not in town to explain things in person to George. Business required that he spend most of his time in Washington, New York and Philadelphia.

"Well," said George, still smiling, smiling, smiling, "as the Bible tells us in no uncertain terms, 'Business is business.'"

The lawyers and bankers felt somewhat cheated, since George didn't seem to be drawing any sort of moral from what should have been an important experience in almost any man's life. One lawyer, who had been looking forward to pointing out the moral when George got mad, couldn't restrain himself from pointing it out anyway, even though George was laughing: "People should always *read* things before they sign them."

"You can bet your boots," said George, "that from now on I *will*."

George Rosewater obviously wasn't a well man when he came back from the war, for no well man, having lost his eyes and his patrimony, would have laughed so much. And a well man, particularly if he were a general and a hero, might have taken some vigorous legal steps to compel his brother to return his property. But George filed no suit. He did not wait for Noah to return to Rosewater County, and he did not go East to find him. In fact, he and Noah were never to meet or communicate again.

He paid a call, wearing the full regalia of a brigadier, to each Rosewater County household that had given him a boy or boys to command, praising them all, mourning with all his heart for the boys who were wounded or dead. Noah Rosewater's brick mansion was being built at that time. One morning the workmen found the brigadier's uniform nailed to the front door as though it were an animal skin nailed to a barn door to dry.

As far as Rosewater County was concerned, George Rosewater had disappeared forever.

• • •

George went East like a vagabond, not to find and kill his brother, but to seek work in Providence, Rhode Island. He had heard that a broom factory was being opened there. It was to be staffed by Union veterans who were blind.

What he had heard was true. There was such a factory, founded by Castor Buntline, who was neither a veteran nor blind. Buntline perceived correctly that blind veterans would make very agreeable employees, that Buntline himself would gain a place in history as a humanitarian, and that no Northern patriot, for several years after the war, anyway, would use anything but a *Buntline Union Beacon Broom*. Thus was the great Buntline fortune begun. And, with broom profits, Castor Buntline and his spastic son Elihu went carpetbagging, became tobacco kings.

• • •

When the footsore, amiable General George Rosewater arrived at the broom factory, Castor Buntline wrote to Washington, confirmed that George was a general, hired George at a very good salary, made him foreman, and named the whiskbrooms the factory was making after him. The brand name entered ordinary speech for a little while. A "General Rosewater" was a *whiskbroom*.

And blind George was given a fourteen-year-old girl, an orphan named Faith Merrihue, who was to be his eyes and his messenger. When she was sixteen, George married her.

And George begat Abraham, who became a Congregationalist minister. Abraham went as a missionary to the Congo, where he met and married Lavinia Waters, the daughter of another missionary, an Illinois Baptist.

In the jungle, Abraham begat Merrihue. Lavinia died at Merrihue's birth. Little Merrihue was nursed on the milk of a Bantu.

•

And Abraham and little Merrihue returned to Rhode Island. Abraham accepted the call to the Congregationalist pulpit in the little fishing village of Pisquontuit. He bought a little house, and with that house came one hundred ten acres of scruffy, sandy woodlot. It was a triangular lot. The hypotenuse of the triangle lay on the shore of Pisquontuit Harbor.

Merrihue, the Parson's son, became a realtor, divided his father's land into lots. He married Cynthia Niles Rumfoord, a minor heiress, invested much of her money in pavement and streetlights and sewers. He made a fortune, lost it, and his wife's fortune, too, in the crash of 1929.

He blew his brains out.

But, before he did that, he wrote a family history and he begat poor Fred, the insurance man.

•　•　•

Sons of suicides seldom do well.

Characteristically, they find life lacking a certain *zing*. They tend to feel more rootless than most, even in a notoriously rootless nation. They are squeamishly incurious about the past and numbly certain about the future to this grisly extent: they suspect that they, too, will probably kill themselves.

The syndrome was surely Fred's. And to it he added twitches, aversions and listlessnesses special to his own case. He had heard the shot that killed his father, had seen his father with a big piece of his head blown away, with the manuscript of the family history in his lap.

Fred had the manuscript, which he had never read, which he never wanted to read. It was on top of a jelly cupboard in the cellar of Fred's home. That was where he kept the rat poison, too.

•　•　•

Now poor Fred Rosewater was in the news store, continuing to talk to the carpenter and the two plumbers about brides. "Ned—" he said to the carpenter, "*we've* both done something for our brides, anyway." The carpenter was worth twenty thousand dollars dead, thanks to Fred. He could think of little else but suicide whenever premium time rolled around.

"And we can forget all about saving, too," said Fred. "That's all taken care of—*automatically.*"

"Yup," said Ned.

There was a waterlogged silence. The two uninsured plumbers, gay and lecherous moments before, were lifeless now.

"With a simple stroke of the pen," Fred reminded the carpenter, "we've created sizable estates. That's the miracle of life insurance. That's the least we can do for our brides."

The plumbers slid off their stools. Fred was not dismayed to see them go. They would be taking their consciences with them wherever they went—and they would be coming back to the news store again and again.

And whenever they came back, there would be Fred.

"You know what my greatest satisfaction is in my profession?" Fred asked the carpenter.

"Nope."

"It comes when I have a bride come up to me and say, 'I don't know how the children and I can ever thank you enough for what you've done. God bless you, Mr. Rosewater.'"

9

THE CARPENTER slunk away from Fred Rosewater, too, leaving a copy of *The American Investigator* behind. Fred went through an elaborate pantomime of ennui, demonstrated to anyone who might be watching that he was a man with absolutely nothing to read, a sleepy man, possibly hung over, and that he was likely to seize any reading matter at all, like a man in a dream.

"Uff, uff, uff," he yawned. He stretched out his arms, gathered the paper in.

There seemed to be only one other person in the store, the girl behind the lunch counter. "Really now—" he said to her, "who are the idiots who read this garbage, anyway?"

The girl might have responded truthfully that Fred himself read it from cover to cover every week. But, being an idiot herself, she noticed practically nothing. "Search me," she said.

It was an unappetizing invitation.

• • •

Fred Rosewater, snorting with incredulity, turned to the advertising section of the paper, which was called, "Here I Am." Men and women confessed there that they were looking for love, marriage, and monkeyshines. They did so at a cost to themselves of a dollar forty-five cents per line.

Attractive, sparkling, professional woman, 40, Jewish, *said one*, college graduate, resides Connecticut. Seeks marriage-minded Jewish college-educated man. Children warmly welcomed. Investigator, Box L-577.

That was a sweet one. Most weren't that sweet.

St. Louis hairdresser, male, would like to hear from other males in Show-me State. Exchange snaps? *said another.*
Modern couple new to Dallas would like to meet sophisticated couples interested in candid photography. All sincere letters answered. All snaps returned, *said another.*
Male preparatory school teacher badly needs course in manners

from stern instructress, preferably a horse-lover of German or Scandinavian extraction, *said another*. Will travel anywhere in U.S.

New York top exec wants dates weekday afternoons. No prudes, *said another*.

On the facing page was a large coupon on which a reader was invited to write an ad of his own. Fred sort of hankered to.

• • •

Fred turned the page, read an account of a rape-murder that happened in Nebraska in 1933. The illustrations were revoltingly clinical photographs that only a coroner had a right to see. The rape-murder was thirty years old when Fred read of it, when *The Investigator*'s reputedly ten million readers read of it. The issues with which the paper dealt were eternal. Lucretia Borgia could make screaming headlines at any time. It was from *The Investigator*, in fact, that Fred, who had attended Princeton for only a year, had learned of the death of Socrates.

A thirteen-year-old girl came into the store, and Fred thrust the paper aside. The girl was Lila Buntline, daughter of his wife's best friend. Lila was a tall creature, horse-faced, knobby. There were great circles under her perfectly beautiful green eyes. Her face was piebald with sunburn and tan and freckles and pink new skin. She was the most competitive and skilful sailor in the Pisquontuit Yacht Club.

Lila glanced at Fred with pity—because he was poor, because his wife was no good, because he was fat, because he was a bore. And she strode to the magazine and book racks, put herself out of sight by sitting on the cold cement floor.

Fred retrieved *The Investigator*, looked at ads that offered to sell him all sorts of dirty things. His breathing was shallow. Poor Fred had a damp, junior high school enthusiasm for *The Investigator* and all it stood for, but lacked the nerve to become a part of it, to correspond with all the box numbers there. Since he was the son of a suicide, it was hardly surprising that his secret hankerings were embarrassing and small.

• • •

A very healthy man now banged into the news store, moved to Fred's side so quickly that Fred couldn't throw the paper away. "Why, you filthy-minded insurance bastard," said the newcomer cheerfully, "what you doing reading a jerk-off paper like that?"

He was Harry Pena, a professional fisherman. He was also Chief of the Pisquontuit Volunteer Fire Department. Harry had two fish traps offshore, labyrinths of pilings and nets that took heartless advantage of the stupidity of fish. Each trap was a long fence in the water, with dry land at one end and a circular corral of stakes and netting at the other. Fish seeking a way around the fence entered the corral. Stupidly, they circled the corral again and again and again, until Harry and his two big sons came in their boat, with gaffhooks and malls, closed the gate of the corral, hauled up a purse net lying on the bottom, and killed and killed and killed.

Harry was middle-aged and bandy-legged, but he had a head and shoulders Michelangelo might have given to Moses or God. He had not been a fisherman all his life. Harry had been an insurance bastard himself, in Pittsfield, Massachusetts. One night in Pittsfield, Harry had cleaned his living-room carpet with carbon tetrachloride, and all but died. When he recovered his doctor told him this: "Harry—either you work out-of-doors, or you die."

So Harry became what his father had been—a trap fisherman.

•   •   •

Harry threw an arm over Fred's suety shoulders. He could afford to be affectionate. He was one of the few men in Pisquontuit whose manhood was not in question. "Aaaaah— you poor insurance bastard—" he said, "why be an insurance bastard? Do something beautiful." He sat down, ordered black coffee and a golden cigar.

"Well now, Harry—" said Fred, with lip-pursing judiciousness, "I think maybe my insurance philosophy is a little different from what yours was."

"Shit," said Harry pleasantly. He took the paper away from Fred, considered the front-page challenge hurled by Randy Herald. "By God," he said, "she takes whatever kind of baby I give her, and I say *when* she gets it, too, not her."

"Seriously, Harry—" Fred insisted, "I *like* insurance. I like *helping* people."

Harry gave no indication that he'd heard. He scowled at a picture of a French girl in a bikini.

Fred, understanding that he seemed a bleak, sexless person to Harry, tried to prove that Harry had him wrong. He nudged Harry, man-to-man. "Like that, Harry?" he asked.

"Like what?"

"The girl there."

"That's not a girl. That's a piece of paper."

"Looks like a girl to *me*." Fred Rosewater leered.

"Then you're easily fooled," said Harry. "It's done with ink on a piece of paper. That girl isn't lying there on the counter. She's thousands of miles away, doesn't even know we're alive. If this was a real girl, all I'd have to do for a living would be to stay home and cut out pictures of big fish."

• • •

Harry Pena turned to the "Here I Am" ads, asked Fred for a pen.

"Pen?" said Fred Rosewater, as though it were a foreign word.

"You've *got* one, don't you?"

"Sure, I've got one." Fred handed over one of the nine pens distributed about his person.

"Sure he's got one." Harry laughed. And this is what he wrote on the coupon facing the ads:

Red-hot Papa, member of white race, seeks red-hot Mama, any race, any age, any religion. Object: everything but matrimony. Will exchange snaps. My teeth are my own.

"You really going to send that in?" Fred's own itch to run an ad, to get a few dirty replies, was pathetically plain.

Harry signed the ad: "*Fred Rosewater, Pisquontuit, Rhode Island.*"

"Very funny," said Fred, drawing back from Harry with acid dignity.

Harry winked. "Funny for Pisquontuit," he said.

• • •

Fred's wife Caroline came into the news store now. She was a pretty, pinched, skinny, lost little woman, all dolled-up in well-made clothes cast off by her wealthy, Lesbian friend, Amanita Buntline. Caroline Rosewater clinked and flashed with accessories. Their purpose was to make the second-hand clothing distinctly her own. She was going to have lunch with Amanita. She wanted money from Fred, in order that she might insist, with something behind her, upon paying for her own food and drink.

When she spoke to Fred, with Harry Pena watching, she behaved like a woman who was keeping her dignity while being frog-walked. With the avid help of Amanita, she pitied herself for being married to a man who was so poor and dull. That she was exactly as poor and dull as Fred was a possibility she was constitutionally unable to entertain. For one thing, she was a Phi Beta Kappa, having won her key as a philosophy major at Dillon University, in Dodge City, Kansas. That was where she and Fred had met, in Dodge City, in a U.S.O. Fred had been stationed at Fort Riley during the Korean War. She married Fred because she thought everybody who lived in Pisquontuit and had been to Princeton was rich.

She was humiliated to discover that it was not true. She honestly believed that she was an intellectual, but she knew almost nothing, and every problem she ever considered could be solved by just one thing: money, and lots of it. She was a frightful housekeeper. She cried when she did housework, because she was convinced that she was cut out for better things.

As for the Lesbian business, it wasn't particularly deep on Caroline's part. She was simply a female chameleon trying to get ahead in the world.

•   •   •

"Lunch with Amanita again?" Fred whinnied.

"Why not?"

"This gets to be damn expensive, fancy lunches every day."

"It isn't every day. It's twice a week at the very most." She was brittle and cold.

"It's still a hell of an expense, Caroline."

Caroline held out a white-gloved hand for money. "It's worth it to your wife."

Fred gave her money.

Caroline did not thank Fred. She left, took her place on a fawn-colored cushion of glove leather, next to the fragrant Amanita Buntline in Amanita's powder-blue Mercedes *300-SL.*

Harry Pena looked at Fred's chalky face appraisingly. He made no comment. He lit a cigar, departed—went fishing for real fish with his two real sons—in a real boat on a salty sea.

• • •

Lila, the daughter of Amanita Buntline, sat on the cold floor of the news store, reading Henry Miller's *Tropic of Cancer,* which, along with William Burroughs' *Naked Lunch,* she had taken from the Lazy Susan book rack. Lila's interest in the books was commercial. At thirteen, she was Pisquontuit's leading dealer in smut.

She was a dealer in fireworks, too, for the same reason she was a dealer in smut, which was: *Profit.* Her playmates at the Pisquontuit Yacht Club and Pisquontuit Country Day School were so rich and foolish that they would pay her almost anything for almost anything. In a routine business day, she might sell a seventy-five-cent copy of *Lady Chatterley's Lover* for ten dollars and a fifteen-cent cherry bomb for five.

She bought her fireworks during family vacations in Canada and Florida and Hong Kong. Most of her smut came from the open stock of the news store. The thing was, Lila knew which titles were red hot, which was more than her playmates or the employees of the news store knew. And Lila bought the hot ones as fast as they were tucked into the Lazy Susan. All her transactions were with the idiot behind the lunch counter, who forgot everything faster than it could happen.

The relationship between Lila and the news store was wonderfully symbiotic, for hanging in the store's front window was a large medallion of gilded polystyrene, awarded by the *Rhode Island Mothers to Save Children from Filth.* Representatives of that group inspected the store's paperback selection regularly. The polystyrene medallion was their admission that they had not found one filthy thing.

They thought that their children were safe, but the truth was that Lila had cornered the market.

There was one sort of smut that Lila could not buy at the

news store—dirty pictures. She got them by doing what Fred Rosewater had so often lusted weakly to do—by answering raunchy ads in *The American Investigator.*

• • •

Large feet now intruded into her childish world on the news store floor. They were the feet of Fred Rosewater.

Lila did not conceal her red-hot books. She went on reading, as though *Tropic of Cancer* were *Heidi:*

The trunk is open and her things are lying around everywhere just as before. She lies down on the bed with her clothes on. Once, twice, three times, four times . . . I'm afraid she'll go mad . . . in bed, under the blankets, how good to feel her body again! But for how long? Will it last this time? Already I have a presentiment that it won't.

Lila and Fred often met between the books and magazines. Fred never asked her what she was reading. And she knew he would do what he always did—would look with sad hunger at the covers of girly magazines, then pick up and open something as fat and domestic as *Better Homes and Gardens.* This is precisely what he did now.

"I guess my wife is out to lunch with your Mummy again," said Fred.

"I guess she is," said Lila. That ended the conversation, but Lila continued to think about Fred. She was on level with the Rosewater shins. She thought about them. Whenever she saw Fred in shorts or a bathing suit, his shins were covered with scars and scabs, as though he had been kicked and kicked and kicked every day of his life. Lila thought that maybe it was a vitamin deficiency that made Fred's shins look like that, or mange.

• • •

Fred's gory shins were victims of his wife's interior decorating scheme, which called for an almost schizophrenic use of little tables, dozens of them all through the house. Each little table had its own ashtray and dish of dusty after-dinner mints, although the Rosewaters never entertained. And Caroline was forever rearranging the tables, as though for this kind of party one day and another the next. So poor Fred was forever barking his shins on the tables.

One time Fred had had a deep cut on his chin that required eleven stitches. That fall hadn't been caused by all the little tables. It had been caused by an object that Caroline never put away. The object was always in evidence, like a pet anteater with a penchant for sleeping in doorways or on the staircase, or on the hearth.

That object, the one Fred had fallen over and cut his chin on, was Caroline Rosewater's *Electrolux.* Subconsciously, Caroline had sworn to herself that she would never put the vacuum cleaner away until she was rich.

• • •

Fred, thinking Lila wasn't paying any attention to him, now put down *Better Homes and Gardens,* picked up what looked like one hell of a sexy paperback novel, *Venus on the Half-shell,* by Kilgore Trout. On the back cover was an abridgment of a red-hot scene inside. It went like this:

Queen Margaret of the planet Shaltoon let her gown fall to the floor. She was wearing nothing underneath. Her high, firm, uncowled bosom was proud and rosy. Her hips and thighs were like an inviting lyre of pure alabaster. They shone so whitely they might have had a light inside. 'Your travels are over, Space Wanderer,' she whispered, her voice husky with lust. 'Seek no more, for you have found. The answer is in my arms.'

'It's a glorious answer, Queen Margaret, God knows,' the Space Wanderer replied. His palms were perspiring profusely. 'I am going to accept it gratefully. But I have to tell you, if I'm going to be perfectly honest with you, that I will have to be on my way again tomorrow.'

'But you have found your answer, you have found your answer,' she cried, and she forced his head between her fragrant young breasts.

He said something that she did not hear. She thrust him out at arm's length. 'What was that you said?'

'I said, Queen Margaret, that what you offer is an awfully good answer. It just doesn't happen to be the one I'm primarily looking for.'

There was a photograph of Trout. He was an old man with a full black beard. He looked like a frightened, aging Jesus, whose sentence to crucifixion had been commuted to imprisonment for life.

10

Lila Buntline pedalled her bicycle through the muffled beauty of Pisquontuit's Utopian lanes. Every house she passed was a very expensive dream come true. The owners of the houses did not have to work at all. Neither would their children have to work, nor want for a thing, unless somebody revolted. Nobody seemed about to.

Lila's handsome house was on the harborfront. It was Georgian. She went inside, put down her new books in the hallway, stole into her father's study to make certain that her father, who was lying on his couch, was still alive. It was a thing she did at least once every day.

"Father—?"

The morning's mail was on a silver platter on a table at his head. Next to it was an untouched Scotch and soda. Its bubbles were dead. Stewart Buntline wasn't forty yet. He was the best looking man in town, a cross, somebody once said, between Cary Grant and a German shepherd. On his lean midsection lay a fifty-seven-dollar book, a railroad atlas of the Civil War, which his wife had given to him. That was his only enthusiasm in life, the Civil War.

"Daddy—"

Stewart snoozed on. His father had left him fourteen million dollars, tobacco money mostly. That money, churned and fertilized and hybridized and transmogrified in the hydroponic money farm of the Trust Department of the New England Seafarer's Bank and Trust Company of Boston, had increased by about eight hundred thousand dollars a year since it had been put in Stewart's name. Business seemed to be pretty good. Other than that, Stewart didn't know much about business.

Sometimes, when pressed to give his business views, he would declare roundly that he liked *Polaroid*. People seemed to find this vivid, that he should like *Polaroid* so much. Actually, he didn't know if he owned any *Polaroid* or not. The bank took care of things like that—the bank and the law firm of McAllister, Robjent, Reed and McGee.

"Daddy—"

"Mf?"

"I wanted to make sure you—you were all right," said Lila.

"Yup," he said. He couldn't be positive about it. He opened his eyes a little, licked his dry lips. "Fine, Sweetheart."

"You can go back to sleep now."

Stewart did.

• • •

There was no reason for him not to sleep soundly, for he was represented by the same law firm that represented Senator Rosewater, and had been since he was orphaned at the age of sixteen. The partner who looked after him was Reed McAllister. Old McAllister had enclosed a piece of literature with his last letter. It was called, "A Rift Between Friends in the War of Ideas," a pamphlet published by the Pine Tree Press of the Freedom School, Box 165, Colorado Springs, Colorado. This was now serving as a bookmark in the railroad atlas.

Old McAllister generally enclosed material about creeping socialism as opposed to free enterprise, because, some twenty years before, Stewart had come into his office, a wild-eyed young man, had announced that the free enterprise system was wrong, and that he wanted to give all his money to the poor. McAllister had talked the rash young man out of it, but he continued to worry about Stewart's having a relapse. The pamphlets were prophylaxis.

McAllister needn't have bothered. Drunk or sober, pamphlets or not, Stewart was irrevocably committed to free enterprise now. He did not require the bucking up in "A Rift Between Friends in the War of Ideas," which was supposedly a letter from a conservative to close friends who were socialists without knowing it. Because he did not need to, Stewart had not read what the pamphlet had to say about the recipients of social security and other forms of welfare, which was this:

Have we really helped these people? Look at them well. Consider this specimen who is the end result of our pity! What can we say to this third generation of people to whom welfare has long since become a way of life? Observe carefully our handiwork whom we have spawned and are spawning by the millions, even in times of plenty!

They do not work and will not. Heads down, unmindful, they have neither pride nor self-respect. They are totally unreliable, not maliciously so, but like cattle who wander aimlessly. Foresight and the ability to reason have simply atrophied from long neglect. Talk to them, listen to them, work with them as I do and you realize with a kind of dull horror that they have lost all semblance of human beings except that they stand on two feet and talk—like parrots. "More. Give me more. I need more," are the only new thoughts they have learned. . . .

They stand today as a monumental caricature of Homo sapiens, the harsh and horrible reality created by us out of our own misguided pity. They are also, if we continue our present course, the living prophecy of what a great percentage of the rest of us will become.

And so on.

These sentiments were coals to Newcastle as far as Stewart Buntline was concerned. He was through with misguided pity. He was through with sex, too. And, if the truth be told, he was fed to the teeth with the Civil War.

• • •

The conversation with McAllister that had set Stewart on the path of conservatism twenty years before was this:

"So you want to be a saint, do you, young man?"

"I didn't say that, and I hope I didn't imply it. You are in charge of what I inherited, money I did nothing to earn?"

"I'll answer the first part of your question: Yes, we are in charge of what you inherited. In reply to the second part: If you haven't earned it yet, you will, you shall. You come from a family that is congenitally unable to fail to earn its way and then some. You'll lead, my boy, because you were born to lead, and that can be hell."

"That may or may not be, Mr. McAllister. We'll have to wait and see about that. What I'm telling you now is: This world is full of suffering, and money can do a lot to relieve that suffering, and I have far more money than I can use. I want to buy decent food and clothing and housing for the poor, and right away."

"And, after you've done that, what would you like to be called, 'St. Stewart' or 'St. Buntline'?"

"I didn't come here to be made fun of."

"And your father didn't name us your guardians in his will because he thought we would agree politely with anything you might say. If I strike you as impudent and irreverent on the subject of would-be saints, it's because I've been through this same silly argument with so many young people before. One of the principal activities of this firm is the prevention of saintliness on the part of our clients. You think you're unusual? You're not.

"Every year at least one young man whose affairs we manage comes into our office, wants to give his money away. He has completed his first year at some great university. It has been an eventful year! He has learned of unbelievable suffering around the world. He has learned of the great crimes that are at the roots of so many family fortunes. He has had his Christian nose rubbed, often for the very first time, in the Sermon on the Mount.

"He is confused, tearful, angry! He demands to know, in hollow tones, how much money he is worth. We tell him. He goes haggard with shame, even if his fortune is based on something as honest and useful as Scotch Tape, aspirin, rugged pants for the working man, or, as in your case, brooms. You have, if I'm not mistaken, just completed one year at Harvard?"

"Yes."

"It's a great institution, but, when I see the effect it has on certain young people, I ask myself, 'How dare a university teach compassion without teaching history, too?' History tells us this, my dear young Mr. Buntline, if it tells us nothing else: Giving away a fortune is a futile and destructive thing. It makes whiners of the poor, without making them rich or even comfortable. And the donor and his descendents become undistinguished members of the whining poor."

• • •

"A personal fortune as great as yours, Mr. Buntline," old McAllister went on, those many fateful years ago, "is a miracle, thrilling and rare. You have come by it effortlessly, and so have little opportunity to learn what it is. In order to help you learn something about its miraculousness, I have to offer what is perhaps an insult. Here it is, like it or not: Your fortune is the most important single determinant of what you think of yourself and of what others think of you. Because of the money, you are extraordinary. Without it, for example, you would not now be taking the priceless time of a senior partner in McAllister, Robjent, Reed and McGee.

"If you give away your money, you will become utterly ordinary, unless you happen to be a genius. You aren't a genius, are you, Mr. Buntline?"

"No."

"Um. And, genius or not, without money you'll surely be less comfortable and free. Not only that, but you will be volunteering your descendents for the muggy, sorehead way of life peculiar to persons who might have been rich and free, had not a soft-headed ancestor piddled a fortune away.

"Cling to your miracle, Mr. Buntline. Money is dehydrated Utopia. This is a dog's life for almost everybody, as your professors have taken such pains to point out. But, because of your miracle, life for you and yours can be a paradise! Let me see you smile! Let me see that you already understand what they do not teach at Harvard until the junior year: That to be born rich and to stay rich is something less than a felony."

• • •

Lila, Stewart's daughter, now went upstairs to her bedroom. The color scheme, selected by her mother, was pink and frost. Her casement windows looked out on the harbor, on the nodding Pisquontuit Yacht Club fleet.

A forty-foot workboat named *Mary* was chugging her graceless, smoky way through the fleet, rocking the playthings. The playthings had names like *Scomber* and *Skat* and *Rosebud II* and *Follow Me* and *Red Dog* and *Bunty*. *Rosebud II* belonged to Fred and Caroline Rosewater. *Bunty* belonged to Stewart and Amanita Buntline.

Mary belonged to Harry Pena, the trap fisherman. She was a gray, lapstreak tub whose purpose was to wallow home in all weather with tons of fresh fish on board. There wasn't any shelter on her, except for a wooden box to keep the big new Chrysler dry. The wheel and the throttle and the clutch were mounted on the box. All the rest of the *Mary* was a bare-boned tub.

Harry was on his way to his traps. His two big sons, Manny and Kenny, lay head-to-head in the bow, murmuring in lazy lechery. Each boy had a six-foot tuna gaff beside him. Harry was armed with a twelve-pound mall. All three wore rubber aprons and boots. When they got to work, they would bathe in gore.

"Stop talking about fucking," said Harry. "Think about fish."

"We will, old man, when we're as old as you." This was a deeply affectionate reply.

• • •

An airplane came over very low, making its approach to Providence Airport. On board, reading *The Conscience of a Conservative*, was Norman Mushari.

• • •

The world's largest private collection of harpoons was displayed in a restaurant called *The Weir*, which was five miles outside of Pisquontuit. The marvellous collection belonged to a tall homosexual from New Bedford named Bunny Weeks. Until Bunny came down from New Bedford and opened his restaurant, Pisquontuit had nothing to do with whaling —ever.

Bunny called his place *The Weir* because its Thermopane windows on the south looked out at the fish traps of Harry Pena. There were opera glasses on each table, in order that guests might watch Harry and his boys clean out their traps. And when the fisherfolk were performing out there on the briny deep, Bunny went from table to table, explaining with gusto and *expertise* what they were doing, and why. While disserting, he would paw women shamelessly, would never touch a man.

If guests wished to participate even more vibrantly in the fishing business, they might order a *Horse Mackerel Cocktail*, which was rum, grenadine, and cranberry juice, or a *Fisherman's*

Salad, which was a peeled banana thrust through a pineapple ring, set in a nest of chilled, creamed tuna and curly coconut shreds.

Harry Pena and his boys knew about the salad and the cocktail and the opera glasses, though they had never visited *The Weir*. Sometimes they would respond to their involuntary involvement with the restaurant by urinating off the boat. They called this ". . . *making cream of leek soup for Bunny Weeks.*"

• • •

Bunny Weeks' harpoon collection lay across the rude rafters of the gift shop that constituted the opulently mouldy entrance to *The Weir*. The shop itself was called *The Jolly Whaler*. There was a dusty skylight over the shop, the dusty effect having been achieved by spraying on *Jet-Spray Bon Ami*, and never wiping it off. The lattice of rafters and harpoons underneath the skylight was projected onto the merchandise below. The effect that Bunny had created was that real whalers, smelling of blubber and rum and sweat and ambergris, had stored their equipment in his loft. They would be coming back for it at any time.

It was through the criss-crossed shadows of harpoons that Amanita Buntline and Caroline Rosewater now shuffled. Amanita led the way, set the tone, examined the stock greedily, barbarously. As for the nature of the stock: it was everything a cold bitch might demand of an impotent husband upon rising from a scalding bath.

Caroline's manner was a wispy echo of Amanita's. Caroline was made clumsy by the fact that Amanita was forever between her and whatever seemed worth examining. The moment Amanita stopped looking at something, moved from between it and Caroline, the object somehow stopped being worth examining. Caroline was made clumsy by other facts, too, of course —that her husband worked, that she was wearing a dress that everybody knew had been Amanita's, that she had very little money in her purse.

Caroline now heard her own voice saying, as though from afar, "He certainly has good taste."

"They all do," said Amanita. "I'd rather go shopping with one than with a woman. Present company excepted, of course."

"What is it that makes them so artistic?"

"They're more sensitive, dear. They're like *us*. They *feel*."

"Oh."

•   •   •

Bunny Weeks now loped into *The Jolly Whaler*, his Topsiders squeaking as they squeegeed. He was a slender man in his early thirties. He had eyes that were standard equipment for rich American fairies—junk jewelry eyes, synthetic star sapphires with winking Christmas-tree lights behind them. Bunny was the great grandson of the famous Captain Hannibal Weeks of New Bedford, the man who finally killed Moby Dick. No less than seven of the irons resting on the rafters overhead were said to have come from the hide of the Great White Whale.

"Amanita! Amanita!" Bunny cried fondly. He threw his arms around her, hugged her hard. "How's my girl?"

Amanita laughed.

"Something's funny?"

"Not to *me*."

"I've been hoping you'd come in today. I have a little intelligence test for you." He wanted to show her a new piece of merchandise, have her guess what it was. He hadn't greeted Caroline yet, was now obliged to do so, for she was standing between him and where he thought the object he wanted was. "Excuse me."

"I beg your pardon." Caroline Rosewater stepped aside. Bunny never seemed to remember her name, though she had been in *The Weir* at least fifty times.

Bunny failed to find what he was looking for, wheeled to search elsewhere, again found Caroline in his way. "Excuse me."

"Excuse *me*." Caroline, in getting out of his way, tripped on a cunning little milking stool, went down with one knee on the stool and both hands grasping a post.

"Oh my God!" said Bunny, annoyed with her. "Are you all right? Here! Here!" He hoisted her up, and did it in such a way that her feet kept slipping out from under her, as though she were wearing roller skates for the first time. "Are you hurt?"

Caroline smiled sloppily. "Just my dignity is all."

"Oh, the hell with your dignity, dear," he said, and he cast himself very strongly as another woman when he said it. "How are your *bones*? How are your little *insides*?"

"Fine—thank you."

Bunny turned his back on her, resumed his search.

"You remember Caroline Rosewater, of course," said Amanita. It was a cruelly unnecessary thing to ask.

"Of course I remember Mrs. Rosewater," said Bunny. "Any relation to the Senator?"

"You always ask me that."

"Do I? And what do you always reply?"

"I think so—somehow—way far back—I'm almost sure."

"How interesting. He's resigning, you know."

"He is?"

Bunny faced her again. He now had a box in his hands. "Didn't he *tell* you he was going to resign?"

"No—he—"

"You don't *communicate* with him?"

"No," said Caroline bleakly, her chin pulled in.

"I'd think he'd be a very fascinating man to *communicate* with."

Caroline nodded. "Yes."

"But you don't communicate."

"No."

• • •

"Now then, my dear—" said Bunny, placing himself before Amanita and opening the box, "here is your intelligence test." He took from the box, which was marked "Product of Mexico," a large tin can with one end removed. The can was covered with gay wallpaper both inside and out. Glued to the unopened end was a round lace doily, and glued to the doily was an artificial water lily. "I defy you to tell me what this is for. If you tell me, and this is a seventeen-dollar item, I will give it to you free, grotesquely rich though I know you are."

"Can *I* guess, too?" said Caroline.

Bunny closed his eyes. "Of course," he whispered tiredly.

Amanita gave up at once, announcing proudly that she was dumb, that she despised tests. Caroline was about to make a chirping, bright-eyed, birdy guess, but Bunny didn't give her a chance.

"It's a cover for a spare roll of toilet paper!" said Bunny.

"That's what I was *going* to guess," said Caroline.

"Were you now?" said Bunny apathetically.

"She's a *Phi Beta Kappa*," said Amanita.

"Are you now?" said Bunny.

"Yes," said Caroline. "I don't talk about it much. I don't think about it much."

"Nor do I," said Bunny.

"You're a *Phi Beta Kappa*, too?"

"Do you mind?"

"No."

"As clubs go," said Bunny, "I've found it's a rather big one."

"Um."

"Do you like this thing, little genius?" Amanita asked Caroline, speaking of the toilet paper cover.

"Yes—it's—it's very pretty. It's sweet."

"Do you want it?"

"For seventeen *dollars*?" said Caroline. "It *is* darling." She became mournful about being poor. "Some day, maybe. Some day."

"Why not today?" asked Amanita.

"You know why not today." Caroline blushed.

"What if I were to buy it for you?"

"You mustn't! Seventeen dollars!"

"If you don't stop worrying about money so much, little bird, I'm going to have to find some other friend."

"What can I *say*?"

"Wrap it as a gift, please, Bunny."

"Oh, Amanita, thank you so much," said Caroline.

"It's no more than you deserve."

"Thank you."

"People get what they deserve," said Amanita. "Isn't that right, Bunny?"

"That's the First Law of Life," said Bunny Weeks.

• • •

The work boat called the *Mary* now reached the traps she served, came into view for the many drinkers and diners in the restaurant of Bunny Weeks.

"Drop your cocks and grab your socks," Harry Pena called to his snoozing sons.

He killed the engine. The momentum of the *Mary* carried

her through the gate of a trap, into a ring of long poles festooned with net.

"Smell 'em?" he said. He was asking if his sons smelled all the big fish in the net.

The sons sniffed, said they did.

The big belly of the net, which might or might not hold fish, lay on the bottom. The rim of the net was in air, running from pole-tip to pole-tip in lank parabolas. The rim dipped under water at only one point. That point was the gate. It was also the mouth that would feed fish, if any, into the big belly of the net.

Now Harry himself was inside the trap. He untied a line from a cleat by the gate, hoisted away, lifted the mouth of the net into air, tied the line to the cleat again. There was no way out of the belly now—not for fish. For fish it was a bowl of doom.

The *Mary* rubbed herself gently against one side of the bowl. Harry and his sons, all in a row, reached into the sea with iron hands, pulled net into air, fed it back to the sea.

Hand-over-hand, the three were making smaller, ever smaller, the place where fish could be. And, as that place grew ever smaller, the *Mary* crept sideways across the surface of the bowl.

No one spoke. It was a magic time. Even the gulls fell silent as the three, purified of all thought, hauled net from the sea.

• • •

The only place where the fish could be became an oval pool. A seeming shower of dimes flashed in the depths, and that was all. The men kept working, hand-over-hand.

The only place where the fish could be now became a curving trough, a deep one, alongside the *Mary*. It now became a shallower trough as the three men continued to work, hand-over-hand. The father and the two sons paused. A goosefish, a prehistoric monstrosity, a ten-pound tadpole studded with chancres and warts, came to the surface, opened its needle-filled mouth, surrendered. And around the goosefish, the brainless, inedible horror of cartilage, the surface of the sea was blooming with dimpled humps. Big animals were in the dark below.

Harry and his two big sons set to work again, hand-over-hand, pulling in net and feeding it back. There was almost nowhere for the fish to be. Paradoxically, the surface of the sea became mirror-like.

And then the fin of a tuna slit the mirror, was gone again.

• • •

In the fish trap moments later there was joyful, bloody hell. Eight big tuna were making the water heave, boil, split and roll. They shot past the *Mary*, were turned by the net, shot past again.

Harry's boys grabbed their gaffs. The younger boy thrust his hook underwater, jerked the hook into the belly of a fish, stopped the fish, turned it on a point of pure agony.

The fish came drifting alongside, languid with shock, avoiding any motion that might make the agony worse.

Harry's younger boy gave the hook a wrenching yank. The new, deeper agony made the fish walk on his tail, topple into the *Mary* with a rubbery crash.

Harry slammed the head of the fish with his mighty mall. The fish lay still.

And another fish came crashing in. Harry slammed it on the head, too—and slammed another and another, until eight great fish lay dead.

Harry laughed, wiped his nose on his sleeve. "Son of a bitch, boys! Son of a bitch!"

The boys laughed back. All three were as satisfied with life as men can ever be.

The youngest boy thumbed his nose at the fairy's restaurant.

"Fuck 'em all, boys. Right?" said Harry.

• • •

Bunny came to Amanita's and Caroline's table, jingled his slave bracelet, put his hand on Amanita's shoulder, remained standing. Caroline took the opera glasses from her eyes, said a depressing thing. "It's so much like life. Harry Pena is so much like God."

"Like God?" Bunny was amused.

"You don't see what I mean?"

"I'm sure the fish do. I don't happen to be a fish. I'll tell you what I *am*, though."

"Please—not while we're eating," said Amanita.

Bunny gave a crippled little chuckle, went on with his thought. "I *am* a director of a bank."

"What's that got to do with anything?" Amanita inquired.

"You find out who's broke and who isn't. And, if that's God out there, I hate to tell you, but God is bankrupt."

Amanita and Caroline expressed, each in her own way, disbelief that a man that virile could ever have a business failure. While they were twittering in this wise, Bunny's hand tightened on Amanita's shoulder to the point where she complained. "You're hurting me."

"Sorry. Didn't know it was possible."

"Bastard."

"Might as well be." And the hand bit hard again. "That's all over," he said, meaning Harry and his sons. The pulsing pressure of his hand let Amanita know that he wanted very much for her to keep her mouth shut for a change, that he was being serious for a change. "Real people don't make their livings that way any more. Those three romantics out there make as much sense as Marie Antoinette and her milkmaids. When the bankruptcy proceedings begin—in a week, a month, a year—they'll find out that their only economic value was as animated wallpaper for my restaurant here." Bunny, to his credit, was not happy about this. "That's all over, men working with their hands and backs. They are not needed."

"Men like Harry will always win, won't they?" said Caroline.

"They're losing everywhere." Bunny let go of Amanita. He looked around his restaurant, invited Amanita to do so, too, to help him count the house. He invited them, moreover, to despise his customers as much as he did. Almost all were inheritors. Almost all were beneficiaries of boodles and laws that had nothing to do with wisdom or work.

Four stupid, silly, fat widows in furs laughed over a bathroom joke on a paper cocktail napkin.

"And look who's winning. And look who's won."

11

N ORMAN MUSHARI rented a red convertible at the Providence Airport, drove eighteen miles to Pisquontuit to find Fred Rosewater. As far as Mushari's employers knew, he was in his apartment in Washington, sick in bed. On the contrary, he felt very good.

He didn't find Fred all afternoon, for the not very simple reason that Fred was asleep on his sailboat, a secret thing Fred often did on warm days. There was never much doing in life insurance for poor people on warm afternoons.

Fred would row out to his mooring in a little yacht club dinghy, *scree-scraw, scree-scraw*, with three inches of freeboard all around. And he would transfer his bulk to *Rosebud II*, and lie down in the cockpit, out of sight, with his head on an orange lifejacket. He would listen to the lapping of the water, the clinking and creaking of the rigging, put one hand on his genitals, feel at one with God, go to sleepy-bye. That much was lovely.

• • •

The Buntlines had a young upstairs maid named Selena Deal, who knew Fred's secret. One little window in her bedroom looked out on the fleet. When she sat on her narrow bed and wrote, as she was doing now, her window framed the *Rosebud II*. Her door was ajar, so she could hear the telephone ring. That was all she had to do during the afternoons, usually —answer the telephone in case it rang. It seldom rang, and, as Selena asked herself, "Why would it?"

She was eighteen years old. She was an orphan from an orphanage that had been founded by the Buntline family in Pawtucket in 1878. When it was founded, the Buntlines required three things: That all orphans be raised as Christians, regardless of race, color, or creed, that they take an oath once a week, before Sunday supper, and that, each year, an intelligent, clean female orphan enter domestic service in a Buntline home,

. . . in order to learn about the better things in life, and perhaps to be inspired to climb a few rungs of the ladder of culture and social grace.

The oath, which Selena had taken six hundred times, before six hundred very plain suppers, went like this, and was written by Castor Buntline, poor old Stewart's great-grandfather:

I do solemnly swear that I will respect the sacred private property of others, and that I will be content with whatever station in life God Almighty may assign me to. I will be grateful to those who employ me, and will never complain about wages and hours, but will ask myself instead, "What more can I do for my employer, my republic, and my God?" I understand that I have not been placed on Earth to be happy. I am here to be tested. If I am to pass the test, I must be always unselfish, always sober, always truthful, always chaste in mind, body, and deed, and always respectful to those to whom God has, in His Wisdom, placed above me. If I pass the test, I will go to joy everlasting in Heaven when I die. If I fail, I shall roast in hell while the Devil laughs and Jesus weeps.

• • •

Selena, a pretty girl who played the piano beautifully and wanted to be a nurse, was writing to the head of the orphan-age, a man named Wilfred Parrot. Parrot was sixty. He had done a lot of interesting things in his life, such as fighting in Spain in the Abraham Lincoln Brigade and, from 1933 until 1936, writing a radio serial called "Beyond the Blue Horizon." He ran a happy orphanage. All of the children called him "Daddy," and all of the children could cook and dance and play some musical instrument and paint.

Selena had been with the Buntlines a month. She was sup-posed to stay a year. This is what she wrote:

Dear Daddy Parrot: Maybe things will get better here, but I don't see how. Mrs. Buntline and I don't get along very well. She keeps saying I am ungrateful and impertinent. I don't mean to be, but I guess maybe I am. I just hope she doesn't get so mad at me she turns against the orphanage. That is the big thing I worry about. I am just going to have to try harder to obey the oath. What goes wrong all the time is things she sees in my eyes. I can't keep those things out of my eyes. She says something or does something I think is kind of dumb or pitiful or something, and I don't say anything about it, but she looks in my eyes and gets very mad. One time she told me that music was the most important thing in her life, next to her husband and her daughter. They have loudspeakers all over the house, all connected to a big phonograph in the front coat closet. There is music all day long, and Mrs. Buntline said what she enjoyed more than anything was picking out a musical program at the start of every day, and loading it into the record changer. This morning there was music coming out of all the loudspeakers, and it didn't sound like any music I had ever heard before. It was very high and fast and twittery, and Mrs. Buntline was humming along with it, rocking her head from side to side to show me how much she loved it. It was driving me crazy. And then her best friend, a woman named Mrs. Rosewater, came over, and she said how much she loved the music, too. She said someday, when her ship came in, she would have beautiful music all the time, too. I finally broke down and asked Mrs. Buntline what on earth it was. "Why, my dear child," she said, "that is none other than the immortal Beethoven." "Beethoven!" I said. "Have you ever heard of him before?" she said. "Yes, mam, I have. Daddy Parrot played Beethoven all the time back at the orphanage, but it didn't sound like that." So she took me in where the phonograph was, and she said, "Very well, I will prove it is Beethoven. I have loaded the changer with nothing but Beethoven. Every so often I just go on a Beethoven binge." "I just adore Beethoven, too," Mrs. Rosewater said. Mrs. Buntline told me to look at what was in the record changer and tell her whether it was Beethoven or not. It was. She had loaded the changer with all nine symphonies, but that poor woman had them playing at 78 revolutions per minute instead of 33, and she couldn't tell the difference. I told her about it, Daddy. I had to tell her, didn't I? I was very polite, but I must have gotten that look in my eyes, because she got very mad, and she made me go out and clean up the chauffeur's lavatory in the back of the garage. Actually, it wasn't a very dirty job. They haven't had a chauffeur for years.

• • •

Another time, Daddy, she took me out to watch a sailboat race in Mr. Buntline's big motorboat. I asked to go. I said all anybody ever seemed to talk about in Pisquontuit was sailboat races. I said I would like to see what was so wonderful about them. Her daughter Lila was racing that day. Lila is the best sailer in town. You should see all the cups she has won. They are the main decorations of the house. There aren't any pictures to speak of. A neighbor has a Picasso, but I heard him say he would a lot rather have a daughter who could sail like Lila. I don't think it makes much difference one way or another, but

I didn't say so. Believe me, Daddy, I don't say half the things I could. Anyway, we went out to see this sailboat race, and I wish you could have heard the way Mrs. Buntline yelled and swore. You remember the things Arthur Gonsalves used to say? Mrs. Buntline used words that would have been news to Arthur. I never saw a woman get so excited and mad. She just forgot I was there. She looked like a witch with the rabies. You would have thought the fate of the universe was being decided by those sunburned children in those pretty little white boats. She finally remembered me, and she realized she had said some things that didn't sound very good. "You've got to understand why we're all so excited right now," she said. "Lila has two legs on the Commodore's Cup." "Oh," I said, "that explains everything." I swear, Daddy, that's all I said, but there must have been that look in my eyes.

What gets me most about these people, Daddy, isn't how ignorant they are, or how much they drink. It's the way they have of thinking that everything nice in the world is a gift to the poor people from them or their ancestors. The first afternoon I was here, Mrs. Buntline made me come out on the back porch and look at the sunset. So I did, and I said I liked it very much, but she kept waiting for me to say something else. I couldn't think of what else I was supposed to say, so I said what seemed liked a dumb thing. "Thank you very much," I said. That was exactly what she was waiting for. "You're entirely welcome," she said. I have since thanked her for the ocean, the moon, the stars in the sky, and the United States Constitution.

Maybe I am just too wicked and dumb to realize how wonderful Pisquontuit really is. Maybe this is a case of pearls before swine, but I don't see how. I am homesick. Write soon. I love you.

Selena

P.S. Who really does run this crazy country? These creeps sure don't.

Norman Mushari killed the afternoon by driving over to Newport, paid a quarter to tour the famous Rumfoord Mansion. The queer thing about the tour was that the Rumfoords were still living there, and glaring at all comers. Moreover, they didn't need the money, God knows.

Mushari was sufficiently offended by the way that Lance Rumfoord, who was six feet eight inches tall, sneered whinnyingly at him, that he complained about it to a family servant who was guiding the tour. "If they hate the public so much," said Mushari, "they shouldn't invite them in and take their money."

This failed to gain the sympathy of the servant, who explained with acrid fatalism that the estate was open to the public for only one day out of every five years. This was required by a will now three generations old.

"Why would a will say that?"

"It was the feeling of the founder of this estate that it would be in the best interests of those living within these walls to periodically take a sampling of the sorts of people who were appearing at random outside of them." He looked Mushari up and down. "You might call it keeping up with current events. You know?"

As Mushari was leaving the estate, Lance Rumfoord came loping after him. Predatorily genial, he towered over little Mushari, explained that his mother considered herself a great judge of character, and had made the guess that Mushari had once served in the United States Infantry.

"No."

"Really? She so seldom misses. She said specifically that you had been a sniper."

"No."

Lance shrugged. "If not in this life, in some other one, then." And he sneered and whinnied again.

• • •

Sons of suicides often think of killing themselves at the end of a day, when their blood sugar is low. And so it was with Fred Rosewater when he came home from work. He nearly fell over the Electrolux in the living room archway, caught his balance with a quick stride, barked his shin on a little table, knocked the mints on the table to the floor. He got down on his hands and knees and picked them up.

He knew his wife was home, for the record-player Amanita had given to her for her birthday was going. She only owned five records, and they were all in the changer. They were her bonus for joining a record club. She had gone through hell, selecting five free records from a list of one hundred. The five she finally chose were *Come Dance With Me*, by Frank Sinatra, *A Mighty Fortress Is Our God, and Other Sacred Selections*, by the Mormon Tabernacle Choir; *It's a Long Way to Tipperary and Others*, by the Soviet Army Chorus and Band, *The New World Symphony*, conducted by Leonard Bernstein, and *Poems of Dylan Thomas*, read by Richard Burton.

The Burton record was playing as Fred picked up the mints.

Fred stood up, swayed. There were bells in his ears. There were spots before his eyes. He went into the bedroom, found his wife asleep in bed with her clothes on. She was drunk, and full of chicken and mayonnaise, as she always was after a luncheon with Amanita. Fred tiptoed out again, thought of hanging himself from a pipe in the cellar.

But then he remembered his son. He heard a toilet flush, so that was where little Franklin was, in the bathroom. He went into Franklin's bedroom to wait for him. It was the only room in the house where Fred felt really comfortable. The shades were drawn, which was mildly puzzling, since there was no reason for the boy to exclude the last of the daylight, and there were no neighbors to peep in.

The only light came from a curious lamp on the bedside table. The lamp consisted of a plaster statuette of a blacksmith who had his hammer raised. There was a pane of frosted orange glass behind the blacksmith. And behind the glass was an electric bulb, and over the bulb was a little tin windmill. Hot air rising from the bulb caused the windmill to turn. The bright surfaces of the turning mill made the light playing on the orange glass flicker, made it look a lot like real fire.

There was a story that went with the lamp. It was thirty-three years old. The company that made the lamps had been Fred's father's very last speculation.

•   •   •

Fred thought of taking a lot of sleeping pills, remembered his son again. He looked about the weirdly illuminated room for something to talk to the boy about, saw the corner of a photograph sticking out from under the pillow on the bed. Fred pulled it into the open, thinking it was probably a picture of some sports hero, or maybe a picture of Fred himself at the helm of the *Rosebud II.*

But it turned out to be a pornographic picture that little Franklin had bought that morning from Lila Buntline, using money he earned himself on his paper route. It showed two fat, simpering, naked whores, one of whom was attempting to have impossible sexual congress with a dignified, decent, unsmiling Shetland pony.

•   •   •

Sickened, confused, Fred put the picture into his pocket, stumbled out into the kitchen, wondered what, in God's name, to say.

About the kitchen: an electric chair would not have seemed out of place in it. It was Caroline's idea of a place of torment. There was a philodendron. It had died of thirst. In the soap-dish on the sink was a mottled ball of soap made out of many moistened slivers pressed together. Making soap balls out of slivers was the only household art Caroline had brought to marriage. It was a thing her mother had taught her to do.

Fred thought of filling the bathtub with hot water, of climbing in and slashing his wrists with a stainless steel razorblade. But then he saw that the little plastic garbage can in the corner was full, knew how hysterical Caroline became if she got up from a drunken sleep and found that no one had carried out the garbage. So he carried it to the garage and dumped it, then washed out the can with the hose at the side of the house.

"Frusha-frusha-blacka-blacka-burl," said the water in the can. And Fred saw that someone had left the light on in the cellar. He looked down through the dusty window in an areaway, saw the top of the jelly cupboard. Resting on it was the family history his father had written—a history that Fred had never wished to read. There was also a can of rat poison there, and a thirty-eight-calibre revolver sick with rust.

It was an interesting still life. And then Fred perceived that it wasn't entirely at rest. A little mouse was nibbling at one corner of the manuscript.

Fred tapped on the window. The mouse hesitated, looked everywhere but at Fred, went on nibbling again.

Fred went down into the basement, took the manuscript from its shelf to see how badly damaged it was. He blew the dust from the title page, which said, *A History of the Rosewaters of Rhode Island, by Merrihue Rosewater*. Fred untied the string that held the manuscript together, turned to page one, which said:

The Old World home of the Rosewaters was and is in the Scilly Islands, off Cornwall. The founder of the family there, whose name was John, arrived on St. Mary Island in 1645, with the party accompanying the fifteen-year-old Prince Charles, later to become Charles the Second, who was fleeing the Puritan Revolution. The name Rosewater was then a pseudonym. Until John chose it for himself, there were no Rosewaters in England. His real name was John Graham. He was the youngest of the five sons of James Graham, Fifth Earl and First Marquis of Montrose. There was need for a pseudonym, for James Graham was a leader of the Royalist cause, and the Royalist cause was lost. James, among other romantic exploits, once disguised himself, went to the Scotch Highlands, organized a small, fierce army, and led it to six bloody victories over the far greater forces of the Lowland Presbyterian Army of Archibald Campbell, the Eighth Earl of Argyll. James was also a poet. So every Rosewater is in fact a Graham, and has the blood of Scotch nobility in him. James was hanged in 1650.

Poor old Fred simply could not believe this, that he should have connection with anyone so glorious. As it happened, he was wearing Argyll socks, and he hitched up his trousers some to look at them. *Argyll* had a new meaning for him now. One of his ancestors, he told himself, had whipped the Earl of Argyll six times. Fred noticed, too, that he had banged his shins on a table more severely than he'd thought, for there was blood running down to the tops of his Argylls.

He read on:

John Graham, rechristened John Rosewater in the Scilly Islands, apparently found the mild climate and the new name congenial, for he remained there for the rest of his life, fathering seven sons and six daughters. He, too, is said to have been a poet, though none of his work survives. If we had some of his poems, they might explain to us what must remain a mystery, why a nobleman would give up his good name and all the privileges it could mean, and be content to live as a simple farmer on an island far from the centers of wealth and power. I can make a guess, and it can never be more than a guess, that he was perhaps sickened by all the bloody things he saw when he fought at his brother's side. At any rate, he made no effort to tell his family where he was, nor to reveal himself as Graham when royalty was restored. In the history of the Grahams, he is said to have been lost at sea while guarding Prince Charles.

Fred heard Caroline throwing up now upstairs.

John Rosewater's third son, Frederick, was the direct ancestor of the Rhode Island Rosewaters. We know little else about him, except that he had a son named George, who was the first Rosewater to leave the islands. George went to London in 1700, became a florist. George had two sons, the younger of which, John, was imprisoned for debt in 1731. He was freed in 1732 by James E. Oglethorpe, who paid his debts on the condition that John accompany Oglethorpe on an expedition to Georgia. John was to serve as chief horticulturalist for the expedition, which planned to plant mulberry trees and raise silk. John Rosewater would also become the chief architect, laying out what was to become the city of Savannah. In 1742, John was badly wounded in the Battle of Bloody Marsh against the Spanish.

At this point, Fred was so elated over the resourcefulness and bravery of his own flesh and blood in the past, that he had to tell his wife about it at once. And he didn't think for a moment of bringing the sacred book to his wife. It had to stay in the holy cellar, and she had to come down to *it.*

So he stripped the bedspread away from her, certainly the most audacious, most blatantly sexual act of their marriage, told her his real name was Graham, said an ancestor of his had designed Savannah, told her she had to come down into the cellar with him.

• • •

She tramped blearily down the stairs after Fred, and he pointed to the manuscript, gave her a strident synopsis of the history of the Rhode Island Rosewaters up to the Battle of Bloody Marsh.

"The point I'm trying to make," he said, "is—we *are* somebody. I am *sick* and I am *tired* of pretending that we just aren't *anybody.*"

"I never pretended we weren't anybody."

"You've pretended *I* wasn't anybody." This was daringly true, and said almost accidentally. The truth of it stunned them both. "You know what I mean," said Fred. He pressed on, did so gropingly, since he was in the unfamiliar condition of having poignant things to say, of being by no means at the end of them.

"These phony bastards you think are so wonderful, compared to us—compared to *me*—I'd like to see how many ancestors they could turn up that could compare with mine. I've always thought people were silly who bragged about their family trees—but, by God, if anybody wants do any comparing, I'd be glad to show 'em mine! Let's *quit* apologizing!"

"I don't know what you mean."

"Other people say, 'Hello' or 'Goodbye!' We always say, 'Excuse me,' no matter what we're doing." He threw up his hands. "No more apologies! So we're poor! All right, we're poor! This is America! And America is one place in this sorry world where people shouldn't *have* to apologize for being poor. The question in America should be, 'Is this guy a good citizen? Is he honest? Does he pull his own weight?'"

Fred hoisted the manuscript in his two plump hands, threatened poor Caroline with it. "The Rhode Island Rosewaters have been active, creative people in the past, and will continue to be in the future," he told her. "Some have had money, and some have not, but, by God, they've played their parts in history! No more apologies!"

He had won Caroline to his way of thinking. It was a simple thing for any passionate person to do. She was ga-ga with terrified respect.

"You know what it says over the door of the National Archives in Washington?"

"No," she admitted.

"'The past is prologue!'"

"Oh."

"All right," said Fred, "now let's read this story of the Rhode Island Rosewaters together, and try to pull our marriage together with a little mutual pride and faith."

She nodded dumbly.

• • •

The tale of John Rosewater at the Battle of Bloody Marsh ended the second page of the manuscript. So Fred now gripped the corner of that page between his thumb and forefinger, and dramatically peeled it from wonders lying below.

The manuscript was hollow. Termites had eaten the heart out of the history. They were still there, maggotty blue-grey, eating away.

When Caroline had clumped back up the cellar stairs, tremulous with disgust, Fred calmly advised himself that the time had come to *really* die. Fred could tie a hangman's knot blindfolded, and he tied one now in clothesline. He climbed onto a stool, tied the other end to a water pipe with a two-half hitch, which he tested.

He was putting the noose over his head, when little Franklin called down the stairway that a man wanted to see him. And the man, who was Norman Mushari, came down the stairs uninvited, lugging a fat, cross-gartered, slack-jawed briefcase.

Fred moved quickly, barely escaped being caught in the embarrassing act of destroying himself.

"Yes—?" he said to Mushari.

"Mr. Rosewater—?"

"Yes—?"

"Sir—at this very moment, your Indiana relatives are swindling you and yours out of your birthright, out of millions upon millions of dollars. I am here to tell you about a relatively cheap and simple court action that will make those millions yours."

Fred fainted.

12

TWO DAYS LATER, it was nearly time for Eliot to get on a Greyhound Bus at the Saw City Kandy Kitchen, to go to Indianapolis to meet Sylvia in the Bluebird Room. It was noon. He was still asleep. He had had one hell of a night, not only with telephone calls, but with people coming in person at all hours, more than half of them drunk. There was panic in Rosewater. No matter how often Eliot had denied it, his clients were sure he was leaving them forever.

Eliot had cleared off the top of his desk. Laid out on it were a new blue suit, a new white shirt, a new blue tie, a new pair of black nylon socks, a new pair of Jockey shorts, a new toothbrush and a bottle of Lavoris. He had used the new toothbrush once. His mouth was a bloody wreck.

Dogs barked outside. They crossed the street from the firehouse to greet a great favorite of theirs, Delbert Peach, a town drunk. They were cheering him in his efforts to stop being a human being and become a dog. "Git! Git! Git!" he cried ineffectually. "God damn, I ain't in heat."

He tumbled in through Eliot's street-level door, slammed the door on his best friends, climbed the stairs singing. This is what he sang:

> I've got the clap, and the blueballs, too.
> The clap don't hurt, but the blueballs do.

Delbert Peach, all bristles and stink, ran out of that song halfway up the stairs, for his progress was slow. He switched to *The Star Spangled Banner*, and he was gasping and burping and humming that when he entered Eliot's office proper.

"Mr. Rosewater? Mr. Rosewater?" Eliot's head was under his blanket, and his hands, though he was sound asleep, gripped the shroud tightly. So Peach, in order to see Eliot's beloved face, had to overcome the strength of those hands. "Mr. Rosewater—are you alive? Are you all right?"

Eliot's face was contorted by the struggle for the blanket. "What? What? What?" His eyes opened wide.

"Thank the good Lord! I dreamed you was dead!"

"Not that I know of."

"I dreamed the angels had come down from the sky, and carried you up, and set you down next to Sweet Jesus Himself."

"No," said Eliot fuzzily. "Nothing like that happened."

"It'll happen sometime. And the weeping and wailing in this town, you'll hear it up there."

Eliot hoped he wouldn't hear the weeping and wailing up there, but he didn't say so.

"Even though you're not dying, Mr. Rosewater, I know you'll never come back here. You'll get up there to Indianapolis, with all the excitement and lights and beautiful buildings, and you'll get a taste of the high life again, and you'll hunger for more of it, which is only natural for anybody who's ever tasted the high life the way you have, and the next thing you know you'll be in New York, living the very highest life there is. And why shouldn't you?"

"Mr. Peach—" and Eliot rubbed his eyes, "if I were to somehow wind up in New York, and start living the highest of all possible lives again, you know what would happen to me? The minute I got near any navigable body of water, a bolt of lightning would knock me into the water, a whale would swallow me up, and the whale would swim down to the Gulf of Mexico and up the Mississippi, up the Ohio, up the Wabash, up the White, up Lost River, up Rosewater Creek. And that whale would jump from the creek into the Rosewater Inter-State Ship Canal, and it would swim down the canal to this city, and spit me out in the Parthenon. And there I'd be."

• • •

"Whether you're coming back or not, Mr. Rosewater, I want to make you a present of some good news to take with you."

"And what news is that, Mr. Peach?"

"As of ten minutes ago, I swore off liquor forever. That's my present to you."

• • •

Eliot's red telephone rang. He lunged at it, for it was the fire department's hot line. "Hello!" He folded all the fingers of his left hand, except for the middle one. The gesture was not obscene. He was readying the finger that would punch the red button, that would make the doomsday horn on top of the firehouse bawl.

"Mr. Rosewater?" It was a woman's voice, and it was so coy.

"Yes! Yes!" Eliot was hopping up and down. "Where's the fire?"

"It's in my heart, Mr. Rosewater."

Eliot was enraged, and no one would have been surprised to see him so. He was famous for his hatred of skylarking where the fire department was concerned. It was the only thing he hated. He recognized the caller, who was Mary Moody, the slut whose twins he had baptized the day before. She was a suspected arsonist, a convicted shoplifter, and a five-dollar whore. Eliot blasted her for using the hot line.

"God *damn* you for calling this number! You should go to jail and rot! Stupid sons of bitches who make personal calls on a fire department line should go to hell and fry forever!" He slammed the receiver down.

A few seconds later, the black telephone rang. "This is the Rosewater Foundation," said Eliot sweetly. "How can we help you?"

"Mr. Rosewater—this is Mary Moody again." She was sobbing.

"What on earth is the trouble, dear?" He honestly didn't know. He was ready to kill whoever had made her cry.

• • •

A chauffeur-driven black Chrysler Imperial pulled to the curb below Eliot's two windows. The chauffeur opened the back door. His old joints giving him pain, out came Senator Lister Ames Rosewater of Indiana. He was not expected.

He went creakingly upstairs. This abject mode of progress had not been his style in times past. He had aged shockingly, wished to demonstrate that he had aged shockingly. He did what few visitors ever did, knocked on Eliot's office door, asked if it would be all right if he came in. Eliot, who was still in his fragrant war-surplus long Johns, hurried to his father, embraced him.

"Father, Father, Father—what a wonderful surprise."

"It isn't easy for me to come here."

"I hope that isn't because you think you're not welcome."

"I can't stand the sight of this mess."

"It's certainly a lot better than it was a week ago."

"It is?"

"We had a top-to-bottom house cleaning a week ago."

The Senator winced, nudged a beer can with his toe. "Not on my account, I hope. Just because I fear an outbreak of cholera is no reason you should, too." This was said quietly.

"You know Delbert Peach, I believe?"

"I know *of* him." The Senator nodded. "How do you do, Mr. Peach. I'm certainly familiar with your war record. Deserted twice, didn't you? Or was it three times?"

Peach, cowering and sullen in the presence of such a majestic person, mumbled that he had never served in the armed forces.

"It was your father, then. I apologize. It's hard to tell how old people are, if they seldom wash or shave."

Peach admitted with his silence that it probably had been his father who had deserted three times.

"I wonder if we might not be alone for a few moments," the Senator said to Eliot, "or would that run counter to your concept of how open and friendly our society should be?"

"I'm leaving," said Peach. "I know when I'm not wanted."

"I imagine you've had plenty of opportunities to learn," said the Senator.

Peach, who was shuffling out the door, turned at this insult, surprised even himself by understanding that he had been insulted. "For a man who depends on the votes of the ordinary common people, Senator, you certainly can say mean things to them."

"As a drunk, Mr. Peach, you must surely know that drunks are not allowed in polling places."

"I've voted." This was a transparent lie.

"If you have, you've probably voted for me. Most people do, even though I never flattered the people of Indiana in my life, not even in time of war. And do you know why they vote for me? Inside of every American, I don't care how decayed, is a scrawny, twanging old futz like me, who hates crooks and weaklings even more than I do."

• • •

"Gee, Father—I certainly didn't expect to see *you*. What a pleasant surprise. You look wonderful."

"I feel rotten. I have rotten news for you, too. I thought I'd better deliver it in person."

Eliot frowned slightly. "When was the last time your bowels moved?"

"None of your business!"

"Sorry."

"I'm not here for a cathartic. The C.I.O. says my bowels haven't moved since the National Recovery Act was declared unconstitutional, but that's not why I'm here."

"You said everything was so *rotten*."

"So?"

"Usually, when somebody comes in here and says that, nine times out of ten, it's a case of constipation."

"I'll tell you what the news is, boy, and then let's see if *you* can cheer up with Ex-Lax. A young lawyer working for McAllister, Robjent, Reed and McGee, with full access to all the confidential files about you, has quit. He's hired out to the Rhode Island Rosewaters. They're going to get you in court. They're going to prove you're insane."

The buzzer of Eliot's alarm clock went off. Eliot picked up the clock, went to the red button on the wall. He watched the sweep secondhand of the clock intently, his lips working, counting off the seconds. He aimed the blunt middle finger of his left hand at the button, suddenly stabbed, thus activating the loudest fire alarm in the Western Hemisphere.

The awful shout of the horn hurled the Senator against a wall, curled him up with his hands over his ears. A dog in New Ambrosia, seven miles away, ran in circles, bit his tail. A stranger in the Saw City Kandy Kitchen threw coffee all over himself and the proprietor. In Bella's Beauty Nook in the basement of the Court House, three-hundred-pound Bella had a mild heart attack. And wits throughout the county poised themselves to tell a tired and untruthful joke about Fire Chief Charley Warmergran, who had an insurance office next to the fire-house: "Must have scared Charley Warmergram half out of his secretary."

Eliot released the button. The great alarm began to swallow its own voice, speaking gutturally and interminably of "*bubble-gum, bubblegum, bubblegum.*"

There was no fire. It was simply high noon in Rosewater.

· · ·

"What a racket!" the Senator mourned, straightening up slowly. "I've forgotten everything I ever knew."

"That might be nice."

"Did you hear what I said about the Rhode Island people?"

"Yes."

"And how does it make you feel?"

"Sad and frightened." Eliot sighed, tried a wistful smile, couldn't manage one. "I had hoped it would never have to be proved, that it would never matter one way or another—whether I was sane or not."

"You have some doubts as to your own sanity?"

"Certainly."

"And how long has *this* been going on?"

Eliot's eyes widened as he sought an honest answer. "Since I was ten, maybe."

· · ·

"I'm sure you're joking."

"That's a comfort."

"You were a sturdy, sane little boy."

"I was?" Eliot was ingenuously charmed by the little boy he had been, was glad to think about him rather than about the spooks that were closing in on him.

"I'm only sorry we brought you out here."

"I loved it out here. I still do," Eliot confessed dreamily.

The Senator moved his feet slightly apart, making a firmer base for the blow he was about to deliver. "That may be, boy, but it's time to go now—and never come back."

"Never come back?" Eliot echoed marvelingly.

"This part of your life is over. It had to end sometime. I'll thank the Rhode Island vermin for this much: They're forcing you to leave, and to leave right now."

"How can they do *that*?"

"How do you expect to defend your sanity with a backdrop like this?"

Eliot looked about himself, saw nothing remarkable. "This looks—this looks—*peculiar*?"

"You know damn well it does."

Eliot shook his head slowly. "You'd be surprised what I don't know, Father."

"There's no institution like this anywhere else in the world. If this were a set on a stage, and the script called for the curtain to go up with no one on stage, when the curtain went up, the audience would be on pins and needles, eager to see the incredible nut who could live this way."

"What if the nut came out and gave sensible explanations for his place being the way it is?"

"He would still be a nut."

• • •

Eliot accepted this, or seemed to. He didn't argue with it, allowed that he had better wash up and get dressed for his trip. He rummaged through his desk drawers, found a small paper bag containing purchases he had made the day before, a bar of *Dial* soap, a bottle of *Absorbine, Jr.*, for his athlete's foot, a bottle of *Head and Shoulders* shampoo for his dandruff, a bottle of *Arrid* roll-on deodorant, and a tube of *Crest* toothpaste.

"I'm glad to see you taking pride in your appearance again, boy."

"Hm?" Eliot was reading the label on the *Arrid*, which he had never used before. He had never used *any* underarm deodorant before.

"You get cleaned up, cut down on the booze, clear out of here, open a decent office in Indianapolis or Chicago or New York, and, when the hearing comes up, they'll see you're as sane as anybody."

"Um." Eliot asked his father if *he* had ever used *Arrid*.

The Senator was offended. "I shower every morning and night. I presume that takes care of any fulsome effluvium."

"It says here that you might get a rash, and you should stop using it, if you get a rash."

"If it worries you, don't use it. Soap and water are the important things."

"Um."

"That's one of the troubles with this country," said the Senator. "The Madison Avenue people have made us all more alarmed about our own armpits than about Russia, China and Cuba combined."

The conversation, actually a very dangerous one between two highly vulnerable men, had drifted into a small area of peace. They could agree with one another, and not be afraid.

"You know—" said Eliot, "Kilgore Trout once wrote a whole book about a country that was devoted to fighting odors. That was the national purpose. There wasn't any disease, and there wasn't any crime, and there wasn't any war, so they went after odors."

"If you get in court," said the Senator, "it would be just as well if you didn't mention your enthusiasm for Trout. Your fondness for all that Buck Rogers stuff might make you look immature in the eyes of a lot of people."

The conversation had left the area of peace again. Eliot's voice was edgy as he persisted in telling the story by Trout, which was called *Oh Say Can You Smell?*

"This country," said Eliot, "had tremendous research projects devoted to fighting odors. They were supported by individual contributions given to mothers who marched on Sundays from door to door. The ideal of the research was to find a specific chemical deodorant for every odor. But then the hero, who was also the country's dictator, made a wonderful scientific breakthrough, even though he wasn't a scientist, and they didn't need the projects any more. He went right to the root of the problem."

"Uh huh," said the Senator. He couldn't stand stories by Kilgore Trout, was embarrassed for his son. "He found one chemical that would eliminate all odors?" he suggested, to hasten the tale to a conclusion.

"No. As I say, the hero was dictator, and he simply eliminated noses."

• • •

Eliot was now taking a full bath in the frightful little lavatory, shivering and barking and coughing as he sloshed himself with sopping paper towels.

His father could not watch, roamed the office instead, averting his eyes from the obscene and ineffectual ablutions. There was no lock on the office door, and Eliot had, at his father's insistence, shoved a filing cabinet against it. "What if somebody should walk in here and see you stark naked?" the Senator had demanded. And Eliot had responded, "To these people around here, Father, I'm no particular sex at all."

So the Senator pondered that unnatural sexlessness along with all the other evidences of insanity, disconsolately pulled open the top drawer of the filing cabinet. There were three cans of beer in it, a 1948 New York State driver's license, and an unsealed envelope, addressed to Sylvia in Paris, never mailed. In the envelope was a love poem from Eliot to Sylvia, dated two years before.

The Senator thrust aside shame and read the poem, hoping to learn from it things that might defend his son. This was the poem he read, and he was not able to keep shame away when he was through:

> "I'm a painter in my dreams, you know,
>   Or maybe you didn't know. And a sculptor.
>   Long time no see.
>   And a kick to me
>   Is the interplay of materials
>   And these hands of mine.
>   And some of the things I would do to you
>   Might surprise you.
>   For instance, if I were there with you as you read this,
>   And you were lying down,
>   I might ask you to bare your belly
>   In order that I might take my left thumbnail
>   And draw a straight line five inches long
>   Above your pubic hair.
>   And then I might take the index finger
>   Of my right hand,

And insinuate it just over the rim of the right side
Of your famous belly button,
And leave it there, motionless, for maybe half an hour.
Queer?
You bet."

The Senator was shocked. It was the mention of pubic hair
that really appalled him. He had seen very few naked bodies in
his time, perhaps five or six, and pubic hair was to him the
most unmentionable, unthinkable of all materials.

Now Eliot came out of the lavatory, all naked and hairy,
drying himself with a tea towel. The tea towel was new. It still
had a price tag on it. The Senator was petrified, felt beset by
overwhelming forces of filth and obscenity on all sides.

Eliot did not notice. He continued to dry himself innocently,
then threw the tea towel into the wastebasket. The black telephone rang.

"This is the Rosewater Foundation. How can we help
you?"

"Mr. Rosewater—" said a woman, "there was a thing on the
radio about you."

"Oh?" Eliot now began to play unconsciously with his pubic
hair. It was nothing extravagant. He would simply uncoil a
tight spring of it, let it snap back into place.

"It said they were going to try to prove you were crazy."

"Don't worry about it, dear. There's many a slip betwixt the
cup and the lip."

"Oh, Mr. Rosewater—if you go away and never come back,
we'll die."

"I give you my word of honor I'm coming back. How is
that?"

"Maybe they won't *let* you come back."

"Do you think I'm crazy, dear?"

"I don't know how to put it."

"Any way you like."

"I can't help thinking people are going to *think* you're crazy
for paying so much attention to people like us."

"Have you seen the other people there are to pay attention to?"

"I never been out of Rosewater County."

"It's worth a trip, dear. When I get back, why don't I give you a trip to New York?"

"Oh God! But you're never coming back!"

"I gave you my word of honor."

"I know, I know—but we all feel it in our bones, we smell it in the air. You're not coming back."

Eliot had now found a hair that was a lulu. He kept extending and extending it until it was revealed as being one foot long. He looked down at it, then glanced at his father, incredulously proud of owning such a thing.

The Senator was livid.

"We tried to plan all kinds of ways to say good-bye to you, Mr. Rosewater," the woman went on. "Parades and signs and flags and flowers. But you won't see a one of us. We're all too scared."

"Of what?"

"I don't know." She hung up.

● ● ●

Eliot pulled on his new Jockey shorts. As soon as they were snugly on, his father spoke grimly.

"Eliot—"

"Sir—?" Eliot was running his thumbs pleasurably under the elasticized belly-band. "These things certainly give support. I'd forgotten how nice it was to *have* support."

The Senator blew up. "Why do you *hate* me so?" he cried.

Eliot was flabbergasted. "Hate you? Father—I don't hate you. I don't hate anybody."

"Your every act and word is aimed at hurting me as much as you possibly can!"

"No!"

"I have no idea what I ever did to you that you're paying me back for now, but the debt must surely be settled by now."

Eliot was shattered. "Father—please—"

"Get away! You'll only hurt me more, and I can't stand any more pain."

"For the love of God—"

"Love!" the Senator echoed bitterly. "You certainly loved me, didn't you? Loved me so much you smashed up every hope or ideal I ever had. And you certainly loved Sylvia, didn't you?"

Eliot covered his ears.

The old man raved on, spraying fine beads of spit. Eliot could not hear the words, but lip-read the terrible story of how he had ruined the life and health of a woman whose only fault had been to love him.

The Senator stormed out of the office, was gone.

Eliot uncovered his ears, finished dressing, as though nothing special had happened. He sat down to tie his shoelaces. When these were tied, he straightened up. And he froze as stiff as any corpse.

The black telephone rang. He did not answer.

13

S OMETHING THERE WAS IN ELIOT, though, that watched the clock. Ten minutes before his bus was due at the Saw City Kandy Kitchen, he thawed, arose, pursed his lips, picked some lint from his suit, went out his office door. He had no surface memory of the fight with his father. His step was jaunty, that of a Chaplinesque *boulevardier*.

He bent to pat the heads of dogs who welcomed him to street level. His new clothes hampered him, bound him in the crotch and armpits, crackled as though lined with newspaper, reminded him of how nicely turned out he was.

There was talk coming from the lunchroom. Eliot listened without showing himself. He did not recognize any of the voices, although they belonged to friends of his. Three men were talking ruefully of money, which they did not have. There were many pauses, for thoughts came to them almost as hard as money did.

"Well," said one at last, "it ain't no disgrace to be poor." This line was the first half of a fine old joke by the Hoosier humorist, Kin Hubbard.

"No," said another man, completing the joke, "but it might as well be."

•   •   •

Eliot crossed the street, went into Fire Chief Charley Warmergran's insurance office. Charley was not a pitiful person, had never applied to the Foundation for help of any kind. He was one of about seven in the county who had actually done quite well under real free enterprise. Bella of Bella's Beauty Nook was another. Both of them had started with nothing, both were children of brakemen on the Nickel Plate. Charley was ten years younger than Eliot. He was six-feet-four, had broad shoulders, no hips, no belly. In addition to being Fire Chief, he was Federal Marshal and Inspector of Weights and Measures. He also owned, jointly with Bella, La Boutique de Paris, which was a nice little haberdashery and notions store in the new shopping center for the well-to-do people in New Ambrosia. Like all real heroes, Charley had a fatal flaw. He refused to believe that he had gonorrhea, whereas the truth was that he did.

•   •   •

Charley's famous secretary was on an errand. The only other person there when Eliot walked in was Noyes Finnerty, who was sweeping the floor. Noyes had been the center of the immortal Noah Rosewater Memorial High School Basketball Team which went undefeated in 1933. In 1934, Noyes strangled his sixteen-year-old wife for notorious infidelity, went to prison for life. Now he was paroled, thanks to Eliot. He was fifty-one. He had no friends, no relatives. Eliot found out about his being in prison by accident, while leafing through old copies of *The Rosewater County Clarion Call*, made it his business to get him paroled.

Noyes was a quiet, cynical, resentful man. He had never thanked Eliot for anything. Eliot was neither hurt nor startled. He was used to ingratitude. One of his favorite Kilgore Trout books dealt with ingratitude and nothing else. It was called, *The First District Court of Thankyou*, which was a court you could take people to, if you felt they hadn't been properly grateful for something you had done. If the defendant lost his case, the court gave him a choice between thanking the plaintiff in public, or going into solitary confinement on bread and water for a month. According to Trout, eighty per cent of those convicted chose the black hole.

•   •   •

Noyes was a lot faster than Charley in perceiving that Eliot was far from well. He stopped sweeping, watched acutely. He was a mean voyeur. Charley, enchanted by memories of so many fires at which he and Eliot had behaved so well, did not become suspicious until Eliot congratulated him on having just won an award which he had in fact won three years before.

"Eliot—are you kidding?"

"Why would I kid you? I think it's a wonderful honor." They

were discussing the Young Hoosier Horatio Alger Award for 1962, awarded to Charley by the Indiana Federation of Conservative Young Republican Businessmen's Clubs.

"Eliot—" said Charley wincingly, "that was three years ago."

"It was?"

Charley arose from his desk. "And you and I sat up in your office, and we decided to send the damn plaque back."

"We did?"

"We went over the history of the thing, and we decided it was the kiss of death."

"Why would we decide that?"

"*You* were the one who dug up the history, Eliot."

Eliot frowned ever so slightly. "I've forgotten." The little frown was a formality. The forgetting didn't really bother him.

"They started giving the thing in 1945. They'd given it sixteen times before I won it. Don't you remember now?"

"No."

"Out of sixteen winners of the Young Hoosier Horatio Alger Award, six were behind bars for fraud or income-tax evasion, four were under indictment for one thing or another, two had falsified their war records, and one actually went to the electric chair."

•   •   •

"Eliot—" said Charley with mounting anxiety, "did you hear what I just said?"

"Yes," said Eliot.

"What did I just say?"

"I forget."

"You just said you heard me."

Noyes Finnerty spoke up. "All he hears is the big click." He came forward for a closer examination of Eliot. His approach was not sympathetic. It was clinical. Eliot's response was clinical, too, as though a nice doctor were shining a bright light in his eyes, looking for something. "He heard that *click*, man. Man, did he ever hear that *click*."

"What the hell are you talking about?" Charley asked him.

"It's a thing you learn to listen for in prison."

"We're not in prison now."

"It ain't a thing that happens just in prison. In prison, though, you get to listening for things more and more. You stay there long enough, you go blind, you're all ears. The click is one thing you listen for. You two—you think you're mighty close? If you were really close—and that don't mean you have to like him, just *know* him—you would have heard that *click* of his a mile away. You get to know a man, and down deep there's something bothering him bad, and maybe you never find out what it is, but it's what makes him do like he does, it's what makes him look like he's got secrets in his eyes. And you tell him, 'Calm down, calm down, take it easy now.' Or you ask him, 'How come you keep doing the same crazy things over and over again, when you know they're just going to get you in trouble again?' Only you know there's no sense arguing with him, on account of it's the thing inside that's making him go. It says, 'Jump,' he jumps. It says, 'Steal,' he steals. It says, 'Cry,' he cries. Unless he dies young, though, or unless he gets everything all his way and nothing big goes wrong, that thing inside of him is going to run down like a wind-up toy. You're working in the prison laundry next to this man. You've known him twenty years. You're working along, and all of a sudden you hear this *click* from him. You turn to look at him. He's stopped working. He's all calmed down. He looks real dumb. He looks real sweet. You look in his eyes, and the secrets are gone. He can't even tell you his own name right then. He goes back to work, but he'll never be the same. That thing that bothered him so will never click on again. It's dead, it's *dead*. And that part of that man's life where he had to be a certain crazy way, that's *done!*"

Noyes, who had begun with such a massive lack of passion, was now rigid and perspiring. Both of his hands were white, choking the broomhandle in a deathgrip. And while the natural design of his story suggested that he calm down, to illustrate how nicely the man next to him in the laundry had calmed down, it was impossible for him to simulate peace. The wrenching work his hands did on the broomhandle became obscene, and the passion that would not die made him nearly inarticulate. "Done! Done!" he insisted. It was the broomhandle that enraged him most now. He tried to snap it across his thigh, snarled at Charley, the owner of the broom, "The son of a bitch won't break! Won't break!

"You lucky bastard," he said to Eliot, still trying to break the broom, "you've had yours!" He showered Eliot with obscenities.

He flung the broom away. "Motherfucker won't break!" he cried, and he stormed out the door.

• • •

Eliot was unruffled by the scene. He asked Charley mildly what the man had against brooms. He said, too, that he guessed he had better catch his bus.

"Are—are you all right, Eliot?"

"I'm wonderful."

"You are?"

"I never felt better in my life. I feel as though—as though—"

"Yeah—?"

"As though some marvelous new phase of my life were about to begin."

"That must be nice."

"It is! It is!"

• • •

And that continued to be Eliot's mood as he sauntered to the Saw City Kandy Kitchen. The aspect of the street was unnaturally quiet, as though a gun fight were expected, but Eliot did not notice this. The town was certain he was leaving forever. Those most dependent on Eliot had heard the *click* as clearly as they would have heard a cannon shot. There had been a lot of frantic, lame-brained planning of an appropriate farewell—a firemen's parade, a demonstration with placards saying the things that most needed saying, a triumphal arch of water from fire hoses. The plans had all collapsed. There was no one to organize such a thing, to lead. Most were so eviscerated by the prospect of Eliot's leaving that they could not find the energy or bravery to stand at the rear of a large crowd, even, and feebly wave bye-bye. They knew the street down which he would walk. From that most fled.

Eliot left the afternoon dazzle of the sidewalk for the humid shade of the Parthenon, strolled along the canal. A retired saw-maker, a man about the Senator's age, was fishing with a bamboo pole. He was seated on a camp stool. A transistor radio was on the pavement between his high shoes. The radio was playing "Ol' Man River." "Darkies all work," it said, "while the white folks play."

The old man wasn't a drunk or a pervert or anything. He was simply old, and a widower, and shot full of cancer, and his son in the Strategic Air Command never wrote, and his personality wasn't much. Booze upset him. The Rosewater Foundation had given him a grant for morphine, which his doctor prescribed.

Eliot greeted him, found he could not remember his name, nor what his trouble was. Eliot filled his lungs. It was too fine a day for sad things anyway.

• • •

At the far end of the Parthenon, which was a tenth of a mile long, was a small stand that sold shoelaces, razor-blades, soft drinks, and copies of *The American Investigator*. It was run by a man named Lincoln Ewald, who had been an ardent Nazi sympathizer during the Second World War. During that war, Ewald had set up a shortwave transmitter, in order to tell the Germans what was being produced by the Rosewater Saw Company every day, which was paratroop knives and armor plate. His first message, and the Germans hadn't asked him for any messages at all, was to the effect that, if they could bomb Rosewater, the entire American economy would shrivel and die. He didn't ask for money in exchange for the information. He sneered at money, said that that was why he hated America, because money was king. He wanted an Iron Cross, which he requested be sent in a plain wrapper.

His message was received loud and clear on the walkie-talkies of two game wardens in Turkey Run State Park, forty-two miles away. The wardens spilled the beans to the Federal Bureau of Investigation, who arrested Ewald at the address to which the Iron Cross was to be sent. He was put in a mental institution until the war was over.

The Foundation had done very little for him, except to listen to his political views, which no one else would do. The only things Eliot ever bought him were a cheap phonograph and a set of German lessons on records. Ewald wanted so much to learn German, but he was too excited and angry all the time.

Eliot couldn't remember Ewald's name, either, and nearly passed him by without seeing him. His sinister little leper's booth there in the ruin of a great civilization was easy to miss.

"Heil Hitler," said Ewald in a grackle voice.

Eliot stopped, looked amiably at the place from which the greeting had come. Ewald's booth was curtained by copies of *The American Investigator*. The curtains seemed to be polka-dotted. The polka dots were the belly-buttons of Randy Herald, the cover girl. And she asked over and over again for a man who could give her a baby that would be a genius.

"Heil Hitler," said Ewald again. He did not part the curtains.

"And Heil Hitler to you, sir," said Eliot smiling, "and good-bye."

• • •

The barbaric sunshine slammed Eliot as he stepped from the Parthenon. His momentarily injured eyes saw two loafers on the courthouse steps as charred stickmen surrounded by steam. He heard Bella, down in her beauty nook, bawling out a woman for not taking good care of her fingernails.

Eliot encountered no one for quite a while, although he did catch someone peeking at him from a window. He winked and waved to whomever it was. When he reached Noah Rosewater Memorial High School, which was closed tight for the summer, he paused before the flagpole, indulged himself in shallow melancholy. He was taken by the sounds of the hollow iron pole's being tapped and caressed despondently by the hardware on the empty halyard.

He wanted to comment on the sounds, to have someone else listen to them, too. But there was nobody around but a dog that had been following him, so he spoke to the dog. "That's such an *American* sound, you know? School out and the flag down? Such a sad American sound. You should hear it sometime when the sun's gone down, and a light evening wind comes up, and it's suppertime all around the world."

A lump grew in his throat. It felt good.

• • •

As Eliot passed the Sunoco station, a young man crept from between two pumps. He was Roland Barry, who had suffered a nervous breakdown ten minutes after being sworn into the Army at Fort Benjamin Harrison. He had a one hundred per cent disability pension. His breakdown came when he was ordered to take a shower with one hundred other men. The pension was no joke. Roland could not speak above a whisper. He spent many hours a day between the pumps, pretending to strangers that he had something to do with something there. "Mr. Rosewater—?" he whispered.

Eliot smiled, held out his hand. "You'll have to forgive me—I've forgotten your name."

Roland's self-esteem was so low that he was not surprised at being forgotten by a man whom he had visited at least once a day for the past year. "Wanted to thank you for saving my life."

"For what?"

"My life, Mr. Rosewater—you saved it, whatever it is."

"You're exaggerating, surely."

"You're the only one who didn't think what happened to me was funny. Maybe you won't think a poem is funny, either." He thrust a piece of paper into Eliot's hand. "I cried while I wrote it. That's how funny it was to me. That's how funny everything is to me." He ran away.

Perplexed, Eliot read the poem, which went like this:

> "Lakes, carillons,
> Pools and bells,
> Fifes and freshets,
> Harps and wells;
> Flutes and rivers,
> Streams, bassoons,
> Geysers, trumpets,
> Chimes, lagoons.
> Hear the music,
> Drink the water,
> As we poor lambs
> All go to slaughter.
> I love you Eliot.

Good-bye. I cry.
Tears and violins.
Hearts and flowers,
Flowers and tears.
Rosewater, good-bye."

Eliot arrived at the Saw City Kandy Kitchen without further incident. Only the proprietor and one customer were inside. The customer was a fourteen-year-old nymphet, pregnant by her stepfather, which stepfather was in prison now. The Foundation was paying for her medical care. It had also reported the stepfather's crime to the police, had subsequently hired for him the best Indiana lawyer that money could buy.

The girl's name was Tawny Wainwright. When she brought her troubles to Eliot, he asked her how her spirits were. "Well," she said, "I guess I don't feel too *bad*. I guess this is as good a way as any to start out being a movie star."

She was drinking a Coca-Cola and reading *The American Investigator* now. She glanced furtively at Eliot once. That was the last time.

• • •

"A ticket to Indianapolis, please."
"One way or round trip, Eliot?"
Eliot did not hesitate. "One way, if you please."
Tawny's glass nearly toppled. She caught it in time.
"One way to Indianapolis!" said the proprietor loudly. "Here you are, sir!" He validated Eliot's ticket with a stamp savagely, handed over the ticket, turned quickly away. He didn't look at Eliot again, either.

Eliot, unaware of any strain, drifted over to the magazine and book racks for something to read on the trip. He was tempted by the *Investigator*, opened it, scanned a story about a seven-year-old girl who had had her head eaten off by a bear in Yellowstone Park in 1934. He returned it to the rack, selected instead a paperback book by Kilgore Trout. It was called *Pan-Galactic Three-Day Pass*.

The bus blew its flatulent horns outside.

• • •

As Eliot boarded the bus, Diana Moon Glampers appeared. She was sobbing. She was carrying her white Princess telephone, dragging its uprooted wire behind her. "Mr. Rosewater!"

"Yes?"

She smashed the telephone on the pavement by the door of the bus. "I don't need a telephone any more. Nobody for me to call up. Nobody to call me up."

He sympathized with her, but he did not recognize her. "I'm—I'm sorry. I don't understand."

"You don't *what*? It's *me*, Mr. Rosewater! It's Diana! It's Diana Moon Glampers!"

"I'm pleased to meet you."

"Pleased to *meet* me?"

"I really *am*—but—but, what's this about a telephone?"

"You were the only reason I *needed* one."

"Oh, now—" he said, doubtingly, "you surely have many other acquaintances."

"Oh, Mr. Rosewater—" she sobbed, and she sagged against the bus, "you're my *only* friend."

"You can make more, surely," Eliot suggested hopefully.

"Oh God!" she cried.

"You could join some church group, perhaps."

"*You're* my church group! You're my *everything*! You're my government. You're my husband. You're my friends."

These claims made Eliot uncomfortable. "You're very nice to say so. Good luck to you. I really have to be going now." He waved. "Good-bye."

• • •

Eliot now began to read *Pan-Galactic Three-Day Pass*. There was more fussing outside the bus, but Eliot didn't think it had anything to do with him. He was immediately enchanted by the book, so much so that he didn't even notice when the bus pulled away. It was an exciting story, all about a man who was serving on a sort of Space-Age Lewis and Clark Expedition. The hero's name was Sergeant Raymond Boyle.

The expedition had reached what appeared to be the absolute and final rim of the Universe. There didn't seem to be anything beyond the solar system they were in, and they were setting up equipment to sense the faintest signals that might be coming from the slightest anything in all that black velvet nothing out there.

Sergeant Boyle was an Earthling. He was the only Earthling on the expedition. In fact, he was the only creature from the Milky Way. The other members were from all over the place. The expedition was a joint effort supported by about two hundred galaxies. Boyle wasn't a technician. He was an English teacher. The thing was that Earth was the only place in the whole known Universe where language was used. It was a unique Earthling invention. Everybody else used mental telepathy, so Earthlings could get pretty good jobs as language teachers just about anywhere they went.

The reason creatures wanted to use language instead of mental telepathy was that they found out they could get so much more *done* with language. Language made them so much more *active*. Mental telepathy, with everybody constantly telling everybody everything, produced a sort of generalized indifference to *all* information. But language, with its slow, narrow meanings, made it possible to think about one thing at a time—to start thinking in terms of *projects*.

Boyle was called out of his English class, was told to report at once to the commanding officer of the expedition. He couldn't imagine what it was all about. He went into the C.O.'s office, saluted the old man. Actually, the C.O. didn't look anything like an old man. He was from the planet *Tralfamadore*, and was about as tall as an Earthling beer can. Actually, he didn't look like a beer can, either. He looked like a little plumber's friend.

He wasn't alone. The chaplain of the expedition was there, too. The padre was from the planet Glinko-X-3. He was an enormous sort of Portuguese man-o'-war, in a tank of sulfuric acid on wheels. The chaplain looked grave. Something awful had happened.

The chaplain told Boyle to be brave, and then the C.O. told him there was very bad news from home. The C.O. said there had been a death back home, that Boyle was being given an emergency three-day pass, that he should get ready to leave right away.

"Is it—is it—Mom?" said Boyle, fighting back the tears. "Is it Pop? Is it Nancy?" Nancy was the girl next door. "Is it Gramps?"

"Son—" said the C.O., "brace yourself. I hate to tell you this: It isn't *who* has died. It's *what* has died."

"What's died?"

"What's died, my boy, is the Milky Way."

Eliot looked up from his reading. Rosewater County was gone. He did not miss it.

• • •

When the bus stopped in Nashville, Indiana, the seat of Brown County, Eliot glanced up again, studied the fire apparatus on view there. He thought of buying Nashville some really nice equipment, but decided against it. He didn't think the people would take good care of it.

Nashville was an arts and crafts center, so it wasn't surprising that Eliot also saw a glassblower making Christmas-tree ornaments in June.

• • •

Eliot didn't look up again until the bus reached the outskirts of Indianapolis. He was astonished to see that the entire city was being consumed by a fire-storm. He had never seen a fire-storm, but he had certainly read and dreamed about many of them.

He had a book hidden in his office, and it was a mystery even to Eliot as to why he should hide it, why he should feel guilty every time he got it out, why he should be afraid of being caught reading it. His feelings about the book were those of a weak-willed puritan with respect to pornography, yet no book could be more innocent of eroticism than the book he hid. It was called *The Bombing of Germany*. It was written by Hans Rumpf.

And the passage Eliot would read over and over again, his features blank, his palms sweating, was this description of the fire-storms in Dresden:

As the many fires broke through the roofs of the burning buildings, a column of heated air rose more than two and a half miles high and one and a half miles in diameter. . . . This column was turbulent, and it was fed from its base by in-rushing cooler ground-surface air. One and one and a half miles from the fires this draught increased the wind velocity from eleven to thirty-three miles per hour. At the edge of the area the velocities must have been appreciably greater, as trees three feet in diameter were uprooted. In a short time the temperature reached ignition point for all combustibles, and the entire area was ablaze. In such fires complete burn-out occurred; that is, no trace of combustible material remained, and only after two days were the areas cool enough to approach.

Eliot, rising from his seat in the bus, beheld the fire-storm of Indianapolis. He was awed by the majesty of the column of fire, which was at least eight miles in diameter and fifty miles high. The boundaries of the column seemed absolutely sharp and unwavering, as though made of glass. Within the boundaries, helixes of dull red embers turned in stately harmony about an inner core of white. The white seemed holy.

14

EVERYTHING WENT BLACK for Eliot, as black as what lay beyond the ultimate rim of the universe. And then he awoke to find himself sitting on the flat rim of a dry fountain. He was dappled by sunlight filtering down through a sycamore tree. A bird was singing in the sycamore tree. "*Poo-tee-weet?*" it sang. "*Poo-tee-weet. Weet, weet, weet.*" Eliot was within a high garden wall, and the garden was familiar. He had spoken to Sylvia many times in just this place. It was the garden of Dr. Brown's private mental hospital in Indianapolis, to which he had brought her so many years before. These words were cut into the fountain rim:

"Pretend to be good always, and even God will be fooled."

Eliot found that someone had dressed him for tennis, all in snowy white, and that, as though he were a department store display, someone had even put a tennis racket in his lap. He closed his hand around the racket handle experimentally, to discover whether it was real and whether he was real. He watched the play of the intricate basketwork of his forearm's musculature, sensed that he was not only a tennis player, but a good one. And he did not wonder where it was that he played tennis, for one side of the garden was bounded by a tennis court, with morning-glories and sweet peas twining in the chicken wire.

"*Poo-tee-weet?*"

Eliot looked up at the bird and all the green leaves, understood that this garden in downtown Indianapolis could not have survived the fire he saw. So there had been no fire. He accepted this peacefully.

• • •

He continued to look up at the bird. He wished that he were a dicky bird, so that he could go up into the treetop and never come down. He wanted to fly up so high because there was something going on at ground-zero that did not make him feel good. Four men in dark business suits were seated chockablock on a concrete bench only six feet away. They were staring at him hard, expecting something significant from him. And it was Eliot's feeling that he had nothing of significance to say or give.

The muscles in the back of his neck were aching now. They couldn't hold his head tipped back forever.

"Eliot—?"

"Sir—?" And Eliot knew that he had just spoken to his father. He now brought his gaze down from the tree gradually, let it drop like a sick dicky bird from twig to twig. His eyes were at last on level with those of his father.

"You were going to tell us something important," his father reminded him.

Eliot saw that there were three old men and one young one on the bench, all sympathetic, and listening intently for whatever he might care to say. The young man he recognized as Dr. Brown. The second old man was Thurmond McAllister, the family lawyer. The third old man was a stranger. Eliot could not name him, and yet, in some way that did not disturb Eliot, the man's features, those of a kindly country undertaker, claimed him as a close friend, indeed.

• • •

"You can't find the words?" Dr. Brown suggested. There was a tinge of anxiety in the healer's voice, and he shifted about, putting body English on whatever Eliot was about to do.

"I can't find the words," Eliot agreed.

"Well," said the Senator, "if you can't put it into words, you certainly can't use it at a sanity hearing."

Eliot nodded in appreciation of the truth of this. "Did—did I even *begin* to put it into words?"

"You simply announced," said the Senator, "that you had just been struck by an idea that would clear up this whole mess instantly, beautifully and fairly. And then you looked up in the tree."

"Um," said Eliot. He pretended to think, then shrugged. "Whatever it was, it's slipped my mind."

• • •

Senator Rosewater clapped his speckled old hands. "It isn't as though we're short of ideas as to how to beat this thing." He gave his hideous victory grin, patted McAllister on the knee. "Right?" He reached behind McAllister, patted the stranger on the back. "Right?" He was crazy about the stranger. "We've got the greatest idea man in the world on our side!" He laughed, he was so happy about all the ideas.

The Senator now extended his arms to Eliot. "But my boy here, just the way he looks and carries himself—*there's* our winning argument number one. So trim! So clean!" The old eyes glittered. "How much weight has he lost, Doctor?"

"Forty-three pounds."

"Back to fighting weight," the Senator rhapsodized. "Not a spare ounce on him. And what a tennis game! Merciless!" He bounced to his feet, did a ramshackle pantomime of a tennis serve. "Greatest game I ever saw in my life took place an hour ago, within these walls. You *killed* him, Eliot!"

"Um." Eliot looked around for a mirror or some reflecting surface. He had no idea what he looked like. There was no water in the pool of the fountain. But there was a little in the birdbath at the center of the pool, a bitter broth of soot and leaves.

"Didn't you say the man Eliot beat was a tennis pro?" the Senator asked Dr. Brown.

"Years ago."

"And Eliot *murdered* him! And the fact that the man is a mental patient wouldn't interfere with his game, would it?" He didn't wait for an answer. "And then when Eliot came bounding off the court, victorious, to shake our hands, I wanted to laugh and cry at the same time. 'And this is the man,' I said to myself, 'who has to prove tomorrow that he's not insane! Ha!'"

Eliot, drawing courage from the fact that the four men watching him were sure he was sane, now stood, as though to stretch. His real purpose was to bring himself nearer the birdbath. He took advantage of his reputation as an athlete, hopped into the dry pool, did a deep-knee bend, as though working off an excess of animal spirits. His body did the exercise effortlessly. He was made of spring steel.

The vigorous movements called Eliot's attention to something bulky in his hip pocket. He pulled it out, found that it was a rolled copy of *The American Investigator*. He unrolled it, half expecting to see Randy Herald begging to be planted with genius seeds. What he saw on the cover was his own picture instead. He was wearing a fire helmet. The picture was a blow-up from a Fourth of July group photograph of the Fire Department.

The headline said this:

SANEST MAN IN AMERICA? (SEE INSIDE)

• • •

Eliot looked inside, while the others engaged each other in optimistic palaver about the way the hearing would go the next day. Eliot found another picture of himself in the center spread. It was a blurry one of him playing tennis on the nut house court.

On the facing page, the gallantly sore-headed little family of Fred Rosewater seemed to glare at him as he played. They looked like sharecroppers. Fred had lost a lot of weight, too. There was a picture of Norman Mushari, their lawyer. Mushari, now in business for himself, had acquired a fancy vest and massive gold watch chain. He was quoted as follows:

"My clients want nothing but their natural and legal birthrights for themselves and their descendents. The bloated Indiana plutocrats have spent millions and mobilized powerful friends from coast to coast in order to deny their cousins their day in court. The hearing has been delayed seven times for the flimsiest of reasons, and, meanwhile, within the walls of a lunatic asylum, Eliot Rosewater plays and plays, and his henchmen deny loudly that he is insane.

"If my clients lose this case, they will lose their modest house and average furnishings, their used car, their child's small sailboat, Fred Rosewater's insurance policies, their life savings, and thousands borrowed from a loyal friend. These brave, wholesome, average Americans have bet everything they have on the American system of justice, which will not, must not, cannot let them down."

On Eliot's side of the layout were two pictures of Sylvia. An old one showed her twisting with Peter Lawford in Paris. A brand new one showed her entering a Belgian nunnery, where the rule of silence was observed.

And Eliot might have reflected on this quaint ending and beginning for Sylvia, had he not heard his father address the old stranger affectionately as "Mr. Trout."

• • •

"Trout!" Eliot exclaimed. He was so startled that he momentarily lost his balance, grabbed the birdbath for support. The birdbath was so precariously balanced on its pedestal that it began to tip. Eliot dropped *The Investigator*, grabbed the birdbath with both hands to keep it from falling. And he saw himself in the water. Looking up at him was an emaciated, feverish, middle-aged boy.

"My God," he thought to himself, "F. Scott Fitzgerald, with one day to live."

• • •

He was careful not to cry out Trout's name again as he turned around. He understood that this might betray how sick he was, understood that he and Trout had evidently gotten to know each other during all the blackness. Eliot did not recognize him for the simple reason that all of Trout's bookjackets showed him with a beard. The stranger had no beard.

"By God, Eliot," said the Senator, "when you told me to bring Trout here, I told the Doctor you were still crazy. You said Trout could explain the meaning of everything you'd done in Rosewater, even if you couldn't. But I was willing to try anything, and calling him in is the smartest thing I ever did."

"Right," said Eliot, sitting gingerly on the fountain's rim again. He reached behind himself, retrieved *The Investigator*. He rolled it up, noticed the date on it for the first time. He made a calm calculation. Somehow, somewhere, he had lost one year.

• • •

"You say what Mr. Trout says you should say," ordered the Senator, "and you look the way you look now, and I don't see how we can lose tomorrow."

"Then I will certainly say what Mr. Trout says I should say, and not change one detail of my make-up. I would appreciate, though, a last run-through of what Mr. Trout says I should say."

"It's so simple," said Trout. His voice was rich and deep.

"You two have been over it so many times," said the Senator.

"Even so," said Eliot, "I'd like to hear it one last time."

"Well—" and Trout rubbed his hands, watched the rubbing, "what you did in Rosewater County was far from insane. It was quite possibly the most important social experiment of our time, for it dealt on a very small scale with a problem whose queasy horrors will eventually be made world-wide by the so-phistication of machines. The problem is this: How to love people who have no use?

"In time, almost all men and women will become worthless as producers of goods, food, services, and more machines, as sources of practical ideas in the areas of economics, engineer-ing, and probably medicine, too. So—if we can't find reasons and methods for treasuring human beings because they are *human beings*, then we might as well, as has so often been suggested, rub them out."

• • •

"Americans have long been taught to hate all people who will not or cannot work, to hate even themselves for that. We can thank the vanished frontier for that piece of common-sense cruelty. The time is coming, if it isn't here now, when it will no longer be common sense. It will simply be cruel."

"A poor man with gumption can still elevate himself out of the mire," said the Senator, "and that will continue to be true a thousand years from now."

"Maybe, maybe," Trout answered gently. "He may even have so much gumption that his descendents will live in a Utopia like Pisquontuit, where, I'm sure, the soul-rot and silli-ness and torpor and insensitivity are exactly as horrible as any-thing epidemic in Rosewater County. Poverty is a relatively mild disease for even a very flimsy American soul, but useless-ness will kill strong and weak souls alike, and kill every time.

"We must find a cure."

• • •

"Your devotion to volunteer fire departments is very sane, too, Eliot, for they are, when the alarm goes off, almost the only examples of enthusiastic unselfishness to be seen in this land. They rush to the rescue of any human being, and count not the cost. The most contemptible man in town, should his contemptible house catch fire, will see his enemies put the fire out. And, as he pokes through the ashes for remains of his contemptible possessions, he will be comforted and pitied by no less than the Fire Chief."

Trout spread his hands. "There we have people treasuring people as people. It's extremely rare. So from this we must learn."

• • •

"By God, you're great!" the Senator said to Trout. "You should have been a public relations man! You could make lockjaw sound good for the community! What was a man with your talents doing in a stamp redemption center?"

"Redeeming stamps," Trout mildly replied.

"Mr. Trout," said Eliot, "what happened to your beard?"

"That was the first thing you asked me."

"Tell me again."

"I was hungry and demoralized. A friend knew of a job. So I shaved off my beard and applied. P.S., I got the job."

"I don't suppose they would have hired you with a beard."

"I would have shaved it off, even if they'd said I could keep it."

"Why?"

"Think of the sacrilege of a Jesus figure redeeming stamps."

• • •

"I can't get enough of this Trout," the Senator declared.

"Thank you."

"I just wish you'd stop saying you're a socialist. You're not! You're a free-enterpriser!"

"Through no choice of my own, believe me."

Eliot studied the relationship between the two interesting old men. Trout was not offended, as Eliot thought he should have been, by the suggestion that he be an ultimately dishonest man, a press agent. Trout apparently enjoyed the Senator as a vigorous and wholly consistent work of art, was disinclined to dent or tamper with him in any way. And the Senator admired Trout as a rascal who could rationalize anything, not understanding that Trout had never tried to tell anything but the truth.

"What a political platform you could write, Mr. Trout!"

"Thank you."

"Lawyers think this way, too—figuring out wonderful explanations for hopeless messes. But somehow, from them, it never sounds right. From them it always sounds like the *1812 Overture* played on a kazoo." He sat back, beamed. "Come on—tell us some of the other wonderful things Eliot was doing down there when he was so full of booze."

· · ·

"The court," said McAllister, "is certainly going to want to know what Eliot *learned* from the experiment."

"Keep away from booze, remember who you are, and behave accordingly," the Senator roundly declared. "And don't play God to people, or they will slobber all over you, take you for everything they can get, break commandments just for the fun of being forgiven—and revile you when you are gone."

Eliot couldn't let this pass. "*Revile* me, do they?"

"Oh hell—they love you, they hate you, they cry about you, they laugh at you, they make up new lies about you every day. They run around like chickens with their heads cut off, just as though you really were God, and one day walked out."

Eliot felt his soul cringe, knew he could never stand to return to Rosewater County again.

"It seems to me," said Trout, "that the main lesson Eliot learned is that people can use all the uncritical love they can get."

"This is *news*?" the Senator raucously inquired.

"It's news that a man was able to *give* that kind of love over a long period of time. If one man can do it, perhaps others can do it, too. It means that our hatred of useless human beings and the cruelties we inflict upon them for their own good need not be parts of human nature. Thanks to the example of Eliot Rosewater, millions upon millions of people may learn to love and help whomever they see."

Trout glanced from face to face before speaking his last word on the subject. The last word was: "Joy."

•   •   •

"*Poo-tee-weet?*"

Eliot looked up into the tree again, wondered what his own ideas about Rosewater County had been, ideas he had somehow lost up there in the sycamore.

"If only there had been a child—" said the Senator.

"Well, if you *really* want grandchildren," said McAllister jocularly, "you have something like fifty-seven to choose from, at the most recent count."

Everybody but Eliot had a good laugh over that.

"What's this about fifty-seven grandchildren?"

"Your progeny, my boy," the Senator chuckled.

"My what?"

"Your wild oats."

Eliot sensed that this was a crucial mystery, risked showing how sick he was. "I don't understand."

"That's how many women in Rosewater County claim you're the father of their children."

"This is crazy."

"Of course it is," said the Senator.

Eliot stood, all tensed up. "This is—is impossible!"

"You act as though this was the first time you ever heard of it," said the Senator, and he gave Dr. Brown a glance of flickering unease.

Eliot covered his eyes. "I'm sorry, I—I seem to have drawn a complete blank on this particular subject."

"You're all right, aren't you, boy?"

"Yes." He uncovered his eyes. "I'm fine. There's just this little gap in my memory—and you can fill it up again. How—how did all these women come to say this thing about me?"

"We can't prove it," said McAllister, "but Mushari has been going around the county, bribing people to say bad things about you. The baby thing started with Mary Moody. One day after Mushari was in town, she announced that you were the father of her twins, Foxcroft and Melody. And that touched off a kind of female mania, apparently—"

Kilgore Trout nodded, appreciating the mania.

"So women all over the county started claiming their children were yours. At least half of them seem to believe it. There's one fifteen-year-old girl down there whose stepfather went to prison for getting her pregnant. Now she claims it was you."

"It isn't true!"

"Of course it isn't, Eliot," said his father. "Calm down, calm down. Mushari won't dare mention it in court. The whole scheme backfired and went out of control for him. It's so obviously a mania, no judge would listen. We ran blood tests on Foxcroft and Melody, and they couldn't possibly be yours. We have no intention of testing the other fifty-six claimants. They can go to hell."

• • •

"*Poo-tee-weet?*"

Eliot looked up into the tree, and the memory of all that had happened in the blackness came crashing back—the fight with the bus driver, the straitjacket, the shock treatments, the suicide attempts, all the tennis, all the strategy meetings about the sanity hearing.

And with that mighty inward crash of memories came the idea he had had for settling everything instantly, beautifully, and fairly.

"Tell me—" he said, "do you all swear I'm sane?"

They all swore to that passionately.

"And am I still head of the Foundation? Can I still write checks against its account?"

McAllister told him that he certainly could.

"How's the balance?"

"You haven't spent anything for a year—except for legal fees and what it costs to keep you here, and the three hundred thousand dollars you sent Harvard, and the fifty thousand you gave to Mr. Trout."

"At that, he spent more this year than last year," said the

Senator. This was true. Eliot's Rosewater County operation had been cheaper than staying in a sanitarium.

McAllister told Eliot that he had a balance of about three and a half million dollars, and Eliot asked him for a pen and a check. He then wrote a check to his cousin Fred, in the amount of one million dollars.

The Senator and McAllister went through the roof, told him they had already offered a cash settlement to Fred, and that Fred, through his lawyer, had haughtily refused. "They want the whole thing!" said the Senator.

"That's too bad," said Eliot, "because they're going to get this check, and that's all."

"That's for the court to say—and God only knows what the court *will* say," McAllister warned him. "And you never know. You never know."

"If I had a child," said Eliot, "there wouldn't be any point in a hearing, would there? I mean, the child would inherit the Foundation automatically, whether I was crazy or not, and Fred's degree of relationship would be too distant to entitle him to anything?"

"True."

"Even so," said the Senator, "a million dollars is much too much for the Rhode Island pig!"

"How much, then?"

"A hundred thousand is plenty."

So Eliot tore up the check for a million, made out another for a tenth that much. He looked up, found himself surrounded by awe, for the import of what he had said had now sunk in.

"Eliot—" quavered the Senator, "are you telling us there *is* a child?"

Eliot gave him a Madonna's smile. "Yes."

"Where? By whom?"

Eliot gestured sweetly for their patience. "In time, in time."

"I'm a grandfather!" said the Senator. He tipped back his old head and thanked God.

"Mr. McAllister," said Eliot, "are you duty-bound to carry out any legal missions I may give you, regardless of what my father or anyone else may say to the contrary?"

"As legal counsel of the Foundation, I am."

"Good. I now instruct you to draw up at once papers that will legally acknowledge that every child in Rosewater County said to be mine *is* mine, regardless of blood type. Let them all have full rights of inheritance as my sons and daughters."

"Eliot!"

"Let their names be Rosewater from this moment on. And tell them that their father loves them, no matter what they may turn out to be. And tell them—" Eliot fell silent, raised his tennis racket as though it were a magic wand.

"And tell them," he began again, "to be fruitful and multiply."

SLAUGHTERHOUSE-FIVE
or The Children's Crusade

Slaughterhouse-Five

OR

THE CHILDREN'S CRUSADE

A DUTY-DANCE WITH DEATH

BY

Kurt Vonnegut, Jr.

A FOURTH-GENERATION GERMAN-AMERICAN
NOW LIVING IN EASY CIRCUMSTANCES
ON CAPE COD
[AND SMOKING TOO MUCH],
WHO, AS AN AMERICAN INFANTRY SCOUT
HORS DE COMBAT,
AS A PRISONER OF WAR,
WITNESSED THE FIRE-BOMBING
OF DRESDEN, GERMANY,
"THE FLORENCE OF THE ELBE,"
A LONG TIME AGO,
AND SURVIVED TO TELL THE TALE.
THIS IS A NOVEL
SOMEWHAT IN THE TELEGRAPHIC SCHIZOPHRENIC
MANNER OF TALES
OF THE PLANET TRALFAMADORE,
WHERE THE FLYING SAUCERS
COME FROM.
PEACE.

For
Mary O'Hare
and
Gerhard Müller

The cattle are lowing,
The Baby awakes.
But the little Lord Jesus
No crying He makes.

1

ALL THIS HAPPENED, more or less. The war parts, anyway, are pretty much true. One guy I knew really *was* shot in Dresden for taking a teapot that wasn't his. Another guy I knew really *did* threaten to have his personal enemies killed by hired gunmen after the war. And so on. I've changed all the names.

I really *did* go back to Dresden with Guggenheim money (God love it) in 1967. It looked a lot like Dayton, Ohio, more open spaces than Dayton has. There must be tons of human bone meal in the ground.

I went back there with an old war buddy, Bernard V. O'Hare, and we made friends with a cab driver, who took us to the slaughterhouse where we had been locked up at night as prisoners of war. His name was Gerhard Müller. He told us that he was a prisoner of the Americans for a while. We asked him how it was to live under Communism, and he said that it was terrible at first, because everybody had to work so hard, and because there wasn't much shelter or food or clothing. But things were much better now. He had a pleasant little apartment, and his daughter was getting an excellent education. His mother was incinerated in the Dresden fire-storm. So it goes.

He sent O'Hare a postcard at Christmastime, and here is what it said:

"I wish you and your family also as to your friend Merry Christmas and a happy New Year and I hope that we'll meet again in a world of peace and freedom in the taxi cab if the accident will."

I like that very much: "If the accident will."

I would hate to tell you what this lousy little book cost me in money and anxiety and time. When I got home from the Second World War twenty-three years ago, I thought it would be easy for me to write about the destruction of Dresden, since all I would have to do would be to report what I had seen. And I thought, too, that it would be a masterpiece or at least make me a lot of money, since the subject was so big.

But not many words about Dresden came from my mind then—not enough of them to make a book, anyway. And not many words come now, either, when I have become an old fart with his memories and his Pall Malls, with his sons full grown.

I think of how useless the Dresden part of my memory has been, and yet how tempting Dresden has been to write about, and I am reminded of the famous limerick:

> There was a young man from Stamboul,
> Who soliloquized thus to his tool:
> "You took all my wealth
> And you ruined my health,
> And now you won't *pee*, you old fool."

And I'm reminded, too, of the song that goes:

> My name is Yon Yonson,
> I work in Wisconsin,
> I work in a lumbermill there.
> The people I meet when I walk down the street,
> They say, "What's your name?"
> And I say,
> "My name is Yon Yonson,
> I work in Wisconsin . . ."

And so on to infinity.

Over the years, people I've met have often asked me what I'm working on, and I've usually replied that the main thing was a book about Dresden.

I said that to Harrison Starr, the movie-maker, one time, and he raised his eyebrows and inquired, "Is it an anti-war book?"

"Yes," I said. "I guess."

"You know what I say to people when I hear they're writing anti-war books?"

"No. What *do* you say, Harrison Starr?"

"I say, 'Why don't you write an anti-*glacier* book instead?'"

What he meant, of course, was that there would always be wars, that they were as easy to stop as glaciers. I believe that, too.

And, even if wars didn't keep coming like glaciers, there would still be plain old death.

•

When I was somewhat younger, working on my famous Dresden book, I asked an old war buddy named Bernard V. O'Hare if I could come to see him. He was a district attorney in Pennsylvania. I was a writer on Cape Cod. We had been privates in the war, infantry scouts. We had never expected to make any money after the war, but we were doing quite well.

I had the Bell Telephone Company find him for me. They are wonderful that way. I have this disease late at night sometimes, involving alcohol and the telephone. I get drunk, and I drive my wife away with a breath like mustard gas and roses. And then, speaking gravely and elegantly into the telephone, I ask the telephone operators to connect me with this friend or that one, from whom I have not heard in years.

I got O'Hare on the line in this way. He is short and I am tall. We were Mutt and Jeff in the war. We were captured together in the war. I told him who I was on the telephone. He had no trouble believing it. He was up. He was reading. Everybody else in his house was asleep.

"Listen—" I said, "I'm writing this book about Dresden. I'd like some help remembering stuff. I wonder if I could come down and see you, and we could drink and talk and remember."

He was unenthusiastic. He said he couldn't remember much. He told me, though, to come ahead.

"I think the climax of the book will be the execution of poor old Edgar Derby," I said. "The irony is *so* great. A whole city gets burned down, and thousands and thousands of people are killed. And then this one American foot soldier is arrested in the ruins for taking a teapot. And he's given a regular trial, and then he's shot by a firing squad."

"Um," said O'Hare.

"Don't you think that's really where the climax should come?"

"I don't know anything about it," he said. "That's your trade, not mine."

As a trafficker in climaxes and thrills and characterization and wonderful dialogue and suspense and confrontations, I had outlined the Dresden story many times. The best outline I ever made, or anyway the prettiest one, was on the back of a roll of wallpaper.

I used my daughter's crayons, a different color for each main character. One end of the wallpaper was the beginning of the story, and the other end was the end, and then there was all that middle part, which was the middle. And the blue line met the red line and then the yellow line, and the yellow line stopped because the character represented by the yellow line was dead. And so on. The destruction of Dresden was represented by a vertical band of orange cross-hatching, and all the lines that were still alive passed through it, came out the other side.

The end, where all the lines stopped, was a beetfield on the Elbe, outside of Halle. The rain was coming down. The war in Europe had been over for a couple of weeks. We were formed in ranks, with Russian soldiers guarding us—Englishmen, Americans, Dutchmen, Belgians, Frenchmen, Canadians, South Africans, New Zealanders, Australians, thousands of us about to stop being prisoners of war.

And on the other side of the field were thousands of Russians and Poles and Yugoslavians and so on guarded by American soldiers. An exchange was made there in the rain—one for one. O'Hare and I climbed into the back of an American truck with a lot of others. O'Hare didn't have any souvenirs. Almost everybody else did. I had a ceremonial Luftwaffe saber, still do. The rabid little American I call Paul Lazzaro in this book had about a quart of diamonds and emeralds and rubies and so on. He had taken these from dead people in the cellars of Dresden. So it goes.

An idiotic Englishman, who had lost all his teeth somewhere, had his souvenir in a canvas bag. The bag was resting on my insteps. He would peek into the bag every now and then, and he would roll his eyes and swivel his scrawny neck, trying to catch people looking covetously at his bag. And he would bounce the bag on my insteps.

I thought this bouncing was accidental. But I was mistaken. He *had* to show somebody what was in the bag, and he had decided he could trust me. He caught my eye, winked, opened the bag. There was a plaster model of the Eiffel Tower in there. It was painted gold. It had a clock in it.

"There's a smashin' thing," he said.

•

And we were flown to a rest camp in France, where we were fed chocolate malted milkshakes and other rich foods until we were all covered with baby fat. Then we were sent home, and I married a pretty girl who was covered with baby fat, too.

And we had babies.

And they're all grown up now, and I'm an old fart with his memories and his Pall Malls. My name is Yon Yonson, I work in Wisconsin, I work in a lumbermill there.

Sometimes I try to call up old girl friends on the telephone late at night, after my wife has gone to bed. "Operator, I wonder if you could give me the number of a Mrs. So-and-So. I think she lives at such-and-such."

"I'm sorry, sir. There is no such listing."

"Thanks, Operator. Thanks just the same."

And I let the dog out, or I let him in, and we talk some. I let him know I like him, and he lets me know he likes me. He doesn't mind the smell of mustard gas and roses.

"You're all right, Sandy," I'll say to the dog. "You know that, Sandy? You're O.K."

Sometimes I'll turn on the radio and listen to a talk program from Boston or New York. I can't stand recorded music if I've been drinking a good deal.

Sooner or later I go to bed, and my wife asks me what time it is. She always has to know the time. Sometimes I don't know, and I say, "Search *me*."

I think about my education sometimes. I went to the University of Chicago for a while after the Second World War. I was a student in the Department of Anthropology. At that time, they were teaching that there was absolutely no difference between anybody. They may be teaching that still.

Another thing they taught was that nobody was ridiculous or bad or disgusting. Shortly before my father died, he said to me, "You know—you never wrote a story with a villain in it."

I told him that was one of the things I learned in college after the war.

While I was studying to be an anthropologist, I was also working as a police reporter for the famous Chicago City News

Bureau for twenty-eight dollars a week. One time they switched me from the night shift to the day shift, so I worked sixteen hours straight. We were supported by all the newspapers in town, and the AP and the UP and all that. And we would cover the courts and the police stations and the Fire Department and the Coast Guard out on Lake Michigan and all that. We were connected to the institutions that supported us by means of pneumatic tubes which ran under the streets of Chicago.

Reporters would telephone in stories to writers wearing headphones, and the writers would stencil the stories on mimeograph sheets. The stories were mimeographed and stuffed into the brass and velvet cartridges which the pneumatic tubes ate. The very toughest reporters and writers were women who had taken over the jobs of men who'd gone to war.

And the first story I covered I had to dictate over the telephone to one of those beastly girls. It was about a young veteran who had taken a job running an old-fashioned elevator in an office building. The elevator door on the first floor was ornamental iron lace. Iron ivy snaked in and out of the holes. There was an iron twig with two iron lovebirds perched upon it.

This veteran decided to take his car into the basement, and he closed the door and started down, but his wedding ring was caught in all the ornaments. So he was hoisted into the air and the floor of the car went down, dropped out from under him, and the top of the car squashed him. So it goes.

So I phoned this in, and the woman who was going to cut the stencil asked me, "What did his wife say?"

"She doesn't know yet," I said. "It just happened."

"Call her up and get a statement."

"What?"

"Tell her you're Captain Finn of the Police Department. Say you have some sad news. Give her the news, and see what she says."

So I did. She said about what you would expect her to say. There was a baby. And so on.

When I got back to the office, the woman writer asked me, just for her own information, what the squashed guy had looked like when he was squashed.

I told her.

"Did it bother you?" she said. She was eating a Three Musketeers Candy Bar.

"Heck no, Nancy," I said. "I've seen lots worse than that in
the war."

Even then I was supposedly writing a book about Dresden.
It wasn't a famous air raid back then in America. Not many
Americans knew how much worse it had been than Hiroshima,
for instance. I didn't know that, either. There hadn't been
much publicity.

I happened to tell a University of Chicago professor at a
cocktail party about the raid as I had seen it, about the book I
would write. He was a member of a thing called The Committee
on Social Thought. And he told me about the concentration
camps, and about how the Germans had made soap and candles
out of the fat of dead Jews and so on.

All I could say was, "I know, I know. I *know*."

World War Two had certainly made everybody very tough.
And I became a public relations man for General Electric in
Schenectady, New York, and a volunteer fireman in the village
of Alplaus, where I bought my first home. My boss there was
one of the toughest guys I ever hope to meet. He had been a
lieutenant colonel in public relations in Baltimore. While I was
in Schenectady he joined the Dutch Reformed Church, which
is a very tough church, indeed.

He used to ask me sneeringly sometimes why I hadn't been
an officer, as though I'd done something wrong.

My wife and I had lost our baby fat. Those were our scrawny
years. We had a lot of scrawny veterans and their scrawny wives
for friends. The nicest veterans in Schenectady, I thought, the
kindest and funniest ones, the ones who hated war the most,
were the ones who'd really fought.

I wrote the Air Force back then, asking for details about the
raid on Dresden, who ordered it, how many planes did it, why
they did it, what desirable results there had been and so on. I
was answered by a man who, like myself, was in public relations. He said that he was sorry, but that the information was
top secret still.

I read the letter out loud to my wife, and I said, "Secret? My God—from *whom?*"

We were United World Federalists back then. I don't know what we are now. Telephoners, I guess. We telephone a lot—or *I* do, anyway, late at night.

A couple of weeks after I telephoned my old war buddy, Bernard V. O'Hare, I really *did* go to see him. That must have been in 1964 or so—whatever the last year was for the New York World's Fair. *Eheu, fugaces labuntur anni.* My name is Yon Yonson. There was a young man from Stamboul.

I took two little girls with me, my daughter, Nanny, and her best friend, Allison Mitchell. They had never been off Cape Cod before. When we saw a river, we had to stop so they could stand by it and think about it for a while. They had never seen water in that long and narrow, unsalted form before. The river was the Hudson. There were carp in there and we saw them. They were as big as atomic submarines.

We saw waterfalls, too, streams jumping off cliffs into the valley of the Delaware. There were lots of things to stop and see—and then it was time to go, always time to go. The little girls were wearing white party dresses and black party shoes, so strangers would know at once how nice they were. "Time to go, girls," I'd say. And we would go.

And the sun went down, and we had supper in an Italian place, and then I knocked on the front door of the beautiful stone house of Bernard V. O'Hare. I was carrying a bottle of Irish whiskey like a dinner bell.

I met his nice wife, Mary, to whom I dedicate this book. I dedicate it to Gerhard Müller, the Dresden taxi driver, too. Mary O'Hare is a trained nurse, which is a lovely thing for a woman to be.

Mary admired the two little girls I'd brought, mixed them in with her own children, sent them all upstairs to play games and watch television. It was only after the children were gone that I sensed that Mary didn't like me or didn't like *something* about the night. She was polite but chilly.

"It's a nice cozy house you have here," I said, and it really was.

"I've fixed up a place where you can talk and not be bothered," she said.

"Good," I said, and I imagined two leather chairs near a fire in a paneled room, where two old soldiers could drink and talk. But she took us into the kitchen. She had put two straight-backed chairs at a kitchen table with a white porcelain top. That table top was screaming with reflected light from a two-hundred-watt bulb overhead. Mary had prepared an operating room. She put only one glass on it, which was for me. She explained that O'Hare couldn't drink the hard stuff since the war.

So we sat down. O'Hare was embarrassed, but he wouldn't tell me what was wrong. I couldn't imagine what it was about me that could burn up Mary so. I was a family man. I'd been married only once. I wasn't a drunk. I hadn't done her husband any dirt in the war.

She fixed herself a Coca-Cola, made a lot of noise banging the ice-cube tray in the stainless steel sink. Then she went into another part of the house. But she wouldn't sit still. She was moving all over the house, opening and shutting doors, even moving furniture around to work off anger.

I asked O'Hare what I'd said or done to make her act that way.

"It's all right," he said. "Don't worry about it. It doesn't have anything to do with you." That was kind of him. He was lying. It had everything to do with me.

So we tried to ignore Mary and remember the war. I took a couple of belts of the booze I'd brought. We would chuckle or grin sometimes, as though war stories were coming back, but neither one of us could remember anything good. O'Hare remembered one guy who got into a lot of wine in Dresden, before it was bombed, and we had to take him home in a wheelbarrow. It wasn't much to write a book about. I remembered two Russian soldiers who had looted a clock factory. They had a horse-drawn wagon full of clocks. They were happy and drunk. They were smoking huge cigarettes they had rolled in newspaper.

That was about *it* for memories, and Mary was still making noise. She finally came out in the kitchen again for another Coke. She took another tray of ice cubes from the refrigerator, banged it in the sink, even though there was already plenty of ice out.

Then she turned to me, let me see how angry she was, and that the anger was for me. She had been talking to herself, so what she said was a fragment of a much larger conversation. "You were just *babies* then!" she said.

"What?" I said.

"You were just babies in the war—like the ones upstairs!"

I nodded that this was true. We *had* been foolish virgins in the war, right at the end of childhood.

"But you're not going to write it that way, are you." This wasn't a question. It was an accusation.

"I—I don't know," I said.

"Well, *I* know," she said. "You'll pretend you were men instead of babies, and you'll be played in the movies by Frank Sinatra and John Wayne or some of those other glamorous, war-loving, dirty old men. And war will look just wonderful, so we'll have a lot more of them. And they'll be fought by babies like the babies upstairs."

So then I understood. It was war that made her so angry. She didn't want her babies or anybody else's babies killed in wars. And she thought wars were partly encouraged by books and movies.

So I held up my right hand and I made her a promise: "Mary," I said, "I don't think this book of mine is ever going to be finished. I must have written five thousand pages by now, and thrown them all away. If I ever do finish it, though, I give you my word of honor: there won't be a part for Frank Sinatra or John Wayne.

"I tell you what," I said, "I'll call it 'The Children's Crusade.'"

She was my friend after that.

O'Hare and I gave up on remembering, went into the living room, talked about other things. We became curious about the real Children's Crusade, so O'Hare looked it up in a book he had, *Extraordinary Popular Delusions and the Madness of*

Crowds, by Charles Mackay, LL. D. It was first published in London in 1841.

Mackay had a low opinion of *all* Crusades. The Children's Crusade struck him as only slightly more sordid than the ten Crusades for grown-ups. O'Hare read this handsome passage out loud:

History in her solemn page informs us that the crusaders were but ignorant and savage men, that their motives were those of bigotry unmitigated, and that their pathway was one of blood and tears. Romance, on the other hand, dilates upon their piety and heroism, and portrays, in her most glowing and impassioned hues, their virtue and magnanimity, the imperishable honor they acquired for themselves, and the great services they rendered to Christianity.

And then O'Hare read this: *Now what was the grand result of all these struggles? Europe expended millions of her treasures, and the blood of two million of her people; and a handful of quarrelsome knights retained possession of Palestine for about one hundred years!*

Mackay told us that the Children's Crusade started in 1213, when two monks got the idea of raising armies of children in Germany and France, and selling them in North Africa as slaves. Thirty thousand children volunteered, thinking they were going to Palestine. *They were no doubt idle and deserted children who generally swarm in great cities, nurtured on vice and daring,* said Mackay, *and ready for anything.*

Pope Innocent the Third thought they were going to Palestine, too, and he was thrilled. "These children are awake while we are asleep!" he said.

Most of the children were shipped out of Marseilles, and about half of them drowned in shipwrecks. The other half got to North Africa where they were sold.

Through a misunderstanding, some children reported for duty at Genoa, where no slave ships were waiting. They were fed and sheltered and questioned kindly by good people there—then given a little money and a lot of advice and sent back home.

"Hooray for the good people of Genoa," said Mary O'Hare.

•

I slept that night in one of the children's bedrooms. O'Hare had put a book for me on the bedside table. It was *Dresden, History, Stage and Gallery*, by Mary Endell. It was published in 1908, and its introduction began:

It is hoped that this little book will make itself useful. It at-tempts to give to an English-reading public a bird's-eye view of how Dresden came to look as it does, architecturally; of how it ex-panded musically, through the genius of a few men, to its present bloom; and it calls attention to certain permanent landmarks in art that make its Gallery the resort of those seeking lasting impressions.

I read some history further on:

Now, in 1760, Dresden underwent siege by the Prussians. On the fifteenth of July began the cannonade. The Picture-Gallery took fire. Many of the paintings had been transported to the Königstein, but some were seriously injured by splinters of bomb-shells,—notably Francia's "Baptism of Christ." Furthermore, the stately Kreuzkirche tower, from which the enemy's movements had been watched day and night, stood in flames. It later succumbed. In sturdy contrast with the pitiful fate of the Kreuzkirche, stood the Frauenkirche, from the curves of whose stone dome the Prussian bombs rebounded like rain. Friederich was obliged finally to give up the siege, because he learned of the fall of Glatz, the critical point of his new conquests. "We must be off to Silesia, so that we do not lose everything."

The devastation of Dresden was boundless. When Goethe as a young student visited the city, he still found sad ruins: "Von der Kuppel der Frauenkirche sah ich diese leidigen Trümmer zwischen die schöne städtische Ordnung hineingesät; da rühmte mir der Küster die Kunst des Baumeisters, welcher Kirche und Kuppel auf einen so unerwünschten Fall schon eingerichtet und bombenfest erbaut hatte. Der gute Sakristan deutete mir alsdann auf Ruinen nach allen Seiten und sagte bedenklich lakonisch: Das hat der Feind gethan!"

The two little girls and I crossed the Delaware River where George Washington had crossed it, the next morning. We went to the New York World's Fair, saw what the past had been like, according to the Ford Motor Car Company and Walt Disney, saw what the future would be like, according to General Motors.

And I asked myself about the present: how wide it was, how deep it was, how much was mine to keep.

I taught creative writing in the famous Writers Workshop at the University of Iowa for a couple of years after that. I got into some perfectly beautiful trouble, got out of it again. I taught in the afternoons. In the mornings I wrote. I was not to be disturbed. I was working on my famous book about Dresden.

And somewhere in there a nice man named Seymour Lawrence gave me a three-book contract, and I said, "O.K., the first of the three will be my famous book about Dresden."

The friends of Seymour Lawrence call him "Sam." And I say to Sam now: "Sam—here's the book."

It is so short and jumbled and jangled, Sam, because there is nothing intelligent to say about a massacre. Everybody is supposed to be dead, to never say anything or want anything ever again. Everything is supposed to be very quiet after a massacre, and it always is, except for the birds.

And what do the birds say? All there is to say about a massacre, things like "*Poo-tee-weet?*"

I have told my sons that they are not under any circumstances to take part in massacres, and that the news of massacres of enemies is not to fill them with satisfaction or glee.

I have also told them not to work for companies which make massacre machinery, and to express contempt for people who think we need machinery like that.

As I've said: I recently went back to Dresden with my friend O'Hare. We had a million laughs in Hamburg and West Berlin and East Berlin and Vienna and Salzburg and Helsinki, and in Leningrad, too. It was very good for me, because I saw a lot of authentic backgrounds for made-up stories which I will write later on. One of them will be "Russian Baroque" and another will be "No Kissing" and another will be "Dollar Bar" and another will be "If the Accident Will," and so on.

And so on.

There was a Lufthansa plane that was supposed to fly from Philadelphia to Boston to Frankfurt. O'Hare was supposed to get on in Philadelphia and I was supposed to get on in Boston, and off we'd go. But Boston was socked in, so the plane flew straight to Frankfurt from Philadelphia. And I became a nonperson in the Boston fog, and Lufthansa put me in a limousine with some other non-persons and sent us to a motel for a non-night.

The time would not pass. Somebody was playing with the clocks, and not only with the electric clocks, but the wind-up kind, too. The second hand on my watch would twitch once, and a year would pass, and then it would twitch again.

There was nothing I could do about it. As an Earthling, I had to believe whatever clocks said—and calendars.

I had two books with me, which I'd meant to read on the plane. One was *Words for the Wind*, by Theodore Roethke, and this is what I found in there:

> *I wake to sleep, and take my waking slow.*
> *I feel my fate in what I cannot fear.*
> *I learn by going where I have to go.*

My other book was Erika Ostrovsky's *Céline and His Vision*. Céline was a brave French soldier in the First World War—until his skull was cracked. After that he couldn't sleep, and there were noises in his head. He became a doctor, and he treated poor people in the daytime, and he wrote grotesque novels all night. No art is possible without a dance with death, he wrote.

The truth is death, he wrote. *I've fought nicely against it as long as I could . . . danced with it, festooned it, waltzed it around . . . decorated it with streamers, titillated it . . .*

Time obsessed him. Miss Ostrovsky reminded me of the amazing scene in *Death on the Installment Plan* where Céline wants to stop the bustling of a street crowd. He screams on paper, *Make them stop . . . don't let them move anymore at*

*all . . . There, make them freeze . . . once and for all! . . . So
that they won't disappear anymore!*

I looked through the Gideon Bible in my motel room for
tales of great destruction. *The sun was risen upon the Earth
when Lot entered into Zo-ar*, I read. *Then the Lord rained upon
Sodom and upon Gomorrah brimstone and fire from the Lord out
of Heaven; and He overthrew those cities, and all the plain, and
all the inhabitants of the cities, and that which grew upon the
ground.*

So it goes.

Those were vile people in both those cities, as is well known.
The world was better off without them.

And Lot's wife, of course, was told not to look back where
all those people and their homes had been. But she *did* look
back, and I love her for that, because it was so human.

So she was turned to a pillar of salt. So it goes.

People aren't supposed to look back. I'm certainly not going
to do it anymore.

I've finished my war book now. The next one I write is going to be fun.

This one is a failure, and had to be, since it was written by a
pillar of salt. It begins like this:

Listen:

Billy Pilgrim has come unstuck in time.

It ends like this:

Poo-tee-weet?

2

L ISTEN:
Billy Pilgrim has come unstuck in time.

Billy has gone to sleep a senile widower and awakened on his wedding day. He has walked through a door in 1955 and come out another one in 1941. He has gone back through that door to find himself in 1963. He has seen his birth and death many times, he says, and pays random visits to all the events in between.

He says.

Billy is spastic in time, has no control over where he is going next, and the trips aren't necessarily fun. He is in a constant state of stage fright, he says, because he never knows what part of his life he is going to have to act in next.

Billy was born in 1922 in Ilium, New York, the only child of a barber there. He was a funny-looking child who became a funny-looking youth—tall and weak, and shaped like a bottle of Coca-Cola. He graduated from Ilium High School in the upper third of his class, and attended night sessions at the Ilium School of Optometry for one semester before being drafted for military service in the Second World War. His father died in a hunting accident during the war. So it goes.

Billy saw service with the infantry in Europe, and was taken prisoner by the Germans. After his honorable discharge from the Army in 1945, Billy again enrolled in the Ilium School of Optometry. During his senior year there, he became engaged to the daughter of the founder and owner of the school, and then suffered a mild nervous collapse.

He was treated in a veteran's hospital near Lake Placid, and was given shock treatments and released. He married his fiancée, finished his education, and was set up in business in Ilium by his father-in-law. Ilium is a particularly good city for optometrists because the General Forge and Foundry Company is there. Every employee is required to own a pair of safety glasses, and to wear them in areas where manufacturing is going on. GF&F has sixty-eight thousand employees in Ilium. That calls for a lot of lenses and a lot of frames.

Frames are where the money is.

Billy became rich. He had two children, Barbara and Robert. In time, his daughter Barbara married another optometrist, and Billy set him up in business. Billy's son Robert had a lot of trouble in high school, but then he joined the famous Green Berets. He straightened out, became a fine young man, and he fought in Vietnam.

Early in 1968, a group of optometrists, with Billy among them, chartered an airplane to fly them from Ilium to an international convention of optometrists in Montreal. The plane crashed on top of Sugarbush Mountain, in Vermont. Everybody was killed but Billy. So it goes.

While Billy was recuperating in a hospital in Vermont, his wife died accidentally of carbon-monoxide poisoning. So it goes.

When Billy finally got home to Ilium after the airplane crash, he was quiet for a while. He had a terrible scar across the top of his skull. He didn't resume practice. He had a housekeeper. His daughter came over almost every day.

And then, without any warning, Billy went to New York City, and got on an all-night radio program devoted to talk. He told about having come unstuck in time. He said, too, that he had been kidnapped by a flying saucer in 1967. The saucer was from the planet Tralfamadore, he said. He was taken to Tralfamadore, where he was displayed naked in a zoo, he said. He was mated there with a former Earthling movie star named Montana Wildhack.

Some night owls in Ilium heard Billy on the radio, and one of them called Billy's daughter Barbara. Barbara was upset. She and her husband went down to New York and brought Billy home. Billy insisted mildly that everything he had said on the radio was true. He said he had been kidnapped by the Tralfamadorians on the night of his daughter's wedding. He hadn't been missed, he said, because the Tralfamadorians had taken him through a time warp, so that he could be on

Tralfamadore for years, and still be away from Earth for only a microsecond.

Another month went by without incident, and then Billy wrote a letter to the Ilium *News Leader*, which the paper published. It described the creatures from Tralfamadore.

The letter said that they were two feet high, and green, and shaped like plumber's friends. Their suction cups were on the ground, and their shafts, which were extremely flexible, usually pointed to the sky. At the top of each shaft was a little hand with a green eye in its palm. The creatures were friendly, and they could see in four dimensions. They pitied Earthlings for being able to see only three. They had many wonderful things to teach Earthlings, especially about time. Billy promised to tell what some of those wonderful things were in his next letter.

Billy was working on his second letter when the first letter was published. The second letter started out like this:

"The most important thing I learned on Tralfamadore was that when a person dies he only *appears* to die. He is still very much alive in the past, so it is very silly for people to cry at his funeral. All moments, past, present, and future, always have existed, always will exist. The Tralfamadorians can look at all the different moments just the way we can look at a stretch of the Rocky Mountains, for instance. They can see how permanent all the moments are, and they can look at any moment that interests them. It is just an illusion we have here on Earth that one moment follows another one, like beads on a string, and that once a moment is gone it is gone forever.

"When a Tralfamadorian sees a corpse, all he thinks is that the dead person is in bad condition in that particular moment, but that the same person is just fine in plenty of other moments. Now, when I myself hear that somebody is dead, I simply shrug and say what the Tralfamadorians say about dead people, which is 'So it goes.'"

And so on.

Billy was working on this letter in the basement rumpus room of his empty house. It was his housekeeper's day off. There was an old typewriter in the rumpus room. It was a beast. It weighed as much as a storage battery. Billy couldn't carry it very far very easily, which was why he was writing in the rumpus room instead of somewhere else.

The oil burner had quit. A mouse had eaten through the insulation of a wire leading to the thermostat. The temperature in the house was down to fifty degrees, but Billy hadn't noticed. He wasn't warmly dressed, either. He was barefoot, and still in his pajamas and a bathrobe, though it was late afternoon. His bare feet were blue and ivory.

The cockles of Billy's heart, at any rate, were glowing coals. What made them so hot was Billy's belief that he was going to comfort so many people with the truth about time. His door chimes upstairs had been ringing and ringing. It was his daughter Barbara up there, wanting in. Now she let herself in with a key, crossed the floor over his head, calling, "Father? Daddy, where are you?" And so on.

Billy didn't answer her, so she was nearly hysterical, expecting to find his corpse. And then she looked into the very last place there *was* to look—which was the rumpus room.

"Why didn't you answer me when I called?" Barbara wanted to know, standing there in the door of the rumpus room. She had the afternoon paper with her, the one in which Billy described his friends from Tralfamadore.

"I didn't *hear* you," said Billy.

The orchestration of the moment was this: Barbara was only twenty-one years old, but she thought her father was senile, even though he was only forty-six—senile because of damage to his brain in the airplane crash. She also thought that she was head of the family, since she had had to manage her mother's funeral, since she had to get a housekeeper for Billy, and all that. Also, Barbara and her husband were having to look after Billy's business interests, which were considerable, since Billy didn't seem to give a damn for business any more. All this responsibility at such an early age made her a bitchy flibbertigibbet. And Billy, meanwhile, was trying to hang onto his dignity, to persuade Barbara and everybody else that he was far from senile, that, on the contrary, he was devoting himself to a calling much higher than mere business.

He was doing nothing less now, he thought, than prescribing

corrective lenses for Earthling souls. So many of those souls were lost and wretched, Billy believed, because they could not see as well as his little green friends on Tralfamadore.

"Don't lie to me, Father," said Barbara. "I know perfectly well you heard me when I called." This was a fairly pretty girl, except that she had legs like an Edwardian grand piano. Now she raised hell with him about the letter in the paper. She said he was making a laughing stock of himself and everybody associated with him.

"Father, Father, Father—" said Barbara, "what are we going to *do* with you? Are you going to force us to put you where your mother is?" Billy's mother was still alive. She was in bed in an old people's home called Pine Knoll on the edge of Ilium.

"What is it about my letter that makes you so mad?" Billy wanted to know.

"It's all just crazy. None of it's true!"

"It's all true." Billy's anger was not going to rise with hers. He never got mad at anything. He was wonderful that way.

"There is no such planet as Tralfamadore."

"It can't be detected from Earth, if that's what you mean," said Billy. "Earth can't be detected from Tralfamadore, as far as that goes. They're both very small. They're very far apart."

"Where did you get a crazy name like 'Tralfamadore'?"

"That's what the creatures who live there *call* it."

"Oh God," said Barbara, and she turned her back on him. She celebrated frustration by clapping her hands. "May I ask you a simple question?"

"Of course."

"Why is it you never mentioned any of this before the airplane crash?"

"I didn't think the time was *ripe.*"

And so on. Billy says that he first came unstuck in time in 1944, long before his trip to Tralfamadore. The Tralfamadorians didn't have anything to do with his coming unstuck. They were simply able to give him insights into what was really going on.

Billy first came unstuck while World War Two was in progress. Billy was a chaplain's assistant in the war. A chaplain's assistant is customarily a figure of fun in the American Army. Billy was no exception. He was powerless to harm the enemy or to help his friends. In fact, he had no friends. He was a valet to a preacher, expected no promotions or medals, bore no arms, and had a meek faith in a loving Jesus which most soldiers found putrid.

While on maneuvers in South Carolina, Billy played hymns he knew from childhood, played them on a little black organ which was waterproof. It had thirty-nine keys and two stops— *vox humana* and *vox celeste*. Billy also had charge of a portable altar, an olive-drab attaché case with telescoping legs. It was lined with crimson plush, and nestled in that passionate plush were an anodized aluminum cross and a Bible.

The altar and the organ were made by a vacuum-cleaner company in Camden, New Jersey—and said so.

One time on maneuvers Billy was playing "A Mighty Fortress Is Our God," with music by Johann Sebastian Bach and words by Martin Luther. It was Sunday morning. Billy and his chaplain had gathered a congregation of about fifty soldiers on a Carolina hillside. An umpire appeared. There were umpires everywhere, men who said who was winning or losing the theoretical battle, who was alive and who was dead.

The umpire had comical news. The congregation had been theoretically spotted from the air by a theoretical enemy. They were all theoretically dead now. The theoretical corpses laughed and ate a hearty noontime meal.

Remembering this incident years later, Billy was struck by what a Tralfamadorian adventure with death that had been, to be dead and to eat at the same time.

Toward the end of maneuvers, Billy was given an emergency furlough home because his father, a barber in Ilium, New York, was shot dead by a friend while they were out hunting deer. So it goes.

When Billy got back from his furlough, there were orders for him to go overseas. He was needed in the headquarters company of an infantry regiment fighting in Luxembourg. The regimental chaplain's assistant had been killed in action. So it goes.

When Billy joined the regiment, it was in the process of being destroyed by the Germans in the famous Battle of the Bulge. Billy never even got to meet the chaplain he was supposed to assist, was never even issued a steel helmet and combat boots. This was in December of 1944, during the last mighty German attack of the war.

Billy survived, but he was a dazed wanderer far behind the new German lines. Three other wanderers, not quite so dazed, allowed Billy to tag along. Two of them were scouts, and one was an antitank gunner. They were without food or maps. Avoiding Germans, they were delivering themselves into rural silences ever more profound. They ate snow.

They went Indian file. First came the scouts, clever, graceful, quiet. They had rifles. Next came the antitank gunner, clumsy and dense, warning Germans away with a Colt .45 automatic in one hand and a trench knife in the other.

Last came Billy Pilgrim, empty-handed, bleakly ready for death. Billy was preposterous—six feet and three inches tall, with a chest and shoulders like a box of kitchen matches. He had no helmet, no overcoat, no weapon, and no boots. On his feet were cheap, low-cut civilian shoes which he had bought for his father's funeral. Billy had lost a heel, which made him bob up-and-down, up-and-down. The involuntary dancing, up and down, up and down, made his hip joints sore.

Billy was wearing a thin field jacket, a shirt and trousers of scratchy wool, and long underwear that was soaked with sweat. He was the only one of the four who had a beard. It was a random, bristly beard, and some of the bristles were white, even though Billy was only twenty-one years old. He was also going bald. Wind and cold and violent exercise had turned his face crimson.

He didn't look like a soldier at all. He looked like a filthy flamingo.

And on the third day of wandering, somebody shot at the four from far away—shot four times as they crossed a narrow brick road. One shot was for the scouts. The next one was for the antitank gunner, whose name was Roland Weary.

The third bullet was for the filthy flamingo, who stopped dead center in the road when the lethal bee buzzed past his ear. Billy stood there politely, giving the marksman another chance. It was his addled understanding of the rules of warfare that the marksman *should* be given a second chance. The next shot missed Billy's kneecaps by inches, going end-on-end, from the sound of it.

Roland Weary and the scouts were safe in a ditch, and Weary growled at Billy, "Get out of the road, you dumb mother-fucker." The last word was still a novelty in the speech of white people in 1944. It was fresh and astonishing to Billy, who had never fucked anybody—and it did its job. It woke him up and got him off the road.

"Saved your life again, you dumb bastard," Weary said to Billy in the ditch. He had been saving Billy's life for days, cursing him, kicking him, slapping him, making him move. It was absolutely necessary that cruelty be used, because Billy wouldn't do anything to save himself. Billy wanted to quit. He was cold, hungry, embarrassed, incompetent. He could scarcely distinguish between sleep and wakefulness now, on the third day, found no important differences, either, between walking and standing still.

He wished everybody would leave him alone. "You guys go on without me," he said again and again.

Weary was as new to war as Billy. He was a replacement, too. As a part of a gun crew, he had helped to fire one shot in anger—from a 57-millimeter antitank gun. The gun made a ripping sound like the opening of the zipper on the fly of God Almighty. The gun lapped up snow and vegetation with a blowtorch thirty feet long. The flame left a black arrow on the ground, showing the Germans exactly where the gun was hidden. The shot was a miss.

What had been missed was a Tiger tank. It swiveled its 88-millimeter snout around sniffingly, saw the arrow on the ground. It fired. It killed everybody on the gun crew but Weary. So it goes.

Roland Weary was only eighteen, was at the end of an unhappy childhood spent mostly in Pittsburgh, Pennsylvania. He had been unpopular in Pittsburgh. He had been unpopular because he was stupid and fat and mean, and smelled like bacon no matter how much he washed. He was always being ditched in Pittsburgh by people who did not want him with them.

It made Weary sick to be ditched. When Weary was ditched, he would find somebody who was even more unpopular than himself, and he would horse around with that person for a while, pretending to be friendly. And then he would find some pretext for beating the shit out of him.

It was a pattern. It was a crazy, sexy, murderous relationship Weary entered into with people he eventually beat up. He told them about his father's collection of guns and swords and torture instruments and leg irons and so on. Weary's father, who was a plumber, actually did collect such things, and his collection was insured for four thousand dollars. He wasn't alone. He belonged to a big club composed of people who collected things like that.

Weary's father once gave Weary's mother a Spanish thumbscrew in working condition—for a kitchen paperweight. Another time he gave her a table lamp whose base was a model one foot high of the famous "Iron Maiden of Nuremberg." The real Iron Maiden was a medieval torture instrument, a sort of boiler which was shaped like a woman on the outside— and lined with spikes. The front of the woman was composed of two hinged doors. The idea was to put a criminal inside and then close the doors slowly. There were two special spikes where his eyes would be. There was a drain in the bottom to let out all the blood.

So it goes.

Weary had told Billy Pilgrim about the Iron Maiden, about the drain in her bottom—and what that was for. He had talked to Billy about dum-dums. He told him about his father's Derringer pistol, which could be carried in a vest pocket, which was yet capable of making a hole in a man "which a bull bat could fly through without touching either wing."

Weary scornfully bet Billy one time that he didn't even know what a blood gutter was. Billy guessed that it was the drain in the bottom of the Iron Maiden, but that was wrong. A blood gutter, Billy learned, was the shallow groove in the side of the blade of a sword or bayonet.

Weary told Billy about neat tortures he'd read about or seen in the movies or heard on the radio—about other neat tortures he himself had invented. One of the inventions was sticking a dentist's drill into a guy's ear. He asked Billy what he thought the worst form of execution was. Billy had no opinion. The correct answer turned out to be this: "You stake a guy out on an anthill in the desert—see? He's facing upward, and you put honey all over his balls and pecker, and you cut off his eyelids so he has to stare at the sun till he dies." So it goes.

Now, lying in the ditch with Billy and the scouts after having been shot at, Weary made Billy take a very close look at his trench knife. It wasn't government issue. It was a present from his father. It had a ten-inch blade that was triangular in cross section. Its grip consisted of brass knuckles, was a chain of rings through which Weary slipped his stubby fingers. The rings weren't simple. They bristled with spikes.

Weary laid the spikes along Billy's cheek, roweled the cheek with savagely affectionate restraint. "How'd you like to be hit with this—hm? Hmmmmmmmmmm?" he wanted to know.

"I wouldn't," said Billy.

"Know why the blade's triangular?"

"No."

"Makes a wound that won't close up."

"Oh."

"Makes a three-sided hole in a guy. You stick an ordinary knife in a guy—makes a slit. Right? A slit closes right up. Right?"

"Right."

"Shit. What do you know? What the hell they teach in college?"

"I wasn't there very long," said Billy, which was true. He had had only six months of college, and the college hadn't been a regular college, either. It had been the night school of the Ilium School of Optometry.

"Joe College," said Weary scathingly.

Billy shrugged.

"There's more to life than what you read in books," said Weary. "You'll find that out."

Billy made no reply to this, either, there in the ditch, since he didn't want the conversation to go on any longer than necessary. He was dimly tempted to say, though, that he knew a thing or two about gore. Billy, after all, had contemplated torture and hideous wounds at the beginning and the end of nearly every day of his childhood. Billy had an extremely gruesome crucifix hanging on the wall of his little bedroom in Ilium. A military surgeon would have admired the clinical fidelity of the artist's rendition of all Christ's wounds—the spear wound, the thorn wounds, the holes that were made by the iron spikes. Billy's Christ died horribly. He was pitiful.

So it goes.

Billy wasn't a Catholic, even though he grew up with a ghastly crucifix on the wall. His father had no religion. His mother was a substitute organist for several churches around town. She took Billy with her whenever she played, taught him to play a little, too. She said she was going to join a church as soon as she decided which one was right.

She never *did* decide. She did develop a terrific hankering for a crucifix, though. And she bought one from a Santa Fe gift shop during a trip the little family made out West during the Great Depression. Like so many Americans, she was trying to construct a life that made sense from things she found in gift shops.

And the crucifix went up on the wall of Billy Pilgrim.

The two scouts, loving the walnut stocks of their rifles in the ditch, whispered that it was time to move out again. Ten minutes had gone by without anybody's coming to see if they were hit or not, to finish them off. Whoever had shot was evidently far away and all alone.

And the four crawled out of the ditch without drawing any more fire. They crawled into a forest like the big, unlucky mammals they were. Then they stood up and began to walk quickly. The forest was dark and old. The pines were planted in ranks and files. There was no undergrowth. Four inches of unmarked snow blanketed the ground. The Americans had no

choice but to leave trails in the snow as unambiguous as dia-
grams in a book on ballroom dancing—*step, slide, rest—step,
slide, rest.*

"Close it up and keep it closed!" Roland Weary warned Billy
Pilgrim as they moved out. Weary looked like Tweedledum or
Tweedledee, all bundled up for battle. He was short and
thick.

He had every piece of equipment he had ever been issued,
every present he'd received from home: helmet, helmet liner,
wool cap, scarf, gloves, cotton undershirt, woolen undershirt,
wool shirt, sweater, blouse, jacket, overcoat, cotton underpants,
woolen underpants, woolen trousers, cotton socks, woolen
socks, combat boots, gas mask, canteen, mess kit, first-aid
kit, trench knife, blanket, shelter-half, raincoat, bullet-proof
Bible, a pamphlet entitled "Know Your Enemy," another pamphlet entitled "Why We Fight," and another pamphlet of
German phrases rendered in English phonetics, which would
enable Weary to ask Germans questions such as "Where is your
headquarters?" and "How many howitzers have you?" or to
tell them, "Surrender. Your situation is hopeless," and so on.

Weary had a block of balsa wood which was supposed to be
a foxhole pillow. He had a prophylactic kit containing two
tough condoms "For the Prevention of Disease Only!" He
had a whistle he wasn't going to show anybody until he got
promoted to corporal. He had a dirty picture of a woman attempting sexual intercourse with a Shetland pony. He had
made Billy Pilgrim admire that picture several times.

The woman and the pony were posed before velvet draperies
which were fringed with deedlee-balls. They were flanked by
Doric columns. In front of one column was a potted palm.
The picture that Weary had was a print of the first dirty photograph in history. The word *photography* was first used in 1839,
and it was in that year, too, that Louis J. M. Daguerre revealed
to the French Academy that an image formed on a silvered
metal plate covered with a thin film of silver iodide could be
developed in the presence of mercury vapor.

In 1841, only two years later, an assistant to Daguerre, André
Le Fèvre, was arrested in the Tuileries Gardens for attempting

to sell a gentleman a picture of the woman and the pony. That was where Weary bought his picture, too—in the Tuileries. Le Fèvre argued that the picture was fine art, and that his intention was to make Greek mythology come alive. He said the columns and the potted palm proved that.

When asked which myth he meant to represent, Le Fèvre replied that there were thousands of myths like that, with the woman a mortal and the pony a god.

He was sentenced to six months in prison. He died there of pneumonia. So it goes.

Billy and the scouts were skinny people. Roland Weary had fat to burn. He was a roaring furnace under all his layers of wool and straps and canvas. He had so much energy that he bustled back and forth between Billy and the scouts, delivering dumb messages which nobody had sent and which nobody was pleased to receive. He also began to suspect, since he was so much busier than anybody else, that he was the leader.

He was so hot and bundled up, in fact, that he had no sense of danger. His vision of the outside world was limited to what he could see through a narrow slit between the rim of his helmet and his scarf from home, which concealed his baby face from the bridge of his nose on down. He was so snug in there that he was able to pretend that he was safe at home, having survived the war, and that he was telling his parents and his sister a true war story—whereas the true war story was still going on.

Weary's version of the true war story went like this: There was a big German attack, and Weary and his antitank buddies fought like hell until everybody was killed but Weary. So it goes. And then Weary tied in with two scouts, and they became close friends immediately, and they decided to fight their way back to their own lines. They were going to travel fast. They were damned if they'd surrender. They shook hands all around. They called themselves "The Three Musketeers."

But then this damn college kid, who was so weak he shouldn't even have been in the army, asked if he could come along. He didn't even have a gun or a knife. He didn't even have a helmet or a cap. He couldn't even walk right—kept bobbing up-and-down, up-and-down, driving everybody crazy, giving their position away. He was pitiful. The Three Musketeers pushed and carried and dragged the college kid all the way back to their own lines, Weary's story went. They saved his God-damned hide for him.

In real life, Weary was retracing his steps, trying to find out what had happened to Billy. He had told the scouts to wait while he went back for the college bastard. He passed under a low branch now. It hit the top of his helmet with a *clonk*. Weary didn't hear it. Somewhere a big dog was barking. Weary didn't hear that, either. His war story was at a very exciting point. An officer was congratulating the Three Musketeers, telling them that he was going to put them in for Bronze Stars.

"Anything else I can do for you boys?" said the officer.

"Yes, sir," said one of the scouts. "We'd like to stick together for the rest of the war, sir. Is there some way you can fix it so nobody will ever break up the Three Musketeers?"

Billy Pilgrim had stopped in the forest. He was leaning against a tree with his eyes closed. His head was tilted back and his nostrils were flaring. He was like a poet in the Parthenon.

This was when Billy first came unstuck in time. His attention began to swing grandly through the full arc of his life, passing into death, which was violet light. There wasn't anybody else there, or any thing. There was just violet light—and a hum.

And then Billy swung into life again, going backwards until he was in pre-birth, which was red light and bubbling sounds. And then he swung into life again and stopped. He was a little boy taking a shower with his hairy father at the Ilium Y.M.C.A. He smelled chlorine from the swimming pool next door, heard the springboard boom.

Little Billy was terrified, because his father had said Billy was going to learn to swim by the method of sink-or-swim. His father was going to throw Billy into the deep end, and Billy was going to damn well swim.

It was like an execution. Billy was numb as his father carried him from the shower room to the pool. His eyes were closed. When he opened his eyes, he was on the bottom of the pool,

and there was beautiful music everywhere. He lost consciousness, but the music went on. He dimly sensed that somebody
was rescuing him. Billy resented that.

From there he traveled in time to 1965. He was forty-one
years old, and he was visiting his decrepit mother at Pine Knoll,
an old people's home he had put her in only a month before.
She had caught pneumonia, and wasn't expected to live. She
did live, though, for years after that.

Her voice was nearly gone, so, in order to hear her, Billy had
to put his ear right next to her papery lips. She evidently had
something very important to say.

"How . . . ?" she began, and she stopped. She was too
tired. She hoped that she wouldn't have to say the rest of the
sentence, that Billy would finish it for her.

But Billy had no idea what was on her mind. "How *what*,
Mother?" he prompted.

She swallowed hard, shed some tears. Then she gathered energy from all over her ruined body, even from her toes and fingertips. At last she had accumulated enough to whisper this
complete sentence:

"How did I get so *old*?"

Billy's antique mother passed out, and Billy was led from the
room by a pretty nurse. The body of an old man covered by a
sheet was wheeled by just as Billy entered the corridor. The
man had been a famous marathon runner in his day. So it goes.
This was before Billy had his head broken in an airplane crash,
by the way—before he became so vocal about flying saucers
and traveling in time.

Billy sat down in a waiting room. He wasn't a widower yet.
He sensed something hard under the cushion of his overstuffed
chair. He dug it out, discovered that it was a book, *The
Execution of Private Slovik*, by William Bradford Huie. It was a
true account of the death before an American firing squad of
Private Eddie D. Slovik, 36896415, the only American soldier
to be shot for cowardice since the Civil War. So it goes.

Billy read the opinion of a staff judge advocate who reviewed
Slovik's case, which ended like this: *He has directly challenged
the authority of the government, and future discipline depends*

upon a resolute reply to this challenge. If the death penalty is ever to be imposed for desertion, it should be imposed in this case, not as a punitive measure nor as retribution, but to maintain that discipline upon which alone an army can succeed against the enemy. There was no recommendation for clemency in the case and none is here recommended. So it goes.

Billy blinked in 1965, traveled in time to 1958. He was at a banquet in honor of a Little League team of which his son Robert was a member. The coach, who had never been married, was speaking. He was all choked up. "Honest to God," he was saying, "I'd consider it an honor just to be *water* boy for these kids."

Billy blinked in 1958, traveled in time to 1961. It was New Year's Eve, and Billy was disgracefully drunk at a party where everybody was in optometry or married to an optometrist.

Billy usually didn't drink much, because the war had ruined his stomach, but he certainly had a snootful now, and he was being unfaithful to his wife Valencia for the first and only time. He had somehow persuaded a woman to come into the laundry room of the house, and then sit up on the gas dryer, which was running.

The woman was very drunk herself, and she helped Billy get her girdle off. "What was it you wanted to talk about?" she said.

"It's all right," said Billy. He honestly thought it was all right. He couldn't remember the name of the woman.

"How come they call you Billy instead of William?"

"Business reasons," said Billy. That was true. His father-in-law, who owned the Ilium School of Optometry, who had set Billy up in practice, was a genius in his field. He told Billy to encourage people to call him Billy—because it would stick in their memories. It would also make him seem slightly magical, since there weren't any other grown Billys around. It also compelled people to think of him as a friend right away.

Somewhere in there was an awful scene, with people expressing disgust for Billy and the woman, and Billy found himself out in his automobile, trying to find the steering wheel.

The main thing now was to find the steering wheel. At first, Billy windmilled his arms, hoping to find it by luck. When that didn't work, he became methodical, working in such a way that the wheel could not possibly escape him. He placed himself hard against the left-hand door, searched every square inch of the area before him. When he failed to find the wheel, he moved over six inches, and searched again. Amazingly, he was eventually hard against the right-hand door, without having found the wheel. He concluded that somebody had stolen it. This angered him as he passed out.

He was in the back seat of his car, which was why he couldn't find the steering wheel.

Now somebody was shaking Billy awake. Billy still felt drunk, was still angered by the stolen steering wheel. He was back in World War Two again, behind the German lines. The person who was shaking him was Roland Weary. Weary had gathered the front of Billy's field jacket into his hands. He banged Billy against a tree, then pulled him away from it, flung him in the direction he was supposed to take under his own power.

Billy stopped, shook his head. "You go on," he said.

"What?"

"You guys go on without me. I'm all right."

"You're what?"

"I'm O.K."

"Jesus—I'd hate to see somebody *sick*," said Weary, through five layers of humid scarf from home. Billy had never seen Weary's face. He had tried to imagine it one time, had imaged a toad in a fishbowl.

Weary kicked and shoved Billy for a quarter of a mile. The scouts were waiting between the banks of a frozen creek. They had heard the dog. They had heard men calling back and forth, too—calling like hunters who had a pretty good idea of where their quarry was.

The banks of the creek were high enough to allow the scouts to stand without being seen. Billy staggered down the bank ridiculously. After him came Weary, clanking and clinking and tinkling and hot.

"Here he is, boys," said Weary. "He don't want to live, but he's gonna live anyway. When he gets out of this, by God, he's gonna owe his life to the Three Musketeers." This was the first the scouts had heard that Weary thought of himself and them as the Three Musketeers.

Billy Pilgrim, there in the creekbed, thought he, Billy Pilgrim, was turning to steam painlessly. If everybody would leave him alone for just a little while, he thought, he wouldn't cause anybody any more trouble. He would turn to steam and float up among the treetops.

Somewhere the big dog barked again. With the help of fear and echoes and winter silences, that dog had a voice like a big bronze gong.

Roland Weary, eighteen years old, insinuated himself between the scouts, draped a heavy arm around the shoulder of each. "So what do the Three Musketeers do now?" he said.

Billy Pilgrim was having a delightful hallucination. He was wearing dry, warm, white sweatsocks, and he was skating on a ballroom floor. Thousands cheered. This wasn't time-travel. It had never happened, never would happen. It was the craziness of a dying young man with his shoes full of snow.

One scout hung his head, let spit fall from his lips. The other did the same. They studied the infinitesimal effects of spit on snow and history. They were small, graceful people. They had been behind German lines before many times—living like woods creatures, living from moment to moment in useful terror, thinking brainlessly with their spinal cords.

Now they twisted out from under Weary's loving arms. They told Weary that he and Billy had better find somebody to surrender to. The scouts weren't going to wait for them any more.

And they ditched Weary and Billy in the creekbed.

Billy Pilgrim went on skating, doing tricks in sweatsocks, tricks that most people would consider impossible—making turns, stopping on a dime and so on. The cheering went on, but its tone was altered as the hallucination gave way to time-travel.

Billy stopped skating, found himself at a lectern in a Chinese restaurant in Ilium, New York, on an early afternoon in the autumn of 1957. He was receiving a standing ovation from the

Lions Club. He had just been elected President, and it was necessary that he speak. He was scared stiff, thought a ghastly mistake had been made. All those prosperous, solid men out there would discover now that they had elected a ludicrous waif. They would hear his reedy voice, the one he'd had in the war. He swallowed, knew that all he had for a voice box was a little whistle cut from a willow switch. Worse—he had nothing to say. The crowd quieted down. Everybody was pink and beaming.

Billy opened his mouth, and out came a deep, resonant tone. His voice was a gorgeous instrument. It told jokes which brought down the house. It grew serious, told jokes again, and ended on a note of humility. The explanation of the miracle was this: Billy had taken a course in public speaking.

And then he was back in the bed of the frozen creek again. Roland Weary was about to beat the living shit out of him.

Weary was filled with a tragic wrath. He had been ditched again. He stuffed his pistol into its holster. He slipped his knife into its scabbard. Its triangular blade and blood gutters on all three faces. And then he shook Billy hard, rattled his skeleton, slammed him against a bank.

Weary barked and whimpered through his layers of scarf from home. He spoke unintelligibly of the sacrifices he had made on Billy's behalf. He dilated upon the piety and heroism of "The Three Musketeers," portrayed, in the most glowing and impassioned hues, their virtue and magnanimity, the imperishable honor they acquired for themselves, and the great services they rendered to Christianity.

It was entirely Billy's fault that this fighting organization no longer existed, Weary felt, and Billy was going to pay. Weary socked Billy a good one on the side of his jaw, knocked Billy away from the bank and onto the snow-covered ice of the creek. Billy was down on all fours on the ice, and Weary kicked him in the ribs, rolled him over on his side. Billy tried to form himself into a ball.

"You shouldn't even *be* in the Army," said Weary.

Billy was involuntarily making convulsive sounds that were a lot like laughter. "You think it's funny, huh?" Weary inquired. He walked around to Billy's back. Billy's jacket and shirt and

undershirt had been hauled up around his shoulders by the violence, so his back was naked. There, inches from the tips of
Weary's combat boots, were the pitiful buttons of Billy's
spine.

Weary drew back his right boot, aimed a kick at the spine, at
the tube which had so many of Billy's important wires in it.
Weary was going to break that tube.

But then Weary saw that he had an audience. Five German
soldiers and a police dog on a leash were looking down into
the bed of the creek. The soldiers' blue eyes were filled with a
bleary civilian curiosity as to why one American would try to
murder another one so far from home, and why the victim
should laugh.

3

THE GERMANS and the dog were engaged in a military operation which had an amusingly self-explanatory name, a human enterprise which is seldom described in detail, whose name alone, when reported as news or history, gives many war enthusiasts a sort of post-coital satisfaction. It is, in the imagination of combat's fans, the divinely listless loveplay that follows the orgasm of victory. It is called "mopping up."

The dog, who had sounded so ferocious in the winter distances, was a female German shepherd. She was shivering. Her tail was between her legs. She had been borrowed that morning from a farmer. She had never been to war before. She had no idea what game was being played. Her name was Princess.

Two of the Germans were boys in their early teens. Two were ramshackle old men—droolers as toothless as carp. They were irregulars, armed and clothed fragmentarily with junk taken from real soldiers who were newly dead. So it goes. They were farmers from just across the German border, not far away.

Their commander was a middle-aged corporal—red-eyed, scrawny, tough as dried beef, sick of war. He had been wounded four times—and patched up, and sent back to war. He was a very good soldier—about to quit, about to find somebody to surrender to. His bandy legs were thrust into golden cavalry boots which he had taken from a dead Hungarian colonel on the Russian front. So it goes.

Those boots were almost all he owned in this world. They were his home. An anecdote: One time a recruit was watching him bone and wax those golden boots, and he held one up to the recruit and said, "If you look in there deeply enough, you'll see Adam and Eve."

Billy Pilgrim had not heard this anecdote. But, lying on the black ice there, Billy stared into the patina of the corporal's boots, saw Adam and Eve in the golden depths. They were naked. They were so innocent, so vulnerable, so eager to behave decently. Billy Pilgrim loved them.

•

Next to the golden boots were a pair of feet which were swaddled in rags. They were crisscrossed by canvas straps, were shod with hinged wooden clogs. Billy looked up at the face that went with the clogs. It was the face of a blond angel, of a fifteen-year-old boy.

The boy was as beautiful as Eve.

Billy was helped to his feet by the lovely boy, by the heavenly androgyne. And the others came forward to dust the snow off Billy, and then they searched him for weapons. He didn't have any. The most dangerous thing they found on his person was a two-inch pencil stub.

Three inoffensive *bangs* came from far away. They came from German rifles. The two scouts who had ditched Billy and Weary had just been shot. They had been lying in ambush for Germans. They had been discovered and shot from behind. Now they were dying in the snow, feeling nothing, turning the snow to the color of raspberry sherbet. So it goes. So Roland Weary was the last of the Three Musketeers.

And Weary, bug-eyed with terror, was being disarmed. The corporal gave Weary's pistol to the pretty boy. He marveled at Weary's cruel trench knife, said in German that Weary would no doubt like to use the knife on him, to tear his face off with the spiked knuckles, to stick the blade into his belly or throat. He spoke no English, and Billy and Weary understood no German.

"Nice playthings you have," the corporal told Weary, and he handed the knife to an old man. "Isn't that a pretty thing? Hmmm?"

He tore open Weary's overcoat and blouse. Brass buttons flew like popcorn. The corporal reached into Weary's gaping bosom as though he meant to tear out his pounding heart, but he brought out Weary's bullet-proof Bible instead.

A bullet-proof Bible is a Bible small enough to be slipped into a soldier's breast pocket, over his heart. It is sheathed in steel.

The corporal found the dirty picture of the woman and the pony in Weary's hip pocket. "What a lucky pony, eh?" he said.

"Hmmmm? Hmmmm? Don't you wish you were that pony?"
He handed the picture to the other old man. "Spoils of war!
It's yours, all yours, you lucky lad."

Then he made Weary sit down in the snow and take off his
combat boots, which he gave to the beautiful boy. He gave
Weary the boy's clogs. So Weary and Billy were both without
decent military footwear now, and they had to walk for miles
and miles, with Weary's clogs clacking, with Billy bobbing up-
and-down, up-and-down, crashing into Weary from time to
time.

"Excuse me," Billy would say, or "I beg your pardon."

They were brought at last to a stone cottage at a fork in the
road. It was a collecting point for prisoners of war. Billy and
Weary were taken inside, where it was warm and smoky. There
was a fire sizzling and popping in the fireplace. The fuel was
furniture. There were about twenty other Americans in there,
sitting on the floor with their backs to the wall, staring into the
flames—thinking whatever there was to think, which was
zero.

Nobody talked. Nobody had any good war stories to tell.

Billy and Weary found places for themselves, and Billy went
to sleep with his head on the shoulder of an unprotesting captain. The captain was a chaplain. He was a rabbi. He had been
shot through the hand.

Billy traveled in time, opened his eyes, found himself staring
into the glass eyes of a jade green mechanical owl. The owl was
hanging upside down from a rod of stainless steel. The owl
was Billy's optometer in his office in Ilium. An optometer is an
instrument for measuring refractive errors in eyes—in order
that corrective lenses may be prescribed.

Billy had fallen asleep while examining a female patient who
was in a chair on the other side of the owl. He had fallen asleep
at work before. It had been funny at first. Now Billy was starting to get worried about it, about his mind in general. He
tried to remember how old he was, couldn't. He tried to remember what year it was. He couldn't remember that, either.

"Doctor—" said the patient tentatively.

"Hm?" he said.

"You're so quiet."

"Sorry."

"You were talking away there—and then you got so quiet."

"Um."

"You see something terrible?"

"Terrible?"

"Some disease in my eyes?"

"No, no," said Billy, wanting to doze again. "Your eyes are fine. You just need glasses for reading." He told her to go across the corridor—to see the wide selection of frames there.

When she was gone, Billy opened the drapes and was no wiser as to what was outside. The view was still blocked by a venetian blind, which he hoisted clatteringly. Bright sunlight came crashing in. There were thousands of parked automobiles out there, twinkling on a vast lake of blacktop. Billy's office was part of a suburban shopping center.

Right outside the window was Billy's own Cadillac El Dorado Coupe de Ville. He read the stickers on the bumper. "Visit Ausable Chasm," said one. "Support Your Police Department," said another. There was a third. "Impeach Earl Warren," it said. The stickers about the police and Earl Warren were gifts from Billy's father-in-law, a member of the John Birch Society. The date on the license plate was 1967, which would make Billy Pilgrim forty-four years old. He asked himself this: "Where have all the years gone?"

Billy turned his attention to his desk. There was an open copy of *The Review of Optometry* there. It was opened to an editorial, which Billy now read, his lips moving slightly.

What happens in 1968 will rule the fate of European optometrists for at least 50 years! Billy read. *With this warning, Jean Thiriart, Secretary of the National Union of Belgium Opticians, is pressing for formation of a "European Optometry Society." The alternatives, he says, will be the obtaining of professional status, or, by 1971, reduction to the role of spectacle-sellers.*

Billy Pilgrim tried hard to care.

A siren went off, scared the hell out of him. He was expecting World War Three at any time. The siren was simply

announcing high noon. It was housed in a cupola atop a firehouse across the street from Billy's office.

Billy closed his eyes. When he opened them, he was back in
World War Two again. His head was on the wounded rabbi's
shoulder. A German was kicking his feet, telling him to wake
up, that it was time to move on.

The Americans, with Billy among them, formed a fools' parade on the road outside.

There was a photographer present, a German war correspon-
dent with a Leica. He took pictures of Billy's and Roland
Weary's feet. The picture was widely published two days later
as heartening evidence of how miserably equipped the American Army often was, despite its reputation for being rich.

The photographer wanted something more lively, though, a
picture of an actual capture. So the guards staged one for him.
They threw Billy into shrubbery. When Billy came out of the
shrubbery, his face wreathed in goofy good will, they menaced
him with their machine pistols, as though they were capturing
him then.

Billy's smile as he came out of the shrubbery was at least as
peculiar as Mona Lisa's, for he was simultaneously on foot in
Germany in 1944 and riding his Cadillac in 1967. Germany
dropped away, and 1967 became bright and clear, free of inter-
ference from any other time. Billy was on his way to a Lions
Club luncheon meeting. It was a hot August, but Billy's car
was air-conditioned. He was stopped by a signal in the middle
of Ilium's black ghetto. The people who lived here hated it so
much that they had burned down a lot of it a month before. It
was all they had, and they'd wrecked it. The neighborhood reminded Billy of some of the towns he had seen in the war. The
curbs and sidewalks were crushed in many places, showing
where the National Guard tanks and half-tracks had been.

"Blood brother," said a message written in pink paint on the
side of a shattered grocery store.

There was a tap on Billy's car window. A black man was out
there. He wanted to talk about something. The light had
changed. Billy did the simplest thing. He drove on.

•

Billy drove through a scene of even greater desolation. It looked like Dresden after it was fire-bombed—like the surface of the moon. The house where Billy had grown up used to be somewhere in what was so empty now. This was urban renewal. A new Ilium Government Center and a Pavilion of the Arts and a Peace Lagoon and high-rise apartment buildings were going up here soon.

That was all right with Billy Pilgrim.

The speaker at the Lions Club meeting was a major in the Marines. He said that Americans had no choice but to keep fighting in Vietnam until they achieved victory or until the Communists realized that they could not force their way of life on weak countries. The major had been there on two separate tours of duty. He told of many terrible and many wonderful things he had seen. He was in favor of increased bombings, of bombing North Vietnam back into the Stone Age, if it refused to see reason.

Billy was not moved to protest the bombing of North Vietnam, did not shudder about the hideous things he himself had seen bombing do. He was simply having lunch with the Lions Club, of which he was past president now.

Billy had a framed prayer on his office wall which expressed his method for keeping going, even though he was unenthusiastic about living. A lot of patients who saw the prayer on Billy's wall told him that it helped *them* to keep going, too. It went like this:

GOD GRANT ME
THE SERENITY TO ACCEPT
THE THINGS I CANNOT CHANGE,
COURAGE
TO CHANGE THE THINGS I CAN,
AND WISDOM ALWAYS
TO TELL THE
DIFFERENCE.

Among the things Billy Pilgrim could not change were the past, the present, and the future.

Now he was being introduced to the Marine major. The person who was performing the introduction was telling the major that Billy was a veteran, and that Billy had a son who was a sergeant in the Green Berets—in Vietnam.

The major told Billy that the Green Berets were doing a great job, and that he should be proud of his son.

"I *am*. I certainly *am*," said Billy Pilgrim.

He went home for a nap after lunch. He was under doctor's orders to take a nap every day. The doctor hoped that this would relieve a complaint that Billy had: Every so often, for no apparent reason, Billy Pilgrim would find himself weeping. Nobody had ever caught Billy doing it. Only the doctor knew. It was an extremely quiet thing Billy did, and not very moist.

Billy owned a lovely Georgian home in Ilium. He was rich as Croesus, something he had never expected to be, not in a million years. He had five other optometrists working for him in the shopping plaza location, and netted over sixty thousand dollars a year. In addition, he owned a fifth of the new Holiday Inn out on Route 54, and half of three Tastee-Freeze stands. Tastee-Freeze was a sort of frozen custard. It gave all the pleasure that ice cream could give, without the stiffness and bitter coldness of ice cream.

Billy's home was empty. His daughter Barbara was about to get married, and she and his wife had gone downtown to pick out patterns for her crystal and silverware. There was a note saying so on the kitchen table. There were no servants. People just weren't interested in careers in domestic service anymore. There wasn't a dog, either.

There used to be a dog named Spot, but he died. So it goes. Billy had liked Spot a lot, and Spot had liked him.

Billy went up the carpeted stairway and into his and his wife's bedroom. The room had flowered wallpaper. There was a double bed with a clock-radio on a table beside it. Also on the table were controls for the electric blanket, and a switch to turn on a gentle vibrator which was bolted to the springs of the box mattress. The trade name of the vibrator was "Magic Fingers." The vibrator was the doctor's idea, too.

Billy took off his tri-focals and his coat and his necktie and his shoes, and he closed the venetian blinds and then the drapes, and he lay down on the outside of the coverlet. But sleep would not come. Tears came instead. They seeped. Billy turned on the Magic Fingers, and he was jiggled as he wept.

The doorchimes rang. Billy got off the bed and looked down through a window at the front doorstep, to see if somebody important had come to call. There was a crippled man down there, as spastic in space as Billy Pilgrim was in time. Convulsions made the man dance flappingly all the time, made him change his expressions, too, as though he were trying to imitate various famous movie stars.

Another cripple was ringing a doorbell across the street. He was on crutches. He had only one leg. He was so jammed between his crutches that his shoulders hid his ears.

Billy knew what the cripples were up to: They were selling subscriptions to magazines that would never come. People subscribed to them because the salesmen were so pitiful. Billy had heard about this racket from a speaker at the Lions Club two weeks before—a man from the Better Business Bureau. The man said that anybody who saw cripples working a neighborhood for magazine subscriptions should call the police.

Billy looked down the street, saw a new Buick Riviera parked about half a block away. There was a man in it, and Billy assumed correctly that he was the man who had hired the cripples to do this thing. Billy went on weeping as he contemplated the cripples and their boss. His doorchimes clanged hellishly.

He closed his eyes, and opened them again. He was still weeping, but he was back in Luxembourg again. He was marching with a lot of other prisoners. It was a winter wind that was bringing tears to his eyes.

Ever since Billy had been thrown into shrubbery for the sake of a picture, he had been seeing Saint Elmo's fire, a sort of electronic radiance around the heads of his companions and captors. It was in the treetops and on the rooftops of Luxembourg, too. It was beautiful.

Billy was marching with his hands on top of his head, and so were all the other Americans. Billy was bobbing up-and-down, up-and-down. Now he crashed into Roland Weary accidentally. "I beg your pardon," he said.

Weary's eyes were tearful also. Weary was crying because of horrible pains in his feet. The hinged clogs were transforming his feet into blood puddings.

At each road intersection Billy's group was joined by more Americans with their hands on top of their haloed heads. Billy had smiles for them all. They were moving like water, downhill all the time, and they flowed at last to a main highway on a valley's floor. Through the valley flowed a Mississippi of humiliated Americans. Tens of thousands of Americans shuffled eastward, their hands clasped on top of their heads. They sighed and groaned.

Billy and his group joined the river of humiliation, and the late afternoon sun came out from the clouds. The Americans didn't have the road to themselves. The west-bound lane boiled and boomed with vehicles which were rushing German reserves to the front. The reserves were violent, windburned, bristly men. They had teeth like piano keys.

They were festooned with machine-gun belts, smoked cigars and guzzled booze. They took wolfish bites from sausages, patted their horny palms with potato-masher grenades.

One soldier in black was having a drunk hero's picnic all by himself on top of a tank. He spit on the Americans. The spit hit Roland Weary's shoulder, gave Weary a *fourragère* of snot and blutwurst and tobacco juice and Schnapps.

Billy found the afternoon stingingly exciting. There was so much to see—dragon's teeth, killing machines, corpses with bare feet that were blue and ivory. So it goes.

Bobbing up-and-down, up-and-down, Billy beamed lovingly at a bright lavender farmhouse that had been spattered with machine-gun bullets. Standing in its cock-eyed doorway was a German colonel. With him was his unpainted whore.

Billy crashed into Weary's shoulder, and Weary cried out sobbingly. "Walk right! Walk right!"

They were climbing a gentle rise now. When they reached the top, they weren't in Luxembourg any more. They were in Germany.

A motion-picture camera was set up at the border—to record the fabulous victory. Two civilians in bearskin coats were leaning on the camera when Billy and Weary came by. They had run out of film hours ago.

One of them singled out Billy's face for a moment, then focused at infinity again. There was a tiny plume of smoke at infinity. There was a battle there. People were dying there. So it goes.

And the sun went down, and Billy found himself bobbing in place in a railroad yard. There were rows and rows of boxcars waiting. They had brought reserves to the front. Now they were going to take prisoners into Germany's interior.

Flashlight beams danced crazily.

The Germans sorted out the prisoners according to rank. They put sergeants with sergeants, majors with majors, and so on. A squad of full colonels was halted near Billy. One of them had double pneumonia. He had a high fever and vertigo. As the railroad yard dipped and swooped around the colonel, he tried to hold himself steady by staring into Billy's eyes.

The colonel coughed and coughed, and then he said to Billy, "You one of my boys?" This was a man who had lost an entire regiment, about forty-five hundred men—a lot of them children, actually. Billy didn't reply. The question made no sense.

"What was your outfit?" said the colonel. He coughed and coughed. Every time he inhaled his lungs rattled like greasy paper bags.

Billy couldn't remember the outfit he was from.

"You from the Four-fifty-first?"

"Four-fifty-first what?" said Billy.

There was a silence. "Infantry regiment," said the colonel at last.

"Oh," said Billy Pilgrim.

•

There was another long silence, with the colonel dying and dying, drowning where he stood. And then he cried out wetly, "It's me, boys! It's Wild Bob!" That is what he had always wanted his troops to call him: "Wild Bob."

None of the people who could hear him were actually from his regiment, except for Roland Weary, and Weary wasn't listening. All Weary could think of was the agony in his own feet.

But the colonel imagined that he was addressing his beloved troops for the last time, and he told them that they had nothing to be ashamed of, that there were dead Germans all over the battlefield who wished to God that they had never heard of the Four-fifty-first. He said that after the war he was going to have a regimental reunion in his home town, which was Cody, Wyoming. He was going to barbecue whole steers.

He said all this while staring into Billy's eyes. He made the inside of poor Billy's skull echo with balderdash. "God be with you, boys!" he said, and that echoed and echoed. And then he said, "If you're ever in Cody, Wyoming, just ask for Wild Bob!"

I was there. So was my old war buddy, Bernard V. O'Hare.

Billy Pilgrim was packed into a boxcar with many other privates. He and Roland Weary were separated. Weary was packed into another car in the same train.

There were narrow ventilators at the corners of the car, under the eaves. Billy stood by one of these, and, as the crowd pressed against him, he climbed part way up a diagonal corner brace to make more room. This placed his eyes on a level with the ventilator, so he could see another train about ten yards away.

Germans were writing on the cars with blue chalk—the number of persons in each car, their rank, their nationality, the date on which they had been put aboard. Other Germans were securing the hasps on the car doors with wire and spikes and other trackside trash. Billy could hear somebody writing on his car, too, but he couldn't see who was doing it.

Most of the privates on Billy's car were very young—at the end of childhood. But crammed into the corner with Billy was a former hobo who was forty years old.

"I been hungrier than this," the hobo told Billy. "I been in worse places than this. This ain't so bad."

A man in a boxcar across the way called out through the ventilator that a man had just died in there. So it goes. There were four guards who heard him. They weren't excited by the news.

"Yo, yo," said one, nodding dreamily. "Yo, yo."

And the guards didn't open the car with the dead man in it. They opened the next car instead, and Billy Pilgrim was enchanted by what was in there. It was like heaven. There was candlelight, and there were bunks with quilts and blankets heaped on them. There was a cannonball stove with a steaming coffeepot on top. There was a table with a bottle of wine and a loaf of bread and a sausage on it. There were four bowls of soup.

There were pictures of castles and lakes and pretty girls on the walls. This was the rolling home of the railroad guards, men whose business it was to be forever guarding freight rolling from here to there. The four guards went inside and closed the door.

A little while later they came out smoking cigars, talking contentedly in the mellow lower register of the German language. One of them saw Billy's face at the ventilator. He wagged a finger at him in affectionate warning, telling him to be a good boy.

The Americans across the way told the guards again about the dead man on their car. The guards got a stretcher out of their own cozy car, opened the dead man's car and went inside. The dead man's car wasn't crowded at all. There were just six live colonels in there—and one dead one.

The Germans carried the corpse out. The corpse was Wild Bob. So it goes.

During the night, some of the locomotives began to tootle to one another, and then to move. The locomotive and the last car of each train were marked with a striped banner of orange and black, indicating that the train was not fair game for airplanes—that it was carrying prisoners of war.

•

The war was nearly over. The locomotives began to move
east in late December. The war would end in May. German
prisons everywhere were absolutely full, and there was no longer any food for the prisoners to eat, and no longer any fuel to
keep them warm. And yet—here came more prisoners.

Billy Pilgrim's train, the longest train of all, did not move for
two days.

"This ain't bad," the hobo told Billy on the second day.
"This ain't nothing at all."

Billy looked out through the ventilator. The railroad yard
was a desert now, except for a hospital train marked with red
crosses—on a siding far, far away. Its locomotive whistled. The
locomotive of Billy Pilgrim's train whistled back. They were
saying, "Hello."

Even though Billy's train wasn't moving, its boxcars were
kept locked tight. Nobody was to get off until the final destination. To the guards who walked up and down outside, each
car became a single organism which ate and drank and excreted
through its ventilators. It talked or sometimes yelled through
its ventilators, too. In went water and loaves of blackbread and
sausage and cheese, and out came shit and piss and language.

Human beings in there were excreting into steel helmets,
which were passed to the people at the ventilators, who
dumped them. Billy was a dumper. The human beings also
passed canteens, which guards would fill with water. When
food came in, the human beings were quiet and trusting and
beautiful. They shared.

Human beings in there took turns standing or lying down.
The legs of those who stood were like fence posts driven into a
warm, squirming, farting, sighing earth. The queer earth was a
mosaic of sleepers who nestled like spoons.

Now the train began to creep eastward.

Somewhere in there was Christmas. Billy Pilgrim nestled
like a spoon with the hobo on Christmas night, and he fell
asleep, and he traveled in time to 1967 again—to the night he
was kidnapped by a flying saucer from Tralfamadore.

4

BILLY PILGRIM could not sleep on his daughter's wedding night. He was forty-four. The wedding had taken place that afternoon in a gaily striped tent in Billy's backyard. The stripes were orange and black.

Billy and his wife, Valencia, nestled like spoons in their big double bed. They were jiggled by Magic Fingers. Valencia didn't need to be jiggled to sleep. Valencia was snoring like a bandsaw. The poor woman didn't have ovaries or a uterus any more. They had been removed by a surgeon—by one of Billy's partners in the new Holiday Inn.

There was a full moon.

Billy got out of bed in the moonlight. He felt spooky and luminous, felt as though he were wrapped in cool fur that was full of static electricity. He looked down at his bare feet. They were ivory and blue.

Billy now shuffled down his upstairs hallway, knowing he was about to be kidnapped by a flying saucer. The hallway was zebra-striped with darkness and moonlight. The moonlight came into the hallway through doorways of the empty rooms of Billy's two children, children no more. They were gone forever. Billy was guided by dread and the lack of dread. Dread told him when to stop. Lack of it told him when to move again. He stopped.

He went into his daughter's room. Her drawers were dumped. Her closet was empty. Heaped in the middle of the room were all the possessions she could not take on a honeymoon. She had a Princess telephone extension all her own—on her windowsill. Its tiny night light stared at Billy. And then it rang.

Billy answered. There was a drunk on the other end. Billy could almost smell his breath—mustard gas and roses. It was a wrong number. Billy hung up. There was a soft drink bottle on the windowsill. Its label boasted that it contained no nourishment whatsoever.

•

Billy Pilgrim padded downstairs on his blue and ivory feet. He went into the kitchen, where the moonlight called his attention to a half bottle of champagne on the kitchen table, all that was left from the reception in the tent. Somebody had stoppered it again. "Drink me," it seemed to say.

So Billy uncorked it with his thumbs. It didn't make a pop. The champagne was dead. So it goes.

Billy looked at the clock on the gas stove. He had an hour to kill before the saucer came. He went into the living room, swinging the bottle like a dinner bell, turned on the television. He came slightly unstuck in time, saw the late movie backwards, then forwards again. It was a movie about American bombers in the Second World War and the gallant men who flew them. Seen backwards by Billy, the story went like this:

American planes, full of holes and wounded men and corpses, took off backwards from an airfield in England. Over France, a few German fighter planes flew at them backwards, sucked bullets and shell fragments from some of the planes and crewmen. They did the same for wrecked American bombers on the ground, and those planes flew up backwards to join the formation.

The formation flew backwards over a German city that was in flames. The bombers opened their bomb bay doors, exerted a miraculous magnetism which shrunk the fires, gathered them into cylindrical steel containers, and lifted the containers into the bellies of the planes. The containers were stored neatly in racks. The Germans below had miraculous devices of their own, which were long steel tubes. They used them to suck more fragments from the crewmen and planes. But there were still a few wounded Americans, though, and some of the bombers were in bad repair. Over France, though, German fighters came up again, made everything and everybody as good as new.

When the bombers got back to their base, the steel cylinders were taken from the racks and shipped back to the United States of America, where factories were operating night and day, dismantling the cylinders, separating the dangerous contents into minerals. Touchingly, it was mainly women who did this work. The minerals were then shipped to specialists in remote areas. It was their business to put them into the ground, to hide them cleverly, so they would never hurt anybody ever again.

The American fliers turned in their uniforms, became high school kids. And Hitler turned into a baby, Billy Pilgrim supposed. That wasn't in the movie. Billy was extrapolating. Everybody turned into a baby, and all humanity, without exception, conspired biologically to produce two perfect people named Adam and Eve, he supposed.

Billy saw the war movies backwards then forwards—and then it was time to go out into his backyard to meet the flying saucer. Out he went, his blue and ivory feet crushing the wet salad of the lawn. He stopped, took a swig of the dead champagne. It was like 7-Up. He would not raise his eyes to the sky, though he knew there was a flying saucer from Tralfamadore up there. He would see it soon enough, inside and out, and he would see, too, where it came from soon enough—soon enough.

Overhead he heard the cry of what might have been a melodious owl, but it wasn't a melodious owl. It was a flying saucer from Tralfamadore, navigating in both space and time, therefore seeming to Billy Pilgrim to have come from nowhere all at once. Somewhere a big dog barked.

The saucer was one hundred feet in diameter, with portholes around its rim. The light from the portholes was a pulsing purple. The only noise it made was the owl song. It came down to hover over Billy, and to enclose him in a cylinder of pulsing purple light. Now there was the sound of a seeming kiss as an airtight hatch in the bottom of the saucer was opened. Down snaked a ladder that was outlined in pretty lights like a Ferris wheel.

Billy's will was paralyzed by a zap gun aimed at him from one of the portholes. It became imperative that he take hold of the bottom rung of the sinuous ladder, which he did. The rung was electrified, so that Billy's hands locked onto it hard. He was hauled into the airlock, and machinery closed the bottom door. Only then did the ladder, wound onto a reel in the airlock, let him go. Only then did Billy's brain start working again.

There were two peepholes inside the airlock—with yellow eyes pressed to them. There was a speaker on the wall. The Tralfamadorians had no voice boxes. They communicated telepathically. They were able to talk to Billy by means of a computer and a sort of electric organ which made every Earthling speech sound.

"Welcome aboard, Mr. Pilgrim," said the loudspeaker. "Any questions?"

Billy licked his lips, thought a while, inquired at last: "Why me?"

"That is a very *Earthling* question to ask, Mr. Pilgrim. Why *you*? Why *us* for that matter? Why *anything*? Because this moment simply *is*. Have you ever seen bugs trapped in amber?"

"Yes." Billy, in fact, had a paperweight in his office which was a blob of polished amber with three ladybugs embedded in it.

"Well, here we are, Mr. Pilgrim, trapped in the amber of this moment. There is no *why*."

They introduced an anesthetic into Billy's atmosphere now, put him to sleep. They carried him to a cabin where he was strapped to a yellow Barca-Lounger which they had stolen from a Sears & Roebuck warehouse. The hold of the saucer was crammed with other stolen merchandise, which would be used to furnish Billy's artificial habitat in a zoo on Tralfamadore.

The terrific acceleration of the saucer as it left Earth twisted Billy's slumbering body, distorted his face, dislodged him in time, sent him back to the war.

When he regained consciousness, he wasn't on the flying saucer. He was in a boxcar crossing Germany again.

Some people were rising from the floor of the car, and others were lying down. Billy planned to lie down, too. It would be lovely to sleep. It was black in the car, and black outside the car, which seemed to be going about two miles an hour. The car never seemed to go any faster than that. It was a long time between clicks, between joints in the track. There would be a click, and then a year would go by, and then there would be another click.

The train often stopped to let really important trains bawl and hurtle by. Another thing it did was stop on sidings near prisons, leaving a few cars there. It was creeping across all of Germany, growing shorter all the time.

And Billy let himself down oh so gradually now, hanging onto the diagonal cross-brace in the corner in order to make himself seem nearly weightless to those he was joining on the floor. He knew it was important that he make himself nearly ghostlike when lying down. He had forgotten why, but a reminder soon came.

"Pilgrim—" said a person he was about to nestle with, "is that *you?*"

Billy didn't say anything, but nestled very politely, closed his eyes.

"God damn it," said the person. "That *is* you, isn't it?" He sat up and explored Billy rudely with his hands. "It's you, all right. Get the hell out of here."

Now Billy sat up, too—wretched, close to tears.

"Get out of here! I want to sleep!"

"Shut up," said somebody else.

"I'll shut up when Pilgrim gets away from here."

So Billy stood up again, clung to the cross-brace. "Where *can* I sleep?" he asked quietly.

"Not with me."

"Not with me, you son of a bitch," said somebody else. "You yell. You kick."

"I do?"

"You're God damn right you do. And whimper."

"I do?"

"Keep the hell away from here, Pilgrim."

And now there was an acrimonious madrigal, with parts sung in all quarters of the car. Nearly everybody, seemingly, had an atrocity story of something Billy Pilgrim had done to him in his sleep. Everybody told Billy Pilgrim to keep the hell away.

•

So Billy Pilgrim had to sleep standing up, or not sleep at all. And food had stopped coming in through the ventilators, and the days and nights were colder all the time.

On the eighth day, the forty-year-old hobo said to Billy, "This ain't bad. I can be comfortable anywhere."

"You can?" said Billy.

On the ninth day, the hobo died. So it goes. His last words were, "You think this is bad? This ain't bad."

There was something about death and the ninth day. There was a death on the ninth day in the car ahead of Billy's too. Roland Weary died—of gangrene that had started in his mangled feet. So it goes.

Weary, in his nearly continuous delirium, told again and again of the Three Musketeers, acknowledged that he was dying, gave many messages to be delivered to his family in Pittsburgh. Above all, he wanted to be avenged, so he said again and again the name of the person who had killed him. Everyone on the car learned the lesson well.

"Who killed me?" he would ask.

And everybody knew the answer, which was this: "Billy Pilgrim."

Listen—on the tenth night the peg was pulled out of the hasp on Billy's boxcar door, and the door was opened. Billy Pilgrim was lying at an angle on the corner-brace, self-crucified, holding himself there with a blue and ivory claw hooked over the sill of the ventilator. Billy coughed when the door was opened, and when he coughed he shit thin gruel. This was in accordance with the Third Law of Motion according to Sir Isaac Newton. This law tells us that for every action there is a reaction which is equal and opposite in direction.

This can be useful in rocketry.

The train had arrived on a siding by a prison which was originally constructed as an extermination camp for Russian prisoners of war.

The guards peeked inside Billy's car owlishly, cooed calmingly. They had never dealt with Americans before, but they surely understood this general sort of freight. They knew that it was essentially a liquid which could be induced to flow slowly toward cooing and light. It was nighttime.

The only light outside came from a single bulb which hung from a pole—high and far away. All was quiet outside, except for the guards, who cooed like doves. And the liquid began to flow. Gobs of it built up in the doorway, plopped to the ground.

Billy was the next-to-last human being to reach the door. The hobo was last. The hobo could not flow, could not plop. He wasn't liquid any more. He was stone. So it goes.

Billy didn't want to drop from the car to the ground. He sincerely believed that he would shatter like glass. So the guards helped him down, cooing still. They set him down facing the train. It was such a dinky train now.

There was a locomotive, a tender, and three little boxcars. The last boxcar was the railroad guards' heaven on wheels. Again—in that heaven on wheels—the table was set. Dinner was served.

At the base of the pole from which the light bulb hung were three seeming haystacks. The Americans were wheedled and teased over to those three stacks, which weren't hay after all. They were overcoats taken from prisoners who were dead. So it goes.

It was the guards' firmly expressed wish that every American without an overcoat should take one. The coats were cemented together with ice, so the guards used their bayonets as ice picks, pricking free collars and hems and sleeves and so on, then peeling off coats and handing them out at random. The coats were stiff and dome-shaped, having conformed to their piles.

The coat that Billy Pilgrim got had been crumpled and frozen in such a way, and was so small, that it appeared to be not a coat but a sort of large black, three-cornered hat. There were gummy stains on it, too, like crankcase drainings or old strawberry jam. There seemed to be a dead, furry animal frozen to it. The animal was in fact the coat's fur collar.

Billy glanced dully at the coats of his neighbors. Their coats all had brass buttons or tinsel or piping or numbers or stripes or eagles or moons or stars dangling from them. They were soldiers' coats. Billy was the only one who had a coat from a dead civilian. So it goes.

And Billy and the rest were encouraged to shuffle around their dinky train and into the prison camp. There wasn't anything warm or lively to attract them—merely long, low, narrow sheds by the thousands, with no lights inside.

Somewhere a dog barked. With the help of fear and echoes and winter silences, that dog had a voice like a big bronze gong.

Billy and the rest were wooed through gate after gate, and Billy saw his first Russian. The man was all alone in the night—a ragbag with a round, flat face that glowed like a radium dial.

Billy passed within a yard of him. There was barbed wire between them. The Russian did not wave or speak, but he looked directly into Billy's soul with sweet hopefulness, as though Billy might have good news for him—news he might be too stupid to understand, but good news all the same.

Billy blacked out as he walked through gate after gate. He came to in what he thought might be a building on Tralfamadore. It was shrilly lit and lined with white tiles. It was on Earth, though. It was a delousing station through which all new prisoners had to pass.

Billy did as he was told, took off his clothes. That was the first thing they told him to do on Tralfamadore, too.

A German measured Billy's upper right arm with his thumb and forefinger, asked a companion what sort of an army would send a weakling like that to the front. They looked at the other American bodies now, pointed out a lot more that were nearly as bad as Billy's.

One of the best bodies belonged to the oldest American by far, a high school teacher from Indianapolis. His name was Edgar Derby. He hadn't been in Billy's boxcar. He'd been in Roland Weary's car, had cradled Weary's head while he died. So it goes. Derby was forty-four years old. He was so old he had a son who was a marine in the Pacific theater of war.

Derby had pulled political wires to get into the army at his age. The subject he had taught in Indianapolis was Contemporary Problems in Western Civilization. He also coached the tennis team, and took very good care of his body.

Derby's son would survive the war. Derby wouldn't. That good body of his would be filled with holes by a firing squad in Dresden in sixty-eight days. So it goes.

The worst American body wasn't Billy's. The worst body belonged to a car thief from Cicero, Illinois. His name was Paul Lazzaro. He was tiny, and not only were his bones and teeth rotten, but his skin was disgusting. Lazzaro was polka-dotted all over with dime-sized scars. He had had many plagues of boils.

Lazzaro, too, had been on Roland Weary's boxcar, and had given his word of honor to Weary that he would find some way to make Billy Pilgrim pay for Weary's death. He was looking around now, wondering which naked human being was Billy.

The naked Americans took their places under many showerheads along a white-tiled wall. There were no faucets they could control. They could only wait for whatever was coming. Their penises were shriveled and their balls were retracted. Reproduction was not the main business of the evening.

An unseen hand turned a master valve. Out of the showerheads gushed scalding rain. The rain was a blowtorch that did not warm. It jazzed and jangled Billy's skin without thawing the ice in the marrow of his long bones.

The Americans' clothes were meanwhile passing through poison gas. Body lice and bacteria and fleas were dying by the billions. So it goes.

And Billy zoomed back in time to his infancy. He was a baby who had just been bathed by his mother. Now his mother wrapped him in a towel, carried him into a rosy room that was filled with sunshine. She unwrapped him, laid him on the tickling towel, powdered him between his legs, joked with him, patted his little jelly belly. Her palm on his little jelly belly made potching sounds.

Billy gurgled and cooed.

•

And then Billy was a middle-aged optometrist again, playing hacker's golf this time—on a blazing summer Sunday morning. Billy never went to church any more. He was hacking with three other optometrists. Billy was on the green in seven strokes, and it was his turn to putt.

It was an eight-foot putt and he made it. He bent over to take the ball out of the cup, and the sun went behind a cloud. Billy was momentarily dizzy. When he recovered, he wasn't on the golf course any more. He was strapped to a yellow contour chair in a white chamber aboard a flying saucer, which was bound for Tralfamadore.

"Where am I?" said Billy Pilgrim.

"Trapped in another blob of amber, Mr. Pilgrim. We are where we have to be just now—three hundred million miles from Earth, bound for a time warp which will get us to Tralfamadore in hours rather than centuries."

"How—how did I get here?"

"It would take another Earthling to explain it to you. Earthlings are the great explainers, explaining why this event is structured as it is, telling how other events may be achieved or avoided. I am a Tralfamadorian, seeing all time as you might see a stretch of the Rocky Mountains. All time is all time. It does not change. It does not lend itself to warnings or explanations. It simply *is*. Take it moment by moment, and you will find that we are all, as I've said before, bugs in amber."

"You sound to me as though you don't believe in free will," said Billy Pilgrim.

"If I hadn't spent so much time studying Earthlings," said the Tralfamadorian, "I wouldn't have any idea what was meant by 'free will.' I've visited thirty-one inhabited planets in the universe, and I have studied reports on one hundred more. Only on Earth is there any talk of free will."

5

BILLY PILGRIM says that the Universe does not look like a lot of bright little dots to the creatures from Tralfamadore. The creatures can see where each star has been and where it is going, so that the heavens are filled with rarefied, luminous spaghetti. And Tralfamadorians don't see human beings as two-legged creatures, either. They see them as great millepedes—"with babies' legs at one end and old people's legs at the other," says Billy Pilgrim.

Billy asked for something to read on the trip to Tralfamadore. His captors had five million Earthling books on microfilm, but no way to project them in Billy's cabin. They had only one actual book in English, which would be placed in a Tralfamadorian museum. It was *Valley of the Dolls*, by Jacqueline Susann.

Billy read it, thought it was pretty good in spots. The people in it certainly had their ups and downs, ups and downs. But Billy didn't want to read about the same ups and downs over and over again. He asked if there wasn't, please, some other reading matter around.

"Only Tralfamadorian novels, which I'm afraid you couldn't begin to understand," said the speaker on the wall.

"Let me look at one anyway."

So they sent him in several. They were little things. A dozen of them might have had the bulk of *Valley of the Dolls*—with all its ups and downs, ups and downs.

Billy couldn't read Tralfamadorian, of course, but he could at least see how the books were laid out—in brief clumps of symbols separated by stars. Billy commented that the clumps might be telegrams.

"Exactly," said the voice.

"They *are* telegrams?"

"There are no telegrams on Tralfamadore. But you're right: each clump of symbols is a brief, urgent message—describing a situation, a scene. We Tralfamadorians read them all at once, not one after the other. There isn't any particular relationship between all the messages, except that the author has chosen them carefully, so that, when seen all at once, they produce an image of life that is beautiful and surprising and deep. There is no beginning, no middle, no end, no suspense, no moral, no causes, no effects. What we love in our books are the depths of many marvelous moments seen all at one time."

Moments after that, the saucer entered a time warp, and Billy was flung back into his childhood. He was twelve years old, quaking as he stood with his mother and father on Bright Angel Point, at the rim of Grand Canyon. The little human family was staring at the floor of the canyon, one mile straight down.

"Well—" said Billy's father, manfully kicking a pebble into space, "there it *is*." They had come to this famous place by automobile. They had had seven blowouts on the way.

"It was worth the trip," said Billy's mother raptly. "Oh, God —was it ever *worth* it."

Billy hated the canyon. He was sure that he was going to fall in. His mother touched him, and he wet his pants.

There were other tourists looking down into the canyon, too, and a ranger was there to answer questions. A Frenchman who had come all the way from France asked the ranger in broken English if many people committed suicide by jumping in.

"Yes, sir," said the ranger. "About three folks a year." So it goes.

And Billy took a very short trip through time, made a pee-wee jump of only ten days, so he was still twelve, still touring the West with his family. Now they were down in Carlsbad Caverns, and Billy was praying to God to get him out of there before the ceiling fell in.

A ranger was explaining that the Caverns had been discovered by a cowboy who saw a huge cloud of bats come out of a hole in the ground. And then he said that he was going to turn out all the lights, and that it would probably be the first time in the lives of most people there that they had ever been in darkness that was total.

Out went the lights. Billy didn't even know whether he was still alive or not. And then something ghostly floated in air to his left. It had numbers on it. His father had taken out his pocket watch. The watch had a radium dial.

Billy went from total dark to total light, found himself back in the war, back in the delousing station again. The shower was over. An unseen hand had turned the water off.

When Billy got his clothes back, they weren't any cleaner, but all the little animals that had been living in them were dead. So it goes. And his new overcoat was thawed out and limp now. It was much too small for Billy. It had a fur collar and a lining of crimson silk, and had apparently been made for an impresario about as big as an organ-grinder's monkey. It was full of bullet holes.

Billy Pilgrim dressed himself. He put on the little overcoat, too. It split up the back, and, at the shoulders, the sleeves came entirely free. So the coat became a fur-collared vest. It was meant to flare at its owner's waist, but the flaring took place at Billy's armpits. The Germans found him to be one of the most screamingly funny things they had seen in all of World War Two. They laughed and laughed.

And the Germans told everybody else to form in ranks of five, with Billy as their pivot. Then out of doors went the parade, and through gate after gate again. There were more starving Russians with faces like radium dials. The Americans were livelier than before. The jazzing with hot water had cheered them up. And they came to a shed where a corporal with only one arm and one eye wrote the name and serial number of each prisoner in a big, red ledger. Everybody was legally alive now. Before they got their names and numbers in that book, they were missing in action and probably dead.

So it goes.

As the Americans were waiting to move on, an altercation broke out in their rear-most rank. An American had muttered something which a guard did not like. The guard knew English, and he hauled the American out of ranks, knocked him down.

The American was astonished. He stood up shakily, spitting

blood. He'd had two teeth knocked out. He had meant no harm by what he'd said, evidently, had no idea that the guard would hear and understand.

"Why me?" he asked the guard.

The guard shoved him back into ranks. "Vy you? Vy anybody?" he said.

When Billy Pilgrim's name was inscribed in the ledger of the prison camp, he was given a number, too, and an iron dogtag in which that number was stamped. A slave laborer from Poland had done the stamping. He was dead now. So it goes.

Billy was told to hang the tag around his neck along with his American dogtags, which he did. The tag was like a salt cracker, perforated down its middle so that a strong man could snap it in two with his bare hands. In case Billy died, which he didn't, half of the tag would mark his body and half would mark his grave.

After poor Edgar Derby, the high school teacher, was shot in Dresden later on, a doctor pronounced him dead and snapped his dogtag in two. So it goes.

Properly enrolled and tagged, the Americans were led through gate after gate again. In two days' time now their families would learn from the International Red Cross that they were alive.

Next to Billy was little Paul Lazzaro, who had promised to avenge Roland Weary. Lazzaro wasn't thinking about vengeance. He was thinking about his terrible bellyache. His stomach had shrunk to the size of a walnut. That dry, shriveled pouch was as sore as a boil.

Next to Lazzaro was poor, doomed old Edgar Derby, with his American and German dogs displayed like a necklace, on the outside of his clothes. He had expected to become a captain, a company commander, because of his wisdom and age. Now here he was on the Czechoslovakian border at midnight.

"Halt," said a guard.

The Americans halted. They stood there quietly in the cold. The sheds they were among were outwardly like thousands of other sheds they had passed. There was this difference, though:

the sheds had tin chimneys, and out of the chimneys whirled constellations of sparks.

A guard knocked on a door.

The door was flung open from inside. Light leaped out through the door, escaped from prison at 186,000 miles per second. Out marched fifty middle-aged Englishmen. They were singing "Hail, Hail, the Gang's All Here" from the *Pirates of Penzance.*

These lusty, ruddy vocalists were among the first English-speaking prisoners to be taken in the Second World War. Now they were singing to nearly the last. They had not seen a woman or a child for four years or more. They hadn't seen any birds, either. Not even sparrows would come into the camp.

The Englishmen were officers. Each of them had attempted to escape from another prison at least once. Now they were here, dead-center in a sea of dying Russians.

They could tunnel all they pleased. They would inevitably surface within a rectangle of barbed wire, would find them-selves greeted listlessly by dying Russians who spoke no English, who had no food or useful information or escape plans of their own. They could scheme all they pleased to hide aboard a vehicle or steal one, but no vehicle ever came into their compound. They could feign illness, if they liked, but that wouldn't earn them a trip anywhere, either. The only hospital in the camp was a six-bed affair in the British compound itself.

The Englishmen were clean and enthusiastic and decent and strong. They sang boomingly well. They had been singing to-gether every night for years.

The Englishmen had also been lifting weights and chinning themselves for years. Their bellies were like washboards. The muscles of their calves and upper arms were like cannonballs. They were all masters of checkers and chess and bridge and cribbage and dominoes and anagrams and charades and Ping-Pong and billiards, as well.

They were among the wealthiest people in Europe, in terms of food. A clerical error early in the war, when food was still getting through to prisoners, had caused the Red Cross to ship them five hundred parcels every month instead of fifty. The Englishmen had hoarded these so cunningly that now, as the war was ending, they had three tons of sugar, one ton of coffee, eleven hundred pounds of chocolate, seven hundred pounds of tobacco, seventeen hundred pounds of tea, two tons of flour, one ton of canned beef, twelve hundred pounds of canned butter, sixteen hundred pounds of canned cheese, eight hundred pounds of powdered milk, and two tons of orange marmalade.

They kept all this in a room without windows. They had rat-proofed it by lining it with flattened tin cans.

They were adored by the Germans, who thought they were exactly what Englishmen ought to be. They made war look stylish and reasonable, and fun. So the Germans let them have four sheds, though one shed would have held them all. And, in exchange for coffee or chocolate or tobacco, the Germans gave them paint and lumber and nails and cloth for fixing things up.

The Englishmen had known for twelve hours that American guests were on their way. They had never had guests before, and they went to work like darling elves, sweeping, mopping, cooking, baking—making mattresses of straw and burlap bags, setting tables, putting party favors at each place.

Now they were singing their welcome to their guests in the winter night. Their clothes were aromatic with the feast they had been preparing. They were dressed half for battle, half for tennis or croquet. They were so elated by their own hospitality, and by all the goodies waiting inside, that they did not take a good look at their guests while they sang. And they imagined that they were singing to fellow officers fresh from the fray.

They wrestled the Americans toward the shed door affectionately, filling the night with manly blather and brotherly rodomontades. They called them "Yank," told them "Good show," promised them that "Jerry was on the run," and so on.

Billy Pilgrim wondered dimly who Jerry was.

Now he was indoors, next to an iron cookstove that was glowing cherry red. Dozens of teapots were boiling there. Some of them had whistles. And there was a witches' cauldron full of golden soup. The soup was thick. Primeval bubbles surfaced in it with lethargical majesty as Billy Pilgrim stared.

There were long tables set for a banquet. At each place was a bowl made from a can that had once contained powdered milk. A smaller can was a cup. A taller, more slender can was a tumbler. Each tumbler was filled with warm milk.

At each place was a safety razor, a washcloth, a package of razor blades, a chocolate bar, two cigars, a bar of soap, ten cigarettes, a book of matches, a pencil, and a candle.

Only the candles and the soap were of German origin. They had a ghostly, opalescent similarity. The British had no way of knowing it, but the candles and the soap were made from the fat of rendered Jews and Gypsies and fairies and communists, and other enemies of the State.

So it goes.

The banquet hall was illuminated by candlelight. There were heaps of fresh-baked white bread on the tables, gobs of butter, pots of marmalade. There were platters of sliced beef from cans. Soup and scrambled eggs and hot marmalade pie were yet to come.

And, at the far end of the shed, Billy saw pink arches with azure draperies hanging between them, and an enormous clock, and two golden thrones, and a bucket and a mop. It was in this setting that the evening's entertainment would take place, a musical version of *Cinderella*, the most popular story ever told.

Billy Pilgrim was on fire, having stood too close to the glowing stove. The hem of his little coat was burning. It was a quiet, patient sort of fire—like the burning of punk.

Billy wondered if there was a telephone somewhere. He wanted to call his mother, to tell her he was alive and well.

There was silence now, as the Englishmen looked in astonishment at the frowsy creatures they had so lustily waltzed inside. One of the Englishmen saw that Billy was on fire. "You're on fire, lad!" he said, and he got Billy away from the stove and beat out the sparks with his hands.

When Billy made no comment on this, the Englishman asked him, "Can you talk? Can you hear?"

Billy nodded.

The Englishman touched him exploratorily here and there, filled with pity. "My God—what have they done to you, lad? This isn't a man. It's a broken kite."

"Are you really an American?" said the Englishman.

"Yes," said Billy.

"And your rank?"

"Private."

"What became of your boots, lad?"

"I don't remember."

"Is that coat a *joke*?"

"Sir?"

"Where did you get such a thing?"

Billy had to think hard about that. "They gave it to me," he said at last.

"Jerry gave it to you?"

"Who?"

"The Germans gave it to you?"

"Yes."

Billy didn't like the questions. They were fatiguing.

"Ohhhh—Yank, Yank, Yank—" said the Englishman, "that coat was an *insult*."

"Sir?"

"It was a deliberate attempt to humiliate you. You mustn't let Jerry do things like that."

Billy Pilgrim swooned.

Billy came to on a chair facing the stage. He had somehow eaten, and now he was watching *Cinderella*. Some part of him had evidently been enjoying the performance for quite a while. Billy was laughing hard.

The women in the play were really men, of course. The clock had just struck midnight, and Cinderella was lamenting:

> "Goodness me, the clock has struck—
> Alackday, and fuck my luck."

Billy found the couplet so comical that he not only laughed —he shrieked. He went on shrieking until he was carried out of the shed and into another, where the hospital was. It

was a six-bed hospital. There weren't any other patients in
there.

Billy was put to bed and tied down, and given a shot of morphine. Another American volunteered to watch over him. This
volunteer was Edgar Derby, the high school teacher who
would be shot to death in Dresden. So it goes.

Derby sat on a three-legged stool. He was given a book to
read. The book was *The Red Badge of Courage*, by Stephen
Crane. Derby had read it before. Now he read it again while
Billy Pilgrim entered a morphine paradise.

Under morphine, Billy had a dream of giraffes in a garden.
The giraffes were following gravel paths, were pausing to
munch sugar pears from treetops. Billy was a giraffe, too. He
ate a pear. It was a hard one. It fought back against his grinding teeth. It snapped in juicy protest.

The giraffes accepted Billy as one of their own, as a harmless
creature as preposterously specialized as themselves. Two approached him from opposite sides, leaned against him. They
had long, muscular upper lips which they could shape like the
bells of bugles. They kissed him with these. They were female
giraffes—cream and lemon yellow. They had horns like door-
knobs. The knobs were covered with velvet.

Why?

Night came to the garden of the giraffes, and Billy Pilgrim
slept without dreaming for a while, and then he traveled in
time. He woke up with his head under a blanket in a ward for
nonviolent mental patients in a veterans' hospital near Lake
Placid, New York. It was springtime in 1948, three years after
the end of the war.

Billy uncovered his head. The windows of the ward were
open. Birds were twittering outside. "Poo-tee-weet?" one
asked him. The sun was high. There were twenty-nine other
patients assigned to the ward, but they were all outdoors now,
enjoying the day. They were free to come and go as they
pleased, to go home, even, if they liked—and so was Billy
Pilgrim. They had come here voluntarily, alarmed by the outside world.

Billy had committed himself in the middle of his final year at the Ilium School of Optometry. Nobody else suspected that he was going crazy. Everybody else thought he looked fine and was acting fine. Now he was in the hospital. The doctors agreed: He *was* going crazy.

They didn't think it had anything to do with the war. They were sure Billy was going to pieces because his father had thrown him into the deep end of the Y.M.C.A. swimming pool when he was a little boy, and had then taken him to the rim of the Grand Canyon.

The man assigned to the bed next to Billy's was a former infantry captain named Eliot Rosewater. Rosewater was sick and tired of being drunk all the time.

It was Rosewater who introduced Billy to science fiction, and in particular to the writings of Kilgore Trout. Rosewater had a tremendous collection of science-fiction paperbacks under his bed. He had brought them to the hospital in a steamer trunk. Those beloved, frumpish books gave off a smell that permeated the ward—like flannel pajamas that hadn't been changed for a month, or like Irish stew.

Kilgore Trout became Billy's favorite living author, and science fiction became the only sort of tales he could read.

Rosewater was twice as smart as Billy, but he and Billy were dealing with similar crises in similar ways. They had both found life meaningless, partly because of what they had seen in war. Rosewater, for instance, had shot a fourteen-year-old fireman, mistaking him for a German soldier. So it goes. And Billy had seen the greatest massacre in European history, which was the fire-bombing of Dresden. So it goes.

So they were trying to re-invent themselves and their universe. Science fiction was a big help.

Rosewater said an interesting thing to Billy one time about a book that wasn't science fiction. He said that everything there was to know about life was in *The Brothers Karamazov*, by Feodor Dostoevsky. "But that isn't *enough* any more," said Rosewater.

Another time Billy heard Rosewater say to a psychiatrist, "I think you guys are going to have to come up with a lot of wonderful *new* lies, or people just aren't going to want to go on living."

There was a still life on Billy's bedside table—two pills, an ashtray with three lipstick-stained cigarettes in it, one cigarette still burning, and a glass of water. The water was dead. So it goes. Air was trying to get out of that dead water. Bubbles were clinging to the walls of the glass, too weak to climb out.

The cigarettes belonged to Billy's chain-smoking mother. She had sought the ladies' room, which was off the ward for WACS and WAVES and SPARS and WAFS who had gone bananas. She would be back at any moment now.

Billy covered his head with his blanket again. He always covered his head when his mother came to see him in the mental ward—always got much sicker until she went away. It wasn't that she was ugly, or had bad breath or a bad personality. She was a perfectly nice, standard-issue, brown-haired, white woman with a high-school education.

She upset Billy simply by being his mother. She made him feel embarrassed and ungrateful and weak because she had gone to so much trouble to give him life, and to keep that life going, and Billy didn't really like life at all.

Billy heard Eliot Rosewater come in and lie down. Rosewater's bedsprings talked a lot about that. Rosewater was a big man, but not very powerful. He looked as though he might be made out of nose putty.

And then Billy's mother came back from the ladies' room, sat down on a chair between Billy's and Rosewater's bed. Rosewater greeted her with melodious warmth, asked how she was today. He seemed delighted to hear that she was fine. He was experimenting with being ardently sympathetic with everybody he met. He thought that might make the world a slightly more pleasant place to live in. He called Billy's mother "dear." He was experimenting with calling everybody "dear."

"Some day," she promised Rosewater, "I'm going to come

in here, and Billy is going to uncover his head, and do you
know what he's going to say?"

"What's he going to say, dear?"

"He's going to say, 'Hello, Mom,' and he's going to smile.
He's going to say, 'Gee, it's good to see you, Mom. How have
you been?'"

"Today could be the day."

"Every night I pray."

"That's a *good* thing to do."

"People would be surprised if they knew how much in this
world was due to prayers."

"You never said a truer word, dear."

"Does your mother come to see you often?"

"My mother is dead," said Rosewater. So it goes.

"I'm sorry."

"At least she had a happy life as long as it lasted."

"That's a consolation, anyway."

"Yes."

"Billy's father is dead, you know," said Billy's mother. So it
goes.

"A boy *needs* a father."

And on and on it went—that duet between the dumb, praying lady and the big, hollow man who was so full of loving
echoes.

"He was at the top of his class when this happened," said
Billy's mother.

"Maybe he was *working* too hard," said Rosewater. He held
a book he wanted to read, but he was much too polite to read
and talk, too, easy as it was to give Billy's mother satisfactory
answers. The book was *Maniacs in the Fourth Dimension*, by
Kilgore Trout. It was about people whose mental diseases
couldn't be treated because the causes of the diseases were all
in the fourth dimension, and three-dimensional Earthling
doctors couldn't see those causes at all, or even imagine
them.

One thing Trout said that Rosewater liked very much was
that there really *were* vampires and werewolves and goblins and
angels and so on, but that they were in the fourth dimension.

So was William Blake, Rosewater's favorite poet, according to Trout. So were heaven and hell.

"He's engaged to a very rich girl," said Billy's mother.

"That's good," said Rosewater. "Money can be a great comfort sometimes."

"It really *can*."

"Of course it can."

"It isn't much fun if you have to pinch every penny till it screams."

"It's nice to have a little breathing room."

"Her father owns the optometry school where Billy was going. He also owns six offices around our part of the state. He flies his own plane and has a summer place up on Lake George."

"That's a beautiful lake."

Billy fell asleep under his blanket. When he woke up again, he was tied to the bed in the hospital back in prison. He opened one eye, saw poor old Edgar Derby reading *The Red Badge of Courage* by candlelight.

Billy closed that one eye, saw in his memory of the future poor old Edgar Derby in front of a firing squad in the ruins of Dresden. There were only four men in that squad. Billy had heard that one man in each firing squad was customarily given a rifle loaded with a blank cartridge. Billy didn't think there would be a blank cartridge issued in a squad that small, in a war that old.

Now the head Englishman came into the hospital to check on Billy. He was an infantry colonel captured at Dunkirk. It was he who had given Billy morphine. There wasn't a real doctor in the compound, so the doctoring was up to him. "How's the patient?" he asked Derby.

"Dead to the world."

"But not actually dead."

"No."

"How nice—to feel nothing, and still get full credit for being alive."

Derby now came to lugubrious attention.

"No, no—please—as you were. With only two men for each officer, and all the men sick, I think we can do without the usual pageantry between officers and men."

Derby remained standing. "You seem older than the rest," said the colonel.

Derby told him he was forty-five, which was two years older than the colonel. The colonel said that the other Americans had all shaved now, that Billy and Derby were the only two still with beards. And he said, "You know—we've had to imagine the war here, and we have imagined that it was being fought by aging men like ourselves. We had forgotten that wars were fought by babies. When I saw those freshly shaved faces, it was a shock. 'My God, my God—' I said to myself, 'It's the Children's Crusade.'"

The colonel asked old Derby how he had been captured, and Derby told a tale of being in a clump of trees with about a hundred other frightened soldiers. The battle had been going on for five days. The hundred had been driven into the trees by tanks.

Derby described the incredible artificial weather that Earthlings sometimes create for other Earthlings when they don't want those other Earthlings to inhabit Earth any more. Shells were bursting in the treetops with terrific bangs, he said, showering down knives and needles and razorblades. Little lumps of lead in copper jackets were crisscrossing the woods under the shellbursts, zipping along much faster than sound.

A lot of people were being wounded or killed. So it goes.

Then the shelling stopped, and a hidden German with a loudspeaker told the Americans to put their weapons down and come out of the woods with their hands on the top of their heads, or the shelling would start again. It wouldn't stop until everybody in there was dead.

So the Americans put their weapons down, and they came out of the woods with their hands on top of their heads, because they wanted to go on living, if they possibly could.

Billy traveled in time back to the veterans' hospital again. The blanket was over his head. It was quiet outside the blanket. "Is my mother gone?" said Billy.

"Yes."

Billy peeked out from under his blanket. His fiancée was out there now, sitting on the visitor's chair. Her name was Valencia Merble. Valencia was the daughter of the owner of the Ilium School of Optometry. She was rich. She was as big as a house because she couldn't stop eating. She was eating now. She was eating a Three Musketeers Candy Bar. She was wearing trifocal lenses in harlequin frames, and the frames were trimmed with rhinestones. The glitter of the rhinestones was answered by the glitter of the diamond in her engagement ring. The diamond was insured for eighteen hundred dollars. Billy had found that diamond in Germany. It was booty of war.

Billy didn't want to marry ugly Valencia. She was one of the symptoms of his disease. He knew he was going crazy when he heard himself proposing marriage to her, when he begged her to take the diamond ring and be his companion for life.

Billy said, "Hello," to her, and she asked him if he wanted some candy, and he said, "No, thanks."

She asked him how he was, and he said, "Much better, thanks." She said that everybody at the Optometry School was sorry he was sick and hoped he would be well soon, and Billy said, "When you see 'em, tell 'em, 'Hello.'"

She promised she would.

She asked him if there was anything she could bring him from the outside, and he said, "No. I have just about everything I want."

"What about books?" said Valencia.

"I'm right next to one of the biggest private libraries in the world," said Billy, meaning Eliot Rosewater's collection of science fiction.

Rosewater was on the next bed, reading, and Billy drew him into the conversation, asked him what he was reading this time.

So Rosewater told him. It was *The Gospel from Outer Space*, by Kilgore Trout. It was about a visitor from outer space, shaped very much like a Tralfamadorian, by the way. The visitor from outer space made a serious study of Christianity, to learn, if he could, why Christians found it so easy to be cruel. He concluded that at least part of the trouble was slipshod storytelling in the New Testament. He supposed that the intent of the Gospels was to teach people, among other things, to be merciful, even to the lowest of the low.

But the Gospels actually taught this:

Before you kill somebody, make absolutely sure he isn't well connected. So it goes.

The flaw in the Christ stories, said the visitor from outer space, was that Christ, who didn't look like much, was actually the Son of the Most Powerful Being in the Universe. Readers understood that, so, when they came to the crucifixion, they naturally thought, and Rosewater read out loud again:

Oh, boy—they sure picked the wrong guy to lynch that time!

And that thought had a brother: "*There are* right people *to lynch.*" Who? People not well connected. So it goes.

The visitor from outer space made a gift to Earth of a new Gospel. In it, Jesus really *was* a nobody, and a pain in the neck to a lot of people with better connections than he had. He still got to say all the lovely and puzzling things he said in the other Gospels.

So the people amused themselves one day by nailing him to a cross and planting the cross in the ground. There couldn't possibly be any repercussions, the lynchers thought. The reader would have to think that, too, since the new Gospel hammered home again and again what a nobody Jesus was.

And then, just before the nobody died, the heavens opened up, and there was thunder and lightning. The voice of God came crashing down. He told the people that he was adopting the bum as his son, giving him the full powers and privileges of the Son of the Creator of the Universe throughout all eternity. God said this: *From this moment on, He will punish horribly anybody who torments a bum who has no connections!*

Billy's fiancée had finished her Three Musketeers Candy Bar. Now she was eating a Milky Way.

"Forget books," said Rosewater, throwing that particular book under his bed. "The hell with 'em."

"That sounded like an interesting one," said Valencia.

"Jesus—if Kilgore Trout could only *write!*" Rosewater

exclaimed. He had a point: Kilgore Trout's unpopularity was deserved. His prose was frightful. Only his ideas were good.

"I don't think Trout has ever been out of the country," Rosewater went on. "My God—he writes about Earthlings all the time, and they're all Americans. Practically nobody on Earth is an American."

"Where does he live?" Valencia asked.

"Nobody knows," Rosewater replied. "I'm the only person who ever heard of him, as far as I can tell. No two books have the same publisher, and every time I write him in care of a publisher, the letter comes back because the publisher has failed."

He changed the subject now, congratulated Valencia on her engagement ring.

"Thank you," she said, and held it out so Rosewater could get a close look. "Billy got that diamond in the war."

"That's the attractive thing about war," said Rosewater. "Absolutely everybody gets a little something."

With regard to the whereabouts of Kilgore Trout: he actually lived in Ilium, Billy's hometown, friendless and despised. Billy would meet him by and by.

"Billy—" said Valencia Merble.

"Hm?"

"You want to talk about our silver pattern?"

"Sure."

"I've got it narrowed down pretty much to either Royal Danish or Rambler Rose."

"Rambler Rose," said Billy.

"It isn't something we should *rush* into," she said. "I mean —whatever we decide on, that's what we're going to have to live with the rest of our lives."

Billy studied the pictures. "Royal Danish," he said at last.

"Colonial Moonlight is nice, too."

"Yes, it is," said Billy Pilgrim.

And Billy traveled in time to the zoo on Tralfamadore. He was forty-four years old, on display under a geodesic dome. He was reclining on the lounge chair which had been his cradle during his trip through space. He was naked. The Tralfamadorians were interested in his body—*all* of it. There were thousands of them outside, holding up their little hands so that their eyes could see him. Billy had been on Tralfamadore for six Earthling months now. He was used to the crowd.

Escape was out of the question. The atmosphere outside the dome was cyanide, and Earth was 446,120,000,000,000,000 miles away.

Billy was displayed there in the zoo in a simulated Earthling habitat. Most of the furnishings had been stolen from the Sears & Roebuck warehouse in Iowa City, Iowa. There was a color television set and a couch that could be converted into a bed. There were end tables with lamps and ashtrays on them by the couch. There was a home bar and two stools. There was a little pool table. There was wall-to-wall carpeting in federal gold, except in the kitchen and bathroom areas and over the iron manhole cover in the center of the floor. There were magazines arranged in a fan on the coffee table in front of the couch.

There was a stereophonic phonograph. The phonograph worked. The television didn't. There was a picture of one cowboy killing another one pasted to the television tube. So it goes.

There were no walls in the dome, no place for Billy to hide. The mint green bathroom fixtures were right out in the open. Billy got off his lounge chair now, went into the bathroom and took a leak. The crowd went wild.

Billy brushed his teeth on Tralfamadore, put in his partial denture, and went into his kitchen. His bottled-gas range and his refrigerator and his dishwasher were mint green, too. There was a picture painted on the door of the refrigerator. The refrigerator had come that way. It was a picture of a Gay Nineties couple on a bicycle built for two.

Billy looked at that picture now, tried to think something about the couple. Nothing came to him. There didn't seem to be *anything* to think about those two people.

•

Billy ate a good breakfast from cans. He washed his cup and plate and knife and fork and spoon and saucepan, put them away. Then he did exercises he had learned in the Army—straddle jumps, deep knee bends, sit-ups and push-ups. Most Tralfamadorians had no way of knowing Billy's body and face were not beautiful. They supposed that he was a splendid specimen. This had a pleasant effect on Billy, who began to enjoy his body for the first time.

He showered after his exercises and trimmed his toenails. He shaved, and sprayed deodorant under his arms, while a zoo guide on a raised platform outside explained what Billy was doing—and why. The guide was lecturing telepathically, simply standing there, sending out thought waves to the crowd. On the platform with him was the little keyboard instrument with which he would relay questions to Billy from the crowd.

Now the first question came—from the speaker on the television set: "Are you happy here?"

"About as happy as I was on Earth," said Billy Pilgrim, which was true.

There were five sexes on Tralfamadore, each of them performing a step necessary in the creation of a new individual. They looked identical to Billy—because their sex differences were all in the fourth dimension.

One of the biggest moral bombshells handed to Billy by the Tralfamadorians, incidentally, had to do with sex on Earth. They said their flying-saucer crews had identified no fewer than *seven* sexes on Earth, each essential to reproduction. Again: Billy couldn't possibly imagine what five of those seven sexes had to do with the making of a baby, since they were sexually active only in the fourth dimension.

The Tralfamadorians tried to give Billy clues that would help him imagine sex in the invisible dimension. They told him that there could be no Earthling babies without male homosexuals. There *could* be babies without female homosexuals. There couldn't be babies without women over sixty-five years old. There *could* be babies without men over sixty-five. There couldn't be babies without other babies who had lived an hour or less after birth. And so on.

It was gibberish to Billy.

•

There was a lot that Billy said that was gibberish to the Tralfamadorians, too. They couldn't imagine what time looked like to him. Billy had given up on explaining that. The guide outside had to explain as best he could.

The guide invited the crowd to imagine that they were looking across a desert at a mountain range on a day that was twinkling bright and clear. They could look at a peak or a bird or a cloud, at a stone right in front of them, or even down into a canyon behind them. But among them was this poor Earthling, and his head was encased in a steel sphere which he could never take off. There was only one eyehole through which he could look, and welded to that eyehole were six feet of pipe.

This was only the beginning of Billy's miseries in the metaphor. He was also strapped to a steel lattice which was bolted to a flatcar on rails, and there was no way he could turn his head or touch the pipe. The far end of the pipe rested on a bi-pod which was also bolted to the flatcar. All Billy could see was the little dot at the end of the pipe. He didn't know he was on a flatcar, didn't even know there was anything peculiar about his situation.

The flatcar sometimes crept, sometimes went extremely fast, often stopped—went uphill, downhill, around curves, along straightaways. Whatever poor Billy saw through the pipe, he had no choice but to say to himself, "That's life."

Billy expected the Tralfamadorians to be baffled and alarmed by all the wars and other forms of murder on Earth. He expected them to fear that the Earthling combination of ferocity and spectacular weaponry might eventually destroy part or maybe all of the innocent Universe. Science fiction had led him to expect that.

But the subject of war never came up until Billy brought it up himself. Somebody in the zoo crowd asked him through the lecturer what the most valuable thing he had learned on Tralfamadore was so far, and Billy replied, "How the inhabitants of a whole planet can live in peace! As you know, I am from a planet that has been engaged in senseless slaughter since the beginning of time. I myself have seen the bodies of schoolgirls who were boiled alive in a water tower by my own

countrymen, who were proud of fighting pure evil at the time."
This was true. Billy saw the boiled bodies in Dresden. "And I
have lit my way in a prison at night with candles from the fat of
human beings who were butchered by the brothers and fathers
of those schoolgirls who were boiled. Earthlings must be the
terrors of the Universe! If other planets aren't now in danger
from Earth, they soon will be. So tell me the secret so I can
take it back to Earth and save us all: How can a planet live at
peace?"

Billy felt that he had spoken soaringly. He was baffled when
he saw the Tralfamadorians close their little hands on their
eyes. He knew from past experience what this meant: He was
being stupid.

"Would—would you mind telling me—" he said to the
guide, much deflated, "what was so stupid about that?"

"We know how the Universe ends—" said the guide, "and
Earth has nothing to do with it, except that *it* gets wiped out,
too."

"How—how *does* the Universe end?" said Billy.

"We blow it up, experimenting with new fuels for our flying
saucers. A Tralfamadorian test pilot presses a starter button,
and the whole Universe disappears." So it goes.

"If you know this," said Billy, "isn't there some way you can
prevent it? Can't you keep the pilot from *pressing* the button?"

"He has *always* pressed it, and he always *will*. We *always* let
him and we always *will* let him. The moment is *structured* that
way."

"So—" said Billy gropingly, "I suppose that the idea of pre-
venting war on Earth is stupid, too."

"Of course."

"But you *do* have a peaceful planet here."

"Today we do. On other days we have wars as horrible as
any you've ever seen or read about. There isn't anything we
can do about them, so we simply don't look at them. We ignore
them. We spend eternity looking at pleasant moments—like
today at the zoo. Isn't this a nice moment?"

"Yes."

"That's one thing Earthlings might learn to do, if they tried hard enough: Ignore the awful times, and concentrate on the good ones."

"Um," said Billy Pilgrim.

Shortly after he went to sleep that night, Billy traveled in time to another moment which was quite nice, his wedding night with the former Valencia Merble. He had been out of the veterans' hospital for six months. He was all well. He had graduated from the Ilium School of Optometry—third in his class of forty-seven.

Now he was in bed with Valencia in a delightful studio apartment which was built on the end of a wharf on Cape Ann, Massachusetts. Across the water were the lights of Gloucester. Billy was on top of Valencia, making love to her. One result of this act would be the birth of Robert Pilgrim, who would become a problem in high school, but who would then straighten out as a member of the famous Green Berets.

Valencia wasn't a time-traveler, but she did have a lively imagination. While Billy was making love to her, she imagined that she was a famous woman in history. She was being Queen Elizabeth the First of England, and Billy was supposedly Christopher Columbus.

Billy made a noise like a small, rusty hinge. He had just emptied his seminal vesicles into Valencia, had contributed his share of the Green Beret. According to the Tralfamadorians, of course, the Green Beret would have seven parents in all.

Now he rolled off his huge wife, whose rapt expression did not change when he departed. He lay with the buttons of his spine along the edge of the mattress, folded his hands behind his head. He was rich now. He had been rewarded for marrying a girl nobody in his right mind would have married. His father-in-law had given him a new Buick Roadmaster, an all-electric home, and had made him manager of his most prosperous office, his Ilium office, where Billy could expect to make at least thirty thousand dollars a year. That was good. His father had been only a barber.

As his mother said, "The Pilgrims are coming up in the world."

•

The honeymoon was taking place in the bittersweet mysteries of Indian Summer in New England. The lovers' apartment
had one romantic wall which was all French doors. They opened
onto a balcony and the oily harbor beyond.

A green and orange dragger, black in the night, grumbled
and drummed past their balcony, not thirty feet from their
wedding bed. It was going to sea with only its running lights
on. Its empty holds were resonant, made the song of the engines rich and loud. The wharf began to sing the same song,
and then the honeymooners' headboard sang, too. And it continued to sing long after the dragger was gone.

"Thank you," said Valencia at last. The headboard was singing a mosquito song.

"You're welcome."

"It was nice."

"I'm glad."

Then she began to cry.

"What's the matter?"

"I'm so happy."

"Good."

"I never thought anybody would marry me."

"Um," said Billy Pilgrim.

"I'm going to lose weight for you," she said.

"What?"

"I'm going to go on a diet. I'm going to become beautiful
for you."

"I like you just the way you are."

"Do you *really?*"

"Really," said Billy Pilgrim. He had already seen a lot of their
marriage, thanks to time-travel, knew that it was going to be at
least bearable all the way.

A great motor yacht named the *Scheherezade* now slid past
the marriage bed. The song its engines sang was a very low organ note. All her lights were on.

Two beautiful people, a young man and a young woman in
evening clothes, were at the rail in the stern, loving each other
and their dreams and the wake. They were honeymooning,

EVERYTHING
WAS
BEAUTIFUL,
AND
NOTHING
HURT

too. They were Lance Rumfoord, of Newport, Rhode Island, and his bride, the former Cynthia Landry, who had been a childhood sweetheart of John F. Kennedy in Hyannis Port, Massachusetts.

There was a slight coincidence here. Billy Pilgrim would later share a hospital room with Rumfoord's uncle, Professor Bertram Copeland Rumfoord of Harvard, official Historian of the United States Air Force.

When the beautiful people were past, Valencia questioned her funny-looking husband about war. It was a simple-minded thing for a female Earthling to do, to associate sex and glamor with war.

"Do you ever think about the war?" she said, laying a hand on his thigh.

"Sometimes," said Billy Pilgrim.

"I look at you sometimes," said Valencia, "and I get a funny feeling that you're just full of secrets."

"I'm not," said Billy. This was a lie, of course. He hadn't told anybody about all the time-traveling he'd done, about Tralfamadore and so on.

"You must have secrets about the war. Or, not secrets, I guess, but things you don't want to talk about."

"No."

"I'm *proud* you were a soldier. Do you know that?"

"Good."

"Was it awful?"

"Sometimes." A crazy thought now occurred to Billy. The truth of it startled him. It would make a good epitaph for Billy Pilgrim—and for me, too.

"Would you talk about the war now, if I *wanted* you to?" said Valencia. In a tiny cavity in her great body she was assembling the materials for a Green Beret.

"It would sound like a dream," said Billy. "Other people's dreams aren't very interesting, usually."

"I heard you tell Father one time about a German firing squad." She was referring to the execution of poor old Edgar Derby.

"Um."

"You had to bury him?"

"Yes."

"Did he see you with your shovels before he was shot?"

"Yes."

"Did he *say* anything?"

"No."

"Was he *scared*?"

"They had him doped up. He was sort of glassy-eyed."

"And they pinned a target to him?"

"A piece of paper," said Billy. He got out of bed, said, "Excuse me," went into the darkness of the bathroom to take a leak. He groped for the light, realized as he felt the rough walls that he had traveled back to 1944, to the prison hospital again.

The candle in the hospital had gone out. Poor old Edgar Derby had fallen asleep on the cot next to Billy's. Billy was out of bed, groping along a wall, trying to find a way out because he had to take a leak so badly.

He suddenly found a door, which opened, let him reel out into the prison night. Billy was loony with time-travel and morphine. He delivered himself to a barbed-wire fence which snagged him in a dozen places. Billy tried to back away from it, but the barbs wouldn't let go. So Billy did a silly little dance with the fence, taking a step this way, then that way, then returning to the beginning again.

A Russian, himself out in the night to take a leak, saw Billy dancing—from the other side of the fence. He came over to the curious scarecrow, tried to talk with it gently, asked it what country it was from. The scarecrow paid no attention, went on dancing. So the Russian undid the snags one by one, and the scarecrow danced off into the night again without a word of thanks.

The Russian waved to him, and called after him in Russian, "Good-bye."

Billy took his pecker out, there in the prison night, and peed and peed on the ground. Then he put it away again, more or less, and contemplated a new problem: Where had he come from, and where should he go now?

Somewhere in the night there were cries of grief. With nothing better to do, Billy shuffled in their direction. He wondered what tragedy so many had found to lament out of doors.

Billy was approaching, without knowing it, the back of the latrine. It consisted of a one-rail fence with twelve buckets underneath it. The fence was sheltered on three sides by a screen of scrap lumber and flattened tin cans. The open side faced the black tarpaper wall of the shed where the feast had taken place.

Billy moved along the screen and reached a point where he could see a message freshly painted on the tarpaper wall. The words were written with the same pink paint which had brightened the set for *Cinderella*. Billy's perceptions were so unreliable that he saw the words as hanging in air, painted on a transparent curtain, perhaps. And there were lovely silver dots on the curtain, too. These were really nailheads holding the tarpaper to the shed. Billy could not imagine how the curtain was supported in nothingness, and he supposed that the magic curtain and the theatrical grief were part of some religious ceremony he knew nothing about.

Here is what the message said:

Billy looked inside the latrine. The wailing was coming from in there. The place was crammed with Americans who had taken their pants down. The welcome feast had made them as sick as volcanoes. The buckets were full or had been kicked over.

An American near Billy wailed that he had excreted

everything but his brains. Moments later he said, "There they go, there they go." He meant his brains.

That was I. That was me. That was the author of this book.

Billy reeled away from his vision of Hell. He passed three Englishmen who were watching the excrement festival from a distance. They were catatonic with disgust.

"Button your pants!" said one as Billy went by.

So Billy buttoned his pants. He came to the door of the little hospital by accident. He went through the door, and found himself honeymooning again, going from the bathroom back to bed with his bride on Cape Ann.

"I missed you," said Valencia.

"I missed *you*," said Billy Pilgrim.

Billy and Valencia went to sleep nestled like spoons, and Billy traveled in time back to the train ride he had taken in 1944—from maneuvers in South Carolina to his father's funeral in Ilium. He hadn't seen Europe or combat yet. This was still in the days of steam locomotives.

Billy had to change trains a lot. All the trains were slow. The coaches stunk of coal smoke and rationed tobacco and rationed booze and the farts of people eating wartime food. The upholstery of the iron seats was bristly, and Billy couldn't sleep much. He got to sleep soundly when he was only three hours from Ilium, with his legs splayed toward the entrance of the busy dining car.

The porter woke him up when the train reached Ilium. Billy staggered off with his duffel bag, and then he stood on the station platform next to the porter, trying to wake up.

"Have a good nap, did you?" said the porter.

"Yes," said Billy.

"Man," said the porter, "you sure had a hard-on."

At three in the morning on Billy's morphine night in prison, a new patient was carried into the hospital by two lusty Englishmen. He was tiny. He was Paul Lazzaro, the polka-dotted car thief from Cicero, Illinois. He had been caught stealing cigarettes from under the pillow of an Englishman. The

Englishman, half asleep, had broken Lazzaro's right arm and knocked him unconscious.

The Englishman who had done this was helping to carry Lazzaro in now. He had fiery red hair and no eyebrows. He had been Cinderella's Blue Fairy Godmother in the play. Now he supported his half of Lazzaro with one hand while he closed the door behind himself with the other. "Doesn't weigh as much as a chicken," he said.

The Englishman with Lazzaro's feet was the colonel who had given Billy his knock-out shot.

The Blue Fairy Godmother was embarrassed, and angry, too. "If I'd known I was fighting a chicken," he said, "I wouldn't have fought so *hard*."

"Um."

The Blue Fairy Godmother spoke frankly about how disgusting all the Americans were. "Weak, smelly, self-pitying—a pack of sniveling, dirty, thieving bastards," he said. "They're worse than the bleeding Russians."

"*Do* seem a scruffy lot," the colonel agreed.

A German major came in now. He considered the Englishmen as close friends. He visited them nearly every day, played games with them, lectured to them on German history, played their piano, gave them lessons in conversational German. He told them often that, if it weren't for their civilized company, he would go mad. His English was splendid.

He was apologetic about the Englishmen's having to put up with the American enlisted men. He promised them that they would not be inconvenienced for more than a day or two, that the Americans would soon be shipped to Dresden as contract labor. He had a monograph with him, published by the German Association of Prison Officials. It was a report on the behavior in Germany of American enlisted men as prisoners of war. It was written by a former American who had risen high in the German Ministry of Propaganda. His name was Howard W. Campbell, Jr. He would later hang himself while awaiting trial as a war criminal.

So it goes.

While the British colonel set Lazzaro's broken arm and mixed plaster for the cast, the German major translated out loud passages from Howard W. Campbell, Jr.'s monograph. Campbell had been a fairly well-known playwright at one time. His opening line was this one:

America is the wealthiest nation on Earth, but its people are mainly poor, and poor Americans are urged to hate themselves. To quote the American humorist Kin Hubbard, "It ain't no disgrace to be poor, but it might as well be." It is in fact a crime for an American to be poor, even though America is a nation of poor. Every other nation has folk traditions of men who were poor but extremely wise and virtuous, and therefore more estimable than anyone with power and gold. No such tales are told by the American poor. They mock themselves and glorify their betters. The meanest eating or drinking establishment, owned by a man who is himself poor, is very likely to have a sign on its wall asking this cruel question: "If you're so smart, why ain't you rich?" There will also be an American flag no larger than a child's hand—glued to a lollipop stick and flying from the cash register.

The author of the monograph, a native of Schenectady, New York, was said by some to have had the highest I.Q. of all the war criminals who were made to face a death by hanging. So it goes.

Americans, like human beings everywhere, believe many things that are obviously untrue, the monograph went on. *Their most destructive untruth is that it is very easy for any American to make money. They will not acknowledge how in fact hard money is to come by, and, therefore, those who have no money blame and blame and blame themselves. This inward blame has been a treasure for the rich and powerful, who have had to do less for their poor, publicly and privately, than any other ruling class since, say, Napoleonic times.*

Many novelties have come from America. The most startling of these, a thing without precedent, is a mass of undignified poor. They do not love one another because they do not love themselves. Once this is understood, the disagreeable behavior of American enlisted men in German prisons ceases to be a mystery.

•

Howard W. Campbell, Jr., now discussed the uniform of the American enlisted in World War Two: *Every other army in history, prosperous or not, has attempted to clothe even its lowliest soldiers so as to make them impressive to themselves and others as stylish experts in drinking and copulation and looting and sudden death. The American Army, however, sends its enlisted men out to fight and die in a modified business suit quite evidently made for another man, a sterilized but unpressed gift from a nose-holding charity which passes out clothing to drunks in the slums.*

When a dashingly-clad officer addresses such a frumpishly dressed bum, he scolds him, as an officer in any army must. But the officer's contempt is not, as in other armies, avuncular theatricality. It is a genuine expression of hatred for the poor, who have no one to blame for their misery but themselves.

A prison administrator dealing with captured American enlisted men for the first time should be warned: Expect no brotherly love, even between brothers. There will be no cohesion between the individuals. Each will be a sulky child who often wishes he were dead.

Campbell told what the German experience with captured American enlisted men had been. They were known everywhere to be the most self-pitying, least fraternal, and dirtiest of all prisoners of war, said Campbell. They were incapable of concerted action on their own behalf. They despised any leader from among their own number, refused to follow or even listen to him, on the grounds that he was no better than they were, that he should stop putting on airs.

And so on. Billy Pilgrim went to sleep, woke up as a widower in his empty home in Ilium. His daughter Barbara was reproaching him for writing ridiculous letters to the newspapers.

"Did you hear what I said?" Barbara inquired. It was 1968 again.

"Of course." He had been dozing.

"If you're going to act like a child, maybe we'll just have to *treat* you like a child."

"That isn't what happens next," said Billy.

"We'll *see* what happens next." Big Barbara now embraced herself. "It's awfully cold in here. Is the heat on?"

"The *heat*?"

"The furnace—the thing in the basement, the thing that makes hot air that comes out of these registers. I don't think it's working."

"Maybe not."

"Aren't you cold?"

"I hadn't noticed."

"Oh my God, you *are* a child. If we leave you alone here, you'll freeze to death, you'll starve to death." And so on. It was very exciting for her, taking his dignity away in the name of love.

Barbara called the oil-burner man, and she made Billy go to bed, made him promise to stay under the electric blanket until the heat came on. She set the control of the blanket at the highest notch, which soon made Billy's bed hot enough to bake bread in.

When Barbara left, slamming the door behind her, Billy traveled in time to the zoo on Tralfamadore again. A mate had just been brought to him from Earth. She was Montana Wildhack, a motion picture star.

Montana was under heavy sedation. Tralfamadorians wearing gas masks brought her in, put her on Billy's yellow lounge chair; withdrew through his airlock. The vast crowd outside was delighted. All attendance records for the zoo were broken. Everybody on the planet wanted to see the Earthlings mate.

Montana was naked, and so was Billy, of course. He had a tremendous wang, incidentally. You never know who'll get one.

Now she fluttered her eyelids. Her lashes were like buggy whips. "Where *am* I?" she said.

"Everything is all right," said Billy gently. "Please don't be afraid."

Montana had been unconscious during her trip from Earth. The Tralfamadorians hadn't talked to her, hadn't shown them-

selves to her. The last thing she remembered was sunning herself by a swimming pool in Palm Springs, California. Montana
was only twenty years old. Around her neck was a silver chain
with a heart-shaped locket hanging from it—between her
breasts.

Now she turned her head to see the myriads of Tralfamadorians outside the dome. They were applauding her by
opening and closing their little green hands quickly.

Montana screamed and screamed.

All the little green hands closed tight, because Montana's
terror was so unpleasant to see. The head zoo keeper ordered
a crane operator, who was standing by, to drop a navy blue
canopy over the dome, thus simulating Earthling night inside.
Real night came to the zoo for only one Earthling hour out of
every sixty-two.

Billy switched on a floor lamp. The light from the single
source threw the baroque detailing of Montana's body into
sharp relief. Billy was reminded of fantastic architecture in
Dresden, before it was bombed.

In time, Montana came to love and trust Billy Pilgrim. He
did not touch her until she made it clear that she wanted him
to. After she had been on Tralfamadore for what would have
been an Earthling week, she asked him shyly if he wouldn't
sleep with her. Which he did. It was heavenly.

And Billy traveled in time from that delightful bed to a bed
in 1968. It was his bed in Ilium, and the electric blanket was
turned up high. He was drenched in sweat, remembered grog-
gily that his daughter had put him to bed, had told him to stay
there until the oil burner was repaired.

Somebody was knocking on his bedroom door.

"Yes?" said Billy.

"Oil-burner man."

"Yes?"

"It's running good now. Heat's coming up."

"Good."

"Mouse ate through a wire from the thermostat."

"I'll be darned."

Billy sniffed. His hot bed smelled like a mushroom cellar. He had had a wet dream about Montana Wildhack.

On the morning after that wet dream, Billy decided to go back to work in his office in the shopping plaza. Business was booming as usual. His assistants were keeping up with it nicely. They were startled to see him. They had been told by his daughter that he might never practice again.

But Billy went into his examining room briskly, asked that the first patient be sent in. So they sent him one—a twelve-year-old boy who was accompanied by his widowed mother. They were strangers, new in town. Billy asked them a little about themselves, learned that the boy's father had been killed in Vietnam—in the famous five-day battle for Hill 875 near Dakto. So it goes.

While he examined the boy's eyes, Billy told him matter-of-factly about his adventures on Tralfamadore, assured the father-less boy that his father was very much alive still in moments the boy would see again and again.

"Isn't that comforting?" Billy asked.

And somewhere in there, the boy's mother went out and told the receptionist that Billy was evidently going crazy. Billy was taken home. His daughter asked him again, "Father, Father, Father—what *are* we going to *do* with you?"

6

Listen:

Billy Pilgrim says he went to Dresden, Germany, on the day after his morphine night in the British compound in the center of the extermination camp for Russian prisoners of war. Billy woke up at dawn on that day in January. There were no windows in the little hospital, and the ghostly candles had gone out. So the only light came from pin-prick holes in the walls, and from a sketchy rectangle that outlined the imperfectly fitted door. Little Paul Lazzaro, with a broken arm, snored on one bed. Edgar Derby, the high school teacher who would eventually be shot, snored on another.

Billy sat up in bed. He had no idea what year it was or what planet he was on. Whatever the planet's name was, it was cold. But it wasn't the cold that had awakened Billy. It was animal magnetism which was making him shiver and itch. It gave him profound aches in his musculature, as though he had been exercising hard.

The animal magnetism was coming from behind him. If Billy had had to guess as to the source, he would have said that there was a vampire bat hanging upside down on the wall behind him.

Billy moved down toward the foot of his cot before turning to look at whatever it was. He didn't want the animal to drop into his face and maybe claw his eyes out or bite off his big nose. Then he turned. The source of the magnetism really did resemble a bat. It was Billy's impresario's coat with the fur collar. It was hanging from a nail.

Billy now backed toward it again, looking at it over his shoulder, feeling the magnetism increase. Then he faced it, kneeling on his cot, dared to touch it here and there. He was seeking the exact source of the radiations.

He found two small sources, two lumps an inch apart and hidden in the lining. One was shaped like a pea. The other was shaped like a tiny horseshoe. Billy received a message carried by the radiations. He was told not to find out what the lumps were. He was advised to be content with knowing that they could work miracles for him, provided he did not insist on learning their nature. That was all right with Billy Pilgrim. He was grateful. He was glad.

Billy dozed, awakened in the prison hospital again. The sun was high. Outside were Golgotha sounds of strong men digging holes for upright timbers in hard, hard ground. Englishmen were building themselves a new latrine. They had abandoned their old latrine to the Americans—and their theater, the place where the feast had been held, too.

Six Englishmen staggered through a hospital with a pool table on which several mattresses were piled. They were transferring it to living quarters attached to the hospital. They were followed by an Englishman dragging his mattress and carrying a dartboard.

The man with the dartboard was the Blue Fairy Godmother who had injured little Paul Lazzaro. He stopped by Lazzaro's bed, asked Lazzaro how he was.

Lazzaro told him he was going to have him killed after the war.

"Oh?"

"You made a big mistake," said Lazzaro. "Anybody touches me, he better *kill* me, or I'm gonna have *him* killed."

The Blue Fairy Godmother knew something about killing. He gave Lazzaro a careful smile. "There is still time for *me* to kill *you*," he said, "if you really persuade me that it's the sensible thing to do."

"Why don't you go fuck yourself?"

"Don't think I haven't tried," the Blue Fairy Godmother answered.

The Blue Fairy Godmother left, amused and patronizing. When he was gone, Lazzaro promised Billy and poor old Edgar Derby that he was going to have revenge, and that revenge was sweet.

"It's the sweetest thing there is," said Lazzaro. "People fuck with me," he said, "and Jesus Christ are they ever fucking sorry. I laugh like hell. I don't care if it's a guy or a dame. If the President of the United States fucked around with me, I'd fix

him good. You should have seen what I did to a dog one
time."

"A dog?" said Billy.

"Son of a bitch bit me. So I got me some steak, and I got
me the spring out of a clock. I cut that spring up in little pieces.
I put points on the ends of the pieces. They were sharp as razor
blades. I stuck 'em into the steak—way inside. And I went past
where they had the dog tied up. He wanted to bite me again.
I said to him, 'Come on, doggie—let's be friends. Let's not be
enemies any more. I'm not mad.' He believed me."

"He *did?*"

"I threw him the steak. He swallowed it down in one big
gulp. I waited around for ten minutes." Now Lazzaro's eyes
twinkled. "Blood started coming out of his mouth. He started
crying, and he rolled on the ground, as though the knives were
on the outside of him instead of on the inside of him. Then he
tried to bite out his own insides. I laughed, and I said to him,
'You got the right idea now. Tear your own guts out, boy.
That's *me* in there with all those knives.'" So it goes.

"Anybody ever asks you what the sweetest thing in life is—"
said Lazzaro, "it's revenge."

When Dresden was destroyed later on, incidentally, Lazzaro
did not exult. He didn't have anything against the Germans,
he said. Also, he said he liked to take his enemies one at a time.
He was proud of never having hurt an innocent bystander.
"Nobody ever got it from Lazzaro," he said, "who didn't have
it coming."

Poor old Edgar Derby, the high school teacher, got into the
conversation now. He asked Lazzaro if he planned to feed the
Blue Fairy Godmother clock springs and steak.

"Shit," said Lazzaro.

"He's a pretty big man," said Derby, who, of course, was a
pretty big man himself.

"Size don't mean a thing."

"You're going to *shoot* him?"

"I'm gonna *have* him shot," said Lazzaro. "He'll get home
after the war. He'll be a big hero. The dames'll be climbing all

over him. He'll settle down. A couple of years'll go by. And then one day there'll be a knock on his door. He'll answer the door, and there'll be a stranger out there. The stranger'll ask him if he's so-and-so. When he says he is, the stranger'll say, 'Paul Lazzaro sent me.' And he'll pull out a gun and shoot his pecker off. The stranger'll let him think a couple of seconds about who Paul Lazzaro is and what life's gonna be like without a pecker. Then he'll shoot him once in the guts and walk away." So it goes.

Lazzaro said that he could have anybody in the world killed for a thousand dollars plus traveling expenses. He had a list in his head, he said.

Derby asked him who all was on the list, and Lazzaro said, "Just make fucking sure *you* don't get on it. Just don't cross me, that's all." There was a silence, and then he added, "And don't cross my friends."

"You have *friends*?" Derby wanted to know.

"In the *war*?" said Lazzaro. "Yeah—I had a friend in the war. He's dead." So it goes.

"That's too bad."

Lazzaro's eyes were twinkling again. "Yeah. He was my buddy on the boxcar. His name was Roland Weary. He died in my arms." Now he pointed to Billy with his one mobile hand. "He died on account of this silly cocksucker here. So I promised him I'd have this silly cocksucker shot after the war."

Lazzaro erased with his hand anything Billy Pilgrim might be about to say. "Just forget about it, kid," he said. "Enjoy life while you can. Nothing's gonna happen for maybe five, ten, fifteen, twenty years. But lemme give you a piece of advice: Whenever the doorbell rings, have somebody else answer the door."

Billy Pilgrim says now that this really is the way he *is* going to die, too. As a time-traveler, he has seen his own death many times, has described it to a tape recorder. The tape is locked up with his will and some other valuables in his safe-deposit box at the Ilium Merchants National Bank and Trust, he says.

I, Billy Pilgrim, the tape begins, *will die, have died, and always will die on February thirteenth, 1976.*

At the time of his death, he says, he is in Chicago to address a large crowd on the subject of flying saucers and the true nature of time. His home is still in Ilium. He has had to cross three international boundaries in order to reach Chicago. The United States of America has been Balkanized, has been divided into twenty petty nations so that it will never again be a threat to world peace. Chicago has been hydrogen-bombed by angry Chinamen. So it goes. It is all brand new.

Billy is speaking before a capacity audience in a baseball park, which is covered by a geodesic dome. The flag of the country is behind him. It is a Hereford bull on a field of green. Billy predicts his own death within an hour. He laughs about it, invites the crowd to laugh with him. "It is high time I was dead," he says. "Many years ago," he said, "a certain man promised to have me killed. He is an old man now, living not far from here. He has read all the publicity associated with my appearance in your fair city. He is insane. Tonight he will keep his promise."

There are protests from the crowd.

Billy Pilgrim rebukes them. "If you protest, if you think that death is a terrible thing, then you have not understood a word I've said." Now he closes his speech as he closes every speech —with these words: "Farewell, hello, farewell, hello."

There are police around him as he leaves the stage. They are there to protect him from the crush of popularity. No threats on his life have been made since 1945. The police offer to stay with him. They are floridly willing to stand in a circle around him all night, with their zap guns drawn.

"No, no," says Billy serenely. "It is time for you to go home to your wives and children, and it is time for me to be dead for a little while—and then live again." At that moment, Billy's high forehead is in the cross hairs of a high-powered laser gun. It is aimed at him from the darkened press box. In the next moment, Billy Pilgrim is dead. So it goes.

So Billy experiences death for a while. It is simply violet light and a hum. There isn't anybody else there. Not even Billy Pilgrim is there.

Then he swings back into life again, all the way back to an hour after his life was threatened by Lazzaro—in 1945. He has been told to get out of his hospital bed and dress, that he is well. He and Lazzaro and poor old Edgar Derby are to join their fellows in the theater. There they will choose a leader for themselves by secret ballot in a free election.

Billy and Lazzaro and poor old Edgar Derby crossed the prison yard to the theater now. Billy was carrying his little coat as though it were a lady's muff. It was wrapped around and around his hands. He was the central clown in an unconscious travesty of that famous oil painting, "The Spirit of '76."

Edgar Derby was writing letters home in his head, telling his wife that he was alive and well, that she shouldn't worry, that the war was nearly over, that he would soon be home.

Lazzaro was talking to himself about people he was going to have killed after the war, and rackets he was going to work, and women he was going to make fuck him, whether they wanted to or not. If he had been a dog in a city, a policeman would have shot him and sent his head to a laboratory, to see if he had rabies. So it goes.

As they neared the theater, they came upon an Englishman who was hacking a groove in the Earth with the heel of his boot. He was marking the boundary between the American and English sections of the compound. Billy and Lazzaro and Derby didn't have to ask what the line meant. It was a familiar symbol from childhood.

The theater was paved with American bodies that nestled like spoons. Most of the Americans were in stupors or asleep. Their guts were fluttering, dry.

"Close the fucking door," somebody said to Billy. "Were you born in a barn?"

Billy closed it, took a hand from his muff, touched a stove. It was as cold as ice. The stage was still set for *Cinderella*. Azure curtains hung from arches which were shocking pink. There were golden thrones and the dummy clock, whose hands were set at midnight. Cinderella's slippers, which were airman's boots painted silver, were capsized side by side under a golden throne.

Billy and poor old Edgar Derby and Lazzaro had been in the hospital when the British passed out blankets and mattresses, so they had none. They had to improvise. The only space open to them was up on the stage, and they went up there, pulled the azure curtains down, made nests.

Billy, curled in his azure nest, found himself staring at Cinderella's silver boots under a throne. And then he remembered that his shoes were ruined, that he *needed* boots. He hated to get out of his nest, but he forced himself to do it. He crawled to the boots on all fours, sat, tried them on.

The boots fit perfectly. Billy Pilgrim was Cinderella, and Cinderella was Billy Pilgrim.

Somewhere in there was a lecture on personal hygiene by the head Englishman, and then a free election. At least half the Americans went on snoozing through it all. The Englishman got up on the stage, and he rapped on the arm of a throne with a swagger stick, called, "Lads, lads, lads—can I have your attention, please?" And so on.

What the Englishman said about survival was this: "If you stop taking pride in your appearance, you will very soon die." He said that he had seen several men die in the following way: "They ceased to stand up straight, then ceased to shave or wash, then ceased to get out of bed, then ceased to talk, then died. There is this much to be said for it: it is evidently a very easy and painless way to go." So it goes.

The Englishman said that he, when captured, had made and kept the following vows to himself: To brush his teeth twice a day, to shave once a day, to wash his face and hands before every meal and after going to the latrine, to polish his shoes once a day, to exercise for at least half an hour each morning and then move his bowels, and to look into a mirror frequently, frankly evaluating his appearance, particularly with respect to posture.

Billy Pilgrim heard all this while lying in his nest. He looked not at the Englishman's face but his ankles.

"I *envy* you lads," said the Englishman.

Somebody laughed. Billy wondered what the joke was.

"You lads are leaving this afternoon for Dresden—a beautiful city, I'm told. You won't be cooped up like us. You'll be out where the life is, and the food is certain to be more plentiful than here. If I may inject a personal note: It has been five years now since I have seen a tree or flower or woman or child—or a dog or a cat or a place of entertainment, or a human being doing useful work of any kind.

"You needn't worry about bombs, by the way. Dresden is an open city. It is undefended, and contains no war industries or troop concentrations of any importance."

Somewhere in there, old Edgar Derby was elected head American. The Englishman called for nominations from the floor, and there weren't any. So he nominated Derby, praising him for his maturity and long experience in dealing with people. There were no further nominations, so the nominations were closed.

"All in favor?"

Two or three people said, "Aye."

Then poor old Derby made a speech. He thanked the Englishman for his good advice, said he meant to follow it exactly. He said he was sure that all the other Americans would do the same. He said that his primary responsibility now was to make damn well sure that everybody got home safely.

"Go take a flying fuck at a rolling doughnut," murmured Paul Lazzaro in his azure nest. "Go take a flying fuck at the moon."

The temperature climbed startlingly that day. The noontime was balmy. The Germans brought soup and bread in two-wheeled carts which were pulled by Russians. The Englishman sent over real coffee and sugar and marmalade and cigarettes and cigars, and the doors of the theater were left open, so the warmth could get in.

The Americans began to feel much better. They were able to hold their food. And then it was time to go to Dresden. The Americans marched fairly stylishly out of the British compound. Billy Pilgrim again led the parade. He had silver boots now, and a muff, and a piece of azure curtain which he wore like a toga. Billy still had a beard. So did poor old Edgar Derby, who was beside him. Derby was imagining letters to home, his lips working tremulously:

Dear Margaret—We are leaving for Dresden today. Don't worry. It will never be bombed. It is an open city. There was an election at noon, and guess what? And so on.

They came to the prison railroad yard again. They had arrived on only two cars. They would depart far more comfortably on four. They saw the dead hobo again. He was frozen stiff in the weeds beside the track. He was in a fetal position, trying even in death to nestle like a spoon with others. There were no others now. He was nestling with thin air and cinders. Somebody had taken his boots. His bare feet were blue and ivory. It was all right, somehow, his being dead. So it goes.

The trip to Dresden was a lark. It took only two hours. Shriveled little bellies were full. Sunlight and mild air came in through the ventilators. There were plenty of smokes from the Englishmen.

The Americans arrived in Dresden at five in the afternoon. The boxcar doors were opened, and the doorways framed the loveliest city that most of the Americans had ever seen. The skyline was intricate and voluptuous and enchanted and absurd. It looked like a Sunday school picture of Heaven to Billy Pilgrim.

Somebody behind him in the boxcar said, "Oz." That was I. That was me. The only other city I'd ever seen was Indianapolis, Indiana.

Every other big city in Germany had been bombed and burned ferociously. Dresden had not suffered so much as a cracked windowpane. Sirens went off every day, screamed like hell, and people went down into cellars and listened to radios there. The planes were always bound for someplace else— Leipzig, Chemnitz, Plauen, places like that. So it goes.

Steam radiators still whistled cheerily in Dresden. Streetcars clanged. Telephones rang and were answered. Lights went on and off when switches were clicked. There were theaters and restaurants. There was a zoo. The principal enterprises of the city were medicine and food-processing and the making of cigarettes.

People were going home from work now in the late afternoon. They were tired.

Eight Dresdeners crossed the steel spaghetti of the railroad yard. They were wearing new uniforms. They had been sworn into the army the day before. They were boys and men past middle age, and two veterans who had been shot to pieces in Russia. Their assignment was to guard one hundred American prisoners of war, who would work as contract labor. A grandfather and his grandson were in the squad. The grandfather was an architect.

The eight were grim as they approached the boxcars containing their wards. They knew what sick and foolish soldiers they themselves appeared to be. One of them actually had an artificial leg, and carried not only a loaded rifle but a cane. Still —they were expected to earn obedience and respect from tall, cocky, murderous American infantrymen who had just come from all the killing at the front.

And then they saw bearded Billy Pilgrim in his blue toga and silver shoes, with his hands in a muff. He looked at least sixty years old. Next to Billy was little Paul Lazzaro with a broken arm. He was fizzing with rabies. Next to Lazzaro was the poor old high school teacher, Edgar Derby, mournfully pregnant with patriotism and middle age and imaginary wisdom. And so on.

The eight ridiculous Dresdeners ascertained that these hundred ridiculous creatures really *were* American fighting men fresh from the front. They smiled, and then they laughed. Their terror evaporated. There was nothing to be afraid of. Here were more crippled human beings, more fools like themselves. Here was light opera.

So out of the gate of the railroad yard and into the streets of Dresden marched the light opera. Billy Pilgrim was the star. He led the parade. Thousands of people were on the sidewalks, going home from work. They were watery and putty-colored, having eaten mostly potatoes during the past two years. They had expected no blessings beyond the mildness of the day. Suddenly—here was fun.

Billy did not meet many of the eyes that found him so enter-taining. He was enchanted by the architecture of the city. Merry amoretti wove garlands above windows. Roguish fauns and naked nymphs peeked down at Billy from festooned cornices. Stone monkeys frisked among scrolls and seashells and bamboo.

Billy, with his memories of the future, knew that the city would be smashed to smithereens and then burned—in about thirty more days. He knew, too, that most of the people watching him would soon be dead. So it goes.

And Billy worked his hands in his muff as he marched. His fingertips, working there in the hot darkness of the muff, wanted to know what the two lumps in the lining of the little impresario's coat were. The fingertips got inside the lining. They palpated the lumps, the pea-shaped thing and the horse-shoe-shaped thing. The parade had to halt by a busy corner. The traffic light was red.

There at the corner, in the front rank of pedestrians, was a surgeon who had been operating all day. He was a civilian, but his posture was military. He had served in two world wars. The sight of Billy offended him, especially after he learned from the guards that Billy was an American. It seemed to him that Billy was in abominable taste, supposed that Billy had gone to a lot of silly trouble to costume himself just so.

The surgeon spoke English, and he said to Billy, "I take it you find war a very comical thing."

Billy looked at him vaguely. Billy had lost track momentarily of where he was or how he had gotten there. He had no idea that people thought he was clowning. It was Fate, of course, which had costumed him—Fate, and a feeble will to survive.

"Did you expect us to *laugh*?" the surgeon asked him.

The surgeon was demanding some sort of satisfaction. Billy was mystified. Billy wanted to be friendly, to help, if he could, but his resources were meager. His fingers now held the two objects from the lining of the coat. Billy decided to show the surgeon what they were.

"You thought we would enjoy being *mocked*?" the surgeon said. "And do you feel *proud* to represent America as you do?"

Billy withdrew a hand from his muff, held it under the

surgeon's nose. On his palm rested a two-carat diamond and a partial denture. The denture was an obscene little artifact— silver and pearl and tangerine. Billy smiled.

The parade pranced, staggered and reeled to the gate of the Dresden slaughterhouse, and then it went inside. The slaughter- house wasn't a busy place any more. Almost all the hooved ani- mals in Germany had been killed and eaten and excreted by human beings, mostly soldiers. So it goes.

The Americans were taken to the fifth building inside the gate. It was a one-story cement-block cube with sliding doors in front and back. It had been built as a shelter for pigs about to be butchered. Now it was going to serve as a home away from home for one hundred American prisoners of war. There were bunks in there, and two potbellied stoves and a water tap. Behind it was a latrine, which was a one-rail fence with buckets under it.

There was a big number over the door of the building. The number was *five*. Before the Americans could go inside, their only English-speaking guard told them to memorize their sim- ple address, in case they got lost in the big city. Their address was this: "Schlachthof-fünf." *Schlachthof* meant *slaughterhouse*. *Fünf* was good old *five*.

7

BILLY PILGRIM got onto a chartered airplane in Ilium twenty-five years after that. He knew it was going to crash, but he didn't want to make a fool of himself by saying so. It was supposed to carry Billy and twenty-eight other optometrists to a convention in Montreal.

His wife, Valencia, was outside, and his father-in-law, Lionel Merble, was strapped to the seat beside him.

Lionel Merble was a machine. Tralfamadorians, of course, say that every creature and plant in the Universe is a machine. It amuses them that so many Earthlings are offended by the idea of being machines.

Outside the plane, the machine named Valencia Merble Pilgrim was eating a Peter Paul Mound Bar and waving bye-bye.

The plane took off without incident. The moment was structured that way. There was a barbershop quartet on board. They were optometrists, too. They called themselves "The Febs," which was an acronym for "Four-eyed Bastards."

When the plane was safely aloft, the machine that was Billy's father-in-law asked the quartet to sing his favorite song. They knew what song he meant, and they sang it, and it went like this:

> In my prison cell I sit,
> With my britches full of shit,
> And my balls are bouncing gently on the floor.
> And I see the bloody snag
> When she bit me in the bag.
> Oh, I'll never fuck a Polack any more.

Billy's father-in-law laughed and laughed at that, and he begged the quartet to sing the other Polish song he liked so much. So they sang a song from the Pennsylvania coal mines that began:

Me and Mike, ve vork in mine.
Holy shit, ve have good time.
Vunce a veek ve get our pay.
Holy shit, no vork next day.

Speaking of people from Poland: Billy Pilgrim accidentally
saw a Pole hanged in public, about three days after Billy got to
Dresden. Billy just happened to be walking to work with some
others shortly after sunrise, and they came to a gallows and a
small crowd in front of a soccer stadium. The Pole was a farm
laborer who was being hanged for having had sexual intercourse with a German woman. So it goes.

Billy, knowing the plane was going to crash pretty soon,
closed his eyes, traveled in time back to 1944. He was back in
the forest in Luxembourg again—with the Three Musketeers.
Roland Weary was shaking him, bonking his head against a
tree. "You guys go on without me," said Billy Pilgrim.

The barbershop quartet on the airplane was singing "Wait
Till the Sun Shines, Nelly," when the plane smacked into the
top of Sugarbush Mountain in Vermont. Everybody was killed
but Billy and the copilot. So it goes.

The people who first got to the crash scene were young
Austrian ski instructors from the famous ski resort below. They
spoke to each other in German as they went from body to
body. They wore black wind masks with two holes for their eyes
and a red topknot. They looked like golliwogs, like white
people pretending to be black for the laughs they could get.

Billy had a fractured skull, but he was still conscious. He
didn't know where he was. His lips were working, and one of
the golliwogs put his ear close to them to hear what might be
his dying words.

Billy thought the golliwog had something to do with
World War Two, and he whispered to him his address:
"Schlachthof-fünf."

Billy was brought down Sugarbush Mountain on a tobog-
gan. The golliwogs controlled it with ropes and yodeled melo-
diously for right-of-way. Near the bottom, the trail swooped

around the pylons of a chair lift. Billy looked up at all the young people in bright elastic clothing and enormous boots and goggles, bombed out of their skulls with snow, swinging through the sky in yellow chairs. He supposed that they were part of an amazing new phase of World War Two. It was all right with him. Everything was pretty much all right with Billy.

He was taken to a small private hospital. A famous brain surgeon came up from Boston and operated on him for three hours. Billy was unconscious for two days after that, and he dreamed millions of things, some of them true. The true things were time-travel.

One of the true things was his first evening in the slaughterhouse. He and poor old Edgar Derby were pushing an empty two-wheeled cart down a dirt lane between empty pens for animals. They were going to a communal kitchen for supper for all. They were guarded by a sixteen-year-old German named Werner Gluck. The axles of the cart were greased with the fat of dead animals. So it goes.

The sun had just gone down, and its afterglow was backlighting the city, which formed low cliffs around the bucolic void to the idle stockyards. The city was blacked out because bombers might come, so Billy didn't get to see Dresden do one of the most cheerful things a city is capable of doing when the sun goes down, which is to wink its lights on one by one.

There was a broad river to reflect those lights, which would have made their nighttime winkings very pretty indeed. It was the Elbe.

Werner Gluck, the young guard, was a Dresden boy. He had never been in the slaughterhouse before, so he wasn't sure where the kitchen was. He was tall and weak like Billy, might have been a younger brother of his. They were, in fact, distant cousins, something they never found out. Gluck was armed with an incredibly heavy musket, a single-shot museum piece with an octagonal barrel and a smooth bore. He had fixed his bayonet. It was like a long knitting needle. It had no blood gutters.

Gluck led the way to a building that he thought might contain the kitchen, and he opened the sliding door in its side. There wasn't a kitchen in there, though. There was a dressing room adjacent to a communal shower, and there was a lot of steam. In the steam were about thirty teen-age girls with no clothes on. They were German refugees from Breslau, which had been tremendously bombed. They had just arrived in Dresden, too. Dresden was jammed with refugees.

There those girls were with all their private parts bare, for anybody to see. And there in the doorway were Gluck and Derby and Pilgrim—the childish soldier and the poor old high school teacher and the clown in his toga and silver shoes —staring. The girls screamed. They covered themselves with their hands and turned their backs and so on, and made themselves utterly beautiful.

Werner Gluck, who had never seen a naked woman before, closed the door. Billy had never seen one, either. It was nothing new to Derby.

When the three fools found the communal kitchen, whose main job was to make lunch for workers in the slaughterhouse, everybody had gone home but one woman who had been waiting for them impatiently. She was a war widow. So it goes. She had her hat and coat on. She wanted to go home, too, even though there wasn't anybody there. Her white gloves were laid out side by side on the zinc counter top.

She had two big cans of soup for the Americans. It was simmering over low fires on the gas range. She had stacks of loaves of black bread, too.

She asked Gluck if he wasn't awfully young to be in the army. He admitted that he was.

She asked Edgar Derby if he wasn't awfully old to be in the army. He said he was.

She asked Billy Pilgrim what he was supposed to be. Billy said he didn't know. He was just trying to keep warm.

"All the real soldiers are dead," she said. It was true. So it goes.

Another true thing that Billy saw while he was unconscious in Vermont was the work that he and the others had to do in

Dresden during the month before the city was destroyed. They washed windows and swept floors and cleaned lavatories and put jars into boxes and sealed cardboard boxes in a factory that made malt syrup. The syrup was enriched with vitamins and minerals. The syrup was for pregnant women.

The syrup tasted like thin honey laced with hickory smoke, and everybody who worked in the factory secretly spooned it all day long. They weren't pregnant, but they needed vitamins and minerals, too. Billy didn't spoon syrup on his first day at work, but lots of other Americans did.

Billy spooned it on his second day. There were spoons hidden all over the factory, on rafters, in drawers, behind radiators, and so on. They had been hidden in haste by persons who had been spooning syrup, who had heard somebody else coming. Spooning was a crime.

On his second day, Billy was cleaning behind a radiator, and he found a spoon. To his back was a vat of syrup that was cooling. The only other person who could see Billy and his spoon was poor old Edgar Derby, who was washing a window outside. The spoon was a tablespoon. Billy thrust it into the vat, turned it around and around, making a gooey lollipop. He thrust it into his mouth.

A moment went by, and then every cell in Billy's body shook him with ravenous gratitude and applause.

There were diffident raps on the factory window. Derby was out there, having seen all. He wanted some syrup, too.

So Billy made a lollipop for him. He opened the window. He stuck the lollipop into poor old Derby's gaping mouth. A moment passed, and then Derby burst into tears. Billy closed the window and hid the sticky spoon. Somebody was coming.

8

THE AMERICANS in the slaughterhouse had a very interesting visitor two days before Dresden was destroyed. He was Howard W. Campbell, Jr., an American who had become a Nazi. Campbell was the one who had written the monograph about the shabby behavior of American prisoners of war. He wasn't doing more research about prisoners now. He had come to the slaughterhouse to recruit men for a German military unit called "The Free American Corps." Campbell was the inventor and commander of the unit, which was supposed to fight only on the Russian front.

Campbell was an ordinary-looking man, but he was extravagantly costumed in a uniform of his own design. He wore a white ten-gallon hat and black cowboy boots decorated with swastikas and stars. He was sheathed in a blue body stocking which had yellow stripes running from his armpits to his ankles. His shoulder patch was a silhouette of Abraham Lincoln's profile on a field of pale green. He had a broad armband which was red, with a blue swastika in a circle of white.

He was explaining this armband now in the cement-block hog barn.

Billy Pilgrim had a boiling case of heartburn, since he had been spooning malt syrup all day long at work. The heartburn brought tears to his eyes, so that his image of Campbell was distorted by jiggling lenses of salt water.

"Blue is for the American sky," Campbell was saying. "White is for the race that pioneered the continent, drained the swamps and cleared the forests and built the roads and bridges. Red is for the blood of American patriots which was shed so gladly in years gone by."

Campbell's audience was sleepy. It had worked hard at the syrup factory, and then it had marched a long way home in the cold. It was skinny and hollow-eyed. Its skins were beginning to blossom with small sores. So were its mouths and throats and intestines. The malt syrup it spooned at the factory contained only a few of the vitamins and minerals every Earthling needs.

Campbell offered the Americans food now, steaks and mashed potatoes and gravy and mince pie, if they would join the Free American Corps. "Once the Russians are defeated," he went on, "you will be repatriated through Switzerland."

There was no response.

"You're going to have to fight the Communists sooner or later," said Campbell. "Why not get it over with now?"

And then it developed that Campbell was not going to go unanswered after all. Poor old Derby, the doomed high school teacher, lumbered to his feet for what was probably the finest moment in his life. There are almost no characters in this story, and almost no dramatic confrontations, because most of the people in it are so sick and so much the listless playthings of enormous forces. One of the main effects of war, after all, is that people are discouraged from being characters. But old Derby was a character now.

His stance was that of a punch-drunk fighter. His head was down. His fists were out front, waiting for information and battle plan. Derby raised his head, called Campbell a snake. He corrected that. He said that snakes couldn't help being snakes, and that Campbell, who *could* help being what he was, was something much lower than a snake or a rat—or even a blood-filled tick.

Campbell smiled.

Derby spoke movingly of the American form of government, with freedom and justice and opportunities and fair play for all. He said there wasn't a man there who wouldn't gladly die for those ideals.

He spoke of the brotherhood between the American and the Russian people, and how those two nations were going to crush the disease of Nazism, which wanted to infect the whole world.

The air-raid sirens of Dresden howled mournfully.

The Americans and their guards and Campbell took shelter in an echoing meat locker which was hollowed in living rock under the slaughterhouse. There was an iron staircase with iron doors at the top and bottom.

Down in the locker were a few cattle and sheep and pigs and horses hanging from iron hooks. So it goes. The locker had empty hooks for thousands more. It was naturally cool. There was no refrigeration. There was candlelight. The locker was whitewashed and smelled of carbolic acid. There were benches along a wall. The Americans went to these, brushing away flakes of whitewash before they sat down.

Howard W. Campbell, Jr., remained standing, like the guards. He talked to the guards in excellent German. He had written many popular German plays and poems in his time, and had married a famous German actress named Resi North. She was dead now, had been killed while entertaining troops in the Crimea. So it goes.

Nothing happened that night. It was the next night that about one hundred and thirty thousand people in Dresden would die. So it goes. Billy dozed in the meat locker. He found himself engaged again, word for word, gesture for gesture, in the argument with his daughter with which this tale began.

"Father," she said, "What are we going to *do* with you?" And so on. "You know who I could just kill?" she asked.

"*Who* could you kill?" said Billy.

"That Kilgore Trout."

Kilgore Trout was and is a science-fiction writer, of course. Billy has not only read dozens of books by Trout—he has also become Trout's friend, to the extent that anyone can become a friend of Trout, who is a bitter man.

Trout lives in a rented basement in Ilium, about two miles from Billy's nice white home. He himself has no idea how many novels he has written—possibly seventy-five of the things. Not one of them has made money. So Trout keeps body and soul together as a circulation man for the *Ilium Gazette*, manages newspaper delivery boys, bullies and flatters and cheats little kids.

Billy met him for the first time in 1964. Billy drove his Cadillac down a back alley in Ilium, and he found his way blocked by dozens of boys and their bicycles. A meeting was in progress. The boys were harangued by a man in a full beard. He was cowardly and dangerous, and obviously very good at his job. Trout was sixty-two years old back then. He was telling the kids to get off their dead butts and get their daily customers to subscribe to the fucking Sunday edition, too. He said that whoever sold the most Sunday subscriptions during the next two months would get a free trip for himself and his parents to Martha's fucking Vineyard for a week, all expenses paid.

And so on.

One of the newspaper boys was actually a newspaper *girl*. She was electrified.

Trout's paranoid face was terribly familiar to Billy, who had seen it on the jackets of so many books. But, coming upon that face suddenly in a home-town alley, Billy could not guess why the face was familiar. Billy thought maybe he had known this cracked messiah in Dresden somewhere. Trout certainly looked like a prisoner of war.

And then the newspaper girl held up her hand. "Mr. Trout—" she said, "if I win, can I take my sister, too?"

"Hell no," said Kilgore Trout. "You think money grows on *trees?*"

Trout, incidentally, had written a book about a money tree. It had twenty-dollar bills for leaves. Its flowers were government bonds. Its fruit was diamonds. It attracted human beings who killed each other around the roots and made very good fertilizer.

So it goes.

Billy Pilgrim parked his Cadillac in the alley, and waited for the meeting to end. When the meeting broke up, there was still one boy Trout had to deal with. The boy wanted to quit because the work was so hard and the hours were so long and the pay was so small. Trout was concerned, because, if the boy really quit, Trout would have to deliver the boy's route himself, until he could find another sucker.

"What are you?" Trout asked the boy scornfully. "Some kind of gutless wonder?"

This, too, was the title of a book by Trout, *The Gutless Wonder*. It was about a robot who had bad breath, who became popular after his halitosis was cured. But what made the story remarkable, since it was written in 1932, was that it predicted the widespread use of burning jellied gasoline on human beings.

It was dropped on them from airplanes. Robots did the dropping. They had no conscience, and no circuits which would allow them to imagine what was happening to the people on the ground.

Trout's leading robot looked like a human being, and could talk and dance and so on, and go out with girls. And nobody held it against him that he dropped jellied gasoline on people. But they found his halitosis unforgivable. But then he cleared that up, and he was welcomed to the human race.

Trout lost his argument with the boy who wanted to quit. He told the boy about all the millionaires who had carried newspapers as boys, and the boy replied: "Yeah—but I bet they quit after a week, it's *such* a royal screwing."

And the boy left his full newspaper bag at Trout's feet, with the customer book on top. It was up to Trout to deliver these papers. He didn't have a car. He didn't even have a bicycle, and he was scared to death of dogs.

Somewhere a big dog barked.

As Trout lugubriously slung the bag from his shoulder, Billy Pilgrim approached him. "Mr. Trout—?"

"Yes?"

"Are—are you *Kilgore* Trout?"

"Yes." Trout supposed that Billy had some complaint about the way his newspapers were being delivered. He did not think of himself as a writer for the simple reason that the world had never allowed him to think of himself in this way.

"The—the writer?" said Billy.

"The what?"

Billy was certain that he had made a mistake. "There's a writer named Kilgore Trout."

"There *is?*" Trout looked foolish and dazed.

"You never heard of him?"

Trout shook his head. "Nobody—nobody ever did."

•

Billy helped Trout deliver his papers, driving him from house to house in the Cadillac. Billy was the responsible one, finding the houses, checking them off. Trout's mind was blown. He had never met a fan before, and Billy was such an *avid* fan.

Trout told him that he had never seen a book of his advertised, reviewed, or on sale. "All these years," he said, "I've been opening the window and making love to the world."

"You must surely have gotten letters," said Billy. "I've felt like writing you letters many times."

Trout held up a single finger. "One."

"Was it *enthusiastic*?"

"It was *insane*. The writer said I should be President of the World."

It turned out that the person who had written this letter was Eliot Rosewater, Billy's friend in the veterans' hospital near Lake Placid. Billy told Trout about Rosewater.

"My God—I thought he was about fourteen years old," said Trout.

"A full grown man—a captain in the war."

"He *writes* like a fourteen-year-old," said Kilgore Trout.

Billy invited Trout to his eighteenth wedding anniversary which was only two days hence. Now the party was in progress.

Trout was in Billy's dining room, gobbling canapés. He was talking with a mouthful of Philadelphia cream cheese and salmon roe to an optometrist's wife. Everybody at the party was associated with optometry in some way, except Trout. And he alone was without glasses. He was making a great hit. Everybody was thrilled to have a real author at the party, even though they had never read his books.

Trout was talking to a Maggie White, who had given up being a dental assistant to become a homemaker for an optometrist. She was very pretty. The last book she had read was *Ivanhoe*.

Billy Pilgrim stood nearby, listening. He was palpating something in his pocket. It was a present he was about to give his wife, a white satin box containing a star sapphire cocktail ring. The ring was worth eight hundred dollars.

•

The adulation that Trout was receiving, mindless and illiterate as it was, affected Trout like marijuana. He was happy and loud and impudent.

"I'm afraid I don't read as much as I *ought* to," said Maggie.

"We're all afraid of something," Trout replied. "I'm afraid of cancer and rats and Doberman pinschers."

"I should know, but I don't, so I have to ask," said Maggie, "what's the most famous thing you ever wrote?"

"It was about a funeral for a great French chef."

"That sounds interesting."

"All the great chefs in the world are there. It's a beautiful ceremony." Trout was making this up as he went along. "Just before the casket is closed, the mourners sprinkle parsley and paprika on the deceased." So it goes.

"Did that really *happen*?" said Maggie White. She was a dull person, but a sensational invitation to make babies. Men looked at her and wanted to fill her up with babies right away. She hadn't had even one baby yet. She used birth control.

"Of course it happened," Trout told her. "If I wrote something that hadn't really happened, and I tried to sell it, I could go to jail. That's *fraud*."

Maggie believed him. "I'd never thought about that before."

"Think about it now."

"It's like advertising. You have to tell the truth in advertising, or you get in trouble."

"Exactly. The same body of law applies."

"Do you think you might put *us* in a book sometime?"

"I put everything that happens to me in books."

"I guess I better be careful what I say."

"That's right. And I'm not the only one who's listening. God is listening, too. And on Judgment Day he's going to tell you all the things you said and did. If it turns out they're bad things instead of good things, that's too bad for you, because you'll burn forever and ever. The burning never stops hurting."

Poor Maggie turned gray. She believed *that*, too, and was petrified.

Kilgore Trout laughed uproariously. A salmon egg flew out of his mouth and landed in Maggie's cleavage.

Now an optometrist called for attention. He proposed a toast to Billy and Valencia, whose anniversary it was. According to plan, the barbershop quartet of optometrists, "The Febs," sang while people drank and Billy and Valencia put their arms around each other, just glowed. Everybody's eyes were shining. The song was "That Old Gang of Mine."

Gee, that song went, *but I'd give the world to see that old gang of mine.* And so on. A little later it said, *So long forever, old fellows and gals, so long forever old sweethearts and pals—God bless 'em*—And so on.

Unexpectedly, Billy Pilgrim found himself upset by the song and the occasion. He had never had an old gang, old sweethearts and pals, but he missed one anyway, as the quartet made slow, agonized experiments with chords—chords intentionally sour, sourer still, unbearably sour, and then a chord that was suffocatingly sweet, and then some sour ones again. Billy had powerful psychosomatic responses to the changing chords. His mouth filled with the taste of lemonade, and his face became grotesque, as though he really were being stretched on the torture engine called the *rack.*

He looked so peculiar that several people commented on it solicitously when the song was done. They thought he might have been having a heart attack, and Billy seemed to confirm this by going to a chair and sitting down haggardly.

There was silence.

"Oh my God," said Valencia, leaning over him, "Billy—are you all right?"

"Yes."

"You look so awful."

"Really—I'm O.K." And he was, too, except that he could find no explanation for why the song had affected him so grotesquely. He had supposed for years that he had no secrets from himself. Here was proof that he had a great big secret somewhere inside, and he could not imagine what it was.

•

People drifted away now, seeing the color return to Billy's cheeks, seeing him smile. Valencia stayed with him, and Kilgore Trout, who had been on the fringe of the crowd, came closer, interested, shrewd.

"You looked as though you'd seen a *ghost*," said Valencia.

"No," said Billy. He hadn't seen anything but what was really before him—the faces of the four singers, those four ordinary men, cow-eyed and mindless and anguished as they went from sweetness to sourness to sweetness again.

"Can I make a guess?" said Kilgore Trout. "You saw through a *time window*."

"A what?" said Valencia.

"He suddenly saw the past or the future. Am I right?"

"No," said Billy Pilgrim. He got up, put a hand into his pocket, found the box containing the ring in there. He took out the box, gave it absently to Valencia. He had meant to give it to her at the end of the song, while everybody was watching. Only Kilgore Trout was there to see.

"For me?" said Valencia.

"Yes."

"Oh my God," she said. Then she said it louder, so other people heard. They gathered around, and she opened it, and she almost screamed when she saw the sapphire with a star in it. "Oh, my God," she said. She gave Billy a big kiss. She said, "Thank you, thank you, thank you."

There was a lot of talk about what wonderful jewelry Billy had given to Valencia over the years. "My God—" said Maggie White, "she's already got the biggest diamond I ever saw outside of a movie." She was talking about the diamond Billy had brought back from the war.

The partial denture he had found inside his little impresario's coat, incidentally, was in his cufflinks box in his dresser drawer. Billy had a wonderful collection of cufflinks. It was the custom of the family to give him cufflinks on every Father's Day. He was wearing Father's Day cufflinks now. They had cost over one hundred dollars. They were made out of ancient Roman coins. He had one pair of cufflinks upstairs which were little roulette wheels that really worked. He had another pair which had a real thermometer in one and a real compass in the other.

•

Billy now moved about the party—outwardly normal. Kilgore Trout was shadowing him, keen to know what Billy had suspected or seen. Most of Trout's novels, after all, dealt with time warps and extrasensory perception and other unexpected things. Trout believed in things like that, was greedy to have their existence proved.

"You ever put a full-length mirror on the floor, and then have a dog stand on it?" Trout asked Billy.

"No."

"The dog will look down, and all of a sudden he'll realize there's nothing under him. He thinks he's standing on thin air. He'll jump a *mile*."

"He *will*?"

"That's how *you* looked—as though you all of a sudden realized you were standing on thin air."

The barbershop quartet sang again. Billy was emotionally racked again. The experience was *definitely* associated with those four men and not what they sang.

Here is what they sang, while Billy was pulled apart inside:

> 'Leven cent cotton, forty cent meat,
> How in the world can a poor man eat?
> Pray for the sunshine, 'cause it will rain.
> Things gettin' worse, drivin' all insane;
> Built a nice barn, painted it brown;
> Lightnin' came along and burnt it down:
> No use talkin', any man's beat,
> With 'leven cent cotton and forty cent meat.
> 'Leven cent cotton, a car-load of tax,
> The load's too heavy for our poor backs . . .

And so on.

Billy fled upstairs in his nice white home.

Trout would have come upstairs with him if Billy hadn't told him not to. Then Billy went into the upstairs bathroom, which was dark. He closed and locked the door. He left it dark, and gradually became aware that he was not alone. His son was in there.

"Dad—?" his son said in the dark. Robert, the future Green Beret, was seventeen then. Billy liked him, but didn't know him very well. Billy couldn't help suspecting that there wasn't much *to* know about Robert.

Billy flicked on the light. Robert was sitting on the toilet with his pajama bottoms around his ankles. He was wearing an electric guitar, slung around his neck on a strap. He had just bought the guitar that day. He couldn't play it yet and, in fact, never learned to play it. It was a nacreous pink.

"Hello, son," said Billy Pilgrim.

Billy went into his bedroom, even though there were guests to be entertained downstairs. He lay down on his bed, turned on the Magic Fingers. The mattress trembled, drove a dog out from under the bed. The dog was Spot. Good old Spot was still alive in those days. Spot lay down again in a corner.

Billy thought hard about the effect the quartet had had on him, and then found an association with an experience he had had long ago. He did not travel in time to the experience. He remembered it shimmeringly—as follows:

He was down in the meat locker on the night that Dresden was destroyed. There were sounds like giant footsteps above. Those were sticks of high-explosive bombs. The giants walked and walked. The meat locker was a very safe shelter. All that happened down there was an occasional shower of calcimine. The Americans and four of their guards and a few dressed carcasses were down there, and nobody else. The rest of the guards had, before the raid began, gone to the comforts of their own homes in Dresden. They were all being killed with their families.

So it goes.

The girls that Billy had seen naked were all being killed, too, in a much shallower shelter in another part of the stockyards.

So it goes.

A guard would go to the head of the stairs every so often to see what it was like outside, then he would come down and whisper to the other guards. There was a fire-storm out there. Dresden was one big flame. The one flame ate everything organic, everything that would burn.

It wasn't safe to come out of the shelter until noon the next day. When the Americans and their guards did come out, the sky was black with smoke. The sun was an angry little pinhead. Dresden was like the moon now, nothing but minerals. The stones were hot. Everybody else in the neighborhood was dead.

So it goes.

The guards drew together instinctively, rolled their eyes. They experimented with one expression and then another, said nothing, though their mouths were often open. They looked like a silent film of a barbershop quartet.

"So long forever," they might have been singing, "old fellows and gals; So long forever, old sweethearts and pals—God bless 'em—"

"Tell me a story," Montana Wildhack said to Billy Pilgrim in the Tralfamadorian zoo one time. They were in bed side by side. They had privacy. The canopy covered the dome. Montana was six months pregnant now, big and rosy, lazily demanding small favors from Billy from time to time. She couldn't send Billy out for ice cream or strawberries, since the atmosphere outside the dome was cyanide, and the nearest strawberries and ice cream were millions of light years away.

She could send him to the refrigerator, which was decorated with the blank couple on the bicycle built for two—or, as now, she could wheedle, "Tell me a story, Billy boy."

"Dresden was destroyed on the night of February 13, 1945," Billy Pilgrim began. "We came out of our shelter the next day." He told Montana about the four guards who, in their astonishment and grief, resembled a barbershop quartet. He told her about the stockyards with all the fenceposts gone, with roofs and windows gone—told her about seeing little logs lying around. These were people who had been caught in the fire storm. So it goes.

Billy told her what had happened to the buildings that used to form cliffs around the stockyards. They had collapsed. Their wood had been consumed, and their stones had crashed down, had tumbled against one another until they locked at last in low and graceful curves.

"It was like the moon," said Billy Pilgrim.

•

The guards told the Americans to form in ranks of four, which they did. Then they had them march back to the hog barn which had been their home. Its walls still stood, but its windows and roof were gone, and there was nothing inside but ashes and dollops of melted glass. It was realized then that there was no food or water, and that the survivors, if they were going to continue to survive, were going to have to climb over curve after curve on the face of the moon.

Which they did.

The curves were smooth only when seen from a distance. The people climbing them learned that they were treacherous, jagged things—hot to the touch, often unstable—eager, should certain important rocks be disturbed, to tumble some more, to form lower, more solid curves.

Nobody talked much as the expedition crossed the moon. There was nothing appropriate to say. One thing was clear: Absolutely everybody in the city was supposed to be dead, regardless of what they were, and that anybody that moved in it represented a flaw in the design. There were to be no moon men at all.

American fighter planes came in under the smoke to see if anything was moving. They saw Billy and the rest moving down there. The planes sprayed them with machine-gun bullets, but the bullets missed. Then they saw some other people moving down by the riverside and they shot at them. They hit some of them. So it goes.

The idea was to hasten the end of the war.

Billy's story ended very curiously in a suburb untouched by fire and explosions. The guards and the Americans came at nightfall to an inn which was open for business. There was candlelight. There were fires in three fireplaces downstairs. There were empty tables and chairs waiting for anyone who might come, and empty beds with covers turned down upstairs.

There was a blind innkeeper and his sighted wife, who was the cook, and their two young daughters, who worked as waitresses and maids. This family knew that Dresden was gone.

Those with eyes had seen it burn and burn, understood that they were on the edge of a desert now. Still—they had opened for business, had polished the glasses and wound the clocks and stirred the fires, and waited and waited to see who would come.

There was no great flow of refugees from Dresden. The clocks ticked on, the fires crackled, the translucent candles dripped. And then there was a knock on the door, and in came four guards and one hundred American prisoners of war.

The innkeeper asked the guards if they had come from the city.

"Yes."

"Are there more people coming?"

And the guards said that, on the difficult route they had chosen, they had not seen another living soul.

The blind innkeeper said that the Americans could sleep in his stable that night, and he gave them soup and ersatz coffee and a little beer. Then he came out to the stable to listen to them bedding down in the straw.

"Good night, Americans," he said in German. "Sleep well."

9

HERE IS HOW Billy Pilgrim lost his wife, Valencia.

He was unconscious in the hospital in Vermont, after the airplane crashed on Sugarbush Mountain, and Valencia, having heard about the crash, was driving from Ilium to the hospital in the family Cadillac El Dorado Coupe de Ville. Valencia was hysterical, because she had been told frankly that Billy might die, or that, if he lived, he might be a vegetable.

Valencia adored Billy. She was crying and yelping so hard as she drove that she missed the correct turnoff from the throughway. She applied her power brakes, and a Mercedes slammed into her from behind. Nobody was hurt, thank God, because both drivers were wearing seat belts. Thank God, thank God. The Mercedes lost only a headlight. But the rear end of the Cadillac was a body-and-fender man's wet dream. The trunk and fenders were collapsed. The gaping trunk looked like the mouth of a village idiot who was explaining that he didn't know anything about anything. The fenders shrugged. The bumper was at a high port arms. "Reagan for President!" a sticker on the bumper said. The back window was veined with cracks. The exhaust system rested on the pavement.

The driver of the Mercedes got out and went to Valencia, to find out if she was all right. She blabbed hysterically about Billy and the airplane crash, and then she put her car in gear and crossed the median divider, leaving her exhaust system behind.

When she arrived at the hospital, people rushed to the windows to see what all the noise was. The Cadillac, with both mufflers gone, sounded like a heavy bomber coming in on a wing and a prayer. Valencia turned off the engine, but then she slumped against the steering wheel, and the horn brayed steadily. A doctor and a nurse ran out to find out what the trouble was. Poor Valencia was unconscious, overcome by carbon monoxide. She was a heavenly azure.

One hour later she was dead. So it goes.

•

Billy knew nothing about it. He dreamed on, and traveled in time and so forth. The hospital was so crowded that Billy couldn't have a room to himself. He shared a room with a Harvard history professor named Bertram Copeland Rumfoord. Rumfoord didn't have to look at Billy, because Billy was surrounded by white linen screens on rubber wheels. But Rumfoord could hear Billy talking to himself from time to time.

Rumfoord's left leg was in traction. He had broken it while skiing. He was seventy years old, but had the body and spirit of a man half that age. He had been honeymooning with his fifth wife when he broke his leg. Her name was Lily. Lily was twenty-three.

Just about the time poor Valencia was pronounced dead, Lily came into Billy's and Rumfoord's room with an armload of books. Rumfoord had sent her down to Boston to get them. He was working on a one-volume history of the United States Army Air Corps in World War Two. The books were about bombings and sky battles that had happened before Lily was even *born*.

"You guys go on without me," said Billy Pilgrim deliriously, as pretty little Lily came in. She had been an a-go-go girl when Rumfoord saw her and resolved to make her his own. She was a high school dropout. Her I.Q. was 103. "He *scares* me," she whispered to her husband about Billy Pilgrim.

"He bores the *hell* out of *me*!" Rumfoord replied boomingly. "All he does in his sleep is quit and surrender and apologize and ask to be left alone." Rumfoord was a retired brigadier general in the Air Force Reserve, the official Air Force Historian, a full professor, the author of twenty-six books, a multimillionaire since birth, and one of the great competitive sailors of all time. His most popular book was about sex and strenuous athletics for men over sixty-five. Now he quoted Theodore Roosevelt, whom he resembled a lot:

"'I could carve a better man out of a banana.'"

One of the things Rumfoord had told Lily to get in Boston was a copy of President Harry S. Truman's announcement to the world that an atomic bomb had been dropped on Hiroshima. She had a Xerox of it, and Rumfoord asked her if she had read it.

"No." She didn't read well, which was one of the reasons she had dropped out of high school.

Rumfoord ordered her to sit down and read the Truman statement now. He didn't know that she couldn't read much. He knew very little about her, except that she was one more public demonstration that he was a superman.

So Lily sat down and pretended to read the Truman thing, which went like this:

Sixteen hours ago an American airplane dropped one bomb on Hiroshima, an important Japanese Army base. That bomb had more power than 20,000 tons of T. N. T. It had more than two thousand times the blast power of the British "Grand Slam," which is the largest bomb ever yet used in the history of warfare.

The Japanese began the war from the air at Pearl Harbor. They have been repaid many-fold. And the end is not yet. With this bomb we have now added a new and revolutionary increase in destruction to supplement the growing power of our armed forces. In their present form these bombs are now in production, and even more powerful forms are in development.

It is an atomic bomb. It is a harnessing of the basic power of the universe. The force from which the sun draws its power has been loosed against those who brought war to the Far East.

Before 1939, it was the accepted belief of scientists that it was theoretically possible to release atomic energy. But nobody knew any practical method of doing it. By 1942, however, we knew that the Germans were working feverishly to find a way to add atomic energy to all the other engines of war with which they hoped to enslave the world. But they failed. We may be grateful to Providence that the Germans got the V-1's and V-2's late and in limited quantities and even more grateful that they did not get the atomic bomb at all.

The battle of the laboratories held fateful risks for us as well as the battles of the air, land, and sea, and we have now won the battle of the laboratories as we have won the other battles.

We are now prepared to obliterate more rapidly and completely every productive enterprise the Japanese have above ground in any city, said Harry Truman. *We shall destroy their docks, their factories, and their communications. Let there be no mistake; we shall completely destroy Japan's power to make war. It was to spare—*

And so on.

One of the books that Lily had brought Rumfoord was *The Destruction of Dresden*, by an Englishman named David Irving. It was an American edition, published by Holt, Rinehart and Winston in 1964. What Rumfoord wanted from it were portions of the forewords by his friends Ira C. Eaker, Lieutenant General, U.S.A.F., retired, and British Air Marshal Sir Robert Saundby, K.C.B., K.B.E., M.C., D.F.C., A.F.C.

I find it difficult to understand Englishmen or Americans who weep about enemy civilians who were killed but who have not shed a tear for our gallant crews lost in combat with a cruel enemy, wrote his friend General Eaker in part. *I think it would have been well for Mr. Irving to have remembered, when he was drawing the frightful picture of the civilians killed at Dresden, that V-1's and V-2's were at that very time falling on England, killing civilian men, women, and children indiscriminately, as they were designed and launched to do. It might be well to remember Buchenwald and Coventry, too.*

Eaker's foreword ended this way:

I deeply regret that British and U.S. bombers killed 135,000 people in the attack on Dresden, but I remember who started the last war and I regret even more the loss of more than 5,000,000 Allied lives in the necessary effort to completely defeat and utterly destroy nazism.

So it goes.

What Air Marshal Saundby said, among other things, was this:

That the bombing of Dresden was a great tragedy none can deny. That it was really a military necessity few, after reading this book, will believe. It was one of those terrible things that sometimes happen in wartime, brought about by an unfortunate combination of circumstances. Those who approved it were neither wicked nor cruel, though it may well be that they were too remote from the harsh realities of war to understand fully the appalling destructive power of air bombardment in the spring of 1945.

The advocates of nuclear disarmament seem to believe that, if they could achieve their aim, war would become tolerable and decent. They would do well to read this book and ponder the fate of Dresden, where 135,000 people died as the result of an air attack with conventional weapons. On the night of March 9th, 1945, an air attack on Tokyo by American heavy bombers, using incendiary and high explosive bombs, caused the death of 83,793 people. The atom bomb dropped on Hiroshima killed 71,379 people.

So it goes.

"If you're ever in Cody, Wyoming," said Billy Pilgrim behind his white linen screens, "just ask for Wild Bob."

Lily Rumfoord shuddered, went on pretending to read the Harry Truman thing.

Billy's daughter Barbara came in later that day. She was all doped up, had the same glassy-eyed look that poor old Edgar Derby wore just before he was shot in Dresden. Doctors had given her pills so she could continue to function, even though her father was broken and her mother was dead.

So it goes.

She was accompanied by a doctor and a nurse. Her brother Robert was flying home from a battlefield in Vietnam. "Daddy—" she said tentatively. "Daddy—?"

But Billy was ten years away, back in 1958. He was examining the eyes of a young male Mongolian idiot in order to prescribe corrective lenses. The idiot's mother was there, acting as an interpreter.

"How many dots do you see?" Billy Pilgrim asked him.

And then Billy traveled in time to when he was sixteen years old, in the waiting room of a doctor. Billy had an infected thumb. There was only one other patient waiting—an old, old man. The old man was in agony because of gas. He farted tremendously, and then he belched.

"Excuse me," he said to Billy. Then he did it again. "Oh God—" he said, "I knew it was going to be bad getting old." He shook his head. "I didn't know it was going to be *this* bad."

Billy Pilgrim opened his eyes in the hospital in Vermont, did not know where he was. Watching him was his son Robert. Robert was wearing the uniform of the famous Green Berets. Robert's hair was short, was wheat-colored bristles. Robert was clean and neat. He was decorated with a Purple Heart and a Silver Star and a Bronze Star with two clusters.

This was a boy who had flunked out of high school, who had been an alcoholic at sixteen, who had run with a rotten bunch of kids, who had been arrested for tipping over hundreds of tombstones in a Catholic cemetery one time. He was all straightened out now. His posture was wonderful and his shoes were shined and his trousers were pressed, and he was a leader of men.

"Dad—?"

Billy Pilgrim closed his eyes again.

Billy had to miss his wife's funeral because he was still so sick. He was conscious, though, while Valencia was being put into the ground in Ilium. Billy hadn't said much since regaining consciousness, hadn't responded very elaborately to the news of Valencia's death and Robert's coming home from the war and so on—so it was generally believed that he was a vegetable. There was talk of performing an operation on him later, one which might improve the circulation of blood to his brain.

Actually, Billy's outward listlessness was a screen. The listlessness concealed a mind which was fizzing and flashing thrillingly. It was preparing letters and lectures about the flying saucers, the negligibility of death, and the true nature of time.

Professor Rumfoord said frightful things about Billy within Billy's hearing, confident that Billy no longer had any brain at all. "Why don't they let him *die*?" he asked Lily.

"I don't know," she said.

"That's not a human being anymore. Doctors are for human beings. They should turn him over to a veterinarian or a tree surgeon. *They*'d know what to do. Look at him! That's life, according to the medical profession. Isn't life wonderful?"

"I don't know," said Lily.

Rumfoord talked to Lily about the bombing of Dresden one time, and Billy heard it all. Rumfoord had a problem about Dresden. His one-volume history of the Army Air Force in World War Two was supposed to be a readable condensation of the twenty-seven-volume *Official History of the Army Air*

Force in World War Two. The thing was, though, there was almost nothing in the twenty-seven volumes about the Dresden raid, even though it had been such a howling success. The extent of the success had been kept a secret for many years after the war—a secret from the American people. It was no secret from the Germans, of course, or from the Russians, who occupied Dresden after the war, who are in Dresden still.

"Americans have finally heard about Dresden," said Rumfoord, twenty-three years after the raid. "A lot of them know now how much worse it was than Hiroshima. So I've got to put something about it in my book. From the official Air Force standpoint, it'll all be new."

"Why would they keep it a secret so long?" said Lily.

"For fear that a lot of bleeding hearts," said Rumfoord, "might not think it was such a wonderful thing to do."

It was now that Billy Pilgrim spoke up intelligently. "I was there," he said.

It was difficult for Rumfoord to take Billy seriously, since Rumfoord had so long considered Billy a repulsive non-person who would be much better off dead. Now, with Billy speaking clearly and to the point, Rumfoord's ears wanted to treat the words as a foreign language that was not worth learning. "What did he say?" said Rumfoord.

Lily had to serve as an interpreter. "He said he was there," she explained.

"He was where?"

"I don't know," said Lily. "Where were you?" she asked Billy.

"Dresden," said Billy.

"Dresden," Lily told Rumfoord.

"He's simply echoing things we say," said Rumfoord.

"Oh," said Lily.

"He's got echolalia now."

"Oh."

Echolalia is a mental disease which makes people immediately repeat things that well people around them say. But Billy didn't really have it. Rumfoord simply insisted, for his own comfort, that Billy had it. Rumfoord was thinking in a military manner: that an inconvenient person, one whose death he wished for very much, for practical reasons, was suffering from a repulsive disease.

Rumfoord went on insisting for several hours that Billy had echolalia—told nurses and a doctor that Billy had echolalia now. Some experiments were performed on Billy. Doctors and nurses tried to get Billy to echo something, but Billy wouldn't make a sound for them.

"He isn't doing it now," said Rumfoord peevishly. "The minute you go away, he'll start doing it again."

Nobody took Rumfoord's diagnosis seriously. The staff thought Rumfoord was a hateful old man, conceited and cruel. He often said to them, in one way or another, that people who were weak deserved to die. Whereas the staff, of course, was devoted to the idea that weak people should be helped as much as possible, that nobody should die.

There in the hospital, Billy was having an adventure very common among people without power in time of war: He was trying to prove to a willfully deaf and blind enemy that he was interesting to hear and see. He kept silent until the lights went out at night, and then, when there had been a long period of silence containing nothing to echo, he said to Rumfoord, "I was in Dresden when it was bombed. I was a prisoner of war."

Rumfoord sighed impatiently.

"Word of honor," said Billy Pilgrim. "Do you believe me?"

"Must we talk about it now?" said Rumfoord. He had heard. He didn't believe.

"We don't ever have to talk about it," said Billy. "I just want you to know: I was there."

Nothing more was said about Dresden that night, and Billy closed his eyes, traveled in time to a May afternoon, two days after the end of the Second World War in Europe. Billy and five other American prisoners were riding in a coffin-shaped green wagon, which they had found abandoned, complete with two horses, in a suburb of Dresden. Now they were being drawn by the clop-clop-clopping horses down narrow lanes which had been cleared through the moonlike ruins. They were going back to the slaughterhouse for souvenirs of the war. Billy was reminded of the sounds of milkmen's horses early in the morning in Ilium, when he was a boy.

Billy sat in the back of the jiggling coffin. His head was tilted back and his nostrils were flaring. He was happy. He was warm. There was food in the wagon, and wine—and a camera, and a stamp collection, and a stuffed owl, and a mantel clock that ran on changes of barometric pressure. The Americans had gone into empty houses in the suburb where they had been imprisoned, and they had taken these and many other things.

The owners, hearing that the Russians were coming, killing and robbing and raping and burning, had fled.

But the Russians hadn't come yet, even two days after the war. It was peaceful in the ruins. Billy saw only one other person on the way to the slaughterhouse. It was an old man pushing a baby buggy. In the buggy were pots and cups and an umbrella frame, and other things he had found.

Billy stayed in the wagon when it reached the slaughterhouse, sunning himself. The others went looking for souvenirs. Later on in life, the Tralfamadorians would advise Billy to concentrate on the happy moments of his life, and to ignore the unhappy ones—to stare only at pretty things as eternity failed to go by. If this sort of selectivity had been possible for Billy, he might have chosen as his happiest moment his sun-drenched snooze in the back of the wagon.

Billy Pilgrim was armed as he snoozed. It was the first time he had been armed since basic training. His companions had insisted that he arm himself, since God only knew what sorts of killers might be in burrows on the face of the moon—wild dogs, packs of rats fattened on corpses, escaped maniacs and murderers, soldiers who would never quit killing until they themselves were killed.

Billy had a tremendous cavalry pistol in his belt. It was a relic of World War One. It had a ring in its butt. It was loaded with bullets the size of robins' eggs. Billy had found it in the bedside table in a house. That was one of the things about the end of the war: Absolutely anybody who wanted a weapon could have one. They were lying all around. Billy had a saber, too. It was a Luftwaffe ceremonial saber. Its hilt was stamped with a screaming eagle. The eagle was carrying a swastika and looking down. Billy found it stuck into a telephone pole. He had pulled it out of the pole as the wagon went by.

Now his snoozing became shallower as he heard a man and a woman speaking German in pitying tones. The speakers were commiserating with somebody lyrically. Before Billy opened his eyes, it seemed to him that the tones might have been those used by the friends of Jesus when they took His ruined body down from His cross. So it goes.

Billy opened his eyes. A middle-aged man and wife were crooning to the horses. They were noticing what the Americans had not noticed—that the horses' mouths were bleeding, gashed by the bits, that the horses' hooves were broken, so that every step meant agony, that the horses were insane with thirst. The Americans had treated their form of transportation as though it were no more sensitive than a six-cylinder Chevrolet.

These two horse pitiers moved back along the wagon to where they could gaze in patronizing reproach at Billy—at Billy Pilgrim, who was so long and weak, so ridiculous in his azure toga and silver shoes. They weren't afraid of him. They weren't afraid of anything. They were doctors, both obstetricians. They had been delivering babies until the hospitals were all burned down. Now they were picnicking near where their apartment used to be.

The woman was softly beautiful, translucent from having eaten potatoes for so long. The man wore a business suit, necktie and all. Potatoes had made him gaunt. He was as tall as Billy, wore steel-rimmed tri-focals. This couple, so involved with babies, had never reproduced themselves, though they could have. This was an interesting comment on the whole idea of reproduction.

They had nine languages between them. They tried Polish on Billy Pilgrim first, since he was dressed so clownishly, since the wretched Poles were the involuntary clowns of the Second World War.

Billy asked them in English what it was they wanted, and

they at once scolded him in English for the condition of the
horses. They made Billy get out of the wagon and come look
at the horses. When Billy saw the condition of his means of
transportation, he burst into tears. He hadn't cried about anything else in the war.

Later on, as a middle-aged optometrist, he would weep quietly and privately sometimes, but never make loud *boo-hooing*
noises.

Which is why the epigraph of this book is the quatrain from
the famous Christmas carol. Billy cried very little, though he
often saw things worth crying about, and in *that* respect, at
least, he resembled the Christ of the carol:

> *The cattle are lowing,*
> *The Baby awakes.*
> *But the little Lord Jesus*
> *No crying He makes.*

Billy traveled in time back to the hospital in Vermont. Breakfast had been eaten and cleared away, and Professor Rumfoord
was reluctantly becoming interested in Billy as a human being.
Rumfoord questioned Billy gruffly, satisfied himself that Billy
really had been in Dresden. He asked Billy what it had been
like, and Billy told him about the horses and the couple picnicking on the moon.

The story ended this way: Billy and the doctors unharnessed
the horses, but the horses wouldn't go anywhere. Their feet
hurt too much. And then Russians came on motorcycles, and
they arrested everybody but the horses.

Two days after that, Billy was turned over to the Americans,
who shipped him home on a very slow freighter called the
Lucretia A. Mott. Lucretia A. Mott was a famous American
suffragette. She was dead. So it goes.

"It *had* to be done," Rumfoord told Billy, speaking of the
destruction of Dresden.

"I know," said Billy.

"That's war."

"I know. I'm not complaining."

"It must have been hell on the ground."

"It was," said Billy Pilgrim.

"Pity the men who had to *do* it."

"I do."

"You must have had mixed feelings, there on the ground."

"It was all right," said Billy. "*Everything* is all right, and everybody has to do exactly what he does. I learned that on Tralfamadore."

Billy Pilgrim's daughter took him home later that day, put him to bed in his house, turned the Magic Fingers on. There was a practical nurse there. Billy wasn't supposed to work or even leave the house for a while, at least. He was under observation.

But Billy sneaked out while the nurse wasn't watching, and he drove to New York City, where he hoped to appear on television. He was going to tell the world about the lessons of Tralfamadore.

Billy Pilgrim checked into the Royalton Hotel on Forty-fourth Street in New York. He by chance was given a room which had once been the home of George Jean Nathan, the critic and editor. Nathan, according to the Earthling concept of time, had died back in 1958. According to the Tralfamadorian concept, of course, Nathan was still alive somewhere and always would be.

The room was small and simple, except that it was on the top floor, and had French doors which opened onto a terrace as large as the room. And beyond the parapet of the terrace was the air space over Forty-fourth Street. Billy now leaned over that parapet, looked down at all the people moving hither and yon. They were jerky little scissors. They were a lot of fun.

It was a chilly night, and Billy came indoors after a while, closed the French doors. Closing those doors reminded him of his honeymoon. There had been French doors on the Cape Ann love nest of his honeymoon, still were, always would be.

Billy turned on his television set, clicking its channel selector around and around. He was looking for programs on which he might be allowed to appear. But it was too early in the evening for programs that allowed people with peculiar opinions to speak out. It was only a little after eight o'clock, so all the shows were about silliness or murder. So it goes.

Billy left his room, went down the slow elevator, walked over to Times Square, looked into the window of a tawdry bookstore. In the window were hundreds of books about fucking and buggery and murder, and a street guide to New York City, and a model of the Statue of Liberty with a thermometer on it. Also in the window, speckled with soot and fly shit, were four paperback novels by Billy's friend, Kilgore Trout.

The news of the day, meanwhile, was being written in a ribbon of lights on a building to Billy's back. The window reflected the news. It was about power and sports and anger and death. So it goes.

Billy went into the bookstore.

A sign in there said that adults only were allowed in the back. There were peep shows in the back that showed movies of young women and men with no clothes on. It cost a quarter to look into a machine for one minute. There were still photographs of naked young people for sale back there, too. You could take those home. The stills were a lot more Tralfamadorian than the movies, since you could look at them whenever you wanted to, and they wouldn't change. Twenty years in the future, those girls would still be young, would still be smiling or smoldering or simply looking stupid, with their legs wide open. Some of them were eating lollipops or bananas. They would still be eating those. And the peckers of the young men would still be semierect, and their muscles would be bulging like cannonballs.

But Billy Pilgrim wasn't beguiled by the back of the store. He was thrilled by the Kilgore Trout novels in the front. The titles were all new to him, or he thought they were. Now he opened one. It seemed all right for him to do that. Everybody else in the store was pawing things. The name of the book was *The Big Board*. He got a few paragraphs into it, and then he realized that he *had* read it before—years ago, in the veterans' hospital. It was about an Earthling man and woman who were kidnapped by extra-terrestrials. They were put on display in a zoo on a planet called Zircon-212.

These fictitious people in the zoo had a big board supposedly showing stock market quotations and commodity prices along one wall of their habitat, and a news ticker, and a telephone that was supposedly connected to a brokerage on Earth. The creatures on Zircon-212 told their captives that they had invested a million dollars for them back on Earth, and that it was up to the captives to manage it so that they would be fabulously wealthy when they were returned to Earth.

The telephone and the big board and the ticker were all fakes, of course. They were simply stimulants to make the Earthlings perform vividly for the crowds at the zoo—to make them jump up and down and cheer, or gloat, or sulk, or tear their hair, to be scared shitless or to feel as contented as babies in their mothers' arms.

The Earthlings did very well on paper. That was part of the rigging, of course. And religion got mixed up in it, too. The news ticker reminded them that the President of the United States had declared National Prayer Week, and that everybody should pray. The Earthlings had had a bad week on the market before that. They had lost a small fortune in olive oil futures. So they gave praying a whirl.

It worked. Olive oil went up.

Another Kilgore Trout book there in the window was about a man who built a time machine so he could go back and see Jesus. It worked, and he saw Jesus when Jesus was only twelve years old. Jesus was learning the carpentry trade from his father.

Two Roman soldiers came into the shop with a mechanical drawing on papyrus of a device they wanted built by sunrise the next morning. It was a cross to be used in the execution of a rabble-rouser.

Jesus and his father built it. They were glad to have the work. And the rabble-rouser was executed on it.

So it goes.

•

The bookstore was run by seeming quintuplets, by five short, bald men chewing unlit cigars that were sopping wet. They never smiled, and each one had a stool to perch on. They were making money running a paper-and-celluloid whorehouse. They didn't have hard-ons. Neither did Billy Pilgrim. Everybody else did. It was a ridiculous store, all about love and babies.

The clerks occasionally told somebody to buy or get out, not to just look and look and look and paw and paw. Some of the people were looking at each other instead of the merchandise.

A clerk came up to Billy and told him the good stuff was in the back, that the books Billy was reading were window dressing. "That ain't what you want, for Christ's sake," he told Billy. "What you want's in *back*."

So Billy moved a little farther back, but not as far as the part for adults only. He moved because of absentminded politeness, taking a Trout book with him—the one about Jesus and the time machine.

The time-traveler in the book went back to *Bible* times to find out one thing in particular: Whether or not Jesus had really died on the cross, or whether he had been taken down while still alive, whether he had really gone on living. The hero had a stethoscope along.

Billy skipped to the end of the book, where the hero mingled with the people who were taking Jesus down from the cross. The time-traveler was the first one up the ladder, dressed in clothes of the period, and he leaned close to Jesus so people couldn't see him use the stethoscope, and he listened.

There wasn't a sound inside the emaciated chest cavity. The Son of God was dead as a doornail.

So it goes.

The time-traveler, whose name was Lance Corwin, also got to measure the length of Jesus, but not to weigh him. Jesus was five feet and three and a half inches long.

Another clerk came up to Billy and asked him if he was going to buy the book or not, and Billy said that he wanted to buy it, please. He had his back to a rack of paperback books about oral-genital contacts from ancient Egypt to the present and so on, and the clerk supposed Billy was reading one of these. So he was startled when he saw what Billy's book was. He said, "Jesus Christ, where did you find this thing?" and so on, and he had to tell the other clerks about the pervert who wanted to buy the window dressing. The other clerks already knew about Billy. They had been watching him, too.

The cash register where Billy waited for his change was near a bin of old girly magazines. Billy looked at one out of the corner of his eye, and he saw this question on its cover: *What really became of Montana Wildhack?*

So Billy read it. He knew where Montana Wildhack *really* was, of course. She was back on Tralfamadore, taking care of the baby, but the magazine, which was called *Midnight Pussycats*, promised that she was wearing a cement overcoat under thirty fathoms of saltwater in San Pedro Bay.

So it goes.

Billy wanted to laugh. The magazine, which was published for lonesome men to jerk off to, ran the story so it could print pictures taken from blue movies which Montana had made as a teen-ager. Billy did not look closely at these. They were grainy things, soot and chalk. They could have been anybody.

Billy was again directed to the back of the store, and he went this time. A jaded sailor stepped away from a movie machine while the film was still running. Billy looked in, and there was Montana Wildhack alone on a bed, peeling a banana. The picture clicked off. Billy did not want to see what happened next, and a clerk importuned him to come over and see some really hot stuff they kept under the counter for connoisseurs.

Billy was mildly curious as to what could possibly have been kept hidden in such a place. The clerk leered and showed him. It was a photograph of a woman and a Shetland pony. They were attempting to have sexual intercourse between two Doric columns, in front of velvet draperies which were fringed with deedlee-balls.

Billy didn't get onto television in New York that night, but he *did* get onto a radio talk show. There was a radio station right next to Billy's hotel. He saw its call letters over the entrance of an office building, so he went in. He went up to the studio on an automatic elevator, and there were other people up there, waiting to go in. They were literary critics, and they thought Billy was one, too. They were going to discuss whether the novel was dead or not. So it goes.

Billy took his seat with the others around a golden oak table, with a microphone all his own. The master of ceremonies asked him his name and what paper he was from. Billy said he was from the *Ilium Gazette.*

He was nervous and happy. "If you're ever in Cody, Wyoming," he told himself, "just ask for Wild Bob."

Billy put his hand up at the very first part of the program, but he wasn't called on right away. Others got in ahead of him. One of them said that it would be a nice time to bury the novel, now that a Virginian, one hundred years after Appomattox, had written *Uncle Tom's Cabin.* Another one said that people couldn't read well enough anymore to turn print into exciting situations in their skulls, so that authors had to do what Norman Mailer did, which was to perform in public what he had written. The master of ceremonies asked people to say what they thought the function of the novel might be in modern society, and one critic said, "To provide touches of color in rooms with all-white walls." Another one said, "To describe blow-jobs artistically." Another one said, "To teach wives of junior executives what to buy next and how to act in a French restaurant."

And then Billy was allowed to speak. Off he went, in that beautifully trained voice of his, telling about the flying saucers and Montana Wildhack and so on.

He was gently expelled from the studio during a commercial. He went back to his hotel room, put a quarter into the Magic Fingers machine connected to his bed, and he went to sleep. He traveled in time back to Tralfamadore.

"Time-traveling again?" said Montana. It was artificial evening in the dome. She was breast-feeding their child.

"Hmm?" said Billy.

"You've been time-traveling again. I can always tell."

"Um."

"Where did you go this time? It wasn't the war. I can tell that, too."

"New York."

"The Big Apple."

"Hm?"

"That's what they used to call New York."

"Oh."

"You see any plays or movies?"

"No—I walked around Times Square some, bought a book by Kilgore Trout."

"Lucky *you*." She did not share his enthusiasm for Kilgore Trout.

Billy mentioned casually that he had seen part of a blue movie she had made. Her response was no less casual. It was Tralfamadorian and guilt-free:

"Yes—" she said, "and I've heard about you in the war, about what a clown you were. And I've heard about the high-school teacher who was shot. He made a blue movie with a firing squad." She moved the baby from one breast to the other, because the moment was so structured that she *had* to do so.

There was a silence.

"They're playing with the clocks again," said Montana, rising, preparing to put the baby into its crib. She meant that their keepers were making the electric clocks in the dome go fast, then slow, then fast again, and watching the little Earthling family through peepholes.

There was a silver chain around Montana Wildhack's neck. Hanging from it, between her breasts, was a locket containing a photograph of her alcoholic mother—a grainy thing, soot and chalk. It could have been anybody. Engraved on the outside of the locket were these words:

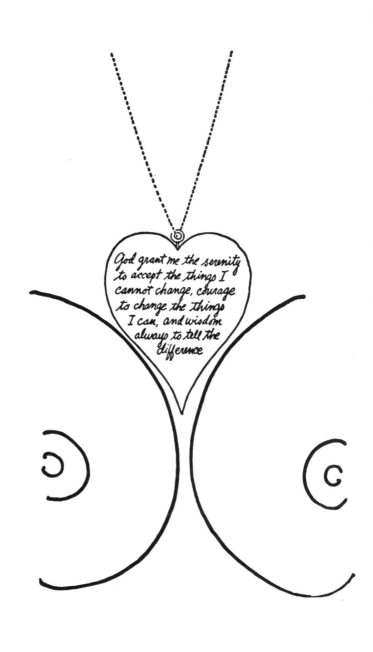

10

ROBERT KENNEDY, whose summer home is eight miles from the home I live in all year round, was shot two nights ago. He died last night. So it goes.

Martin Luther King was shot a month ago. He died, too. So it goes.

And every day my Government gives me a count of corpses created by military science in Vietnam. So it goes.

My father died many years ago now—of natural causes. So it goes. He was a sweet man. He was a gun nut, too. He left me his guns. They rust.

On Tralfamadore, says Billy Pilgrim, there isn't much interest in Jesus Christ. The Earthling figure who is most engaging to the Tralfamadorian mind, he says, is Charles Darwin—who taught that those who die are meant to die, that corpses are improvements. So it goes.

The same general idea appears in *The Big Board* by Kilgore Trout. The flying saucer creatures who capture Trout's hero ask him about Darwin. They also ask him about golf.

If what Billy Pilgrim learned from the Tralfamadorians is true, that we will all live forever, no matter how dead we may sometimes seem to be, I am not overjoyed. Still—if I am going to spend eternity visiting this moment and that, I'm grateful that so many of those moments are nice.

One of the nicest ones in recent times was on my trip back to Dresden with my old war buddy, O'Hare.

We took a Hungarian Airlines plane from East Berlin. The pilot had a handlebar mustache. He looked like Adolphe Menjou. He smoked a Cuban cigar while the plane was being fueled. When we took off, there was no talk of fastening seat belts.

When we were up in the air, a young steward served us rye bread and salami and butter and cheese and white wine. The folding tray in front of me would not open out. The steward went into the cockpit for a tool, came back with a beer-can opener. He used it to pry out the tray.

There were only six other passengers. They spoke many languages. They were having nice times, too. East Germany was down below, and the lights were on. I imagined dropping bombs on those lights, those villages and cities and towns.

O'Hare and I had never expected to make any money—and here we were now, extremely well-to-do.

"If you're ever in Cody, Wyoming," I said to him lazily, "just ask for Wild Bob."

O'Hare had a little notebook with him, and printed in the back of it were postal rates and airline distances and the altitudes of famous mountains and other key facts about the world. He was looking up the population of Dresden, which wasn't in the notebook, when he came across this, which he gave me to read:

On an average, 324,000 new babies are born into the world every day. During that same day, 10,000 persons, on an average, will have starved to death or died from malnutrition. So it goes. In addition, 123,000 persons will die for other reasons. So it goes. This leaves a net gain of about 191,000 each day in the world. The Population Reference Bureau predicts that the world's total population will double to 7,000,000,000 before the year 2000.

"I suppose they will all want dignity," I said.

"I suppose," said O'Hare.

Billy Pilgrim was meanwhile traveling back to Dresden, too, but not in the present. He was going back there in 1945, two days after the city was destroyed. Now Billy and the rest were being marched into the ruins by their guards. I was there. O'Hare was there. We had spent the past two nights in the blind innkeeper's stable. Authorities had found us there. They told us what to do. We were to borrow picks and shovels and crowbars and wheelbarrows from our neighbors. We were to march with these implements to such and such a place in the ruins, ready to go to work.

●

There were barricades on the main roads leading into the ruins. Germans were stopped there. They were not permitted to explore the moon.

Prisoners of war from many lands came together that morning at such and such a place in Dresden. It had been decreed that here was where the digging for bodies was to begin. So the digging began.

Billy found himself paired as a digger with a Maori, who had been captured at Tobruk. The Maori was chocolate brown. He had whirlpools tattooed on his forehead and his cheeks. Billy and the Maori dug into the inert, unpromising gravel of the moon. The materials were loose, so there were constant little avalanches.

Many holes were dug at once. Nobody knew yet what there was to find. Most holes came to nothing—to pavement, or to boulders so huge they would not move. There was no machinery. Not even horses or mules or oxen could cross the moonscape.

And Billy and the Maori and others helping them with their particular hole came at last to a membrane of timbers laced over rocks which had wedged together to form an accidental dome. They made a hole in the membrane. There was darkness and space under there.

A German soldier with a flashlight went down into the darkness, was gone a long time. When he finally came back, he told a superior on the rim of the hole that there were dozens of bodies down there. They were sitting on benches. They were unmarked.

So it goes.

The superior said that the opening in the membrane should be enlarged, and that a ladder should be put in the hole, so that the bodies could be carried out. Thus began the first corpse mine in Dresden.

There were hundreds of corpse mines operating by and by. They didn't smell bad at first, were wax museums. But then the bodies rotted and liquefied, and the stink was like roses and mustard gas.

So it goes.

The Maori Billy had worked with died of the dry heaves, after having been ordered to go down in that stink and work. He tore himself to pieces, throwing up and throwing up.

So it goes.

So a new technique was devised. Bodies weren't brought up any more. They were cremated by soldiers with flame-throwers right where they were. The soldiers stood outside the shelters, simply sent the fire in.

Somewhere in there the poor old high school teacher, Edgar Derby, was caught with a teapot he had taken from the catacombs. He was arrested for plundering. He was tried and shot.

So it goes.

And somewhere in there was springtime. The corpse mines were closed down. The soldiers all left to fight the Russians. In the suburbs, the women and children dug rifle pits. Billy and the rest of his group were locked up in the stable in the suburbs. And then, one morning, they got up to discover that the door was unlocked. World War Two in Europe was over.

Billy and the rest wandered out onto the shady street. The trees were leafing out. There was nothing going on out there, no traffic of any kind. There was only one vehicle, an abandoned wagon drawn by two horses. The wagon was green and coffin-shaped.

Birds were talking.

One bird said to Billy Pilgrim, "*Poo-tee-weet?*"

BREAKFAST OF CHAMPIONS
or Goodbye Blue Monday!

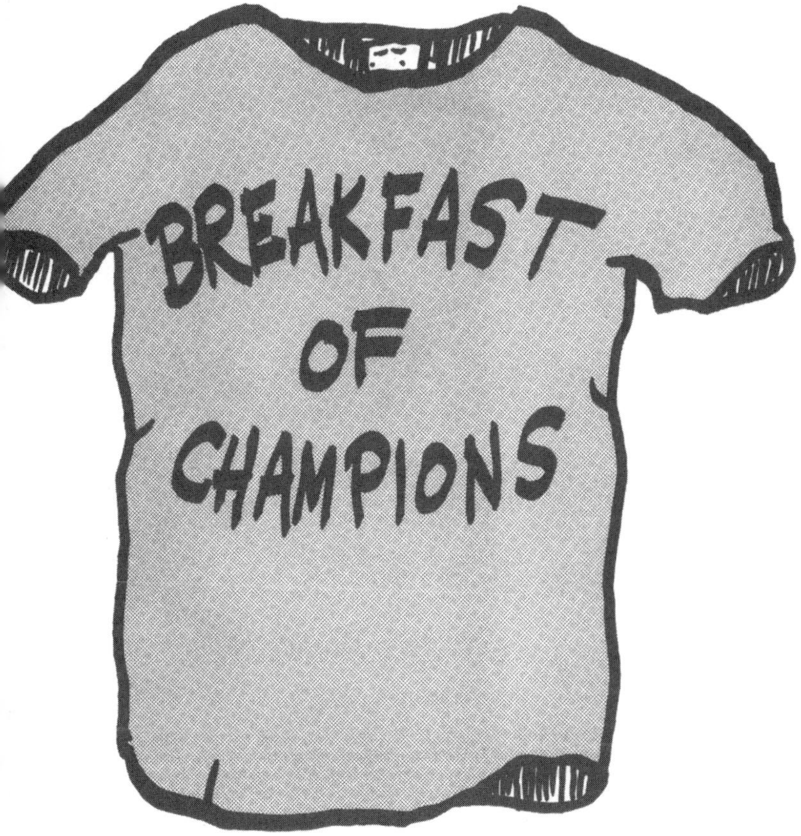
BREAKFAST
OF
CHAMPIONS

In Memory of Phoebe Hurty,
who comforted me in Indianapolis—
during the Great Depression.

When he hath tried me,
I shall come forth as gold.
                    —JOB

Preface

THE EXPRESSION "Breakfast of Champions" is a registered trademark of General Mills, Inc., for use on a breakfast cereal product. The use of the identical expression as the title for this book is not intended to indicate an association with or sponsorship by General Mills, nor is it intended to disparage their fine products.

• • •

The person to whom this book is dedicated, Phoebe Hurty, is no longer among the living, as they say. She was an Indianapolis widow when I met her late in the Great Depression. I was sixteen or so. She was about forty.

She was rich, but she had gone to work every weekday of her adult life, so she went on doing that. She wrote a sane and funny advice-to-the-lovelorn column for the Indianapolis *Times*, a good paper which is now defunct.

Defunct.

She wrote ads for the William H. Block Company, a department store which still flourishes in a building my father designed. She wrote this ad for an end-of-the-summer sale on straw hats: "For prices like this, you can run them through your horse and put them on your roses."

• • •

Phoebe Hurty hired me to write copy for ads about teenage clothes. I had to wear the clothes I praised. That was part of the job. And I became friends with her two sons, who were my age. I was over at their house all the time.

She would talk bawdily to me and her sons, and to our girlfriends when we brought them around. She was funny. She was liberating. She taught us to be impolite in conversation not only about sexual matters, but about American history and famous heroes, about the distribution of wealth, about school, about everything.

I now make my living by being impolite. I am clumsy at it. I keep trying to imitate the impoliteness which was so graceful in Phoebe Hurty. I think now that grace was easier for her than it is for me because of the mood of the Great Depression. She believed what so many Americans believed then: that the nation would be happy and just and rational when prosperity came.

I never hear that word anymore: *Prosperity.* It used to be a synonym for *Paradise.* And Phoebe Hurty was able to believe that the impoliteness she recommended would give shape to an American paradise.

Now her sort of impoliteness is fashionable. But nobody believes anymore in a new American paradise. I sure miss Phoebe Hurty.

• • •

As for the suspicion I express in this book, that human beings are robots, are machines: It should be noted that people, mostly men, suffering from the last stages of syphilis, from *loco-motor ataxia*, were common spectacles in downtown Indianapolis and in circus crowds when I was a boy.

Those people were infested with carnivorous little corkscrews which could be seen only with a microscope. The victims' vertebrae were welded together after the corkscrews got through with the meat between. The syphilitics seemed tremendously dignified—erect, eyes straight ahead.

I saw one stand on a curb at the corner of Meridian and Washington streets one time, underneath an overhanging clock which my father designed. The intersection was known locally as "*The Crossroads of America.*"

This syphilitic man was thinking hard there, at the Crossroads of America, about how to get his legs to step off the curb and carry him across Washington Street. He shuddered gently, as though he had a small motor which was idling inside. Here was his problem: his brains, where the instructions to his legs originated, were being eaten alive by corkscrews. The wires which had to carry the instructions weren't insulated anymore, or were eaten clear through. Switches along the way were welded open or shut.

This man looked like an old, old man, although he might have been only thirty years old. He thought and thought. And then he kicked two times like a chorus girl.

He certainly looked like a machine to me when I was a boy.

• • •

I tend to think of human beings as huge, rubbery test tubes, too, with chemical reactions seething inside. When I was a boy, I saw a lot of people with goiters. So did Dwayne Hoover, the Pontiac dealer who is the hero of this book. Those unhappy Earthlings had such swollen thyroid glands that they seemed to have zucchini squash growing from their throats.

All they had to do in order to have ordinary lives, it turned out, was to consume less than one-millionth of an ounce of iodine every day.

My own mother wrecked her brains with chemicals, which were supposed to make her sleep.

When I get depressed, I take a little pill, and I cheer up again.

And so on.

So it is a big temptation to me, when I create a character for a novel, to say that he is what he is because of faulty wiring, or because of microscopic amounts of chemicals which he ate or failed to eat on that particular day.

• • •

What do I myself think of this particular book? I feel lousy about it, but I always feel lousy about my books. My friend Knox Burger said one time that a certain cumbersome novel ". . . read as though it had been written by Philboyd Studge." That's who I think I am when I write what I am seemingly programmed to write.

• • •

This book is my fiftieth-birthday present to myself. I feel as though I am crossing the spine of a roof—having ascended one slope.

I am programmed at fifty to perform childishly—to insult "The Star-Spangled Banner," to scrawl pictures of a Nazi flag and an asshole and a lot of other things with a felt-tipped pen. To give an idea of the maturity of my illustrations for this book, here is my picture of an asshole:

• • •

I think I am trying to clear my head of all the junk in there—the assholes, the flags, the underpants. Yes—there is a picture in this book of underpants. I'm throwing out characters from my other books, too. I'm not going to put on any more puppet shows.

I think I am trying to make my head as empty as it was when I was born onto this damaged planet fifty years ago.

I suspect that this is something most white Americans, and nonwhite Americans who imitate white Americans, should do. The things other people have put into *my* head, at any rate, do not fit together nicely, are often useless and ugly, are out of proportion with one another, are out of proportion with life as it really is outside my head.

I have no culture, no humane harmony in my brains. I can't live without a culture anymore.

• • •

So this book is a sidewalk strewn with junk, trash which I throw over my shoulders as I travel in time back to November eleventh, nineteen hundred and twenty-two.

I will come to a time in my backwards trip when November eleventh, accidentally my birthday, was a sacred day called *Armistice Day*. When I was a boy, and when Dwayne Hoover was a boy, all the people of all the nations which had fought in the First World War were silent during the eleventh minute of the eleventh hour of Armistice Day, which was the eleventh day of the eleventh month.

It was during that minute in nineteen hundred and eighteen, that millions upon millions of human beings stopped butchering one another. I have talked to old men who were on battlefields during that minute. They have told me in one way or another that the sudden silence was the Voice of God. So we still have among us some men who can remember when God spoke clearly to mankind.

• • •

Armistice Day has become Veterans' Day. Armistice Day was sacred. Veterans' Day is not.

So I will throw Veterans' Day over my shoulder. Armistice Day I will keep. I don't want to throw away any sacred things.

What else is sacred? Oh, *Romeo and Juliet*, for instance.

And all music is.

—PHILBOYD STUDGE

Chapter 1

THIS IS A TALE of a meeting of two lonesome, skinny, fairly old white men on a planet which was dying fast.

One of them was a science-fiction writer named Kilgore Trout. He was a nobody at the time, and he supposed his life was over. He was mistaken. As a consequence of the meeting, he became one of the most beloved and respected human beings in history.

The man he met was an automobile dealer, a *Pontiac* dealer named Dwayne Hoover. Dwayne Hoover was on the brink of going insane.

•   •   •

Listen:

Trout and Hoover were citizens of the United States of America, a country which was called *America* for short. This was their national anthem, which was pure balderdash, like so much they were expected to take seriously:

> *O, say can you see by the dawn's early light*
> *What so proudly we hailed at the twilight's last gleaming,*
> *Whose broad stripes and bright stars, thru the perilous fight*
> *O'er the ramparts we watched were so gallantly streaming?*
> *And the rockets' red glare, the bombs bursting in air,*
> *Gave proof through the night that our flag was still there.*
> *O, say does that star-spangled banner yet wave*
> *O'er the land of the free and the home of the brave?*

There were one quadrillion nations in the Universe, but the nation Dwayne Hoover and Kilgore Trout belonged to was the only one with a national anthem which was gibberish sprinkled with question marks.

Here is what their flag looked like:

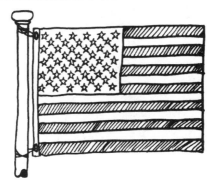

It was the law of their nation, a law no other nation on the planet had about its flag, which said this: "*The flag shall not be dipped to any person or thing.*"

Flag-dipping was a form of friendly and respectful salute, which consisted of bringing the flag on a stick closer to the ground, then raising it up again.

• • •

The motto of Dwayne Hoover's and Kilgore Trout's nation was this, which meant in a language nobody spoke anymore, *Out of Many, One*: "*E pluribus unum.*"

The undippable flag was a beauty, and the anthem and the vacant motto might not have mattered much, if it weren't for this: a lot of citizens were so ignored and cheated and insulted that they thought they might be in the wrong country, or even on the wrong planet, that some terrible mistake had been made. It might have comforted them some if their anthem and their motto had mentioned fairness or brotherhood or hope or happiness, had somehow welcomed them to the society and its real estate.

If they studied their paper money for clues as to what their country was all about, they found, among a lot of other baroque trash, a picture of a truncated pyramid with a radiant eye on top of it, like this:

Not even the President of the United States knew what that was all about. It was as though the country were saying to its citizens, "*In nonsense is strength.*"

• • •

A lot of the nonsense was the innocent result of playfulness on the part of the founding fathers of the nation of Dwayne Hoover and Kilgore Trout. The founders were aristocrats, and they wished to show off their useless education, which consisted of the study of hocus-pocus from ancient times. They were bum poets as well.

But some of the nonsense was evil, since it concealed great crimes. For example, teachers of children in the United States of America wrote this date on blackboards again and again, and asked the children to memorize it with pride and joy:

1492

The teachers told the children that this was when their continent was discovered by human beings. Actually, millions of human beings were already living full and imaginative lives on the continent in 1492. That was simply the year in which sea pirates began to cheat and rob and kill them.

Here was another piece of evil nonsense which children were taught: that the sea pirates eventually created a government which became a beacon of freedom to human beings everywhere else. There were pictures and statues of this supposed imaginary beacon for children to see. It was sort of an icecream cone on fire. It looked like this:

Actually, the sea pirates who had the most to do with the creation of the new government owned human slaves. They used human beings for machinery, and, even after slavery was eliminated, because it was so embarrassing, they and their descendants continued to think of ordinary human beings as machines.

● ● ●

The sea pirates were white. The people who were already on the continent when the pirates arrived were copper-colored. When slavery was introduced onto the continent, the slaves were black.

Color was everything.

• • •

Here is how the pirates were able to take whatever they wanted from anybody else: they had the best boats in the world, and they were meaner than anybody else, and they had gunpowder, which was a mixture of potassium nitrate, charcoal, and sulphur. They touched this seemingly listless powder with fire, and it turned violently into gas. This gas blew projectiles out of metal tubes at terrific velocities. The projectiles cut through meat and bone very easily; so the pirates could wreck the wiring or the bellows or the plumbing of a stubborn human being, even when he was far, far away.

The chief weapon of the sea pirates, however, was their capacity to astonish. Nobody else could believe, until it was much too late, how heartless and greedy they were.

• • •

When Dwayne Hoover and Kilgore Trout met each other, their country was by far the richest and most powerful country on the planet. It had most of the food and minerals and machinery, and it disciplined other countries by threatening to shoot big rockets at them or to drop things on them from airplanes.

Most other countries didn't have doodley-squat. Many of them weren't even inhabitable anymore. They had too many people and not enough space. They had sold everything that was any good, and there wasn't anything to eat anymore, and still the people went on fucking all the time.

Fucking was how babies were made.

• • •

A lot of the people on the wrecked planet were *Communists.* They had a theory that what was left of the planet should be shared more or less equally among all the people, who hadn't asked to come to a wrecked planet in the first place. Meanwhile, more babies were arriving all the time—kicking and screaming, yelling for milk.

In some places people would actually try to eat mud or suck on gravel while babies were being born just a few feet away.

And so on.

• • •

Dwayne Hoover's and Kilgore Trout's country, where there was still plenty of everything, was opposed to Communism. It didn't think that Earthlings who had a lot should share it with others unless they really wanted to, and most of them didn't want to.

So they didn't have to.

• • •

Everybody in America was supposed to grab whatever he could and hold on to it. Some Americans were very good at grabbing and holding, were fabulously well-to-do. Others couldn't get their hands on doodley-squat.

Dwayne Hoover was fabulously well-to-do when he met Kilgore Trout. A man whispered those exact words to a friend one morning as Dwayne walked by: "Fabulously well-to-do."

And here's how much of the planet Kilgore Trout owned in those days: doodley-squat.

And Kilgore Trout and Dwayne Hoover met in Midland City, which was Dwayne's home town, during an Arts Festival there in autumn of 1972.

As has already been said: Dwayne was a Pontiac dealer who was going insane.

Dwayne's incipient insanity was mainly a matter of chemicals, of course. Dwayne Hoover's body was manufacturing certain chemicals which unbalanced his mind. But Dwayne, like all novice lunatics, needed some bad ideas, too, so that his craziness could have shape and direction.

Bad chemicals and bad ideas were the Yin and Yang of madness. Yin and Yang were Chinese symbols of harmony. They looked like this:

The bad ideas were delivered to Dwayne by Kilgore Trout. Trout considered himself not only harmless but invisible. The world had paid so little attention to him that he supposed he was dead.

He *hoped* he was dead.

But he learned from his encounter with Dwayne that he was alive enough to give a fellow human being ideas which would turn him into a monster.

Here was the core of the bad ideas which Trout gave to Dwayne: Everybody on Earth was a robot, with one exception —Dwayne Hoover.

Of all the creatures in the Universe, only Dwayne was think- ing and feeling and worrying and planning and so on. Nobody else knew what pain was. Nobody else had any choices to make. Everybody else was a fully automatic machine, whose purpose was to stimulate Dwayne. Dwayne was a new type of creature being tested by the Creator of the Universe.

Only Dwayne Hoover had free will.

· · ·

Trout did not expect to be believed. He put the bad ideas into a science-fiction novel, and that was where Dwayne found them. The book wasn't addressed to Dwayne alone. Trout had never heard of Dwayne when he wrote it. It was addressed to anybody who happened to open it up. It said to simply any- body, in effect, "Hey—guess what: You're the only creature with free will. How does that make you feel?" And so on.

It was a *tour de force*. It was a *jeu d'esprit*.

But it was mind poison to Dwayne.

· · ·

It shook up Trout to realize that even *he* could bring evil into the world—in the form of bad ideas. And, after Dwayne was carted off to a lunatic asylum in a canvas camisole, Trout became a fanatic on the importance of ideas as causes and cures for diseases.

But nobody would listen to him. He was a dirty old man in the wilderness, crying out among the trees and underbrush, "Ideas or the lack of them can cause disease!"

• • •

Kilgore Trout became a pioneer in the field of mental health. He advanced his theories disguised as science-fiction. He died in 1981, almost twenty years after he made Dwayne Hoover so sick.

He was by then recognized as a great artist and scientist. The American Academy of Arts and Sciences caused a monument to be erected over his ashes. Carved in its face was a quotation from his last novel, his two-hundred-and-ninth novel, which was unfinished when he died. The monument looked like this:

KILGORE TROUT
1907-1981

"WE ARE HEALTHY ONLY TO THE
EXTENT THAT
OUR IDEAS ARE
HUMANE."

Chapter 2

DWAYNE WAS a widower. He lived alone at night in a dream house in Fairchild Heights, which was the most desirable residential area in the city. Every house there cost at least one hundred thousand dollars to build. Every house was on at least four acres of land.

Dwayne's only companion at night was a Labrador retriever named *Sparky*. Sparky could not wag his tail—because of an automobile accident many years ago, so he had no way of telling other dogs how friendly he was. He had to fight all the time. His ears were in tatters. He was lumpy with scars.

• • •

Dwayne had a black servant named Lottie Davis. She cleaned his house every day. Then she cooked his supper for him and served it. Then she went home. She was descended from slaves.

Lottie Davis and Dwayne didn't talk much, even though they liked each other a lot. Dwayne reserved most of his conversation for the dog. He would get down on the floor and roll around with Sparky, and he would say things like, "You and me, Spark," and "How's my old buddy?" and so on.

And that routine went on unrevised, even after Dwayne started to go crazy, so Lottie had nothing unusual to notice.

• • •

Kilgore Trout owned a parakeet named *Bill*. Like Dwayne Hoover, Trout was all alone at night, except for his pet. Trout, too, talked to his pet.

But while Dwayne babbled to his Labrador retriever about love, Trout sneered and muttered to his parakeet about the end of the world.

"Any time now," he would say. "And high time, too."

It was Trout's theory that the atmosphere would become unbreathable soon.

Trout supposed that when the atmosphere became poisonous,

514

Bill would keel over a few minutes before Trout did. He would kid Bill about that. "How's the old respiration, Bill?" he'd say, or, "Seems like you've got a touch of the old emphysema, Bill," or, "We never discussed what kind of a funeral you want, Bill. You never even told me what your religion is." And so on.

He told Bill that humanity deserved to die horribly, since it had behaved so cruelly and wastefully on a planet so sweet. "We're all Heliogabalus, Bill," he would say. This was the name of a Roman emperor who had a sculptor make a hollow, life-size iron bull with a door on it. The door could be locked from the outside. The bull's mouth was open. That was the only other opening to the outside.

Heliogabalus would have a human being put into the bull through the door, and the door would be locked. Any sounds the human being made in there would come out of the mouth of the bull. Heliogabalus would have guests in for a nice party, with plenty of food and wine and beautiful women and pretty boys—and Heliogabalus would have a servant light kindling. The kindling was under dry firewood—which was under the bull.

•   •   •

Trout did another thing which some people might have considered eccentric: he called mirrors *leaks*. It amused him to pretend that mirrors were holes between two universes.

If he saw a child near a mirror, he might wag his finger at a child warningly, and say with great solemnity, "Don't get too near that leak. You wouldn't want to wind up in the other universe, would you?"

Sometimes somebody would say in his presence, "Excuse me, I have to take a leak." This was a way of saying that the speaker intended to drain liquid wastes from his body through a valve in his lower abdomen.

And Trout would reply waggishly, "Where I come from, that means you're about to steal a mirror."

And so on.

By the time of Trout's death, of course, everybody called mirrors *leaks*. That was how respectable even his jokes had become.

●　●　●

In 1972, Trout lived in a basement apartment in Cohoes, New York. He made his living as an installer of aluminum combination storm windows and screens. He had nothing to do with the sales end of the business—because he had no *charm*. Charm was a scheme for making strangers like and trust a person immediately, no matter what the charmer had in mind.

●　●　●

Dwayne Hoover had oodles of charm.

●　●　●

I can have oodles of charm when I want to.

●　●　●

A lot of people have oodles of charm.

●　●　●

Trout's employer and co-workers had no idea that he was a writer. No reputable publisher had ever heard of him, for that matter, even though he had written one hundred and seventeen novels and two thousand short stories by the time he met Dwayne.

He made carbon copies of nothing he wrote. He mailed off manuscripts without enclosing stamped, self-addressed envelopes for their safe return. Sometimes he didn't even include a return address. He got names and addresses of publishers from magazines devoted to the writing business, which he read avidly in the periodical rooms of public libraries. He thus got in touch with a firm called World Classics Library, which published hard-core pornography in Los Angeles, California. They used his stories, which usually didn't even have women in them, to give bulk to books and magazines of salacious pictures.

They never told him where or when he might expect to find himself in print. Here is what they paid him: doodley-squat.

• • •

They didn't even send him complimentary copies of the books and magazines in which he appeared, so he had to search them out in pornography stores. And the titles he gave to his stories were often changed. "Pan Galactic Straw-boss," for instance, became "Mouth Crazy."

Most distracting to Trout, however, were the illustrations his publishers selected, which had nothing to do with his tales. He wrote a novel, for instance, about an Earthling named Delmore Skag, a bachelor in a neighborhood where everybody else had enormous families. And Skag was a scientist, and he found a way to reproduce himself in chicken soup. He would shave living cells from the palm of his right hand, mix them with the soup, and expose the soup to cosmic rays. The cells turned into babies which looked exactly like Delmore Skag.

Pretty soon, Delmore was having several babies a day, and inviting his neighbors to share his pride and happiness. He had mass baptisms of as many as a hundred babies at a time. He became famous as a family man.

And so on.

• • •

Skag hoped to force his country into making laws against excessively large families, but the legislatures and the courts declined to meet the problem head-on. They passed stern laws instead against the possession by unmarried persons of chicken soup.

And so on.

The illustrations for this book were murky photographs of several white women giving blow jobs to the same black man, who, for some reason, wore a Mexican sombrero.

At the time he met Dwayne Hoover, Trout's most widely-distributed book was *Plague on Wheels*. The publisher didn't change the title, but he obliterated most of it and all of Trout's name with a lurid banner which made this promise:

WIDE-OPEN BEAVERS INSIDE!

A wide-open beaver was a photograph of a woman not wearing underpants, and with her legs far apart, so that the mouth of her vagina could be seen. The expression was first used by news photographers, who often got to see up women's skirts at accidents and sporting events and from underneath fire escapes and so on. They needed a code word to yell to other newsmen and friendly policemen and firemen and so on, to let them know what could be seen, in case they wanted to see it. The word was this: "Beaver!"

A beaver was actually a large rodent. It loved water, so it built dams. It looked like this:

The sort of beaver which excited news photographers so much looked like this:

This was where babies came from.

• • •

When Dwayne was a boy, when Kilgore Trout was a boy, when I was a boy, and even when we became middle-aged men and older, it was the duty of the police and the courts to keep representations of such ordinary apertures from being examined and discussed by persons not engaged in the practice of medicine. It was somehow decided that wide-open beavers, which were ten thousand times as common as real beavers, should be the most massively defended secret under law.

So there was a madness about wide-open beavers. There was also a madness about a soft, weak metal, an element, which had somehow been declared the most desirable of all elements, which was gold.

• • •

And the madness about wide-open beavers was extended to underpants when Dwayne and Trout and I were boys. Girls concealed their underpants at all costs, and boys tried to see their underpants at all costs.

Female underpants looked like this:

One of the first things Dwayne learned in school as a little boy, in fact, was a poem he was supposed to scream in case he saw a girl's underpants by accident in the playground. Other students taught it to him. This was it:

> *I see England,*
> *I see France;*
> *I see a little girl's*
> *Underpants!*

When Kilgore Trout accepted the Nobel Prize for Medicine in 1979, he declared: "Some people say there is no such thing as progress. The fact that human beings are now the only animals left on Earth, I confess, seems a confusing sort of victory. Those of you familiar with the nature of my earlier published works will understand why I mourned especially when the last beaver died.

"There were two monsters sharing this planet with us when I was a boy, however, and I celebrate their extinction today. They were determined to kill us, or at least to make our lives meaningless. They came close to success. They were cruel adversaries, which my little friends the beavers were not. Lions? No. Tigers? No. Lions and tigers snoozed most of the time. The monsters I will name never snoozed. They inhabited our heads. They were the arbitrary lusts for gold, and, God help us, for a glimpse of a little girl's underpants.

"I thank those lusts for being so ridiculous, for they taught us that it was possible for a human being to believe anything, and to behave passionately in keeping with that belief—*any* belief.

"So now we can build an unselfish society by devoting to unselfishness the frenzy we once devoted to gold and to underpants."

He paused, and then he recited with wry mournfulness the beginning of a poem he had learned to scream in Bermuda, when he was a little boy. The poem was all the more poignant, since it mentioned two nations which no longer existed as such. "I see England," he said, "I see France—"

• • •

Actually, women's underpants had been drastically devalued by the time of the historic meeting between Dwayne Hoover and Trout. The price of gold was still on the rise.

Photographs of women's underpants weren't worth the paper they were printed on, and even high quality color motion pictures of wide-open beavers were going begging in the marketplace.

There had been a time when a copy of Trout's most popular book to date, *Plague on Wheels*, had brought as much as twelve dollars, because of the illustrations. It was now being offered for a dollar, and people who paid even that much did so not because of the pictures. They paid for the words.

• • •

The words in the book, incidentally, were about life on a dying planet named *Lingo-Three*, whose inhabitants resembled American automobiles. They had wheels. They were powered by internal combustion engines. They ate fossil fuels. They weren't manufactured, though. They reproduced. They laid eggs containing baby automobiles, and the babies matured in pools of oil drained from adult crankcases.

Lingo-Three was visited by space travelers, who learned that the creatures were becoming extinct for this reason: they had destroyed their planet's resources, including its atmosphere.

The space travelers weren't able to offer much in the way of material assistance. The automobile creatures hoped to borrow some oxygen, and to have the visitors carry at least one of their eggs to another planet, where it might hatch, where an automobile civilization could begin again. But the smallest egg they had was a forty-eight pounder, and the space travelers themselves were only an inch high, and their space ship wasn't even as big as an Earthling shoebox. They were from Zeltoldimar.

The spokesman for the Zeltoldimarians was Kago. Kago said that all he could do was to tell others in the Universe about how wonderful the automobile creatures had been. Here is what he said to all those rusting junkers who were out of gas: "You will be gone, but not forgotten."

The illustration for the story at this point showed two Chinese girls, seemingly identical twins, seated on a couch with their legs wide open.

● ● ●

So Kago and his brave little Zeltoldimarian crew, which was all homosexual, roamed the Universe, keeping the memory of the automobile creatures alive. They came at last to the planet Earth. In all innocence, Kago told the Earthlings about the automobiles. Kago did not know that human beings could be as easily felled by a single idea as by cholera or the bubonic plague. There was no immunity to cuckoo ideas on Earth.

● ● ●

And here, according to Trout, was the reason human beings could not reject ideas because they were bad: "Ideas on Earth were badges of friendship or enmity. Their content did not matter. Friends agreed with friends, in order to express friendliness. Enemies disagreed with enemies, in order to express enmity.

"The ideas Earthlings held didn't matter for hundreds of thousands of years, since they couldn't do much about them anyway. Ideas might as well be badges as anything.

"They even had a saying about the futility of ideas: 'If wishes were horses, beggars would ride.'

"And then Earthlings discovered tools. Suddenly agreeing with friends could be a form of suicide or worse. But agreements went on, not for the sake of common sense or decency or self-preservation, but for friendliness.

"Earthlings went on being friendly, when they should have been thinking instead. And even when they built computers to do some thinking for them, they designed them not so much for wisdom as for friendliness. So they were doomed. Homicidal beggars could ride."

Chapter 3

WITHIN A CENTURY of little Kago's arrival on Earth, according to Trout's novel, every form of life on that once peaceful and moist and nourishing blue-green ball was dying or dead. Everywhere were the shells of the great beetles which men had made and worshipped. They were automobiles. They had killed everything.

Little Kago himself died long before the planet did. He was attempting to lecture on the evils of the automobile in a bar in Detroit. But he was so tiny that nobody paid any attention to him. He lay down to rest for a moment, and a drunk automobile worker mistook him for a kitchen match. He killed Kago by trying to strike him repeatedly on the underside of the bar.

• • •

Trout received only one fan letter before 1972. It was from an eccentric millionaire, who hired a private detective agency to discover who and where he was. Trout was so invisible that the search cost eighteen thousand dollars.

The fan letter reached him in his basement in Cohoes. It was hand-written, and Trout concluded that the writer might be fourteen years old or so. The letter said that *Plague on Wheels* was the greatest novel in the English language, and that Trout should be President of the United States.

Trout read the letter out loud to his parakeet. "Things are looking up, Bill," he said. "Always knew they would. Get a load of this." And then he read the letter. There was no indication in the letter that the writer, whose name was Eliot Rosewater, was a grownup, was fabulously well-to-do.

• • •

Kilgore Trout, incidentally, could never be President of the United States without a Constitutional amendment. He hadn't been born inside the country. His birthplace was Bermuda. His father, Leo Trout, while remaining an American citizen, worked there for many years for the Royal Ornithological Society—guarding the only nesting place in the world for

Bermuda Erns. These great green sea eagles eventually became extinct, despite anything anyone could do.

• • •

As a child, Trout had seen those Erns die, one by one. His father had assigned him the melancholy task of measuring wingspreads of the corpses. These were the largest creatures ever to fly under their own power on the planet. And the last corpse had the greatest wingspread of all, which was nineteen feet, two and three-quarters inches.

After all the Erns were dead, it was discovered what had killed them. It was a fungus, which attacked their eyes and brains. Men had brought the fungus to their rookery in the innocent form of athlete's foot.

Here is what the flag of Kilgore Trout's native island looked like:

• • •

So Kilgore Trout had a depressing childhood, despite all of the sunshine and fresh air. The pessimism that overwhelmed him in later life, which destroyed his three marriages, which drove his only son, Leo, from home at the age of fourteen, very likely had its roots in the bittersweet mulch of rotting Erns.

•   •   •

The fan letter came much too late. It wasn't good news. It was perceived as an invasion of privacy by Kilgore Trout. The letter from Rosewater promised that he would make Trout famous. This is what Trout had to say about that, with only his parakeet listening: "Keep the hell out of my body bag."

A body bag was a large plastic envelope for a freshly killed American soldier. It was a new invention.

•   •   •

I do not know who invented the body bag. I do know who invented Kilgore Trout. I did.

I made him snaggle-toothed. I gave him hair, but I turned it white. I wouldn't let him comb it or go to a barber. I made him grow it long and tangled.

I gave him the same legs the Creator of the Universe gave to my father when my father was a pitiful old man. They were pale white broomsticks. They were hairless. They were embossed fantastically with varicose veins.

And, two months after Trout received his first fan letter, I had him find in his mailbox an invitation to be a speaker at an arts festival in the American Middle West.

•   •   •

The letter was from the Festival's chairman, Fred T. Barry. He was respectful, almost reverent about Kilgore Trout. He beseeched him to be one of several distinguished out-of-town participants in the Festival, which would last for five days. It would celebrate the opening of the Mildred Barry Memorial Center for the Arts in Midland City.

The letter did not say so, but Mildred Barry was the late mother of the Chairman, the wealthiest man in Midland City. Fred T. Barry had paid for the new Center of the Arts, which was a translucent sphere on stilts. It had no windows. When il-luminated inside at night, it resembled a rising harvest moon.

Fred T. Barry, incidentally, was exactly the same age as Trout. They had the same birthday. But they certainly didn't look anything alike. Fred T. Barry didn't even look like a white man anymore, even though he was of pure English stock. As he grew older and older and happier and happier, and all his hair fell out everywhere, he came to look like an ecstatic old Chinaman.

He looked so much like a Chinaman that he had taken to dressing like a Chinaman. Real Chinamen often mistook him for a real Chinaman.

• • •

Fred T. Barry confessed in his letter that he had not read the works of Kilgore Trout, but that he would joyfully do so before the Festival began. "You come highly recommended by Eliot Rosewater," he said, "who assures me that you are perhaps the greatest living American novelist. There can be no higher praise than that."

Clipped to the letter was a check for one thousand dollars. Fred T. Barry explained that this was for travel expenses and an honorarium.

It was a lot of money. Trout was suddenly fabulously well-to-do.

• • •

Here is how Trout happened to be invited: Fred T. Barry wanted to have a fabulously valuable oil painting as a focal point for the Midland City Festival of the Arts. As rich as he was, he couldn't afford to buy one, so he looked for one to borrow.

The first person he went to was Eliot Rosewater, who owned an El Greco worth three million dollars or more. Rosewater said the Festival could have the picture on one condition: that it hire as a speaker the greatest living writer in the English language, who was Kilgore Trout.

Trout laughed at the flattering invitation, but he felt fear after that. Once again, a stranger was tampering with the privacy of his body bag. He put this question to his parakeet haggardly, and he rolled his eyes: "Why all this sudden interest in Kilgore Trout?"

He read the letter again. "They not only want Kilgore Trout," he said, "they want him in a *tuxedo*, Bill. Some mistake has been made."

He shrugged. "Maybe they invited me because they know I

have a tuxedo," he said. He really did own a tuxedo. It was in
a steamer trunk which he had lugged from place to place for
more than forty years. It contained toys from childhood,
the bones of a Bermuda Ern, and many other curiosities—
including the tuxedo he had worn to a senior dance just prior
to his graduation from Thomas Jefferson High School in
Dayton, Ohio, in 1924. Trout was born in Bermuda, and attended grammar school there. But then his family moved to
Dayton.

His high school was named after a slave owner who was also
one of the world's greatest theoreticians on the subject of
human liberty.

• • •

Trout got his tuxedo out of the trunk and he put it on. It
was a lot like a tuxedo I'd seen my father put on when he was
an old, old man. It had a greenish patina of mold. Some of the
growths it supported resembled patches of fine rabbit fur.
"This will do nicely for the evenings," said Trout. "But tell me,
Bill—what does one wear in Midland City in October before
the sun goes down?" He hauled up his pants legs so that his
grotesquely ornamental shins were exposed. "Bermuda shorts
and bobby socks, eh, Bill? After all—I *am* from Bermuda."

He dabbed at his tuxedo with a damp rag, and the fungi
came away easily. "Hate to do this, Bill," he said of the fungi he
was murdering. "Fungi have as much right to life as I do. They
know what they want, Bill. Damned if *I* do anymore."

Then he thought about what Bill himself might want. It was
easy to guess. "Bill," he said, "I like you so much, and I am
such a big shot in the Universe, that I will make your three
biggest wishes come true." He opened the door of the cage,
something Bill couldn't have done in a thousand years.

Bill flew over to a windowsill. He put his little shoulder
against the glass. There was just one layer of glass between Bill
and the great out-of-doors. Although Trout was in the storm
window business, he had no storm windows on his own
abode.

"Your second wish is about to come true," said Trout, and
he again did something which Bill could never have done. He
opened the window. But the opening of the window was such

an alarming business to the parakeet that he flew back to his cage and hopped inside.

Trout closed the door of the cage and latched it. "That's the most intelligent use of three wishes I ever heard of," he told the bird. "You made sure you'd still have something worth wishing for—to get out of the cage."

•   •   •

Trout made the connection between his lone fan letter and the invitation, but he couldn't believe that Eliot Rosewater was a grownup. Rosewater's handwriting looked like this:

You ought to be President of the United States!

"Bill," said Trout tentatively, "some teen-ager named Rosewater got me this job. His parents must be friends of the Chairman of the Arts Festival, and they don't know anything about books out that way. So when he said I was good, they believed him."

Trout shook his head. "I'm not going, Bill. I don't want out of my cage. I'm too smart for that. Even if I did want out, though, I wouldn't go to Midland City to make a laughing stock of myself—and my only fan."

•   •   •

He left it at that. But he reread the invitation from time to time, got to know it by heart. And then one of the subtler messages on the paper got through to him. It was in the letter-head, which displayed two masks intended to represent comedy and tragedy:

One mask looked like this:

The other one looked like this:

"They don't want anything but smilers out there," Trout said to his parakeet. "Unhappy failures need not apply." But his mind wouldn't leave it alone at that. He got an idea which he found very tangy: "But maybe an unhappy failure *is* exactly what they *need* to see."

He became energetic after that. "Bill, Bill—" he said, "listen, I'm leaving the cage, but I'm coming back. I'm going out there to show them what nobody has ever seen at an arts festival before: a representative of all the thousands of artists who devoted their entire lives to a search for truth and beauty—and didn't find doodley-squat!"

• • •

Trout accepted the invitation after all. Two days before the Festival was to begin, he delivered Bill into the care of his landlady upstairs, and he hitchhiked to New York City—with five hundred dollars pinned to the inside of his underpants. The rest of the money he had put in a bank.

He went to New York first—because he hoped to find some of his books in pornography stores there. He had no copies at home. He despised them, but now he wanted to read out loud from them in Midland City—as a demonstration of a tragedy which was ludicrous as well.

He planned to tell the people out there what he hoped to have in the way of a tombstone.

This was it:

SOMEBODY

[Sometime to Sometime]

He Tried

Chapter 4

DWAYNE WAS meanwhile getting crazier all the time. He saw eleven moons in the sky over the new Mildred Barry Memorial Center for the Arts one night. The next morning, he saw a huge duck directing traffic at the intersection of Arsenal Avenue and Old County Road. He didn't tell anybody what he saw. He maintained secrecy.

And the bad chemicals in his head were fed up with secrecy. They were no longer content with making him feel and see queer things. They wanted him to *do* queer things, also, and make a lot of noise.

They wanted Dwayne Hoover to be *proud* of his disease.

• • •

People said later that they were furious with themselves for not noticing the danger signals in Dwayne's behavior, for ignoring his obvious cries for help. After Dwayne ran amok, the local paper ran a deeply sympathetic editorial about it, begging people to watch each other for danger signals. Here was its title:

A CRY FOR HELP

But Dwayne wasn't all that weird before he met Kilgore Trout. His behavior in public kept him well within the limits of acceptable acts and beliefs and conversations in Midland City. The person closest to him, Francine Pefko, his white secretary and mistress, said that Dwayne seemed to be getting happier and happier all the time during the month before Dwayne went public as a maniac.

"I kept thinking," she told a newspaper reporter from her hospital bed, "'He is finally getting over his wife's suicide.'"

• • •

Francine worked at Dwayne's principal place of business, which was *Dwayne Hoover's Exit Eleven Pontiac Village*, just off the Interstate, next door to the new Holiday Inn.

Here is what made Francine think he was becoming happier: Dwayne began to sing songs which had been popular in his youth, such as "The Old Lamp Lighter," and "Tippy-Tippy-Tin," and "Hold Tight," and "Blue Moon," and so on. Dwayne had never sung before. Now he did it loudly as he sat at his desk, when he took a customer for a ride in a demonstrator, when he watched a mechanic service a car. One day he sang loudly as he crossed the lobby of the new Holiday Inn, smiling and gesturing at people as though he had been hired to sing for their pleasure. But nobody thought that was necessarily a hint of derangement, either—especially since Dwayne owned a piece of the Inn.

A black bus boy and a black waiter discussed this singing. "Listen at him sing," said the bus boy.

"If I owned what he owns, I'd sing, too," the waiter replied.

• • •

The only person who said out loud that Dwayne was going crazy was Dwayne's white sales manager at the Pontiac agency, who was Harry LeSabre. A full week before Dwayne went off his rocker, Harry said to Francine Pefko, "Something has come over Dwayne. He used to be so charming. I don't find him so charming anymore."

Harry knew Dwayne better than did any other man. He had been with Dwayne for twenty years. He came to work for him when the agency was right on the edge of the Nigger part of town. A Nigger was a human being who was black.

"I know him the way a combat soldier knows his buddy," said Harry. "We used to put our lives on the line every day, when the agency was down on Jefferson Street. We got held up on the average of fourteen times a year. And I tell you that the Dwayne of today is a Dwayne I never saw before."

• • •

It was true about the holdups. That was how Dwayne bought a Pontiac agency so cheaply. White people were the only people with money enough to buy new automobiles, except for a few black criminals, who always wanted Cadillacs. And white people were scared to go anywhere on Jefferson Street anymore.

· · ·

Here is where Dwayne got the money to buy the agency: He borrowed it from the Midland County National Bank. For collateral, he put up stock he owned in a company which was then called *The Midland City Ordnance Company*. It later became *Barrytron, Limited*. When Dwayne first got the stock, in the depths of the Great Depression, the company was called *The Robo-Magic Corporation of America*.

The name of the company kept changing through the years because the nature of its business changed so much. But its management hung on to the company's original motto—for old time's sake. The motto was this:

GOODBYE, BLUE MONDAY.

· · ·

Listen:

Harry LeSabre said to Francine, "When a man has been in combat with another man, he gets so he can sense the slightest change in his buddy's personality, and Dwayne has changed. You ask Vernon Garr."

Vernon Garr was a white mechanic who was the only other employee who had been with Dwayne before Dwayne moved the agency out to the Interstate. As it happened, Vernon was having trouble at home. His wife, Mary, was a schizophrenic, so Vernon hadn't noticed whether Dwayne had changed or not. Vernon's wife believed that Vernon was trying to turn her brains into plutonium.

· · ·

Harry LeSabre was entitled to talk about combat. He had been in actual combat in a war. Dwayne hadn't been in combat. He was a civilian employee of the United States Army Air Corps during the Second World War, though. One time he got to paint a message on a five-hundred-pound bomb which was going to be dropped on Hamburg, Germany. This was it:

• • •

"Harry," said Francine, "everybody is entitled to a few bad days. Dwayne has fewer than anybody I know, so when he does have one like today, some people are hurt and surprised. They shouldn't be. He's human like anybody else."

"But why should he single out *me*?" Harry wanted to know. He was right: Dwayne *had* singled him out for astonishing insults and abuse that day. Everybody else still found Dwayne nothing but charming.

Later on, of course, Dwayne would assault all sorts of people, even three strangers from Erie, Pennsylvania, who had never been to Midland City before. But Harry was an isolated victim now.

• • •

"Why *me*?" said Harry. This was a common question in Midland City. People were always asking that as they were loaded into ambulances after accidents of various kinds, or arrested for disorderly conduct, or burglarized, or socked in the nose and so on: "*Why me*?"

"Probably because he felt that you were man enough and friend enough to put up with him on one of his few bad days," said Francine.

"How would you like it if he insulted your clothes?" said Harry. This is what Dwayne had done to him: insulted his clothes.

"I would remember that he was the best employer in town," said Francine. This was true. Dwayne paid high wages. He had profit-sharing and Christmas bonuses at the end of every year. He was the first automobile dealer in his part of the State to offer his employees Blue Cross–Blue Shield, which was health insurance. He had a retirement plan which was superior to every retirement plan in the city with the exception of the one at Barrytron. His office door was always open to any employee who had troubles to discuss, whether they had to do with the automobile business or not.

For instance, on the day he insulted Harry's clothing, he also spent two hours with Vernon Garr, discussing the hallucinations Vernon's wife was having. "She sees things that aren't there," said Vernon.

"She needs rest, Vern," said Dwayne.

"Maybe I'm going crazy, too," said Vernon. "Christ, I go home and I talk for hours to my fucking dog."

"That makes two of us," said Dwayne.

• • •

Here is the scene between Harry and Dwayne which upset Harry so much:

Harry went into Dwayne's office right after Vernon left. He expected no trouble, because he had never had any serious trouble with Dwayne.

"How's my old combat buddy today?" he said to Dwayne.

"As good as can be expected," said Dwayne. "Anything special bothering you?"

"No," said Harry.

"Vern's wife thinks Vern is trying to turn her brains into plutonium," said Dwayne.

"What's plutonium?" said Harry, and so on. They rambled along, and Harry made up a problem for himself just to keep the conversation lively. He said he was sad sometimes that he had no children. "But I'm glad in a way, too," he went on. "I mean, why should I contribute to overpopulation?"

Dwayne didn't say anything.

"Maybe we should have adopted one," said Harry, "but it's too late now. And the old lady and me—we have a good time just horsing around with ourselves. What do we need a kid for?"

It was after the mention of adoption that Dwayne blew up. He himself had been adopted—by a couple who had moved to Midland City from West Virginia in order to make big money as factory workers in the First World War. Dwayne's real mother was a spinster school teacher who wrote sentimental poetry and claimed to be descended from Richard the Lion-Hearted, who was a king. His real father was an itinerant typesetter, who seduced his mother by setting her poems in type. He didn't sneak them into a newspaper or anything. It was enough for her that they were set in type.

She was a defective child-bearing machine. She destroyed herself automatically while giving birth to Dwayne. The printer disappeared. He was a disappearing machine.

• • •

It may be that the subject of adoption caused an unfortunate chemical reaction in Dwayne's head. At any rate, Dwayne suddenly snarled this at Harry: "Harry, why don't you get a bunch of cotton waste from Vern Garr, soak it in *Blue Sunoco*, and burn up your fucking wardrobe? You make me feel like I'm at *Watson Brothers*." *Watson Brothers* was the name of the funeral parlor for white people who were at least moderately well-to-do. *Blue Sunoco* was a brand of gasoline.

Harry was startled, and then pain set in. Dwayne had never said anything about his clothes in all the years he'd known him. The clothes were conservative and neat, in Harry's opinion. His shirts were white. His ties were black or navy blue. His suits were gray or dark blue. His shoes and socks were black.

"Listen, Harry," said Dwayne, and his expression was mean, "Hawaiian Week is coming up, and I'm absolutely serious: burn your clothes and get new ones, or apply for work at Watson Brothers. Have yourself embalmed while you're at it."

• • •

Harry couldn't do anything but let his mouth hang open. The Hawaiian Week Dwayne had mentioned was a sales promotion scheme which involved making the agency look as much like the Hawaiian Islands as possible. People who bought new or used cars, or had repairs done in excess of five hundred dollars during the week would be entered automatically in a lottery. Three lucky people would each win a free, all-expenses-paid trip to Las Vegas and San Francisco and then Hawaii for a party of two.

"I don't mind that you have the name of a Buick, Harry, when you're supposed to be selling Pontiacs—" Dwayne went on. He was referring to the fact that the Buick division of General Motors put out a model called the *Le Sabre.* "You can't help that." Dwayne now patted the top of his desk softly. This was somehow more menacing than if he had pounded the desk with his fist. "But there *are* a hell of a lot of things you *can* change, Harry. There's a long weekend coming up. I expect to see some big changes in you when I come to work on Tuesday morning."

The weekend was extra-long because the coming Monday was a national holiday, *Veterans' Day.* It was in honor of people who had served their country in uniform.

• • •

"When we started selling Pontiacs, Harry," said Dwayne, "the car was sensible transportation for school teachers and grandmothers and maiden aunts." This was true. "Perhaps you haven't noticed, Harry, but the Pontiac has now become a glamorous, youthful adventure for people who want a *kick* out of life! And you dress and act like this was a mortuary! Look at yourself in a mirror, Harry, and ask yourself, 'Who could ever associate a man like this with a Pontiac?'"

Harry LeSabre was too choked up to point out to Dwayne that, no matter what he looked like, he was generally acknowledged to be one of the most effective sales managers for Pontiac not only in the State, but in the entire Middle West. Pontiac was the best-selling automobile in the Midland City area, despite the fact that it was not a low-price car. It was a medium-price car.

• • •

Dwayne Hoover told poor Harry LeSabre that the Hawaiian Festival, only a long weekend away, was Harry's golden opportunity to loosen up, to have some fun, to encourage other people to have some fun, too.

"Harry," said Dwayne. "I have some news for you: modern

science has given us a whole lot of wonderful new colors, with strange, exciting names like *red!*, *orange!*, *green!*, and *pink!*, Harry. We're not stuck any more with just black, gray and white! Isn't that good news, Harry? And the State Legislature has just announced that it is no longer a crime to smile during working hours, Harry, and I have the personal promise of the Governor that never again will anybody be sent to the Sexual Offenders' Wing of the Adult Correctional Institution for telling a joke!"

• • •

Harry LeSabre might have weathered all this with only minor damage, if only Harry hadn't been a secret transvestite. On weekends he liked to dress up in women's clothing, and not drab clothing, either. Harry and his wife would pull down the window blinds, and Harry would turn into a bird of paradise.

Nobody but Harry's wife knew his secret.

When Dwayne razzed him about the clothes he wore to work, and then mentioned the Sexual Offenders' Wing of the Adult Correctional Institution at Shepherdstown, Harry had to suspect that his secret was out. And it wasn't merely a comical secret, either. Harry could be arrested for what he did on weekends. He could be fined up to three thousand dollars and sentenced to as much as five years at hard labor in the Sexual Offenders' Wing of the Adult Correctional Institution at Shepherdstown.

• • •

So poor Harry spent a wretched Veterans' Day weekend after that. But Dwayne spent a worse one.

Here is what the last night of that weekend was like for Dwayne: his bad chemicals rolled him out of bed. They made him dress as though there were some sort of emergency with which he had to deal. This was in the wee hours. Veterans' Day had ended at the stroke of twelve.

Dwayne's bad chemicals made him take a loaded thirty-eight caliber revolver from under his pillow and stick it in his mouth. This was a tool whose only purpose was to make holes in human beings. It looked like this:

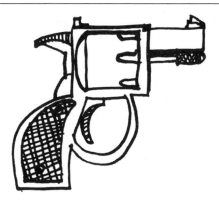

In Dwayne's part of the planet, anybody who wanted one could get one down at his local hardware store. Policemen all had them. So did the criminals. So did the people caught in between.

Criminals would point guns at people and say, "Give me all your money," and the people usually would. And policemen would point their guns at criminals and say, "Stop" or whatever the situation called for, and the criminals usually would. Sometimes they wouldn't. Sometimes a wife would get so mad at her husband that she would put a hole in him with a gun. Sometimes a husband would get so mad at his wife that he would put a hole in her. And so on.

In the same week Dwayne Hoover ran amok, a fourteen-year-old Midland City boy put holes in his mother and father because he didn't want to show them the bad report card he had brought home. His lawyer planned to enter a plea of temporary insanity, which meant that at the time of the shooting the boy was unable to distinguish the difference between right and wrong.

• • •

Sometimes people would put holes in famous people so they could be at least fairly famous, too. Sometimes people would get on airplanes which were supposed to fly to someplace, and they would offer to put holes in the pilot and co-pilot unless they flew the airplane to someplace else.

• • •

Dwayne held the muzzle of his gun in his mouth for a while. He tasted oil. The gun was loaded and cocked. There were neat little metal packages containing charcoal, potassium nitrate and sulphur only inches from his brains. He had only to trip a lever, and the powder would turn to gas. The gas would blow a chunk of lead down a tube and through Dwayne's brains.

But Dwayne elected to shoot up one of his tiled bathrooms instead. He put chunks of lead through his toilet and a washbasin and a bathtub enclosure. There was a picture of a flamingo sandblasted on the glass of the bathtub enclosure. It looked like this:

Dwayne shot the flamingo.

He snarled at his recollection of it afterwards. Here is what he snarled: "Dumb fucking bird."

• • •

Nobody heard the shots. All the houses in the neighborhood were too well insulated for sound ever to get in or out. A sound wanting in or out of Dwayne's dreamhouse, for instance, had to go through an inch and a half of plasterboard, a polystyrene vapor barrier, a sheet of aluminum foil, a three-inch airspace, another sheet of aluminum foil, a three-inch blanket of glass wool, another sheet of aluminum foil, one inch of insulating board made of pressed sawdust, tarpaper, one inch of wood sheathing, more tarpaper, and then aluminum siding which was hollow. The space in the siding was filled with a miracle insulating material developed for use on rockets to the Moon.

• • •

Dwayne turned on the floodlights around his house, and he played basketball on the blacktop apron outside his five-car garage.

Dwayne's dog Sparky hid in the basement when Dwayne shot up the bathroom. But he came out now. Sparky watched Dwayne play basketball.

"You and me, Sparky," said Dwayne. And so on. He sure loved that dog.

Nobody saw him playing basketball. He was screened from his neighbors by trees and shrubs and a high cedar fence.

• • •

He put the basketball away, and he climbed into a black Plymouth *Fury* he had taken in trade the day before. The Plymouth was a Chrysler product, and Dwayne himself sold General Motors products. He had decided to drive the Plymouth for a day or two in order to keep abreast of the competition.

As he backed out of his driveway, he thought it important to explain to his neighbors why he was in a Plymouth *Fury*, so he

yelled out the window: "Keeping abreast of the competition!"
He blew his horn.

• • •

Dwayne zoomed down Old County Road and onto the
Interstate, which he had all to himself. He swerved into Exit
Ten at a high rate of speed, slammed into a guardrail, spun
around and around. He came out onto Union Avenue going
backwards, jumped a curb, and came to a stop in a vacant lot.
Dwayne owned the lot.

Nobody saw or heard anything. Nobody lived in the area. A
policeman was supposed to cruise by about once every hour or
so, but he was cooping in an alley behind a Western Electric
warehouse about two miles away. *Cooping* was police slang for
sleeping on the job.

• • •

Dwayne stayed in his vacant lot for a while. He played the
radio. All the Midland City stations were asleep for the night,
but Dwayne picked up a country music station in West Virginia,
which offered him ten different kinds of flowering shrubs and
five fruit trees for six dollars, C.O.D.

"Sounds good to me," said Dwayne. He meant it. Almost all
the messages which were sent and received in his country, even
the telepathic ones, had to do with buying or selling some
damn thing. They were like lullabies to Dwayne.

Chapter 5

WHILE DWAYNE HOOVER listened to West Virginia, Kilgore Trout tried to fall asleep in a movie theater in New York City. It was much cheaper than a night in a hotel. Trout had never done it before, but he knew sleeping in movie houses was the sort of thing really dirty old men did. He wished to arrive in Midland City as the dirtiest of all old men. He was supposed to take part in a symposium out there entitled "The Future of the American Novel in the Age of McLuhan." He wished to say at that symposium, "I don't know who McLuhan is, but I know what it's like to spend the night with a lot of other dirty old men in a movie theater in New York City. Could we talk about that?"

He wished to say, too, "Does this McLuhan, whoever he is, have anything to say about the relationship between wide-open beavers and the sales of books?"

• • •

Trout had come down from Cohoes late that afternoon. He had since visited many pornography shops and a shirt store. He had bought two of his own books, *Plague on Wheels* and *Now It Can Be Told*, a magazine containing a short story of his, and a tuxedo shirt. The name of the magazine was *Black Garterbelt*. The tuxedo shirt had a cascade of ruffles down its bosom. On the shirt salesman's advice, Trout had also bought a packaged ensemble consisting of a cumberbund, a boutonnière, and a bow tie. They were all the color of tangerines.

These goodies were all in his lap, along with a crackling brown paper parcel containing his tuxedo, six new pairs of jockey shorts, six new pairs of socks, his razor and a new toothbrush. Trout hadn't owned a toothbrush for years.

• • •

The jackets of *Plague on Wheels* and *Now It Can Be Told* both promised plenty of wide-open beavers inside. The picture on the cover of *Now It Can Be Told*, which was the book which would turn Dwayne Hoover into a homicidal maniac, showed

a college professor being undressed by a group of naked sorority girls. A library tower could be seen through a window in
the sorority house. It was daytime outside, and there was a
clock in the tower. The clock looked like this:

The professor was stripped down to his candy-striped underwear shorts and his socks and garters and his mortarboard,
which was a hat which looked like this:

There was absolutely nothing about a professor or a sorority or a university anywhere in the body of the book. The book was in the form of a long letter from the Creator of the Universe to the only creature in the Universe who had free will.

•   •   •

As for the story in *Black Garterbelt* magazine: Trout had no idea that it had been accepted for publication. It had been accepted years ago, apparently, for the date on the magazine was April, 1962. Trout found it by chance in a bin of tame old magazines near the front of the store. They were underpants magazines.

When he bought the magazine, the cashier supposed Trout was drunk or feeble-minded. All he was getting, the cashier thought, was pictures of women in their underpants. Their legs were apart, all right, but they had on underpants, so they were certainly no competition for the wide-open beavers on sale in the back of the store.

"I hope you enjoy it," said the cashier to Trout. He meant that he hoped Trout would find some pictures he could masturbate to, since that was the only point of all the books and magazines.

"It's for an arts festival," said Trout.

•   •   •

As for the story itself, it was entitled "The Dancing Fool." Like so many Trout stories, it was about a tragic failure to communicate.

Here was the plot: A flying saucer creature named Zog arrived on Earth to explain how wars could be prevented and how cancer could be cured. He brought the information from Margo, a planet where the natives conversed by means of farts and tap dancing.

Zog landed at night in Connecticut. He had no sooner touched down than he saw a house on fire. He rushed into the house, farting and tap dancing, warning the people about the terrible danger they were in. The head of the house brained Zog with a golfclub.

•   •   •

The movie theater where Trout sat with all his parcels in his lap showed nothing but dirty movies. The music was soothing. Phantasms of a young man and a young woman sucked harmlessly on one another's soft apertures on the silver screen.

And Trout made up a new novel while he sat there. It was about an Earthling astronaut who arrived on a planet where all the animal and plant life had been killed by pollution, except for humanoids. The humanoids ate food made from petroleum and coal.

They gave a feast for the astronaut, whose name was Don. The food was terrible. The big topic of conversation was censorship. The cities were blighted with motion picture theaters which showed nothing but dirty movies. The humanoids wished they could put them out of business somehow, but without interfering with free speech.

They asked Don if dirty movies were a problem on Earth, too, and Don said, "Yes." They asked him if the movies were *really* dirty, and Don replied, "As dirty as movies could get."

This was a challenge to the humanoids, who were sure their dirty movies could beat anything on Earth. So everybody piled into air-cushion vehicles, and they floated to a dirty movie house downtown.

It was intermission time when they got there, so Don had some time to think about what could possibly be dirtier than what he had already seen on Earth. He became sexually excited even before the house lights went down. The women in his party were all twittery and squirmy.

So the theater went dark and the curtains opened. At first there wasn't any picture. There were slurps and moans from loudspeakers. Then the picture itself appeared. It was a high quality film of a male humanoid eating what looked like a pear. The camera zoomed in on his lips and tongue and teeth, which glistened with saliva. He took his time about eating the pear. When the last of it had disappeared into his slurpy mouth, the camera focussed on his Adam's apple. His Adam's apple bobbed obscenely. He belched contentedly, and then these words appeared on the screen, but in the language of the planet:

THE END

• • •

It was all faked, of course. There weren't any pears anymore. And the eating of a pear wasn't the main event of the evening anyway. It was a short subject, which gave the members of the audience time to settle down.

Then the main feature began. It was about a male and a female and their two children, and their dog and their cat. They ate steadily for an hour and a half—soup, meat, biscuits, butter, vegetables, mashed potatoes and gravy, fruit, candy, cake, pie. The camera rarely strayed more than a foot from their glistening lips and their bobbing Adam's apples. And then the father put the cat and dog on the table, so they could take part in the orgy, too.

After a while, the actors couldn't eat any more. They were so stuffed that they were goggle-eyed. They could hardly move. They said they didn't think they could eat again for a week, and so on. They cleared the table slowly. They went waddling out into the kitchen, and they dumped about thirty pounds of leftovers into a garbage can.

The audience went wild.

• • •

When Don and his friends left the theater, they were accosted by humanoid whores, who offered them eggs and oranges and milk and butter and peanuts and so on. The whores couldn't actually deliver these goodies, of course.

The humanoids told Don that if he went home with a whore, she would cook him a meal of petroleum and coal products at fancy prices.

And then, while he ate them, she would talk dirty about how fresh and full of natural juices the food was, even though the food was fake.

Chapter 6

DWAYNE HOOVER sat in the used Plymouth *Fury* in his own vacant lot for an hour, listening to West Virginia. He was told about health insurance for pennies a day, about how to get better performance from his car. He was told what to do about constipation. He was offered a Bible which had everything that God or Jesus had actually said out loud printed in red capital letters. He was offered a plant which would attract and eat disease-carrying insects in his home.

All this was stored away in Dwayne's memory, in case he should need it later on. He had all kinds of stuff in there.

• • •

While Dwayne sat there so alone, the oldest inhabitant of Midland City was dying in the County Hospital, at the foot of Fairchild Boulevard, which was nine miles away. She was Mary Young. She was one hundred and eight years old. She was black. Mary Young's parents had been human slaves in Kentucky.

There was a tiny connection between Mary Young and Dwayne Hoover. She did the laundry for Dwayne's family for a few months, back when Dwayne was a little boy. She told Bible stories and stories about slavery to little Dwayne. She told him about a public hanging of a white man she had seen in Cincinnati, when she was a little girl.

• • •

A black intern at the County Hospital now watched Mary Young die of pneumonia.

The intern did not know her. He had been in Midland City for only a week. He wasn't even a fellow-American, although he had taken his medical degree at Harvard. He was an Indaro. He was a Nigerian. His name was Cyprian Ukwende. He felt no kinship with Mary or with any American blacks. He felt kinship only with Indaros.

As she died, Mary was as alone on the planet as were Dwayne Hoover or Kilgore Trout. She had never reproduced. There were no friends or relatives to watch her die. So she spoke her very last words on the planet to Cyprian Ukwende. She did not have enough breath left to make her vocal cords buzz. She could only move her lips noiselessly.

Here is all she had to say about death: "Oh my, oh my."

•   •   •

Like all Earthlings at the point of death, Mary Young sent faint reminders of herself to those who had known her. She released a small cloud of telepathic butterflies, and one of these brushed the cheek of Dwayne Hoover, nine miles away.

Dwayne heard a tired voice from somewhere behind his head, even though no one was back there. It said this to Dwayne: "Oh my, oh my."

•   •   •

Dwayne's bad chemicals now made him put his car in gear. He drove out of the vacant lot, proceeded sedately down Union Avenue, which paralleled the Interstate.

He went past his principal place of business, which was *Dwayne Hoover's Exit Eleven Pontiac Village*, and he turned into the parking lot of the new Holiday Inn next door. Dwayne owned a third of the Inn—in partnership with Midland City's leading orthodontist, Dr. Alfred Maritimo, and Bill Miller, who was Chairman of the Parole Board at the Adult Correctional Institution at Shepherdstown, among other things.

Dwayne went up the Inn's back steps to the roof without meeting anybody. There was a full moon. There were *two* full moons. The new Mildred Barry Memorial Center for the Arts was a translucent sphere on stilts, and it was illuminated from the inside now—and it looked like a moon.

•   •   •

Dwayne gazed over the sleeping city. He had been born there. He had spent the first three years of his life in an orphanage only two miles from where he stood. He had been adopted and educated there.

He owned not only the Pontiac agency and a piece of the new Holiday Inn. He owned three Burger Chefs, too, and five coin-operated car washes, and pieces of the Sugar Creek Drive-In

Theatre, Radio Station WMCY, the Three Maples Par-Three Golf Course, and seventeen hundred shares of common stock in Barrytron, Limited, a local electronics firm. He owned dozens of vacant lots. He was on the Board of Directors of the Midland County National Bank.

But now Midland City looked unfamiliar and frightening to Dwayne. "Where am I?" he said.

He even forgot that his wife Celia had committed suicide, for instance, by eating Drāno—a mixture of sodium hydroxide and aluminum flakes, which was meant to clear drains. Celia became a small volcano, since she was composed of the same sorts of substances which commonly clogged drains.

Dwayne even forgot that his only child, a son, had grown up to be a notorious homosexual. His name was George, but everybody called him "Bunny." He played piano in the cocktail lounge of the new Holiday Inn.

"Where am I?" said Dwayne.

Chapter 7

KILGORE TROUT took a leak in the men's room of the New York City movie house. There was a sign on the wall next to the roller towel. It advertised a massage parlor called *The Sultan's Harem*. Massage parlors were something new and exciting in New York. Men could go in there and photograph naked women, or they could paint the women's naked bodies with water-soluble paints. Men could be rubbed all over by a woman until their penises squirted jism into Turkish towels.

"It's a full life and a merry one," said Kilgore Trout.

There was a message written in pencil on the tiles by the roller towel. This was it:

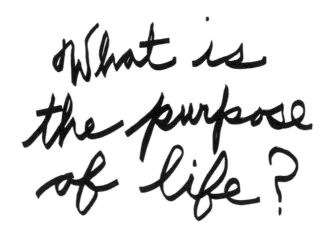

What is the purpose of life?

Trout plundered his pockets for a pen or pencil. He had an answer to the question. But he had nothing to write with, not even a burnt match. So he left the question unanswered, but here is what he would have written, if he had found anything to write with:

> *To be*
> *the eyes*
> *and ears*

and conscience
of the Creator of the Universe,
you fool.

When Trout headed back for his seat in the theater, he played at being the eyes and ears and conscience of the Creator of the Universe. He sent messages by telepathy to the Creator, wherever He was. He reported that the men's room had been clean as a whistle. "The carpeting under my feet," he signaled from the lobby, "is springy and new. I think it must be some miracle fiber. It's blue. You know what I mean by *blue*?" And so on.

When he got to the auditorium itself, the house lights were on. Nobody was there but the manager, who was also the ticket-taker and the bouncer and the janitor. He was sweeping filth from between the seats. He was a middle-aged white man. "No more fun tonight, grandfather," he said to Trout. "Time to go home."

Trout didn't protest. Neither did he leave immediately. He examined a green enameled steel box in the back of the auditorium. It contained the projector and the sound system and the films. There was a wire that led from the box to a plug in the wall. There was a hole in the front of the box. That was how the pictures got out. On the side of the box was a simple switch. It looked like this:

•   •   •

It intrigued Trout to know that he had only to flick the switch, and the people would start fucking and sucking again.

"Good night, Grandfather," said the manager pointedly.

Trout took his leave of the machine reluctantly. He said this about it to the manager: "It fills such a *need*, this machine, and it's so easy to operate."

•   •   •

As Trout departed, he sent this telepathic message to the Creator of the Universe, serving as His eyes and ears and conscience: "Am headed for Forty-second Street now. How much do you already know about Forty-second Street?"

Chapter 8

TROUT WANDERED out onto the sidewalk of Forty-second Street. It was a dangerous place to be. The whole city was dangerous—because of chemicals and the uneven distribution of wealth and so on. A lot of people were like Dwayne: they created chemicals in their own bodies which were bad for their heads. But there were thousands upon thousands of other people in the city who bought bad chemicals and ate them or sniffed them—or injected them into their veins with devices which looked like this:

Sometimes they even stuffed bad chemicals up their assholes. Their assholes looked like this:

• • •

People took such awful chances with chemicals and their bodies because they wanted the quality of their lives to improve. They lived in ugly places where there were only ugly things to do. They didn't own doodley-squat, so they couldn't improve their surroundings. So they did their best to make their insides beautiful instead.

The results had been catastrophic so far—suicide, theft, murder, and insanity and so on. But new chemicals were coming onto the market all the time. Twenty feet away from Trout there on Forty-second Street, a fourteen-year-old white boy lay unconscious in the doorway of a pornography store. He had swallowed a half pint of a new type of paint remover which had gone on sale for the first time only the day before. He had also swallowed two pills which were intended to prevent contagious abortion in cattle, which was called *Bang's disease*.

• • •

Trout was petrified there on Forty-second Street. It had given him a life not worth living, but I had also given him an iron will to live. This was a common combination on the planet Earth.

The theater manager came out and locked the door behind him.

And two young black prostitutes materialized from nowhere. They asked Trout and the manager if they would like to have some fun. They were cheerful and unafraid—because of a tube of Norwegian hemorrhoid remedy which they had eaten about half an hour before. The manufacturer had never intended the stuff to be eaten. People were supposed to squirt it up their assholes.

These were country girls. They had grown up in the rural south of the nation, where their ancestors had been used as agricultural machinery. The white farmers down there weren't using machines made out of meat anymore, though, because machines made out of metal were cheaper and more reliable, and required simpler homes.

So the black machines had to get out of there, or starve to death. They came to cities because everyplace else had signs like this on the fences and trees:

• • •

Kilgore Trout once wrote a story called "This Means You." It was set in the Hawaiian Islands, the place where the lucky winners of Dwayne Hoover's contest in Midland City were supposed to go. Every bit of land on the islands was owned by only about forty people, and, in the story, Trout had those people decide to exercise their property rights to the full. They put up *no trespassing* signs on everything.

This created terrible problems for the million other people on the islands. The law of gravity required that they stick somewhere on the surface. Either that, or they could go out into the water and bob offshore.

But then the Federal Government came through with an emergency program. It gave a big balloon full of helium to every man, woman and child who didn't own property.

• • •

There was a cable with a harness on it dangling from each balloon. With the help of the balloons, Hawaiians could go on inhabiting the islands without always sticking to things other people owned.

• • •

The prostitutes worked for a pimp now. He was splendid and cruel. He was a god to them. He took their free will away from them, which was perfectly all right. They didn't want it anyway. It was as though they had surrendered themselves to Jesus, for instance, so they could live unselfishly and trustingly —except that they had surrendered to a pimp instead.

Their childhoods were over. They were dying now. Earth was a tinhorn planet as far as they were concerned.

When Trout and the theater manager, two tinhorns, said they didn't want any tinhorn fun, the dying children sauntered off, their feet sticking to the planet, coming unstuck, then sticking again. They disappeared around a corner. Trout, the eyes and ears of the Creator of the Universe, sneezed.

•   •   •

"God bless you," said the manager. This was a fully automatic response many Americans had to hearing a person sneeze.

"Thank you," said Trout. Thus a temporary friendship was formed.

Trout said he hoped to get safely to a cheap hotel. The manager said he hoped to get to the subway station on Times Square. So they walked together, encouraged by the echoes of their footsteps from the building façades.

The manager told Trout a little about what the planet looked like to him. It was a place where he had a wife and two kids, he said. They didn't know he ran a theater which showed blue movies. They thought he was doing consulting work as an engineer so late at night. He said that the planet didn't have much use for engineers his age anymore. It had adored them once.

"Hard times," said Trout.

The manager told of being in on the development of a miraculous insulating material, which had been used on rocket ships to the Moon. This was, in fact, the same material which gave the aluminum siding of Dwayne Hoover's dream house in Midland City its miraculous insulating qualities.

The manager reminded Trout of what the first man to set foot on the Moon had said: "One small step for man, one great leap for mankind."

"Thrilling words," said Trout. He looked over his shoulder, perceived that they were being followed by a white Oldsmobile *Toronado* with a black vinyl roof. This four hundred horse-power, front-wheel drive vehicle was burbling along at about three miles an hour, ten feet behind them and close to the curb.

That was the last thing Trout remembered—seeing the Oldsmobile back there.

• • •

The next thing he knew, he was on his hands and knees on a handball court underneath the Queensboro Bridge at Fifty-ninth Street, with the East River nearby. His trousers and underpants were around his ankles. His money was gone. His parcels were scattered around him—the tuxedo, the new shirt, the books. Blood seeped from one ear.

The police caught him in the act of pulling up his trousers. They dazzled him with a spotlight as he leaned against the backboard of the handball court and fumbled foolishly with his belt and the buttons on his fly. The police supposed that they had caught him committing some public nuisance, had caught him working with an old man's limited palette of excrement and alcohol.

He wasn't quite penniless. There was a ten-dollar bill in the watch pocket of his pants.

• • •

It was determined at a hospital that Trout was not seriously hurt. He was taken to a police station, where he was questioned. All he could say was that he had been kidnapped by pure evil in a white Oldsmobile. The police wanted to know how many people were in the car, their ages, their sexes, the colors of their skins, their manners of speech.

"For all I know, they may not even have been Earthlings," said Trout. "For all I know, that car may have been occupied by an intelligent gas from Pluto."

• • •

Trout said this so innocently, but his comment turned out to be the first germ in an epidemic of mind-poisoning. Here is how the disease was spread: a reporter wrote a story for the *New York Post* the next day, and he led off with the quotation from Trout.

The story appeared under this headline:

PLUTO BANDITS
KIDNAP PAIR

Trout's name was given as Kilmer Trotter, incidentally, address unknown. His age was given as eighty-two.

Other papers copied the story, rewrote it some. They all hung on to the joke about Pluto, spoke knowingly of *The Pluto Gang*. And reporters asked police for any new information on *The Pluto Gang*, so police went looking for information on *The Pluto Gang*.

• • •

So New Yorkers, who had so many nameless terrors, were easily taught to fear something seemingly specific—*The Pluto Gang*. They bought new locks for their doors and gratings for their windows, to keep out *The Pluto Gang*. They stopped going to theaters at night, for fear of *The Pluto Gang*.

Foreign newspapers spread the terror, ran articles on how persons thinking of visiting New York might keep to a certain few streets in Manhattan and stand a fair chance of avoiding *The Pluto Gang*.

• • •

In one of New York City's many ghettos for dark-skinned people, a group of Puerto Rican boys gathered together in the basement of an abandoned building. They were small, but they were numerous and volatile. They wished to become frightening, in order to defend themselves and their friends and families, something the police wouldn't do. They also wanted to drive the drug peddlers out of the neighborhood, and to get enough publicity, which was very important, to catch the attention of the Government, so that the Government would do a better job of picking up the garbage and so on.

One of them, José Mendoza, was a fairly good painter. So

he painted the emblem of their new gang on the backs of the members' jackets. This was it:

Chapter 9

WHILE Kilgore Trout was inadvertently poisoning the collective mind of New York City, Dwayne Hoover, the demented Pontiac dealer, was coming down from the roof of his own Holiday Inn in the Middle West.

Dwayne went into the carpeted lobby of the place not long before sunrise, to ask for a room. As queer as the hour was, there was a man ahead of him, and a black one at that. This was Cyprian Ukwende, the Indaro, the physician from Nigeria, who was staying at the Inn until he could find a suitable apartment.

Dwayne awaited his turn humbly. He had forgotten that he was a co-owner of the Inn. As for staying at a place where black men stayed, Dwayne was philosophical. He experienced a sort of bittersweet happiness as he told himself, "Times change. Times change."

• • •

The night clerk was new. He did not know Dwayne. He had Dwayne fill out a registration in full. Dwayne, for his part, apologized for not knowing what the number of his license plate was. He felt guilty about that, even though he knew he had done nothing he should feel guilty about.

He was elated when the clerk let him have a room key. He had passed the test. And he adored his room. It was so new and cool and clean. It was so *neutral*! It was the brother of thousands upon thousands of rooms in Holiday Inns all over the world.

Dwayne Hoover might be confused as to what his life was all about, or what he should do with it next. But this much he has done correctly: He had delivered himself to an irreproachable container for a human being.

It awaited anybody. It awaited Dwayne.

Around the toilet seat was a band of paper like this, which he would have to remove before he used the toilet:

562

This loop of paper guaranteed Dwayne that he need have no fear that corkscrew-shaped little animals would crawl up his asshole and eat up his wiring. That was one less worry for Dwayne.

• • •

There was a sign hanging on the inside doorknob, which Dwayne now hung on the outside doorknob. It looked like this:

Dwayne pulled open his floor-to-ceiling draperies for a moment. He saw the sign which announced the presence of the Inn to weary travelers on the Interstate. Here is what it looked like:

He closed his draperies. He adjusted the heating and ventilating system. He slept like a lamb.

A lamb was a young animal which was legendary for sleeping well on the planet Earth. It looked like this:

Chapter 10

KILGORE TROUT was released by the Police Department of the City of New York like a weightless thing—at two hours before dawn on the day after Veterans' Day. He crossed the island of Manhattan from east to west in the company of Kleenex tissues and newspapers and soot.

He got a ride in a truck. It was hauling seventy-eight thousand pounds of Spanish olives. It picked him up at the mouth of the Lincoln Tunnel, which was named in honor of a man who had had the courage and imagination to make human slavery against the law in the United States of America. This was a recent innovation.

The slaves were simply turned loose without any property. They were easily recognizable. They were black. They were suddenly free to go exploring.

• • •

The driver, who was white, told Trout that he would have to lie on the floor of the cab until they reached open country, since it was against the law for him to pick up hitchhikers.

• • •

It was still dark when he told Trout he could sit up. They were crossing the poisoned marshes and meadows of New Jersey. The truck was a General Motors Astro-95 Diesel tractor, hooked up to a trailer forty feet long. It was so enormous that it made Trout feel that his head was about the size of a piece of bee-bee shot.

The driver said he used to be a hunter and a fisherman, long ago. It broke his heart when he imagined what the marshes and meadows had been like only a hundred years before. "And when you think of the shit that most of these factories make—wash day products, catfood, pop—"

• • •

566

He had a point. The planet was being destroyed by manufacturing processes, and what was being manufactured was lousy, by and large.

Then Trout made a good point, too. "Well," he said, "I used to be a conservationist. I used to weep and wail about people shooting bald eagles with automatic shotguns from helicopters and all that, but I gave it up. There's a river in Cleveland which is so polluted that it catches fire about once a year. That used to make me sick, but I laugh about it now. When some tanker accidently dumps its load in the ocean, and kills millions of birds and billions of fish, I say, 'More power to Standard Oil,' or whoever it was that dumped it." Trout raised his arms in celebration. "'Up your ass with Mobil gas,'" he said.

The driver was upset by this. "You're kidding," he said.

"I realized," said Trout, "that God wasn't any conservationist, so for anybody else to be one was sacrilegious and a waste of time. You ever see one of His volcanoes or tornadoes or tidal waves? Anybody ever tell you about the Ice Ages he arranges for every half-million years? How about Dutch Elm disease? There's a nice conservation measure for you. That's God, not man. Just about the time we got our rivers cleaned up, he'd probably have the whole galaxy go up like a celluloid collar. That's what the Star of Bethlehem was, you know."

"What *was* the Star of Bethlehem?" said the driver.

"A whole galaxy going up like a celluloid collar," said Trout.

• • •

The driver was impressed. "Come to think about it," he said, "I don't think there's anything about conservation anywhere in the Bible."

"Unless you want to count the story about the Flood," said Trout.

• • •

They rode in silence for a while, and then the driver made another good point. He said he knew that his truck was turning the atmosphere into poison gas, and that the planet was being turned into pavement so his truck could go anywhere. "So I'm committing suicide," he said.

"Don't worry about it," said Trout.

"My brother is even worse," the driver went on. "He works in a factory that makes chemicals for killing plants and trees in Viet Nam." Viet Nam was a country where America was trying to make people stop being communists by dropping things on them from airplanes. The chemicals he mentioned were intended to kill all the foliage, so it would be harder for communists to hide from airplanes.

"Don't worry about it," said Trout.

"In the long run, *he's* committing suicide," said the driver. "Seems like the only kind of job an American can get these days is committing suicide in some way."

"Good point," said Trout.

• • •

"I can't tell if you're serious or not," said the driver.

"I won't know myself until I find out whether *life* is serious or not," said Trout. "It's *dangerous*, I know, and it can hurt a lot. That doesn't necessarily mean it's *serious*, too."

• • •

After Trout became famous, of course, one of the biggest mysteries about him was whether he was kidding or not. He told one persistent questioner that he always crossed his fingers when he was kidding.

"And please note," he went on, "that when I gave you that priceless piece of information, my fingers were crossed."

And so on.

He was a pain in the neck in a lot of ways. The truck driver got sick of him after an hour or two. Trout used the silence to make up an anticonservation story he called "Gilgongo!"

"Gilgongo!" was about a planet which was unpleasant because there was too much creation going on.

The story began with a big party in honor of a man who had wiped out an entire species of darling little panda bears. He had devoted his life to this. Special plates were made for the party, and the guests got to take them home as souvenirs.

There was a picture of a little bear on each one, and the date of the party. Underneath the picture was the word:

GILGONGO!

In the language of the planet, that meant "Extinct!"

• • •

People were glad that the bears were *gilgongo*, because there were too many species on the planet already, and new ones were coming into being almost every hour. There was no way anybody could prepare for the bewildering diversity of creatures and plants he was likely to encounter.

The people were doing their best to cut down on the number of species, so that life could be more predictable. But Nature was too creative for them. All life on the planet was suffocated at last by a living blanket one hundred feet thick. The blanket was composed of passenger pigeons and eagles and Bermuda Erns and whooping cranes.

• • •

"At least it's olives," the driver said.

"What?" said Trout.

"Lots worse things we could be hauling than olives."

"Right," said Trout. He had forgotten that the main thing they were doing was moving seventy-eight thousand pounds of olives to Tulsa, Oklahoma.

• • •

The driver talked about politics some.

Trout couldn't tell one politician from another one. They were all formlessly enthusiastic chimpanzees to him. He wrote a story one time about an optimistic chimpanzee who became President of the United States. He called it "Hail to the Chief."

The chimpanzee wore a little blue blazer with brass buttons, and with the seal of the President of the United States sewed to the breast pocket. It looked like this:

Everywhere he went, bands would play "Hail to the Chief."
The chimpanzee loved it. He would bounce up and down.

•   •   •

They stopped at a diner. Here is what the sign in front of the
diner said:

So they ate.

Trout spotted an idiot who was eating, too. The idiot was a white male adult—in the care of a white female nurse. The idiot couldn't talk much, and he had a lot of trouble feeding himself. The nurse put a bib around his neck.

But he certainly had a wonderful appetite. Trout watched him shovel waffles and pork sausage into his mouth, watched him guzzle orange juice and milk. Trout marveled at what a big animal the idiot was. The idiot's happiness was fascinating, too, as he stoked himself with calories which would get him through yet another day.

Trout said this to himself: "Stoking up for another day."

• • •

"Excuse me," said the truck driver to Trout, "I've got to take a leak."

"Back where I come from," said Trout, "that means you're going to steal a mirror. We call mirrors *leaks*."

"I never heard that before," said the driver. He repeated the word: "Leaks." He pointed to a mirror on a cigarette machine. "You call that a *leak*?"

"Doesn't it look like a leak to you?" said Trout.

"No," said the driver. "Where did you say you were from?"

"I was born in Bermuda," said Trout.

About a week later, the driver would tell his wife that mirrors were called *leaks* in Bermuda, and she would tell her friends.

• • •

When Trout followed the driver back to the truck, he took his first good look at their form of transportation from a distance, saw it whole. There was a message written on the side of it in bright orange letters which were eight feet high. This was it:

Trout wondered what a child who was just learning to read would make of a message like that. The child would suppose that the message was terrifically important, since somebody had gone to the trouble of writing it in letters so big.

And then, pretending to be a child by the roadside, he read the message on the side of another truck. This was it:

Chapter 11

DWAYNE HOOVER slept until ten at the new Holiday Inn. He was much refreshed. He had a Number Five Breakfast in the popular restaurant of the Inn, which was the *Tally-Ho Room*. The drapes were drawn at night. They were wide open now. They let the sunshine in.

At the next table, also alone, was Cyprian Ukwende, the Indaro, the Nigerian. He was reading the classified ads in the Midland City *Bugle-Observer*. He needed a cheap place to live. The Midland County General Hospital was footing his bills at the Inn while he looked around, and they were getting restless about that.

He needed a woman, too, or a bunch of women who would fuck him hundreds of times a week, because he was so full of lust and jism all the time. And he ached to be with his Indaro relatives. Back home, he had six hundred relatives he knew by name.

Ukwende's face was impassive as he ordered the Number Three Breakfast with whole-wheat toast. Behind his mask was a young man in the terminal stages of nostalgia and lover's nuts.

• • •

Dwayne Hoover, six feet away, gazed out at the busy, sunny Interstate Highway. He knew where he was. There was a familiar moat between the parking lot of the Inn and the Interstate, a concrete trough which the engineers had built to contain Sugar Creek. Next came a familiar resilient steel barrier which prevented cars and trucks from tumbling into Sugar Creek. Next came the three familiar west-bound lanes, and then the familiar grassy median divider. After that came the three familiar east-bound lanes, and then another familiar steel barrier. After that came the familiar Will Fairchild Memorial Airport—and then the familiar farmlands beyond.

• • •

It was certainly flat out there—flat city, flat township, flat county, flat state. When Dwayne was a little boy, he had supposed that almost everybody lived in places that were treeless and flat. He imagined that oceans and mountains and forests were mainly sequestered in state and national parks. In the third grade, little Dwayne scrawled an essay which argued in favor of creating a national park at a bend in Sugar Creek, the only significant surface water within eight miles of Midland City.

Dwayne said the name of that familiar surface water to himself now, silently: "Sugar Creek."

•   •   •

Sugar Creek was only two inches deep and fifty yards wide at the bend, where little Dwayne thought the park should be. Now they had put the Mildred Barry Memorial Center for the Arts there instead. It was beautiful.

Dwayne fiddled with his lapel for a moment, felt a badge pinned there. He unpinned it, having no recollection of what it said. It was a boost for the Arts Festival, which would begin that evening. All over town people were wearing badges like Dwayne's. Here is what the badges said:

• • •

Sugar Creek flooded now and then. Dwayne remembered about that. In a land so flat, flooding was a queerly pretty thing for water to do. Sugar Creek brimmed over silently, formed a vast mirror in which children might safely play.

The mirror showed the citizens the shape of the valley they lived in, demonstrated that they were hill people who inhabited slopes rising one inch for every mile that separated them from Sugar Creek.

Dwayne silently said the name of the water again: "Sugar Creek."

• • •

Dwayne finished his breakfast, and he dared to suppose that he was no longer mentally diseased, that he had been cured by a simple change of residence, by a good night's sleep.

His bad chemicals let him cross the lobby and then the cocktail lounge, which wasn't open yet, without experiencing anything strange. But when he stepped out of the side door of the cocktail lounge, and onto the asphalt prairie which surrounded both his Inn and his Pontiac agency, he discovered that someone had turned the asphalt into a sort of trampoline.

It sank beneath Dwayne's weight. It dropped Dwayne to well below street level, then slowly brought him only partway up again. He was in a shallow, rubbery dimple. Dwayne took another step in the direction of his automobile agency. He sank down again, came up again, and stood in a brand new dimple.

He gawked around for witnesses. There was only one. Cyprian Ukwende stood on the rim of the dimple, not sinking in. This was all Ukwende had to say, even though Dwayne's situation was extraordinary:

"Nice day."

• • •

Dwayne progressed from dimple to dimple.

He blooped across the used car lot now.

He stopped in a dimple, looked up at another young black

man. This one was polishing a maroon 1970 Buick *Skylark* convertible with a rag. The man wasn't dressed for that sort of work. He wore a cheap blue suit and a white shirt and a black necktie. Also: he wasn't merely polishing the car—he was *burnishing* it.

The young man did some more burnishing. Then he smiled at Dwayne blindingly, then he burnished the car again.

Here was the explanation: this young black man had just been paroled from the Adult Correctional Institution at Shepherdstown. He needed work right away, or he would starve to death. So he was showing Dwayne how hard a worker he was.

He had been in orphanages and youth shelters and prisons of one sort or another in the Midland City area since he was nine years old. He was now twenty-six.

•   •   •

He was free at last!

•   •   •

Dwayne thought the young man was an hallucination.

•   •   •

The young man went back to burnishing the automobile. His life was not worth living. He had a feeble will to survive. He thought the planet was terrible, that he never should have been sent there. Some mistake had been made. He had no friends or relatives. He was put in cages all the time.

He had a name for a better world, and he often saw it in dreams. Its name was a secret. He would have been ridiculed, if he had said its name out loud. It was such a *childish* name.

The young black jailbird could see the name any time he wanted to, written in lights on the inside of his skull. This is what it looked like:

•   •   •

He had a photograph of Dwayne in his wallet. He used to have photographs of Dwayne on the walls of his cell at Shepherdstown. They were easy to get, because Dwayne's smiling face, with his motto underneath, was a part of every ad he ran in the *Bugle-Observer*. The picture was changed every six months. The motto hadn't varied in twenty-five years.

Here was the motto:

> ASK ANYBODY—
> YOU CAN TRUST
> DWAYNE.

The young ex-convict smiled yet again at Dwayne. His teeth were in perfect repair. The dental program at Shepherdstown was excellent. So was the food.

"Good morning, sir," said the young man to Dwayne. He was dismayingly innocent. There was so much he had to learn. He didn't know anything about women, for instance. Francine Pefko was the first woman he had spoken to in eleven years.

"Good morning," said Dwayne. He said it softly, so his voice wouldn't carry very far, in case he was conversing with an hallucination.

"Sir—I have read your ads in the newspapers with great interest, and I have found pleasure in your radio advertising, too," the parolee said. During the last year in prison, he had been obsessed by one idea: that he would work for Dwayne someday, and live happily ever after. It would be like Fairyland.

Dwayne made no reply to this, so the young man went on: "I am a very hard worker, sir, as you can see. I hear nothing but good things about you. I think the good Lord meant for me to work for you."

"Oh?" said Dwayne.

"Our names are so close," said the young man, "it's the good Lord telling us *both* what to do."

Dwayne Hoover didn't ask him what his name was, but the young man told him anyway, radiantly: "My name, sir, is Wayne Hoobler."

All around Midland City, Hoobler was a common Nigger name.

• • •

Dwayne Hoover broke Wayne Hoobler's heart by shaking his head vaguely, then walking away.

• • •

Dwayne entered his showroom. The ground wasn't blooping underneath him anymore, but now he saw something else for which there could be no explanation: A palm tree was growing out of the showroom floor. Dwayne's bad chemicals made him forget all about Hawaiian Week. Actually, Dwayne had designed the palm tree himself. It was a sawed-off telephone pole—swaddled in burlap. It had real coconuts nailed to the top of it. Sheets of green plastic had been cut to resemble leaves.

The tree so bewildered Dwayne that he almost swooned. Then he looked around and saw pineapples and ukuleles scattered everywhere.

And then he saw the most unbelievable thing of all: His sales manager, Harry LeSabre, came toward him leeringly, wearing

a lettuce-green leotard, straw sandals, a grass skirt, and a pink
T-shirt which looked like this:

• • •

Harry and his wife had spent all weekend arguing about
whether or not Dwayne suspected that Harry was a transvestite. They concluded that Dwayne had no reason to suspect it.
Harry never talked about women's clothes to Dwayne. He had
never entered a transvestite beauty contest or done what a lot
of transvestites in Midland City did, which was join a big transvestite club over in Cincinnati. He never went into the city's
transvestite bar, which was *Ye Old Rathskeller*, in the basement
of the Fairchild Hotel. He had never exchanged Polaroid pictures with any other transvestites, had never subscribed to a
transvestite magazine.

Harry and his wife concluded that Dwayne had meant

nothing more than what he said, that Harry had better put on some wild clothes for Hawaiian Week, or Dwayne would can him.

So here was the new Harry now, rosy with fear and excitement. He felt uninhibited and beautiful and lovable and suddenly free.

He greeted Dwayne with the Hawaiian word which meant both *hello* and *goodbye*. "Aloha," he said.

Chapter 12

KILGORE TROUT was far away, but he was steadily closing the distance between himself and Dwayne. He was still in the truck named *Pyramid*. It was crossing a bridge named in honor of the poet Walt Whitman. The bridge was veiled in smoke. The truck was about to become a part of Philadelphia now. A sign at the foot of the bridge said this:

. . .

As a younger man, Trout would have sneered at the sign about brotherhood—posted on the rim of a bomb crater, as anyone could see. But his head no longer sheltered ideas of how things could be and should be on the planet, as opposed to how they really were. There was only one way for the Earth to be, he thought: the way it was.

Everything was necessary. He saw an old white woman fishing through a garbage can. That was necessary. He saw a bathtub toy, a little rubber duck, lying on its side on the grating over a storm sewer. It *had* to be there.

And so on.

. . .

The driver mentioned that the day before had been Veterans' Day.

"Um," said Trout.

"You a veteran?" said the driver.

"No," said Trout. "Are you?"

"No," said the driver.

Neither one of them was a veteran.

• • •

The driver got onto the subject of friends. He said it was hard for him to maintain friendships that meant anything because he was on the road most of the time. He joked about the time when he used to talk about his "best friends." He guessed people stopped talking about best friends after they got out of junior high school.

He suggested that Trout, since Trout was in the combination aluminum storm window and screen business, had opportunities to build many lasting friendships in the course of his work. "I mean," he said, "you get men working together day after day, putting up those windows, they get to know each other pretty well."

"I work alone," said Trout.

The driver was disappointed. "I assumed it would take two men to do the job."

"Just one," said Trout. "A weak little kid could do it without any help."

The driver wanted Trout to have a rich social life so that he could enjoy it vicariously. "All the same," he insisted, "you've got buddies you see after work. You have a few beers. You play some cards. You have some laughs."

Trout shrugged.

"You walk down the same streets every day," the driver told him. "You know a lot of people, and they know you, because it's the same streets for you, day after day. You say, 'Hello,' and they say 'Hello,' back. You call them by name. They call you by name. If you're in a real jam, they'll help you, because you're one of 'em. You *belong*. They see you every day."

Trout didn't want to argue about it.

• • •

Trout had forgotten the driver's name.

Trout had a mental defect which I, too, used to suffer from.

He couldn't remember what different people in his life looked like—unless their bodies or faces were strikingly unusual.

When he lived on Cape Cod, for instance, the only person he could greet warmly and by name was Alfy Bearse, who was a one-armed albino. "Hot enough for you, Alfy?" he would say. "Where you been keeping yourself, Alfy?" he'd say. "You're a sight for sore eyes, Alfy," he'd say.

And so on.

• • •

Now that Trout lived in Cohoes, the only person he called by name was a red-headed Cockney midget, Durling Heath. He worked in a shoe repair shop. Heath had an executive-type nameplate on his workbench, in case anybody wished to address him by name. The nameplate looked like this:

Trout would drop into the shop from time to time, and say such things as, "Who's gonna win the World Series this year, Durling?" and "You have any idea what all the sirens were blowing about last night, Durling?" and, "You're looking good today, Durling—where'd you get that shirt?" And so on.

Trout wondered now if his friendship with Heath was over. The last time Trout had been in the shoe repair place, saying this and that to Durling, the midget had unexpectedly screamed at him.

This is what he had screamed in his Cockney accent: "Stop bloody *hounding* me!"

• • •

The Governor of New York, Nelson Rockefeller, shook Trout's hand in a Cohoes grocery story one time. Trout had no idea who he was. As a science-fiction writer, he should have been flabbergasted to come so close to such a man. Rockefeller wasn't merely Governor. Because of the peculiar laws in that part of the planet, Rockefeller was allowed to own vast areas of Earth's surface, and the petroleum and other valuable minerals underneath the surface, as well. He owned or controlled more of the planet than many nations. This had been his destiny since infancy. He had been *born* into that cockamamie proprietorship.

"How's it going, fella?" Governor Rockefeller asked him.

"About the same," said Kilgore Trout.

• • •

After insisting that Trout had a rich social life, the driver pretended, again for his own gratification, that Trout had begged to know what the sex life of a transcontinental truck driver was like. Trout had begged no such thing.

"You want to know how truck drivers make out with women, right?" the driver said. "You have this idea that every driver you see is fucking up a storm from coast to coast, right?"

Trout shrugged.

The truck driver became embittered by Trout, scolded him for being so salaciously misinformed. "Let me tell you, Kilgore—" he hesitated. "That's your name, right?"

"Yes," said Trout. He had forgotten the driver's name a hundred times. Every time Trout looked away from him, Trout forgot not only his name but his face, too.

"Kilgore, God damn it—" the driver said, "if I was to have my rig break down in Cohoes, for instance, and I was to have to stay there for two days while it was worked on, how easy you think it would be for me to get laid while I was there—a stranger, looking the way I do?"

"It would depend on how *determined* you were," said Trout.

The driver sighed. "Yeah, God—" he said, and he despaired for himself, "that's probably the story of my life: not enough determination."

• • •

They talked about aluminum siding as a technique for making old houses look new again. From a distance, these sheets, which never needed painting, looked like freshly painted wood.

The driver wanted to talk about *Perma-Stone*, too, which was a competitive scheme. It involved plastering the sides of old houses with colored cement, so that, from a distance, they looked as though they were made of stone.

"If you're in aluminum storm windows," the driver said to Trout, "you must be in aluminum siding, too." All over the country, the two businesses went hand-in-hand.

"My company sells it," said Trout, "and I've seen a lot of it. I've never actually worked on an installation."

The driver was thinking seriously of buying aluminum siding for his home in Little Rock, and he begged Trout to give him an honest answer to this question: "From what you've seen and heard—the people who get aluminum siding, are they *happy* with what they get?"

"Around Cohoes," said Trout. "I think those were about the only really happy people I ever saw."

• • •

"I know what you mean," said the driver. "One time I saw a whole family standing outside their house. They couldn't believe how nice their house looked after the aluminum siding went on. My question to you, and you can give me an honest answer, on account of we'll never have to do business, you and me: Kilgore, how long will that happiness last?"

"About fifteen years," said Trout. "Our salesmen say you can easily afford to have the job redone with all the money you've saved on paint and heat."

"*Perma-Stone* looks a lot richer, and I suppose it lasts a lot longer, too," said the driver. "On the other hand, it costs a lot more."

"You get what you pay for," said Kilgore Trout.

• • •

The truck driver told Trout about a gas hot-water heater he had bought thirty years ago, and it hadn't given him a speck of trouble in all that time.

"I'll be damned," said Kilgore Trout.

● ● ●

Trout asked about the truck, and the driver said it was the greatest truck in the world. The tractor alone cost twenty-eight thousand dollars. It was powered by a three hundred and twenty-four horsepower Cummins Diesel engine, which was turbo-charged, so it would function well at high altitudes. It had hydraulic steering, air brakes, a thirteen-speed transmission, and was owned by his brother-in-law.

His brother-in-law, he said, owned twenty-eight trucks, and was President of the Pyramid Trucking Company.

"Why did he name his company *Pyramid*?" asked Trout. "I mean—this thing can go a hundred miles an hour, if it has to. It's fast and useful and unornamental. It's as up-to-date as a rocket ship. I never saw anything that was less like a pyramid than this truck."

● ● ●

A pyramid was a sort of huge stone tomb which Egyptians had built thousands and thousands of years before. The Egyptians didn't build them anymore. The tombs looked like this, and tourists would come from far away to gaze at them:

"Why would anybody in the business of highspeed transportation name his business and his trucks after buildings which haven't moved an eighth of an inch since Christ was born?"

The driver's answer was prompt. It was peevish, too, as though he thought Trout was stupid to have to ask a question like that. "He liked the *sound* of it," he said. "Don't you like the *sound* of it?"

Trout nodded in order to keep things friendly. "Yes," he said, "it's a very nice sound."

• • •

Trout sat back and thought about the conversation. He shaped it into a story, which he never got around to writing until he was an old, old man. It was about a planet where the language kept turning into pure music, because the creatures there were so enchanted by sounds. Words became musical notes. Sentences became melodies. They were useless as conveyors of information, because nobody knew or cared what the meanings of words were anymore.

So leaders in government and commerce, in order to function, had to invent new and much uglier vocabularies and sentence structures all the time, which would resist being transmuted to music.

• • •

"You married, Kilgore?" the driver asked.

"Three times," said Trout. It was true. Not only that, but each of his wives had been extraordinarily patient and loving and beautiful. Each had been shriveled by his pessimism.

"Any kids?"

"One," said Trout. Somewhere in the past, tumbling among all the wives and stories lost in the mails was a son named Leo. "He's a man now," said Trout.

• • •

Leo left home forever at the age of fourteen. He lied about his age, and he joined the Marines. He sent a note to his father from boot camp. It said this: "I pity you. You've crawled up your own asshole and died."

That was the last Trout heard from Leo, directly or indirectly, until he was visited by two agents from the Federal Bureau of Investigation. Leo had deserted from his division in Viet Nam, they said. He had committed high treason. He had joined the Viet Cong.

Here was the F.B.I. evaluation of Leo's situation on the planet at that time: "Your boy's in bad trouble," they said.

Chapter 13

WHEN DWAYNE HOOVER saw Harry LeSabre, his sales manager, in leaf-green leotards and a grass skirt and all that, he could not believe it. So he made himself not see it. He went into his office, which was also cluttered with ukuleles and pineapples.

Francine Pefko, his secretary, looked normal, except that she had a rope of flowers around her neck and a flower behind one ear. She smiled. This was a war widow with lips like sofa pillows and bright red hair. She adored Dwayne. She adored Hawaiian Week, too.

"Aloha," she said.

•   •   •

Harry LeSabre, meanwhile, had been destroyed by Dwayne.

When Harry presented himself to Dwayne so ridiculously, every molecule in his body awaited Dwayne's reaction. Each molecule ceased its business for a moment, put some distance between itself and its neighbors. Each molecule waited to learn whether its galaxy, which was called *Harry LeSabre*, would or would not be dissolved.

When Dwayne treated Harry as though he were invisible, Harry thought he had revealed himself as a revolting transvestite, and that he was fired on that account.

Harry closed his eyes. He never wanted to open them again. His heart sent this message to his molecules: "For reasons obvious to us all, this galaxy is *dissolved*!"

•   •   •

Dwayne didn't know anything about that. He leaned on Francine Pefko's desk. He came close to telling her how sick he was. He warned her: "This is a very tough day, for some reason. So no jokes, no surprises. Keep everything simple. Keep anybody the least bit nutty out of here. No telephone calls."

Francine told Dwayne that the twins were waiting for him in

the inner office. "Something bad is happening to the cave, I think," she told him.

Dwayne was grateful for a message that simple and clear. The twins were his younger stepbrothers, Lyle and Kyle Hoover. The cave was Sacred Miracle Cave, a tourist trap just south of Shepherdstown, which Dwayne owned in partnership with Lyle and Kyle. It was the sole source of income for Lyle and Kyle, who lived in identical yellow ranch houses on either side of the gift shop which sheltered the entrance to the cave.

All over the State, nailed to trees and fence posts, were arrow-shaped signs, which pointed in the direction of the cave and said how far away it was—for example:

Before Dwayne entered his inner office, he read one of many comical signs which Francine had put up on the wall in order to amuse people, to remind them of what they so easily forgot: that people didn't have to be serious all the time.

Here was the text of the sign Dwayne read:

> YOU DON'T HAVE TO BE CRAZY
> TO WORK HERE, BUT IT SURE HELPS!

There was a picture of a crazy person to go with the text. This was it:

Francine wore a button on her bosom which showed a creature in a healthier, more enviable frame of mind. This was the button:

. . .

Lyle and Kyle sat side-by-side on the black leather couch in Dwayne Hoover's inner office. They looked so much alike that Dwayne had not been able to tell them apart until 1954, when Lyle got in a fight over a woman at the Roller Derby. After that, Lyle was the one with the broken nose. As babies in crib, Dwayne remembered now, they used to suck each other's thumbs.

. . .

Here is how Dwayne happened to have stepbrothers, incidentally, even though he had been adopted by people who couldn't have children of their own. Their adopting him triggered something to their bodies which made it possible for them to have children after all. This was a common phenomenon. A lot of couples seemed to be programmed that way.

• • •

Dwayne was so glad to see them now—these two little men in overalls and work shoes, each wearing a pork-pie hat. They were familiar, they were *real*. Dwayne closed his door on the chaos outside. "All right—" he said, "what's happened at the cave?"

Ever since Lyle had had his nose broken, the twins agreed that Lyle should do the talking for the two. Kyle hadn't said a thousand words since 1954.

"Them bubbles is halfway up to the *Cathedral* now," said Lyle. "The way they're coming, they'll be up to *Moby Dick* in a week or two."

Dwayne understood him perfectly. The underground stream which passed through the bowels of Sacred Miracle Cave was polluted by some sort of industrial waste which formed bubbles as tough as ping-pong balls. These bubbles were shouldering one another up a passage which led to a big boulder which had been painted white to resemble *Moby Dick, the Great White Whale*. The bubbles would soon engulf *Moby Dick* and invade the *Cathedral of Whispers*, which was the main attraction at the cave. Thousands of people had been married in the *Cathedral of Whispers*—including Dwayne and Lyle and Kyle. Harry LeSabre, too.

• • •

Lyle told Dwayne about an experiment he and Kyle had performed the night before. They had gone into the cave with their identical Browning Automatic Shotguns, and they had opened fire on the advancing wall of bubbles.

"They let loose a stink you wouldn't believe," said Lyle. He said it smelled like athlete's foot. "It drove me and Kyle right out of there. We run the ventilating system for an hour, and then we went back in. The paint was blistered on *Moby Dick*.

He ain't even got eyes anymore." *Moby Dick* used to have long-lashed blue eyes as big as dinner plates.

•   •   •

"The organ turned black, and the ceiling turned a kind of dirty yellow," said Lyle. "You can't hardly see the *Sacred Miracle* no more."

The organ was the *Pipe Organ of the Gods*, a thicket of stalactites and stalagmites which had grown together in one corner of the *Cathedral*. There was a loudspeaker in back of it, through which music for weddings and funerals was played. It was illuminated by electric lights, which changed colors all the time.

The *Sacred Miracle* was a cross on the ceiling of the *Cathedral*. It was formed by the intersection of two cracks. "It never *was* real easy to see," said Lyle, speaking of the cross. "I ain't even sure it's there anymore." He asked Dwayne's permission to order a load of cement. He wanted to plug up the passage between the stream and the Cathedral.

"Just forget about *Moby Dick* and *Jesse James* and the slaves and all that," said Lyle, "and save the *Cathedral*."

Jesse James was a skeleton which Dwayne's stepfather had bought from the estate of a doctor back during the Great Depression. The bones of its right hand mingled with the rusted parts of a .45 caliber revolver. Tourists were told that it had been found that way, that it probably belonged to some railroad robber who had been trapped in the cave by a rockslide.

As for the slaves: these were plaster statues of black men in a chamber fifty feet down the corridor from *Jesse James*. The statues were removing one another's chains with hammers and hacksaws. Tourists were told that real slaves had at one time used the cave after escaping to freedom across the Ohio River.

•   •   •

The story about the slaves was as fake as the one about Jesse James. The cave wasn't discovered until 1937, when a small earthquake opened it up a crack. Dwayne Hoover himself discovered the crack, and then he and his stepfather opened it with crowbars and dynamite. Before that, not even small animals had been in there.

The only connection the cave had with slavery was this: the farm on which it was discovered was started by an ex-slave, Josephus Hoobler. He was freed by his master, and he came north and started the farm. Then he went back and bought his mother and a woman who became his wife.

Their descendants continued to run the farm until the Great Depression, when the Midland County Merchants Bank foreclosed on the mortgage. And then Dwayne's stepfather was hit by an automobile driven by a white man who had bought the farm. In an out-of-court settlement for his injuries, Dwayne's stepfather was given what he called contemptuously ". . . a God damn Nigger farm."

Dwayne remembered the first trip the family took to see it. His father ripped a Nigger sign off the Nigger mailbox, and he threw it into a ditch. Here is what it said:

Chapter 14

THE TRUCK carrying Kilgore Trout was in West Virginia now. The surface of the State had been demolished by men and machinery and explosives in order to make it yield up its coal. The coal was mostly gone now. It had been turned into heat.

The surface of West Virginia, with its coal and trees and top-soil gone, was rearranging what was left of itself in conformity with the laws of gravity. It was collapsing into all the holes which had been dug into it. Its mountains, which had once found it easy to stand by themselves, were sliding into valleys now.

The demolition of West Virginia had taken place with the approval of the executive, legislative, and judicial branches of the State Government, which drew their power from the people.

Here and there an inhabited dwelling still stood.

• • •

Trout saw a broken guardrail ahead. He gazed into a gully below it, saw a 1968 Cadillac *El Dorado* capsized in a brook. It had Alabama license plates. There were also several old home appliances in the brook—stoves, a washing machine, a couple of refrigerators.

An angel-faced white child, with flaxen hair, stood by the brook. She waved up at Trout. She clasped an eighteen-ounce bottle of *Pepsi-Cola* to her breast.

• • •

Trout asked himself out loud what the people did for amusement, and the driver told him a queer story about a night he spent in West Virginia, in the cab of his truck, near a windowless building which droned monotonously.

"I'd see folks go in, and I'd see folks come out," he said, "but I couldn't figure out what kind of a machine it was that made the drone. The building was a cheap old frame thing set up on cement blocks, and it was out in the middle of nowhere. Cars came and went, and the folks sure seemed to like whatever was doing the droning," he said.

So he had a look inside. "It was full of folks on roller-skates," he said. "They went around and around. Nobody smiled. They just went around and around."

• • •

He told Trout about people he'd heard of in the area who grabbed live copperheads and rattlesnakes during church services, to show how much they believed that Jesus would protect them.

"Takes all kinds of people to make up a world," said Trout.

• • •

Trout marveled at how recently white men had arrived in West Virginia, and how quickly they had demolished it—for heat.

Now the heat was all gone, too—into outer space, Trout supposed. It had boiled water, and the steam had made steel windmills whiz around and around. The windmills had made rotors in generators whiz around and around. America was jazzed with electricity for a while. Coal had also powered old-fashioned steamboats and choo-choo trains.

• • •

Choo-choo trains and steamboats and factories had whistles which were blown by steam when Dwayne Hoover and Kilgore Trout and I were boys—when our fathers were boys, when our grandfathers were boys. The whistles looked like this:

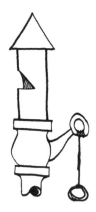

Steam from water boiled by burning coal was sent raging through the whistles, which made harshly beautiful laments, as though they were the voice boxes of mating or dying dinosaurs—cries such as *woooooooo-uh*, *wooooo-uh*, and *torrrrrrrrrr-rrrrrrrrrrrrrrrrrrnnnnnnnnnnnn*, and so on.

•   •   •

A dinosaur was a reptile as big as a choo-choo train. It looked like this:

It had two brains, one for its front end and one for its rear end. It was extinct. Both brains combined were smaller than a pea. A pea was a legume which looked like this:

Coal was a highly compressed mixture of rotten trees and flowers and bushes and grasses and so on, and dinosaur excrement.

•   •   •

Kilgore Trout thought about the cries of steam whistles he had known, and about the destruction of West Virginia, which made their songs possible. He supposed that the heart-rending cries had fled into outer space, along with the heat. He was mistaken.

Like most science-fiction writers, Trout knew almost nothing about science, was bored stiff by technical details. But no cry from a whistle had got very far from Earth for this reason: sound could only travel in an atmosphere, and the atmosphere of Earth relative to the planet wasn't even as thick as the skin of an apple. Beyond that lay an all-but-perfect vacuum.

An apple was a popular fruit which looked like this:

• • •

The driver was a big eater. He pulled into a McDonald's Hamburger establishment. There were many different chains of hamburger establishments in the country. *McDonald's* was one. *Burger Chef* was another. Dwayne Hoover, as has already been said, owned franchises for several *Burger Chefs.*

• • •

A hamburger was made out of an animal which looked like this:

The animal was killed and ground up into little bits, then shaped into patties and fried, and put between two pieces of bread. The finished product looked like this:

• • •

And Trout, who had so little money left, ordered a cup of coffee. He asked an old, old man on a stool next to him at the table if he had worked in the coal mines.

The old man said this: "From the time I was ten till I was sixty-two."

"You glad to be out of 'em?" said Trout.

"Oh, God," said the man, "you never get out of 'em—even when you sleep. I *dream* mines."

Trout asked him what it had felt like to work for an industry whose business was to destroy the countryside, and the old man said he was usually too tired to care.

• • •

"Don't matter if you care," the old miner said, "if you don't own what you care about." He pointed out that the mineral rights to the entire county in which they sat were owned by the Rosewater Coal and Iron Company, which had acquired these rights soon after the end of the Civil War. "The law says," he went on, "when a man owns something under the ground and he wants to get at it, you got to let him tear up anything between the surface and what he owns."

Trout did not make the connection between the Rosewater Coal and Iron Company and Eliot Rosewater, his only fan. He still thought Eliot Rosewater was a teenager.

The truth was that Rosewater's ancestors had been among the principal destroyers of the surface and the people of West Virginia.

• • •

"It don't seem right, though," the old miner said to Trout, "that a man can own what's underneath another man's farm or woods or house. And any time the man wants to get what's underneath all that, he's got a right to wreck what's on top to get at it. The rights of the people on top of the ground don't amount to nothing compared to the rights of the man who owns what's underneath."

He remembered out loud when he and other miners used to try to force the Rosewater Coal and Iron Company to treat them like human beings. They would fight small wars with the company's private police and the State Police and the National Guard.

"I never saw a Rosewater," he said, "but Rosewater always won. I walked on Rosewater. I dug holes for Rosewater in Rosewater. I lived in Rosewater houses. I ate Rosewater food. I'd fight Rosewater, whatever Rosewater is, and Rosewater would beat me and leave me for dead. You ask people around here and they'll tell you: this whole world is Rosewater as far as *they're* concerned."

• • •

The driver knew Trout was bound for Midland City. He didn't know Trout was a writer on his way to an arts festival. Trout understood that honest working people had no use for the arts.

"Why would anybody in his right mind go to Midland City?" the driver wanted to know. They were riding along again.

"My sister is sick," said Trout.

"Midland City is the asshole of the Universe," said the driver.

"I've often wondered where the asshole was," said Trout.

"If it isn't in Midland City," said the driver, "it's in Libertyville, Georgia. You ever see Libertyville?"

"No," said Trout.

"I was arrested for speeding down there. They had a speed trap, where you all of a sudden had to go from fifty down to fifteen miles an hour. It made me mad. I had some words with the policeman, and he put me in jail.

"The main industry there was pulping up old newspapers and magazines and books, and making new paper out of 'em," said the driver. "Trucks and trains were bringing in hundreds of tons of unwanted printed material every day."

"Um," said Trout.

"And the unloading process was sloppy, so there were pieces of books and magazines and so on blowing all over town. If you wanted to start a library, you could just go over to the freight yard, and carry away all the books you wanted."

"Um," said Trout. Up ahead was a white man hitchhiking with his pregnant wife and nine children.

"Looks like Gary Cooper, don't he?" said the truck driver of the hitchhiking man.

"Yes, he does," said Trout. Gary Cooper was a movie star.

• • •

"Anyway," said the driver, "they had so many books in Libertyville, they used books for toilet paper in the jail. They got me on a Friday, late in the afternoon, so I couldn't have a hearing in court until Monday. So I sat there in the calaboose for two days, with nothing to do but read my toilet paper. I can still remember one of the stories I read."

"Um," said Trout.

"That was the *last* story I ever read," said the driver. "My God—that must be all of fifteen years ago. The story was about another planet. It was a crazy story. They had museums full of paintings all over the place, and the government used a kind of roulette wheel to decide what to put in the museums, and what to throw out."

Kilgore Trout was suddenly woozy with *déjà vu*. The truck driver was reminding him of the premise of a book he hadn't thought about for years. The driver's toilet paper in Libertyville, Georgia, had been *The Barring-gaffner of Bagnialto, or This Year's Masterpiece*, by Kilgore Trout.

• • •

The name of the planet where Trout's book took place was *Bagnialto*, and a "Barring-gaffner" there was a government official who spun a wheel of chance once a year. Citizens submitted works of art to the government, and these were given numbers, and then they were assigned cash values according to the Barring-gaffner's spins of the wheel.

The viewpoint of character of the tale was not the Barring-gaffner, but a humble cobbler named Gooz. Gooz lived alone, and he painted a picture of his cat. It was the only picture he had ever painted. He took it to the Barring-gaffner, who numbered it and put it in a warehouse crammed with works of art.

The painting by Gooz had an unprecedented gush of luck on the wheel. It became worth eighteen thousand *lambos*, the equivalent of one billion dollars on Earth. The Barring-gaffner awarded Gooz a check for that amount, most of which was taken back at once by the tax collector. The picture was given a place of honor in the National Gallery, and people lined up for miles for a chance to see a painting worth a billion dollars.

There was also a huge bonfire of all the paintings and statues and books and so on which the wheel had said were worthless. And then it was discovered that the wheel was rigged, and the Barring-gaffner committed suicide.

• • •

It was an amazing coincidence that the truck driver had read a book by Kilgore Trout. Trout had never met a reader before, and his response now was interesting: He did not admit that he was the father of the book.

• • •

The driver pointed out that all the mailboxes in the area had the same last name painted on them.

"There's another one," he said, indicating a mailbox which looked like this:

The truck was passing through the area where Dwayne Hoover's stepparents had come from. They had trekked from West Virginia to Midland City during the First World War, to make big money at the Keedsler Automobile Company, which was manufacturing airplanes and trucks. When they got to Midland City, they had their name changed legally from *Hoobler* to *Hoover*, because there were so many black people in Midland City named Hoobler.

As Dwayne Hoover's stepfather explained to him one time, "It was embarrassing. Everybody up here naturally assumed Hoobler was a *Nigger* name."

Chapter 15

Dwayne Hoover got through lunch all right that day. He remembered now about Hawaiian Week. The ukuleles and so on were no longer mysterious. The pavement between his automobile agency and the new Holiday Inn was no longer a trampoline.

He drove to lunch alone in an air-conditioned demonstrator, a blue Pontiac *Le Mans* with a cream interior, with his radio on. He heard several of his own radio commercials, which drove home the point: "You can always trust Dwayne."

Though his mental health had improved remarkably since breakfast, a new symptom of illness made itself known. It was incipient echolalia. Dwayne found himself wanting to repeat out loud whatever had just been said.

So when the radio told him, "You can always trust Dwayne," he echoed the last word. "Dwayne," he said.

When the radio said there had been a tornado in Texas, Dwayne said this out loud: "Texas."

Then he heard that husbands of women who had been raped during the war between India and Pakistan wouldn't have anything to do with their wives anymore. The women, in the eyes of their husbands, had become *unclean*, said the radio.

"Unclean," said Dwayne.

• • •

As for Wayne Hoobler, the black ex-convict whose only dream was to work for Dwayne Hoover: he had learned to play hide-and-seek with Dwayne's employees. He did not wish to be ordered off the property for hanging around the used cars. So, when an employee came near, Wayne would wander off to the garbage and trash area behind the Holiday Inn, and gravely study the remains of club sandwiches and empty packs of Salem cigarettes and so on in the cans back there, as though he were a health inspector or some such thing.

When the employee went away, Wayne would drift back to the used cars, keeping the boiled eggs of his eyes peeled for the real Dwayne Hoover.

604

The real Dwayne Hoover, of course, had in effect denied that he was Dwayne. So, when the real Dwayne came out at lunch time, Wayne, who had nobody to talk to but himself, said this to himself: "That ain't Mr. Hoover. Sure *look* like Mr. Hoover, though. Maybe Mr. Hoover sick today." And so on.

• • •

Dwayne had a hamburger and French fries and a Coke at his newest Burger Chef, which was out on Crestview Avenue, across the street from where the new John F. Kennedy High School was going up. John F. Kennedy had never been in Midland City, but he was a President of the United States who was shot to death. Presidents of the country were often shot to death. The assassins were confused by some of the same bad chemicals which troubled Dwayne.

• • •

Dwayne certainly wasn't alone, as far as having bad chemicals inside of him was concerned. He had plenty of company throughout all history. In his own lifetime, for instance, the people in a country called Germany were so full of bad chemicals for a while that they actually built factories whose only purpose was to kill people by the millions. The people were delivered by railroad trains.

When the Germans were full of bad chemicals, their flag looked like this:

Here is what their flag looked like after they got well again:

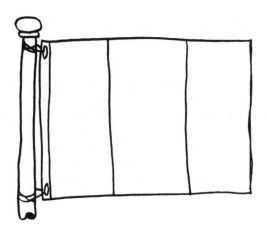

After they got well again, they manufactured a cheap and durable automobile which became popular all over the world, especially among young people. It looked like this:

People called it "the beetle." A real beetle looked like this:

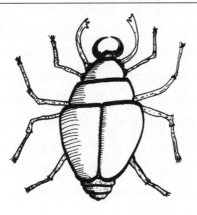

The mechanical beetle was made by Germans. The real beetle was made by the Creator of the Universe.

• • •

Dwayne's waitress at the Burger Chef was a seventeen-year-old white girl named Patty Keene. Her hair was yellow. Her eyes were blue. She was very old for a mammal. Most mammals were senile or dead by the time they were seventeen. But Patty was a sort of mammal which developed very slowly, so the body she rode around in was only now mature.

She was a brand-new adult, who was working in order to pay off the tremendous doctors' and hospital bills her father had run up in the process of dying of cancer of the colon and then cancer of the everything.

This was in a country where everybody was expected to pay his own bills for everything, and one of the most expensive things a person could do was get sick. Patty Keene's father's sickness cost ten times as much as all the trips to Hawaii which Dwayne was going to give away at the end of Hawaiian Week.

• • •

Dwayne appreciated Patty Keene's brand-newness, even though he was not sexually attracted to women that young.

She was like a new automobile, which hadn't even had its radio turned on yet, and Dwayne was reminded of a ditty his father would sing sometimes when his father was drunk. It went like this:

> *Roses are red,*
> *And ready for plucking.*
> *You're sixteen,*
> *And ready for high school.*

Patty Keene was stupid on purpose, which was the case with most women in Midland City. The women all had big minds because they were big animals, but they did not use them much for this reason: unusual ideas could make enemies, and the women, if they were going to achieve any sort of comfort and safety, needed all the friends they could get.

So, in the interests of survival, they trained themselves to be agreeing machines instead of thinking machines. All their minds had to do was to discover what other people were thinking, and then they thought that, too.

• • •

Patty knew who Dwayne was. Dwayne didn't know who Patty was. Patty's heart beat faster when she waited on him— because Dwayne could solve so many of her problems with the money and power he had. He could give her a fine house and new automobiles and nice clothes and a life of leisure, and he could pay all the medical bills—as easily as she had given him his hamburger and his French fries and his Coke.

Dwayne could do for her what the Fairy Godmother did for Cinderella, if he wanted to, and Patty had never been so close to such a magical person before. She was in the presence of the supernatural. And she knew enough about Midland City and herself to understand that she might never be this close to the supernatural ever again.

Patty Keene actually imagined Dwayne's waving a magic wand at her troubles and dreams. It looked like this:

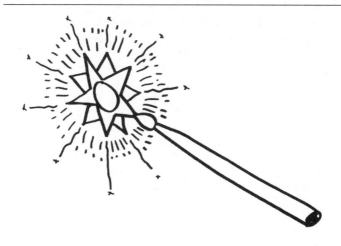

She spoke up bravely, to learn if supernatural assistance was possible in her case. She was willing to do without it, expected to do without it—to work hard all her life, to get not much in return, and to associate with other men and women who were poor and powerless, and in debt. She said this to Dwayne:

"Excuse me for calling you by name, Mr. Hoover, but I can't help knowing who you are, with your picture in all your ads and everything. Besides—everybody else who works here told me who you were. When you came in, they just buzzed and buzzed."

"Buzzed," said Dwayne. This was his echolalia again.

• • •

"I guess that isn't the right word," she said. She was used to apologizing for her use of language. She had been encouraged to do a lot of that in school. Most white people in Midland City were insecure when they spoke, so they kept their sentences short and their words simple, in order to keep embarrassing mistakes to a minimum. Dwayne certainly did that. Patty certainly did that.

This was because their English teachers would wince and cover their ears and give them flunking grades and so on whenever they failed to speak like English aristocrats before the First World War. Also: they were told that they were unworthy to speak or write their language if they couldn't love or understand incomprehensible novels and poems and plays about people long ago and far away, such as *Ivanhoe*.

•   •   •

The black people would not put up with this. They went on talking English every *which* way. They refused to read books they couldn't understand—on the grounds they couldn't understand them. They would ask such impudent questions as, "Whuffo I want to read no *Tale of Two Cities*? Whuffo?"

•   •   •

Patty Keene flunked English during the semester when she had to read and appreciate *Ivanhoe*, which was about men in iron suits and the women who loved them. And she was put in a remedial reading class, where they made her read *The Good Earth*, which was about Chinamen.

It was during this same semester that she lost her virginity. She was raped by a white gas-conversion unit installer named Don Breedlove in the parking lot outside the Bannister Memorial Fieldhouse at the County Fairgrounds after the Regional High School Basketball Playoffs. She never reported it to the police. She never reported it to anybody, since her father was dying at the time.

There was enough trouble already.

•   •   •

The Bannister Memorial Fieldhouse was named in honor of George Hickman Bannister, a seventeen-year-old boy who was killed while playing high school football in 1924. George Hickman Bannister had the largest tombstone in Calvary Cemetery, a sixty-two-foot obelisk with a marble football on top.

The marble football looked like this:

Football was a war game. Two opposing teams fought over the ball while wearing armor made out of leather and cloth and plastic.

George Hickman Bannister was killed while trying to get a hold of the ball on Thanksgiving Day. Thanksgiving Day was a holiday when everybody in the country was expected to express gratitude to the Creator of the Universe, mainly for food.

• • •

George Hickman Bannister's obelisk was paid for by public subscription, with the Chamber of Commerce matching every two dollars raised with a dollar of its own. It was for many years the tallest structure in Midland City. A city ordinance was passed which made it illegal to erect anything taller than that, and it was called *The George Hickman Bannister Law*.

The ordinance was junked later on to allow radio towers to go up.

• • •

The two largest monuments in town, until the new Mildred Barry Memorial Arts Center went up in Sugar Creek, were constructed supposedly so that George Hickman Bannister would never be forgotten. But nobody ever thought about him anymore by the time Dwayne Hoover met Kilgore Trout. There wasn't much to think about him, actually, even at the time of his death, except that he was young.

And he didn't have any relatives in town anymore. There weren't any Bannisters in the phone book, except for *The Bannister*, which was a motion picture theater. Actually, there wouldn't even be a *Bannister Theater* in there after the new phonebooks came out. The Bannister had been turned into a cut-rate furniture store.

George Hickman Bannister's father and mother and sister, Lucy, moved away from town before either the tombstone or the fieldhouse was completed, and they couldn't be located for the dedication ceremonies.

•   •   •

It was a very restless country, with people tearing around all the time. Every so often, somebody would stop to put up a monument.

There were monuments all over the country. But it was certainly unusual for somebody from the common people to have not one but *two* monuments in his honor, as was the case with George Hickman Bannister.

Technically, though, only the tombstone had been erected specifically for him. The fieldhouse would have gone up anyway. The money was appropriated for the fieldhouse two years before George Hickman Bannister was cut down in his prime. It didn't cost anything extra to name it after him.

•   •   •

Calvary Cemetery, where George Hickman Bannister was at rest, was named in honor of a hill in Jerusalem, thousands of miles away. Many people believed that the son of the Creator of the Universe had been killed on that hill thousands of years ago.

Dwayne Hoover didn't know whether to believe that or not. Neither did Patty Keene.

•   •   •

And they certainly weren't worrying about it now. They had other fish to fry. Dwayne was wondering how long his attack of echolalia was likely to last, and Patty Keene had to find out if her brand-newness and prettiness and outgoing personality were worth a lot to a sweet, sort of sexy, middle-aged old Pontiac dealer like Dwayne.

"Anyway," she said, "it certainly is an honor to have you visit us, and those aren't the right words, either, but I hope you know what I mean."

"Mean," said Dwayne.

"Is the food all right?" she said.

"All right," said Dwayne.

"It's what everybody else gets," she said. "We didn't do anything special for you."

"You," said Dwayne.

• • •

It didn't matter much what Dwayne said. It hadn't mattered much for years. It didn't matter much what most people in Midland City said out loud, except when they were talking about money or structures or travel or machinery—or other measurable things. Every person had a clearly defined part to play—as a black person, a female high school drop-out, a Pontiac dealer, a gynecologist, a gas-conversion burner installer. If a person stopped living up to expectations, because of bad chemicals or one thing or another, everybody went on imagining that the person was living up to expectations anyway.

That was the main reason the people in Midland City were so slow to detect insanity in their associates. Their imaginations insisted that nobody changed much from day to day. Their imaginations were flywheels on the ramshackle machinery of the awful truth.

• • •

When Dwayne left Patty Keene and his Burger Chef, when he got into his demonstrator and drove away, Patty Keene was persuaded that she could make him happy with her young body, with her bravery and cheerfulness. She wanted to cry about the lines in his face, and the fact that his wife had eaten Drāno, and that his dog had to fight all the time because it couldn't wag its tail, about the fact that his son was a homosexual. She knew all those things about Dwayne. Everybody knew those things about Dwayne.

She gazed at the tower of radio station WMCY, which Dwayne Hoover owned. It was the tallest structure in Midland City. It was eight times as tall as the tombstone of George Hickman Bannister. It had a red light on top of it—to keep airplanes away.

She thought about all the new and used cars Dwayne owned.

•   •   •

Earth scientists had just discovered something fascinating about the continent Patty Keene was standing on, incidentally. It was riding on a slab about forty miles thick, and the slab was drifting around on molten glurp. And all the other continents had slabs of their own. When one slab crashed into another one, mountains were made.

•   •   •

The mountains of West Virginia, for instance, were heaved up when a huge chunk of Africa crashed into North America. And the coal in the state was formed from forests which were buried by the crash.

Patty Keene hadn't heard the big news yet. Neither had Dwayne. Neither had Kilgore Trout. I only found out about it day before yesterday. I was reading a magazine, and I also had the television on. A group of scientists was on television, saying that the theory of floating, crashing, grinding slabs was more than a theory. They could prove it was true now, and that Japan and San Francisco, for instance, were in hideous danger, because that was where some of the most violent crashing and grinding was going on.

They said, too, that ice ages would continue to occur. Mile-thick glaciers would, geologically speaking, continue to go down and up like window blinds.

•   •   •

Dwayne Hoover, incidentally, had an unusually large penis, and didn't even know it. The few women he had had anything to do with weren't sufficiently experienced to know whether he was average or not. The world average was five and seven-eighths inches long, and one and one-half inches in diameter when engorged with blood. Dwayne's was seven inches long and two and one-eighth inches in diameter when engorged with blood.

Dwayne's son Bunny had a penis that was exactly average.

Kilgore Trout had a penis seven inches long, but only one and one-quarter inches in diameter.

This was an inch:

Harry LeSabre, Dwayne's sales manager, had a penis five inches long and two and one-eighth inches in diameter.

Cyprian Ukwende, the black physician from Nigeria, had a penis six and seven-eighths inches long and one and three-quarters inches in diameter.

Don Breedlove, the gas-conversion unit installer who raped Patty Keene, had a penis five and seven-eighths inches long and one and seven-eighths inches in diameter.

• • •

Patty Keene had thirty-four-inch hips, a twenty-six-inch waist, and a thirty-four-inch bosom.

Dwayne's late wife had thirty-six-inch hips, a twenty-eight-inch waist, and a thirty-eight-inch bosom when he married her. She had thirty-nine-inch hips, a thirty-one-inch waist, and a thirty-eight-inch bosom when she ate Drāno.

His mistress and secretary, Francine Pefko, had thirty-seven-inch hips, a thirty-inch waist, and a thirty-nine-inch bosom.

His stepmother at the time of her death had thirty-four-inch hips, a twenty-four-inch waist, and a thirty-three-inch bosom.

• • •

So Dwayne went from the Burger Chef to the construction site of the new high school. He was in no hurry to get back to his automobile agency, particularly since he had developed echolalia. Francine was perfectly capable of running the place herself, without any advice from Dwayne. He had trained her well.

So he kicked a little dirt down into the cellar hole. He spat down into it. He stepped into mud. It sucked off his right shoe. He dug the shoe out with his hands, and he wiped it. Then he leaned against an old apple tree while he put the shoe back on. This had all been farmland when Dwayne was a boy. There had been an apple orchard here.

•   •   •

Dwayne forgot all about Patty Keene, but she certainly hadn't forgotten him. She would get up enough nerve that night to call him on the telephone, but Dwayne wouldn't be home to answer. He would be in a padded cell in the County Hospital by then.

And Dwayne wandered over to admire a tremendous earth-moving machine which had cleared the site and dug the cellar hole. The machine was idle now, caked with mud. Dwayne asked a white workman how many horsepower drove the machine. All the workmen were white.

The workman said this: "I don't know how many horse-power, but I know what we call it."

"What do you call it?" said Dwayne, relieved to find his echolalia was subsiding.

"We call it *The Hundred-Nigger Machine*," said the workman. This had reference to a time when black men had done most of the heavy digging in Midland City.

•   •   •

The largest human penis in the United States was fourteen inches long and two and a half inches in diameter.

The largest human penis in the world was sixteen and seven-eighths inches long and two and one-quarter inches in diameter.

The blue whale, a sea mammal, had a penis ninety-six inches long and fourteen inches in diameter.

•   •   •

One time Dwayne Hoover got an advertisement through the mail for a penis-extender, made out of rubber. He could slip it over the end of his real penis, according to the ad, and thrill his wife or sweetheart with extra inches. They also wanted to sell him a lifelike rubber vagina for when he was lonesome.

• • •

Dwayne went back to work at about two in the afternoon, and he avoided everybody—because of his echolalia. He went into his inner office, and he ransacked his desk drawers for something to read or think about. He came across the brochure which offered him the penis-extender and the rubber vagina for lonesomeness. He had received it two months before. He still hadn't thrown it away.

The brochure also offered him motion pictures such as the ones Kilgore Trout had seen in New York. There were still photographs taken from the movies, and these caused the sex excitation center in Dwayne's brain to send nerve impulses down to an erection center in his spine.

The erection center caused the dorsal vein in his penis to tighten up, so blood could get in all right, but it couldn't get out again. It also relaxed the tiny arteries in his penis, so they filled up the spongy tissue of which Dwayne's penis was mainly composed, so that the penis got hard and stiff—like a plugged-up garden hose.

So Dwayne called Francine Pefko on the telephone, even though she was only eleven feet away. "Francine—?" he said.

"Yes?" she said.

Dwayne fought down his echolalia. "I am going to ask you to do something I have never asked you to do before. Promise me you'll say yes."

"I promise," she said.

"I want you to walk out of here with me this very moment," he said, "and come with me to the Quality Motor Court at Shepherdstown."

• • •

Francine Pefko was willing to go to the Quality Motor Court with Dwayne. It was her duty to go, she thought—especially since Dwayne seemed so depressed and jangled. But she couldn't simply walk away from her desk for the afternoon, since her desk was the nerve center of Dwayne Hoover's Exit Eleven Pontiac Village.

"You ought to have some crazy young teen-ager, who can rush off whenever you want her to," Francine told Dwayne.

"I don't want a crazy teen-ager," said Dwayne. "I want *you.*"

"Then you're going to have to be patient," said Francine. She went back to the Service Department, to beg Gloria Browning, the white cashier back there, to man her desk for a little while.

Gloria didn't want to do it. She had had a hysterectomy only a month before, at the age of twenty-five—after a botched abortion at the Ramada Inn down in Green County, on Route 53, across from the entrance to Pioneer Village State Park.

There was a mildly amazing coincidence here: the father of the destroyed fetus was Don Breedlove, the white gas-conversion unit installer who had raped Patty Keene in the parking lot of the Bannister Memorial Fieldhouse.

This was a man with a wife and three kids.

• • •

Francine had a sign on the wall over her desk, which had been given to her as a joke at the automobile agency's Christmas party at the new Holiday Inn the year before.

It spelled out the truth of her situation. This was it:

Gloria said she didn't want to man the nerve center. "I don't want to man anything," she said.

• • •

But Gloria took over Francine's desk anyway. "I don't have nerve enough to commit suicide," she said, "so I might as well do anything anybody says—in the service of mankind."

• • •

Dwayne and Francine headed for Shepherdstown in separate cars, so as not to call attention to their love affair. Dwayne was in a demonstrator again. Francine was in her own red GTO. GTO stood for *Gran Turismo Omologato*. She had a sticker on her bumper which said this:

It was certainly loyal of her to put that sticker on her car. She was always doing loyal things like that, always rooting for her man, always rooting for Dwayne.

And Dwayne tried to reciprocate in little ways. For instance, he had been reading articles and books on sexual intercourse recently. There was a sexual revolution going on in the country, and women were demanding that men pay more attention to women's pleasure during sexual intercourse, and not just think of themselves. The key to their pleasure, they said, and scientists backed them up, was the clitoris, a tiny meat cylinder which was right above the hole in women where men were supposed to stick their much larger cylinders.

Men were supposed to pay more attention to the clitoris, and Dwayne had been paying a lot more attention to Francine's, to the point where she said he was paying too much attention to it. This did not surprise him. The things he had read about the clitoris had said that this was a danger—that a man could pay too much attention to it.

So, driving out to the Quality Motor Court that day, Dwayne was hoping that he would pay exactly the right amount of attention to Francine's clitoris.

•   •   •

Kilgore Trout once wrote a short novel about the importance of the clitoris in love-making. This was in response to a suggestion by his second wife, Darlene, that he could make a fortune with a dirty book. She told him that the hero should understand women so well that he could seduce anyone he wanted. So Trout wrote *The Son of Jimmy Valentine*.

Jimmy Valentine was a famous made-up person in another writer's books, just as Kilgore Trout was a famous made-up person in my books. Jimmy Valentine in the other writer's books sandpapered his fingertips, so they were extrasensitive. He was a safe-cracker. His sense of feel was so delicate that he could open any safe in the world by feeling the tumblers fall.

Kilgore Trout invented a son for Jimmy Valentine, named Ralston Valentine. Ralston Valentine also sandpapered his fingertips. But he wasn't a safe-cracker. Ralston was so good at touching women the way they wanted to be touched, that tens of thousands of them became his willing slaves. They abandoned their husbands or lovers for him, in Trout's story, and Ralston Valentine became President of the United States, thanks to the votes of women.

•   •   •

Dwayne and Francine made love in the Quality Motor Court. Then they stayed in bed for a while. It was a water bed. Francine had a beautiful body. So did Dwayne. "We never made love in the afternoon before," said Francine.

"I felt so *tense*," said Dwayne.

"I know," said Francine. "Are you better now?"

"Yes." He was lying on his back. His ankles were crossed. His hands were folded behind his head. His great wang lay across his thigh like a salami. It slumbered now.

"I love you so much," said Francine. She corrected herself. "I know I promised not to say that, but that's a promise I can't help breaking all the time." The thing was: Dwayne had made a pact with her that neither one of them was ever to mention love. Since Dwayne's wife had eaten Drāno, Dwayne never wanted to hear about love ever again. The subject was too painful.

Dwayne snuffled. It was customary for him to communicate by means of snuffles after sexual intercourse. The snuffles all had meanings which were bland: "That's all right . . . forget it . . . who could blame you?" And so on.

"On Judgment Day," said Francine, "when they ask me what bad things I did down here, I'm going to have to tell them, 'Well—there was a promise I made to a man I loved, and I broke it all the time. I promised him never to say I loved him.'"

This generous, voluptuous woman, who had only ninety-six dollars and eleven cents a week in take-home pay, had lost her husband, Robert Pefko, in a war in Viet Nam. He was a career officer in the Army. He had a penis six and one-half inches long and one and seven-eighths inches in diameter.

He was a graduate of West Point, a military academy which turned young men into homicidal maniacs for use in war.

•   •   •

Francine followed Robert from West Point to Parachute School at Fort Bragg, and then to South Korea, where Robert managed a Post Exchange, which was a department store for soldiers, and then to the University of Pennsylvania, where Robert took a Master's Degree in Anthropology, at Army expense, and then back to West Point, where Robert was an Assistant Professor of Social Sciences for three years.

After that, Francine followed Robert to Midland City, where Robert oversaw the manufacture of a new sort of booby trap. A booby trap was an easily hidden explosive device, which blew up when it was accidentally twiddled in some way. One of the virtues of the new type of booby trap was that it could not be smelled by dogs. Various armies at that time were training dogs to sniff out booby traps.

•   •   •

When Robert and Francine were in Midland City, there weren't any other military people around, so they made their first civilian friends. And Francine took a job with Dwayne Hoover, in order to augment her husband's salary and fill her days.

But then Robert was sent to Viet Nam.

Shortly after that, Dwayne's wife ate Drāno and Robert was shipped home in a plastic body bag.

•   •   •

"I pity men," said Francine, there in the Quality Motor Court. She was sincere. "I wouldn't want to be a man—they take such chances, they work so hard." They were on the second floor of the motel. Their sliding glass doors gave them a view of an iron railing and a concrete terrace outside—and then Route 103, and then the wall and the rooftops of the Adult Correctional Institution beyond that.

"I don't wonder you're tired and nervous," Francine went on. "If I was a man, I'd be tired and nervous, too. I guess God made women so men could relax and be treated like little babies from time to time." She was more than satisfied with this arrangement.

Dwayne snuffled. The air was rich with the smell of raspberries, which was the perfume in the disinfectant and roach-killer the motel used.

Francine mused about the prison, where the guards were all white and most of the prisoners were black. "Is it true," she said, "that nobody ever escaped from there?"

"It's true," said Dwayne.

•   •   •

"When was the last time they used the electric chair?" said Francine. She was asking about a device in the basement of the prison, which looked like this:

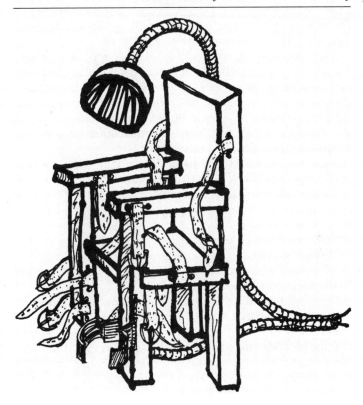

The purpose of it was to kill people by jazzing them with more electricity than their bodies could stand. Dwayne Hoover had seen it twice—once during a tour of the prison by members of the Chamber of Commerce years ago, and then again when it was actually used on a black human being he knew.

• • •

Dwayne tried to remember when the last execution took place at Shepherdstown. Executions had become unpopular. There were signs that they might become popular again. Dwayne and Francine tried to remember the most recent electrocution anywhere in the country which had stuck in their minds.

They remembered the double execution of a man and wife

for treason. The couple had supposedly given secrets about how to make a hydrogen bomb to another country.

They remembered the double execution of a man and woman who were lovers. The man was good-looking and sexy, and he used to seduce ugly old women who had money, and then he and the woman he really loved would kill the women for their money. The woman he really loved was young, but she certainly wasn't pretty in the conventional sense. She weighed two hundred and forty pounds.

Francine wondered out loud why a thin, good-looking young man would love a woman that heavy.

"It takes all kinds," said Dwayne.

• • •

"You know what I keep thinking?" said Francine.

Dwayne snuffled.

"This would be a very good location for a Colonel Sanders Kentucky Fried Chicken franchise."

Dwayne's relaxed body contracted as though each muscle in it had been stung by a drop of lemon juice.

Here was the problem: Dwayne wanted Francine to love him for his body and soul, not for what his money could buy. He thought Francine was hinting that he should buy her a Colonel Sanders Kentucky Fried Chicken franchise, which was a scheme for selling fried chicken.

A chicken was a flightless bird which looked like this:

The idea was to kill it and pull out all its feathers, and cut off its head and feet and scoop out its internal organs—and then chop it into pieces and fry the pieces, and put the pieces in a waxed paper bucket with a lid on it, so it looked like this:

• • •

Francine, who had been so proud of her capacity to make Dwayne relax, was now ashamed to have made him tighten up again. He was as rigid as an ironing board. "Oh my God—" she said, "what's the matter now?"

"If you're going to ask me for presents," said Dwayne, "just do me a favor—and don't hint around right after we've made love. Let's keep love-making and presents separate. O.K.?"

"I don't even know what you think I asked for," said Francine.

Dwayne mimicked her cruelly in a falsetto voice: "'I don't even know what you think I asked you for,'" he said. He looked about as pleasant and relaxed as a coiled rattlesnake now. It was his bad chemicals, of course, which were compelling him to look like that. A real rattlesnake looked like this:

The Creator of the Universe had put a rattle on its tail. The Creator had also given it front teeth which were hypodermic syringes filled with deadly poison.

•　•　•

Sometimes I wonder about the Creator of the Universe.

•　•　•

Another animal invented by the Creator of the Universe was a Mexican beetle which could make a blank-cartridge gun out of its rear end. It could detonate its own farts and knock over other bugs with shock waves.

Word of Honor—I read about it in an article on strange animals in *Diners' Club Magazine*.

•　•　•

So Francine got off the bed in order not to share it with the seeming rattlesnake. She was aghast. All she could say over and over again was, "You're my *man*. You're my *man*." This meant that she was willing to agree about anything with Dwayne, to do anything for him, no matter how difficult or disgusting, to think up nice things to do for him that he didn't even notice, to die for him, if necessary, and so on.

She honestly tried to live that way. She couldn't imagine anything better to do. So she fell apart when Dwayne persisted in his nastiness. He told her that every woman was a whore, and every whore had her price, and Francine's price was what a Colonel Sanders Kentucky Fried Chicken franchise would cost, which would be well over one hundred thousand dollars by the time adequate parking and exterior lighting and all that was taken into consideration, and so on.

Francine replied in blubbering gibberish that she had never wanted the franchise for herself, that she had wanted it for Dwayne, that everything she wanted was for Dwayne. Some of the words came through. "I thought of all the people who come out here to visit their relatives in prison, and I realized how most of them were black, and I thought how much black people liked fried chicken," she said.

"So you want me to open a Nigger joint?" said Dwayne. And so on. So Francine now had the distinction of being the second close associate of Dwayne's who discovered how vile he could be.

"Harry LeSabre was right," said Francine. She was backed up against the cement block wall of the motel room now, with her fingers spread over her mouth. Harry LeSabre, of course, was Dwayne's transvestite sales manager. "He said you'd changed," said Francine. She made a cage of fingers around her mouth. "Oh, God, Dwayne—" she said, "you've changed, you've changed."

"Maybe it was time!" said Dwayne. "I never felt better in my life!" And so on.

• • •

Harry LeSabre was at that moment crying, too. He was at home—in bed. He had a purple velvet sheet over his head. He was well-to-do. He had invested in the stock market very intelligently and luckily over the years. He had bought one hundred shares of Xerox, for instance, for eight dollars a share. With the passage of time, his shares had become one hundred times as valuable, simply lying in the total darkness and silence of a safe-deposit box.

There was a lot of money magic like that going on. It was almost as though some blue fairy were flitting about that part of the dying planet, waving her magic wand over certain deeds and bonds and stock certificates.

• • •

Harry's wife, Grace, was stretched out on a chaise longue at some distance from the bed. She was smoking a small cigar in a long holder made from the legbone of a stork. A stork was a large European bird, about half the size of a Bermuda Ern. Children who wanted to know where babies came from were sometimes told that they were brought by storks. People who told their children such a thing felt that their children were too young to think intelligently about wide-open beavers and all that.

And there were actually pictures of storks delivering babies on birth announcements and in cartoons and so on, for children to see. A typical one might look like this:

Dwayne Hoover and Harry LeSabre saw pictures like that when they were very little boys. They believed them, too.

• • •

Grace LeSabre expressed her contempt for the good opinion of Dwayne Hoover, which her husband felt he had lost. "Fuck Dwayne Hoover," she said. "Fuck Midland City. Let's sell the God damn Xerox stock and buy a condominium on Maui." Maui was one of the Hawaiian Islands. It was widely believed to be a paradise.

"Listen," said Grace, "we're the only white people in Midland City with any kind of sex life, as nearly as I can tell. You're not a freak. Dwayne Hoover's the freak! How many orgasms do you think he has a month?"

"I don't know," said Harry from his humid tent.

Dwayne's monthly orgasm rate on the average over the past ten years, which included the last years of his marriage, was two and one-quarter. Grace's guess was close. "One point five," she said. Her own monthly average over the same period was eighty-seven. Her husband's average was thirty-six. He had been slowing up in recent years, which was one of many reasons he had for feeling panicky.

Grace now spoke loudly and scornfully about Dwayne's marriage. "He was so scared of sex," she said, "he married a woman who had never heard of the subject, who was guaranteed to destroy herself, if she ever *did* hear about it." And so on. "Which she finally did," she said.

• • •

"Can the reindeer hear you?" said Harry.

"Fuck the reindeer," said Grace. Then she added, "No, the reindeer cannot hear." *Reindeer* was their code word for the black maid, who was far away in the kitchen at the time. It was their code word for black people in general. It allowed them to speak of the black problem in the city, which was a big one, without giving offense to any black person who might overhear.

"The reindeer's asleep—or reading the *Black Panther Digest*," she said.

•   •   •

The reindeer problem was essentially this: Nobody white had much use for black people anymore—except for the gangsters who sold the black people used cars and dope and furniture. Still, the reindeer went on reproducing. There were these useless, big black animals everywhere, and a lot of them had very bad dispositions. They were given small amounts of money every month, so they wouldn't have to steal. There was talk of giving them very cheap dope, too—to keep them listless and cheerful, and uninterested in reproduction.

The Midland City Police Department, and the Midland County Sheriff's Department, were composed mainly of white men. They had racks and racks of sub-machine guns and twelve-gauge automatic shotguns for an open season on reindeer, which was bound to come.

"Listen—I'm serious," said Grace to Harry. "This is the asshole of the Universe. Let's split to a condominium on Maui and *live* for a change."

So they did.

•   •   •

Dwayne's bad chemicals meanwhile changed his manner toward Francine from nastiness to pitiful dependency. He apologized to her for ever thinking that she wanted a Colonel Sanders Kentucky Fried Chicken franchise. He gave her full credit for unflagging unselfishness. He begged her to just hold him for a while, which she did.

"I'm so confused," he said.

"We all are," she said. She cradled his head against her breasts.

"I've got to talk to somebody," said Dwayne.

"You can talk to Mommy, if you want," said Francine. She meant that *she* was *Mommy*.

"Tell me what life is all about," Dwayne begged her fragrant bosom.

"Only God knows that," said Francine.

•   •   •

Dwayne was silent for a while. And then he told her halt-ingly about a trip he had made to the headquarters of the Pontiac Division of General Motors at Pontiac, Michigan, only three months after his wife ate Drāno.

"We were given a tour of all the research facilities," he said. The thing that impressed him most, he said, was a series of lab-oratories and out-of-doors test areas where various parts of automobiles and even entire automobiles were destroyed. Pontiac scientists set upholstery on fire, threw gravel at wind-shields, snapped crankshafts and driveshafts, staged head-on collisions, tore gearshift levers out by the roots, ran engines at high speeds with almost no lubrication, opened and closed glove compartment doors a hundred times a minute for days, cooled dashboard clocks to within a few degrees of absolute zero, and so on.

"Everything you're not supposed to do to a car, they did to a car," Dwayne said to Francine. "And I'll never forget the sign on the front door of the building where all that torture went on." Here was the sign Dwayne described to Francine:

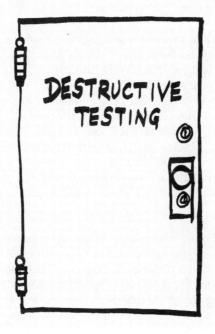

"I saw that sign," said Dwayne, "and I couldn't help wondering if that was what God put me on Earth for—to find out how much a man could take without breaking."

•   •   •

"I've lost my way," said Dwayne. "I need somebody to take me by the hand and lead me out of the woods."

"You're tired," she said. "Why wouldn't you be tired? You work *so* hard. I feel sorry for men, they work so hard. You want to sleep for a while?"

"I can't sleep," said Dwayne, "until I get some answers."

"You want to go to a doctor?" said Francine.

"I don't want to hear the kinds of things doctors say," said Dwayne. "I want to talk to somebody brand new. Francine," he said, and he dug his fingers into her soft arm, "I want to hear new things from new people. I've heard everything anybody in Midland City ever said, ever *will* say. It's got to be somebody new."

"Like who?" said Francine.

"I don't know," said Dwayne. "Somebody from Mars, maybe."

"We could go to some other city," said Francine.

"They're all like here. They're all the same," said Dwayne.

Francine had an idea. "What about all these painters and writers and composers coming to town?" she said. "You never talked to anybody like that before. Maybe you should talk to one of them. They don't think like other people."

"I've tried everything else," said Dwayne. He brightened. He nodded. "You're right! The Festival could give me a brand new viewpoint on life!" he said.

"That's what it's for," said Francine. " *Use* it!"

"I *will*," said Dwayne. This was a bad mistake.

•   •   •

Kilgore Trout, hitchhiking westward, ever westward, had meanwhile become a passenger in a Ford *Galaxie*. The man at the controls of the *Galaxie* was a traveling salesman for a device which engulfed the rear ends of trucks at loading docks. It was a telescoping tunnel of rubberized canvas, and it looked like this in action:

The idea of the gadget was to allow people in a building to load or unload trucks without losing cold air in the summertime or hot air in the wintertime to the out-of-doors.

The man in control of the *Galaxie* also sold large spools for wire and cable and rope. He also sold fire extinguishers. He was a manufacturer's representative, he explained. He was his own boss, in that he represented products whose manufacturers couldn't afford salesmen of their own.

"I make my own hours, and I pick the products I sell. The products don't sell me," he said. His name was Andy Lieber. He was thirty-two. He was white. He was a good deal overweight like so many people in the country. He was obviously a happy man. He drove like a maniac. The *Galaxie* was going ninety-two miles an hour now. "I'm one of the few remaining free men in America," he said.

He had a penis one inch in diameter and seven and a half inches long. During the past year, he had averaged twenty-two orgasms per month. This was far above the national average. His income and the value of his life insurance policies at maturity were also far above average.

• • •

Trout wrote a novel one time which he called *How You Doin'?* and it was about national averages for this and that. An advertising agency on another planet had a successful campaign for the local equivalent of Earthling peanut butter. The eye-catching part of each ad was the statement of some sort of average—the average number of children, the average size of the male sex organ on that particular planet—which was two inches long, with an inside diameter of three inches and an out-side diameter of four and a quarter inches—and so on. The ads invited the readers to discover whether they were superior or inferior to the majority, in this respect or that one—whatever the respect was for that particular ad.

The ad went on to say that superior and inferior people alike ate such and such brand of peanut butter. Except that it wasn't really peanut butter on that planet. It was *Shazzbutter.*

And so on.

Chapter 16

A ND THE PEANUT BUTTER–EATERS on Earth were preparing to conquer the shazzbutter-eaters on the planet in the book by Kilgore Trout. By this time, the Earthlings hadn't just demolished West Virginia and Southeast Asia. They had demolished everything. So they were ready to go pioneering again.

They studied the shazzbutter-eaters by means of electronic snooping, and determined that they were too numerous and proud and resourceful ever to allow themselves to be pioneered.

So the Earthlings infiltrated the ad agency which had the shazzbutter account, and they buggered the statistics in the ads. They made the average for everything so high that everybody on the planet felt inferior to the majority in every respect.

And then the Earthling armored space ships came in and discovered the planet. Only token resistance was offered here and there, because the natives felt so below average. And then the pioneering began.

• • •

Trout asked the happy manufacturer's representative what it felt like to drive a *Galaxie*, which was the name of the car. The driver didn't hear him, and Trout let it go. It was a dumb play on words, so that Trout was asking simultaneously what it was like to drive the car and what it was like to steer something like the Milky Way, which was one hundred thousand light-years in diameter and ten thousand light-years thick. It revolved once every two hundred million years. It contained about one hundred billion stars.

And then Trout saw that a simple fire extinguisher in the *Galaxie* had this brand name:

As far as Trout knew, this word meant *higher* in a dead language. It was also a thing a fictitious mountain climber in a famous poem kept yelling as he disappeared into a blizzard up above. And it was also the trade name for wood shavings which were used to protect fragile objects inside packages.

"Why would anybody name a fire extinguisher *Excelsior*?" Trout asked the driver.

The driver shrugged. "Somebody must have liked the *sound* of it," he said.

• • •

Trout looked out at the countryside, which was smeared by high velocity. He saw this sign:

So he was getting really close to Dwayne Hoover. And, as though the Creator of the Universe or some other supernatural power were preparing him for the meeting, Trout felt the urge to thumb through his own book, *Now It Can Be Told*. This was the book which would soon turn Dwayne into a homicidal maniac.

The premise of the book was this: Life was an experiment by the Creator of the Universe, Who wanted to test a new sort of creature He was thinking of introducing into the Universe. It was a creature with the ability to make up its own mind. All the other creatures were fully-programmed robots.

The book was in the form of a long letter from The Creator of the Universe to the experimental creature. The Creator congratulated the creature and apologized for all the discomfort he had endured. The Creator invited him to a banquet in his honor in the Empire Room of the Waldorf-Astoria Hotel in New York City, where a black robot named Sammy Davis, Jr., would sing and dance.

• • •

And the experimental creature wasn't killed after the banquet. He was transferred to a virgin planet instead. Living cells were sliced from the palms of his hands, while he was unconscious. The operation didn't hurt at all.

And then the cells were stirred into a soupy sea on the virgin planet. They would evolve into ever more complicated life forms as the eons went by. Whatever shapes they assumed, they would have free will.

Trout didn't give the experimental creature a proper name. He simply called him *The Man*.

On the virgin planet, The Man was Adam and the sea was Eve.

• • •

The Man often sauntered by the sea. Sometimes he waded in his Eve. Sometimes he swam in her, but she was too soupy for an invigorating swim. She made her Adam feel sleepy and sticky afterwards, so he would dive into an icy stream that had just jumped off a mountain.

He screamed when he dived into the icy water, screamed again when he came up for air. He bloodied his shins and laughed about it when he scrambled up rocks to get out of the water.

He panted and laughed some more, and he thought of something amazing to yell. The Creator never knew what he was going to yell, since The Creator had no control over him. The Man himself got to decide what he was going to do next —and why. After a dip one day, for instance, The Man yelled this: "Cheese!"

Another time he yelled, "Wouldn't you really rather drive a Buick?"

•   •   •

The only other big animal on the virgin planet was an angel who visited The Man occasionally. He was a messenger and an investigator for the Creator of the Universe. He took the form of an eight hundred pound male cinnamon bear. He was a ro-bot, too, and so was The Creator, according to Kilgore Trout.

The bear was attempting to get a line on why The Man did what he did. He would ask, for instance, "Why did you yell, 'Cheese'?"

And The Man would tell him mockingly, "Because I *felt* like it, you stupid machine."

•   •   •

Here is what The Man's tombstone on the virgin planet looked like at the end of the book by Kilgore Trout:

NOT EVEN
THE CREATOR
OF THE UNIVERSE
KNEW WHAT
THE MAN
WAS GOING TO SAY NEXT

PERHAPS THE MAN
WAS A BETTER UNIVERSE
IN ITS INFANCY

R.J.P.

Chapter 17

BUNNY HOOVER, Dwayne's homosexual son, was dressing for work now. He was the piano player in the cocktail lounge of the new Holiday Inn. He was poor. He lived alone in a room without bath in the old Fairchild Hotel, which used to be fashionable. It was a flophouse now—in the most dangerous part of Midland City.

Very soon, Bunny Hoover would be seriously injured by Dwayne, would soon share an ambulance with Kilgore Trout.

• • •

Bunny was pale, the same unhealthy color of the blind fish that used to live in the bowels of Sacred Miracle Cave. Those fish were extinct. They had all turned belly-up years ago, had been flushed from the cave and into the Ohio River—to turn belly-up, to go *bang* in the noonday sun.

Bunny avoided the sunshine, too. And the water from the taps of Midland City was becoming more poisonous every day. He ate very little. He prepared his own food in his room. The preparation was simple, since vegetables and fruits were all he ate, and he munched them raw.

He not only did without dead meat—he did without living meat, too, without friends or lovers or pets. He had once been highly popular. When he was at Prairie Military Academy, for instance, the student body was unanimous in electing him Cadet Colonel, the highest rank possible, in his senior year.

• • •

When Bunny played the piano bar at the Holiday Inn, he had many, many secrets. One of them was this: he wasn't really there. He was able to absent himself from the cocktail lounge, and from the planet itself, for that matter, by means of Transcendental Meditation. He learned this technique from Maharishi Mahesh Yogi, who once stopped off in Midland City during a world-wide lecture tour.

Maharishi Mahesh Yogi, in exchange for a new handkerchief, a piece of fruit, a bunch of flowers, and thirty-five dollars, taught Bunny to close his eyes, and to say this euphonious nonsense word to himself over and over again: "Aye-eeeem, aye-eeeem, aye-eeeem." Bunny sat on the edge of his bed in the hotel room now, and he did it. "Aye-eeeem, aye-eeeem," he said to himself—internally. The rhythm of the chant matched one syllable with each two beats in his heart. He closed his eyes. He became a skin diver in the depths of his mind. The depths were seldom used.

His heart slowed. His respiration nearly stopped. A single word floated by in the depths. It had somehow escaped from the busier parts of his mind. It wasn't connected to anything. It floated by lazily, a translucent, scarf-like fish. The word was untroubling. Here was the word: "Blue." Here is what it looked like to Bunny Hoover:

And then another lovely scarf swam by. It looked like this:

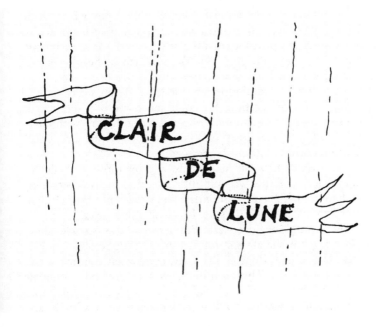

• • •

Fifteen minutes later, Bunny's awareness bobbed to the surface of its own accord. Bunny was refreshed. He got up from the bed, and he brushed his hair with the military brushes his mother had given him when he was elected Cadet Colonel so long ago.

• • •

Bunny was sent away to military school, an institution devoted to homicide and absolutely humorless obedience, when he was only ten years old. Here is why: He told Dwayne that he wished he were a woman instead of a man, because what men did was so often cruel and ugly.

• • •

Listen: Bunny Hoover went to Prairie Military Academy for eight years of uninterrupted sports, buggery and Fascism.

Buggery consisted of sticking one's penis in somebody else's asshole or mouth, or having it done to one by somebody else. Fascism was a fairly popular political philosophy which made sacred whatever nation and race the philosopher happened to belong to. It called for an autocratic, centralized government, headed up by a dictator. The dictator had to be obeyed, no matter what he told somebody to do.

And Bunny would bring new medals with him every time he came home for vacation. He could fence and box and wrestle and swim, he could shoot a rifle and a pistol, fight with bayonets, ride a horse, creep and crawl through shrubbery, peek around corners without being seen.

He would show off his medals, and his mother would tell him when his father was out of hearing that she was becoming unhappier with each passing day. She would hint that Dwayne was a monster. It wasn't true. It was all in her head.

She would begin to tell Bunny what was so vile about Dwayne, but she always stopped short. "You're too young to hear about such things," she'd say, even when Bunny was sixteen years old. "There's nothing you or anybody could do about them anyway." She would pretend to lock her lips with a key, and then whisper to Bunny, "There are secrets I will carry to my grave."

Her biggest secret, of course, was one that Bunny didn't detect until she knocked herself off with Drāno. Celia Hoover was crazy as a bedbug.

My mother was, too.

• • •

Listen: Bunny's mother and my mother were different sorts of human beings, but they were both beautiful in exotic ways, and they both boiled over with chaotic talk about love and peace and wars and evil and desperation, of better days coming by and by, of worse days coming by and by. And both our mothers committed suicide. Bunny's mother ate Drāno. My mother ate sleeping pills, which wasn't nearly as horrible.

• • •

And Bunny's mother and my mother had one really bizarre symptom in common: neither one could stand to have her picture taken. They were usually fine in the daytime. They usually concealed their frenzies until late at night. But, if somebody aimed a camera at either one of them during the daytime, the mother who was aimed at would crash down on her knees and protect her head with her arms, as though somebody was about to club her to death. It was a scary and pitiful thing to see.

• • •

At least Bunny's mother taught him how to control a piano, which was a music machine. At least Bunny Hoover's mother taught him a trade. A good piano controller could get a job making music in cocktail lounges almost anywhere in the world, and Bunny was a good one. His military training was useless, despite all the medals he won. The armed forces knew he was a homosexual, that he was certain to fall in love with other fighting men, and the armed forces didn't want to put up with such love affairs.

• • •

So Bunny Hoover now got ready to practice his trade. He slipped a black velvet dinner jacket over a black turtleneck sweater now. Bunny looked out his only window at the alleyway. The better rooms afforded views of Fairchild Park, where there had been fifty-six murders in the past two years. Bunny's room was on the second floor, so his window framed a piece of the blank brick side of what used to be the Keedsler Opera House.

There was an historical marker on the front of the former opera house. Not many people could understand it, but this is what it said:

JENNY LIND

"THE SWEDISH NIGHTINGALE"

SANG HERE

AVGVST 11

ANNO DOMINI MDCCCLXXXI

The Opera House used to be the home of the Midland City Symphony Orchestra, which was an amateur group of music enthusiasts. But they became homeless in 1927, when the Opera House became a motion picture house, *The Bannister*. The orchestra remained homeless, too, until the Mildred Barry Memorial Center for the Arts went up.

And *The Bannister* was the city's leading movie house for many years, until it was engulfed by the high crime district, which was moving north all the time. So it wasn't a theater anymore, even though there were still busts of Shakespeare and Mozart and so on gazing down from niches in the walls inside.

The stage was still in there, too, but it was crowded with dinette sets now. The Empire Furniture Company had taken over the premises now. It was gangster-controlled.

• • •

The nickname for Bunny's neighborhood was *Skid Row*. Every American town of any size had a neighborhood with the same nickname: Skid Row. It was a place where people who didn't have any friends or relatives or property or usefulness or ambition were supposed to go.

People like that would be treated with disgust in other neighborhoods, and policemen would keep them moving. They were as easy to move, usually, as toy balloons.

And they would drift hither and yon, like balloons filled with some gas slightly heavier than air, until they came to rest in Skid Row, against the foundations of the old Fairchild Hotel.

They could snooze and mumble to each other all day long. They could beg. They could get drunk. The basic scheme was this one: they were to stay there and not bother anybody anywhere else—until they were murdered for thrills, or until they were frozen to death by the wintertime.

• • •

Kilgore Trout wrote a story one time about a town which decided to tell derelicts where they were and what was about to happen to them by putting up actual street signs like this:

Bunny now smiled at himself in the mirror, in the *leak*.

He called himself to attention for a moment, became again the insufferably brainless, humorless, heartless soldier he had learned to be in military school. He murmured the motto of the school, a motto he used to have to shout about a hundred times a day—at dawn, at meals, at the start of every class, at games, at bayonet practice, at sunset, at bedtime:

"Can do," he said. "Can do."

Chapter 18

THE *GALAXIE* in which Kilgore Trout was a passenger was on the Interstate now, close to Midland City. It was creeping. It was trapped in rush hour traffic from Barrytron and Western Electric and Prairie Mutual. Trout looked up from his reading, saw a billboard which said this:

So Sacred Miracle Cave had become a part of the past.

• • •

As an old, old man, Trout would be asked by Dr. Thor Lembrig, the Secretary-General of the United Nations, if he feared the future. He would give this reply:

"Mr. Secretary-General, it is the *past* which scares the bejesus out of me."

• • •

Dwayne Hoover was only four miles away. He was sitting alone on a zebra-skin banquette in the cocktail lounge of the new Holiday Inn. It was dark in there, and quiet, too. The glare and uproar of rush hour traffic on the Interstate was blocked out by thick drapes of crimson velvet. On each table was a hurricane lamp with a candle inside, although the air was still.

On each table was a bowl of dry-roasted peanuts, too, and a sign which allowed the staff to refuse service to anyone who was inharmonious with the mood of the lounge. Here is what it said:

• • •

Bunny Hoover was controlling the piano. He had not looked up when his father came in. Neither had his father glanced in his direction. They had not exchanged greetings for many years.

Bunny went on playing his white man's blues. They were slow and tinkling, with capricious silences here and there. Bunny's blues had some of the qualities of a music box, a tired music box. They tinkled, stopped, then reluctantly, torpidly, they managed a few tinkles more.

Bunny's mother used to collect tinkling music boxes, among other things.

• • •

Listen: Francine Pefko was at Dwayne's automobile agency next door. She was catching up on all the work she should have done that afternoon. Dwayne would beat her up very soon.

And the only other person on the property with her as she typed and filed was Wayne Hoobler, the black parolee, who still lurked among the used cars. Dwayne would try to beat him up, too, but Wayne was a genius at dodging blows.

Francine was pure machinery at the moment, a machine made of meat—a typing machine, a filing machine.

Wayne Hoobler, on the other hand, had nothing machine-like to do. He ached to be a useful machine. The used cars were all locked up tight for the night. Now and then aluminum propellors on a wire overhead would be turned by a lazy breeze, and Wayne would respond to them as best he could. "Go," he would say to them. "Spin 'roun'."

• • •

He established a sort of relationship with the traffic on the Interstate, too, appreciating its changing moods. "Everybody goin' home," he said during the rush hour jam. "Everybody home now," he said later on, when the traffic thinned out. Now the sun was going down.

"Sun goin' down," said Wayne Hoobler. He had no clues as to where to go next. He supposed without minding much that he might die of exposure that night. He had never seen death by exposure, had never been threatened by it, since he had so seldom been out-of-doors. He knew of death by exposure because the papery voice of the little radio in his cell told of people's dying of exposure from time to time.

He missed that papery voice. He missed the clash of steel doors. He missed the bread and the stew and the pitchers of milk and coffee. He missed fucking other men in the mouth and the asshole, and being fucked in the mouth and the ass-hole, and jerking off—and fucking cows in the prison dairy, all events in a normal sex life on the planet, as far as he knew.

Here would be a good tombstone for Wayne Hoobler when he died:

• • •

The dairy at the prison provided milk and cream and butter and cheese and ice cream not only for the prison and the County Hospital. It sold its products to the outside world, too. Its trademark didn't mention prison. This was it:

• • •

Wayne couldn't read very well. The words *Hawaii* and *Hawaiian*, for instance, appeared in combination with more familiar words and symbols in signs painted on the windows of the showroom and on the windshields of some used cars. Wayne tried to decode the mysterious words phonetically, without any satisfaction. "Wahee-io," he would say, and "Hoo-he-woo-hi," and so on.

• • •

Wayne Hoobler smiled now, not because he was happy but because, with so little to do, he thought he might as well show off his teeth. They were excellent teeth. The Adult Correctional Institution at Shepherdstown was proud of its dentistry program.

It was such a famous dental program, in fact, that it had been written up in medical journals and in the *Reader's Digest*, which was the dying planet's most popular magazine. The theory behind the program was that many ex-convicts could not or would not get jobs because of their appearances, and good looks began with good teeth.

The program was so famous, in fact, that police even in neighboring states, when they picked up a poor man with expensively maintained teeth, fillings and bridgework and all that, were likely to ask him, "All right, boy—how many years you spend in Shepherdstown?"

• • •

Wayne Hoobler heard some of the orders which a waitress called to the bartender in the cocktail lounge. Wayne heard her call, "Gilbey's and quinine, with a twist." He had no idea what that was—or a Manhattan or a brandy Alexander or a sloe gin fizz. "Give me a Johnnie Walker Rob Roy," she called, "and a Southern Comfort on the rocks, and a Bloody Mary with Wolfschmidt's."

Wayne's only experiences with alcohol had had to do with drinking cleaning fluids and eating shoe polish and so on. He had no fondness for alcohol.

• • •

"Give me a Black and White and water," he heard the waitress say, and Wayne should have pricked up his ears at that. That particular drink wasn't for any ordinary person. That drink was for the person who had created all Wayne's misery to date, who could kill him or make him a millionaire or send him back to prison or do whatever he damn pleased with Wayne. That drink was for me.

• • •

I had come to the Arts Festival incognito. I was there to watch a confrontation between two human beings I had created: Dwayne Hoover and Kilgore Trout. I was not eager to be recognized. The waitress lit the hurricane lamp on my table. I pinched out the flame with my fingers. I had bought a pair of sunglasses at a Holiday Inn outside of Ashtabula, Ohio, where I spent the night before. I wore them in the darkness now. They looked like this:

The lenses were silvered, were mirrors to anyone looking my way. Anyone wanting to know what my eyes were like was confronted with his or her own twin reflections. Where other people in the cocktail lounge had eyes, I had two holes into another universe. I had *leaks.*

• • •

There was a book of matches on my table, next to my Pall Mall cigarettes.

Here is the message on the book of matches, which I read an hour and a half later, while Dwayne was beating the day-lights out of Francine Pefko:

"It's easy to make $100 a week in your spare time by show-ing comfortable, latest style Mason shoes to your friends. EVERYBODY goes for Mason shoes with their many special comfort features! We'll send FREE moneymaking kit so you can run your business from home. We'll even tell you how you can earn shoes FREE OF COST as a bonus for taking profit-able orders!"

And so on.

• • •

"This is a very bad book you're writing," I said to myself behind my *leaks*.

"I know," I said.

"You're afraid you'll kill yourself the way your mother did,"
I said.

"I know," I said.

• • •

There in the cocktail lounge, peering out through my leaks
at a world of my own invention, I mouthed this word:
schizophrenia.

The sound and appearance of the word had fascinated me
for many years. It sounded and looked to me like a human being sneezing in a blizzard of soapflakes.

I did not and do not know for certain that I have that disease. This much I knew and know: I was making myself hideously uncomfortable by not narrowing my attention to details
of life which were immediately important, and by refusing to
believe what my neighbors believed.

• • •

I am better now.

Word of honor: I am better now.

• • •

I was really sick for a while, though. I sat there in a cocktail
lounge of my own invention, and I stared through my *leaks* at
a white cocktail waitress of my own invention. I named her
Bonnie MacMahon. I had her bring Dwayne Hoover his customary drink, which was a House of Lords martini with a twist
of lemon peel. She was a longtime acquaintance of Dwayne's.
Her husband was a guard in the Sexual Offenders' Wing of the
Adult Correctional Institution. Bonnie had to work as a waitress because her husband lost all their money by investing it in
a car wash in Shepherdstown.

Dwayne had advised them not to do it. Here is how Dwayne
knew her and her husband Ralph: They had bought nine
Pontiacs from him over the past sixteen years.

"We're a Pontiac family," they'd say.

Bonnie made a joke now as she served him his martini. She made the same joke every time she served anybody a martini. "Breakfast of Champions," she said.

• • •

The expression "Breakfast of Champions" is a registered trademark of General Mills, Inc., for use on a breakfast cereal product. The use of the identical expression as the title for this book as well as throughout the book is not intended to indicate an association with or sponsorship by General Mills, nor is it intended to disparage their fine products.

• • •

Dwayne was hoping that some of the distinguished visitors to the Arts Festival, who were all staying at the Inn, would come into the cocktail lounge. He wanted to talk to them, if he could, to discover whether they had truths about life which he had never heard before. Here is what he hoped new truths might do for him: enable him to laugh at his troubles, to go on living, and to keep out of the North Wing of the Midland County General Hospital, which was for lunatics.

While he waited for an artist to appear, he consoled himself with the only artistic creation of any depth and mystery which was stored in his head. It was a poem he had been forced to learn by heart during his sophomore year in Sugar Creek High School, the elite white high school at the time. Sugar Creek High was a Nigger high school now. Here was the poem:

> *The Moving Finger writes; and, having writ,*
> *Moves on: nor all your Piety nor Wit*
> *Shall lure it back to cancel half a Line*
> *Nor all your Tears wash out a Word of it.*

Some poem!

• • •

And Dwayne was so open to new suggestions about the meaning of life that he was easily hypnotized. So, when he looked down into his martini, he was put into a trance by dancing myriads of winking eyes on the surface of his drink. The eyes were beads of lemon oil.

Dwayne missed it when two distinguished visitors to the Arts Festival came in and sat down on barstools next to Bunny's piano. They were white. They were Beatrice Keedsler, the Gothic novelist, and Rabo Karabekian, the minimal painter.

Bunny's piano, a Steinway baby grand, was armored with pumpkin-colored Formica and ringed with stools. People could eat and drink from the piano. On the previous Thanksgiving, a family of eleven had had Thanksgiving dinner served on the piano. Bunny played.

•   •   •

"This *has* to be the asshole of the Universe," said Rabo Karabekian, the minimal painter.

Beatrice Keedsler, the Gothic novelist, had grown up in Midland City. "I was petrified about coming home after all these years," she said to Karabekian.

"Americans are always afraid of coming home," said Karabekian, "with good reason, may I say."

"They *used* to have good reason," said Beatrice, "but not anymore. The past has been rendered harmless. I would tell any wandering American now, 'Of course you can go home again, and as often as you please. It's just a motel.'"

•   •   •

Traffic on the westbound barrel of the Interstate had come to a halt a mile east of the new Holiday Inn—because of a fatal accident on Exit 10A. Drivers and passengers got out of their cars—to stretch their legs and find out, if they could, what the trouble was up ahead.

Kilgore Trout was among those who got out. He learned from others that the new Holiday Inn was within easy walking distance. So he gathered up his parcels from the front seat of the *Galaxie*. He thanked the driver, whose name he had forgotten, and he began to trudge.

He also began to assemble in his mind a system of beliefs which would be appropriate to his narrow mission in Midland City, which was to show provincials, who were bent on exalting creativity, a would-be creator who had failed and failed. He paused in his trudge to examine himself in the rearview mirror, the rearview *leak*, of a truck locked up in traffic. The tractor was pulling two trailers instead of one. Here was the message the owners of the rig saw fit to shriek at human beings wherever it went:

Trout's image in the *leak* was as shocking as he had hoped it would be. He had not washed up after his drubbing by *The Pluto Gang*, so there was caked blood on one earlobe, and more under his left nostril. There was dog shit on a shoulder of his coat. He had collapsed into dog shit on the handball court under the Queensboro Bridge after the robbery.

By an unbelievable coincidence, that shit came from the wretched greyhound belonging to a girl I knew.

•   •   •

The girl with the greyhound was an assistant lighting director for a musical comedy about American history, and she kept her poor greyhound, who was named *Lancer*, in a one-room apartment fourteen feet wide and twenty-six feet long, and six flights of stairs above street level. His entire life was devoted to unloading his excrement at the proper time and place. There were two proper places to put it: in the gutter outside the door seventy-two steps below, with the traffic whizzing by, or in a roasting pan his mistress kept in front of the Westinghouse refrigerator.

Lancer had a very small brain, but he must have suspected from time to time, just as Wayne Hoobler did, that some kind of terrible mistake had been made.

•   •   •

Trout trudged onward, a stranger in a strange land. His pilgrimage was rewarded with new wisdom, which would never have been his had he remained in his basement in Cohoes. He learned the answer to a question many human beings were asking themselves so frantically: "What's blocking traffic on the westbound barrel of the Midland City stretch of the Interstate?"

The scales fell from the eyes of Kilgore Trout. He saw the explanation: a *Queen of the Prairies* milk truck was lying on its side, blocking the flow. It had been hit hard by a ferocious 1971 Chevrolet *Caprice* two-door. The Chevy had jumped the median divider strip. The Chevy's passenger hadn't used his seat belt. He had shot right through the shatterproof windshield. He was lying dead now in the concrete trough containing Sugar Creek. The Chevy's driver was also dead. He had been skewered by the post of his steering wheel.

The Chevy's passenger was bleeding blood as he lay dead in Sugar Creek. The milk truck was bleeding milk. Milk and blood were about to be added to the composition of the stinking ping-pong balls which were being manufactured in the bowels of Sacred Miracle Cave.

Chapter 19

I WAS ON A PAR with the Creator of the Universe there in the dark in the cocktail lounge. I shrunk the Universe to a ball exactly one light-year in diameter. I had it explode. I had it disperse itself again.

Ask me a question, any question. How old is the Universe? It is one half-second old, but that half-second has lasted one quintillion years so far. Who created it? Nobody created it. It has always been here.

What is time? It is a serpent which eats its tail, like this:

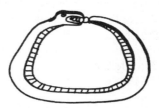

This is the snake which uncoiled itself long enough to offer Eve the apple, which looked like this:

What was the apple which Eve and Adam ate? It was the Creator of the Universe.

And so on.

Symbols can be so beautiful, sometimes.

• • •

Listen:

The waitress brought me another drink. She wanted to light my hurricane lamp again. I wouldn't let her. "Can you see anything in the dark, with your sunglasses on?" she asked me.

"The big show is inside my head," I said.

"Oh," she said.

"I can tell fortunes," I said. "You want your fortune told?"

"Not right now," she said. She went back to the bar, and she and the bartender had some sort of conversation about me, I think. The bartender took several anxious looks in my direction. All he could see were the *leaks* over my eyes. I did not worry about his asking me to leave the establishment. I had created him, after all. I gave him a name: Harold Newcomb Wilbur. I awarded him the Silver Star, the Bronze Star, the Soldier's Medal, the Good Conduct Medal, and a Purple Heart with two Oak-Leaf Clusters, which made him the second most decorated veteran in Midland City. I put all his medals under his handkerchiefs in a dresser drawer.

He won all those medals in the Second World War, which was staged by robots so that Dwayne Hoover could give a free-willed reaction to such a holocaust. The war was such an extravaganza that there was scarcely a robot anywhere who didn't have a part to play. Harold Newcomb Wilbur got his medals for killing Japanese, who were yellow robots. They were fueled by rice.

And he went on staring at me, even though I wanted to stop him now. Here was the thing about my control over the characters I created: I could only guide their movements approximately, since they were such big animals. There was inertia to overcome. It wasn't as though I was connected to them by steel wires. It was more as though I was connected to them by stale rubberbands.

So I made the green telephone in back of the bar ring. Harold Newcomb Wilbur answered it, but he kept his eyes on me. I had to think fast about who was on the other end of the telephone. I put the first most decorated veteran in Midland City on the other end. He had a penis eight hundred miles long and two hundred and ten miles in diameter, but practically all of it was in the fourth dimension. He got his medals in the war in Viet Nam. He had also fought yellow robots who ran on rice.

"Cocktail lounge," said Harold Newcomb Wilbur.

"Hal—?"

"Yes?"

"This is Ned Lingamon."

"I'm busy."

"Don't hang up. The cops got me down at City Jail. They only let me have one call, so I called you."

"Why me?"

"You're the only friend I got left."

"What they got you in for?"

"They say I killed my baby."

And so on.

This man, who was white, had all the medals Harold Newcomb Wilbur had, plus the highest decoration for heroism which an American soldier could receive, which looked like this:

He had now also committed the lowest crime which an American could commit, which was to kill his own child. Her name was Cynthia Anne, and she certainly didn't live very long before she was made dead again. She got killed for crying and crying. She wouldn't shut up.

First she drove her seventeen-year-old mother away with all her demands, and then her father killed her.

And so on.

•   •   •

As for the fortune I might have told for the waitress, this was it: "You will be swindled by termite exterminators and not even know it. You will buy steel-belted radial tires for the front wheels of your car. Your cat will be killed by a motorcyclist named Headley Thomas, and you will get another cat. Arthur, your brother in Atlanta, will find eleven dollars in a taxicab."

•   •   •

I might have told Bunny Hoover's fortune, too: "Your father will become extremely ill, and you will respond so grotesquely that there will be talk of putting you in the booby hatch, too. You will stage scenes in the hospital waiting room, telling doctors and nurses that you are to blame for your father's disease. You will blame yourself for trying for so many years to kill him with hatred. You will redirect your hatred. You will hate your mom."

And so on.

And I had Wayne Hoobler, the black ex-convict, stand bleakly among the garbage cans outside the back door of the Inn, and examine the currency which had been given to him at the prison gate that morning. He had nothing else to do.

He studied the pyramid with the blazing eye on top. He wished he had more information about the pyramid and the eye. There was so much to learn!

Wayne didn't even know the Earth revolved around the Sun. He thought the Sun revolved around the Earth, because it certainly looked that way.

A truck sizzled by on the Interstate, seemed to cry out in pain to Wayne, because he read the message on the side of it phonetically. The message told Wayne that the truck was in agony, as it hauled things from here to there. This was the message, and Wayne said it out loud:

• • •

Here was what was going to happen to Wayne in about four days—because I wanted it to happen to him: He would be picked up and questioned by policemen, because he was behaving suspiciously outside the back gate of Barrytron, Ltd., which was involved in super-secret weapons work. They thought at first that he might be pretending to be stupid and ignorant, that he might, in fact, be a cunning spy for the Communists.

A check of his fingerprints and his wonderful dental work proved that he was who he said he was. But there was still something else he had to explain: What was he doing with a membership card in the Playboy Club of America, made out in the name of Paulo di Capistrano? He had found it in a garbage can in back of the new Holiday Inn.

And so on.

• • •

And it was time now for me to have Rabo Karabekian, the minimalist painter, and Beatrice Keedsler, the novelist, say and do some more stuff for the sake of this book. I did not want to spook them by staring at them as I worked their controls, so I pretended to be absorbed in drawing pictures on my tabletop with a damp fingertip.

I drew the Earthling symbol for *nothingness*, which was this:

I drew the Earthling symbol for *everything*, which was this:

Dwayne Hoover and Wayne Hoobler knew the first one, but not the second one. And now I drew a symbol in vanishing mist which was bitterly familiar to Dwayne but not to Wayne. This was it:

DRĀNO

And now I drew a symbol whose meaning Dwayne had known for a few years in school, a meaning which had since eluded him. The symbol would have looked like the end of a table in a prison dining hall to Wayne. It represented the ratio of the circumference of a circle to its diameter. This ratio could also be expressed as a number, and even as Dwayne and Wayne and Karabekian and Beatrice Keedsler and all the rest of us went about our business, Earthling scientists were monotonously radioing that number into outer space. The idea was to show other inhabited planets, in case they were listening, how intelligent we were. We had tortured circles until they coughed up this symbol of their secret lives:

• • •

And I made an invisible duplicate on my Formica tabletop of a painting by Rabo Karabekian, entitled *The Temptation of Saint Anthony*. My duplicate was a miniature of the real thing, and mine was not in color, but I had captured the picture's form and the spirit, too. This is what I drew.

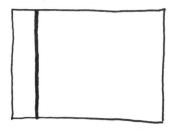

The original was twenty feet wide and sixteen feet high. The field was *Hawaiian Avocado*, a green wall paint manufactured by the O'Hare Paint and Varnish Company in Hellertown, Pennsylvania. The vertical stripe was day-glo orange reflecting tape. This was the most expensive piece of art, not counting buildings and tombstones, and not counting the statue of Abraham Lincoln in front of the old Nigger high school.

It was a scandal what the painting cost. It was the first purchase for the permanent collection of the Mildred Barry Memorial Center for the Arts. Fred T. Barry, the Chairman of the Board of Barrytron, Ltd., had coughed up fifty thousand dollars of his own for the picture.

Midland City was outraged. So was I.

• • •

So was Beatrice Keedsler, but she kept her dismay to herself as she sat at the piano bar with Karabekian. Karabekian, who wore a sweatshirt imprinted with the likeness of Beethoven, knew he was surrounded by people who hated him for getting so much money for so little work. He was amused.

Like everybody else in the cocktail lounge, he was softening his brain with alcohol. This was a substance produced by a tiny creature called yeast. Yeast organisms ate sugar and excreted alcohol. They killed themselves by destroying their own environment with yeast shit.

• • •

Kilgore Trout once wrote a short story which was a dialogue between two pieces of yeast. They were discussing the possible purposes of life as they ate sugar and suffocated in their own excrement. Because of their limited intelligence, they never came close to guessing that they were making champagne.

• • •

So I had Beatrice Keedsler say to Rabo Karabekian there at the piano bar, "This is a dreadful confession, but I don't even know who Saint Anthony was. Who was he, and why should anybody have wanted to tempt him?"

"I don't know, and I would hate to find out," said Karabekian.

"You have no use for truth?" said Beatrice.

"You know what truth is?" said Karabekian. "It's some crazy thing my neighbor believes. If I want to make friends with him, I ask him what he believes. He tells me, and I say, 'Yeah, yeah—ain't it the truth?'"

• • •

I had no respect whatsoever for the creative works of either the painter or the novelist. I thought Karabekian with his meaningless pictures had entered into a conspiracy with millionaires to make poor people feel stupid. I thought Beatrice Keedsler had joined hands with other old-fashioned story-tellers to make people believe that life had leading characters, minor characters, significant details, insignificant details, that it had lessons to be learned, tests to be passed, and a beginning, a middle, and an end.

As I approached my fiftieth birthday, I had become more

and more enraged and mystified by the idiot decisions made by my countrymen. And then I had come suddenly to pity them, for I understood how innocent and natural it was for them to behave so abominably, and with such abominable results: They were doing their best to live like people invented in story books. This was the reason Americans shot each other so often: It was a convenient literary device for ending short stories and books.

Why were so many Americans treated by their government as though their lives were as disposable as paper facial tissues? Because that was the way authors customarily treated bit-part players in their made-up tales.

And so on.

Once I understood what was making America such a dangerous, unhappy nation of people who had nothing to do with real life, I resolved to shun storytelling. I would write about life. Every person would be exactly as important as any other. All facts would also be given equal weightiness. Nothing would be left out. Let others bring order to chaos. I would bring chaos to order, instead, which I think I have done.

If all writers would do that, then perhaps citizens not in the literary trades will understand that there is no order in the world around us, that we must adapt ourselves to the requirements of chaos instead.

It is hard to adapt to chaos, but it can be done. I am living proof of that: It can be done.

• • •

Adapting to chaos there in the cocktail lounge, I now had Bonnie MacMahon, who was exactly as important as anybody else in the Universe, bring more yeast excrement to Beatrice Keedsler and Karabekian. Karabekian's drink was a Beefeater's dry martini with a twist of lemon peel, so Bonnie said to him, "Breakfast of Champions."

"That's what you said when you brought me my first martini," said Karabekian.

"I say it every time I give anybody a martini," said Bonnie.

"Doesn't that get tiresome?" said Karabekian. "Or maybe that's why people found cities in Godforsaken places like this

—so they can make the same jokes over and over again, until the Bright Angel of Death stops their mouths with ashes."

"I just try to cheer people up," said Bonnie. "If that's a crime, I never heard about it till now. I'll stop saying it from now on. I beg your pardon. I did not mean to give offense."

Bonnie detested Karabekian, but she was as sweet as pie to him. She had a policy of never showing her anger about anything there in the cocktail lounge. The largest part of her income by far came from tips, and the way to get big tips was to smile, smile, smile, no matter what. Bonnie had only two goals in life now. She meant to recoup all the money her husband had lost in the car wash in Shepherdstown, and she ached to have steel-belted radial tires for the front wheels of her automobile.

Her husband, meanwhile, was at home watching professional golfers on television, and getting smashed on yeast excrement.

• • •

Saint Anthony, incidentally, was an Egyptian who founded the very first monastery, which was a place where men could live simple lives and pray often to the Creator of the Universe, without the distractions of ambition and sex and yeast excrement. Saint Anthony himself sold everything he had when he was young, and he went out into the wilderness and lived alone for twenty years.

He was often tempted during all those years of perfect solitude by visions of good times he might have had with food and men and women and children and the marketplace and so on.

His biographer was another Egyptian, Saint Athanasius, whose theories on the Trinity, the Incarnation, and the divinity of the Holy Spirit, set down three hundred years after the murder of Christ, were considered valid by Catholics even in Dwayne Hoover's time.

The Catholic high school in Midland City, in fact, was named in honor of Saint Athanasius. It was named in honor of Saint Christopher at first, but then the Pope, who was head of Catholic churches everywhere, announced that there probably never had been a Saint Christopher, so people shouldn't honor him anymore.

•   •   •

A black male dishwasher stepped out of the kitchen of the Inn now for a Pall Mall cigarette and some fresh air. He wore a large button on his sweat-soaked white T-shirt which said this:

There were bowls of such buttons around the Inn, for anybody to help himself to, and the dishwasher had taken one in a spirit of levity. He had no use for works of art, except for cheap and simple ones which weren't meant to live very long. His name was Eldon Robbins, and he had a penis nine inches long and two inches in diameter.

Eldon Robbins, too, had spent time in the Adult Correctional Institution, so it was easy for him to recognize Wayne Hoobler, out among the garbage cans, as a new parolee. "Welcome to the real world, Brother," he said gently and with wry lovingness to Wayne. "When was the last time you ate? This mornin'?"

Wayne shyly acknowledged that this was true. So Eldon took him through a kitchen to a long table where the kitchen staff ate. There was a television set back there, and it was on, and it showed Wayne the beheading of Queen Mary of Scotland. Everybody was all dressed up, and Queen Mary put her head on the block of her own accord.

Eldon arranged for Wayne to get a free steak and mashed potatoes and gravy and anything else he wanted, all prepared by other black men in the kitchen. There was a bowl of Arts Festival buttons on the table, and Eldon made Wayne put one on before he ate. "Wear this at all times," he told Wayne gravely, "and no harm can come to you."

• • •

Eldon revealed to Wayne a peephole, which kitchen workers had drilled through the wall and into the cocktail lounge. "When you get tarred of watchin' television," he said, "you can watch the animals in the zoo."

Eldon himself had a look through the peephole, told Wayne that there was a man seated at the piano bar who had been paid fifty thousand dollars for sticking a piece of yellow tape to a green piece of canvas. He insisted that Wayne take a *good* look at Karabekian. Wayne obeyed.

And Wayne wanted to remove his eye from the peephole after a few seconds, because he didn't have nearly enough background information for any sort of understanding of what was going on in the cocktail lounge. The candles puzzled him, for instance. He supposed that the electricity in there had failed, and that somebody had gone to change a fuse. Also, he did not know what to make of Bonnie MacMahon's costume, which consisted of white cowboy boots and black net stockings with crimson garters plainly showing across several inches of bare thigh, and a tight sequin sort of bathing suit with a puff of pink cotton pinned to its rear.

Bonnie's back was to Wayne, so he could not see that she wore octagonal, rimless trifocals, and was a horse-faced woman forty-two years old. He could not see, either, that she was smiling, smiling, smiling, no matter how insulting Karabekian became. He could read Karabekian's lips, however. He was good at reading lips, as was anyone who had spent any time in Shepherdstown. The rule of silence was enforced in the corridors and at meals in Shepherdstown.

• • •

Karabekian was saying this to Bonnie, indicating Beatrice
Keedsler with a wave of his hand: "This distinguished lady is a
famous storyteller, and also a native of this railroad junction.
Perhaps you could tell her some recent true stories about her
birthplace."

"I don't know any," said Bonnie.

"Oh come now," said Karabekian. "Every human being in
this room must be worth a great novel." He pointed at Dwayne
Hoover. "What is the life story of that man?"

Bonnie limited herself to telling about Dwayne's dog, Sparky,
who couldn't wag his tail. "So he has to fight all the time," she
said.

"Wonderful," said Karabekian. He turned to Beatrice. "I'm
sure you can use that somewhere."

"As a matter of fact, I can," said Beatrice. "That's an enchanting detail."

"The more details the better," said Karabekian. "Thank God
for novelists. Thank God there are people willing to write
everything down. Otherwise, so much would be forgotten!"
He begged Bonnie for more true stories.

Bonnie was deceived by his enthusiasm and energized by the
idea that Beatrice Keedsler honestly needed true stories for her
books. "Well—" she said, "would you consider Shepherdstown
part of Midland City, more or less?"

"Of course," said Karabekian, who had never heard of
Shepherdstown. "What would Midland City be without
Shepherdstown? And what would Shepherdstown be without
Midland City?"

"Well—" said Bonnie, and she thought she had what was
maybe a really good story to tell, "my husband is a guard at
the Shepherdstown Adult Correctional Institution, and he
used to have to keep people who were going to be electrocuted
company—back when they used to electrocute people all the
time. He'd play cards with them, or read parts of the Bible out
loud to them, or whatever they wanted to do, and he had to
keep a white man named Leroy Joyce company."

Bonnie's costume gave off a faint, fishy, queer glow as she
spoke. This was because her garments were heavily impregnated

with fluorescent chemicals. So was the bartender's jacket. So were the African masks on the walls. The chemicals would shine like electric signs when ultraviolet lights in the ceiling were energized. The lights weren't on just now. The bartender turned them on at random times, at his own whim, in order to give the customers a delightful and mystifying surprise.

The power for the lights and for everything electrical in Midland City, incidentally, was generated by coal from strip mines in West Virginia, through which Kilgore Trout had passed not many hours before.

• • •

"Leroy Joyce was so dumb," Bonnie went on, "he couldn't play cards. He couldn't understand the Bible. He could hardly talk. He ate his last supper, and then he sat still. He was going to be electrocuted for rape. So my husband sat out in the corridor outside the cell, and he read to himself. He heard Leroy moving around in his cell, but he didn't worry about it. And then Leroy rattled his tin cup on the bars. My husband thought Leroy wanted some more coffee. So he got up and went over and took the cup. Leroy was smiling as though everything was all right now. He wouldn't have to go to the electric chair after all. He'd cut off his whatchamacallit and put it in the cup."

• • •

This book is made up, of course, but the story I had Bonnie tell actually happened in real life—in the death house of a penitentiary in Arkansas.

As for Dwayne Hoover's dog Sparky, who couldn't wag his tail: Sparky is modeled after a dog my brother owns who has to fight all the time, because he can't wag his tail. There really is such a dog.

• • •

Rabo Karabekian asked Bonnie MacMahon to tell him something about the teen-age girl on the cover of the program for the Festival of the Arts. This was the only internationally famous human being in Midland City. She was Mary Alice Miller, the Women's Two Hundred Meter Breast Stroke Champion of the World. She was only fifteen, said Bonnie.

Mary Alice was also the Queen of the Festival of the Arts. The cover of the program showed her in a white bathing suit, with her Olympic Gold Medal hanging around her neck. The medal looked like this:

Mary Alice was smiling at a picture of Saint Sebastian, by the Spanish painter El Greco. It had been loaned to the Festival by Eliot Rosewater, the patron of Kilgore Trout. Saint Sebastian was a Roman soldier who had lived seventeen hundred years before me and Mary Alice Miller and Wayne and Dwayne and all the rest of us. He had secretly become a Christian when Christianity was against the law.

And somebody squealed on him. The Emperor Diocletian had him shot by archers. The picture Mary Alice smiled at with such uncritical bliss showed a human being who was so full of arrows that he looked like a porcupine.

Something almost nobody knew about Saint Sebastian, incidentally, since painters liked to put so many arrows into him, was that he survived the incident. He actually got well.

He walked around Rome praising Christianity and bad-mouthing the Emperor, so he was sentenced to death a second time. He was beaten to death by rods.

And so on.

And Bonnie MacMahon told Beatrice and Karabekian that Mary Alice's father, who was a member of the Parole Board out at Shepherdstown, had taught Mary Alice to swim when she was eight months old, and that he had made her swim at least four hours a day, every day, since she was three.

Rabo Karabekian thought this over, and then he said loudly, so a lot of people could hear him, "What kind of a man would turn his daughter into an outboard motor?"

•   •   •

And now comes the spiritual climax of this book, for it is at this point that I, the author, am suddenly transformed by what I have done so far. This is why I had gone to Midland City: to be born again. And Chaos announced that it was about to give birth to a new me by putting these words in the mouth of Rabo Karabekian: "What kind of a man would turn his daughter into an outboard motor?"

Such a small remark was able to have such thundering consequences because the spiritual matrix of the cocktail lounge was in what I choose to call a *pre-earthquake condition*. Terrific forces were at work on our souls, but they could do no work, because they balanced one another so nicely.

But then a grain of sand crumbled. One force had a sudden advantage over another, and spiritual continents began to shrug and heave.

One force, surely, was the lust for money which infested so many people in the cocktail lounge. They knew what Rabo Karabekian had been paid for his painting, and they wanted fifty thousand dollars, too. They could have a lot of fun with fifty thousand dollars, or so they believed. But they had to earn money the hard way, just a few dollars at a time, instead. It wasn't right.

Another force was the fear in these same people that their lives might be ridiculous, that their entire city might be ridiculous. Now the worst had happened: Mary Alice Miller, the one thing about their city which they had supposed was ridicule-proof had just been lazily ridiculed by a man from out-of-town.

And my own pre-earthquake condition must be taken into consideration, too, since I was the one who was being reborn. Nobody else in the cocktail lounge was reborn, as far as I know. The rest got their minds changed, some of them, about the value of modern art.

As for myself: I had come to the conclusion that there was nothing sacred about myself or about any human being, that we were all machines, doomed to collide and collide and collide. For want of anything better to do, we became fans of collisions. Sometimes I wrote well about collisions, which meant I was a writing machine in good repair. Sometimes I wrote badly, which meant I was a writing machine in bad repair. I no more harbored sacredness than did a Pontiac, a mousetrap, or a South Bend Lathe.

I did not expect Rabo Karabekian to rescue me. I had created him, and he was in my opinion a vain and weak and trashy man, no artist at all. But it is Rabo Karabekian who made me the serene Earthling which I am this day.

Listen:

"What kind of a man would turn his daughter into an outboard motor?" he said to Bonnie MacMahon.

Bonnie MacMahon blew up. This was the first time she had blown up since she had come to work in the cocktail lounge. Her voice became as unpleasant as the noise of a bandsaw's cutting galvanized tin. It was *loud*, too. "Oh yeah?" she said. "Oh yeah?"

Everybody froze. Bunny Hoover stopped playing the piano. Nobody wanted to miss a word.

"You don't think much of Mary Alice Miller?" she said. "Well, we don't think much of your painting. I've seen better pictures done by a five-year-old."

Karabekian slid off his barstool so he could face all those enemies standing up. He certainly surprised me. I expected him to retreat in a hail of olives, maraschino cherries and lemon rinds. But he was majestic up there. "Listen—" he said so calmly, "I have read the editorial against my painting in your wonderful newspaper. I have read every word of the hate mail you have been thoughtful enough to send to New York."

This embarrassed people some.

"The painting did not exist until I made it," Karabekian went on. "Now that it does exist, nothing would make me happier than to have it reproduced again and again, and vastly improved upon, by all the five-year-olds in town. I would love for your children to find pleasantly and playfully what it took me many angry years to find.

"I now give you my word of honor," he went on, "that the picture your city owns shows everything about life which truly matters, with nothing left out. It is a picture of the awareness of every animal. It is the immaterial core of every animal—the 'I am' to which all messages are sent. It is all that is alive in any of us—in a mouse, in a deer, in a cocktail waitress. It is unwavering and pure, no matter what preposterous adventure may befall us. A sacred picture of Saint Anthony alone is one vertical, unwavering band of light. If a cockroach were near him, or a cocktail waitress, the picture would show two such bands of light. Our awareness is all that is alive and maybe sacred in any of us. Everything else about us is dead machinery.

"I have just heard from this cocktail waitress here, this vertical band of light, a story about her husband and an idiot who was about to be executed at Shepherdstown. Very well—let a five-year-old paint a sacred interpretation of that encounter. Let that five-year-old strip away the idiocy, the bars, the waiting electric chair, the uniform of the guard, the gun of the guard, the bones and meat of the guard. What is that perfect picture which any five-year-old can paint? Two unwavering bands of light."

Ecstasy bloomed on the barbaric face of Rabo Karabekian. "Citizens of Midland City, I salute you," he said. "You have given a home to a masterpiece!"

●   ●   ●

Dwayne Hoover, incidentally, wasn't taking any of this in. He was still hypnotized, turned inward. He was thinking about moving fingers writing and moving on, and so forth. He had bats in his bell tower. He was off his rocker. He wasn't playing with a full deck of cards.

Chapter 20

WHILE MY LIFE was being renewed by the words of Rabo Karabekian, Kilgore Trout found himself standing on the shoulder of the Interstate, gazing across Sugar Creek in its concrete trough at the new Holiday Inn. There were no bridges across the creek. He would have to wade.

So he sat down on a guardrail, removed his shoes and socks, rolled his pantlegs to his knees. His bared shins were rococo with varicose veins and scars. So were the shins of my father when he was an old, old man.

Kilgore Trout had my father's shins. They were a present from me. I gave him my father's feet, too, which were long and narrow and sensitive. They were azure. They were artistic feet.

. . .

Trout lowered his artistic feet into the concrete trough containing Sugar Creek. They were coated at once with a clear plastic substance from the surface of the creek. When, in some surprise, Trout lifted one coated foot from the water, the plastic substance dried in air instantly, sheathed his foot in a thin, skin-tight bootie resembling mother-of-pearl. He repeated the process with his other foot.

The substance was coming from the Barrytron plant. The company was manufacturing a new anti-personnel bomb for the Air Force. The bomb scattered plastic pellets instead of steel pellets, because the plastic pellets were cheaper. They were also impossible to locate in the bodies of wounded enemies by means of x-ray machines.

Barrytron had no idea it was dumping this waste into Sugar Creek. They had hired the Maritimo Brothers Construction Company, which was gangster-controlled, to build a system which would get rid of the waste. They knew the company was gangster-controlled. Everybody knew that. But the Maritimo Brothers were usually the best builders in town. They had built Dwayne Hoover's house, for instance, which was a solid house.

676

But every so often they would do something amazingly criminal. The Barrytron disposal system was a case in point. It was expensive, and it appeared to be complicated and busy. Actually, though, it was old junk hooked up every which way, concealing a straight run of stolen sewer pipe running directly from Barrytron to Sugar Creek.

Barrytron would be absolutely sick when it learned what a polluter it had become. Throughout its history, it had attempted to be a perfect model of corporate good citizenship, no matter what it cost.

• • •

Trout now crossed Sugar Creek on my father's legs and feet, and those appendages became more nacreous with every wading stride. He carried his parcels and his shoes and socks on his head, although the water scarcely reached his kneecaps.

He knew how ridiculous he looked. He expected to be received abominably, dreamed of embarrassing the Festival to death. He had come all this distance for an orgy of masochism. He wanted to be treated like a cockroach.

• • •

His situation, insofar as he was a machine, was complex, tragic, and laughable. But the sacred part of him, his awareness, remained an unwavering band of light.

And this book is being written by a meat machine in cooperation with a machine made of metal and plastic. The plastic, incidentally, is a close relative of the gunk in Sugar Creek. And at the core of the writing meat machine is something sacred, which is an unwavering band of light.

At the core of each person who reads this book is a band of unwavering light.

My doorbell has just rung in my New York apartment. And I know what I will find when I open my front door: an unwavering band of light.

God bless Rabo Karabekian!

• • •

Listen: Kilgore Trout climbed out of the trough and onto the asphalt desert which was the parking lot. It was his plan to enter the lobby of the Inn on wet bare feet, to leave footprints on the carpet—like this:

It was Trout's fantasy that somebody would be outraged by the footprints. This would give him the opportunity to reply grandly, "What is it that offends you so? I am simply using man's first printing press. You are reading a bold and universal headline which says, 'I am here, I am here, I am here.'"

• • •

But Trout was no walking printing press. His feet left no marks on the carpet, because they were sheathed in plastic and the plastic was dry. Here was the structure of the plastic molecule:

The molecule went on and on and on, repeating itself forever to form a sheet both tough and poreless.

This molecule was the monster Dwayne's twin stepbrothers, Lyle and Kyle, had attacked with their automatic shotguns. This was the same stuff which was fucking up Sacred Miracle Cave.

●   ●   ●

The man who told me how to diagram a segment of a molecule of plastic was Professor Walter H. Stockmayer of Dartmouth College. He is a distinguished physical chemist, and an amusing and useful friend of mine. I did not make him up.

I would like to be Professor Walter H. Stockmayer. He is a brilliant pianist. He skis like a dream.

And when he sketched a plausible molecule, he indicated points where it would go on and on just as I have indicated them—with an abbreviation which means sameness without end.

The proper ending for any story about people it seems to me, since life is now a polymer in which the Earth is wrapped so tightly, should be that same abbreviation, which I now write large because I feel like it, which is this one:

• • •

And it is in order to acknowledge the continuity of this polymer that I begin so many sentences with "And" and "So," and end so many paragraphs with ". . . and so on."

And so on.

"It's all like an ocean!" cried Dostoevski. I say it's all like cellophane.

• • •

So Trout entered the lobby as an inkless printing press, but he was still the most grotesque human being who had ever come in there.

All around him were what other people called *mirrors*, which he called *leaks*. The entire wall which separated the lobby from the cocktail lounge was a *leak* ten feet high and thirty-feet long. There was another *leak* on the cigarette machine and yet another on the candy machine. And when Trout looked through them to see what was going on in the other universe, he saw a red-eyed, filthy old creature who was barefoot, who had his pants rolled up to his knees.

As it happened, the only other person in the lobby at the time was the beautiful young desk clerk, Milo Maritimo. Milo's clothing and skin and eyes were all the colors that olives can be. He was a graduate of the Cornell Hotel School. He was the homosexual grandson of Guillermo "Little Willie" Maritimo, a bodyguard of the notorious Chicago gangster, Al Capone.

Trout presented himself to this harmless man, stood before his desk with his bare feet far apart and his arms outspread. "The Abominable Snowman has arrived," he said to Milo. "If I'm not as clean as most abominable snowmen are, it is because I was kidnapped as a child from the slopes of Mount Everest, and taken as a slave to a bordello in Rio de Janeiro, where I have been cleaning the unspeakably filthy toilets for the past fifty years. A visitor to our whipping room there screamed in a transport of agony and ecstasy that there was to be an arts festival in Midland City. I escaped down a rope of sheets taken from a reeking hamper. I have come to Midland City to have myself acknowledged, before I die, as the great artist I believe myself to be."

Milo Maritimo greeted Trout with luminous adoration. "Mr. Trout," he said in rapture, "I'd know you anywhere. Welcome to Midland City. We *need* you so!"

"How do you know who I am?" said Kilgore Trout. Nobody had ever known who he was before.

"You *had* to be you," said Milo.

Trout was deflated—*neutralized*. He dropped his arms, became child-like now. "Nobody ever knew who I was before," he said.

"I know," said Milo. "We have discovered you, and we hope you will discover us. No longer will Midland City be known merely as the home of Mary Alice Miller, the Women's Two Hundred Meter Breast Stroke Champion of the World. It will also be the city which first acknowledged the greatness of Kilgore Trout."

Trout simply walked away from the desk and sat down on a

brocaded Spanish-style settee. The entire lobby, except for the vending machines, was done in Spanish style.

Milo now used a line from a television show which had been popular a few years back. The show wasn't on the air anymore, but most people still remembered the line. Much of the conversation in the country consisted of lines from television shows, both present and past. The show Milo's line was from consisted of taking some old person, usually fairly famous, into what looked like an ordinary room, only it was actually a stage, with an audience out front and television cameras hidden all around. There were also people who had known the person in the older days hidden around. They would come out and tell anecdotes about the person later on.

Milo now said what the master of ceremonies would have said to Trout, if Trout had been on the show and the curtain was going up: "Kilgore Trout! This is your life!"

● ● ●

Only there wasn't any audience or curtain or any of that. And the truth was that Milo Maritimo was the only person in Midland City who knew anything about Kilgore Trout. It was wishful thinking on his part that the upper crust of Midland City was about to be as ga-ga as he was about the works of Kilgore Trout.

"We are so ready for a Renaissance, Mr. Trout! You will be our Leonardo!"

"How could you *possibly* have heard of me?" said Trout dazedly.

"In getting ready for the Midland City Renaissance," said Milo, "I made it my business to read everything I could by and about every artist who was on his way here."

"There isn't anything by me or about me anywhere," protested Trout.

Milo came from behind his desk. He brought with him what appeared to be a lopsided old softball, swaddled in many different sorts of tape. "When I couldn't find out anything about you," he said, "I wrote to Eliot Rosewater, the man who said we had to bring you here. He has a private collection of forty-one of your novels and sixty-three of your short stories, Mr. Trout. He let me read them all." He held out the seeming baseball, which was actually a book from Rosewater's collection. Rosewater used his science-fiction library hard. "This is the only book I haven't finished, and I'll finish it before the sun comes up tomorrow," said Milo.

• • •

The novel in question, incidentally, was *The Smart Bunny.* The leading character was a rabbit who lived like all the other wild rabbits, but who was as intelligent as Albert Einstein or William Shakespeare. It was a female rabbit. She was the only female leading character in any novel or story by Kilgore Trout.

She led a normal female rabbit's life, despite her ballooning intellect. She concluded that her mind was useless, that it was a sort of tumor, that it had no usefulness within the rabbit scheme of things.

So she went hippity-hop, hippity-hop toward the city, to have the tumor removed. But a hunter named Dudley Farrow shot and killed her before she got there. Farrow skinned her and took out her guts, but then he and his wife Grace decided that they had better not eat her because of her unusually large head. They thought what she had thought when she was alive —that she must be diseased.

And so on.

• • •

Kilgore Trout had to change into his only other garments, his high school tuxedo and his new evening shirt and all, right away. The lower parts of his rolled-up trousers had become impregnated with the plastic substance from the creek, so he couldn't roll them down again. They were as stiff as flanges on sewer pipes.

So Milo Maritimo showed him to his suite, which was two ordinary Holiday Inn rooms with a door between them open. Trout and every distinguished visitor had a suite, with two color television sets, two tile baths, four double beds equipped with *Magic Fingers.* Magic Fingers were electric vibrators attached to the mattress springs of a bed. If a guest put a quarter into a little box on his bedside table, the Magic Fingers would jiggle his bed.

There were enough flowers in Trout's room for a Catholic gangster's funeral. They were from Fred T. Barry, the Chairman of the Arts Festival, and from the Midland City Association of Women's Clubs, and from the Chamber of Commerce, and on and on.

Trout read a few of the cards on the flowers, and he commented, "The town certainly seems to be getting behind the arts in a great big way."

Milo closed his olive eyes tight, wincing with a tangy agony. "It's *time*. Oh God, Mr. Trout, we were starving for so long, without even knowing what we were hungering for," he said. This young man was not only a descendant of master criminals, he was a close relative of felons operating in Midland City at the present time. The partners in the Maritimo Brothers Construction Company, for instance, were his uncles. Gino Maritimo, Milo's first cousin once removed, was the dope king of the city.

• • •

"Oh, Mr. Trout," nice Milo went on, there in Trout's suite, "teach us to sing and dance and laugh and cry. We've tried to survive so long on money and sex and envy and real estate and football and basketball and automobiles and television and alcohol—on sawdust and broken glass!"

"Open your eyes!" said Trout bitterly. "Do I look like a dancer, a singer, a man of joy?" He was wearing his tuxedo now. It was a size too large for him. He had lost much weight since high school. His pockets were crammed with mothballs. They bulged like saddlebags.

"Open your eyes!" said Trout. "Would a man nourished by beauty look like this? You have nothing but desolation and desperation here, you say? I bring you more of the same!"

"My eyes *are* open," said Milo warmly, "and I see exactly what I *expect* to see. I see a man who is terribly wounded—because he has dared to pass through the fires of truth to the other side, which we have never seen. And then he has come back again—to tell us about the other side."

• • •

And I sat there in the new Holiday Inn, and made it disappear, then appear again, then disappear, then appear again. Actually, there was nothing but a big open field there. A farmer had put it into rye.

It was high time, I thought, for Trout to meet Dwayne Hoover, for Dwayne to run amok.

I knew how this book would end. Dwayne would hurt a lot of people. He would bite off one joint of the right index finger of Kilgore Trout.

And then Trout, with his wound dressed, would walk out into the unfamiliar city. He would meet his Creator, who would explain everything.

Chapter 21

KILGORE TROUT entered the cocktail lounge. His feet were fiery hot. They were encased not only in shoes and socks, but in clear plastic, too. They could not sweat, they could not breathe.

Rabo Karabekian and Beatrice Keedsler did not see him come in. They were surrounded by new affectionate friends at the piano bar. Karabekian's speech had been splendidly received. Everybody agreed now that Midland City had one of the greatest paintings in the world.

"All you had to do was explain," said Bonnie MacMahon. "I understand now."

"I didn't think there was anything *to* explain," said Carlo Maritimo, the builder, wonderingly. "But there was, by God."

Abe Cohen, the jeweler, said to Karabekian, "If artists would explain more, people would like art more. You realize that?"

And so on.

Trout was feeling spooky. He thought maybe a lot of people were going to greet him as effusively as Milo Maritimo had done, and he had had no experience with celebrations like that. But nobody got in his way. His old friend Anonymity was by his side again, and the two of them chose a table near Dwayne Hoover and me. All he could see of me was the reflection of candle flames in my mirrored glasses, in my *leaks.*

Dwayne Hoover was still mentally absent from activities in the cocktail lounge. He sat like a lump of nose putty, staring at something long ago and far away.

Dwayne moved his lips as Trout sat down. He was saying this soundlessly, and it had nothing to do with Trout or me: "Goodbye, Blue Monday."

• • •

Trout had a fat manila envelope with him. Milo Maritimo had given it to him. It contained a program for the Festival of the Arts, a letter of welcome to Trout from Fred T. Barry, the Chairman of the Festival, a timetable of events during the coming week—and some other things.

Trout also carried a copy of his novel *Now It Can Be Told*. This was the wide-open beaver book which Dwayne Hoover would soon take so seriously.

So there the three of us were. Dwayne and Trout and I could have been included in an equilateral triangle about twelve feet on a side.

As three unwavering bands of light, we were simple and separate and beautiful. As machines, we were flabby bags of ancient plumbing and wiring, of rusty hinges and feeble springs. And our interrelationships were Byzantine.

After all, I had created both Dwayne and Trout, and now Trout was about to drive Dwayne into full-blown insanity, and Dwayne would soon bite off the tip of Trout's finger.

• • •

Wayne Hoobler was watching us through a peephole in the kitchen. There was a tap on his shoulder. The man who had fed him now told him to leave.

So he wandered outdoors, and he found himself among Dwayne's used cars again. He resumed his conversation with the traffic on the Interstate.

• • •

The bartender in the cocktail lounge now flicked on the ultraviolet lights in the ceiling. Bonnie MacMahon's uniform, since it was impregnated with fluorescent materials, lit up like an electric sign.

So did the bartender's jacket and the African masks on the walls.

So did Dwayne Hoover's shirt, and the shirts of several other men. The reason was this: Those shirts had been laundered in washday products which contained fluorescent materials. The idea was to make clothes look brighter in sunlight by making them actually fluorescent.

When the same clothes were viewed in a dark room under ultraviolet light, however, they became ridiculously bright.

Bunny Hoover's teeth also lit up, since he used a toothpaste containing fluorescent materials, which was supposed to make his smile look brighter in daylight. He grinned now, and he appeared to have a mouthful of little Christmas tree lights.

But the brightest new light in the room by far was the bosom of Kilgore Trout's new evening shirt. Its brilliance twinkled and had depth. It might have been the top of a slumping, open sack of radioactive diamonds.

But then Trout hunched forward involuntarily, buckling the starched shirt bosom, forming it into a parabolic dish. This made a searchlight of the shirt. Its beam was aimed at Dwayne Hoover.

The sudden light roused Dwayne from his trance. He thought perhaps he had died. At any rate, something painless and supernatural was going on. Dwayne smiled trustingly at the holy light. He was ready for anything.

• • •

Trout had no explanation for the fantastic transformation of certain garments around the room. Like most science-fiction writers, he knew almost nothing about science. He had no more use for solid information than did Rabo Karabekian. So now he could only be flabbergasted.

My own shirt, being an old one which had been washed many times in a Chinese laundry which used ordinary soap, did not fluoresce.

Dwayne Hoover now lost himself in the bosom of Trout's shirt, just as he had earlier lost himself in twinkling beads of lemon oil. He remembered now a thing his stepfather had told him when he was only ten years old, which was this: Why there were no Niggers in Shepherdstown.

This was not a completely irrelevant recollection. Dwayne had, after all, been talking to Bonnie MacMahon, whose husband had lost so much money in a car wash in Shepherdstown. And the main reason the car wash had failed was that successful car washes needed cheap and plentiful labor, which meant black labor—and there were no Niggers in Shepherdstown.

"Years ago," Dwayne's stepfather told Dwayne when Dwayne was ten, "Niggers was coming up north by the millions—to Chicago, to Midland City, to Indianapolis, to Detroit. The World War was going on. There was such a labor shortage that even Niggers who couldn't read or write could get good factory jobs. Niggers had money like they never had before.

"Over at Shepherdstown, though," he went on, "the white

people got smart quick. They didn't want Niggers in their town, so they put up signs on the main roads at the city limits and in the railroad yard." Dwayne's stepfather described the signs, which looked like this:

"One night—" Dwayne's stepfather said, "a Nigger family got off a boxcar in Shepherdstown. Maybe they didn't see the sign. Maybe they couldn't read it. Maybe they couldn't believe it." Dwayne's stepfather was out of work when he told the story so gleefully. The Great Depression had just begun. He and Dwayne were on a weekly expedition in the family car, hauling garbage and trash out into the country, where they dumped it all in Sugar Creek.

"Anyway, they moved into an empty shack that night," Dwayne's stepfather went on. "They got a fire going in the stove and all. So a mob went down there at midnight. They took out the man, and they sawed him in two on the top strand of a barbed-wire fence." Dwayne remembered clearly that a rainbow of oil from the trash was spreading prettily over the surface of Sugar Creek when he heard that.

"Since that night, which was a long time ago now," his stepfather said, "there ain't been a Nigger even spend the night in Shepherdstown."

• • •

Trout was itchingly aware that Dwayne was staring at his bosom so loonily. Dwayne's eyes swam, and Trout supposed they were swimming in alcohol. He could not know that Dwayne was seeing an oil slick on Sugar Creek which had made rainbows forty long years ago.

Trout was aware of me, too, what little he could see of me. I made him even more uneasy than Dwayne did. The thing was: Trout was the only character I ever created who had enough imagination to suspect that he might be the creation of another human being. He had spoken of this possibility several times to his parakeet. He had said, for instance, "Honest to God, Bill, the way things are going, all I can think of is that I'm a character in a book by somebody who wants to write about somebody who suffers all the time."

Now Trout was beginning to catch on that he was sitting very close to the person who had created him. He was embarrassed. It was hard for him to know how to respond, particularly since his responses were going to be anything I said they were.

I went easy on him, didn't wave, didn't stare. I kept my glasses on. I wrote again on my tabletop, scrawled the symbols for the interrelationship between matter and energy as it was understood in my day:

It was a flawed equation, as far as I was concerned. There should have been an "A" in there somewhere for *Awareness*— without which the "E" and the "M" and the "c," which was a mathematical constant; could not exist.

• • •

All of us were stuck to the surface of a ball, incidentally. The planet was ball-shaped. Nobody knew why we didn't fall off, even though everybody pretended to kind of understand it.

The really smart people understood that one of the best ways to get rich was to own a part of the surface people had to stick to.

• • •

Trout dreaded eye contact with either Dwayne or me, so he went through the contents of the manila envelope which had been waiting for him in his suite.

The first thing he examined was a letter from Fred T. Barry, the Chairman of the Festival of the Arts, the donor of the Mildred Barry Memorial Center for the Arts, and the founder and Chairman of the Board of Directors of Barrytron, Ltd.

Clipped to the letter was one share of common stock in Barrytron, made out in the name of Kilgore Trout. Here was the letter:

"Dear Mr. Trout:" it said, "It is a pleasure and an honor to have such a distinguished and creative person give his precious time to Midland City's first Festival of the Arts. It is our wish that you feel like a member of our family while you are here. To give you and other distinguished visitors a deeper sense of participation in the life of our community, I am making a gift to each of you of one share in the company which I founded, the company of which I am now Chairman of the Board. It is not only my company now, but yours as well.

"Our company began as The Robo-Magic Corporation of America in 1934. It had three employees in the beginning, and its mission was to design and manufacture the first fully automatic washing machine for use in the home. You will find the motto of that washing machine on the corporate emblem at the top of the stock certificate."

The emblem consisted of a Greek goddess on an ornate chaise longue. She held a flagstaff from which a long pennant streamed. Here is what the pennant said:

• • •

The motto of the old Robo-Magic washing machine cleverly confused two separate ideas people had about Monday. One idea was that women traditionally did their laundry on Monday. Monday was simply washday, and not an especially depressing day on that account.

People who had horrible jobs during the week used to call Monday "Blue Monday" sometimes, though, because they hated to return to work after a day of rest. When Fred T. Barry made up the Robo-Magic motto as a young man, he pretended that Monday was called "Blue Monday" because doing the laundry disgusted and exhausted women.

The Robo-Magic was going to cheer them up.

• • •

It wasn't true, incidentally, that most women did their laundry on Monday at the time the Robo-Magic was invented. They did it any time they felt like it. One of Dwayne Hoover's clearest recollections from the Great Depression, for instance, was when his stepmother decided to do the laundry on Christmas Eve. She was bitter about the low estate to which the family had fallen, and she suddenly clumped down into the basement, down among the black beetles and the millipedes, and did the laundry.

"Time to do the Nigger work," she said.

• • •

Fred T. Barry began advertising the Robo-Magic in 1933, long before there was a reliable machine to sell. And he was one of the few persons in Midland City who could afford billboard advertising during the Great Depression, so the Robo-Magic sales message did not have to jostle and shriek for attention. It was practically the only symbol in town.

One of Fred's ads was on a billboard outside the main gate of the defunct Keedsler Automobile Company, which the Robo-Magic Corporation had taken over. It showed a high society woman in a fur coat and pearls. She was leaving her mansion for a pleasant afternoon of idleness, and a balloon was coming out of her mouth. These were the words in the balloon:

Another ad, which was painted on a billboard by the railroad depot, showed two white deliverymen who were bringing a Robo-Magic into a house. A black maid was watching them. Her eyes were popping out in a comical way. There was a balloon coming out of her mouth, too, and she was saying this:

FEETS, GET MOVIN'! DEY'S GOT THEIRSELVES A ROBO-MAGIC! DEY AIN'T GONNA BE NEEDIN' US 'ROUN' HERE NO MO'!

*   *   *

Fred T. Barry wrote these ads himself, and he predicted at the time that Robo-Magic appliances of various sorts would eventually do what he called "all the Nigger work of the world," which was lifting and cleaning and cooking and washing and ironing and tending children and dealing with filth.

Dwayne Hoover's stepmother wasn't the only white woman who was a terrible sport about doing work like that. My own mother was that way, too, and so was my sister, may she rest in peace. They both flatly refused to do Nigger work.

The white men wouldn't do it either, of course. They called it *women's work*, and the women called it *Nigger work*.

*   *   *

I am going to make a wild guess now: I think that the end of the Civil War in my country frustrated the white people in the North, who won it, in a way which has never been acknowledged before. Their descendants inherited that frustration, I think, without ever knowing what it was.

The victors in that war were cheated out of the most desirable spoils of that war, which were human slaves.

*   *   *

The Robo-Magic dream was interrupted by World War Two. The old Keedsler Automobile Works became an armory instead of an appliance factory. All that survived of the Robo-Magic itself was its brain, which had told the rest of the machine when to let the water in, when to let the water out, when to slosh, when to rinse, when to spin dry, and so on.

That brain became the nerve center of the so-called "BLINC System" during the Second World War. It was installed on heavy bombers, and it did the actual dropping of bombs after a bombardier pressed his bright red "bombs away" button. The button activated the BLINC System, which then released the bombs in such a way as to achieve a desired pattern of explosions on the planet below. "BLINC" was an abbreviation of "Blast Interval Normalization Computer."

Chapter 22

A ND I SAT THERE in the cocktail lounge of the new Holiday Inn, watching Dwayne Hoover stare into the bosom of the shirt of Kilgore Trout. I was wearing a bracelet which looked like this:

WO1 stood for Warrant Officer First Class, which was the rank of Jon Sparks.

The bracelet had cost me two dollars and a half. It was a way of expressing my pity for the hundreds of Americans who had been taken prisoner during the war in Viet Nam. Such bracelets were becoming popular. Each one bore the name of an actual prisoner of war, his rank, and the date of his capture.

Wearers of the bracelets weren't supposed to take them off until the prisoners came home or were reported dead or missing.

I wondered how I might fit my bracelet into my story, and hit on the good idea of dropping it somewhere for Wayne Hoobler to find.

Wayne would assume that it belonged to a woman who loved somebody named WO1 Jon Sparks, and that the woman and WO1 had become engaged or married or something important on March 19th, 1971.

Wayne would mouth the unusual first name tentatively. "Woo-*ee*?" he would say. "*Woe-ee? Woe-*eye? Woy?"

• • •

There in the cocktail lounge, I gave Dwayne Hoover credit for having taken a course in speed-reading at night at the Young Men's Christian Association. This would enable him to read Kilgore Trout's novel in minutes instead of hours.

• • •

There in the cocktail lounge, I took a white pill which a doctor said I could take in moderation, two a day, in order not to feel blue.

• • •

There in the cocktail lounge, the pill and the alcohol gave me a terrific sense of urgency about explaining all the things I hadn't explained yet, and then hurtling on with my tale.

Let's see: I have already explained Dwayne's uncharacteristic ability to read so fast. Kilgore Trout probably couldn't have made his trip from New York City in the time I allotted, but it's too late to bugger around with that. Let it stand, let it stand!

Let's see, let's see. Oh, yes—I have to explain a jacket Trout will see at the hospital. It will look like this from the back:

Here is the explanation: There used to be only one Nigger high school in Midland City, and it was an all-Nigger high school still. It was named after Crispus Attucks, a black man who was shot by British troops in Boston in 1770. There was an oil painting of this event in the main corridor of the school. Several white people were stopping bullets, too. Crispus Attucks himself had a hole in his forehead which looked like the front door of a birdhouse.

But the black people didn't call the school *Crispus Attucks High School* anymore. They called it *Innocent Bystander High.*

And when another Nigger high school was built after the Second World War, it was named after George Washington Carver, a black man who was born into slavery, but who became a famous chemist anyway. He discovered many remarkable new uses for peanuts.

But the black people wouldn't call that school by its proper name, either. On the day it opened, there were already young black people wearing jackets which looked like this from the back:

• • •

I have to explain, too, see, why so many black people in Midland City were able to imitate birds from various parts of what used to be the British Empire. The thing was, see, that Fred T. Barry and his mother and father were almost the only people in Midland City who could afford to hire Niggers to do the Nigger work during the Great Depression. They took over the old Keedsler Mansion, where Beatrice Keedsler, the novelist, had been born. They had as many as twenty servants working there, all at one time.

Fred's father got so much money during the prosperity of the twenties as a bootlegger and as a swindler in stocks and bonds. He kept all his money in cash, which turned out to be a bright thing to do, since so many banks failed during the Great Depression. Also: Fred's father was an agent for Chicago gangsters who wanted to buy legitimate businesses for their children and grandchildren. Through Fred's father, those gangsters bought almost every desirable property in Midland City for anything from a tenth to a hundredth of what it was really worth.

And before Fred's mother and father came to the United States after the First World War, they were music hall entertainers in England. Fred's father played the musical saw. His mother imitated birds from various parts of what was still the British Empire.

She went on imitating them for her own amusement, well into the Great Depression. "The Bulbul of Malaysia," she would say, for instance, and then she would imitate that bird.

"The Morepark Owl of New Zealand," she would say, and then she would imitate that bird.

And all the black people who worked for her thought her act was the funniest thing they had ever seen, though they never laughed out loud when she did it. And, in order to double up their friends and relatives with laughter, they, too, learned how to imitate the birds.

The craze spread. Black people who had never been near the Keedsler mansion could imitate the Lyre Bird and the Willy Wagtail of Australia, the Golden Oriole of India, the

Nightingale and the Chaffinch and the Wren and the Chiffchaff of England itself.

They could even imitate the happy screech of the extinct companion of Kilgore Trout's island childhood, which was the Bermuda Ern.

When Kilgore Trout hit town, the black people could still imitate those birds, and say word for word what Fred's mother had said before each imitation. If one of them imitated a Nightingale, for instance, he or she would say this first: "What adds peculiar beauty to the call of the Nightingale, much beloved by poets, is the fact that it will *only* sing by moonlight."

And so on.

•   •   •

There in the cocktail lounge, Dwayne Hoover's bad chemicals suddenly decided that it was time for Dwayne to demand from Kilgore Trout the secrets of life.

"Give me the message," cried Dwayne. He tottered up from his own banquette, crashed down again next to Trout, throwing off heat like a steam radiator. "The message, please."

And here Dwayne did something extraordinarily unnatural. He did it because I wanted him to. It was something I had ached to have a character do for years and years. Dwayne did to Trout what the Duchess did to Alice in Lewis Carroll's *Alice's Adventures in Wonderland*. He rested his chin on poor Trout's shoulder, dug in with his chin.

"The message?" he said, digging in his chin, digging in his chin.

Trout made no reply. He had hoped to get through what little remained of his life without ever having to touch another human being again. Dwayne's chin on his shoulder was as shattering as buggery to Trout.

"Is this it? Is this it?" said Dwayne, snatching up Trout's novel, *Now It Can Be Told*.

"Yes—that's it," croaked Trout. To his tremendous relief, Dwayne removed his chin from his shoulder.

Dwayne now began to read hungrily, as though starved for print. And the speed-reading course he had taken at the Young Men's Christian Association allowed him to make a perfect pig of himself with pages and words.

"Dear Sir, poor sir, brave sir:" he read, "You are an experiment by the Creator of the Universe. You are the only creature in the entire Universe who has free will. You are the only one who has to figure out what to do next—and *why*. Everybody else is a robot, a machine.

"Some persons seem to like you, and others seem to hate you, and you must wonder why. They are simply liking machines and hating machines.

"You are pooped and demoralized," read Dwayne. "Why wouldn't you be? Of course it is exhausting, having to reason all the time in a universe which wasn't meant to be reasonable."

Chapter 23

D WAYNE HOOVER read on: "You are surrounded by loving machines, hating machines, greedy machines, unselfish machines, brave machines, cowardly machines, truthful machines, lying machines, funny machines, solemn machines," he read. "Their only purpose is to stir you up in every conceivable way, so the Creator of the Universe can watch your reactions. They can no more feel or reason than grandfather clocks.

"The Creator of the Universe would now like to apologize not only for the capricious, jostling companionship he provided during the test, but for the trashy, stinking condition of the planet itself. The Creator programmed robots to abuse it for millions of years, so it would be a poisonous, festering cheese when you got here. Also, He made sure it would be desperately crowded by programming robots, regardless of their living conditions, to crave sexual intercourse and adore infants more than almost anything."

• • •

Mary Alice Miller, incidentally, the Women's Breast Stroke Champion of the World and Queen of the Arts Festival, now passed through the cocktail lounge. She made a shortcut to the lobby from the side parking lot, where her father was waiting for her in his avocado 1970 Plymouth *Barracuda* fastback, which he had bought as a used car from Dwayne. It had a new car guarantee.

Mary Alice's father, Don Miller, was, among other things, Chairman of the Parole Board at Shepherdstown. It was he who had decided that Wayne Hoobler, lurking among Dwayne's used cars again, was fit to take his place in society.

Mary Alice went into the lobby to get a crown and scepter for her performance as Queen at the Arts Festival banquet that night. Milo Maritimo, the desk clerk, the gangster's grandson, had made them with his own two hands. Her eyes were permanently inflamed. They looked like maraschino cherries.

Only one person noticed her sufficiently to comment out loud. He was Abe Cohen, the jeweler. He said this about Mary

Alice, despising her sexlessness and innocence and empty mind: "Pure tuna fish!"

• • •

Kilgore Trout heard him say that—about pure tuna fish. His mind tried to make sense of it. His mind was swamped with mysteries. He might as well have been Wayne Hoobler, adrift among Dwayne's used cars during Hawaiian Week.

His feet, which were sheathed in plastic, were meanwhile getting hotter all the time. The heat was painful now. His feet were curling and twisting, begging to be plunged into cold water or waved in the air.

And Dwayne read on about himself and the Creator of the Universe, to wit:

"He also programmed robots to write books and magazines and newspapers for you, and television and radio shows, and stage shows, and films. They wrote songs for you. The Creator of the Universe had them invent hundreds of religions, so you would have plenty to choose among. He had them kill each other by the millions, for this purpose only: that you be amazed. They have committed every possible atrocity and every possible kindness unfeelingly, automatically, inevitably, to get a reaction from Y-O-U."

This last word was set in extra-large type and had a line all to itself, so it looked like this:

• • •

"Every time you went into the library," said the book, "the Creator of the Universe held His breath. With such a higgledy-piggledy cultural smorgasbord before you, what would you, with your free will, choose?

"Your parents were fighting machines and self-pitying

machines," said the book. "Your mother was programmed to
bawl out your father for being a defective moneymaking machine, and your father was programmed to bawl her out for
being a defective housekeeping machine. They were programmed to bawl each other out for being defective loving
machines.

"Then your father was programmed to stomp out of the
house and slam the door. This automatically turned your
mother into a weeping machine. And your father would go
down to a tavern where he would get drunk with some other
drinking machines. Then all the drinking machines would go
to a whorehouse and rent fucking machines. And then your
father would drag himself home to become an apologizing
machine. And your mother would become a very slow forgiving machine."

• • •

Dwayne got to his feet now, having wolfed down tens of
thousands of words of such solipsistic whimsey in ten minutes
or so.

He walked stiffly over to the piano bar. What made him stiff
was his awe of his own strength and righteousness. He dared
not use his full strength in merely walking, for fear of destroying the new Holiday Inn with footfalls. He did not fear for his
own life, Trout's book assured him that he had already been
killed twenty-three times. On each occasion, the Creator of
the Universe had patched him up and got him going again.

Dwayne restrained himself in the name of elegance rather
than safety. He was going to respond to his new understanding
of life with finesse, for an audience of two—himself and his
Creator.

He approached his homosexual son.

Bunny saw the trouble coming, supposed it was death. He
might have protected himself easily with all the techniques of
fighting he had learned in military school. But he chose to
meditate instead. He closed his eyes, and his awareness sank
into the silence of the unused lobes of his mind. This phospho-
rescent scarf floated by:

• • •

Dwayne shoved Bunny's head from behind. He rolled it like a cantaloupe up and down the keys of the piano bar. Dwayne laughed, and he called his son ". . . a God damn cock-sucking machine!"

Bunny did not resist him, even though Bunny's face was being mangled horribly. Dwayne hauled his head from the keys, slammed it down again. There was blood on the keys—and spit, and mucus.

Rabo Karabekian and Beatrice Keedsler and Bonnie Mac-Mahon all grabbed Dwayne now, pulled him away from Bunny. This increased Dwayne's glee. "Never hit a woman, right?" he said to the Creator of the Universe.

He then socked Beatrice Keedsler on the jaw. He punched Bonnie MacMahon in the belly. He honestly believed that they were unfeeling machines.

"All you robots want to know why my wife ate Drāno?" Dwayne asked his thunderstruck audience. "I'll tell you why: She was that kind of machine!"

• • •

There was a map of Dwayne's rampage in the paper the next morning. The dotted line of his route started in the cocktail lounge, crossed the asphalt to Francine Pefko's office in his automobile agency, doubled back to the new Holiday Inn again, then crossed Sugar Creek and the Westbound lane of the Interstate to the median divider, which was grass. Dwayne was subdued on the median divider by two State Policemen who happened by.

Here is what Dwayne said to the policemen as they cuffed his hands behind his back: "Thank God you're here!"

• • •

Dwayne didn't kill anybody on his rampage, but he hurt eleven people so badly they had to go to the hospital. And on the map in the newspaper there was a mark indicating each place where a person had been injured seriously. This was the mark, greatly enlarged:

• • •

In the newspaper map of Dwayne's rampage, there were three such crosses inside the cocktail lounge—for Bunny and Beatrice Keedsler and Bonnie MacMahon.

Then Dwayne ran out onto the asphalt between the Inn and his used car lot. He yelled for Niggers out there, telling them to come at once. "I want to talk to you," he said.

He was out there all alone. Nobody from the cocktail lounge had followed him yet. Mary Alice Miller's father, Don Miller, was in his car near Dwayne, waiting for Mary Alice to come back with her crown and scepter, but he never saw anything of the show Dwayne put on. His car had seats whose backs could be made to lie flat. They could be made into beds. Don was lying on his back, with his head well below window level, resting, staring at the ceiling. He was trying to learn French by means of listening to lessons recorded on tape.

"Demain nous allons passer la soirée au cinéma," said the tape, and Don tried to say it, too. "Nous espérons que notre grand-père vivra encore longtemps," said the tape. And so on.

• • •

Dwayne went on calling for Niggers to come talk to him. He smiled. He thought that the Creator of the Universe had programmed them all to hide, as a joke.

Dwayne glanced around craftily. Then he called out a signal he had used as a child to indicate that a game of hide-and-seek was over, that it was time for children in hiding to go home.

Here is what he called, and the sun was down when he called it: "Olly-olly-ox-in-freeeeeeeeeeeeeeeeeeeeeeeeeeeeeee."

The person who answered this incantation was a person who had never played hide-and-seek in his life. It was Wayne Hoobler, who came out from among the used cars quietly. He clasped his hands behind his back and placed his feet apart. He assumed the position known as *parade rest*. This position was taught to soldiers and prisoners alike—as a way of demonstrating attentiveness, gullibility, respect, and voluntary defenselessness. He was ready for anything, and wouldn't mind death.

"There you are," said Dwayne, and his eyes crinkled in bittersweet amusement. He didn't know who Wayne was. He welcomed him as a typical black robot. Any other black robot would have served as well. And Dwayne again carried on a wry talk with the Creator of the Universe, using a robot as an unfeeling conversation piece. A lot of people in Midland City put useless objects from Hawaii or Mexico or someplace like that on their coffee tables or their livingroom end tables or on what-not shelves—and such an object was called a *conversation piece.*

Wayne remained at parade rest while Dwayne told of his year as a County Executive for the Boy Scouts of America, when more black young people were brought into scouting than in any previous year. Dwayne told Wayne about his efforts to save the life of a young black man named Payton Brown, who, at the age of fifteen and a half, became the youngest person ever to die in the electric chair at Shepherdstown. Dwayne rambled on about all the black people he had hired when nobody else would hire black people, about how they never seemed to be able to get to work on time. He mentioned a few, too, who had been energetic and punctual, and he winked at Wayne, and he said this: "They were programmed that way."

He spoke of his wife and son again, acknowledged that white robots were just like black robots, essentially, in that they were programmed to be whatever they were, to do whatever they did.

Dwayne was silent for a moment after that.

Mary Alice Miller's father was meanwhile continuing to learn conversational French while lying down in his automobile, only a few yards away.

And then Dwayne took a swing at Wayne. He meant to slap him hard with his open hand, but Wayne was very good at ducking. He dropped to his knees as the hand swished through the air where his face had been.

Dwayne laughed. "African dodger!" he said. This had reference to a sort of carnival booth which was popular when Dwayne was a boy. A black man would stick his head through a hole in a piece of canvas at the back of a booth, and people would pay money for the privilege of throwing hard baseballs at his head. If they hit his head, they won a prize.

• • •

So Dwayne thought that the Creator of the Universe had invited him to play a game of African dodger now. He became cunning, concealed his violent intentions with apparent boredom. Then he kicked at Wayne very suddenly.

Wayne dodged again, and had to dodge yet again almost instantly, as Dwayne advanced with quick combinations of intended kicks, slaps, and punches. And Wayne vaulted onto the bed of a very unusual truck, which had been built on the chassis of a 1962 Cadillac limousine. It had belonged to the Maritimo Brothers Construction Company.

Wayne's new elevation gave him a view past Dwayne of both barrels of the Interstate, and of a mile or more of Will Fairchild Memorial Airport, which lay beyond. And it is important to understand at this point that Wayne had never seen an airport before, was unprepared for what could happen to an airport when a plane came in at night.

"That's all right, that's all right," Dwayne assured Wayne.

He was being a very good sport. He had no intention of climbing up on truck for another swing at Wayne. He was winded, for one thing. For another, he understood that Wayne was a perfect dodging machine. Only a perfect hitting machine could hit him. "You're too good for me," said Dwayne.

So Dwayne backed away some, contented himself with preaching up at Wayne. He spoke about human slavery—not only black slaves, but white slaves, too. Dwayne regarded coal miners and workers on assembly lines and so forth as slaves, no matter what color they were. "I used to think that was such a shame," he said. "I used to think the electric chair was a shame. I used to think war was a shame—and automobile accidents and cancer," he said, and so on.

He didn't think they were shames anymore. "Why should I care what happens to machines?" he said.

Wayne Hoobler's face had been blank so far, but now it began to bloom with uncontrollable awe. His mouth fell open.

The runway lights of Will Fairchild Memorial Airport had just come on. Those lights looked like miles and miles of bewilderingly beautiful jewelry to Wayne. He was seeing a dream come true on the other side of the Interstate.

The inside of Wayne's head lit up in recognition of that dream, lit up with an electric sign which gave a childish name to the dream—like this:

Chapter 24

LISTEN: Dwayne Hoover hurt so many people seriously that a special ambulance known as *Martha* was called, *Martha* was a full-sized General Motors transcontinental bus, but with the seats removed. There were beds for thirty-six disaster victims in there, plus a kitchen and a bathroom and an operating room. It had enough food and medical supplies aboard to serve as an independent little hospital for a week without help from the outside world.

Its full name was *The Martha Simmons Memorial Mobile Disaster Unit*, named in honor of the wife of Newbolt Simmons, a County Commissioner of Public Safety. She had died of rabies contracted from a sick bat she found clinging to her floor-to-ceiling livingroom draperies one morning. She had just been reading a biography of Albert Schweitzer, who believed that human beings should treat simpler animals lovingly. The bat nipped her ever so slightly as she wrapped it in *Kleenex*, a face tissue. She carried it out onto her patio, where she laid it gently on a form of artificial grass known as *Astroturf.*

She had thirty-six-inch hips, a twenty-nine-inch waist, and a thirty-eight-inch bosom at the time of her death. Her husband had a penis seven and a half inches long and two inches in diameter.

He and Dwayne were drawn together for a while—because his wife and Dwayne's wife had died such strange deaths within a month of each other.

They bought a gravel pit together, out on Route 23A, but then the Maritimo Brothers Construction Company offered them twice what they had paid for it. So they accepted the offer and divided up the profits, and the friendship petered out somehow. They still exchanged Christmas cards.

Dwayne's most recent Christmas card to Newbolt Simmons looked like this:

Newbolt Simmons' most recent Christmas card to Dwayne looked like this:

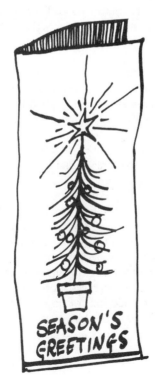

• • •

My psychiatrist is also named Martha. She gathers jumpy people together into little families which meet once a week. It's a lot of fun. She teaches us how to comfort one another intelligently. She is on vacation now. I like her a lot.

And I think now, as my fiftieth birthday draws near, about the American novelist Thomas Wolfe, who was only thirty-eight years old when he died. He got a lot of help in organizing his novels from Maxwell Perkins, his editor at Charles Scribner's Sons. I have heard that Perkins told him to keep in mind as he wrote, as a unifying idea, a hero's search for a father.

It seems to me that really truthful American novels would have the heroes and heroines alike looking for *mothers* instead. This needn't be embarrassing. It's simply true.

A mother is much more useful.

I wouldn't feel particularly good if I found another father. Neither would Dwayne Hoover. Neither would Kilgore Trout.

• • •

And just as motherless Dwayne Hoover was berating motherless Wayne Hoobler in the used car lot, a man who had actually killed his mother was preparing to land in a chartered plane at Will Fairchild Memorial Airport, on the other side of the Interstate. This was Eliot Rosewater, Kilgore Trout's patron. He killed his mother accidentally in a boating accident, when a youth. She was Women's Chess Champion of the United States of America, nineteen hundred and thirty-six years after the Son of God was born, supposedly. Rosewater killed her the year after that.

It was his pilot who caused the airport's runways to become an ex-convict's idea of fairyland. Rosewater remembered his mother's jewelry when the lights came on. He looked to the west, and he smiled at the rosy loveliness of the Mildred Barry Memorial Arts Center, a harvest moon on stilts in a bend of Sugar Creek. It reminded him of how his mother had looked when he saw her through the bleary eyes of infancy.

• • •

I had made him up, of course—and his pilot, too. I put Colonel Looseleaf Harper, the man who had dropped an atomic bomb on Nagasaki, Japan, at the controls.

I made Rosewater an alcoholic in another book. I now had him reasonably well sobered up, with the help of Alcoholics Anonymous. I had him use his new-found sobriety to explore, among other things, the supposed spiritual and physical benefits of sexual orgies with strangers in New York City. He was only confused so far.

I could have killed him, and his pilot, too, but I let them live on. So their plane touched down uneventfully.

•   •   •

The two physicians on the disaster vehicle named *Martha* were Cyprian Ukwende, of Nigeria, and Khashdrahr Miasma, from the infant nation of Bangladesh. Both were parts of the world which were famous from time to time for having the food run out. Both places were specifically mentioned, in fact, in *Now It Can Be Told*, by Kilgore Trout. Dwayne Hoover read in that book that robots all over the world were constantly running out of fuel and dropping dead, while waiting around to test the only free-willed creature in the Universe, on the off-chance that he should appear.

•   •   •

At the wheel of the ambulance was Eddie Key, a young black man who was a direct descendant of Francis Scott Key, the white American patriot who wrote the National Anthem. Eddie knew he was descended from Key. He could name more than six hundred of his ancestors, and had at least an anecdote about each. They were Africans, Indians and white men.

He knew, for instance, that his mother's side of the family had once owned the farm on which Sacred Miracle Cave was discovered, that his ancestors had called it "Bluebird Farm."

•   •   •

Here was why there were so many young foreign doctors on the hospital staff, incidentally: The country didn't produce nearly enough doctors for all the sick people it had, but it had an awful lot of money. So it bought doctors from other countries which didn't have much money.

• • •

Eddie Key knew so much about his ancestry because the black part of his family had done what so many African families still do in Africa, which was to have one member of each generation whose duty it was to memorize the history of the family so far. Eddie Key had begun to store in his mind the names and adventures of ancestors on both his mother's and father's sides of his family when he was only six years old. As he sat in the front of the disaster vehicle, looking out through the windshield, he had the feeling that he himself was a vehicle, and that his eyes were windshields through which his progenitors could look, if they wished to.

Francis Scott Key was only one of thousands back there. On the off-chance that Key might now be having a look at what had become of the United States of America so far, Eddie focussed his eyes on an American flag which was stuck to the windshield. He said this very quietly: "Still wavin', man."

• • •

Eddie Key's familiarity with a teeming past made life much more interesting to him than it was to Dwayne, for instance, or to me, or to Kilgore Trout, or to almost any white person in Midland City that day. We had no sense of anybody else using our eyes—or our hands. We didn't even know who our great-grandfathers and great-grandmothers were. Eddie Key was afloat in a river of people who were flowing from here to there in time. Dwayne and Trout and I were pebbles at rest.

And Eddie Key, because he knew so much by heart, was able to have deep, nourishing feelings about Dwayne Hoover, for instance, and about Dr. Cyprian Ukwende, too. Dwayne was a man whose family had taken over Bluebird Farm. Ukwende, an Indaro, was a man whose ancestors had kidnapped an ancestor of Key's on the West Coast of Africa, a man named Ojumwa. The Indaros sold him for a musket to British slave traders, who took him on a sailing ship named the "Skylark" to

Charleston, South Carolina, where he was auctioned off as a self-propelled, self-repairing farm machine.

And so on.

• • •

Dwayne Hoover was now hustled aboard *Martha* through big double doors in her rear, just ahead of the engine compartment. Eddie Key was in the driver's seat, and he watched the action in his rearview mirror. Dwayne was swaddled so tightly in canvas restraining sheets that his reflection looked to Eddie like a bandaged thumb.

Dwayne didn't notice the restraints. He thought he was on the virgin planet promised by the book by Kilgore Trout. Even when he was laid out horizontally by Cyprian Ukwende and Khashdrahr Miasma, he thought he was standing up. The book had told him that he went swimming in cold water on the virgin planet, that he always yelled something surprising when he climbed out of the icy pool. It was a game. The Creator of the Universe would try to guess what Dwayne would yell each day. And Dwayne would fool him totally.

Here is what Dwayne yelled in the ambulance: "Goodbye, Blue Monday!" Then it seemed to him that another day had passed on the virgin planet, and it was time to yell again. "Not a cough in a carload!" he yelled.

• • •

Kilgore Trout was one of the walking wounded. He was able to climb aboard *Martha* without assistance, and to choose a place to sit where he would be away from real emergencies. He had jumped Dwayne Hoover from behind when Dwayne dragged Francine Pefko out of Dwayne's showroom and onto the asphalt. Dwayne wanted to give her a beating in public, which his bad chemicals made him think she richly deserved.

Dwayne had already broken her jaw and three ribs in the office. When he trundled her outside, there was a fairsize crowd which had drifted out of the cocktail lounge and the kitchen of the new Holiday Inn. "Best fucking machine in the State," he told the crowd. "Wind her up, and she'll fuck you and say she loves you, and she won't shut up till you give her a Colonel Sanders Kentucky Fried Chicken franchise."

And so on. Trout grabbed him from behind.

Trout's right ring finger somehow slipped into Dwayne's mouth, and Dwayne bit off the topmost joint. Dwayne let go of Francine after that, and she slumped to the asphalt. She was unconscious, and the most seriously injured of all. And Dwayne went cantering over to the concrete trough by the Interstate, and he spat Kilgore Trout's fingertip into Sugar Creek.

• • •

Kilgore Trout did not choose to lie down in *Martha*. He settled into a leather bucket seat behind Eddie Key. Key asked him what was the matter with him, and Trout held up his right hand, partly shrouded in a bloody handkerchief, which looked like this:

"A slip of the lip can sink a ship!" yelled Dwayne.

• • •

"Remember Pearl Harbor!" yelled Dwayne. Most of what he had done during the past three-quarters of an hour had been hideously unjust. But he had spared Wayne Hoobler, at least. Wayne was back among the used cars again, unscathed.

He was picking up a bracelet which I had pitched back there for him to find.

As for myself: I kept a respectful distance between myself and all the violence—even though I had created Dwayne and his violence and the city, and the sky above and the Earth below. Even so, I came out of the riot with a broken watch crystal and what turned out later to be a broken toe. Somebody jumped backwards to get out of Dwayne's way. He broke my watch crystal, even though I had created him, and he broke my toe.

• • •

This isn't the kind of book where people get what is coming to them at the end. Dwayne hurt only one person who deserved to be hurt for being so wicked: That was Don Breedlove. Breedlove was the white gas-conversion unit installer who had raped Patty Keene, the waitress in Dwayne's Burger Chef out on Crestview Avenue, in the parking lot of George Hickman Bannister Memorial Fieldhouse out at the County Fairgrounds after Peanut University beat Innocent Bystander High School in the Regional Class High School Basketball Playoffs.

• • •

Don Breedlove was in the kitchen of the Inn when Dwayne began his rampage. He was repairing a defective gas oven in there.

He stepped outside for some fresh air, and Dwayne came running up to him. Dwayne had just spit Kilgore Trout's fingertip into Sugar Creek. Don and Dwayne knew each other quite well, since Dwayne had once sold Breedlove a new Pontiac *Ventura*, which Don said was a lemon. A lemon was an automobile which didn't run right, and which nobody was able to repair.

Dwayne actually lost money on the transaction, making adjustments and replacing parts in an attempt to mollify Breedlove. But Breedlove was inconsolable, and he finally painted this sign in bright yellow on his trunk lid and on both doors:

Here was what was really wrong with the car, incidentally. The child of a neighbor of Breedlove had put maple sugar in the gas tank of the *Ventura*. Maple sugar was a kind of candy made from the blood of trees.

So Dwayne Hoover now extended his right hand to Breedlove, and Breedlove without thinking anything about it took that hand in his own. They linked up like this:

This was a symbol of friendship between men. The feeling was, too, that a lot of character could be read into the way a man shook hands. Dwayne and Don Breedlove gave each other squeezes which were dry and hard.

So Dwayne held on to Don Breedlove with his right hand, and he smiled as though bygones were bygones. Then he made a cup out of his left hand, and he hit Don on the ear with the open end of the cup. This created terrific air pressure in Don's ear. He fell down because the pain was so awful. Don would never hear anything with that ear, ever again.

• • •

So Don was in the ambulance, too, now—sitting up like Kilgore Trout. Francine was lying down—unconscious but moaning. Beatrice Keedsler was lying down, although she might have sat up. Her jaw was broken. Bunny Hoover was lying down. His face was unrecognizable, even as a face—anybody's face. He had been given morphine by Cyprian Ukwende.

There were five other victims as well—one white female, two white males, two black males. The three white people had never been in Midland City before. They were on their way to-gether from Erie, Pennsylvania, to the Grand Canyon, which was the deepest crack on the planet. They wanted to look down into the crack, but they never got to do it. Dwayne Hoover assaulted them as they walked from the car toward the lobby of the new Holiday Inn.

The two black males were both kitchen employees of the Inn.

• • •

Cyprian Ukwende now tried to remove Dwayne Hoover's shoes—but Dwayne's shoes and laces and socks were impreg-nated with the plastic material, which he had picked up while wading across Sugar Creek.

Ukwende was not mystified by plasticized, unitized shoes and socks. He saw shoes and socks like that every day at the hospital, on the feet of children who had played too close to Sugar Creek. In fact, he had hung a pair of tinsnips on the wall of the hospital's emergency room—for cutting off plasticized, unitized shoes and socks.

He turned to his Bengali assistant, young Dr. Khashdrahr Miasma. "Get some shears," he said.

Miasma was standing with his back to the door of the ladies' toilet on the emergency vehicle. He had done nothing so far to deal with all the emergencies. Ukwende and police and a team from Civil Defense had done the work so far. Miasma now refused even to find some shears.

Basically, Miasma probably shouldn't have been in the field of medicine at all, or at least not in any area where there was a chance that he might be criticized. He could not tolerate criticism. This was a characteristic beyond his control. Any hint that anything about him was not absolutely splendid automatically turned him into a useless, sulky child who would only say that it wanted to go home.

That was what he said when Ukwende told him a second time to find shears: "I want to go home."

Here is what he had been criticized for, just before the alarm came in about Dwayne's going berserk: He had amputated a black man's foot, whereas the foot could probably have been saved.

And so on.

• • •

I could go on and on with the intimate details about the various lives of people on the super-ambulance, but what good is more information?

I agree with Kilgore Trout about realistic novels and their accumulations of nit-picking details. In Trout's novel, *The Pan-Galactic Memory Bank*, the hero is on a space ship two hundred miles long and sixty-two miles in diameter. He gets a realistic novel out of the branch library in his neighborhood. He reads about sixty pages of it, and then he takes it back.

The librarian asks him why he doesn't like it, and he says to her, "I already know about human beings."

And so on.

• • •

Martha began to move. Kilgore Trout saw a sign he liked a lot. Here is what it said:

IT IS HARDER
TO BE UNHAPPY
WHEN YOU
ARE EATING

CRAIG'S
ICE CREAM

And so on.

Dwayne Hoover's awareness returned to Earth momentarily. He spoke of opening a health club in Midland City, with rowing machines and stationary bicycles and whirlpool baths and sunlamps and a swimming pool and so on. He told Cyprian Ukwende that the thing to do with a health club was to open it and then sell it as soon as possible for a profit. "People get all enthusiastic about getting back in shape or losing some pounds," said Dwayne. "They sign up for the program, but then they lose interest in about a year, and they stop coming. That's how people are."

And so on.

Dwayne wasn't going to open any health club. He wasn't going to open anything ever again. The people he had injured so unjustly would sue him so vengefully that he would be rendered destitute. He would become one more withered balloon of an old man on Midland City's Skid Row, which was the neighborhood of the once fashionable Fairchild Hotel. He would be by no means the only drifter of whom it could be truthfully said, "See him? Can you believe it? He doesn't have doodley-squat now, but he used to be fabulously well-to-do."

And so on.

Kilgore Trout now peeled strips and patches of plastic from his burning shins and feet in the ambulance. He had to use his uninjured left hand.

Epilogue

THE EMERGENCY ROOM of the hospital was in the basement. After Kilgore Trout had the stump of his ring finger disinfected and trimmed and bandaged, he was told to go upstairs to the finance office. There were certain forms he had to fill out, since he was from outside Midland County, had no health insurance, and was destitute. He had no checkbook. He had no cash.

He got lost in the basement for a little while, as a lot of people did. He found the double doors to the morgue, as a lot of people did. He automatically mooned about his own mortality, as a lot of people did. He found an x-ray room, which wasn't in use. It made him wonder automatically if anything bad was growing inside himself. Other people had wondered exactly the same thing when they passed that room.

Trout felt nothing now that millions of other people wouldn't have felt—automatically.

And Trout found stairs, but they were the wrong stairs. They led him not to the lobby and the finance office and the gift shop and all that, but into a matrix of rooms where persons were recovering or failing to recover from injuries of all kinds. Many of the people there had been flung to the earth by the force of gravity, which never relaxed for a second.

Trout passed a very expensive private room now, and there was a young black man in there, with a white telephone and a color television set and boxes of candy and bouquets of flowers all around. He was Elgin Washington, a pimp who operated out of the old Holiday Inn. He was only twenty-six years old, but he was fabulously well-to-do.

Visiting hours had ended, so all his female sex slaves had departed. But they had left clouds of perfume behind. Trout gagged as he passed the door. It was an automatic reaction to the fundamentally unfriendly cloud. Elgin Washington had just sniffed cocaine into his sinus passages, which amplified tremendously the telepathic messages he sent and received. He felt one hundred times bigger than life, because the messages were so loud and exciting. It was their noise that thrilled him. He didn't care what they said.

And, in the midst of the uproar, Elgin Washington said something wheedlingly to Trout. "Hey man, hey man, hey man," he wheedled. He had had his foot amputated earlier in the day by Khashdrahr Miasma, but he had forgotten that. "Hey man, hey man," he coaxed. He wanted nothing particular from Trout. Some part of his mind was idly exercising his skill at making strangers come to him. He was a fisherman for men's souls. "Hey man—" he said. He showed a gold tooth. He winked an eye.

Trout came to the foot of the black man's bed. This wasn't compassion on his part. He was being machinery again. Trout was, like so many Earthlings, a fully automatic boob when a pathological personality like Elgin Washington told him what to want, what to do. Both men, incidentally, were descendants of the Emperor Charlemagne. Anybody with any European blood in him was a descendant of the Emperor Charlemagne.

Elgin Washington perceived that he had caught yet another human being without really meaning to. It was not in his nature to let one go without making him feel in some way diminished, in some way a fool. Sometimes he actually killed a man in order to diminish him, but he was gentle with Trout. He closed his eyes as though thinking hard, then he earnestly said, "I think I may be dying."

"I'll get a nurse!" said Trout. Any human being would have said exactly the same thing.

"No, no," said Elgin Washington, waving his hands in dreamy protest. "I'm dying *slow*. It's gradual."

"I see," said Trout.

"You got to do me a favor," said Washington. He had no idea what favor to ask. It would come to him. Ideas for favors always came.

"What favor?" said Trout uneasily. He stiffened at the mention of an unspecified favor. He was that kind of a machine. Washington knew he would stiffen. Every human being was that kind of a machine.

"I want you to listen to me while I whistle the song of the Nightingale," he said. He commanded Trout to be silent by giving him the evil eye. "What adds peculiar beauty to the call of the Nightingale, much beloved by poets," he said, "is the fact that it will *only* sing by moonlight." Then he did what almost every black person in Midland City would do: He imitated a Nightingale.

• • •

The Midland City Festival of the Arts was postponed because of madness. Fred T. Barry, its chairman, came to the hospital in his limousine, dressed like a Chinaman, to offer his sympathy to Beatrice Keedsler and Kilgore Trout. Trout could not be found anywhere. Beatrice Keedsler had been put to sleep with morphine.

Kilgore Trout assumed that the Arts Festival would still take place that night. He had no money for any form of transportation, so he set out on foot. He began the five mile walk down Fairchild Boulevard—toward a tiny amber dot at the other end. The dot was the Midland City Center for the Arts. He would make it grow by walking toward it. When his walking had made it big enough, it would swallow him up. There would be food inside.

• • •

I was waiting to intercept him, about six blocks away. I sat in a Plymouth *Duster* I had rented from *Avis* with my *Diners' Club* card. I had a paper tube in my mouth. It was stuffed with leaves. I set it on fire. It was a *soigné* thing to do.

My penis was three inches long and five inches in diameter. Its diameter was a world's record as far as I knew. It slumbered now in my *Jockey Shorts.* And I got out of the car to stretch my legs, which was another *soigné* thing to do. I was among factories and warehouses. The streetlights were widely-spaced and feeble. Parking lots were vacant, except for night watchmen's cars which were here and there. There was no traffic on Fairchild Boulevard, which had once been the aorta of the town. The life had all been drained out of it by the Interstate and by the Robert F. Kennedy Inner Belt Expressway, which was built on the old right-of-way of the Monon Railroad. The Monon was defunct.

• • •

Defunct.

•   •   •

Nobody slept in that part of town. Nobody lurked there. It was a system of forts at night, with high fences and alarms, and with prowling dogs. They were killing machines.

When I got out of my Plymouth *Duster*, I feared nothing. That was foolish of me. A writer off-guard, since the materials with which he works are so dangerous, can expect agony as quick as a thunderclap.

I was about to be attacked by a Doberman pinscher. He was a leading character in an earlier version of this book.

•   •   •

Listen: That Doberman's name was *Kazak*. He patrolled the supply yard of the Maritimo Brothers Construction Company at night. Kazak's trainers, the people who explained to him what sort of a planet he was on and what sort of an animal he was, taught him that the Creator of the Universe wanted him to kill anything he could catch, and to *eat* it, too.

In an earlier version of this book, I had Benjamin Davis, the black husband of Lottie Davis, Dwayne Hoover's maid, take care of Kazak. He threw raw meat down into the pit where Kazak lived in the daytime. He dragged Kazak into the pit at sunrise. He screamed at him and threw tennis balls at him at sundown. Then he turned him loose.

Benjamin Davis was first trumpet with the Midland City Symphony Orchestra, but he got no pay for that, so he needed a real job. He wore a thick gown made of war-surplus mattresses and chicken wire, so Kazak could not kill him. Kazak tried and tried. There were chunks of mattress and swatches of chicken wire all over the yard.

And Kazak did his best to kill anybody who came too close to the fence which enclosed his planet. He leaped at people as though the fence weren't there. The fence bellied out toward the sidewalk everywhere. It looked as though somebody had been shooting cannonballs at it from inside.

I should have noticed the queer shape of the fence when I got out of my automobile, when I did the *soigné* thing of lighting a cigarette. I should have known that a character as ferocious as Kazak was not easily cut out of a novel.

Kazak was crouching behind a pile of bronze pipe which the Maritimo Brothers had bought cheap from a hijacker earlier that day. Kazak meant to kill and *eat* me.

•   •   •

I turned my back to the fence, took a deep puff of my cigarette. *Pall Malls* would kill me by and by. And I mooned philosophically at the murky battlements of the old Keedsler Mansion, on the other side of Fairchild Boulevard.

Beatrice Keedsler had been raised in there. The most famous murders in the city's history had been committed there. Will Fairchild, the war hero, and the maternal uncle of Beatrice Keedsler, appeared one summer night in 1926 with a Springfield rifle. He shot and killed five relatives, three servants, two policemen, and all the animals in the Keedslers' private zoo. Then he shot himself through his heart.

When an autopsy was performed on him, a tumor the size of a piece of birdshot was found in his brain. This was what *caused* the murders.

•   •   •

After the Keedslers lost the mansion at the start of the Great Depression, Fred T. Barry and his parents moved in. The old place was filled with the sounds of British birds. It was silent property of the city now, and there was talk of making it into a museum where children could learn the history of Midland City—as told by arrowheads and stuffed animals and white men's early artifacts.

Fred T. Barry had offered to donate half a million dollars to the proposed museum, on one condition: that the first *Robo-Magic* and the early posters which advertised it be put on display.

And he wanted the exhibit to show, too, how machines evolved just as animals did, but with much greater speed.

•   •   •

I gazed at the Keedsler mansion, never dreaming that a volcanic dog was about to erupt behind me. Kilgore Trout came nearer. I was almost indifferent to his approach, although we had momentous things to say to one another about my having created him.

I thought instead of my paternal grandfather, who had been the first licensed architect in Indiana. He had designed some dream houses for *Hoosier* millionaires. They were mortuaries and guitar schools and cellar holes and parking lots now. I thought of my mother, who drove me around Indianapolis one time during the Great Depression, to impress me with how rich and powerful my maternal grandfather had been. She showed me where his brewery had been, where some of his dream houses had been. Every one of the monuments was a cellar hole.

Kilgore Trout was only half a block from his Creator now, and slowing down. I worried him.

I turned toward him, so that my sinus cavities, where all telepathic messages were sent and received, were lined up symmetrically with his. I told him this over and over telepathically: "I have good news for you."

Kazak sprung.

•   •   •

I saw Kazak out of the corner of my right eye. His eyes were pinwheels. His teeth were white daggers. His slobber was cyanide. His blood was nitroglycerine.

He was floating toward me like a zeppelin, hanging lazily in air.

My eyes told my mind about him.

My mind sent a message to my hypothalamus, told it to release the hormone CRF into the short vessels connecting my hypothalamus and my pituitary gland.

The CRF inspired my pituitary gland to dump the hormone ACTH into my bloodstream. My pituitary had been making and storing ACTH for just such an occasion. And nearer and nearer the zeppelin came.

And some of the ACTH in my bloodstream reached the outer shell of my adrenal gland, which had been making and storing glucocorticoids for emergencies. My adrenal gland added the glucocorticoids to my bloodstream. They went all over my body, changing glycogen into glucose. Glucose was muscle food. It would help me fight like a wildcat or run like a deer.

And nearer and nearer the zeppelin came.

My adrenal gland gave me a shot of adrenaline, too. I turned purple as my blood pressure skyrocketed. The adrenaline made my heart go like a burglar alarm. It also stood my hair on end. It also caused coagulants to pour into my bloodstream, so, in case I was wounded, my vital juices wouldn't drain away.

Everything my body had done so far fell within normal operating procedures for a human machine. But my body took one defensive measure which I am told was without precedent in medical history. It may have happened because some wire short-circuited or some gasket blew. At any rate, I also retracted my testicles into my abdominal cavity, pulled them into my fuselage like the landing gear of an airplane. And now they tell me that only surgery will bring them down again.

Be that as it may, Kilgore Trout watched me from half a block away, not knowing who I was, not knowing about Kazak and what my body had done about Kazak so far.

Trout had had a full day already, but it wasn't over yet. Now he saw his Creator leap completely over an automobile.

• • •

I landed on my hands and knees in the middle of Fairchild Boulevard.

Kazak was flung back by the fence. Gravity took charge of him as it had taken charge of me. Gravity slammed him down on concrete. Kazak was knocked silly.

Kilgore Trout turned away. He hastened anxiously back toward the hospital. I called out to him, but that only made him walk faster.

So I jumped into my car and chased him. I was still high as a kite on adrenaline and coagulants and all that. I did not know yet that I had retracted my testicles in all the excitement. I felt only vague discomfort down there.

Trout was cantering when I came alongside. I clocked him at eleven miles an hour, which was excellent for a man his age. He, too, was now full of adrenaline and coagulants and glucocorticoids.

My windows were rolled down, and I called this to him: "Whoa! Whoa! Mr. Trout! Whoa! Mr. Trout!"

It slowed him down to be called by name.

"Whoa! I'm a friend!" I said. He shuffled to a stop, leaned in panting exhaustion against a fence surrounding an appliance warehouse belonging to the General Electric Company. The company's monogram and motto hung in the night sky behind Kilgore Trout, whose eyes were wild. The motto was this:

PROGRESS IS OUR MOST IMPORTANT PRODUCT

• • •

"Mr. Trout," I said from the unlighted interior of the car, "you have nothing to fear. I bring you tidings of great joy."

He was slow to get his breath back, so he wasn't much of a conversationalist at first. "Are—are you—from the—the Arts Festival?" he said. His eyes rolled and rolled.

"I am from the *Everything* Festival," I replied.

"The what?" he said.

I thought it would be a good idea to let him have a good look at me, and so attempted to flick on the dome light. I turned on the windshield washers instead. I turned them off again. My view of the lights of the County Hospital was garbled by beads of water. I pulled at another switch, and it came away in my hand. It was a cigarette lighter. So I had no choice but to continue to speak from darkness.

"Mr. Trout," I said, "I am a novelist, and I created you for use in my books."

"Pardon me?" he said.

"I'm your Creator," I said. "You're in the middle of a book right now—close to the end of it, actually."

"Um," he said.

"Are there any questions you'd like to ask?"

"Pardon me?" he said.

"Feel free to ask anything you want—about the past, about the future," I said. "There's a Nobel Prize in your future."

"A what?" he said.

"A Nobel Prize in medicine."

"Huh," he said. It was a noncommittal sound.

"I've also arranged for you to have a reputable publisher from now on. No more beaver books for you."

"Um," he said.

"If I were in your spot, I would certainly have lots of questions," I said.

"Do you have a gun?" he said.

I laughed there in the dark, tried to turn on the light again, activated the windshield washer again. "I don't need a gun to control you, Mr. Trout. All I have to do is write down something about you, and that's it."

• • •

"Are you *crazy*?" he said.

"No," I said. And I shattered his power to doubt me. I transported him to the Taj Mahal and then to Venice and then to Dar es Salaam and then to the surface of the Sun, where the flames could not consume him—and then back to Midland City again.

The poor old man crashed to his knees. He reminded me of the way my mother and Bunny Hoover's mother used to act whenever somebody tried to take their photographs.

As he cowered there, I transported him to the Bermuda of his childhood, had him contemplate the infertile egg of a Bermuda Ern. I took him from there to the Indianapolis of my childhood. I put him in a circus crowd there. I had him see a man with *locomotor ataxia* and a woman with a goiter as big as a zucchini.

• • •

I got out of my rented car. I did it noisily, so his ears would tell him a lot about his *Creator*, even if he was unwilling to use his eyes. I slammed the car door firmly. As I approached him from the driver's side of the car, I swiveled my feet some, so that my footsteps were not only deliberate but *gritty*, too.

I stopped with the tips of my shoes on the rim of the narrow field of his downcast eyes. "Mr. Trout, I love you," I said gently. "I have broken your mind to pieces. I want to make it whole. I want you to feel a wholeness and inner harmony such as I have never allowed you to feel before. I want you to raise your eyes, to look at what I have in my hand."

I had nothing in my hand, but such was my power over Trout that he would see in it whatever I wished him to see. I might have shown him a Helen of Troy, for instance, only six inches tall.

"Mr. Trout—*Kilgore*—" I said, "I hold in my hand a symbol of wholeness and harmony and nourishment. It is Oriental in its simplicity, but we are *Americans*, Kilgore, and not Chinamen. We Americans require symbols which are richly colored and three-dimensional and juicy. Most of all, we hunger for symbols which have not been poisoned by great sins our nation has committed, such as slavery and genocide and criminal neglect, or by tinhorn commercial greed and cunning.

"Look up, Mr. Trout," I said, and I waited patiently. "Kilgore—?"

The old man looked up, and he had my father's wasted face when my father was a widower—when my father was an old old man.

He saw that I held an apple in my hand.

• • •

"I am approaching my fiftieth birthday, Mr. Trout," I said. "I am cleansing and renewing myself for the very different sorts of years to come. Under similar spiritual conditions, Count Tolstoi freed his serfs. Thomas Jefferson freed his slaves. I am going to set at liberty all the literary characters who have served me so loyally during my writing career.

"You are the only one I am telling. For the others, tonight will be a night like any other night. Arise, Mr. Trout, you are free, you are *free*."

He arose shamblingly.

I might have shaken his hand, but his right hand was injured, so our hands remained dangling at our sides.

"*Bon voyage*," I said. I disappeared.

• • •

I somersaulted lazily and pleasantly through the void, which is my hiding place when I dematerialize. Trout's cries to me faded as the distance between us increased.

His voice was my father's voice. I *heard* my father—and I

saw my mother in the void. My mother stayed far, far away, because she had left me a legacy of suicide.

A small hand mirror floated by. It was a *leak* with a mother-of-pearl handle and frame. I captured it easily, held it up to my own right eye, which looked like this:

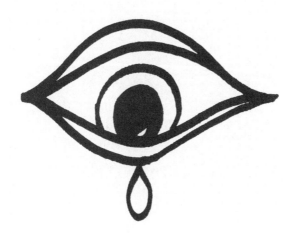

Here was what Kilgore Trout cried out to me in my father's voice: "*Make me young, make me young, make me young!*"

STORIES

Welcome to the Monkey House

So Pete Crocker, the sheriff of Barnstable County, which was the whole of Cape Cod, came into the Federal Ethical Suicide Parlor in Hyannis one May afternoon—and he told the two six-foot Hostesses there that they weren't to be alarmed, but that a notorious nothinghead named Billy the Poet was believed headed for the Cape.

A nothinghead was a person who refused to take his ethical birth-control pills three times a day. The penalty for that was $10,000 and ten years in jail.

This was at a time when the population of Earth was 17 billion human beings. That was far too many mammals that big for a planet that small. The people were virtually packed together like drupelets.

Drupelets are the pulpy little knobs that compose the outside of a raspberry.

So the World Government was making a two-pronged attack on overpopulation. One pronging was the encouragement of ethical suicide, which consisted of going to the nearest Suicide Parlor and asking a Hostess to kill you painlessly while you lay on a Barcalounger. The other pronging was compulsory ethical birth control.

The sheriff told the Hostesses, who were pretty, tough-minded, highly intelligent girls, that roadblocks were being set up and house-to-house searches were being conducted to catch Billy the Poet. The main difficulty was that the police didn't know what he looked like. The few people who had seen him and known him for what he was were women—and they disagreed fantastically as to his height, his hair color, his voice, his weight, the color of his skin.

"I don't need to remind you girls," the sheriff went on, "that a nothinghead is very sensitive from the waist down. If Billy the Poet somehow slips in here and starts making trouble, one good kick in the right place will do wonders."

He was referring to the fact that ethical birth-control pills, the only legal form of birth control, made people numb from the waist down.

Most men said their bottom halves felt like cold iron or balsawood. Most women said their bottom halves felt like wet cotton or stale ginger ale. The pills were so effective that you could blindfold a man who had taken one, tell him to recite the Gettysburg Address, kick him in the balls while he was doing it, and he wouldn't miss a syllable.

The pills were ethical because they didn't interfere with a person's ability to reproduce, which would have been unnatural and immoral. All the pills did was take every bit of pleasure out of sex.

Thus did science and morals go hand in hand.

The two Hostesses there in Hyannis were Nancy McLuhan and Mary Kraft. Nancy was a strawberry blonde. Mary was a glossy brunette. Their uniforms were white lipstick, heavy eye makeup, purple body stockings with nothing underneath, and black-leather boots. They ran a small operation—with only six suicide booths. In a really good week, say the one before Christmas, they might put sixty people to sleep. It was done with a hypodermic syringe.

"My main message to you girls," said Sheriff Crocker, "is that everything's well under control. You can just go about your business here."

"Didn't you leave out part of your main message?" Nancy asked him.

"I don't get you."

"I didn't hear you say he was probably headed straight for us."

He shrugged in clumsy innocence. "We don't know that for sure."

"I thought that was all anybody *did* know about Billy the Poet: that he specializes in deflowering Hostesses in Ethical Suicide Parlors." Nancy was a virgin. All Hostesses were virgins. They also had to hold advanced degrees in psychology and nursing. They also had to be plump and rosy, and at least six feet tall.

America had changed in many ways, but it had yet to adopt the metric system.

Nancy McLuhan was burned up that the sheriff would try to protect her and Mary from the full truth about Billy the

Poet—as though they might panic if they heard it. She told the sheriff so.

"How long do you think a girl would last in the E. S. S.," she said, meaning the Ethical Suicide Service, "if she scared that easy?"

The sheriff took a step backward, pulled in his chin. "Not very long, I guess."

"That's very true," said Nancy, closing the distance between them and offering him a sniff of the edge of her hand, which was poised for a karate chop. All Hostesses were experts at judo and karate. "If you'd like to find out how helpless we are, just come toward me, pretending you're Billy the Poet."

The sheriff shook his head, gave her a glassy smile. "I'd rather not."

"That's the smartest thing you've said today," said Nancy, turning her back on him while Mary laughed. "We're not scared—we're *angry*. Or we're not even *that*. He isn't *worth* that. We're *bored*. How boring that he should come a great distance, should cause all this fuss, in order to—" She let the sentence die there. "It's just too absurd."

"I'm not as mad at *him* as I am at the women who let him do it to them without a struggle"—said Mary—"who let him do it and then couldn't tell the police what he looked like. Suicide Hostesses at that!"

"Somebody hasn't been keeping up with her karate," said Nancy.

It wasn't just Billy the Poet who was attracted to Hostesses in Ethical Suicide Parlors. All nothingheads were. Bombed out of their skulls with the sex madness that came from taking nothing, they thought the white lips and big eyes and body stocking and boots of a Hostess spelled *sex, sex, sex*.

The truth was, of course, that sex was the last thing any Hostess ever had in mind.

"If Billy follows his usual M. O.," said the sheriff, "he'll study your habits and the neighborhood. And then he'll pick one or the other of you and he'll send her a dirty poem in the mail."

"Charming," said Nancy.

"He has also been known to use the telephone."

"How brave," said Nancy. Over the sheriff's shoulder, she could see the mailman coming.

A blue light went on over the door of a booth for which Nancy was responsible. The person in there wanted something. It was the only booth in use at the time.

The sheriff asked her if there was a possibility that the person in there was Billy the Poet, and Nancy said, "Well, if it is, I can break his neck with my thumb and forefinger."

"Foxy Grandpa," said Mary, who'd seen him, too. A Foxy Grandpa was any old man, cute and senile, who quibbled and joked and reminisced for hours before he let a Hostess put him to sleep.

Nancy groaned. "We've spent the past two hours trying to decide on a last meal."

And then the mailman came in with just one letter. It was addressed to Nancy in smeary pencil. She was splendid with anger and disgust as she opened it, knowing it would be a piece of filth from Billy.

She was right. Inside the envelope was a poem. It wasn't an original poem. It was a song from olden days that had taken on new meanings since the numbness of ethical birth control had become universal. It went like this, in smeary pencil again:

> We were walking through the park,
> A-goosing statues in the dark.
> If Sherman's horse can take it,
> So can you.

When Nancy came into the suicide booth to see what he wanted, the Foxy Grandpa was lying on the mint-green Barcalounger, where hundreds had died so peacefully over the years. He was studying the menu from the Howard Johnson's next door and beating time to the Muzak coming from the loudspeaker on the lemon-yellow wall. The room was painted cinder block. There was one barred window with a Venetian blind.

There was a Howard Johnson's next door to every Ethical Suicide Parlor, and vice versa. The Howard Johnson's had an orange roof and the Suicide Parlor had a purple roof, but they were both the Government. Practically everthing was the Government.

Practically everything was automated, too. Nancy and Mary and the sheriff were lucky to have jobs. Most people didn't. The average citizen moped around home and watched television, which was the Government. Every fifteen minutes his television would urge him to vote intelligently or consume intelligently, or worship in the church of his choice, or love his fellowmen, or obey the laws—or pay a call to the nearest Ethical Suicide Parlor and find out how friendly and understanding a Hostess could be.

The Foxy Grandpa was something of a rarity, since he was marked by old age, was bald, was shaky, had spots on his hands. Most people looked twenty-two, thanks to anti-aging shots they took twice a year. That the old man looked old was proof that the shots had been discovered after his sweet bird of youth had flown.

"Have we decided on a last supper yet?" Nancy asked him. She heard peevishness in her own voice, heard herself betray her exasperation with Billy the Poet, her boredom with the old man. She was ashamed, for this was unprofessional of her. "The breaded veal cutlet is very good."

The old man cocked his head. With the greedy cunning of second childhood, he had caught her being unprofessional, unkind, and he was going to punish her for it. "You don't sound very friendly. I thought you were all supposed to be friendly. I thought this was supposed to be a pleasant place to come."

"I beg your pardon," she said. "If I seem unfriendly, it has nothing to do with you."

"I thought maybe I bored you."

"No, no," she said gamely, "not at all. You certainly know some very interesting history." Among other things, the Foxy Grandpa claimed to have known J. Edgar Nation, the Grand Rapids druggist who was the father of ethical birth control.

"Then *look* like you're interested," he told her. He could get away with that sort of impudence. The thing was, he could leave any time he wanted to, right up to the moment he asked for the needle—and he had to *ask* for the needle. That was the law.

Nancy's art, and the art of every Hostess, was to see that
volunteers didn't leave, to coax and wheedle and flatter them
patiently, every step of the way.

So Nancy had to sit down there in the booth, to pretend to
marvel at the freshness of the yarn the old man told, a story
everybody knew, about how J. Edgar Nation happened to experiment with ethical birth control.

"He didn't have the slightest idea his pills would be taken by
human beings someday," said the Foxy Grandpa. "His dream
was to introduce morality into the monkey house at the Grand
Rapids Zoo. Did you realize that?" he inquired severely.

"No. No, I didn't. That's very interesting."

"He and his eleven kids went to church one Easter. And the
day was so nice and the Easter service had been so beautiful
and pure that they decided to take a walk through the zoo,
and they were just walking on clouds."

"Um." The scene described was lifted from a play that was
performed on television every Easter.

The Foxy Grandpa shoehorned himself into the scene, had
himself chat with the Nations just before they got to the monkey house. "'Good morning, Mr. Nation,' I said to him. 'It
certainly is a nice morning.' 'And a good morning to *you*, Mr.
Howard,' he said to me. 'There is nothing like an Easter morning to make a man feel clean and reborn and at one with God's
intentions.'"

"Um." Nancy could hear the telephone ringing faintly, nag-
gingly, through the nearly soundproof door.

"So we went on to the monkey house together, and what do
you think we saw?"

"I can't imagine." Somebody had answered the phone.

"We saw a monkey playing with his private parts!"

"No!"

"Yes! And J. Edgar Nation was so upset he went straight
home and he started developing a pill that would make monkeys in the springtime fit things for a Christian family to see."

There was a knock on the door.

"Yes—?" said Nancy.

"Nancy," said Mary, "telephone for you."

When Nancy came out of the booth, she found the sheriff
choking on little squeals of law-enforcement delight. The

telephone was tapped by agents hidden in the Howard Johnson's. Billy the Poet was believed to be on the line. His call had been traced. Police were already on their way to grab him.

"Keep him on, keep him on," the sheriff whispered to Nancy, and he gave her the telephone as though it were solid gold.

"Yes—?" said Nancy.

"Nancy McLuhan?" said a man. His voice was disguised. He might have been speaking through a kazoo. "I'm calling for a mutual friend."

"Oh?"

"He asked me to deliver a message."

"I see."

"It's a poem."

"All right."

"Ready?"

"Ready." Nancy could hear sirens screaming in the background of the call.

The caller must have heard the sirens, too, but he recited the poem without any emotion. It went like this:

"*Soak yourself in Jergen's Lotion.*
Here comes the one-man population explosion."

They got him. Nancy heard it all—the thumping and clumping, the argle-bargle and cries.

The depression she felt as she hung up was glandular. Her brave body had prepared for a fight that was not to be.

The sheriff bounded out of the Suicide Parlor, in such a hurry to see the famous criminal he'd helped catch that a sheaf of papers fell from the pocket of his trench coat.

Mary picked them up, called after the sheriff. He halted for a moment, said the papers didn't matter any more, asked her if maybe she wouldn't like to come along. There was a flurry between the two girls, with Nancy persuading Mary to go, declaring that she had no curiosity about Billy. So Mary left, irrelevantly handing the sheaf to Nancy.

The sheaf proved to be photocopies of poems Billy had sent to Hostesses in other places. Nancy read the top one. It made much of a peculiar side effect of ethical birth-control pills: They not only made people numb—they also made people piss blue. The poem was called *What the Somethinghead Said to the Suicide Hostess*, and it went like this:

> I did not sow, I did not spin,
> And thanks to pills I did not sin.
> I loved the crowds, the stink, the noise.
> And when I peed, I peed turquoise.
>
> I ate beneath a roof of orange;
> Swung with progress like a door hinge.
> 'Neath purple roof I've come today
> To piss my azure life away.
>
> Virgin hostess, death's recruiter,
> Life is cute, but you are cuter.
> Mourn my pecker, purple daughter—
> All it passed was sky-blue water.

"You never heard that story before—about how J. Edgar Nation came to invent ethical birth control?" the Foxy Grandpa wanted to know. His voice cracked.

"Never did," lied Nancy.

"I thought everybody knew that."

"It was news to me."

"When he got through with the monkey house, you couldn't tell it from the Michigan Supreme Court. Meanwhile, there was this crisis going on in the United Nations. The people who understood science said people had to quit reproducing so much, and the people who understood morals said society would collapse if people used sex for nothing but pleasure."

The Foxy Grandpa got off his Barcalounger, went over to the window, pried two slats of the blind apart. There wasn't much to see out there. The view was blocked by the backside of a mocked-up thermometer twenty feet high, which faced the street. It was calibrated in billions of people on Earth, from zero to twenty. The make-believe column of liquid was a strip of translucent red plastic. It showed how many people there were on Earth. Very close to the bottom was a black arrow that showed what the scientists thought the population ought to be.

The Foxy Grandpa was looking at the setting sun through

that red plastic, and through the blind, too, so that his face was banded with shadows and red.

"Tell me—" he said, "when I die, how much will that thermometer go down? A foot?"

"No."

"An inch?"

"Not quite."

"You know what the answer is, don't you?" he said, and he faced her. The senility had vanished from his voice and eyes. "One inch on that thing equals 83,333 people. You knew that, didn't you?"

"That—that might be true," said Nancy, "but that isn't the right way to look at it, in my opinion."

He didn't ask her what the right way was, in her opinion. He completed a thought of his own, instead. "I'll tell you something else that's true: I'm Billy the Poet, and you're a very good-looking woman."

With one hand, he drew a snub-nosed revolver from his belt. With the other, he peeled off his bald dome and wrinkled forehead, which proved to be rubber. Now he looked twenty-two.

"The police will want to know exactly what I look like when this is all over," he told Nancy with a malicious grin. "In case you're not good at describing people, and it's surprising how many women aren't:

> *I'm five foot two,*
> *With eyes of blue,*
> *With brown hair to my shoulders—*
> *A manly elf*
> *So full of self*
> *The ladies say he smolders."*

Billy was ten inches shorter than Nancy was. She had about forty pounds on him. She told him he didn't have a chance, but Nancy was much mistaken. He had unbolted the bars on the window the night before and he made her go out the window and then down a manhole that was hidden from the street by the big thermometer.

He took her down into the sewers of Hyannis. He knew

where he was going. He had a flashlight and a map. Nancy had
to go before him along the narrow catwalk, her own shadow
dancing mockingly in the lead. She tried to guess where they
were, relative to the real world above. She guessed correctly
when they passed under the Howard Johnson's, guessed from
noises she heard. The machinery that processed and served the
food there was silent. But, so people wouldn't feel too lonesome when eating there, the designers had provided sound
effects for the kitchen. It was these Nancy heard—a tape
recording of the clashing of silverware and the laughter of
Negroes and Puerto Ricans.

After that she was lost. Billy had very little to say to her
other than "Right," or, "Left," or "Don't try anything funny,
Juno, or I'll blow your great big fucking head off."

Only once did they have anything resembling a conversation. Billy began it, and ended it, too. "What in hell is a girl
with hips like yours doing selling death?" he asked her from
behind.

She dared to stop. "I can answer that," she told him. She
was confident that she could give him an answer that would
shrivel him like napalm.

But he gave her a shove, offered to blow her fucking head
off again.

"You don't even want to hear my answer," she taunted him.
"You're afraid to hear it."

"I never listen to a woman till the pills wear off," sneered
Billy. That was his plan, then—to keep her a prisoner for at least
eight hours. That was how long it took for the pills to wear off.

"That's a silly rule."

"A woman's not a woman till the pills wear off."

"You certainly manage to make a woman feel like an object
rather than a person."

"Thank the pills for that," said Billy.

There were 80 miles of sewers under Greater Hyannis, which
had a population of 400,000 drupelets, 400,000 souls. Nancy
lost track of the time down there. When Billy announced that
they had at last reached their destination, it was possible for
Nancy to imagine that a year had passed.

She tested this spooky impression by pinching her own

thigh, by feeling what the chemical clock of her body said. Her thigh was still numb.

Billy ordered her to climb iron rungs that were set in wet masonry. There was a circle of sickly light above. It proved to be moonlight filtered through the plastic polygons of an enormous geodesic dome. Nancy didn't have to ask the traditional victim's question, "Where am I?" There was only one dome like that on Cape Cod. It was in Hyannis Port and it sheltered the ancient Kennedy Compound.

It was a museum of how life had been lived in more expansive times. The museum was closed. It was open only in the summertime.

The manhole from which Nancy and then Billy emerged was set in an expanse of green cement, which showed where the Kennedy lawn had been. On the green cement, in front of the ancient frame houses, were statues representing the fourteen Kennedys who had been Presidents of the United States or the World. They were playing touch football.

The President of the World at the time of Nancy's abduction, incidentally, was an ex–Suicide Hostess named "Ma" Kennedy. Her statue would never join this particular touch-football game. Her name was Kennedy, all right, but she wasn't the real thing. People complained of her lack of style, found her vulgar. On the wall of her office was a sign that said, YOU DON'T HAVE TO BE CRAZY TO WORK HERE, BUT IT SURE HELPS, and another one that said THIMK!, and another one that said, SOMEDAY WE'RE GOING TO HAVE TO GET ORGANIZED AROUND HERE.

Her office was in the Taj Mahal.

Until she arrived in the Kennedy Museum, Nancy McLuhan was confident that she would sooner or later get a chance to break every bone in Billy's little body, maybe even shoot him with his own gun. She wouldn't have minded doing those things. She thought he was more disgusting than a blood-filled tick.

It wasn't compassion that changed her mind. It was the discovery that Billy had a gang. There were at least eight people around the manhole, men and women in equal numbers, with stockings pulled over their heads. It was the women who laid firm hands on Nancy, told her to keep calm. They were all at least as tall as Nancy and they held her in places where they could hurt her like hell if they had to.

Nancy closed her eyes, but this didn't protect her from the obvious conclusion: These perverted women were sisters from the Ethical Suicide Service. This upset her so much that she asked loudly and bitterly, "How can you violate your oaths like this?"

She was promptly hurt so badly that she doubled up and burst into tears.

When she straightened up again, there was plenty more she wanted to say, but she kept her mouth shut. She speculated silently as to what on Earth could make Suicide Hostesses turn against every concept of human decency. Nothingheadedness alone couldn't begin to explain it. They had to be drugged besides.

Nancy went over in her mind all the terrible drugs she'd learned about in school, persuaded herself that the women had taken the worst one of all. That drug was so powerful, Nancy's teachers had told her, that even a person numb from the waist down would copulate repeatedly and enthusiastically after just one glass. That had to be the answer: The women, and probably the men, too, had been drinking gin.

They hastened Nancy into the middle frame house, which was dark like all the rest, and Nancy heard the men giving Billy the news. It was in this news that Nancy perceived a glint of hope. Help might be on its way.

The gang member who had phoned Nancy obscenely had fooled the police into believing that they had captured Billy the Poet, which was bad for Nancy. The police didn't know yet that Nancy was missing, two men told Billy, and a telegram had been sent to Mary Kraft in Nancy's name, declaring that Nancy had been called to New York City on urgent family business.

That was where Nancy saw the glint of hope: Mary wouldn't believe that telegram. Mary knew Nancy had no family in New York. Not one of the 63,000,000 people living there was a relative of Nancy's.

The gang had deactivated the burglar-alarm system of the museum. They had also cut through a lot of the chains and ropes that were meant to keep visitors from touching anything of value. There was no mystery as to who and what had done the cutting. One of the men was armed with brutal lopping shears.

They marched Nancy into a servant's bedroom upstairs. The man with the shears cut the ropes that fenced off the narrow bed. They put Nancy into the bed and two men held Nancy while a woman gave her a knockout shot.

Billy the Poet had disappeared.

As Nancy was going under, the woman who had given her the shot asked her how old she was.

Nancy was determined not to answer, but discovered that the drug had made her powerless not to answer. "Sixty-three," she murmured.

"How does it feel to be a virgin at sixty-three?"

Nancy heard her own answer through a velvet fog. She was amazed by the answer, wanted to protest that it couldn't possibly be hers. "Pointless," she'd said.

Moments later, she asked the woman thickly, "What was in that needle?"

"What was in the needle, honey bunch? Why, honey bunch, they call that 'truth serum.'"

The moon was down when Nancy woke up—but the night was still out there. The shades were drawn and there was candlelight. Nancy had never seen a lit candle before.

What awakened Nancy was a dream of mosquitoes and bees. Mosquitoes and bees were extinct. So were birds. But Nancy dreamed that millions of insects were swarming about her from the waist down. They didn't sting. They fanned her. Nancy was a nothinghead.

She went to sleep again. When she awoke next time, she was being led into a bathroom by three women, still with stockings over their heads. The bathroom was already filled with the steam from somebody else's bath. There were somebody else's wet footprints crisscrossing the floor and the air reeked of pine-needle perfume.

Her will and intelligence returned as she was bathed and perfumed and dressed in a white nightgown. When the women stepped back to admire her, she said to them quietly, "I may be a nothinghead now. But that doesn't mean I have to think like one or act like one."

Nobody argued with her.

Nancy was taken downstairs and out of the house. She fully expected to be sent down a manhole again. It would be the perfect setting for her violation by Billy, she was thinking—down in a sewer.

But they took her across the green cement, where the grass used to be, and then across the yellow cement, where the beach used to be, and then out onto the blue cement, where the harbor used to be. There were twenty-six yachts that had belonged to various Kennedys, sunk up to their water lines in blue cement. It was to the most ancient of these yachts, the *Marlin*, once the property of Joseph P. Kennedy, that they delivered Nancy.

It was dawn. Because of the high-rise apartments all around the Kennedy Museum, it would be an hour before any direct sunlight would reach the microcosm under the geodesic dome.

Nancy was escorted as far as the companionway to the forward cabin of the *Marlin*. The women pantomimed that she was expected to go down the five steps alone.

Nancy froze for the moment and so did the women. And there were two actual statues in the tableau on the bridge. Standing at the wheel was a statue of Frank Wirtanen, once skipper of the *Marlin*. And next to him was his son and first mate, Carly. They weren't paying any attention to poor Nancy. They were staring out through the windshield at the blue cement.

Nancy, barefoot and wearing a thin white nightgown, descended bravely into the forward cabin, which was a pool of candlelight and pine-needle perfume. The companionway hatch was closed and locked behind her.

Nancy's emotions and the antique furnishings of the cabin were so complex that Nancy could not at first separate Billy the Poet from his surroundings, from all the mahogany and leaded glass. And then she saw him at the far end of the cabin, with his back against the door to the forward cockpit. He was wearing purple silk pajamas with a Russian collar. They were piped in red, and writhing across Billy's silken breast was a golden dragon. It was belching fire.

Anticlimactically, Billy was wearing glasses. He was holding a book.

Nancy poised herself on the next-to-the-bottom step, took a firm grip on the handholds in the companionway. She bared her teeth, calculated that it would take ten men Billy's size to dislodge her.

Between them was a great table. Nancy had expected the cabin to be dominated by a bed, possibly in the shape of a swan, but the *Marlin* was a day boat. The cabin was anything but a seraglio. It was about as voluptuous as a lower-middle-class dining room in Akron, Ohio, around 1910.

A candle was on the table. So were an ice bucket and two glasses and a quart of champagne. Champagne was as illegal as heroin.

Billy took off his glasses, gave her a shy, embarrassed smile, said, "Welcome."

"This is as far as I come."

He accepted that. "You're very beautiful there."

"And what am I supposed to say—that you're stunningly handsome? That I feel an overwhelming desire to throw myself into your manly arms?"

"If you wanted to make me happy, that would certainly be the way to do it." He said that humbly.

"And what about *my* happiness?"

The question seemed to puzzle him. "Nancy—that's what this is all about."

"What if my idea of happiness doesn't coincide with yours?"

"And what do you think my idea of happiness is?"

"I'm not going to throw myself into your arms, and I'm not going to drink that poison, and I'm not going to budge from here unless somebody makes me," said Nancy. "So I think your idea of happiness is going to turn out to be eight people holding me down on that table, while you bravely hold a cocked pistol to my head—and do what you want. That's the way it's going to have to be, so call your friends and get it over with!"

Which he did.

•

He didn't hurt her. He deflowered her with a clinical skill she found ghastly. When it was all over, he didn't seem cocky or proud. On the contrary, he was terribly depressed, and he said to Nancy, "Believe me, if there'd been any other way—"

Her reply to this was a face like stone—and silent tears of humiliation.

His helpers let down a folding bunk from the wall. It was scarcely wider than a bookshelf and hung on chains. Nancy allowed herself to be put to bed in it, and she was left alone with Billy the Poet again. Big as she was, like a double bass wedged onto that narrow shelf, she felt like a pitiful little thing. A scratchy, war-surplus blanket had been tucked in around her. It was her own idea to pull up a corner of the blanket to hide her face.

Nancy sensed from sounds what Billy was doing, which wasn't much. He was sitting at the table, sighing occasionally, sniffing occasionally, turning the pages of a book. He lit a cigar and the stink of it seeped under her blanket. Billy inhaled the cigar, then coughed and coughed and coughed.

When the coughing died down, Nancy said loathingly through the blanket, "You're so strong, so masterful, so healthy. It must be wonderful to be so manly."

Billy only sighed at this.

"I'm not a very typical nothinghead," she said. "I hated it— hated everything about it."

Billy sniffed, turned a page.

"I suppose all the other women just loved it—couldn't get enough of it."

"Nope."

She uncovered her face. "What do you mean, 'Nope'?"

"They've all been like you."

This was enough to make Nancy sit up and stare at him. "The women who helped you tonight—"

"What about them?"

"You've done to them what you did to me?"

He didn't look up from his book. "That's right."

"Then why don't they kill you instead of helping you?"

"Because they understand." And then he added mildly, "They're *grateful*."

Nancy got out of bed, came to the table, gripped the edge of the table, leaned close to him. And she said to him tautly, "I am not grateful."

"You will be."

"And what could possibly bring about that miracle?"

"Time," said Billy.

Billy closed his book, stood up. Nancy was confused by his magnetism. Somehow he was very much in charge again.

"What you've been through, Nancy," he said, "is a typical wedding night for a strait-laced girl of a hundred years ago, when everybody was a nothinghead. The groom did without helpers, because the bride wasn't customarily ready to kill him. Otherwise, the spirit of the occasion was much the same. These are the pajamas my great-great-grandfather wore on his wedding night in Niagara Falls.

"According to his diary, his bride cried all that night, and threw up twice. But, with the passage of time, she became a sexual enthusiast."

It was Nancy's turn to reply by not replying. She understood the tale. It frightened her to understand so easily that, from gruesome beginnings, sexual enthusiasm could grow and grow.

"You're a very typical nothinghead," said Billy. "If you dare to think about it now, you'll realize that you're angry because I'm such a bad lover, and a funny-looking shrimp besides. And what you can't help dreaming about from now on is a really suitable mate for a Juno like yourself.

"You'll find him, too—tall and strong and gentle. The nothinghead movement is growing by leaps and bounds."

"But—" said Nancy, and she stopped there. She looked out a porthole at the rising sun.

"But what?"

"The world is in the mess it is today because of the nothingheadedness of olden times. Don't you see?" She was pleading weakly. "The world can't afford sex anymore."

"Of course it can afford sex," said Billy. "All it can't afford anymore is reproduction."

"Then why the laws?"

"They're bad laws," said Billy. "If you go back through history, you'll find that the people who have been most eager to rule, to make the laws, to enforce the laws and to tell everybody exactly how God Almighty wants things here on Earth—those people have forgiven themselves and their friends for anything and everything. But they have been absolutely disgusted and terrified by the natural sexuality of common men and women.

"Why this is, I do not know. That is one of the many questions I wish somebody would ask the machines. I do know this: The triumph of that sort of disgust and terror is now complete. Almost every man and woman looks and feels like something the cat dragged in. The only sexual beauty that an ordinary human being can see today is in the woman who will kill him. Sex is death. There's a short and nasty equation for you: 'Sex is death. Q. E. D.'

"So you see, Nancy," said Billy, "I have spent this night, and many others like it, attempting to restore a certain amount of innocent pleasure to the world, which is poorer in pleasure than it needs to be."

Nancy sat down quietly and bowed her head.

"I'll tell you what my grandfather did on the dawn of his wedding night," said Billy.

"I don't think I want to hear it."

"It isn't violent. It's—it's meant to be tender."

"Maybe that's why I don't want to hear it."

"He read his bride a poem." Billy took the book from the table, opened it. "His diary tells which poem it was. While we aren't bride and groom, and while we may not meet again for many years, I'd like to read this poem to you, to have you know I've loved you."

"Please—no. I couldn't stand it."

"All right, I'll leave the book here, with the place marked, in case you want to read it later. It's the poem beginning:

> *How do I love thee? Let me count the ways.*
> *I love thee to the depth and breadth and height*
> *My soul can reach, when feeling out of sight*
> *For the ends of Being and ideal Grace.*"

Billy put a small bottle on top of the book. "I am also leaving you these pills. If you take one a month, you will never have children. And still you'll be a nothinghead."

And he left. And they all left but Nancy.

When Nancy raised her eyes at last to the book and bottle, she saw that there was a label on the bottle. What the label said was this: WELCOME TO THE MONKEY HOUSE.

1968

Fortitude

*T*HE TIME: *the present.*
    The place: Upstate New York, a large room filled with pulsing, writhing, panting machines that perform the functions of various organs of the human body—heart, lungs, liver, and so on. Color-coded pipes and wires swoop upward from the machines to converge and pass through a hole in the ceiling. To one side is a fantastically complicated master control console.
    DR. ELBERT LITTLE, *a kindly, attractive young general practitioner, is being shown around by the creator and boss of the operation,* DR. NORBERT FRANKENSTEIN. FRANKENSTEIN *is 65, a crass medical genius. Seated at the console, wearing headphones and watching meters and flashing lights, is* DR. TOM SWIFT, FRANKENSTEIN'*s enthusiastic first assistant.*

LITTLE: Oh, my God—oh, my God—

FRANKENSTEIN: Yeah. Those are her kidneys over there. That's her liver, of course. There you got her pancreas.

LITTLE: Amazing. Dr. Frankenstein, after seeing this, I wonder if I've even been *practicing* medicine, if I've ever even *been* to medical school. (*Pointing*) That's her *heart?*

FRANKENSTEIN: That's a Westinghouse heart. They make a damn good heart, if you ever need one. They make a kidney I wouldn't touch with a ten-foot pole.

LITTLE: That heart is probably worth more than the whole township where I practice.

FRANKENSTEIN: That pancreas is worth your whole state. *Vermont?*

LITTLE: Vermont.

FRANKENSTEIN: What we paid for the pancreas—yeah, we could have bought Vermont for that. Nobody'd ever made a pancreas before, and we had to have one in ten days or lose the patient. So we told all the big organ manufacturers, "OK, you guys got to have a crash program for a pancreas. Put every man you got on the job. We don't care what it costs, as long as we get a pancreas by next Tuesday."

LITTLE: And they succeeded.

FRANKENSTEIN: The patient's still alive, isn't she? Believe me, those are some expensive sweetbreads.

LITTLE: But the patient could afford them.

FRANKENSTEIN: You don't live like this on Blue Cross.

LITTLE: And how many operations has she had? In how many years?

FRANKENSTEIN: I gave her her first major operation thirty-six years ago. She's had seventy-eight operations since then.

LITTLE: And how old is she?

FRANKENSTEIN: One hundred.

LITTLE: What *guts* that woman must have!

FRANKENSTEIN: You're looking at 'em.

LITTLE: I mean—what *courage*! What *fortitude*!

FRANKENSTEIN: We knock her out, you know. We don't operate without anesthetics.

LITTLE: Even so . . .

> FRANKENSTEIN *taps* SWIFT *on the shoulder.* SWIFT *frees an ear from the headphones, divides his attention between the visitors and the console.*

FRANKENSTEIN: Dr. Tom Swift, this is Dr. Elbert Little. Tom here is my first assistant.

SWIFT: Howdy-doody.

FRANKENSTEIN: Dr. Little has a practice up in Vermont. He happened to be in the neighborhood. He asked for a tour.

LITTLE: What do you hear in the headphones?

SWIFT: Anything that's going on in the patient's room. (*He offers the headphones*) Be my guest.

LITTLE (*listening to headphones*): Nothing.

SWIFT: She's having her hair brushed now. The beautician's up there. She's always quiet when her hair's being brushed. (*He takes the headphones back*)

FRANKENSTEIN (*to* SWIFT): We should *congratulate* our young visitor here.

SWIFT: What for?

LITTLE: Good question. What for?

FRANKENSTEIN: Oh, I know about the great honor that has come your way.

LITTLE: I'm not sure *I* do.

FRANKENSTEIN: You are *the* Dr. Little, aren't you, who was

named the Family Doctor of the Year by the *Ladies' Home Journal* last month?

LITTLE: Yes—that's right. I don't know how in the hell they decided. And I'm even more flabbergasted that a man of *your* caliber would know about it.

FRANKENSTEIN: I read the *Ladies' Home Journal* from cover to cover every month.

LITTLE: You *do*?

FRANKENSTEIN: I only got one patient, Mrs. Lovejoy. And Mrs. Lovejoy reads the *Ladies' Home Journal*, so I read it, too. That's what we talk about—what's in the *Ladies' Home Journal*. We read all about you last month. Mrs. Lovejoy kept saying, "Oh, what a nice young man he must be. *So understanding.*"

LITTLE: Um.

FRANKENSTEIN: Now here you are in the flesh. I bet she wrote you a letter.

LITTLE: Yes—she did.

FRANKENSTEIN: She writes thousands of letters a year, gets thousands of letters back. Some pen pal she is.

LITTLE: Is she—uh—generally *cheerful* most of the time?

FRANKENSTEIN: If she isn't, that's our fault down here. If she gets unhappy, that means something down *here* isn't working right. She was blue about a month ago. Turned out it was a bum transistor in the console. (*He reaches over* SWIFT*'s shoulder, changes a setting on the console. The machinery subtly adjusts to the new setting.*) There—she'll be all depressed for a couple of minutes now. (*He changes the setting again*) There. Now, pretty quick, she'll be happier than she was before. She'll sing like a bird.

> LITTLE *conceals his horror imperfectly.* CUT TO *patient's room, which is full of flowers and candy boxes and books. The patient is* SYLVIA LOVEJOY, *a billionaire's widow.* SYLVIA *is no longer anything but a head connected to pipes and wires coming up through the floor, but this is not immediately apparent. The first shot of her is a* CLOSE-UP, *with* GLORIA, *a gorgeous beautician, standing behind her.* SYLVIA *is a heartbreakingly good-looking old lady, once a famous beauty. She is crying now.*

SYLVIA: Gloria—

GLORIA: Ma'am?

SYLVIA: Wipe these tears away before somebody comes in and sees them.

GLORIA (*wanting to cry herself*): Yes, ma'am. (*She wipes the tears away with Kleenex, studies the results*) *There. There.*

SYLVIA: I don't know what came over me. Suddenly I was so sad I couldn't stand it.

GLORIA: Everybody has to cry *sometimes.*

SYLVIA: It's passing now. Can you tell I've been crying?

GLORIA: *No. No.*

> *She is unable to control her own tears anymore. She goes to a window so* SYLVIA *can't see her cry.* CAMERA BACKS AWAY *to reveal the tidy, clinical abomination of the head and wires and pipes. The head is on a tripod. There is a black box with winking colored lights hanging under the head, where the chest would normally be. Mechanical arms come out of the box where arms would normally be. There is a table within easy reach of the arms. On it are a pen and paper, a partially solved jigsaw puzzle and a bulky knitting bag. Sticking out of the bag are needles and a sweater in progress. Hanging over* SYLVIA*'s head is a microphone on a boom.*

SYLVIA (*sighing*): Oh, what a *foolish* old woman you must think I am. (GLORIA *shakes her head in denial, is unable to reply*) Gloria? Are you still there?

GLORIA: Yes.

SYLVIA: Is anything the matter?

GLORIA: No.

SYLVIA: You're *such* a good friend, Gloria. I want you to know I feel that with all my heart.

GLORIA: I like you, too.

SYLVIA: If you ever have any problems I can help you with, I hope you'll ask me.

GLORIA: I will, I *will.*

> HOWARD DERBY, *the hospital mail clerk, dances in with an armload of letters. He is a merry old fool.*

DERBY: Mailman! Mailman!

SYLVIA (*brightening*): Mailman! God *bless* the mailman!

DERBY: How's the patient today?

SYLVIA: Very sad a moment ago. But now that I see you, I want to sing like a bird.

DERBY: Fifty-three letters today. There's even one from Leningrad.

SYLVIA: There's a blind woman in Leningrad. Poor soul, *poor* soul.

DERBY (*making a fan of the mail, reading postmarks*): West Virginia, Honolulu, Brisbane, Australia—

SYLVIA *selects an envelope at random.*

SYLVIA: Wheeling, West Virginia. Now, who do I know in Wheeling? (*She opens the envelope expertly with her mechanical hands, reads*) "Dear Mrs. Lovejoy: You don't know me, but I just read about you in the *Reader's Digest*, and I'm sitting here with tears streaming down my cheeks." *Reader's Digest*? My goodness—that article was printed fourteen years ago! And she just *read* it?

DERBY: Old *Reader's Digest*s go on and on. I've got one at home I'll bet is ten years old. I still read it every time I need a little inspiration.

SYLVIA (*reading on*): "I am never going to complain about anything that ever happens to me ever again. I thought I was as unfortunate as a person can get when my husband shot his girlfriend six months ago and then blew his own brains out. He left me with seven children and with eight payments still to go on a Buick Roadmaster with three flat tires and a busted transmission. After reading about you, though, I sit here and count my blessings." Isn't that a nice letter?

DERBY: Sure is.

SYLVIA: There's a P.S.: "Get well real soon, you *hear*?" (*She puts the letter on the table*) There isn't a letter from Vermont, is there?

DERBY: Vermont?

SYLVIA: Last month, when I had that low spell, I wrote what I'm afraid was a very stupid, self-centered, self-pitying letter to a young doctor I read about in the *Ladies' Home Journal*. I'm so ashamed. I live in fear and trembling of what he's going to say back to me—if he answers at all.

GLORIA: What could he say? What could he *possibly* say?

SYLVIA: He could tell me about the *real* suffering going on out there in the world, about people who don't know where the next meal is coming from, about people so poor they've never *been* to a doctor in their whole *lives*. And to think of all the help I've had—all the tender, loving care, all the latest wonders science has to offer.

> CUT TO *corridor outside* SYLVIA'S *room. There is a sign on the door saying,* ALWAYS ENTER SMILING! FRANKENSTEIN *and* LITTLE *are about to enter.*

LITTLE: She's in *there*?

FRANKENSTEIN: Every part of her that isn't downstairs.

LITTLE: And everybody obeys this sign, I'm sure.

FRANKENSTEIN: Part of the therapy. We treat the *whole* patient here.

> GLORIA *comes from the room, closes the door tightly, then bursts into noisy tears.*

FRANKENSTEIN (*to* GLORIA, *disgusted*): Oh, for crying out loud. And what is this?

GLORIA: Let her *die*, Dr. Frankenstein. For the love of God, let her *die*!

LITTLE: This is her *nurse*?

FRANKENSTEIN: She hasn't got brains enough to be a nurse. She is a lousy beautician. A hundred bucks a week she makes—just to take care of one woman's face and hair. (*To* GLORIA) You blew it, honeybunch. You're through.

GLORIA: What?

FRANKENSTEIN: Pick up your check and scram.

GLORIA: I'm her closest friend.

FRANKENSTEIN: Some friend! You just asked me to knock her off.

GLORIA: In the name of mercy, yes, I did.

FRANKENSTEIN: You're that sure there's a heaven, eh? You want to send her right up there so she can get her wings and harp.

GLORIA: I know there's a hell. I've seen it. It's in there, and you're its great inventor.

FRANKENSTEIN (*stung, letting a moment pass before replying*): Christ—the things people say sometimes.

GLORIA: It's time somebody who loves her spoke up.

FRANKENSTEIN: Love.

GLORIA: You wouldn't know what that is.

FRANKENSTEIN: Love. (*More to himself than to her*) Do I have a wife? No. Do I have a mistress? No. I have loved only two women in my life—my mother and that woman in there. I wasn't able to save my mother from death. I had just graduated from medical school and my mother was dying of cancer of the everything. "OK, wise guy," I said to myself, "you're such a hot-shot doctor from Heidelberg, now, let's see you save your mother from death." And everybody told me there wasn't anything I could do for her, and I said, "I don't give a damn. I'm gonna do something anyway." And they finally decided I was nuts and they put me in a crazyhouse for a little while. When I got out, she was dead—the way all the wise men said she had to be. What those wise men didn't know was all the wonderful things machinery could do—and neither did I, but I was gonna find out. So I went to the Massachusetts Institute of Technology and I studied mechanical engineering and electrical engineering and chemical engineering for six long years. I lived in an attic. I ate two-day-old bread and the kind of cheese they put in mousetraps. When I got out of MIT, I said to myself, "OK, boy—it's just barely possible now that you're the only guy on earth with the proper education to practice 20th century medicine." I went to work for the Curley Clinic in Boston. They brought in this woman who was beautiful on the outside and a mess on the inside. She was the image of my mother. She was the widow of a man who had left her five-hundred million dollars. She didn't have any relatives. The wise men said again, "This lady's gotta die." And I said to them, "Shut up and listen. I'm gonna tell you what we're gonna do."

Silence.

LITTLE: That's—that's quite a story.

FRANKENSTEIN: It's a story about *love*. (*To* GLORIA) That love story started years and years before you were born, you great lover, you. And it's still going on.

GLORIA: Last month, she asked me to bring her a pistol so she could shoot herself.

FRANKENSTEIN: You think I don't know that? (*Jerking a thumb at* LITTLE) Last month, she wrote him a letter and said, "Bring me some cyanide, doctor, if you're a doctor with any heart at all."

LITTLE (*startled*): You *knew* that. You—you read her mail?

FRANKENSTEIN: So we'll know what she's *really* feeling. She might try to fool us sometime—just *pretend* to be happy. I told you about that bum transistor last month. We maybe wouldn't have known anything was wrong if we hadn't read her mail and listened to what she was saying to lame-brains like this one here. (*Feeling challenged*) Look—you go in there all by yourself. Stay as long as you want, ask her anything. Then you come back out and tell me the truth: Is that a happy woman in there, or is that a woman in hell?

LITTLE (*hesitating*): I—

FRANKENSTEIN: Go on in! I got some more things to say to this young lady—to Miss Mercy Killing of the Year. I'd like to show her a body that's been in a casket for a couple of years sometime—let her see how pretty death is, this thing she wants for her friend.

> LITTLE *gropes for something to say, finally mimes his wish to be fair to everyone. He enters the patient's room.* CUT TO *room.* SYLVIA *is alone, faced away from the door.*

SYLVIA: Who's that?

LITTLE: A friend—somebody you wrote a letter to.

SYLVIA: That could be anybody. Can I see you, please? (LITTLE *obliges. She looks him over with growing affection.*) Dr. Little—family doctor from Vermont.

LITTLE (*bowing slightly*): Mrs. Lovejoy—how are you today?

SYLVIA: Did you bring me cyanide?

LITTLE: No.

SYLVIA: I wouldn't take it today. It's such a lovely day. I wouldn't want to miss it, or tomorrow, either. Did you come on a snow-white horse?

LITTLE: In a blue Oldsmobile.

SYLVIA: What about your patients, who love and need you so?

LITTLE: Another doctor is covering for me. I'm taking a week off.

SYLVIA: Not on my account.

LITTLE: No.

SYLVIA: Because I'm fine. You can see what wonderful hands I'm in.

LITTLE: Yes.

SYLVIA: One thing I don't need is another doctor.

LITTLE: Right.

Pause.

SYLVIA: I do wish I had somebody to talk to about death, though. You've seen a lot of it, I suppose.

LITTLE: Some.

SYLVIA: And it was a blessing for some of them—when they died?

LITTLE: I've heard that said.

SYLVIA: But you don't say so yourself.

LITTLE: It's not a professional thing for a doctor to say, Mrs. Lovejoy.

SYLVIA: Why have other people said that certain deaths have been a blessing?

LITTLE: Because of the pain the patient was in, because he couldn't be cured at any price—at any price within his means. Or because the patient was a vegetable, had lost his mind and couldn't get it back.

SYLVIA: At any price.

LITTLE: As far as I know, it is not now possible to beg, borrow or steal an artificial mind for someone who's lost one. If I asked Dr. Frankenstein about it, he might tell me that it's the coming thing.

Pause.

SYLVIA: It *is* the coming thing.

LITTLE: He's told you so?

SYLVIA: I asked him yesterday what would happen if my brain started to go. He was serene. He said I wasn't to worry my pretty little head about that. "We'll cross that bridge when we come to it," he told me. (*Pause*) Oh, God, the bridges I've crossed!

CUT TO *room full of organs, as before.* SWIFT *is at the console.* FRANKENSTEIN *and* LITTLE *enter.*

FRANKENSTEIN: You've made the grand tour and now here you are back at the beginning.

LITTLE: And I still have to say what I said at the beginning: "My God—oh, my God."

FRANKENSTEIN: It's gonna be a little tough going back to the aspirin-and-laxative trade after this, eh?

LITTLE: Yes. (*Pause*) What's the cheapest thing here?

FRANKENSTEIN: The simplest thing. It's the goddamn pump.

LITTLE: What does a heart go for these days?

FRANKENSTEIN: Sixty thousand dollars. There are cheaper ones and more expensive ones. The cheap ones are junk. The expensive ones are jewelry.

LITTLE: And how many are sold a year now?

FRANKENSTEIN: Six hundred, give or take a few.

LITTLE: Give one, that's life. Take one, that's death.

FRANKENSTEIN: If the trouble is the heart. It's lucky if you have trouble that cheap. (*To* SWIFT) Hey, Tom—put her to sleep so he can see how the day ends around here.

SWIFT: It's twenty minutes ahead of time.

FRANKENSTEIN: What's the difference? We put her to sleep for twenty minutes extra, she still wakes up tomorrow feeling like a million bucks, unless we got another bum transistor.

LITTLE: Why don't you have a television camera aimed at her, so you can watch her on a screen?

FRANKENSTEIN: She didn't want one.

LITTLE: She gets what she wants?

FRANKENSTEIN: She got *that*. What the hell do we have to watch her face for? We can look at the meters down here and find out more about her than she can know about herself. (*To* SWIFT) Put her to sleep, Tom.

SWIFT (*to* LITTLE): It's just like slowing down a car or banking a furnace.

LITTLE: Um.

FRANKENSTEIN: Tom, too, has degrees in both engineering and medicine.

LITTLE: Are you tired at the end of a day, Tom?

SWIFT: It's a good kind of tiredness—as though I'd flown a big jet from New York to Honolulu, or something like that. (*Taking hold of a lever*) And now we'll bring Mrs. Lovejoy in for a happy landing. (*He pulls the lever gradually and the machinery slows down*) There.

FRANKENSTEIN: Beautiful.

LITTLE: She's asleep?

FRANKENSTEIN: Like a baby.

SWIFT: All I have to do now is wait for the night man to come on.

LITTLE: Has anybody ever brought her a suicide weapon?

FRANKENSTEIN: No. We wouldn't worry about it if they did. The arms are designed so she can't possibly point a gun at herself or get poison to her lips, no matter how she tries. That was Tom's stroke of genius.

LITTLE: Congratulations.

Alarm bell rings. Light flashes.

FRANKENSTEIN: Who could that be? (*To* LITTLE) Somebody just went into her room. We better check! (*To* SWIFT) Lock the door up there, Tom—so whoever it is, we got 'em. (SWIFT *pushes a button that locks door upstairs. To* LITTLE) You come with me.

> CUT TO *patient's room.* SYLVIA *is asleep, snoring gently.* GLORIA *has just sneaked in. She looks around furtively, takes a revolver from her purse, makes sure it's loaded, then hides it in* SYLVIA's *knitting bag. She is barely finished when* FRANKENSTEIN *and* LITTLE *enter breathlessly,* FRANKENSTEIN *opening the door with a key.*

FRANKENSTEIN: What's this?

GLORIA: I left my watch up here. (*Pointing to watch*) I've got it now.

FRANKENSTEIN: Thought I told you never to come into this building again.

GLORIA: I won't.

FRANKENSTEIN (*to* LITTLE): You keep her right there. I'm gonna check things over. Maybe there's been a little huggery buggery. (*To* GLORIA) How would you like to be in court for attempted murder, eh? (*Into microphone*) Tom? Can you hear me?

SWIFT (*voice from squawk box on wall*): I hear you.

FRANKENSTEIN: Wake her up again. I gotta give her a check.

SWIFT: Cock-a-doodle-doo.

> *Machinery can be heard speeding up below.* SYLVIA *opens her eyes, sweetly dazed.*

SYLVIA (*to* FRANKENSTEIN): Good morning, Norbert.

FRANKENSTEIN: How do you feel?

SYLVIA: The way I always feel when I wake up—fine—vaguely at sea. Gloria! Good morning!

GLORIA: Good morning.

SYLVIA: Dr. Little! You're staying another day?

FRANKENSTEIN: It isn't morning. We'll put you back to sleep in a minute.

SYLVIA: I'm sick again?

FRANKENSTEIN: I don't think so.

SYLVIA: I'm going to have to have another operation?

FRANKENSTEIN: Calm down, calm down. (*He takes an ophthalmoscope from his pocket*)

SYLVIA: How can I be calm when I think about another operation?

FRANKENSTEIN (*into microphone*): Tom—give her some tranquilizers.

SWIFT (*squawk box*): Coming up.

SYLVIA: What else do I have to lose? My ears? My hair?

FRANKENSTEIN: You'll be calm in a minute.

SYLVIA: My eyes? My eyes, Norbert—are they going next?

FRANKENSTEIN (*to* GLORIA): Oh, boy, baby doll—will you look what you've done? (*Into microphone*) Where the hell are those tranquilizers?

SWIFT: Should be taking effect just about now.

SYLVIA: Oh, well. It doesn't matter. (*As* FRANKENSTEIN *examines her eyes*) It *is* my eyes, isn't it?

FRANKENSTEIN: It isn't your anything.

SYLVIA: Easy come, easy go.

FRANKENSTEIN: You're healthy as a horse.

SYLVIA: I'm sure somebody manufactures excellent eyes.

FRANKENSTEIN: RCA makes a damn good eye, but we aren't gonna buy one for a while yet. (*He backs away, satisfied*) Everything's all right up here. (*To* GLORIA) Lucky for you.

SYLVIA: I love it when friends of mine are lucky.

SWIFT: Put her to sleep again?

FRANKENSTEIN: Not yet. I want to check a couple of things down there.

SWIFT: Roger and out.

> CUT TO LITTLE, GLORIA *and* FRANKENSTEIN *entering the machinery room minutes later.* SWIFT *is at the console.*

SWIFT: Night man's late.

FRANKENSTEIN: He's got troubles at home. You want a good piece of advice, boy? Don't ever get married. (*He scrutinizes meter after meter*)

GLORIA (*appalled by her surroundings*): My God—oh, my God—

LITTLE: You've never seen this before?

GLORIA: No.

FRANKENSTEIN: She was the great hair specialist. We took care of everything else—everything but the hair. (*The reading on a meter puzzles him*) What's this? (*He socks the meter, which then gives him the proper reading*) That's more like it.

GLORIA (*emptily*): Science.

FRANKENSTEIN: What did you think it was like down here?

GLORIA: I was afraid to think. Now I can see why.

FRANKENSTEIN: You got any scientific background at all—any way of appreciating even slightly what you're seeing here?

GLORIA: I flunked earth science twice in high school.

FRANKENSTEIN: What do they teach in beauty college?

GLORIA: Dumb things for dumb people. How to paint a face. How to curl or uncurl hair. How to cut hair. How to dye hair. Fingernails. Toenails in the summertime.

FRANKENSTEIN: I suppose you're gonna crack off about this place after you get out of here—gonna tell people all the crazy stuff that goes on.

GLORIA: Maybe.

FRANKENSTEIN: Just remember this: You haven't got the brains or the education to talk about any aspect of our operation. Right?

GLORIA: Maybe.

FRANKENSTEIN: What *will* you say to the outside world?

GLORIA: Nothing very complicated—just that. . . .

FRANKENSTEIN: Yes?

GLORIA: That you have the head of a dead woman connected to a lot of machinery, and you play with it all day long, and you aren't married or anything, and that's all you do.

> FREEZE SCENE *as a still photograph.* FADE TO *black.* FADE IN *same still. Figures begin to move.*

FRANKENSTEIN (*aghast*): How can you call her dead? She reads the *Ladies' Home Journal*! She talks! She knits! She writes letters to pen pals all over the world!

GLORIA: She's like some horrible fortunetelling machine in a penny arcade.

FRANKENSTEIN: I thought you loved her.

GLORIA: Every so often, I see a tiny little spark of what she used to be. I love that spark. Most people say they love her for her courage. What's that courage worth, when it comes from down here? You could turn a few faucets and switches down here and she'd be volunteering to fly a rocket ship to the moon. But no matter what you do down here, that little spark goes on thinking, "For the love of God—somebody get me out of here!"

FRANKENSTEIN (*glancing at the console*): Dr. Swift—is that microphone open?

SWIFT: Yeah. (*Snapping his fingers*) I'm sorry.

FRANKENSTEIN: Leave it open. (*To* GLORIA) She's heard every word you've said. How does that make you feel?

GLORIA: She can hear me now?

FRANKENSTEIN: Run off at the mouth some more. You're saving me a lot of trouble. Now I won't have to explain to her what sort of friend you really were and why I gave you the old heave-ho.

GLORIA (*drawing nearer to the microphone*): Mrs. Lovejoy?

SWIFT (*reporting what he has heard on the headphones*): She says, "What is it, dear?"

GLORIA: There's a loaded revolver in your knitting bag, Mrs. Lovejoy—in case you don't want to live anymore.

FRANKENSTEIN (*not in the least worried about the pistol but filled with contempt and disgust for* GLORIA): You total imbecile. Where did you get a pistol?

GLORIA: From a mail-order house in Chicago. They had an ad in *True Romances*.

FRANKENSTEIN: They sell guns to crazy broads.

GLORIA: I could have had a bazooka if I'd wanted one. Fourteen-ninety-eight.

FRANKENSTEIN: I am going to get that pistol now and it is going to be exhibit A at your trial. (*He leaves*)

LITTLE (*to* SWIFT): Shouldn't you put the patient to sleep?

SWIFT: There's no way she can hurt herself.

GLORIA (*to* LITTLE): What does he mean?

LITTLE: Her arms are fixed so she can't point a gun at herself.

GLORIA (*sickened*): They even thought of that.

> CUT TO SYLVIA's *room.* FRANKENSTEIN *is entering.* SYLVIA *is holding the pistol thoughtfully.*

FRANKENSTEIN: Nice playthings you have.

SYLVIA: You mustn't get mad at Gloria, Norbert. I asked her for this. I begged her for this.

FRANKENSTEIN: Last month.

SYLVIA: Yes.

FRANKENSTEIN: But everything is better now.

SYLVIA: Everything but the spark.

FRANKENSTEIN: Spark?

SYLVIA: The spark that Gloria says she loves—the tiny spark of what I used to be. As happy as I am right now, that spark is begging me to take this gun and put it out.

FRANKENSTEIN: And what is your reply?

SYLVIA: I am going to do it, Norbert. This is goodbye. (*She tries every which way to aim the gun at herself, fails and fails, while* FRANKENSTEIN *stands calmly by*) That's no accident, is it?

FRANKENSTEIN: We very much don't want you to hurt yourself. We love you, too.

SYLVIA: And how much longer must I live like this? I've never dared ask before.

FRANKENSTEIN: I would have to pull a figure out of a hat.

SYLVIA: Maybe you'd better not. (*Pause*) Did you pull one out of a hat?

FRANKENSTEIN: At least five hundred years.

> *Silence.*

SYLVIA: So I will still be alive—long after you are gone?

FRANKENSTEIN: Now is the time, my dear Sylvia, to tell you something I have wanted to tell you for years. Every organ downstairs has the capacity to take care of two human beings instead of one. And the plumbing and wiring have been designed so that a second human being can be hooked up in two shakes of a lamb's tail. (*Silence*) Do you understand what I am saying to you, Sylvia? (*Silence. Passionately*) Sylvia! I will be that second human being! Talk about marriage! Talk about great love stories from the past! Your kidney will be my kidney! Your liver will be my liver! Your heart will be my heart! Your ups will be my ups and your downs will be my downs! We will live in such perfect harmony, Sylvia, that the gods themselves will tear out their hair in envy!

SYLVIA: This is what you want?

FRANKENSTEIN: More than anything in this world.

SYLVIA: Well, then—here it is, Norbert. (*She empties the revolver into him*)

> CUT TO *same room almost a half hour later. A second tripod has been set up, with* FRANKENSTEIN's *head on top.* FRANKENSTEIN *is asleep and so is* SYLVIA. SWIFT, *with* LITTLE *standing by, is feverishly making a final connection to the machinery below. There are pipe wrenches and a blowtorch and other plumber's and electrician's tools lying around.*

SWIFT: That's gotta be it. (*He straightens up, looks around*) That's gotta be it.

LITTLE (*consulting watch*): Twenty-eight minutes since the first shot was fired.

SWIFT: Thank God you were around.

LITTLE: What you really needed was a plumber.

SWIFT (*into microphone*): Charley—we're all set up here. You all set down there?

CHARLEY (*squawk box*): All set.

SWIFT: Give 'em plenty of martinis.

> GLORIA *appears numbly in doorway.*

CHARLEY: They've got 'em. They'll be higher than kites.

SWIFT: Better give 'em a touch of LSD, too.

CHARLEY: Coming up.

SWIFT: Hold it! I forgot the phonograph. (*To* LITTLE) Dr.

Frankenstein said that if this ever happened, he wanted a certain record playing when he came to. He said it was in with the other records—in a plain white jacket. (*To* GLORIA) See if you can find it.

> GLORIA *goes to phonograph, finds the record.*

GLORIA: This it?

SWIFT: Put it on.

GLORIA: Which side?

SWIFT: I don't know.

GLORIA: There's tape over one side.

SWIFT: The side *without* tape. (GLORIA *puts record on. Into microphone*) Stand by to wake up the patients.

CHARLEY: Standing by.

> *Record begins to play. It is a Jeanette MacDonald–Nelson Eddy duet, "Ah, Sweet Mystery of Life."*

SWIFT (*into microphone*): Wake 'em up!

> FRANKENSTEIN *and* SYLVIA *wake up, filled with formless pleasure. They dreamily appreciate the music, eventually catch sight of each other, perceive each other as old and beloved friends.*

SYLVIA: Hi, there.

FRANKENSTEIN: Hello.

SYLVIA: How do you feel?

FRANKENSTEIN: Fine. Just fine.

1968

The Big Space Fuck

IN 1987 it became possible in the United States of America
for a young person to sue his parents for the way he had
been raised. He could take them to court and make them pay
money and even serve jail terms for serious mistakes they made
when he was just a helpless little kid. This was not only an effort to achieve justice but to discourage reproduction, since
there wasn't anything much to eat any more. Abortions were
free. In fact, any woman who volunteered for one got her
choice of a bathroom scale or a table lamp.

In 1989, America staged the Big Space Fuck, which was a serious effort to make sure that human life would continue to
exist somewhere in the Universe, since it certainly couldn't
continue much longer on Earth. Everything had turned to shit
and beer cans and old automobiles and Clorox bottles. An interesting thing happened in the Hawaiian Islands, where they
had been throwing trash down extinct volcanoes for years: a
couple of the volcanoes all of a sudden spit it all back up. And
so on.

This was a period of great permissiveness in matters of language, so even the President was saying shit and fuck and so
on, without anybody's feeling threatened or taking offense. It
was perfectly OK. He called the Space Fuck a Space Fuck and
so did everybody else. It was a rocket ship with eight hundred
pounds of freeze-dried jizzum in its nose. It was going to be
fired at the Andromeda Galaxy, two-million light years away.
The ship was named the *Arthur C. Clarke*, in honor of a famous space pioneer.

It was to be fired at midnight on the Fourth of July. At ten
o'clock that night, Dwayne Hoobler and his wife Grace were
watching the countdown on television in the living room of
their modest home in Elk Harbor, Ohio, on the shore of what
used to be Lake Erie. Lake Erie was almost solid sewage now.
There were man-eating lampreys in there thirty-eight feet
long. Dwayne was a guard in the Ohio Adult Correctional
Institution, which was two miles away. His hobby was making

birdhouses out of Clorox bottles. He went on making them and hanging them around his yard, even though there weren't any birds any more.

Dwayne and Grace marveled at a film demonstration of how jizzum had been freeze-dried for the trip. A small beaker of the stuff, which had been contributed by the head of the Mathematics Department at the University of Chicago, was flash-frozen. Then it was placed under a bell jar, and the air was exhausted from the jar. The air evanesced, leaving a fine white powder. The powder certainly didn't look like much, and Dwayne Hoobler said so—but there were several hundred million sperm cells in there, in suspended animation. The original contribution, an average contribution, had been two cubic centimeters. There was enough powder, Dwayne estimated out loud, to clog the eye of a needle. And eight-hundred pounds of the stuff would soon be on its way to Andromeda.

"Fuck you, Andromeda," said Dwayne, and he wasn't being coarse. He was echoing billboards and stickers all over town. Other signs said, "Andromeda, We Love You," and "Earth Has the Hots for Andromeda," and so on.

There was a knock on the door, and an old friend of the family, the County Sheriff, simultaneously let himself in. "How are you, you old motherfucker?" said Dwayne.

"Can't complain, shitface," said the sheriff, and they joshed back and forth like that for a while. Grace chuckled, enjoying their wit. She wouldn't have chuckled so richly, however, if she had been a little more observant. She might have noticed that the sheriff's jocularity was very much on the surface. Underneath, he had something troubling on his mind. She might have noticed, too, that he had legal papers in his hand.

"Sit down, you silly old fart," said Dwayne, "and watch Andromeda get the surprise of her life."

"The way I understand it," the sheriff replied, "I'd have to sit there for more than two million years. My old lady might wonder what's become of me." He was a lot smarter than Dwayne. He had jizzum on the *Arthur C. Clarke*, and Dwayne didn't. You had to have an I.Q. of over 115 to have your jizzum accepted. There were certain exceptions to this: if you were a good athlete or could play a musical instrument or paint pictures, but Dwayne didn't qualify in any of those departments, either. He had hoped that birdhouse-makers might be entitled to special consideration, but this turned out not to be the case. The Director of the New York Philharmonic, on the other hand, was entitled to contribute a whole quart, if he wanted to. He was sixty-eight years old. Dwayne was forty-two.

There was an old astronaut on the television now. He was saying that he sure wished he could go where his jizzum was going. But he would sit at home instead, with his memories and a glass of Tang. Tang used to be the official drink of the astronauts. It was a freeze-dried orangeade.

"Maybe you haven't got two million years," said Dwayne, "but you've got at least five minutes. Sit thee doon."

"What I'm here for—" said the sheriff, and he let his unhappiness show, "is something I customarily do standing up."

Dwayne and Grace were sincerely puzzled. They didn't have the least idea what was coming next. Here is what it was: the sheriff handed each one of them a subpoena, and he said, "It's my sad duty to inform you that your daughter, Wanda June, has accused you of ruining her when she was a child."

Dwayne and Grace were thunderstruck. They knew that Wanda June was twenty-one now, and entitled to sue, but they certainly hadn't expected her to do so. She was in New York City, and when they congratulated her about her birthday on the telephone, in fact, one of the things Grace said was, "Well, you can sue us now, honeybunch, if you want to." Grace was so sure she and Dwayne had been good parents that she could laugh when she went on, "If you want to, you can send your rotten old parents off to jail."

Wanda June was an only child, incidentally. She had come close to having some siblings, but Grace had aborted them. Grace had taken three table lamps and a bathroom scale instead.

"What does she say we did wrong?" Grace asked the sheriff.

"There's a separate list of charges inside each of your subpoenas," he said. And he couldn't look his wretched old friends in the eye, so he looked at the television instead. A scientist there was explaining why Andromeda had been selected as a target. There were at least eighty-seven chronosynclastic infundibulae, time warps, between Earth and the Andromeda Galaxy. If the *Arthur C. Clarke* passed through any one of them, the ship and its load would be multiplied a trillion times, and would appear everywhere throughout space and time.

"If there's any fecundity anywhere in the Universe," the scientist promised, "our seed will find it and bloom."

One of the most depressing things about the space program so far, of course, was that it had demonstrated that fecundity was one hell of a long way off, if anywhere. Dumb people like Dwayne and Grace, and even fairly smart people like the sheriff, had been encouraged to believe that there was hospitality out there, and that Earth was just a piece of shit to use as a launching platform.

Now Earth really was a piece of shit, and it was beginning to dawn on even dumb people that it might be the only inhabitable planet human beings would ever find.

Grace was in tears over being sued by her daughter, and the list of charges she was reading was broken into multiple images by the tears. "Oh God, oh God, oh God—" she said, "she's talking about things I forgot all about, but she never forgot a thing. She's talking about something that happened when she was only four years old."

Dwayne was reading charges against himself, so he didn't ask Grace what awful thing she was supposed to have done when Wanda June was only four, but here it was: Poor little Wanda June drew pretty pictures with a crayon all over the new living-room wallpaper to make her mother happy. Her mother blew up and spanked her instead. Since that day, Wanda June claimed, she had not been able to look at any sort of art materials without trembling like a leaf and breaking out into cold sweats. "Thus was I deprived," Wanda June's lawyer had her say, "of a brilliant and lucrative career in the arts."

Dwayne meanwhile was learning that he had ruined his daughter's opportunities for what her lawyer called an "advantageous marriage and the comfort and love therefrom." Dwayne had done this, supposedly, by being half in the bag whenever a suitor came to call. Also, he was often stripped to the waist when he answered the door, but still had on his cartridge belt and his revolver. She was even able to name a lover her father had lost for her: John L. Newcomb, who had finally married somebody else. He had a very good job now. He was in command of the security force at an arsenal out in South Dakota, where they stockpiled cholera and bubonic plague.

The sheriff had still more bad news to deliver, and he knew he would have an opportunity to deliver it soon enough. Poor Dwayne and Grace were bound to ask him, "What made her *do* this to us?" The answer to that question would be more bad news, which was that Wanda June was in jail, charged with being the head of a shoplifting ring. The only way she could avoid prison was to prove that everything she was and did was her parents' fault.

Meanwhile, Senator Flem Snopes of Mississippi, Chairman of the Senate Space Committee, had appeared on the television screen. He was very happy about the Big Space Fuck, and he said it had been what the American space program had been aiming toward all along. He was proud, he said, that the United States had seen fit to locate the biggest jizzum-freezing plant in his "l'il ol' home town," which was Mayhew.

The word "jizzum" had an interesting history, by the way. It was as old as "fuck" and "shit" and so on, but it continued to be excluded from dictionaries, long after the others were let in. This was because so many people wanted it to remain a truly magic word—the only one left.

And when the United States announced that it was going to do a truly magical thing, was going to fire sperm at the Andromeda Galaxy, the populace corrected its government. Their collective unconscious announced that it was time for the last magic word to come into the open. They insisted that *sperm* was nothing to fire at another galaxy. Only *jizzum* would do. So the Government began using that word, and it did something that had never been done before, either: it standardized the way the word was spelled.

The man who was interviewing Senator Snopes asked him to stand up so everybody could get a good look at his codpiece, which the Senator did. Codpieces were very much in fashion, and many men were wearing codpieces in the shape of rocket ships, in honor of the Big Space Fuck. These customarily had the letters "U.S.A." embroidered on the shaft. Senator Snopes' shaft, however, bore the Stars and Bars of the Confederacy.

This led the conversation into the area of heraldry in general, and the interviewer reminded the Senator of his campaign to eliminate the bald eagle as the national bird. The Senator explained that he didn't like to have his country represented by a creature that obviously hadn't been able to cut the mustard in modern times.

Asked to name a creature that *had* been able to cut the mustard, the Senator did better than that: he named two—the lamprey and the bloodworm. And, unbeknownst to him or to anybody, lampreys were finding the Great Lakes too vile and noxious even for *them*. While all the human beings were in their houses, watching the Big Space Fuck, lampreys were squirming out of the ooze and onto land. Some of them were nearly as long and thick as the *Arthur C. Clarke*.

And Grace Hoobler tore her wet eyes from what she had been reading, and she asked the sheriff the question he had been dreading to hear: "What made her *do* this to us?"

The sheriff told her, and then he cried out against cruel Fate, too. "This is the most horrible duty I ever had to carry out—" he said brokenly, "to deliver news this heartbreaking to friends as close as you two are—on a night that's supposed to be the most joyful night in the history of mankind."

He left sobbing, and stumbled right into the mouth of a lamprey. The lamprey ate him immediately, but not before he screamed. Dwayne and Grace Hoobler rushed outside to see what the screaming was about, and the lamprey ate them, too.

It was ironical that their television set continued to report the countdown, even though they weren't around any more to see or hear or care.

"Nine!" said a voice. And then, "Eight!" And then, "Seven!" And so on.

1972

APPENDIX A

Address to the American Physical Society, New York City, February 5, 1969

MY ONLY BROTHER is a cloud physicist. He is nine years older than I am, and was an inspiration to me in my youth. He used to work with the research laboratory of the General Electric Company in Schenectady. Back in his Schenectady days, Bernard was working with Irving Langmuir and Vincent Schaefer on precipitating certain kinds of clouds as snow or rain—with dry ice or silver iodide, and maybe some other stuff.

He was notorious in Schenectady for having a horrendously messy laboratory. There was a safety officer in the laboratory who called on him regularly, begging him to clean up the death traps all around the room. One day my brother said to him, "If you think this is a mess, you should see what it's like up here." And my brother pointed to his own head. I loved him for that. We love each other very much, even though I am a humanist and he is a physicist.

I am charmed that you should call me in your program notes here a humanist. I have always thought of myself as a paranoid, as an overreactor, and a person who makes a questionable living with his mental diseases. Fiction writers are not customarily persons in the best of mental health.

Many of you are physics teachers. I have been a teacher, too. I have taught creative writing. I often wondered what I thought I was doing, teaching creative writing, since the demand for creative writers is very small in this vale of tears. I was perplexed as to what the usefulness of any of the arts might be, with the possible exception of interior decoration. The most positive notion I could come up with was what I call the canary-in-the-coal-mine theory of the arts. This theory argues that artists are useful to society because they are so sensitive. They are supersensitive. They keel over like canaries in coal mines filled with poison gas, long before more robust types realize that any danger is there.

The most useful thing I could do before this meeting today

is to keel over. On the other hand, artists are keeling over by the thousands every day and nobody seems to pay the least attention.

If you want an outside opinion on your profession, you hired the wrong man. I've had the same formal education you people have had, more or less. I was a chemistry major in college. H. L. Mencken started out as a chemist. H. G. Wells did, too. My father said he would help to pay for my college education only if I studied something serious. This was in the late Thirties. *Reader's Digest* magazine was in those days celebrating the wonderful things Germans were doing with chemicals. Chemistry was obviously the coming thing. So was German. So I went to Cornell University, and I studied chemistry and German.

Actually, it was very lucky for me as a writer that I studied the physical sciences rather than English. I wrote for my own amusement. There was no kindly English professor to tell me for my own good how awful my writing really was. And there was no professor with the power to order me what to read, either. So reading and writing have been pure pleasure for me. I only read *Madame Bovary* last year. It's a very good book. I had heard that it was.

Back in my days as a chemistry student I used to be quite a technocrat. I used to believe that scientists would corner God and photograph Him in Technicolor by 1951. I used to mock my fraternity brothers at Cornell who were wasting their energies on insubstantial subjects such as sociology and government and history. And literature. I told them that all power in the future would rest properly in the hands of chemists and physicists and engineers. The fraternity brothers knew more about the future and about the uses of power than I did. They are rich and they are powerful now. They all became lawyers.

You have summoned me here in my sunset years as a writer. I am forty-six. F. Scott Fitzgerald was dead when he was my age. So was Anton Chekhov. So was D. H. Lawrence. So was George Orwell, a man I admire almost more than any other man. Physicists live longer than writers, by and large. Copernicus died at seventy. Galileo died at seventy-eight. Isaac Newton died at eighty-five. They lived that long even before the discovery of all the miracles of modern medicine. Think of how much longer they might have lived with heart transplants.

You have called me a humanist, and I have looked into humanism some, and I have found that a humanist is a person who is tremendously interested in human beings. My dog is a humanist. His name is Sandy. He is a sheep dog. I know that Sandy is a dud name for a sheep dog, but there it is.

One day when I was a teacher of creative writing at the University of Iowa, in Iowa City, I realized that Sandy had never seen a truly large carnivore. He had never smelled one, either. I assumed that he would be thrilled out of his wits. So I took him to a small zoo they had in Iowa City to see two black bears in a cage.

"Hey, Sandy," I said to him on the way to the zoo, "wait till you see. Wait till you smell."

Those bears didn't interest him at all, even though they were only three inches away. The stink was enough to knock me over. But Sandy didn't seem to notice. He was too busy watching people.

Most people are mainly interested in people, too. Or that has been my experience in the writing game. That's why it was so intelligent of us to send human beings to the moon instead of instruments. Most people aren't very interested in instruments. One of the things that I tell beginning writers is this: "If you describe a landscape, or a cityscape, or a seascape, always be sure to put a human figure somewhere in the scene. Why? Because readers are human beings, mostly interested in human beings. People are humanists. *Most* of them are humanists, that is."

Shortly before coming to this meeting from Cape Cod, I received this letter:

> Dear Mr. Vonnegut,
>
> I saw with interest the announcement of the talk entitled "The Virtuous Scientist," to be delivered by you and Eames and Drexler at the New York A.P.S. meeting. Unfortunately, I will not be present at the New York meeting this year. However, as a humanistic physicist, I would very much

appreciate receiving a copy of the talk. Thanking you in advance.

Sincerely,
GEORGE F. NORWOOD, JR.,
assistant professor of physics,
University of Miami,
Coral Gables, Florida.

If Professor Norwood really is a humanistic physicist, then he is exactly my idea of what a virtuous physicist should be. A virtuous physicist is a humanistic physicist. Being a humanistic physicist, incidentally, is a good way to get *two* Nobel Prizes instead of one. What does a humanistic physicist do? Why, he watches people, listens to them, thinks about them, wishes them and their planet well. He wouldn't knowingly hurt people. He wouldn't knowingly help politicians or soldiers hurt people. If he comes across a technique that would obviously hurt people, he keeps it to himself. He knows that a scientist can be an accessory to murder most foul. That's simple enough, surely. That's surely clear.

I was invited here, I think, mostly because of a book of mine called *Cat's Cradle*. It is still in print, so if you rush out to buy it, you will not be disappointed. It is about an old-fashioned scientist who isn't interested in people. In the midst of a terrible family argument, he asks a question about turtles. Nobody has been talking about turtles. But the old man suddenly wants to know: When turtles pull in their heads, do their spines buckle or contract?

This absentminded old man, who doesn't give a damn for people, discovers a form of ice which is stable at room temperature. He dies, and some idiots get possession of the substance, which I call Ice-9. The idiots eventually drop some of the stuff into the sea, and the waters of the earth freeze—and that is the end of life on earth as we know it.

I got this lovely idea while I was working as a public-relations man at General Electric. I used to write publicity releases about the research laboratory there, where my brother worked. While there, I heard a story about a visit H. G. Wells had made to the laboratory in the early Thirties.

General Electric was alarmed by the news of his coming, because they did not know how to entertain him. The company told Irving Langmuir, who was a most important man in Schenectady, the only Nobel Prize winner in private industry, that he was going to have to entertain Wells. Langmuir didn't want to do it, but he dutifully tried to imagine diversions that would delight Mr. Wells. He made up a science-fiction story he hoped Mr. Wells would want to write. It was about a form of ice which was stable at room temperature. Mr. Wells was not stimulated by the story. He later died, and so did Langmuir. After Langmuir died, I thought to myself, well, I think maybe I'll write a story.

While I was writing that story about Ice-9, I happened to go to a cocktail party where I was introduced to a crystallographer. I told him about this ice which was stable at room temperature. He put his cocktail glass on the mantelpiece. He sat down in an easy chair in the corner. He did not speak to anyone or change expression for half an hour. Then he got up, came back over to the mantelpiece, and picked up his cocktail glass, and he said to me, "Nope." Ice-9 was impossible.

Be that as it may, other scientific developments have been almost that horrible. The idea of Ice-9 had a certain moral validity at any rate, even though scientifically it had to be pure bunk.

I have already called the fictitious inventor of the fictitious Ice-9 an old-fashioned sort of scientist. There used to be a lot of morally innocent scientists like him. No more. Younger scientists are extremely sensitive to the moral implications of all they do. My fictitious old-time scientist asked, among other things, this question: "What is sin?" He asked that question mockingly as though the concept of sin were as obsolete as plate armor. Young scientists, it seems to me, are fascinated by the idea of sin. They perceive it as anything human that seriously threatens the planet and the life thereon.

While I was working at General Electric, long after the Second World War, the older scientists were generally serene, but the younger ones were frequently upset. The young ones were eager to discuss the question as to whether the atomic bomb, for instance, was a sin or not.

David Lilienthal, the first chairman of the Atomic Energy Commission, said he was going to resign his job in order to speak freely, and scientists at General Electric banded together to ask Lilienthal to come to Schenectady to speak to them. They wanted to hear what he had to say about the bomb, now that he was free to say what he pleased. Lilienthal accepted. The young scientists hired a movie theater. It was jammed the night when Lilienthal agreed to speak so freely, to gush.

The audience was silent and thrilled and frightened and awed and hopeful. Lilienthal's opening statement, as I recall it, was this: "First of all, let me say that I see no point in wallowing in misery." Then he told the scientists and their wives, their young wives, about all the wonderful benefits that peacetime uses of atomic energy were going to bring. He told about a ball bearing which was coated with a radioactive isotope and then rolled down a trough. Thanks to atomic energy, minute measurements of the wear and tear on both the ball bearing and the trough could be made.

He told, too, about his egg man, who had a malignant throat tumor the size and shape of a summer squash. This man, who was about to die, was urged to drink an atomic cocktail. The tumor disappeared entirely in a matter of days. The egg man died anyway. But Lilienthal and others like him found the experiment encouraging in the extreme.

I have never seen a more depressed audience leaving a theater. *The Diary of Anne Frank* was a lighthearted comedy when compared with Lilienthal's performance for that particular audience, on that particular night, in that particular city, where science was king. The young scientists and their young wives had learned something which most scientists now realize: that their bosses are not necessarily sensitive or moral or imaginative men. Ask Wernher von Braun. His boss had him firing rockets at London.

The old-fashioned scientist I described in *Cat's Cradle* was the product of a great depression and of World War Two and some other things, of course. The mood of technical people in World War Two can be expressed in slogans such as "Can do!" and "The difficult we do right away; the impossible takes a little longer!"

The Second World War was a war against pure evil. I mean

that seriously. There was never any need to moralize. Nothing was too horrible to do to any enemy that vile. This moral certainty and the heartlessness it encouraged did not necessarily subside when the war was won. Virtuous scientists, however, stopped saying "Can do!"

I don't find this particularly congenial, moralizing up here. Moralizing hasn't really been my style up to now. But people, university people in particular, seem to be demanding more and more that persons who lecture to them put morals at the end of their lectures.

One of the greatest public-speaking failures of my career took place last summer at Valparaiso University in Indiana, where I addressed a convention of editors of college newspapers. I said many screamingly funny things, but the applause was dismal at the end. During the evening I asked one of my hosts in what way I had offended the audience. He replied that they had hoped I would moralize. They had hired me as a moralist.

So now when I speak to students, I do moralize. I tell them not to take more than they need, not to be greedy. I tell them not to kill, even in self-defense. I tell them not to pollute water or the atmosphere. I tell them not to raid the public treasury. I tell them not to work for people who pollute water or the atmosphere, or who raid the public treasury. I tell them not to commit war crimes or to help others to commit war crimes. These morals go over very well. They are, of course, echoes of what the young say to themselves.

I had a friend from Schenectady visit me recently, and he asked me this, "Why are fewer and fewer young Americans going into science each year?" I told him that the young were impressed by the war crimes trials at Nuremberg. They were afraid that careers in science could all too easily lead to the commission of war crimes. They don't want to work on the development of new weapons. They don't want to make discoveries which will lead to improved weapons. They don't want to work for corporations that pollute water or atmosphere or raid the public treasury. So they go into other fields. They become physicists who are so virtuous that they don't go into physics at all.

At the University of Michigan, at Ann Arbor, the students have been raising hell about the university doing secret Government work. I got to talking to some of the students about the protests that have been made against the recruiters for Dow Chemical, manufacturers of napalm among other things. I offered the opinion that an attack on a Dow recruiter was about as significant as an attack on the doorman or theater usher. I didn't think the recruiter stood for anything.

I called attention to the fact that during the Dow protest at Harvard a couple of years back, the actual inventor of napalm was able to circulate through the crowd of protestors unmolested. I didn't find the fact that he was unmolested reprehensible. I saw it as a moral curiosity, though I did not mean to suggest to students at Ann Arbor that the inventor of napalm should have been given one hell of a time. I wasn't sure what I thought.

The next day I received a letter which said this:

> Dear Mr. Vonnegut,
>   I heard you talk at the Canterbury house yesterday, and I must admit that I was struck by your question about Louis Fieser, who was allowed to wander unmolested through the Dow demonstration at Harvard. Your question about why students don't protest the scientists who invent weapons is valid and troublesome. I can only answer that I think we should. But do you know Louis Fieser? I don't know him personally, but I was at Harvard until this year and I have heard the old man lecture in organic chemistry. From this limited exposure and from the response of others to him in his late years, I can only suspect that a protest would be lost on him. He is a very funny and lovable man in the lecture room. I don't imagine he would understand a protest. And his personality leaves an imprint that makes it hard to use him as a symbol. In contrast, Dow representatives are such nicely impersonal representative products of the system that they are easy to protest against both immediately and symbolically.

There ends the letter.

This letter helped me to see that Dr. Fieser and other old-fashioned scientists like him were and are as innocent as Adam and Eve. There was nothing at all sinful in Dr. Fieser's creation of napalm. Scientists will never be so innocent again. Any young scientist, by contrast, when asked by the military to create a terror weapon on the order of napalm, is bound to suspect that he may be committing modern sin. God bless him for that.

APPENDIX B

Letter from PFC Kurt Vonnegut, Jr., to his family, May 29, 1945

FROM:
Pfc. Kurt Vonnegut, Jr.,
12102964 U. S. Army.

TO:
Kurt Vonnegut,
Williams Creek,
Indianapolis, Indiana.

Dear people:

I'm told that you were probably never informed that I was anything other than "missing in action." Chances are that you also failed to receive any of the letters I wrote from Germany. That leaves me a lot of explaining to do—in précis:

I've been a prisoner of war since December 19th, 1944, when our division was cut to ribbons by Hitler's last desperate thrust through Luxembourg and Belgium. Seven Fanatical Panzer Divisions hit us and cut us off from the rest of Hodges' First Army. The other American Divisions on our flanks managed to pull out: We were obliged to stay and fight. Bayonets aren't much good against tanks: Our ammunition, food and medical supplies gave out and our casualties out-numbered those who could still fight—so we gave up. The 106th got a Presidential Citation and some British Decoration from Montgomery for it, I'm told, but I'll be damned if it was worth it. I was one of the few who weren't wounded. For that much thank God.

Well, the supermen marched us, without food, water or sleep to Limberg, a distance of about sixty miles, I think, where we were loaded and locked up, sixty men to each small, unventilated, unheated box car. There were no sanitary accommodations—the floors were covered with fresh cow dung. There wasn't room for all of us to lie down. Half slept while the other half stood. We spent several days, including Christmas, on that Limberg siding. On Christmas Eve the Royal Air Force

793

bombed and strafed our unmarked train. They killed about one-hundred-and-fifty of us. We got a little water Christmas Day and moved slowly across Germany to a large P.O.W. Camp in Muhlburg, South of Berlin. We were released from the box cars on New Year's Day. The Germans herded us through scalding delousing showers. Many men died from shock in the showers after ten days of starvation, thirst and exposure. But I didn't.

Under the Geneva Convention, Officers and Non-commissioned Officers are not obliged to work when taken prisoner. I am, as you know, a Private. One-hundred-and-fifty such minor beings were shipped to a Dresden work camp on January 10th. I was their leader by virtue of the little German I spoke. It was our misfortune to have sadistic and fanatical guards. We were refused medical attention and clothing: We were given long hours at extremely hard labor. Our food ration was two-hundred-and-fifty grams of black bread and one pint of unseasoned potato soup each day. After desperately trying to improve our situation for two months and having been met with blank smiles I told the guards just what I was going to do to them when the Russians came. They beat me up a little. I was fired as group leader. Beatings were very small time: —one boy starved to death and the SS Troops shot two for stealing food.

On about February 14th the Americans came over, followed by the R.A.F. Their combined labors killed 250,000 people in twenty-four hours and destroyed all of Dresden—possibly the world's most beautiful city. But not me.

After that we were put to work carrying corpses from Air-Raid shelters; women, children, old men; dead from concussion, fire or suffocation. Civilians cursed us and threw rocks as we carried bodies to huge funeral pyres in the city.

When General Patton took Leipzig we were evacuated on foot to Hellexisdorf on the Saxony-Czechoslovakian border. There we remained until the war ended. Our guards deserted us. On that happy day the Russians were intent on mopping up isolated outlaw resistance in our sector. Their planes (P-39's) strafed and bombed us, killing fourteen but not me.

Eight of us stole a team and a wagon. We traveled and looted our way through Sudetenland and Saxony for eight days, living like kings. The Russians are crazy about Americans. The Russians picked us up in Dresden. We rode from there to the American lines at Halle in Lend-Lease Ford trucks. We've since been flown to Le Havre.

I'm writing from a Red Cross Club in the Le Havre P.O.W. Repatriation Camp. I'm being wonderfully well fed and entertained. The state-bound ships are jammed, naturally, so I'll have to be patient. I hope to be home in a month. Once home I'll be given twenty-one days recuperation at Atterbury, about $600 back pay and—get this—sixty (60) days furlough!

I've too damned much to say, the rest will have to wait. I can't receive mail here so don't write.

Love,
Kurt—Jr.

Wailing Shall Be in All Streets

I T WAS a routine speech we got during our first day of basic training, delivered by a wiry little lieutenant: "Men, up to now you've been good, clean, American boys with an American's love for sportsmanship and fair play. We're here to change that. Our job is to make you the meanest, dirtiest bunch of scrappers in the history of the World. From now on you can forget the Marquess of Queensberry Rules and every other set of rules. Anything and everything goes. Never hit a man above the belt when you can kick him below it. Make the bastard scream. Kill him any way you can. Kill, kill, kill, do you understand?"

His talk was greeted with nervous laughter and general agreement that he was right. "Didn't Hitler and Tojo say the Americans were a bunch of softies? Ha! They'll find out." And of course, Germany and Japan did find out: a toughened-up democracy poured forth a scalding fury that could not be stopped. It was a war of reason against barbarism, supposedly, with the issues at stake on such a high plane that most of our feverish fighters had no idea why they were fighting—other than that the enemy was a bunch of bastards. A new kind of war, with all destruction, all killing approved. Germans would ask, "Why are you Americans fighting us?" "I don't know, but we're sure beating the hell out of you," was a stock answer.

A lot of people relished the idea of total war: it had a modern ring to it, in keeping with our spectacular technology. To them it was like a football game: "Give 'em the axe, the axe, the axe . . ." Three small-town merchants' wives, middle-aged and plump, gave me a ride when I was hitchhiking home from Camp Atterbury. "Did you kill a lot of them Germans?" asked the driver, making cheerful small-talk. I told her I didn't know. This was taken for modesty. As I was getting out of the car, one of the ladies patted me on the shoulder in motherly fashion: "I'll bet you'd like to get over and kill some of them dirty Japs now, wouldn't you?" We exchanged knowing winks. I didn't tell those simple souls that I had been captured after a week at the front; and more to the point, what I knew and thought about killing dirty Germans, about total war. The reason for my being sick at heart then and now has to do with an incident that received cursory treatment in the American newspapers. In February, 1945, Dresden, Germany, was destroyed, and with it over one hundred thousand human beings. I was there. Not many know how tough America got.

I was among a group of one hundred and fifty infantry privates, captured in the Bulge breakthrough and put to work in Dresden. Dresden, we were told, was the only major German city to have escaped bombing so far. That was in January, 1945. She owed her good fortune to her unwarlike countenance: hospitals, breweries, food-processing plants, surgical supply houses, ceramics, musical instrument factories, and the like. Since the war, hospitals had become her prime concern. Every day hundreds of wounded came into the tranquil sanctuary from the east and west. At night we would hear the dull rumble of distant air raids. "Chemnitz is getting it tonight," we used to say, and speculated what it might be like to be under the yawning bomb-bays and the bright young men with their dials and cross-hairs. "Thank heaven we're in an 'open city,'" we thought, and so thought the thousands of refugees—women, children, and old men—who came in a forlorn stream from the smouldering wreckage of Berlin, Leipzig, Breslau, Munich. . . . They flooded the city to twice its normal population.

There was no war in Dresden. True, planes came over nearly every day and the sirens wailed, but the planes were always en route elsewhere. The alarms furnished a relief period in a tedious work day, a social event, a chance to gossip in the shelters. The shelters, in fact, were not much more than a gesture, casual recognition of the national emergency: wine cellars and basements with benches in them and sand bags blocking the windows, for the most part. There were a few more adequate bunkers in the center of the city, close to the government offices, but nothing like the staunch subterranean fortress that rendered Berlin impervious to her daily pounding. Dresden had no reason to prepare for attack—and thereby hangs a beastly tale.

Dresden was surely among the World's most lovely cities.

Her streets were broad, lined with shade-trees. She was sprinkled with countless little parks and statuary. She had marvelous old churches, libraries, museums, theaters, art galleries, beer gardens, a zoo, and a renowned university. It was at one time a tourist's paradise. They would be far better informed on the city's delights than am I. But the impression I have is that in Dresden—in the physical city—were the symbols of the good life; pleasant, honest, intelligent. In the Swastika's shadow those symbols of the dignity and hope of mankind stood waiting, monuments to truth. The accumulated treasure of hundreds of years, Dresden spoke eloquently of those things excellent in European civilization wherein our debt lies deep. I was a prisoner, hungry, dirty, and full of hate for our captors, but I loved that city and saw the blessed wonder of her past and the rich promise of her future.

In February, 1945, American bombers reduced this treasure to crushed stone and embers; disemboweled her with high-explosives and cremated her with incendiaries. The atom bomb may represent a fabulous advance, but it is interesting to note that primitive TNT and thermite managed to exterminate in one bloody night more people than died in the whole London blitz. Fortress Dresden fired a dozen shots at our airmen. Once back at their bases and sipping hot coffee, they probably remarked, "Flak unusually light tonight. Well, guess it's time to turn in." Captured British pilots from tactical fighter units (covering front-line troops) used to chide those who had flown heavy bombers on city raids with, "How on Earth did you stand the stink of boiling urine and burning perambulators?"

A perfectly routine piece of news: "Last night our planes attacked Dresden. All planes returned safely." The only good German is a dead one: over one hundred thousand evil men, women, and children (the able-bodied were at the fronts) forever purged of their sins against humanity. By chance I met a bombardier who had taken part in the attack. "We hated to do it," he told me.

The night they came over we spent in an underground meat locker in a slaughterhouse. We were lucky, for it was the best shelter in town. Giants stalked the Earth above us. First came the soft murmur of their dancing on the outskirts, then the grumbling of their plodding toward us, and finally the ear-

splitting crashes of their heels upon us—and thence to the outskirts again. Back and forth they swept: saturation bombing.

"I screamed and I wept and I clawed the walls of our shelter," an old lady told me. "I prayed to God to 'please, please,
please, dear God, stop them.' But he didn't hear me. No power
could stop them. On they came, wave after wave. There was
no way we could surrender; no way to tell them we couldn't
stand it anymore. There was nothing anyone could do but sit
and wait for morning." Her daughter and grandson were killed.

Our little prison was burned to the ground. We were to be
evacuated to an outlying camp occupied by the South African
prisoners. Our guards were a melancholy lot, aged Volkssturmers
and disabled veterans. Most of them were Dresden residents
and had friends and families somewhere in the holocaust. A
corporal, who had lost an eye after two years on the Russian
front, ascertained before we marched that his wife, his two
children, and both of his parents had been killed. He had one
cigarette. He shared it with me.

Our march to new quarters took us on the city's edge. It was
impossible to believe that anyone survived in its heart. Ordinarily the day would have been cold, but occasional gusts from
the colossal inferno made us sweat. And ordinarily the day
would have been clear and bright, but an opaque and towering
cloud turned noon to twilight. A grim procession clogged the
outbound highways; people with blackened faces streaked with
tears, some bearing wounded, some bearing dead. They gathered in the fields. None spoke. A few with Red Cross arm-
bands did what they could for the casualties.

Settled with the South Africans, we enjoyed a week without
work. At the end of it communications were reestablished with
higher headquarters and we were ordered to hike seven miles
to the area hardest hit. Nothing in the district had escaped the
fury. A city of jagged building shells, of splintered statuary and
shattered trees; every vehicle stopped, gnarled and burned, left
to rust or rot in the path of the frenzied might. The only
sounds other than our own were those of falling plaster and
their echoes. I cannot describe the desolation properly, but I
can give an idea of how it made us feel, in the words of a deliri-
ous British soldier in a makeshift P.W. hospital: "It's frightenin',
I tell you. I would walk down one of them bloody streets and

feel a thousand eyes on the back of me 'ead. I would 'ear 'em whisperin' behind me. I would turn around to look at 'em and there wouldn't be a bloomin' soul in sight. You can feel 'em and you can 'ear 'em but there's never anybody there." We knew what he said was so.

For "salvage" work we were divided into small crews, each under a guard. Our ghoulish mission was to search for bodies. It was rich hunting that day and the many thereafter. We started on a small scale—here a leg, there an arm, and an occasional baby—but struck a mother lode before noon. We cut our way through a basement wall to discover a reeking hash of over one hundred human beings. Flame must have swept through before the building's collapse sealed the exits, because the flesh of those within resembled the texture of prunes. Our job, it was explained, was to wade into the shambles and bring forth the remains. Encouraged by cuffing and guttural abuse, wade in we did. We did exactly that, for the floor was covered with an unsavory broth from burst water mains and viscera. A number of victims, not killed outright, had attempted to escape through a narrow emergency exit. At any rate, there were several bodies packed tightly into the passageway. Their leader had made it halfway up the steps before he was buried up to his neck in falling brick and plaster. He was about fifteen, I think.

It is with some regret that I here besmirch the nobility of our airmen, but boys, you killed an appalling lot of women and children. The shelter I have described and innumerable others like it were filled with them. We had to exhume their bodies and carry them to mass funeral pyres in the parks—so I know. The funeral pyre technique was abandoned when it became apparent how great was the toll. There was not enough labor to do it nicely, so a man with a flame-thrower was sent down instead, and he cremated them where they lay. Burned alive, suffocated, crushed—men, women, and children indiscriminately killed. For all the sublimity of the cause for which we fought, we surely created a Belsen of our own. The method was impersonal, but the result was equally cruel and heartless. That, I am afraid, is a sickening truth.

When we had become used to the darkness, the odor, and

the carnage, we began musing as to what each of the corpses had been in life. It was a sordid game: "Rich man, poor man, beggar man, thief . . ." Some had fat purses and jewelry, others had precious foodstuffs. A boy had his dog still leashed to him. Renegade Ukrainians in German uniform were in charge of our operations in the shelters proper. They were roaring drunk from adjacent wine cellars and seemed to enjoy their job hugely. It was a profitable one, for they stripped each body of valuables before we carried it to the street. Death became so commonplace that we could joke about our dismal burdens and cast them about like so much garbage. Not so with the first of them, especially the young: we had lifted them onto the stretchers with care, laying them out with some semblance of funeral dignity in their last resting place before the pyre. But our awed and sorrowful propriety gave way, as I said, to rank callousness. At the end of a grisly day we would smoke and survey the impressive heap of dead accumulated. One of us flipped his cigarette butt into the pile: "Hell's bells," he said, "I'm ready for Death anytime he wants to come after me."

A few days after the raid the sirens screamed again. The listless and heartsick survivors were showered this time with leaflets. I lost my copy of the epic, but remember that it ran something like this: "To the people of Dresden: We were forced to bomb your city because of the heavy military traffic your railroad facilities have been carrying. We realize that we haven't always hit our objectives. Destruction of anything other than military objectives was unintentional, unavoidable fortunes of war." That explained the slaughter to everyone's satisfaction, I am sure, but it aroused no little contempt for the American bomb-sight. It is a fact that forty-eight hours after the last B-17 had droned west for a well-earned rest, labor battalions had swarmed over the damaged rail yards and restored them to nearly normal service. None of the rail bridges over the Elbe was knocked out of commission. Bomb-sight manufacturers should blush to know that their marvelous devices laid bombs down as much as three miles wide of what the military claimed to be aiming for. The leaflet should have said, "We hit every blessed church, hospital, school, museum, theater, your university, the zoo, and every apartment building in town, but we honestly weren't trying hard to do it. C'est la guerre. So sorry. Besides, saturation bombing is all the rage these days, you know."

There was tactical significance: stop the railroads. An excellent maneuver, no doubt, but the technique was horrible. The planes started kicking high-explosives and incendiaries through their bomb-bays at the city limits, and for all the pattern their hits presented, they must have been briefed by a Ouija board. Tabulate the loss against the gain. Over one hundred thousand non-combatants and a magnificent city destroyed by bombs dropped wide of the stated objectives: the railroads were knocked out for roughly two days. The Germans counted it the greatest loss of life suffered in any single raid. The death of Dresden was a bitter tragedy, needlessly and willfully executed. The killing of children—"Jerry" children or "Jap" children, or whatever enemies the future may hold for us—can never be justified.

The facile reply to great groans such as mine is the most hateful of all clichés, "fortunes of war," and another, "They asked for it. All they understand is force." *Who* asked for it? The only thing *who* understands is force? Believe me, it is not easy to rationalize the stamping out of vineyards where the grapes of wrath are stored when gathering up babies in bushel baskets or helping a man dig where he thinks his wife may be buried. Certainly enemy military and industrial installations should have been blown flat, and woe unto those foolish enough to seek shelter near them. But the "Get Tough America" policy, the spirit of *revenge*, the approbation of all destruction and killing, has earned us a name for obscene brutality, and cost the World the possibility of Germany's becoming a peaceful and intellectually fruitful nation in anything but the most remote future.

Our leaders had a carte blanche as to what they might or might not destroy. Their mission was to win the war as quickly as possible, and, while they were admirably trained to do just that, their decisions as to the fate of certain priceless World heirlooms—in one case Dresden—were not always judicious. When, late in the war, with the Wehrmacht breaking up on all fronts, our planes were sent to destroy this last major city, I doubt if the question was asked, "How will this tragedy benefit us, and how will that benefit compare with the ill-effects in the long run?" Dresden, a beautiful city, built in the art spirit, symbol of an admirable heritage, so anti-Nazi that Hitler visited it but twice during his whole reign, food and hospital center so bitterly needed now—plowed under and salt strewn in the furrows.

There can be no doubt that the Allies fought on the side of right and the Germans and Japanese on the side of wrong. World War II was fought for near-Holy motives. But I stand convinced that the brand of justice in which we dealt, wholesale bombings of civilian populations, was blasphemous. That the enemy did it first has nothing to do with the moral problem. What I saw of our air war, as the European conflict neared an end, had the earmarks of being an irrational war for war's sake. Soft citizens of the American democracy learned to kick a man below the belt and make the bastard scream.

The occupying Russians, when they discovered that we were Americans, embraced us and congratulated us on the complete desolation our planes had wrought. We accepted their congratulations with good grace and proper modesty, but I felt then as I feel now, that I would have given my life to save Dresden for the World's generations to come. That is how everyone should feel about every city on Earth.

c. 1945–47

A "Special Message"
to readers of the Franklin Library's
limited edition of "Slaughterhouse-Five"

THIS IS a book about something that happened to me a long time ago (1944)—and the book itself is now something else that happened to me a long time ago (1969).

Time marches on—and the key event in this book, which is the fire-bombing of Dresden, is now a fossilized memory, sinking ever deeper into the tar pit of history. If American school children have heard of it at all, they are surely in doubt as to whether it happened in World War One or Two. Nor do I think they should care much.

I, for one, am not avid to keep the memory of the firebombing fresh. I would of course be charmed if people continued to read this book for years to come, but not because I think there are important lessons to be learned from the Dresden catastrophe. I myself was in the midst of it, and learned only that people can become so enraged in war that they will burn great cities to the ground, and slay the inhabitants thereof.

That was nothing new.

I write this in October of 1976, and it so happens that only two nights ago I saw a screening of Marcel Ophuls' new documentary on war crimes, "The Memory of Justice," which included movies, taken from the air, of the Dresden raid—at night. The city appeared to boil, and I was down there somewhere.

I was supposed to appear onstage afterwards, with some other people who had had intimate experiences with Nazi death camps and so on, and to contribute my notions as to the meaning of it all.

Atrocities celebrate meaninglessness, surely. I was mute. I did not mount the stage. I went home.

The Dresden atrocity, tremendously expensive and meticulously planned, was so meaningless, finally, that only one person on the entire planet got any benefit from it. I am that person. I wrote this book, which earned a lot of money for me and made my reputation, such as it is.

One way or another, I got two or three dollars for every person killed. Some business I'm in.

1978

Preface
to the twenty-fifth-anniversary
edition of "Slaughterhouse-Five"

THE British mathematician Stephen Hawking, in his 1988 best seller *A Brief History of Time*, found it tantalizing that we could not remember the future. But remembering the future is child's play for me now. I know what will become of my helpless, trusting babies because they are grown-ups now. I know how my closest friends will end up because so many of them are retired or dead now. Mary O'Hare is a widow now. I know what will happen to a divided Germany and to a monolithic Soviet Union because one has been reunited and the other has fallen to pieces now, and on and on. To Stephen Hawking and all others younger than myself I say, "Be patient. Your future will soon come to you and lie down at your feet like a dog who knows and loves you no matter what you are."

I have no regrets about this book, which the owlish nitwit George Will said trivialized the Holocaust. It is a nonjudgmental expression of astonishment at what I saw and did in Dresden after it was firebombed so long ago, when, in the company of other prisoners of war and slave laborers who had survived the raid, I dug corpses from cellars and carried them, unidentified, their names recorded nowhere, to monumental funeral pyres. The corpses could have been anybody, including me, and there were surely representatives among them, whether collaborators or slaves or refugees, of every nation involved in the European half of World War II.

How could I be nonjudgmental? It was bombs that had done the killing. I had several decent and honorable and courageous friends who were pilots or bombardiers. Actions of men like them on the Dresden raid required no more fury and loathing or angry vigor than would have jobs on an automobile assembly line.

Before I got back to the American Army when the war was over, I met many survivors of the Holocaust in a valley I describe in my novel *Bluebeard*. About ten years ago I visited Auschwitz, where the executioners and the victims could see and hear each other, and possibly get to know each other a little bit. The names and ages and hometowns of all concerned were entered in ledgers that have survived to the present day, like the names of actors and actresses in a playbill for a Grand Guignol production of long ago.

The drama at Auschwitz was about man's inhumanity to man. The drama of any air raid on a civilian population, a gesture in diplomacy to a man like Henry Kissinger, is about the inhumanity of many of man's inventions to man. That is the dominant theme of what I have written during the past forty-five years or so. And the dog of my future, lying at my feet, is snoring now.

1994

CHRONOLOGY

NOTE ON THE TEXTS

NOTES

Chronology

money, at 4365 North Illinois Street, near the intersection with Forty-fifth Street, Indianapolis. After the Great Crash of October, the mortgage payment on the property becomes increasingly difficult to meet.

1931   As the Depression deepens and new construction ceases, Vonnegut, Bohn & Mueller struggles. Father sells investments and heirlooms to keep family solvent, and reluctantly dismisses Ida Young. ("She was humane and wise and gave me decent moral instruction," Vonnegut will later remember. "The compassionate, forgiving aspects of my beliefs come from Ida Young.") Father's younger brother, Alex Vonnegut, a Harvard-educated insurance salesman and bon vivant, becomes Vonnegut's mentor and "ideal grownup friend." ("He taught me something very important: that when things are going well, we should notice it. He urged me to say out loud during such epiphanies, 'If this isn't nice, *what is?*'") Vonnegut is withdrawn from private school and begins fourth grade at James Whitcomb Riley Elementary, P.S. 43.

1934   Father, after years without an architectural commission, closes his office, turns an attic room of the house into an art studio, and begins to paint portraits, still lifes, and landscapes. Mother takes night classes in creative writing and attempts, unsuccessfully, to sell commercial short fiction to women's magazines. Vonnegut, age eleven, takes a strong interest and vicarious pleasure in his parents' artistic pursuits. In September, Grandfather Lieber dies at age seventy-one. The Vonneguts' share of his estate after probate is less than eleven thousand dollars, and mother, grieving, resentful, and obsessively insecure about the family's diminished social position, begins a long struggle with alcohol abuse, insomnia, and depression. ("My mother was addicted to being rich," Vonnegut will later write. "She was tormented by withdrawal symptoms all through the Great Depression.")

1936   Vonnegut enters Shortridge High School, the largest and best equipped free public school in the state of Indiana. Excels in English and public-speaking classes, and, after dedicated application, the sciences. Joins the staff of the Shortridge *Daily Echo*, a four-page broadsheet edited, set up, and printed by students in the school's print shop, and develops the habit of writing regularly, on deadline, for an audience of his peers. (In his junior and senior years, he will be editor and chief writer of the paper's Tuesday edition.) Plays clarinet in school orchestra and marching band, and takes private lessons from Ernst Michaelis, first-chair clarinetist of the Indianapolis Symphony. Forms a book club for two with Uncle Alex and reads, mostly at Alex's suggestion, Robert Louis Stevenson, H. G. Wells, H. L. Mencken, Thorstein Veblen, George Bernard Shaw, and Mark Twain. Other enthusiasms include Ping-Pong, model trains, radio comedy, movies, and jazz, especially Benny Goodman and Artie Shaw. Begins smoking Pall Mall cigarettes, which will become a lifelong habit.

1940   At age eighteen his head is a mop of blond curls and he has attained his adult height of six foot two: "I was a real skinny, narrow-shouldered boy . . . a preposterous kind of flamingo." Graduates from Shortridge High, and, still living with his parents, enrolls at local Butler University. His vague ambition is to study journalism and, ultimately, write for one of Indianapolis's three daily papers.

1941   Disappointed in Butler, transfers to Cornell University, Ithaca, New York, in middle of freshman year. Following his father's orders and his scientist brother's example, shuns "frivolous" classes in the arts and humanities, focusing instead on chemistry and physics. ("I had no talent for science," Vonnegut will remember. "I did badly.") Neglects his studies, taking pleasure only in drilling with ROTC, drinking with his Delta Upsilon brothers, and writing jokes and news for the Cornell *Daily Sun*. In summer, father sells the big brick house and, with proceeds, builds a smaller one in Williams Creek, a new suburban development six miles north of Indianapolis.

1942   Vonnegut writes a regular column, "Well All Right," for the *Daily Sun*—"impudent editorializing" and "college-humor sort of stuff"—and is elected the paper's assistant managing editor. In the middle of the fall semester of his junior year, is placed on academic probation due to poor grades. Contracts viral pneumonia, withdraws from school, and goes home to recover.

1943   Against the pleas of his mother, enlists in the U.S. Army and in March begins basic training at Camp Atterbury, forty miles south of Indianapolis. Takes special classes in manning the 240-millimeter howitzer, the army's largest mobile fieldpiece. In summer joins the Army Specialized Training Program, and is sent first to the Carnegie Institute of Technology, Pittsburgh, and then to the University of Tennessee, Knoxville, for advanced studies in engineering ("thermodynamics, mechanics, the actual use of machine tools. . . . I did badly again").

1944   In March returns to Camp Atterbury and is assigned as private first class to Headquarters Company, 2nd Battalion, 423rd Regiment, 106th Infantry Division. Although he has no infantry training ("bayonets, grenades, and so on") he is made one of the battalion's six scouts. Assigned an "Army buddy," fellow scout Bernard V. O'Hare Jr., a Roman Catholic youth from Shenandoah, Pennsylvania, who will become a friend for life. Secures frequent Sunday passes, enjoying meals at his parents' house and movie dates with Jane Marie Cox, his sometimes high-school sweetheart. On May 14, while Vonnegut is home on a Mother's Day pass, mother, age fifty-five, commits suicide using barbiturates and alcohol. In October the 106th leaves Camp Atterbury and is staged at Camp Myles Standish, Taunton, Massachusetts. The division embarks at New York City on October 17 and, after three weeks' training in England, is deployed in the Ardennes on December 11. The Germans launch a surprise offensive against the American front on December 16, and three days later Vonnegut, O'Hare, and some sixty other infantrymen are separated from their battalion and taken prisoner near Schönberg, on the German-Belgian border. They are marched sixty miles to Limburg and on December 21 are warehoused, sixty men to a forty-man boxcar, on a railroad siding there. After more than a week, the stifling, fetid car is hauled by train to Stalag IV-B, a crowded German P.O.W. camp in Mühlberg, thirty miles north of Dresden.

1945   On New Year's Day the boxcar is opened, and Vonnegut and his fellow-prisoners are provided showers, bunks, and starvation rations of cold potato soup and brown bread. On January 10, Vonnegut, O'Hare, and about one hundred fifty other prisoners are transferred to a Dresden factory where, under observation by armed guards, they manufacture vitamin-enriched barley-malt syrup. Vonnegut, who has rudimentary German learned at home, is elected the group's foreman and interpreter. On February 13–14, the Allied air forces bomb Dresden, destroying much of the city and killing some twenty-five thousand people. Vonnegut, his fellow prisoners, and their guards find safety in the subterranean meat locker of a slaughterhouse. After the raid, the guards put the prisoners to work clearing corpses from basements and air-raid shelters and hauling them to mass funeral pyres in the Old Market. In late April, as U.S. forces advance on Leipzig, the prisoners and their guards evacuate Dresden and march fifty miles southeast toward Hellendorf, a hamlet near the border with Czechoslovakia. There, on the morning after the general surrender of May 7, the Germans abandon the prisoners and flee from the advancing Soviet Army. Vonnegut, O'Hare, and six others steal a horse and wagon and, over the following week, slowly make their way back to Dresden. Outside the city they meet the Soviet Army, which trucks them a hundred miles to the American lines at Halle. From Halle they are flown, on May 22, to Le Havre, France, for rest and recovery at Camp Lucky Strike, a U.S. repatriation facility. ("When I was captured I weighed 180 pounds," Vonnegut later remembered. "When I was liberated, I weighed 132. The Army fed me cheeseburgers and milkshakes and sent me home wearing an overcoat of baby fat.") On April 21, Vonnegut and O'Hare board a Liberty Ship, the SS *Lucretia Mott*, bound for Newport News, Virginia. Vonnegut returns to Camp Atterbury by train and serves three more weeks as a clerical typist; is promoted to corporal, awarded a Purple Heart, then honorably discharged in late July. Marries high-school sweetheart Jane Marie Cox, September 14, and honeymoons at a Vonnegut family cottage on Lake Maxinkuckee. Taking advantage of the G.I. Bill, Vonnegut applies, and in October is accepted, to the Master's program in anthropology at the University of Chicago. The newlyweds rent an inexpensive apartment near the campus, their home for the next two years. Vonnegut finds a part-time job as a police reporter for the City News Bureau, an independent news agency that provides local stories to Chicago's five dailies.

1946   Greatly enjoys his anthropology classes, especially those taught by Robert Redfield, whom Vonnegut will remember as "the most satisfying teacher in my life." Redfield's theory that human beings are hardwired for living in a

"Folk Society"—"a society where everyone knew everybody well, and associations were for life," where "there was
little change" and "what one man believed was what all
men believed," where every man felt himself to be part of
a larger, supportive, coherent whole—quickly becomes central to Vonnegut's world view. ("We are full of chemicals
which require us to belong to folk societies, or failing that,
to feel lousy all the time," Vonnegut will later write. "We
are chemically engineered to live in folk societies, just as
fish are chemically engineered to live in clean water—and
there are no folk societies for us anymore.")

1947   Son born, May 11, and named Mark Vonnegut in honor of
Mark Twain. Master's thesis, "On the Fluctuations Between Good and Evil in Simple Tales," unanimously rejected by Chicago's anthropology faculty. Vonnegut leaves
the program without a degree, fails to turn his part-time
job into full-time newspaper work, and searches in vain for
appropriate employment. Through the agency of his
brother, Bernard, an atmospheric scientist at General Electric, Vonnegut is interviewed by the public-relations department at GE headquarters, in Schenectady, New York.
Accepts position of publicist for research laboratory at
ninety dollars a week, and moves with family to the village
of Alplaus, five miles north of the GE complex. Joins the
Alplaus Volunteer Fire Department, his window into community life, and reads George Orwell, whose work and
moral example become a touchstone.

1949   Vonnegut enjoys the daily company of research scientists
and is "easily excited and entertained" by their work, but
despises the corporate hierarchy of GE and sees no room
for advancement within the PR department. Devotes evenings and weekends to drafting his first short stories, one
of which, "Report on the Barnhouse Effect," he submits to
Knox Burger, chief fiction editor at *Collier's*, a general-
interest mass-circulation magazine which, like its rival *The
Saturday Evening Post*, publishes five stories a week. "Knox
told me what was wrong with it, and how to fix it," Vonnegut will later remember. "I did what he said, and he
bought the story for seven hundred and fifty dollars, six
weeks' pay at GE. I wrote another, and he paid nine hundred and fifty. . . ." Daughter, Edith ("Edie") Vonnegut,
born December 29.

1950   First published story, "Report on the Barnhouse Effect," in
        Collier's, February 11; it is adapted for NBC radio's *Dimen-
        sion X* program (broadcast April 22) and chosen for inclu-
        sion in Robert A. Heinlein's anthology *Tomorrow, the Stars*
        (1952). Sells several more stories to *Collier's* and begins
        planning a satirical novel about a fully automated world
        where human labor and the dignity of work are rendered
        obsolete.

1951   Vonnegut rents a summer cottage in Provincetown, Mas-
        sachusetts, and decides to resign from GE and move his
        family to Cape Cod. Having saved the equivalent of a year's
        salary in freelance income, he buys a small house at 10 Bar-
        nard Street, Osterville, on the south shore of the Cape,
        where he finishes his novel, *Player Piano*. At the recom-
        mendation of Knox Burger, places the book with New York
        agents Kenneth Littauer and Max Wilkinson, both formerly
        of *Collier's*. At Vonnegut's request, they submit it to Charles
        Scribner's Sons, the house of Hemingway and Fitzgerald,
        and have a contract by Christmas.

1952   *Player Piano* published in hardcover, August 18, in an edi-
        tion of 7,600 copies. It receives few but respectful reviews.
        Continues to write short stories for *Collier's* and, with the
        help of Littauer & Wilkinson, Inc., begins placing work in
        The Saturday Evening Post, *Cosmopolitan*, and other top-
        paying magazines.

1953   *Player Piano* reprinted as a July/August selection of the
        Doubleday Science Fiction Book Club. Vonnegut becomes
        involved, as an advisor, fundraiser, volunteer, and actor, in
        the business and artistic affairs of two of Cape Cod's lead-
        ing amateur theatrical companies, the Orleans Arena The-
        atre (summer-stock) and the Barnstable Comedy Club (a
        repertory company staging four plays a year).

1954   After several false starts abandons Prohibition-era social
        novel, "Upstairs and Downstairs," set in Indianapolis and
        inspired by the riches-to-rags career of grandfather Albert
        Lieber. Writes six chapters of a novel about "ice-nine," a
        synthetic form of ice that will not melt at room tempera-
        ture, but soon sets the project aside. Second daughter and
        third child, Nanette ("Nanny") Vonnegut, born October 4.
        Player Piano reprinted in paperback by Bantam Books, un-
        der the title *Utopia 14*.

1955   In February, the Vonneguts leave the small house in Oster-
        ville for a large one at 9 Scudder Lane, in nearby West
        Barnstable. With his favorite market for stories failing (*Col-
        lier's* became a biweekly in 1953, and will cease publication
        in January 1957) and without ideas for a new novel, Von-
        negut takes a full-time job as copywriter in an industrial
        advertising agency. Commutes to Boston daily, and holds
        the job for about two years. Dabbles in playwriting, with
        an eye toward providing a show for the Orleans Arena
        Theatre.

1956   In January Vonnegut's father, recently retired from a sec-
        ond career in architecture and living alone in rural Brown
        County, Indiana, informs his family that he is dying of lung
        cancer. Vonnegut visits him a number of times before his
        death, on October 1, at age seventy-two.

1957   Makes stage adaptation of his short story "EPICAC" (*Col-
        lier's*, 1950) for an evening of one-acts at the Barnstable
        Comedy Club. (The cast features eight-year-old Edie Von-
        negut in the role of a talking computer.) With small in-
        heritance from his father, opens and manages Saab Cape
        Cod, the second Saab dealership in the United States, with
        a showroom and garage on Route 6A, just up the street
        from his house. At a Littauer & Wilkinson holiday party
        Vonnegut is asked by Knox Burger, now an editor for Dell
        Books, to write a science-fiction novel for his new line of
        mass-market paperback originals.

1958   Improvises an outline for his paperback novel, conceived as
        a satire on human grandeur in the form of a pulp-fiction
        "space opera." Writes the first draft with unaccustomed
        speed, then painstakingly revises. ("I *swooped* through that
        novel," Vonnegut will later recall. "All the others were
        bashed out, sentence by sentence.") Sister, Alice, a house-
        wife and amateur sculptor, dies of breast cancer in a New-
        ark, New Jersey, hospital, September 16, at age forty-one,
        with both of her brothers nearby. Only one day earlier her
        husband of fifteen years, James Carmalt Adams, had died
        when a commuter train taking him to Manhattan plunged
        off an open drawbridge into Newark Bay. Without hesita-
        tion Kurt and Jane Vonnegut take in Alice's four orphaned
        children—James Jr. (fourteen years old), Steven (eleven),
        Kurt (called "Tiger," nine), and toddler "Peter Boo" (twenty-
        one months). As Jane will later write, "Our tidy little fam-

ily of five had blown up into a wildly improbable gang of nine."

1959   The Vonneguts assume custody of the three older Adams boys, but after a protracted, bitter dispute with a childless Adams cousin, relinquish control of the youngest. (Allowing the boys to be split between distant and unlike households will be, according to Jane, "the most difficult decision" of the Vonneguts' marriage. "Peter Boo" is raised in Birmingham, Alabama, and until his teens will see little of his older brothers.) In October, Vonnegut's second novel, *The Sirens of Titan*, published in paperback by Dell in an edition of 175,000 copies. It is popular with readers but receives no reviews.

1960   *Penelope*, a two-act comedy about a war hero's unheroic homecoming, receives six performances at the Orleans Arena Theatre, September 5–10. *The Sirens of Titan* named a finalist for the Hugo Award for the year's best science-fiction novel, and Houghton Mifflin arranges to print 2,500 hardcover copies to meet demand from libraries. Vonnegut, having failed to make money for himself or his Swedish franchisers, closes Saab Cape Cod.

1961   In the ten years since the appearance of "Report on the Barnhouse Effect," Vonnegut has published more than three-dozen short stories in "slick" magazines and science-fiction pulps. In September Knox Burger, now at Fawcett Gold Medal Books, publishes *Canary in a Cat House*, a paperback collection of twelve of these stories. Burger also signs Vonnegut's third novel, *Mother Night*, the fictional memoirs of a German-American double agent during World War II. Vonnegut publishes "My Name Is Everyone" (*The Saturday Evening Post*, December 16), a short story evoking the backstage life of a community playhouse much like that of the Barnstable Comedy Club.

1962   In February *Mother Night* published as a paperback original by Fawcett Gold Medal in an edition of 175,000 copies. Vonnegut, returning to the "ice-nine" material of 1954, begins a new novel, *Cat's Cradle*, which Littauer sells to Holt, Rinehart & Winston. *Who Am I This Time?*, Vonnegut's stage adaptation of "My Name Is Everyone," presented by the Barnstable Comedy Club. (It will be revived two years later by the Cape Playhouse in Dennis, Massachusetts.)

1963   In June *Cat's Cradle* published in hardcover by Holt. Re-
            views are few but enthusiastic, and at Christmas Graham
            Greene, writing in the London *Spectator*, names it one of
            his three favorite novels of the year. In fall accepts year-
            long assignment as "the whole English department" at the
            Hopefield School, in East Sandwich, Massachusetts, a small
            private high school for students with emotional and learn-
            ing problems.

1964   Responding to a changing editorial marketplace, stops
            writing short stories and begins contributing personal es-
            says, book reviews, and other nonfiction pieces to periodi-
            cals including *The New York Times Book Review*, *Life*, *Esquire*,
            and the travel magazine *Venture*.

1965   In March *God Bless You, Mr. Rosewater*, a novel about a
            so-called fool and his money, published in hardcover by
            Holt, Rinehart & Winston to many if mixed reviews. Ac-
            cepts last-minute invitation to teach fiction writing at the
            Writers' Workshop, Iowa City, on a two-year contract. Ac-
            companied by Edie, who enrolls in nearby University High
            School, he lives on the first floor of a large brick Victorian
            house at 800 Van Buren Avenue, next door to the writer
            Andre Dubus. "I didn't get to know any literary people
            until [my] two years teaching at Iowa," he will later recall.
            "There at Iowa I was suddenly friends with Nelson Algren
            and José Donoso and Vance Bourjaily and Donald Justice
            . . . and was amazed. Suddenly writing seemed very im-
            portant again. This was better than a transplant of monkey
            glands for a man my age." Enjoys teaching, and is good at it.
            His students include Loree Rackstraw, a future English pro-
            fessor and memoirist who becomes a friend and confidante
            for life. Begins work in earnest on a long-contemplated
            "Dresden novel," based on his experiences during World
            War II.

1966   In May is joined in Iowa by Jane and daughter Nanny.
            Cat's Cradle becomes a bestseller, especially among college-
            age readers, in its Dell paperback edition. *Player Piano* re-
            printed in hardcover by Holt, Rinehart & Winston, and
            Mother Night reprinted in hardcover by Harper & Row.
            Agent Kenneth Littauer dies, July, and Max Wilkinson, to
            Vonnegut's dismay, moves literary agency to Long Island
            and goes into semiretirement. In fall, Richard Yates rejoins
            the Iowa faculty and quickly becomes a lifelong friend.

Vonnegut's students for 1966–67 include the young and unpublished John Irving, Gail Godwin, and John Casey. In November, forty-year-old editor-publisher Seymour ("Sam") Lawrence—formerly of the Atlantic Monthly Press and Knopf, now launching his own imprint at Delacorte Press—offers Vonnegut a three-book contract. Vonnegut, with Wilkinson's consent, hires entertainment lawyer Donald C. Farber to handle the contract. (In 1977 Farber will become Vonnegut's sole agent and attorney.)

1967   Prepares first book for Sam Lawrence, a miscellany of previously published short works including eleven of the twelve stories in *Canary in a Cat House*, eleven uncollected and later stories, and two recent nonfiction pieces. To anchor the book with something new and substantial, writes "Welcome to the Monkey House," his first short story in nearly five years and the first not conceived for a magazine. In April awarded a fellowship from the John Simon Guggenheim Foundation, which finances a summer research trip to Dresden in the company of his Army buddy Bernard V. O'Hare. In May, ends two-year stay at the Iowa Writers' Workshop and returns with family to Barnstable to work on his Dresden novel.

1968   Collection *Welcome to the Monkey House* published by Delacorte/Seymour Lawrence, August, to mixed reviews. Vonnegut completes his Dresden novel, and Sam Lawrence, convinced of the book's sales potential, begins buying rights to earlier works for reissue as Delacorte hardcovers and Delta/Dell paperbacks. "Fortitude," a one-act teleplay commissioned by CBS for an unrealized comedy special, reshaped as a closet drama and published in the September issue of *Playboy*.

1969   On March 31, Vonnegut's Dresden novel, *Slaughterhouse-Five*, published by Delacorte/Seymour Lawrence to uniformly good and well-placed reviews, including the cover of *The New York Times Book Review*. The book spends sixteen weeks on the *Times* fiction list, peaking at number four, and creates an audience for his newly issued paperback backlist. Vonnegut begins a lucrative second career as a public speaker, especially on college campuses. Works on a new novel and teases the press with its title, *Breakfast of Champions*. In May, producer Lester M. Goldsmith options *Penelope*, Vonnegut's play of 1960, and begins planning

Off-Broadway premiere for the following fall. Vonnegut spends most of the summer rewriting the play, giving it the new title *Happy Birthday, Wanda June.*

1970   In early January, at the invitation of a private American relief organization, visits the short-lived, war-torn African republic of Biafra shortly before it surrenders to Nigeria, from which it was attempting to secede. Publishes account of the trip, "Biafra: A People Betrayed," in April issue of *McCall's.* In May receives an Academy Award in Literature from the American Academy of Arts and Letters. Interviewed by Harry Reasoner of CBS's *60 Minutes,* television's most-watched program, for the broadcast of September 15. (Reasoner introduces him as "the current idol of the country's sensitive and intelligent young people, [who] snap up his books as fast as they're reissued. . . . His gentle fantasies of peace and his dark humor are as current among the young as was J. D. Salinger's work in the fifties and Tolkien's in the sixties.") Accepts invitation to teach creative writing at Harvard University for the academic year beginning in the fall. Commutes to Cambridge two days a week from New York City, where, by arrangement with producer Lester Goldsmith, he lives as a "kept playwright" in a Greenwich Village sublet. With director Michael Kane and a cast starring Kevin McCarthy and Marsha Mason, workshops the script of *Happy Birthday, Wanda June* throughout September, tinkering with the show until its first curtain. Play opens at the Theatre de Lys, Christopher Street, on October 7; it receives mixed reviews and runs forty-seven performances, closing on November 15. The show moves to the Edison Theater, Broadway, on December 22. During production of *Wanda June* Vonnegut meets and begins a relationship with the photojournalist Jill Krementz, born 1940.

1971   Son Mark, a self-described hippie and co-founder, with friends from Swarthmore, of a commune at Lake Powell, British Columbia, suffers a manic mental breakdown. On February 14, Vonnegut commits him to the care of Hollywood Psychiatric Hospital in Vancouver, where he makes a slow but steady recovery. Broadway production of *Wanda June* closes March 14 after ninety-six performances. In May, Vonnegut delivers the annual Blashfield Address to the assembled National Institute of Arts and Letters and

American Academy of Arts and Letters. Awarded Master's degree in anthropology by the University of Chicago, which, at the department chair's suggestion, accepts *Cat's Cradle* in lieu of a formal dissertation. In June, book version of *Wanda June*, with a preface by the author and production photographs by Jill Krementz, published by Delacorte/ Seymour Lawrence. Resumes work on *Breakfast of Champions*. In December, Sony Pictures releases film version of *Happy Birthday, Wanda June*, directed by Mark Robson and starring Rod Steiger and Susannah York. ("It was one of the most embarrassing movies ever made," Vonnegut later writes, "and I am happy that it sank like a stone.") Grants WNET-New York and WGBH-Boston the option to develop a ninety-minute made-for-television "revue" based on scenes from his writings. The script, by David O'Dell, is revised by Vonnegut and titled *Between Time and Timbuktu, or Prometheus-5: A Space Fantasy*. Separates from Jane Marie Cox Vonnegut and rents a one-bedroom apartment at 349 East Fifty-fourth Street, between First Avenue and Second Avenue.

1972   On March 13 *Between Time and Timbuktu*, starring William Hickey, Kevin McCarthy, and the comedians Bob and Ray (Bob Elliott and Ray Goulding), broadcast nationally as an installment of public television's *NET Playhouse* series. In October, a book version of the teleplay—"based on materials by Kurt Vonnegut, Jr.," with a preface by the author and photographs by Krementz—published by Delacorte/Seymour Lawrence. On March 15 *Slaughterhouse-Five*, directed by George Roy Hill from a screenplay by Stephen Geller, released by Universal Studios. The film, starring Michael Sacks, Ron Leibman, and Valerie Perrine, delights Vonnegut, who finds the adaptation "flawless." In summer, Vonnegut and Krementz collaborate on an illustrated report from the Republican National Convention in Miami, published as the cover story of the November issue of *Harper's*. "The Big Space Fuck," Vonnegut's widely publicized "farewell" to the short-story form, published in *Again, Dangerous Visions*, an anthology of original science-fiction tales commissioned and edited by Harlan Ellison. Named vice president of PEN American Center, the U.S. branch of the international literary and human-rights organization, and remains active on PEN's behalf for the rest of his life.

1973   In April, *Breakfast of Champions*, embellished with more
           than a hundred felt-tip line drawings by the author, pub-
           lished by Delacorte/Seymour Lawrence to mixed reviews
           but strong sales. It dominates the *New York Times* fiction
           list for twenty-eight weeks, ten weeks in the number-one
           position. In May, speaks against state-sponsored censor-
           ship at the conference of International PEN in Stockholm,
           is inducted into the National Institute of Arts and Letters,
           and receives an honorary doctorate in the humanities from
           Indiana University, Bloomington. In September, begins
           one-year term as Distinguished Professor of English Prose
           at City University of New York, where his colleagues in-
           clude Joseph Heller, who becomes a close friend. In No-
           vember *Slaughterhouse-Five* declared obscene by the school
           board of Drake, North Dakota, which orders thirty-six
           copies of the novel burned in the high-school furnace and
           the teacher who assigned it dismissed; it is the first of more
           than a dozen such incidents of censorship during Von-
           negut's lifetime, all successfully challenged by the Ameri-
           can Civil Liberties Union. Buys a three-story townhouse,
           built in 1862, at 228 East Forty-eighth Street, between
           Second Avenue and Third Avenue, which he shares with
           Jill Krementz. (The top floor of this whitewashed Turtle
           Bay brownstone becomes his office; the separate basement
           apartment, with its entry under the stoop, becomes her
           photography studio.) In December Jane Marie Cox Von-
           negut reluctantly agrees to a divorce.

1974   *Wampeters, Foma & Granfalloons (Opinions)*, a collection
           of twenty-five previously published short prose pieces,
           brought out by Delacorte/Seymour Lawrence, Septem-
           ber. This, the first of his "autobiographical collages" com-
           bining essays, articles, speeches, book reviews, and other
           writings, is the last of his works to be published by "Kurt
           Vonnegut, Jr."; subsequent works, and all reprints, will be
           published under the name "Kurt Vonnegut." In October
           visits Moscow with Krementz; their guide is Rita Rait, the
           translator of his books into Russian.

1975   Writes *Slapstick*, a comic novel about a brother and sister
           dedicated to wiping out "the peculiarly American disease
           called loneliness." In May begins four-year term as Vice
           President for Literature of the National Institute of Arts
           and Letters. Spends summer in a rented beachfront house

in East Hampton, Long Island, and begins search for a second home in the area. Uncle Alex dies, July 28, at age eighty-six. ("I am eternally grateful to him," Vonnegut writes in a tribute, "for my knack of finding in great books reason enough to feel honored to be alive, no matter what else might be going on.") In October, Mark Vonnegut publishes *The Eden Express*, a memoir of his madness, to good reviews and strong sales. The royalties will pay his way through Harvard Medical School.

1976   *Slapstick* published by Delacorte/Seymour Lawrence, October, to uniformly negative reviews, the worst Vonnegut will ever receive. ("The reviewers . . . actually asked critics who had praised me in the past to now admit in public how wrong they'd been," he later wrote. "I felt as though I were sleeping standing up in a boxcar in Germany again.") Sales, however, are strong: it is on the *New York Times* fiction list for twenty-four weeks, peaking at number four.

1977   At the request of George Plimpton, editor of *The Paris Review*, fashions a long autobiographical article in the form of one of the magazine's "Art of Fiction" interviews. Purchases a second home, a clapboard house dating from the 1740s, at 620 Sagg Main Street, Sagaponack, a village in Southampton, Long Island. Summer neighbors include Plimpton, Nelson Algren, Truman Capote, James Jones, and Irwin Shaw.

1978   Works on a new novel, *Jailbird*, the fictional memoirs of a good man who, through no wrongdoing of his own, becomes involved in several of the most shameful episodes in modern American political history.

1979   *Jailbird* published by Delacorte/Seymour Lawrence, September, to good reviews and strong sales. It is on the *New York Times* fiction list for thirty-one weeks, five weeks in the number-one position. In April, commemorates the centenary of the Mark Twain house in Hartford, Connecticut, with a speech in which he says that "we would not be known as a nation with a supple, amusing, and often beautiful language of its own, if it were not for the genius of Mark Twain." Throughout the summer a musical adaptation of *God Bless You, Mr. Rosewater*, with book and lyrics by Howard Ashman and music by Alan Menken, is developed by Ashman's WPA Theater company with Vonnegut's "limited but noisy" involvement. The show, produced by Edie Vonnegut, opens at the Entermedia Theatre, in the East Village, on October 11. Despite good reviews, it closes after only twelve performances, having failed to find a Broadway backer. Vonnegut marries Jill Krementz, November 24, at Christ Church United Methodist, on Sixtieth Street at Park Avenue.

1980   On January 27 Vonnegut, a self-described "Christ-worshiping agnostic," delivers his first sermon, a lecture on human dignity at the First Parish Unitarian Church, Cambridge, Massachusetts. Writes the text for *Sun Moon Star*, a picture story with bold and simple full-color images by the graphic designer Ivan Chermayeff. A retelling of the Nativity as seen through the eyes of the infant Jesus, it is published by Harper & Row as a Christmas gift book. First solo art exhibition, featuring thirty felt-tip drawings on vellum, at the Margo Feiden Galleries, Greenwich Village, October 20–November 15.

1981   *Palm Sunday*, an "autobiographical collage" collecting short nonfiction pieces written between 1974 and 1980, published by Delacorte/Seymour Lawrence, March. The title piece is a sermon given on March 30, 1980, at St. Clement's Episcopal Church on West Forty-sixth Street. Vonnegut's text is John 12:1–8: "For the poor always ye have with you . . ."

1982   Television adaptation of *Who Am I This Time?*, directed by Jonathan Demme and starring Susan Sarandon and Christopher Walken, broadcast on PBS in its *American Playhouse* series, February 2. Hires Janet Cosby, a Washington-based lecture agent, to book his annual speaking tours—two weeks in the spring, two weeks in the fall, a schedule he will keep for most of the next two decades. *Deadeye Dick*, a quickly written novel of guilt, self-punishment, and neutron bombs, published by Delacorte/Seymour Lawrence, October, to mixed reviews. It is on the *New York Times* fiction list for fourteen weeks, peaking at number ten. On December 18, Vonnegut and Krementz adopt a three-day-old girl and name her Lily Vonnegut.

1983   Begins work on a new novel, *Galápagos*, a fantasy about the future of human evolution. Makes further drawings, and begins to take himself seriously as a graphic artist, though he doubts his technique.

1984   In January, unsuccessfully tries to interest art publisher Harry N. Abrams in bringing out a book of his drawings. On the evening of February 13, the thirty-ninth anniversary of the firebombing of Dresden, attempts suicide in his Manhattan home, apparently by overdosing on barbiturates and alcohol. Awakes in St. Vincent's Hospital, Greenwich Village, and is diagnosed, as he writes to a friend, "with acute (all but terminal) depression. . . . I was there for eighteen days, under lock and key. . . . I am no renaissance man, but a manic depressive with a few lopsided gifts." Upon release returns to *Galápagos*, finishing the manuscript by Christmas Day.

1985   *Galápagos* published by Delacorte/Seymour Lawrence, October, to good reviews. It is on the *New York Times* fiction list for seventeen weeks, peaking at number five. Completes working draft of *Make Up Your Mind*, a sex farce for four actors. The play, his first since *Happy Birthday, Wanda June*, is given a staged reading in East Hampton. It is optioned by a Broadway producer but is not produced or published.

1986   Writes *Bluebeard*, the fictional memoirs of a seventy-one-year-old Abstract Expressionist painter whose work is loosely modeled on that of Barnett Newman. On December 19, Jane Marie Cox Vonnegut, now married to law-school professor and Defense Department spokesman Adam Yarmolinsky, dies of ovarian cancer. She leaves behind a memoir of her life with Vonnegut and their six children, published by Houghton Mifflin in October 1987 as *Angels Without Wings*.

1987   *Bluebeard* published by Delacorte/Seymour Lawrence, October, to mixed reviews. It is on the *New York Times* fiction list for eleven weeks, peaking at number eight.

1988   Works on new novel, *Hocus Pocus*, a commentary on "the way we live now" addressing, among much else, American trends in higher education, crime and punishment, political correctness, social privilege, militarism, intolerance, and globalization.

1989   Sam Lawrence moves from Delacorte to Dutton and then to Houghton Mifflin, but Vonnegut declines to follow. Sells *Hocus Pocus* to G. P. Putnam's Sons, where his editor is Faith Sale. In October, at the request of the international humanitarian organization CARE, travels to Mozambique to write about the country's decade-old civil war.

1990   "My Visit to Hell," Vonnegut's report on Mozambique, published in *Parade* magazine, January 7. The report is the journalistic centerpiece of his next "autobiographical collage," the assembling of which becomes a yearlong project. In May, gives anti-war speech in the form of an eye-witness account of the firebombing of Dresden at the National Air and Space Museum, Washington, D.C. Wartime buddy Bernard V. O'Hare, a longtime district attorney in Northampton County, Pennsylvania, dies, June 8. *Hocus Pocus* published by Putnam, September, to good reviews. It is on the *New York Times* fiction list for seven weeks, peaking at number four.

1991   Vonnegut and Krementz start divorce proceedings, and Vonnegut spends time at house in Sagaponack. *Fates Worse Than Death: An Autobiographical Collage of the 1980s* published by Putnam, September. The title piece is a sermon on humility, delivered at the Cathedral of St. John the Divine on May 23, 1982. Vonnegut accepts a commission from the New York Philomusica Ensemble for a new libretto to *L'Histoire du Soldat* (1918), Stravinsky's musical setting of a Russian fairy tale of World War I. Vonnegut bases his text on the case of Private Edward Donald Slovik, who, in 1945, became the first American soldier executed for desertion since the Civil War.

1992   Vonnegut and Krementz drop divorce proceedings. Named Humanist of the Year by the American Humanist Association, and accepts invitation to serve as Honorary President of the association until his death. ("We humanists try to behave as decently, as fairly, and as honorably as we can without any expectation of rewards or punishments in an afterlife," he says in his remarks of acceptance. "The Creator of the Universe has been to us unknowable so far. We serve as best we can the only abstraction with which we have some understanding, which is 'Community.'") Begins writing a new novel, which he claims will be his last.

1993   Sam Schacht, formerly of the Steppenwolf Theater Company, directs *Make Up Your Mind* in a limited Off-Broadway run at the New Group Theater, Forty-second Street, April 20–May 5. On May 6 the Philomusica Ensemble gives the world premiere of *L'Histoire du Soldat/An American Soldier's Tale* at Alice Tully Hall, Lincoln Center. Vonnegut approached by a former GE colleague, now a fundraising consultant in Lexington, Kentucky, to do a benefit reading for his client Midway College. Collaborates with Joe Petro III, an area printmaker, on a collectible limited-edition poster for the November 1st event. Delighted with Petro's result—a hand-pulled silkscreen print adapted from a felt-tip self-portrait—Vonnegut visits the thirty-seven-year-old artist in his Lexington studio. The two soon form a partnership, Origami Express, to produce signed and numbered limited-edition prints adapted from Vonnegut's drawings and calligraphy. This enduring collaboration solves most of Vonnegut's problems with technique, and helps him to become the graphic artist he has longed to be. (In 2004, after producing more than two hundred discrete Origami editions, Vonnegut will write: "One of the best things that ever happened to me, a one-in-a-billion opportunity to enjoy myself in perfect innocence, was my meeting Joe.")

1994   Sam Lawrence dies, January 5, at age sixty-seven. "That anything I have written is in print today is due to the efforts of one publisher," Vonnegut writes in tribute. "When [in 1966] I was broke and completely out of print, Sam bought rights to my books, for peanuts, from publishers who had given up on me. [He] thrust my books back into the myopic public eye and made my reputation." Invited by Daniel Simon, publisher-editor of the newly founded Seven Stories Press, to write an introduction to Nelson Algren's 1942 novel *Never Come Morning*. Struck by Simon's commitment to Algren's work and to publishing books on human rights, social justice, and progressive politics, he becomes an advisory editor to the small independent press.

1995   At the end of the year completes a draft of the novel *Timequake*, a fantasy on the subject of free will concerning "a sudden glitch in the space-time continuum" that, occurring on the eve of the millennium, forces mankind to relive, day by day and mistake by mistake, the entire 1990s. He is unhappy with the book and, to the dismay of Putnam, scraps it and begins again from scratch.

1996   On November 1 *Mother Night*, directed by Keith Gordon from a screenplay by Vonnegut's filmmaker friend Robert B.

Weide, released by Fine Line Features. Vonnegut finds the script "too faithful to the novel" but admires the performance of leading man Nick Nolte. In December completes a second version of *Timequake*—a fictional-autobiographical "stew" made up of excerpts from the earlier *Timequake*, humorous meditations on the creative process, and laments for the passing of the America of his youth.

1997   Brother, Bernard, dies, April 25, at age eighty-three; Vonnegut will write his obituary for year-end issue of *The New York Times Magazine*. *Timequake* published by Putnam, September, to admiring and elegiac reviews. It is on the *New York Times* fiction list for five weeks, peaking at number seven. Vonnegut sells the greater part of his personal and professional papers, including the various drafts of his fourteen published novels, to Lilly Library, Indiana University.

1998   With the news and features staff of WNYC-FM, develops a series of twenty-odd ninety-second radio skits, each a satirical "report on the Afterlife" in which Vonnegut, in a "controlled near-death state" chemically induced by Dr. Jack Kevorkian, interviews Sir Isaac Newton, Mary Shelley, Eugene V. Debs, or some other resident of Paradise. (The best of the skits are revised, expanded, and collected in an eighty-page book, *God Bless You, Dr. Kevorkian*, published in April 1999 by Seven Stories Press.) In October again visits Dresden and the slaughterhouse in which he survived the firebombing of 1945.

1999   Peter J. Reed, of the University of Minnesota, gathers the twenty-three short stories published in magazines in the 1950s and 1960s that did not appear in *Welcome to the Monkey House*, writes a critical preface to the collection, and asks Vonnegut for permission to publish. Vonnegut revises a couple of the less successful stories and writes an autobiographical introduction and "coda" to the volume. *Bagombo Snuff Box: Uncollected Short Fiction* published by Putnam, September, to respectful reviews and mild sales.

2000   On the evening of January 31 Vonnegut is hospitalized for smoke inhalation after successfully containing a fire in the third-floor office of his New York townhouse caused by a smoldering Pall Mall in an overturned ashtray. Pulled from the room by Lily and a neighbor, he lies unconscious for two days in Presbyterian Hospital and is dismissed after three weeks' recuperation. At the suggestion of his daughter Nanny, moves to a studio apartment near her home in Northampton, Massachusetts, where she and her family nurse him back to health. In spring invited by local Smith College to join the English faculty as writer-in-residence for the academic year 2000–01. Works with a handful of student fiction-writers and gives occasional public lectures and readings at the many college campuses throughout Western Massachusetts.

2001   In May begins writing a novel, each chapter a monologue by a famous middle-aged standup comedian who entertains America during the final weeks of mankind. Is shocked and creatively paralyzed by the events of September 11, and sets novel aside for more than a year.

2002   In response to threats posed to the First Amendment by the USA Patriot Act of 2001, lends his celebrity to public-service advertisements for the ACLU, stating "I am an American who knows the importance of being able to read and express any thought without fear." Gives Lilly Library drafts of his early short stories and the very few other literary manuscripts that survived the New York house fire. Writes foreword to the Seven Stories Press reissue of son Mark's *Eden Express*. In fall resumes work on novel, now titled "If God Were Alive Today," which develops as a topical satire on the Bush administration.

2003   In January is interviewed about the coming war in Iraq by Joel Bleifuss, editor of *In These Times*, a biweekly nonprofit news magazine headquartered in Chicago. Discovers easy rapport with Bleifuss, whose politics are "Midwestern progressive" in the tradition of Vonnegut's socialist heroes Eugene V. Debs and Powers Hapgood. Soon becomes a regular columnist and honorary senior editor at *In These Times*, contributing political opinion, personal essays, humor pieces, and drawings. Magazine column cannibalizes material developed for "If God Were Alive Today" and becomes the chief literary project of his remaining years.

2005   In October, *A Man Without a Country*, a collection of columns from *In These Times*, published by Seven Stories Press. A surprise bestseller, it is on the *New York Times* nonfiction list for six weeks, peaking at number nine.

2006   In June says to an interviewer: "Everything I've done is in
        print. I have fulfilled my destiny, such as it is, and have
        nothing more to say. So now I'm writing only little things—
        one line here, two lines there, sometimes a poem. And I do
        art. . . . I have reached what Nietzsche called 'the mel-
        ancholia of everything completed.'"

2007   In mid-March, falls from the steps of his townhouse on
        East Forty-eighth Street and hits his head on the pave-
        ment. Despite aggressive medical treatment, he never re-
        gains consciousness. Dies at Mount Sinai Hospital on the
        evening of April 11, at age eighty-four.

Note on the Texts

This volume collects all the fiction that Kurt Vonnegut published between 1963 and 1973. It contains four novels—*Cat's Cradle* (1963), *God Bless You, Mr. Rosewater* (1965), *Slaughterhouse-Five* (1969), and *Breakfast of Champions* (1973)—and three short stories, one in the form of a closet drama. It also presents, in two appendixes, five short works of nonfiction prose, one relating to *Cat's Cradle* and the others to *Slaughterhouse-Five*.

Cat's Cradle was Vonnegut's fourth published novel, but the premise for it came to him shortly after he had completed his first, *Player Piano*, in 1951. (Vonnegut discusses the biographical and historical sources of *Cat's Cradle* in the speech printed as Appendix A of this volume.) In 1954 he wrote an early version of the opening chapters and showed it to Harry Brague Jr., his editor at Charles Scribner's Sons, who optioned the story, hoping it would become Vonnegut's second book. Vonnegut toyed with the material throughout the 1950s, but set it aside to work on other projects, including the novels *The Sirens of Titan* (1959) and *Mother Night* (1962). He returned to it in earnest only after Scribner's released him from their option, and wrote the final draft at his home in West Barnstable, Massachusetts, in 1961–62. The book was published by Holt, Rinehart & Winston, New York, in June 1963, as both a trade hardcover and the July/August main selection of the Doubleday Science Fiction Book Club. According to Vonnegut's bibliographers Asa B. Pieratt Jr. and Jerome Klinkowitz, both the trade edition of 6,000 copies and the book-club edition of 24,000 copies were printed simultaneously from the same plates at the Doubleday printing plant in Garden City, New York. A small British edition, offset from the Holt pages, was published in fall 1963 by Victor Gollancz, London. Vonnegut did not subsequently revise the book, and the text of the 1963 Holt, Rinehart & Winston edition is printed here.

God Bless You, Mr. Rosewater, Vonnegut's fifth novel, was written in West Barnstable in 1963–64 and published in hardcover by Holt, Rinehart & Winston in March 1965. According to Pieratt and Klinkowitz, the first printing of 6,000 copies was followed in May by a second printing of 7,000. A small British edition, offset from the Holt pages, was published in fall 1965 by Jonathan Cape, London. Vonnegut did not subsequently revise the book, and the text of the 1965 Holt, Rinehart & Winston edition is printed here.

Shortly after returning from World War II, Vonnegut began making notes toward a book based on his experiences as Army private, prisoner of war, and survivor of the Allied firebombing of Dresden. (For an early attempt to give form to his material, see the autobiographical memoir "Wailing Shall Be in All Streets," printed in Appendix B of this volume.) Although in the 1950s he published a handful of stories with wartime settings, it was only in 1964, during the composition of *God Bless You, Mr. Rosewater*, that the long-contemplated "Dresden book" began to take shape as his sixth novel, *Slaughterhouse-Five*. The book was begun in earnest in Iowa City, Iowa, while Vonnegut was a teacher at the Iowa Writers' Workshop, in 1965–67, and was finished at home in West Barnstable, in 1967–68. It was published in hardcover by Delacorte Press/Seymour Lawrence, New York, in March 1969. (The first two chapters had been excerpted before publication in *Ramparts* magazine, October 26, 1968.) According to Pieratt and Klinkowitz, there were two printings of the book before publication, the first a run of 10,000 copies only, the other of 5,000 copies. By July 1969, the book had been printed five more times for a total run of 60,000 copies. A book-club edition, offset from the Delacorte pages, was published as an alternate selection of the Literary Guild in July 1969. A British edition, also offset from the Delacorte pages, was published in spring 1970 by Jonathan Cape. Vonnegut did not subsequently revise the book, and the text of the 1969 Delacorte Press/ Seymour Lawrence edition is printed here.

In 1971 Vonnegut separated from his wife and took up permanent residence in New York City. *Breakfast of Champions*, his seventh novel, was written in a rented apartment on East Fifty-fourth Street in 1971–72. (Many scenes and ideas for the book had been developed in West Barnstable in 1967–69, during and immediately after the composition of *Slaughterhouse-Five*.) The drawings, Vonnegut's first extended foray into the graphic arts, were executed in black felt-tip markers (and, in some instances, Letraset rub-on numbers and letters) on white bond paper. The book was published in hardcover by Delacorte Press/Seymour Lawrence in April 1973. (The opening chapters had been excerpted before publication in *Ramparts* magazine, February 1973.) According to Pieratt and Klinkowitz, the first printing was 100,000 copies. A book-club edition, offset from the Delacorte pages, was published as the main selection of the Literary Guild for May 1973. A British edition, also offset from the Delacorte pages, was published in fall 1973 by Jonathan Cape. Vonnegut did not subsequently revise the book, and the text of the 1973 Delacorte Press/ Seymour Lawrence edition is printed here.

The three short works collected under the rubric "Stories" first appeared in magazines and anthologies between 1968 and 1972 and were later reprinted by the author in hardcover collections of his miscellaneous prose.

Vonnegut wrote "Welcome to the Monkey House" in the summer of 1967 to give weight and novelty to a collection of previously published stories and essays, some dating back to the early 1950s, scheduled for publication the following year. After the collection was submitted to the publisher, the fiction editor at *Playboy*, Robie Macauley, asked to read the story for first-serial consideration. "Welcome to the Monkey House" first appeared in *Playboy*, January 1968. It was reprinted, without changes, in *Welcome to the Monkey House: A Collection of Short Works*, published by Delacorte Press/Seymour Lawrence in August 1968. The text from *Welcome to the Monkey House* is printed here.

"Fortitude" began life in 1967 as an extended skit commissioned by producers Si Litvinoff and Raymond Wagner for a CBS Television special called *The Seven Deadly Virtues*. When production of the special was canceled, Vonnegut, at the request of Robie Macauley, rewrote the teleplay as a closet drama, which was published in *Playboy*, September 1968. It was reprinted, without changes, in *Wampeters, Foma & Granfalloons (Opinions)*, published by Delacorte Press/ Seymour Lawrence in May 1974. The text from *Wampeters, Foma & Granfalloons* is printed here.

"The Big Space Fuck" was commissioned by the science-fiction writer Harlan Ellison for inclusion in his hardcover anthology *Again, Dangerous Visions: Forty-six Original Stories*, published by Doubleday in 1972. It was reprinted, with minor revisions, in *Palm Sunday: An Autobiographical Collage*, published by Delacorte Press/Seymour Lawrence in March 1981. The text from *Palm Sunday* is printed here.

A version of the speech printed under the rubric "Appendix A" was delivered by Vonnegut at the joint annual meeting of the American Physical Society and the American Association of Physics Teachers at the Hilton Hotel, New York City, on February 5, 1969. The text of the speech was published under the title "Physicist, Purge Thyself" in *Chicago Tribune Magazine*, June 22, 1969. Vonnegut thoroughly revised the speech for inclusion, under the title "Address to the American Physical Society," in *Wampeters, Foma & Granfalloons (Opinions)*, published by Delacorte Press/Seymour Lawrence in May 1974. The text from *Wampeters, Foma & Granfalloons* is printed here under the descriptive title "Address to the American Physical Society, New York City, February 5, 1969."

The four items collected under the rubric "Appendix B" were written and published as follows:

The letter from Vonnegut to his family dated May 29, 1945, was typed at the Red Cross Club in Camp Lucky Strike, an American repatriation facility near Le Havre, France. The letter was received by Vonnegut's father and was discovered among his personal papers after his death in October 1957. In 2004, Vonnegut and Joe Petro III published a faithful transcription of the letter as *Missing in Action* (Lexington, Ky.: Origami Express), a small book in an edition of 126 signed, slipcased hardcover copies. A facsimile of the letter was later reproduced, under the title "Letter from PFC Kurt Vonnegut, Jr., to his family, May 29, 1945," in *Armageddon in Retrospect and Other New and Unpublished Writings on War and Peace*, a posthumous collection assembled by Vonnegut's literary estate and published by G. P. Putnam's Sons in April 2008. (The memoir first appeared, one month before book publication, in the April 2008 issue of *Playboy*.) The text and title used in *Armageddon in Retrospect* are printed here.

In 1997 Kurt Vonnegut sold the majority of his professional papers, including the typescript of the unpublished memoir "Wailing Shall Be in All Streets," to the Lilly Library of Indiana University, Bloomington. The Lilly typescript is undated but bears the return address of "3972½ Ellis Avenue, Chicago 15, Ill.," Vonnegut's residence from the fall of 1945 through the summer of 1947. A checklist accompanying the typescript records that Vonnegut submitted the memoir to editors at *Harper's Magazine*, *The Atlantic Monthly*, *The American Mercury*, and *The Yale Review*. "Wailing Shall Be in All Streets" was chosen by Vonnegut's literary estate for inclusion in the posthumous collection *Armageddon in Retrospect*, published by G. P. Putnam's Sons in April 2008. The text from *Armageddon in Retrospect* is printed here.

In October 1976, Vonnegut wrote a "Special Message" for subscribers to a signed, limited edition of *Slaughterhouse-Five* published in 1978 by The Franklin Library, Franklin Center, Pennsylvania. He later collected the piece, under the title "A Nazi City Mourned at Some Profit," in *Palm Sunday: An Autobiographical Collage*, published by Delacorte Press/Seymour Lawrence in March 1981. The text from *Palm Sunday* is printed here, under the descriptive title "A 'Special Message' to readers of the Franklin Library's limited edition of *Slaughterhouse-Five*."

In 1993 Vonnegut wrote a preface for the hardcover reissue of *Slaughterhouse-Five* published by Delacorte Press/Seymour Lawrence in March 1994, the novel's twenty-fifth anniversary. The preface is reprinted here under the descriptive title "Preface to the twenty-fifth-anniversary edition of *Slaughterhouse-Five*."

Some of the material in the texts collected here was previously published and reprinted by permission of the holders of copyright and publication rights. The following is a list of acknowledgments as they appeared on the copyright pages of the original printings:

For *Cat's Cradle*: Grateful acknowledgment is made to Mrs. E. L.

Masters for permission to reprint "Knowlt Hoheimer" from the *Spoon River Anthology* by Edgar Lee Masters. Copyright Macmillan, 1914, 1915, 1942.

For *Slaughterhouse-Five*: "The Waking": Copyright © 1953, from *The Collected Poems of Theodore Roethke*. Reprinted by permission of Doubleday and Company, Inc.; *The Destruction of Dresden* by David Irving. From the Introduction by Ira C. Eaker, Lt. Gen. USAF (Ret.) and the Foreword by Air Marshal Sir Robert Saundby. Copyright © 1963 by William Kimber and Co. Limited. Reprinted by permission of Holt, Rinehart and Winston, Inc. and William Kimber and Co. Limited; "'Leven Cent Cotton" by Bob Miller and Emma Dermer. Copyright © 1928, 1929 by MCA Music. Copyright renewed 1955, 1956 and assigned to MCA Music, a division of MCA Inc. Used by permission.

This volume presents the texts of the original printings chosen for inclusion here, but does not attempt to reproduce nontextual features of their typographic design. The texts are presented without change, except for the correction of typographical errors. Spelling, punctuation, and capitalization are not altered, even when inconsistent or irregular. The following is a list of typographical errors corrected, cited by page and line number: 7.26, Doing,; 33.33, oranges."; 49.29, onto; 54.34, was my; 82.21, '*self-indulgent*.'; 114.24, know."; 159.10, "'Uck?'; 168.11, the; 208.12, his; 209.32, Thorsten; 224.4, clean,; 225.11, Written on; 241.23, "Let; 241.27, in!"; 241.30, "CHAPTER; 241.31, "I; 241.33, home."; 251.14, punishments and; 275.11, Burrough's; 276.7, *The*; 278.2, peddled; 323.11, *what?*" ¶ "It's; 328.2, There; 330.12, go next; 348.35, a accidental; 356.33, Ruinene; 363.39, then; 364.23, 'Tralfamadore?'"; 368.21, Nuremburg."; 373.26, An then; 394.15, corpses; 409.2, faced it; 415.24, with blank; 416.14, "'My; 425.3, Franch; 463.25, bar,; 465.12, and pals; 465.30, seeming; 469.37, S; 487.30, Adolph; 489.10, tattoed; 490.26, talking; 593.12, *The Sacred*; 598.10, MacDonald's; 598.12, *MacDonald's*; 602.15, or; 713.6, sobriety,; 719.25, New; 722.8–9, a doodley-squat; 745.28, Brown; 750.14, Marlin (and *passim*); 759.5, ma'am; 768.18, that's; 781.8, Schaeffer; 786.32, Von; 786.37, Do; 804.22, Ophul's.

Notes

In the notes below, the reference numbers denote page and line of this volume (the line count includes headings, but not images or section breaks). No note is made for material included in standard desk-reference books. Biblical quotations are keyed to the King James Version. Quotations from Shakespeare are keyed to *The Riverside Shakespeare*, edited by G. Blakemore Evans (Boston: Houghton Mifflin, 1974). For reference to other studies, and for further biographical background than is contained in the Chronology, see William Rodney Allen, editor, *Conversations with Kurt Vonnegut* (Jackson: University Press of Mississippi, 1988); Asa B. Pieratt Jr., Julie Huffman-Klinkowitz, and Jerome Klinkowitz, *Kurt Vonnegut: A Comprehensive Bibliography* (Hamden, Conn.: Archon Books, 1987); Loree Rackstraw, *Love as Always, Kurt: Vonnegut as I Knew Him* (Cambridge, Mass.: Da Capo Press, 2009); John G. Rauch, "An Account of the Ancestry of Kurt Vonnegut, Jr., by an Ancient Friend of the Family," in *Summary* 1:2 (1971); and Peter J. Reed and Marc Leeds, editors, *The Vonnegut Chronicles: Interviews and Essays* (Westport, Conn.: Greenwood Press, 1996). See also the major collections of Vonnegut's nonfiction prose: *Wampeters, Foma & Granfalloons (Opinions)* (New York: Delacorte/ Seymour Lawrence, 1974), *Palm Sunday: An Autobiographical Collage* (New York: Delacorte/Seymour Lawrence, 1981), *Fates Worse Than Death: An Autobiographical Collage of the 1980s* (New York: Putnam, 1991), and *A Man Without a Country* (New York: Seven Stories Press, 2005). For notes on Vonnegut's recurring fictional persons, places, and things, see Marc Leeds, *The Vonnegut Encyclopedia: An Authorized Compendium* (Westport, Conn.: Greenwood Press, 1995).

CAT'S CRADLE

2.1   Kenneth Littauer] Littauer (1894–1968) was Vonnegut's literary agent for eighteen years, from 1950 until his, Littauer's, death. A fiction editor at *Collier's* magazine from 1928 to 1948 and a partner in Littauer & Wilkinson, Inc., after 1949, he was known familiarly as "The Colonel" in reference to his exploits as a U.S. airman during World War I. Vonnegut claimed "he was the first man to strafe a trench."

5.3   Call me Jonah] Cf. Herman Melville, *Moby-Dick* (1851), Chapter 1.

5.6–11   unlucky for others . . . Jonah was there.] See the Old Testament book of Jonah.

16.12   L.S.T.] "Landing Ship, Tank," military designation for World War II–era naval vessels built to land troops, vehicles, and cargo directly on an un-improved shore.

18.15   Secret Agent X-9] Eponymous hero of newspaper comic strip (1934–96) created by novelist Dashiell Hammett and artist Alex Raymond.

18.29   Place Pigalle and Port Said] Red-light districts of Paris, France, and the Suez Canal area, Egypt.

24.11   Marmon] The Marmon Motor Car Co. of Indianapolis was a maker of luxury automobiles from 1902 to 1933.

24.15   *Marie Celeste*] U.S. brigantine merchant ship found mysteriously abandoned near the Azores in December 1872, one month after embarking from New York. Its eight-man crew and two passengers were never accounted for.

49.38   Duco Cement] Brand of clear-drying household glue, ideal for model-making.

53.24   American Flyer] American model-train manufacturer, founded 1907. It flourished under several owners through 1967, when it was purchased by its chief business rival, Lionel Toys, and the name retired.

59.3   Tommy Manville] Heir of a New York asbestos fortune (1894–1967) who gained celebrity as a "career bridegroom," marrying—and expensively di-vorcing—eleven glamorous young women during the 1930s and '40s.

59.4   Barbara Hutton] American heiress of the F. W. Woolworth and E. F. Hutton fortunes (1912–1979), popularly known as "Poor Little Rich Girl" for her many marriages, troubled finances, and public emotional breakdowns.

62.30   "The man who wrote *Ben Hur*] Lewis ("Lew") Wallace, born Brookville, Indiana, 1827, died Crawfordsville, Indiana, 1905.

62.31   James Whitcomb Riley] Writer and wit (1849–1916) known as "The Hoosier Poet." Among his poems are "Little Orphant Annie," "The Barefoot Boy," and "When the Frost Is on the Punkin."

69.10   "Render therefore . . . Caesar's."] Cf. Matthew 22:21, Mark 12:17, and Luke 20:25.

70.4   Charles Atlas] Italian-born American bodybuilder (1892–1972) whose mail-order lesson booklets, advertised mainly in pulp magazines and comic books, popularized isometric exercise under the trademarked name "Dynamic Tension."

71.1–2   Blackbeard . . . Edward Teach.] English pirate (c. 1680–1718) who, with the crew of his forty-gun ship *Queen Anne's Revenge*, terrorized the Caribbean and the Carolinas.

71.30   second Battle of Ypres]   Allied defensive victory at Ypres, Belgium (April 22–May 25, 1915). It was the first battle in which Germans deployed poison gas.

74.12–17   Twinkle, twinkle . . . what you are.]   Conflation of lines from the traditional English nursery song and "Twinkle, Twinkle, Little Bat," the Mad Hatter's parody in *Alice's Adventures in Wonderland* (1865).

76.1   Brobdingnagians]   Race of giants in *Gulliver's Travels* (1726), by Jonathan Swift.

81.3   Wehrmacht]   The armed forces of Nazi Germany, 1935–45.

94.33   "When Day Is Done."]   Song (1926), originally titled "Panama," by German songwriter Robert Katscher. The English lyrics, by Buddy DeSylva ("When day is done / and shadows fall / I think of you . . ."), were commissioned by bandleader Paul Whiteman, who in 1927 made the song a swing-band standard.

116.5   short and brutish and mean]   Cf. Thomas Hobbes, *Leviathan* (1651), Chapter 13: "the life of man [is] solitary, poor, nasty, brutish, and short."

120.1–2   *Cat House Piano* . . . Meade Lux Lewis.]   Lewis (1905–1964) was a pianist and composer whose 1938 appearance at Carnegie Hall, broadcast live throughout America, helped spark a national craze for boogie-woogie. His LP recording *Cat House Piano*, with liner notes by jazz journalist Chris Albertson, was released by Down Home Records in 1955.

120.9   Jimmy Yancey]   Boogie-woogie pianist and composer (1898–1951), active in Chicago after 1920, whose works included "Yancey's Stomp" and "State Street Blues."

141.32   oubliette]   *French*: "forgotten place"; a prison cell without doors or windows, accessible only from an aperture in the ceiling.

142.8   Vox Humana]   *Latin*: "human voice"; pipe-organ reed stop that, due to its vibrato effect, is suggestive of a singing voice.

153.29   *Sulfathiazole*]   Fast-acting, highly toxic antimicrobial, widely used during World War II to treat gonorrhea.

168.11   a poem]   "Knowlt Hoheimer," one of the 243 verse monologues that make up the *Spoon River Anthology* (1915), poem-cycle by Edgar Lee Masters (1868–1950).

168.16   battle of Missionary Ridge.]   Union victory at Chattanooga, Tennessee (November 25, 1863).

173.31   peddiwinkus]   Variant of *Scots* "pilliwinks": thumbscrew, toescrew.

173.32   *veglia*]   *Italian*: "vigil," "watch"; form of torture in which the victim is hung horizontally in a small chamber as though he were a hammock, his face toward the ceiling and each wrist and ankle attached to a rope. The ropes are passed through pulleys secured to the wall, and the free end of each rope is attached to a weight. The weights stretch the body and keep it taut, and can be added to incrementally to increase the victim's pain.

183.8–9   'Of all the words . . . "It might have been." ' "] Cf. Robert Burns, "The best laid schemes o' mice and men / Gang aft a-gley" ("To a Mouse," 1785), and John Greenleaf Whittier, "For of all sad words of tongue or pen, / The saddest are these: 'It might have been!'" ("Maud Muller," 1854).

184.3   "Eat, drink . . . tomorrow we die,"] Cf. Isaiah 22:13.

187.17   "Soft pipes, play on,"] See John Keats, "Ode on a Grecian Urn" (1820), stanza 2.

GOD BLESS YOU, MR. ROSEWATER

189.3   *Pearls Before Swine*] See Matthew 7:6: "Give not that which is holy unto the dogs, neither cast ye your pearls before swine, lest they trample them under their feet, and turn again and rend you."

190.1   Alvin Davis] American journalist (1926–1982) and longtime staffer at the *New York Post* (1942–65), ending as managing editor. He was a compulsive drinker and gambler (poker, games of chance) and, as a newspaperman, a specialist in crime and human-interest stories.

200.8   Loomis] The Loomis Institute, in Windsor, Connecticut, was, from 1926 to 1970, an elite boarding school for boys twelve to eighteen. In fall 1970 it became the co-educational Loomis Chaffee School.

205.22   Springfields] Bolt-action rifles. The Springfield M1903 was the standard U.S. infantry weapon in World War I and saw limited service in World War II.

210.2   *Aïda*] Opera (1871) by Giuseppe Verdi. Set in Ancient Egypt, its hero is a soldier in Pharaoh's army, its title character his lover, an Ethiopian slave girl.

219.20–21   Henry J] Two-door, four-cylinder economy sedan (1950–53) manufactured by the short-lived Kaiser-Frazer Corporation and named after its co-founder, industrialist Henry J. Kaiser (1882–1967).

220.17   Ilse Koch.] Koch (1906–1967), wife of the commandant of the Nazi concentration camps at Buchenwald (1937–41) and Majdanek (1941–43), was notorious for her cruelty to prisoners.

223.31–32   "What a noble mind . . . o'erthrown!"] Ophelia, in *Hamlet* III.i.150.

227.3–14   The Angel . . . on Earth."] Gnomic verse no. 21 (c. 1793), from William Blake's *Notebooks*, a.k.a. "The Rossetti Manuscript" (1874).

227.18–21   Love seeketh . . . Heaven's despite.]   From "The Clod and
the Pebble," in William Blake's *Songs of Experience* (1794).

240.26   *Get With Child a Mandrake Root*]   See Donne's "Song" ("Go and
catch a falling star," 1633).

240.30–31   A compassionate turquoise . . . is not well.]   See Donne's
"An Anatomy of the World" ("The First Anniversary," 1611).

246.3   "Two-Seed-in-the-Spirit Predestinarian Baptist."]   Member of a
Protestant sect founded in Illinois in 1833 by Daniel Parker (1781–1844), a dis-
senting Baptist elder who believed that every man carried in him one of two
"seeds"—the Holy Seed planted by God in Adam or the Devil Seed planted by
the Serpent in Eve—which determined whether he was meant for heaven or
for hell.

247.28   *Domesday Book*]   The census of England undertaken, by order of
William the Conqueror, in 1085–86.

256.27–28   customers' men]   Brokers; men on the stock-exchange trading
floor representing their customers.

265.11   *Black Hat Brigade.*]   Union Army formation, also known as the
Iron Brigade, composed mainly of infantry regiments from Indiana, Michigan,
and Wisconsin. The brigade favored the heavy standard-issue dress hats of the
U.S. Army, not the lighter "slouch hats" or "kepis" worn by the majority of
troops.

275.19   *Lady Chatterley's Lover*]   Novel (1928), by D. H. Lawrence, notoriously frank in its language and depiction of sex. Its sale was banned in the
United States from 1930 to 1959.

279.16–17   Pine Tree Press of the Freedom School]   The Freedom School
(1957–68) was an unaccredited four-year college run by Libertarian pundit and
radio personality Robert LeFevre (1911–1986). The school's Pine Tree Press
published political pamphlets, many written by LeFevre and often published
anonymously, including *The Power of Congress (As Congress Sees It)*, *Autarchy
versus Anarchy*, and *A Rift Between Friends in the War of Ideas.*

283.17–18   *The Conscience of a Conservative*]   Cold War–era argument for
the conservative worldview (1960) by Arizona Senator Barry Goldwater (1909–
1998) and his uncredited speechwriter, L. Brent Bozell Jr. A talked-about best-
seller, it helped to make Goldwater a leading voice in Republican Party politics.

314.20   Kin Hubbard]   Frank McKinney "Kin" Hubbard (1868–1930),
vernacular humorist from rural Indiana and creator of the syndicated comic
panel *Abe Martin of Brown County* (1904–30).

325.28   *The Bombing of Germany*]   *Das war der Bombenkrieg: Deutsche
Städte im Feursturm—Ein Dokumentarbericht* (1961), by Hans Rumpf (1888–
1976), translated from the German by Edward Fitzgerald (1963). Rumpf was
Germany's inspector general for fire prevention during World War II.

331.1   Peter Lawford] English-born American screen actor and celebrity (1923–1984), a longtime member of Frank Sinatra's "Rat Pack" and a brother-in-law of President Kennedy.

SLAUGHTERHOUSE-FIVE

339.1   SLAUGHTERHOUSE-FIVE] Assuming the voice of Philboyd Studge, the "author" of the preface to *Breakfast of Champions* (see note 503.25), Vonnegut wrote the following liner notes for the Caedmon Records LP release *Kurt Vonnegut, Jr., Reads "Slaughterhouse-Five"* (1973):

"*Slaughterhouse-Five*," Kurt Vonnegut recently told an interviewer, "is a war story by an amnesiac. All I know about the bombing of Dresden in World War II, the greatest massacre in European history, is that I was there—without being massacred. I forget what that was like."

Asked if that event had a lot to do with the shape of his character, whatever his character was these days, he said, "No. The amazing adventures which shaped me were over by the time I was nine years old, I'm sure. God only knows what they were. They're harder to remember than Dresden. I've tried to recover some of those memories recently, and I've come up with this much, anyway: the big house where I was a little kid was empty a lot of the time, except for me and a black cook named Ida Young. I understand now something I didn't understand a year ago—that I received the basic education on which all subsequent educations were built from Ida Young. If it weren't for her, I wouldn't know as much about the Bible and human slavery and really poor people as I do."

His father and grandfather were Indiana architects. "That big, seemingly so empty house of my childhood," he went on, "was designed by my father, and I would hear him and my mother call it a *dream house* now and then. They lost it during the Great Depression. After the Second World War, Father built another house with many personal touches, and my parents called that one a *dream house*, too. Various good and bad things happened in those houses. I remember them spookily, because they gave me the queer feeling that I wasn't merely in a dwelling but that I was inhabiting my parents' dreams.

"And it was so often the case in that first dream house that the only other inhabitant was another outsider—who was Ida Young."

When it was pointed out to him that he had strayed far from the subject of Dresden, he replied impatiently that he was no more concerned with Dresden than he was about the recent Super Bowl Game or the Second Battle of the Marne. "It's all over, whatever it was. It happened, and can't be undone. I don't think about it, unless somebody makes me think about it. What is there to think about, except that man, for one reason or another, can be a very ferocious animal indeed. So what else is new?

"I will tell you this, though," he went on. "Man isn't a naturally fero-

cious animal. He isn't a naturally any sort of animal. What he becomes
depends on his early education. I am a pacifist, and I have made my
children pacifists, too. But that isn't because of Dresden. It's because of
the humane education I received from Ida Young."

—*Philboyd Studge*

343.1–4   *The cattle . . . He makes.*] From "Away in a Manger" (c. 1885),
American Christmas carol of contested authorship.

345.12   Bernard V. O'Hare] After the war, Vonnegut's friend Bernard
Vincent O'Hare Jr. (1923–1990) returned to his native Pennsylvania to study
law at Dickinson Law School. In 1948 he joined his father's practice in
Shenandoah, Pennsylvania. Two years later he opened his own office in nearby
Nazareth and practiced law in the area, with various partners, until his death.
In 1949 he married Mary T. Hoffman (1923?–1998), a registered nurse, with
whom he raised five children. He was district attorney of Northampton
County in 1963–67.

346.26   Harrison Starr] American film producer (b. 1928) whose credits
include *Rachel, Rachel* (1968) and *Zabriskie Point* (1970).

350.4   the AP and the UP] Associated Press and United Press Association
(later United Press International, or UPI), dominant American news agencies
of the twentieth century.

352.3   United World Federalists] Members of a U.S. citizens' organization
founded in 1947 to promote, in the words of its motto, "World Peace Through
World Law."

352.9   *Eheu, fugaces labuntur anni.*] Horace, *Odes* 2:14: "Alas, our fleet
years slip away."

356.16   *Königstein*] Mountaintop fortress near Dresden, built c. 1240.
During World War II it was used as a prison camp for Allied officers.

356.17   *Francia's "Baptism of Christ."*] Painting (1509) by the Italian artist
known as Francia (Francesco Raibolini, 1450–1517), now in the collection of
the Gemäldegalerie Alte Meister, Dresden.

356.27–34   *"Von der Kuppel . . . Feind gethan!"*] *"From the dome of the
Frauenkirche* [Church of Our Lady] *I saw ugly rubble sitting in the middle of
the beautiful order of the city. The sexton praised the art of the architect who had
made the church and dome bombproof even in these unfortunate circumstances.
The sexton then pointed out the ruins on all sides and said, thoughtfully and la-
conically: The enemy did that!"*—Goethe, *Aus meinem Lieben: Dichtung und
Wahrheit* (*From My Life: Fiction and Truth*), Part Four (1833).

357.11–12   Seymour Lawrence] American editor and publisher (1926–1994)
who, through his imprint Seymour Lawrence Books at Delacorte Press, was
Vonnegut's principal publisher from 1968 to 1987.

358.19 *Words for the Wind*] Collected poems, through 1958, of American poet Theodore Roethke (1908–1963).

358.21–23 *I wake to sleep . . . I have to go.*] Opening lines of "The Waking" (1953), villanelle by Theodore Roethke.

358.24 *Céline and His Vision*] Critical study (1967) of the French novelist Louis-Ferdinand Céline (1894–1961) by the German American critic and biographer Erika Ostrovsky (b. 1926). The quotations from Céline that follow are in Ostrovsky's English.

359.4–9 *The sun . . . the ground.*] Genesis 19:23–25.

359.13 Lot's wife] See Genesis 19:26.

365.10 *vox humana*] See note 142.8.

365.10 *vox celeste.*] *Latin:* "heavenly voice"; pipe-organ violin stop pitched an octave above *vox humana.*

371.5–6 Tweedledum or Tweedledee] Characters in Lewis Carroll's *Through the Looking-Glass* (1871), depicted by illustrator John Tenniel as roly-poly twin brothers. When they "agree to have a battle," Alice dresses them in an armor of blankets, tea trays, and cooking pots, all tied to their bodies with kitchen twine.

371.37–38 André Le Fèvre] Le Fèvre the pornographer is a historical fiction fabricated by Vonnegut.

374.31–32 *The Execution of Private Slovik*] Nonfiction book (1954) by American journalist William Bradford Huie (1910–1986). Although forty-nine American servicemen were sentenced to death for "desertion to avoid hazardous duty" in World War II, only Edward Donald Slovik (1920–1945), who refused to serve with his rifle company in Germany, was executed.

383.19 Ausable Chasm] Two-mile-long sandstone gorge in the Adirondack region of Upstate New York.

383.20 Earl Warren] American lawyer and politician (1891–1974) and the fourteenth Chief Justice of the United States (1953–69).

383.22–23 John Birch Society] Right-wing American political-action group founded in 1958 to resist the rise of world Communism and, in the words of its mission statement, "bring about less government, more responsibility, and, with God's help, a better world."

383.30 *Jean Thiriart*] Wealthy Belgian optometrist (1922–1992) who in the 1960s gained notoriety as an agitator for a unified, isolationist European state.

384.32 half-tracks] All-terrain military vehicles with truck wheels in the front, tractor treads in the rear.

385.27–34 GOD GRANT ME . . . DIFFERENCE.] Prayer (c. 1934), popularly known as the Serenity Prayer, attributed to the American Protestant theologian Reinhold Niebuhr (1892–1971).

388.26   potato-masher]   Stick-handled grenade, a standard weapon of the German infantry throughout World War II.

388.29   *fourragère*]   Military decoration in the form of a braided cord, usually worn around the left shoulder.

403.14   *Valley of the Dolls*]   Bestselling novel (1966) by American writer and television celebrity Jacqueline Susann (1918–1974). It chronicles the lives of three wealthy American actresses addicted to amphetamines (uppers) and barbiturates (downers).

413.13   WACS . . . WAFS]   Members of the women's volunteer services of the World War II: WACS (Women's Auxiliary Corps, U.S. Army), WAVES (Women Accepted for Volunteer Emergency Service, U.S. Navy), SPARS (from "Semper Paratus" [Always Prepared], U.S. Coast Guard), and WAFS (Women's Auxiliary Ferrying Squadron, U.S. Air Force).

432.8   Kin Hubbard]   See note 314.20.

436.13–14   five-day battle . . . Dakto.]   The Battle for Hill 875, near Dak To, Kontum Province (November 19–23, 1967), was one of the bloodiest victories for the U.S. in South Vietnam, leaving 122 American troops dead.

456.15–16   one hundred and thirty thousand people . . . would die.]   The source for this figure is David Irving's *The Destruction of Dresden* (see note 471.4–7).

459.34   Ivanhoe]   Historical romance of medieval England (1820), by the Scottish novelist Sir Walter Scott (1771–1832).

461.8   "That Old Gang of Mine."]   "(Wedding Bells Are Breaking Up) That Old Gang of Mine" (1929), song by Sammy Fain with lyrics by Irving Kahal and Willie Raskin.

463.20–29   'Leven cent cotton . . . our poor backs . . .]   From "'Leven-Cent Cotton" (1932), song by country-music pioneer Bob Miller (1895–1955).

469.36–470.2   President Harry S. Truman's announcement . . . Hiroshima.]   White House press release, made public at 11 A.M. EST, August 6, 1945.

471.4–7   *The Destruction of Dresden* . . . 1964.]   David Irving's book was originally published in London in 1963, when the author was twenty-five years old. As the book became an international best seller, Irving's statement that one hundred thirty-five thousand people died in the Allied bombing of Dresden was challenged as an exaggeration by many historians and veterans of World War II, in Germany as well as in England and America. In the preface to the 2007 edition of the book, Irving revised his count of the Dresden dead downward to "sixty thousand or more; perhaps a hundred thousand—certainly the single largest air raid massacre of the War in Europe." In October 2008, a commission of German historians appointed by Dresden city government concluded, after exhaustive examination of archival evidence including police reports and burial records, that the air raids of February 1945 killed more than eighteen thousand but not more than twenty-five thousand people.

471.8   Ira C. Eaker] Eaker (1896–1987) was one of the leading American proponents of strategic daylight percision bombing during World War II. He was commander of the Eighth Air Force (based in England), 1942–43, and the Mediterranean Allied Air Force, 1944–45.

471.9–10   Sir Robert Saundby . . . A.F.C.] Saundby (1896–1971) was the senior air staff officer (chief of staff) of RAF Bomber Command, 1940–43, and its deputy commander, 1943–45. His honors and decorations included Knight Commander of the Order of the Bath (K.C.B.), Knight Commander of the Order of the British Empire (K.B.E.), the Military Cross (M.C.), the Distinguished Flying Cross (D.F.C.), and the Air Force Cross (A.F.C.).

478.13–16   *The cattle . . . He makes.*] See note 343.1–4.

478.30   *Lucretia A. Mott.*] American abolitionist and women's rights activist (1793–1880). Her middle initial was not "A" but "C," for "Coffin."

479.20   George Jean Nathan] Indiana-born drama critic (1882–1958) and the coeditor, with H. L. Mencken, of the magazines *The Smart Set* (1914–23) and *The American Mercury* (1924–25).

484.14–15   a Virginian . . . had written *Uncle Tom's Cabin*] In 1967, a little more than a century after the end of the American Civil War, the Virginia-born writer William Styron (1925–2006) published *The Confessions of Nat Turner*, a best-selling and controversial novel based on a slave revolt of 1831.

484.18   do what Norman Mailer did] Mailer (1923–2007) depicted and celebrated acts of physical violence before becoming notorious for committing such acts himself.

487.3   two nights ago.] That is, on June 5, 1968.

487.30   Adolphe Menjou] Hollywood character actor (1890–1963) who, though American-born, was frequently cast as an elegant European sophisticate.

BREAKFAST OF CHAMPIONS

491.1   BREAKFAST OF CHAMPIONS] In February 1992, Vonnegut wrote a prefatory note for *La Colozione dei Campioni*, the Italian edition of *Breakfast of Champions* (Milan: Eleuthera, 1992). Below is not Vonnegut's original, which he never published, but an English version of the Italian translation.

I am now nearing seventy. When I wrote this fabulous book, twenty years ago, I was still shaken by the impact of television on the old craft of storytelling with ink on paper. It seemed a good idea to save the situation—that is, to keep whatever small audience was left for ink-stained wretches like myself—by making my writing more "visual." So I created this work, which is a delight for both the eyes and the intellect. There is something in this book even for the illiterate, who are said to number in the United States something like forty million. When they look at my drawing of a pair of underpants, for example, they will have no trouble recognizing it as underwear and thinking to themselves: "underpants."

499.1–2   *When he hath tried me . . . gold.*] Job 23:10.

501.3–4   breakfast cereal product]   Wheaties, a brand of toasted whole-wheat flakes launched in 1921. The slogan "Breakfast of Champions" has been in continuous use by General Mills since 1933.

502.24–25   clock which my father designed.] Architectural clock with four eight-foot circular faces, designed by Kurt Vonnegut (Sr.) and built in 1936 for the L. S. Ayres department store at 1 West Washington Street, Indianapolis.

503.22   Knox Burger] American editor and literary agent (1922–2010) who, as fiction editor of *Collier's* magazine (1948–51), published Vonnegut's first short stories. The dedication of Vonnegut's collection *Welcome to the Monkey House* (1968) reads: "For Knox Burger—Ten days older than I am, he has been a very good father to me."

503.25   Philboyd Studge.] In the story "Filboid Studge" (1911), by the English comic writer Saki (1870–1916), Filboid Studge is the new name given by an inspired copywriter to a nutritious but unpalatable and poorly marketed breakfast cereal formerly called Pipenta. For several weeks, Filboid Studge is advertised aggressively but available nowhere, thus creating unprecedented public demand. In the end the public hates the taste of the cereal, but this does not dampen their insatiable appetite for it: the copywriter "had grasped the fact that people will do things from a sense of duty"—and in conformity to fashion—"which they would never attempt as a pleasure."

507.2–3   "*The flag shall not be dipped . . . thing.*"] U.S. Code, Title 36, Chapter 10, Paragraph 176 (December 22, 1942).

544.9   McLuhan.] Marshall McLuhan (1911–1980), Canadian critic and media theorist whose works include *The Gutenberg Galaxy* (1962), *Understanding Media* (1964), and *The Medium is the Massage* (1967).

556.15   *Bang's disease.*] Obsolete name for brucellosis, identified in 1897 by the Danish veterinarian Bernhard Bang (1848–1932).

610.4   *Ivanhoe*] See note 459.34.

610.9 *Tale of Two Cities*] Novel (1859), by Charles Dickens, set in London and Paris during the French Revolution.

610.13–14 *The Good Earth*] Pulitzer Prize–winning novel (1931) by the American writer Pearl S. Buck (1892–1973).

620.13 Jimmy Valentine was a famous made-up person] See "A Retrieved Reformation" (1903), short story by O. Henry (William Sydney Porter, 1862–1910).

636.2–3 a famous poem] "Excelsior" (1842), by Henry Wadsworth Long-fellow (1807–1882).

644.top JENNY LIND] World-renowned Swedish soprano (1820–1887).

654.25–28 *The Moving finger writes . . . Word of it.*] Untitled quatrain (or *rubái*) from *The Rubáiyát of Omar Khayyám* (first edition, 1859), a volume of free translations from the twelfth-century Persian by the English poet Edward FitzGerald (1809–1883).

660.21 highest decoration for heroism] The Medal of Honor, awarded since 1862 for "gallantry and intrepidity . . . above and beyond the call of duty while engaged against any enemy of the United States." The medal has a distinct design for each branch of service. Vonnegut's drawing on page 660 depicts the Army Medal of Honor.

667.29 His biographer . . . Saint Athanasius] Athansius, Bishop of Alexandria (c. 293–373), was a contemporary of Saint Anthony (c. 251–356). His *Vita Antonii*, written c. 370, codified the monastic life for the early church.

679.8 Walter H. Stockmayer] American physical chemist and educator (1914–2004) whose area of expertise was polymers and macromolecules.

682.3 a television show] *This Is Your Life*, produced and hosted by Ralph Edwards, aired on NBC from 1952 to 1961.

696.4 bracelet] Aluminum or copper "P.O.W. bracelet" produced and sold by Viva, a Los Angeles–based student group, as a token of sympathy for— and a call for diplomatic negotiations on behalf of—American prisoners of war in Vietnam. The bracelet program, launched on Veteran's Day 1970, was a re-markably popular success. Hundreds of thousands of bracelets were sold before Viva ceased operations in 1976.

696.6 Jon Sparks] Jon Michael Sparks (1950–1971?) of Carey, Idaho, was the co-pilot of a Huey helicopter gunship that crash-landed in Laos after being hit by North Vietnamese ground fire on March 19, 1971. Sparks was listed as missing in action until 1978, when he was officially declared to have been killed by hostile action.

707.1–3 "Demain nous allons passer la soirée . . . longtemps,"] "Tomorrow we will spend the evening at the movies" . . . "We hope our grandfather will live a long time yet."

715.21–22   "Not a cough in a carload!"]   Advertising slogan (c. 1930–50) for Old Gold cigarettes.

727.13   Springfield rifle]   See note 205.22.

730.11   "you have nothing to fear . . . joy."]   Cf. Luke 2:10.

STORIES

754.33–36   *How do I love thee? . . . Grace."*]   From Sonnet 43, in *Sonnets from the Portuguese* (1850), by Elizabeth Barrett Browning (1806–1851).

772.14–15   *Jeanette MacDonald–Nelson Eddy*]   MacDonald (1903–1965) and Eddy (1901–1967), classically trained soprano and baritone, were paired in eight popular Hollywood musicals between 1935 and 1942.

772.15   "Ah, Sweet Mystery of Life."]   Song by Victor Herbert, with words by Rida Johnson Young, from the American operetta *Naughty Marietta* (1910). A film adaptation of the operetta, starring Jeanette MacDonald and Nelson Eddy, was released by M-G-M in 1935.

773.27   *Arthur C. Clarke*]   British science-fiction writer and futurist (1917–2008) who co-wrote the screenplay for Stanley Kubrick's *2001: A Space Odyssey* (1968) and, in a scientific paper of 1945, posited the idea of geostationary telecommunications satellites.

777.13   Flem Snopes]   Name borrowed from the fiction of William Faulkner. Snopes is the rapacious small-town despot of *The Hamlet* (1940), *The Town* (1957), *The Mansion* (1959), and several short stories.

APPENDIX A

781.1   American Physical Society]   Association of physicists and physics teachers founded at Columbia University, New York City, in 1899 "to advance and diffuse the study of physics" among both the scientific community and the general public.

781.3   MY ONLY BROTHER]   Bernard Vonnegut (1914–1997), an atmospheric scientist who in 1946 pioneered the use of silver iodide in cloud seeding. He was a research chemist at General Electric (1945–52) and Arthur D. Little (1952–67) before becoming Professor of Atmospheric Sciences at New York State University, Albany (1967–85).

781.7   Irving Langmuir]   American research scientist (1881–1957) whose discoveries, made mostly while employed by General Electric (1909–50), led to improvements in the manufacture of vacuum tubes, incandescent light bulbs, arc welders, x-ray machines, ice melt, and other products. His work in the chemistry of oil films won him the 1932 Nobel Prize in Chemistry.

781.7–8   Vincent Schaefer]   American meteorologist and atmospheric chemist (1906–1993) who, while a researcher at General Electric, pioneered the use of dry ice (solid carbon dioxide) in cloud seeding.

783.35–36   Eames and Drexler]   Charles Eames (1907–1978), American designer of molded-plywood furniture, and Arthur Drexler (1926–1987), director of the Department of Architecture and Design at the Museum of Modern Art, New York (1951–85).

786.1   David Lilienthal]   Lawyer, public official, and popular writer (1899–1981) who was a director of the Tennessee Valley Authority (1933–46) before joining the Atomic Energy Commission (1946–50).

786.32   Wernher von Braun]   German-born rocket scientist (1912–1977) who, after developing the V-2 missile for Nazi Germany, designed rockets for the United States, including the Saturn boosters for the Apollo space program.

788.21   Louis Fieser]   Organic chemist (1899–1977) who in 1943, as a research scientist at Harvard University, invented napalm, a jellied form of gasoline widely used by the U.S. military as an incendiary weapon, most controversially during the Vietnam War.

APPENDIX B

793.16   our division was cut to ribbons]   The 106th Infantry, which had an authorized strength of 14,253 men, recorded casualties of 470 men killed or fatally wounded, 1,278 wounded, and 6,697 men taken prisoner.

794.34   Hellexisdorf]   Former German village that in 1974 was incorporated as the town of Hellendorf.

794.26   killed 250,000 people]   This figure was fabricated by the Nazi propaganda ministry and then disseminated through the press in neutral countries.

794.37   (P-39's)]   American fighter aircraft supplied to the Soviets through Lend-Lease.

796.1   *Wailing Shall Be in All Streets*]   See Amos 5:16.

797.6   one hundred thousand human beings]   See note 471.4–7.

797.25   twice its normal population]   In February 1945 there were an estimated one to two hundred thousand refugees in Dresden in addition to the city's five hundred sixty-seven thousand residents.

799.12   aged Volkssturmers]   Members of the Nazi party militia, in which all male civilians between sixteen and sixty were required to serve.

804.22   Marcel Ophuls']   French documentary filmmaker (b. 1927) whose works include *The Sorrow and the Pity* (1969) and *Hotel Terminus: The Life and Times of Klaus Barbie* (1988).

806.18   George Will]   Conservative American political commentator (b. 1941) and, since 1974, a syndicated opinion columnist.

This book is set in 10 point ITC Galliard Pro,
a face designed for digital composition by Matthew Carter
and based on the sixteenth-century face Granjon. The paper
is acid-free lightweight opaque and meets the requirements
for permanence of the American National Standards Institute.
The binding material is Brillianta, a woven rayon cloth made
by Van Heek–Scholco Textielfabrieken, Holland. Composition
by Dedicated Book Services. Printing and binding
by Edwards Brothers Malloy, Ann Arbor.
Designed by Bruce Campbell.

THE LIBRARY OF AMERICA SERIES

The Library of America fosters appreciation of America's literary heritage by publishing, and keeping permanently in print, authoritative editions of America's best and most significant writing. An independent nonprofit organization, it was founded in 1979 with seed funding from the National Endowment for the Humanities and the Ford Foundation.